DEVIL'S PACT

Samantha Cruise

EROTIC ROMANCE

Siren Publishing, Inc.
www.SirenPublishing.com

A SIREN PUBLISHING BOOK
IMPRINT: Erotic Romance

DEVIL'S PACT
Copyright © 2008 by Samantha Cruise
ISBN-10: 1-60601-004-2
ISBN-13: 978-1-60601-004-4

First Printing, March 2008

PUBLISHER
Siren Publishing, Inc.
www.SirenPublishing.com

DEVIL'S PACT

SAMANTHA CRUISE
Copyright © 2008

Chapter 1

When Devin first spotted the wanted poster, that peculiar feeling he dubbed his "best friend" crept up on him. What a man wouldn't do for that much gold. Ten thousand was a hell of a lot of reward for just one man.

Bemusedly, he patted the missive in the pocket of his buckskin jacket.

It would necessitate more backbone than brains to go after that bounty. He was half tempted himself.

Only problem, it was him the law wanted. The Devil's Spawn.

From the looks of it, they wanted him alive. That in itself was implausible, cause for circumspection. No one in his right mind would dare try to take him alive. *Why not dead?* Then any young buck out to make a name for himself, money-hungry bounty hunter, or plum crazy old coot would be after his high-priced blood. Sneak up on him in the dead of night while he slept, perhaps shoot him in the back from high atop a mountain, or, if they had a large enough posse, chase him down.

Regardless the ceremony, they'd be buzzard pickins before they ever saw him. He grinned with assurance.

For now, Devin didn't know whether to be flattered, shocked, or amused. Definitely not scared or worried. Few men in life were born without a scared bone in their bodies. He was one of the elite few— exceptional in more ways than the simple fact he knew no fear. Perhaps there was some sort of sentimental gene that eluded him.

Not that he would blame God for the deficiency due to religious beliefs. More like he stopped believing in the divinity all told. Same time, he stopped living like a normal human being at the ripe old age of ten. Nineteen years later and no less roughshod, there was no way in the infernal fires of damnation the name 'God' ever passed his lips.

What he lacked in sentimentality, he gained in other ways. His senses were sharpened to a heightened awareness that kept him alive when he should have died many times over. His strength, size, and agility were not that of any normal man. Whether an asset or curse, it was his lot in life to make the average man flinch upon staring into his eyes, mothers snatch their children off streets whenever he rode into town, or women coil in fear at the sight of his nakedness. He dealt with the latter best he could. The rest, he didn't give a damn.

The past three years, he stayed away from civilization. Roamed the wilderness alone, ventured into towns when the need to rut grew so intense, he could no longer control the lust. Finding the nearest brothel, he'd pay handsomely to every willing prostitute brave enough to take on "The Cannon." After long absences without a woman, he would ride them hard, fast, and merciless.

Unlike most men, he took what he wanted only after he gave them what they needed. And the women always looked grateful to see him walk through the door, going so far as fight for his attention sometimes. He was eager to fire up "The Cannon," nicknamed by the girls at the Titillate Trove, his favorite whorehouse in Montana Territory. The only nickname he was partial to.

Having been called every name imaginable to go along with the tales attached didn't bother him none, mainly because the tales were true.

He was often described as pure evil. They claimed he murdered so-called innocent men in cold blood, simply because they crossed his path. Of course, that was after he helped himself to gold, money, horses, weapons, or whatever they had that he wanted.

Flat on his stomach, hidden in the dense brush overlooking the river, he stared down at his hands, half expecting to see dried-up blood or some trace of the melee that always followed wherever he went. He had no inkling as to what the fuss was about. As far as he could tell, his hands were just like the next fellow—perhaps a mite larger and faster than most, but two just the same, with four fingers and a thumb on each.

He recalled the same unshakable feeling gripping him when he heard the news about his father. The gut warning had little to do with learning his father was ailing in the worst way possible.

Every man's father died sooner or later. It was a fact of life. Nothing changed that. Same could be said about marriages and births. Only exception was, word about Devin's kinfolk was non-existent. No one suspected the devil had kin. And he liked it that way. Since word traveled to Comanche territory, it was especially peculiar.

For the past month, he lived with the Comanche, spent the winter with the Cheyenne, and roamed the wilderness before that. Two weeks ago, a weasel of a trader doing business with the Indians mentioned an old man by the name of Reed Spawn, who lived in the Tejas Territory.

"Dangled one foot in ground," the scalawag said. He dared enough to ask if the old man was any kin of his.

Detached, he listened to the account and neither confirmed nor denied it. Devin rode out as soon as the trader left the village. Two weeks of hard riding in the saddle, only stopping long enough to rest and feed Deuce, his sidekick, sole confidant, and whom he considered his only family in the world, brought him to this point. He was hidden in the brush, ignoring the poster in his pocket, and admiring the exquisite apparition in front of him.

He pushed all thoughts of the bounty aside along with every feeling other than the one rock hard and aching between his legs. In front of him, not more than ninety yards, swam the prettiest female form he had laid eyes on in a long time. He'd watched her play in the river without a stitch on for the last forty minutes. Grimacing, aware his over indulgent arousal was now a painful need, he tried to remember the last time he buried deep into the lusty wetness between two plump thighs.

With the sun long departed beyond the horizon, the sky streaked with hues of blue, pink and purple, darkness would soon set in. His vision strained to make out the fine details of every exposed feature on the luscious vision before him.

In water to the bottom curve of her buttocks, she stood, her long, sandy-blonde hair clinging to her heart-shaped backside and one wet lock covering a perfectly cone-shaped breast.

She brushed the hair off her shoulder with the sweep of a hand. He guessed the movement grazed the indiscernible nipple, for her body suddenly quivered as though an arousing sensation swept through her.

Much to his surprise and delight, her hands slowly and sensuously ran down her slender hips, then back up her flat stomach and finally cupped her small breasts. If he didn't know any better, he would think she was no longer bathing or swimming, but actually taking pleasure in exploring her young, budding body.

Was it his imagination?

Was it wishful thinking?

Only whores took pleasure in sex, not respectable women. And this pretty little gal couldn't be a whore. She looked too pure and innocent, like a fine porcelain figurine. A far cry from the women he encountered in brothels.

If judged by pubic hair so sparse, it looked as though it just sprouted or else been plucked, he guessed she was fifteen or sixteen, not a day over seventeen. Old enough for marriage, but not old enough to fend for herself against four-legged predators, much less the more dangerous two-legged variety.

His throat went dry when she caressed her breasts, rolling her fingers over the faintly colored tips that almost blended with her milky complexion. Licking her lips, her right hand slowly descended lower, lower, and lower over the soft curves of her skin, until a single finger disappeared between her dampened thighs. He swore he heard a breathy moan escape her lips, and her head fell back when the hand covering the damp golden curls on her mound seemed to move up and down or more like in and out.

Devin let out a low, pained groan as the woman's legs drew slightly apart, and he imagined her fingers tunneling through the slick, hot flesh, pulsing with her own desire. He would give anything to sink a finger, tongue, cock—hell, he didn't care what he sank between those legs, just as long as he could taste, touch, smell or suck on that sweet pussy. It seemed an awful waste for such a pretty young thing to resort to self-pleasure alone in the woods. Whoever the man, husband or father, to leave such an alluringly sensuous female alone was one ace shy of a full deck.

To his dismay, she was rather frail looking and very petite. Her rib cage was well defined and her breasts pathetically small with faint tips. Her hipbones stuck out prominently. If a strong wind blew, he swore she would break in half, or else take to the air.

He was aware girls much younger worked the bawdy crib houses. Personally, he stayed away from little lassies and forced the raucous men he used to lead to do the same. She was nothing like the robust women he preferred. Well-built to withstand the dark desires he craved, full breasts to sink his teeth into, plump thighs to ride him all night long, and a strong back. Oh, hell, yes, they definitely needed strength to withstand the hard-core sex he demanded from his partners.

Prim and proper ladies never appealed to him, either. A good thing, considering he seldom ran across any in the wilderness—at least, until now. There was something about her that tempted him beyond reason, despite the fact it had been too damned long since he coupled with a warm body.

When he came upon the river, he planned to take a bath before heading to his father's ranch. Scrape off two weeks of frontier dust and grime. Instead, he found a bathing beauty who aroused feelings in him distinctly out of the ordinary. Normally, he would have ventured further down the river, leaving the little lady to her privacy, as was his custom whenever he stumbled across the Indian women in the village bathing with their children, but he was drawn to her, rooted to the ground, unable to move or look away.

He was imagining all sorts of ways to make an exception to his one virtue, compliments of growing up with two elderly aunts. Innocent women and children were off-limits.

With a mind of its own, his rioting erection grew more and more convincing when she suddenly fell backwards and floated away. A rough groan escaped his dry throat, and his entire body stiffened.

Like a creamy white log, she now drifted along the river, a treasure trove of deep gold floating around her head.

He shifted his hips, attempting to find a more comfortable position as his cock grew painfully hard to the point of bursting, crushing the bed of dried pine needles beneath him. He reflected on the groove a tracker would find in the event someone trailed him. He'd laugh if he weren't already struggling to breathe.

It wasn't until she floated spread-eagled atop the water, baring her pussy for the world to see—or at least, for him and the other forest animals—that he hunched on all fours in a swift silent motion. He was too far. He had to get closer. He wanted, needed a better look at what was shielded by the curls and sunless shadows between her legs.

Of all the rivers, lakes, and ponds he'd come across during the past two weeks, why did he have to find her in Tejas of all places?

Long ago, he made an unspoken oath to himself. Never start any trouble in Tejas as long as his father lived. Every other territory or state was his to plunder. Tejas Territory was off limits.

Sweet little missy was going to have to wait until some other randy cowboy put her out of her misery.

Anywhere else, he couldn't care less. Already wanted in almost every state and territory, what was one more infraction?

But he was in Tejas, and if he couldn't have her, at least he could wake a snake. He made his way to the tree stump a good distance from the single horse-drawn wagon, where he spotted her dress neatly folded. He was careful not to startle the animal and alert her to his presence. He knew that for a man his size, he moved stealthily and generated no sound in his moccasins.

He reached the area as she waded out of the river. Via the cover of the shadows of the fading light, he took two steps from behind a large tree, reached out, and grabbed her dress in a rapid motion while she leaned over to retrieve the shift she'd discarded earlier on the bank.

He became more intrigued by the young girl, watching from the concealment behind the wide tree trunk in the duskiness as she flapped her shift in the air to rid it of any trace of dirt before tossing the frayed garment over her head. Had she been waiting for a lover who obviously failed to appear, or was she awakening her lust, to be satisfied soon in waiting arms when she returned home? From the lack of a clearly identifiable reaction to an orgasm, she hadn't made herself come.

Oddly, he couldn't help but wonder what she would have looked like in the throes of passion, her skin flush, eyes glazed with arousal, and her body trembling as her orgasm washed over her. Was she a screamer who liked to dig her nails in her lover's back, or did she close her eyes and whimper softly? It would be a helluva shame if she were one of them prissy girls who just lay there while her man huffed and puffed.

With a shake of his head, he decided that was out of the question. A gal horny enough to stick her fingers up her twat out in the open had to know the ins and outs of passion.

Despite her age, she behaved like no virgin.

He thought the whole situation downright odd. If someone started something, may as well go whole hog. She could have come in the river, again at home, and if it were up to him, on the way home to boot.

His tenet for carnality: anywhere, any time, any way.

* * * *

Megan felt refreshed. She looked up at the faint moon in the darkening blue and pink sky and inhaled deeply as the twilight air whipped softly around the green canopy above. She exhaled, then chuckled. Funny, she thought as she peered toward the river once more, how a swim could make her feel clean, guilty, and naughty. A small luxury seldom afforded, privacy, time alone, and a bit of indulgence.

For a moment, her eyes followed a passing tree branch carried downstream by the lazy current. She turned away and sighed, wondering what it felt like to be swept away, have no worries or cares, travel along an unguided path with only faith and heart to guide her.

She glanced at the worn-out buckboard with rusty springs and her old gray mare hitched to it and smiled. With one or two exceptions, her life was better than most. There wasn't anywhere else in the world she would rather be than right here, right now.

Heading toward the tree stump to retrieve her dress, Megan glanced behind her at her long, wet trail in the cool earth. She wrung out her hair between her hands, drained what she could from the soaked strands that hung over her shoulders and down her back. Rivulets drenched her shift, causing goose flesh in the evening breeze as the damp, oversized shift clung to her.

As shivers ran through her, she shook her head in an attempt to wring more water from her hair before wrapping it in a loose bun at the nape of her neck, the most sensible style for the thick, unruly hip-length ringlets. Long, wayward strands hung over her shoulders and down her back.

Within a few feet from the stump, she frowned. She crossed her arms against the chill of the wet gown, fanned by the light breeze ruffling through the leaves in the tall trees, and her gaze swept the area. Her eyes darted to the wagon. No, she thought, certain she didn't leave her dress in the wagon.

"It has to be here," she muttered aloud to herself. She stepped closer to the stump, thinking it must have fallen off in a swift breeze. Nervousness began to creep in. The early spring winds weren't strong enough to blow her dress away. If Shelby or Emma had woken up and meant to play a trick on her, she would have noticed, since her gaze instinctively went to the buckboard every few minutes.

Alarm ripped through her at the realization of the only other possibility.

Megan froze at the ominous figure emerging from behind the tree.

"Is this what you're looking for?" The deep resonate voice was hauntingly low and utterly menacing. The owner of that intimidating voice held her dress up in his right hand, his left thumb hooked over his double holster, strapped low on his waist and tied-down the way gunslingers wore their belts. His fingers strummed casually over his left pistol, a long dagger sheathed by its side.

She gaped, and as she studied the huge bear of a man, transcendent fear rose in her. It gripped her heart so fast, she thought she was going to die where she stood. At around what must be six-nine, he towered over her four-eleven frame, and even seemed to dwarf the hundred-year-old elm tree he stood beside.

A wide-brimmed charcoal grey hat sat low on his forehead, completely shading his eyes. Dark wavy hair hung over the collar of his buckskin-fringed jacket. His sun-faded black shirt with the buttons undone midway revealed hard, bronzed flesh underneath and a spattering of dark curls across an impressively wide chest. Well-worn buckskins clung to his long, massive thighs and legged moccasins that reached his knees, where a hunting knife was strapped to both sides of each calf.

The huge trespasser looked every bit as dangerous as he sounded.

Quickly, she weighed her options, concluded there were none.

She drew in a deep breath. Her first thought was the children. Hopefully, it wouldn't be her last. She needed to think quickly if they were to survive.

She eyed him defiantly, squaring her shoulders for the forthcoming battle. Her death, if it came to that, would not be that of a coward. She dropped her arms to her side, unconcerned the wet homespun shift now molded her body, transparent thanks to the river water dribbling from her soaked hair.

A grin curled the corner of his lips, as if he derived enjoyment from unnerving her. She glared at him as her heart thundered.

"Seems I am in possession of a calico, and you have need of one."

She willed herself not to move, run, or show fear, holding her ground with great difficulty. Despite the shadow concealing his eyes, the heat of his scrutiny was apparent. She could see the outline of his cock twitching beneath his buckskins. She wanted to scream bloody murder and bring about every man in the territory, gun in hand to shoot the brazen heathen. It was impossible. If she screamed, no one was around for miles to hear. Only Shelby and Emma, sound asleep in the back of the wagon, would come to her aid. What could two small children do but only add to the harrowing quandary?

"Sir, I'm much obliged you found my dress." Her tense-free tone came as quite a shock considering her limbs were unsteady. Mindful charitable sorts offered, not pilfered, she held out her hand. Bold. Foolish. It was a risk worth taking.

"Oh, no, missy, it ain't gonna be that easy," he replied in a tone hinged with a self-indulged diversion, a warning of sorts. Her eyes widened as he took a predatory step closer, lofty and menacing.

She yanked her hand back instantly. Her wildly beating heart plummeted to her stomach. A chill of terror grated over her body. She gaped up into the dark shadow concealing his face and could only blink at the blatant insinuation.

"It's gonna cost you." He waved the dress in his hand and narrowed the gap in two broad strides.

"Sir, I have no money with me," she responded in an unwavering tone, staggering backward. She feigned an ease she did not feel as her innards quivered by the nearness of such a powerful body. "If you follow me…"

His deep chuckle caused her to falter for a brief moment.

"…follow me home, I'll pay. Name your price." She didn't have any money, even at home. Doc, and his assistant, Caleb, were waiting for her.

They would pay, or better yet, shoot him on sight. Silently, she prayed it would be the latter.

* * * *

Devin studied her up close, her hazel brown eyes and long, sweeping lashes. Her soaked hair, he imagined when dry, would be the color of fiery gold. Her straight nose, with a few freckles across the bridge and high cheeks bones, were delicately carved.

She had a very appealing mouth, a delightfully sinful mouth with full, pink lips. With a quick intake of breath, he visualized those perfectly lined lips on his and other places as well. His cock jerked in response.

An oval face framed exquisite features, her only flaws were the shadows under her eyes, which he suspected were from the daylight fading fast behind the dense canopy of trees.

And with a voice so soft and melodious, it sounded as if she were singing rather than speaking. It suited her perfectly, as did the dimples sparking near the corners of her lips.

This little lady wasn't pretty. Rather, she was a dream come alive. Downright the most beautiful lassie he ever laid eyes on, and that was saying a lot.

He stood close enough to witness the fear in her eyes, despite the notable calm in her tone. She was definitely afraid of him, and with good reason. If she knew who he was, she would have turned tail long ago. Strangely, he wondered why she hadn't made a run thus far.

This woman definitely intrigued him.

"Little miss, I don't want your money."

A sharp gasp escaped her gaped mouth, which she abruptly clinched. Her eyes darted frantically around, as if looking for an escape.

"If you want my horse, take it and ride on out," she urged, her voice quavering slightly.

He didn't answer right away. Instead, his steady gaze bore into her. Her entire body trembled with fright—of that, he was certain. Nevertheless, she stood, facing him with her arms by her sides. Chin held high. She was not making a move to cover herself. She no doubt knew full well he could see right through the thin wet garment that clung to her every curve.

The woman had balls of stone, which was more than he could say about most men he came across. His were hard as stone and ready to crack any second.

"If that ol' mare was worth more than half a red cent, I would've taken it long ago."

"I have nothing else of value."

His gaze traveled over her trim figure, the outline of her breast clearly visible, the taut nipples straining against the soaked fabric, calling out to him. Impulsively, he licked his lower lip as his sights rested on the dark wet hair shielding her mound. His cock twitched for freedom, aching for the glory between those thighs.

He fought to hold onto the scrap of control that remained. It had been too damn long. He silently cursed himself for not stopping at the nearest brothel along the way. The way he felt now, he could come just by staring. Shit, six months without a woman could do that to a man.

"From where I stand, you got plenty assets."

"I…I…"

"I mean you no harm. If I wanted to molest or kill you, I would have done so by now." He could see her fear of imminent ravishment in her eyes.

"Wha—what then?" She looked fairly relieved.

Her relief was short-lived.

"A kiss."

She watched as he tossed aside her dress. The calico with the pretty green floral pattern landed near the tree stump.

With his hands on the butt of each six-shooter, he waited patiently. He felt his rock-hard cock twitch as he imagined what they could be doing right now. How her small body would writhe beneath him as he held her slender hips and buried his cock between those slender thighs. Damn it! Why weren't they anywhere else but Tejas? He'd have to settle for a meager kiss.

That was, if she was willing.

Thanks to the damned teachings on the proper treatment of the dainty gender ingrained in his subconscious by his two spinster aunts, if this dandelion said no, then by golly, it had to be no.

Shit!

He stood firm, looming out of the dark brush like an indomitable sequoia, ensuring she had no doubt that if he wanted, he could easily change his mind and kill her on the spot, though he never would.

Leaving her no choice but to eventually accept.

The tense silence lengthened.

"One kiss?" It was a breathy, nervous utterance.

"Yes." Though her consent came as clear victory on his part, his voice remained without inflection.

"And you'll leave us, *me* alone." She bit her lip quickly.

"Just drifting, I'll be on my way...*after*." He held his grin at bay. This was not going to be his first kiss. He was no green boy. Hell, he was doing more than kissing grown women at a tender age, so why the sudden excitement and anticipation of a simple kiss from half a sliver of a young lady a step outside of puberty?

Judging from the size of her apple-sized breasts, impossibly tiny waist, slight roundness of what he didn't even want to refer to as hips, and the fresh innocence in her hazel eyes, he figured she couldn't be well into her teens yet.

If only she were a little older...

"I have your word as a gentleman. One kiss and you'll leave?"

"Hell, yes, you have my word as a gentleman," he said firmly and let out a slight chuckle. He'd been called plenty of things in his life, but a gentleman was never one of them.

Before she could utter another word, he tossed his hat in the vicinity of her dress and closed the short gap between them. He encircled her waist, amazed his long fingers overlapped. He lifted her. She weighed nothing at all.

"What are you doing?" she shrieked as her feet left the ground. Her hands barely curled over his forearms as she grabbed onto him. She was a tiny thing. He walked toward several boulders a few feet away, holding her at arms' length.

He stood her on the closest boulder, keeping his hands on her waist until she steadied herself. Calmly, he explained, "So I don't strain my neck bending down so far."

Barely reaching mid-chest when firmly planted on the ground, the added height of the boulder brought her to within a few inches of his towering height.

She closed her eyes, inhaled deeply as if to ease her nerves. The subtle move caused her breasts to rise and fall in a beguiling way that caught his appreciative attention.

He cleared his parched throat and wondered how he was going to get though this in one piece. "Don't worry. I won't hurt you," he offered, more as a reminder to himself.

* * * *

Megan repeated to herself, she could do this. One minuscule indiscretion, a simple kiss from a brute she doubted ever kissed a woman in his life. If one judged from his squalid clothes and unkempt whiskers, no decent woman would dare near him. Perhaps if she kept her eyes closed and thought of someone else. With her pistol hidden in the pocket of her dress yards away, there was no other choice. *For the children*, she replayed in her mind.

She felt a gentle brush of his hand against her cheek.

"You're beautiful."

Her eyes darted open at his unexpected touch, the softness in his tone and the honesty in those two words. For the first time, she gazed into piercing silvery gray eyes. She witnessed a torrent of emotions and lust flaming in the darkening depths that stole her breath.

She realized there was every reason to fear this man. More so than the guns, knives, and sheer brute strength of his size, which clearly proved he was a man capable of murder. The glimpse into the depths of his very soul revealed a brutality of one possessed by the devil himself.

Her heart skipped a beat, and her mouth fell open in awe as she continued to peer into deep caverns of granite that mesmerized and beckoned her.

"Do I frighten you?"

Whatever it was she felt, it wasn't fear. Yet she was frightened—not by him, but by the way she was responding to him.

Slowly, she nodded her head as she held a trembling hand to squelch the fluttering low in her belly. She tried not to notice the blatant desire in his silver gaze, the invitingly sensuous, full lips parting in anticipation, surrounded by the sable brown beard and mustache that matched his wavy, shoulder-length hair.

She couldn't believe or deny the instantaneous thrill of the forbidden rushing through her veins, igniting every nerve while he ran his thumb along her jaw in a smooth caress that seared an indelible path in her skin. A simple touch beckoned the wanton woman in her. That sinful nature Mrs. Walker warned she was cursed with.

"Don't be. I won't hurt you," he promised in a husky, pained tone as though he was the one compromised.

For some unknown reason, she believed him. A huge, powerful, and formidable man with piercing eyes that seemed to read her deepest thoughts. Long-forgotten urges made her ache with desire.

It was true.

Everything they said about her was true. Respectable women weren't supposed to take pleasure in mating with a man. Yet here she was with a complete stranger, the epitome of evil, touching her, about to kiss her, and her body was coming alive, tingled with lustful awareness, a warm gush of liquid settled between her thighs.

With her arms by her side, she clinched her hands into tight fists as he twined his fingers in her soaked hair, disturbing the bun she just made. His warm breath against her ear sent currents of heated blood surging to her toes.

"I'll be gentle," he whispered as his fingers curled in her hair and drew her yielding body close with his other hand.

Before she could say or do anything, his lips covered hers in a surprisingly soft, warm, and inviting kiss.

Megan groaned, caught off-guard by his sweet lips, talented and persuasive. His rugged, musky scent of fresh pine, baked sweat, trail dust, and ferine male arousal drugged her. She grew dizzy. Her head spun as his hands moved down the length of her back, pressing her body into a hard wall of rippled muscle.

Foreign sensations coursed through her body as he boldly swept his tongue over her lips, asking, probing, caressing, and tempting an invitation to a state of complete bliss—paradise.

She melted against his strength and clutched his jacket to keep from falling as her legs turned to mush. He nipped her lower lip between his teeth and bottom lip. Her mouth opened with a small startled gasp, and his tongue slid into her mouth, tasting every inch, exploring every crevice, teasing her senses.

Instead of pulling away and breaking the illicit kiss, she found herself responding willingly. Deepening the kiss, she captured and began to suck on his tongue.

In return, he devoured her mouth with his own hunger that took her unawares. His lips were firm, yet passionately demanding, too sensuous to resist. His velvet tongue was greedy, influencing her traitorous body to submit mercifully as she surrendered to the incredible sensual pleasure he roused in her.

Unable to resist, her hands draped around his neck, splayed across his back as she pressed closer to his body. The bulging heat beneath his buckskins pressed against her belly, and she felt a flame of arousal race down her spine and flare deep in her core.

He slid his hands lower and cupped her buttocks, lifting her off the rock, pulling her body tightly against his. He easily positioned her mound against the engorged head of his cock without breaking their bond. Slowly, he started to move her flushed body up and down, rubbing the tender flesh against his cock. She couldn't distinguish his groans from her moans.

The heat of his hard cock building a roaring fire between her throbbing legs made her want to wrap them around him. She clung to his neck, her nipples growing harder, breasts flat against his massive chest. Her breathing grew uneven as her entire body writhed in his grasp. She ground her hips against the solid flesh jutting between them and allowed the burning ache to transcend any trace of reality, every aspect of decency, surrendering to the exquisite torture he deftly inflicted.

* * * *

What in the hell was he doing? Devin thought. If he kept this up, he was going to either spend in his buckskins or rape her any second.

"Shit," he growled, unprepared for the sheer force of a single kiss. Never had a need so great consumed him with the capacity to hinder his self-restraint. He was unable to get enough of her, as though his skin wanted to breathe her into his pores, brand her body to his. Senses inundated with furious intensity, he used every last drop of willpower to lower her feet back to the boulder. His chest heaved with each rasping breath, and the Cannon throbbed at the violent denial, so close to erupting. He was in physical, bone-searing pain.

As he straightened, a pitiful sigh of protest escaped her. She sounded as if she wanted more.

His hands went to the back of his neck to loosen her unrelenting stronghold. At that moment, she pulled him closer. She stared wide-eyed and hopeful into his eyes, bewildered and darkened with unsatisfied, fiery lust.

"Don't stop," she pleaded breathlessly.

He stared at her for the briefest of moments. A flood of emotions clouded her glazed eyes. Whatever it was she struggled with, her red-hot desire was stronger and he wasn't about to disappoint her.

It wasn't rape if she asked for it. Lady or not, Tejas or not, young'un or not, he wasn't about to pass up the raw hunger blazing in her eyes.

She wanted him as badly as he wanted her.

Hell, maybe even more.

It wasn't too often he came across a woman like her. Those luminous hazel eyes revealed a ravenous sexual appetite capable of fulfilling his darkest needs and carnal demands.

* * * *

Megan reeled from an unspoken promise broken. She was unable to believe he actually stopped after one long, passionate kiss that boiled her blood, aroused her lust, and left her desiring more.

She rose on her toes. Her lips possessed his in a kiss so passionate it was almost savage in intensity as his arms wrapped around her. Her fingers clutched his hair as she moved against him. Her tongue asked, begged, and demanded what she could not.

Something had come over her. Never would she be able to explain it. Perhaps the truth suddenly became all too real. Maybe it was the simple fact he said she was beautiful, the heat of his silken touch, or her shameless disappointment.

Maybe it was a combination of everything, including too many years going without love or closeness, for fear of what might happen. Fear of her doubts, her sexuality of everything she'd been taught about the sins of the flesh.

Whatever it was, it overpowered her completely.

This was her only chance to experience what she'd witnessed all those years working at Madame Jazelle's whorehouse. To bring consciousness to what caused her so much shame and sent her life spiraling out of control years ago.

With this stranger, consequences mattered little.

Long after they found his dead body, no one would ever suspect her.

The opportunity he presented was a revelation, a newfound freedom, a sexual awakening.

Empowered, her hand found its way underneath his holster and into the front of his buckskins. An impossible heat burned her skin as her fingers touched silky smoothness and something incredibly hard and large.

It couldn't possibly be?

* * * *

"Dang, woman, slow down," Devin groaned. Apparently, his reputation as the fastest two-handed slinger throughout the western frontier wasn't quick enough for her. Normally, he would be the last man to ever tell a woman no, but as it was, he was 'bout ready to burst.

In a flash, he swept her up into his arms. He carried her closer to the river where the trees were not as dense, allowing the grass to flourish into an ideal green carpet for what he intended.

He laid her down and knelt beside her slightly parted thighs. Anxiously, he lifted her thin, dampened shift above her breasts. His gaze took in the delectable feast before him. She might have been pint-sized, but what she packed was pure prime.

Like a wild coyote about to feast on its kill, he licked his lips and splayed a dark hand over her young, firm breasts, dragging his fingers impatiently over her smooth, soft belly, skimming down slowly until his fingers covered the sparse curls on her mound. She closed her eyes, arched her body to meet his heated caresses while strangled moans escaped from her throat.

Half mad with desire, he no longer cared how old she was. Perhaps only a sawed-off shotgun to the head above his shoulders could stop him, 'cause nothing was stopping the throbbing head below. He dipped his thumb between her swollen labia, barely touched the sensitive nub. She cried out with open delight. Spurred by her obvious eagerness, his fingers separated the saturated lips. His breath caught as her legs fell further apart. So hot and so hard, he fought to maintain control upon seeing her hips arch instinctively.

"Is this what you want?" Not waiting for a reply, he stroked her silky folds with a knowing touch. She gasped for breath as he teased the slick entrance just enough to stir the fire to keep her arousal on edge. After she glimpsed what he kept hidden from her view and didn't want her to touch, she may get a hankering to not only change her mind but run for the hills.

He smiled. One look at what raged beneath his buckskins, even flaccid, and ladies would clamp their legs out of sheer fright. Another reason he paid handsomely for his deviant pleasure.

This little lady had no idea what she was in for. Propped on an elbow, he stretched out beside her, maintained their intimate contact. He took her mouth in another hungry kiss.

This time, she responded without hesitation, parting her lips readily. Her arms clutched his neck and pulled him down. It fired his blood when she boldly swept her tongue over his lips, against his teeth, down his throat. Like a little vixen, she tasted him, explored his mouth, tempting urges he could no longer resist.

Careful not to put his weight on her, he held himself up on his forearm. His leg was draped over her thigh, keeping her legs open for what was soon to come. She panted breathlessly in his mouth while his fingers stroked and probed her intimate, drenched flesh and built the fiery need that glazed her eyes.

"Damn, you're too tight," he groaned roughly against her mouth as he tried to nudge a finger into the depths of her wet pussy to test her readiness. She whimpered with pleasure into his mouth and arched her hips to meet him.

It wasn't going to be easy. Already near the edge of madness, her body was soft, inviting, and tempting—too tempting as he fought to hold back the raw, explosive dark desires. He imagined his cock thrusting in wet, dripping flesh tighter than his fist, milking him dry. If he didn't hurry, they would both be out of luck.

He withdrew his finger and quickly untied his buckskins while he kept her distracted in a long, deep kiss that was hard and demanding.

* * * *

A lusty moan rose from her throat as Megan gave herself over to him completely. She felt on fire. His kiss, his touch, the potent heat of his strength was all powerful. The attraction sizzling between them was undeniable. She played a dangerous game with a complete stranger, but somehow, she knew with utmost certainty he could satisfy the burning passion he aroused with a mere look, a warm touch, and a soft word.

She did not know him. She did not desire him. She did not even want him. Nonetheless, she needed him desperately, just as assuredly as her very survival was dependent upon the sunrise tomorrow.

He moved between her parted thighs. With his free hand, he spread her legs farther apart. She felt her pussy throb, and a rush of fluid seeped between her bare thighs. If he was as skilled at lovemaking as he was at kissing, she was eager to experience pleasure and forget past dissatisfactions.

"This may hurt. I'll go slowly." His tone resonated with a dark primal hunger, a hint of warning as he nibbled along the curve of her throat. She felt his erection at the entrance to her untutored body.

Her eyes flared open as she tried to comprehend his meaning.

While working at Jazelle's brothel, they forced her to look through the peephole at the girls with every man who had the price to pay for their body.

She'd learned secondhand all about sexual relations between a man and woman. Somehow relegated to a mechanical process where a woman would climb on top and grind a fella until he felt lucky if he lasted a full two minutes. A few seemed to enjoy what they did with the men, though most never seemed to suffer distress.

Was sex supposed to be pleasurable, or merely an endurable means to absorb the excess lust of men?

Or was Mrs. Walker correct with her morally righteous ideals that all coupling other than the necessity of child bearing was a lewd act, painful and degrading to sinners who partook in lustful desires of the flesh?

Surely Mrs. Walker was wrong.

Whatever her dark, mysterious stranger touched her with felt like heaven, wonderful. There was no pain, only unbelievable pleasure. Never did she imagine something could feel so incredible and tantalizing—even his sensuous, dominant kisses took her breath away.

A sudden consciousness radiated through her, a sense of panic, as she felt something hot and very large touch her throbbing vagina.

"Oh, you want it bad." His voice rolled deep from his throat.

She shuddered beneath him. Her breath caught as she felt his cock stroke the slick folds of her pussy as if teasing her, tempting her entrance with the conquest to come.

"So hot and wet."

Megan ignored his brazen comments, feeling her all but virginal skin start to stretch impossibly wide. Alarm burst through her system. She stared down where his flesh nudged hers.

"Ready for me." He suddenly groaned, his face taut with the insane, lust-driven need to fuck that she also had given in to.

Her entire body tensed as her mouth opened, then clamped shut, catching the scream trying to escape between her now-clenched teeth. She ground her teeth and grimaced. Withheld each scream as the pain roared from between her thighs to every panicking nerve in her body. Desperate, she buckled against the painful intruder in an attempt to throw him off her, every muscle clenched in protest. It was like a duckling trying to topple a mountain with its tail feathers. He didn't budge, and another tortuous shot pierced through her as the first inch pried her apart.

"Don't rush." His voice sounded strangled as if he too were desperate, but for an entirely different reason. "Take it easy. Relax."

The man was crazy, absolutely crazy. He thought she encouraged his barbarism. As though she wanted to be split in two. The destroying intensity of the pain was too much for her weakened state to fight against, let alone understand why his dominance excited her, heated her blood.

Her mind was telling her one thing and the need throbbing between her thighs another. She could feel hot liquid spilling out of her. Despite the pain and the pleasure she wouldn't admit to, she felt each quivering muscles stretch around his thickness, more than willing to accept him. Ashamed at how easily he could bend her to his will, she wanted to scream at the sinful depravity pouring over her.

* * * *

Devin used every shred of control to ease the head inside, but it wasn't easy. That small contact alone had him seeping from the tip and pulsating in her grip. It wasn't even halfway in yet, and she was already rushing, tightening on him and coating his cock with her hot cream as she arched into him. He could easily tear her apart if he pummeled into her. But damn, she felt so good, so fucking fantastic. Tightest, sweetest, prettiest pink piece of cunt he ever had. He wanted to give it all to her in one hard thrust, send her careening out of control. Make her scream. Beg.

Next time, he'd do all of that and more, certain there was going to be a next time.

He felt her body tighten and knew any tighter and his near-bursting cock wouldn't last another minute. His hand smoothed upward to caress a breast until the little peak was pebble hard. He kissed the tendon along the base of her throat and felt her body soften. When she moaned into his kiss after his lips found hers once more, he sank another inch into her tight wetness.

Her face contorted with observable pain as he drove into her tight heat. She squeezed her eyes shut, breaking their contact. He watched amazed how her tiny body let him in, heels bolstered in the grass to arch her hips to accept him.

"Oh, yeah," he rasped tightly, pulling away slightly as his gaze dropped between her thighs. "We're almost there. Get the feel of me." The bulky mushroom-shaped head was buried within the tightest wet heat imaginable, so hot it seared his flesh. Her vaginal muscles clamped around his hard flesh—so silky tight, he was ready to come. The sight of his twelve-inch, thick, red cock wedged between two slender thighs of pale cream was maddening to his control. It was a challenge to restrain his impetuous need to plunge into her with a reckless fury.

"Damn, you're so tight." The tight pinch of her cunt bordered on a sharp edge of pain and pleasure, burning him alive as he slowly worked his cock further into her sensitive tissue. He knew she was going to be tight, but he felt like he was drilling into a fiery hole. He felt her tremble as her slick, hot, inner muscles stretched around him. "Does it feel good?"

He stilled, breathing hard, fast, waiting for the urge to thrust pass. For a rare moment, he wished they were somewhere else. A bed would be nice, or at least four walls and a roof for privacy. Anywhere else, where she would be comfortable as he rammed his steel rod into her tight pussy.

Oh well, can't have everything. At least out here in the woods, when she screamed, the only ones to hear her would be the birds, squirrels, deer, and other animals, him included.

He ran his tongue along the hollow of her shoulder, tried impatiently to inch a little deeper. She moved against him, her head thrashing in the grass. A low, throaty moan escaped her lips. Hungrily, he sought her mouth again. "You can't wait to be fucked, can you?"

Quickly, he brushed aside her hair and captured her mouth with his. He drove his tongue deep, mimicking the motions he longed for. His fingers, plucking, teased the already hard nipple roughly on her swollen breast until she whimpered in his mouth.

* * * *

Dear God, no. Megan refused to allow herself to surrender to his madness, to be ripped apart because her lascivious nature had a weak mind of its own. She had to clear her mind and free her body of the growing haze of sinful pleasure. To do that she had to break the phenomenal kiss as the agonizing pain of being plundered shattered every nerve ending. She wiggled her hips attempting to break free from his restrictive grasp. Unable to see through the tangled mass of hair covering her face, she shook her head. Who in their right mind would let him kiss her or touch her with whatever he possessed between his legs? Her only thought was to escape the brutal assault on her senses.

Gasping, she clenched her fist into the front of his jacket, hating herself for being vulnerable and weak as she felt her depraved flesh dripping over him, tightening, begging to be filled. Beneath her tresses, her eyes widened catching sight of the wild fire in his darkening gaze. She realized with amazement this was but a glimpse into the overwhelming strength of his passion, the force of which seemed too powerful for even him to govern.

Her body trembled with renewed fear as her heart pounded in her chest. Underestimating his power of seduction she'd allowed his skilled kiss in the first place. Her traitorous body thrived on the sharp bite of pain. Like a demon she could not rule, her body wanted this stranger to take her, no matter the consequences.

Heaven help her, the man was dangerous on so many levels.

"I'm inside. Don't move," he demanded in a strangled tone as he moved his hand to steady her hips. His cock jerked sharply. "Damn, did you feel that?"

The burning heat, intense ache, throbbing need, tunneling inside was a sensation unmatched, seemingly intolerable as her muscles stretched around the hard flesh lodged between her thighs. Through half-lidded eyes, she watched him as he seemed to struggle. That strained expression on his face she'd seen before. It matched those of men desperate to withhold their beckoning climax, eager to get their money's worth, one she spied often at Jazelle's. If he was too close to the edge, thanks to the frank talk among women, she knew what to do to free her body of this depraved misery.

Suddenly, she felt another inch of his thick shaft force its way into the confines of her trembling moisture. A jolt of unbearable pain tore at her sensitive flesh once again as she clenched her teeth on the scream bubbling in her throat. The violent charge whipped through her body. In a last feeble attempt to break his strong hold on her, deny further entry to the foreign invader wedged snuggly within her weakened body, she twisted her hips side to side. She clenched her inner muscles around his cock and began to milk him.

* * * *

"Nooo," Devin growled in torment, throwing his head back. That slight movement of her tight muscles gripping the sensitive underside of the embedded head sent his essence exploding into her in long, hot spurts. His body shuddered from the magnitude of the force that slammed into him. His angry cock, so long denied, was no match for such a young, hot-blooded temptress, now hidden behind a tangled mass of damp hair.

In agony, he braced his weight over hers and convulsed uncontrollably as a seemingly endless stream erupted from the head of his cock throbbing within the tight confines of her pussy. Each spurting jet of his seed was detrimental to his strength, weakening him until he lowered himself over her frail body.

With only the head jammed into her hot depths, he was frustrated, mad as hell that he lost control, unable to hold back his release. Every instinct told him to thrust in her tight inferno, take his pleasure freely as he had done so many times. He knew he needed to hurry, and yet, he waited too damned long. It didn't do her a damn bit of good. It left him lusting for more.

Content in knowing he would soon be ready to go again, and for much longer, now that the ravenous hunger was satisfied, he nestled his face in her hair and caught his breath. Perspiration beading his forehead, and he delighted in her rosy scent and reveled in her frailty beneath him while his heartbeat eased.

Chapter 2

The only discord spoiling the serene, deep blue sky and still cool water of the mountain-fed river was his ragged breathing. Moments afterward, to her shame, Megan added a sniffling noise. He opened his eyes, and she tried to avert his gaze, hide her weakness and humiliation by turning her face from his. She felt his eyes burn into her, and she knew her attempt at bravado would be all for naught if she cried. Heaven help her, she couldn't hold back the single tear that ran down her cheek.

Gradually, he lifted his arm as though it weighed a ton, and brushed away the damp hair matted around her face. "Sorry if I hurt ya. Next time, it will be all about you. We'll do it right."

Next time! Next time! Her fitful emotions went into overdrive at the unabashed arrogant statement. There wouldn't be a next time. There wasn't even supposed to be this time. What had she done? She had to get away. Carefully, her hand made its way to his hip. Whomever this stranger was who lay on top of her, poured his seed into her, she was about to make sure he knew there would never be a next time.

She felt his body scarcely tense at the recognizable clicking sound of a hammer being cocked as the cold, hard steel in her hand pressed into his ribs. A dark shadow flickered in his silver gaze. His eyes locked with hers, yet he didn't make a move, didn't say a word.

"Get off me," she demanded in a low, firm tone as she pressed his pistol further into his side.

"Said I was sorry," he replied in a tone that undermined the fact a gun was pressed in his gut. His gaze softened somewhat, which only irritated her more.

"And I said get off me. Now!"

He shook his head slowly. "I've never seen a woman so fired up for not getting hers. Don't worry little lady, I'll guarantee you come next time," he pledged in a tone more amused than apologetic, bracing his arms on either side of her shoulders as though he was about to rise off her. Instead, he looked down into her eyes and thrust his hips forward. The head of his diminished cock slid several inches into her well-lubricated passage.

She gasped, eyes flaring wide. All pain momentarily forgotten as she reveled in the erotic delirium of such a captivating sensation. Her cheeks heated, and she actually felt her inner muscles grip him, welcoming his flesh. She hated herself, her body, her lapse of control over the flagrant sexual urges tormenting her and for nearly begging him not to stop—again.

With a wicked glint in his gaze, he shifted to his knees and slowly withdrew, as if giving her a chance to enjoy every thick, slick, heated inch. The arrogant bastard was doing it intentionally. She fought for breath, fought the pleasure building in her body and the temptation to wrap her legs around him.

Through clenched teeth, she fought back the moan of pleasure deep in her throat. Her body quivered as she felt her muscles clutch his flesh to keep him buried deep inside. The intoxicating extent of the carnal sensations made her want to cry out for more, much, much more as her hips instinctively arched upward slightly, following his departure wantonly as he pushed to his feet.

He straightened to his full, formidable height, hands on his wide hips and faced her. She scrambled to her feet, breathing a tad easier. Her eyes never left his. *Stay strong.* She held the gun leveled at his broad chest and readjusted her crinkled, dampened shift, which had bunched into her underarms.

Her pulse raced. Between ragged breaths, she ordered him to raise his hands, which he obliged with a silly smirk on his face. She held the gun, so why did he appear amused by the transfer of power? There wasn't an ounce of fear in the man. He wasn't normal. Good God, who or what was he?

"I don't know who you are mister, but there won't be a next time." She hoped she sounded convincing, because her tingling body sure as heck didn't concur. She smoothed the grass-stained shift with long sweeping strokes. A hot, sticky fluid trickled down her thighs, his seed. At that betraying reminder, she clamped her legs together.

"Well little lady, I usually ask for my partner's name before I fuck them…not after."

"I...you..." Turning beat red from her roots to her toes she shook the gun at him. Dear God, she wanted to shoot him dead so bad.

"I only asked for a kiss. You're the one who went reaching for my cock."

As if on cue, her eyes strayed to his glistening penis and testicles, coated with his release and her lubrication and dangling heavily out of his opened fly. It jerked in response to her gaze and came to life. The specimen of manhood rose to a full, glorious sight in a matter of seconds. It stood straight out of its dark hairy nest, pointed directly at her. Helplessly, she couldn't drag her gaze away as he shifted his weight from one leg to the next, thrusting his hips forward slightly in the process, as though daring her to speak, look away, or spread her legs. Her body throbbed with carnal desire, hot and intense.

"See, dimples, it likes you."

Before she knew what happened, he was in front of her, removing the gun from her grasp. Mortified, she looked up at him in disbelief. Confidently, he used that thing jutting out of his groin surrounded by lush dark curls to distract her. Harlot that she was, she fell for it. And because she was drawn to it, she lowered her mesmerized gaze once more.

She licked her lips.

Just like him, it was enormous. Never before had she seen a man built so large and she'd witnessed quite a few. She shuddered at the mental picture of him trying to put that *thing* inside her. Where would it all go? It would probably take both her small hands to span its girth, and its head was the size of her fist.

Oh, my God.

It was dark red, thickly veined in blue, very long and so very, very tempting. Dear God, Oh Lord, Mother Mary, she wanted to touch it. The burning ache, outlandishly occurring with increased regularity since she'd first kissed the wickedly alluring stranger, spread through her, renewed the wetness between her thighs.

There was no other way to explain it. She was a wanton, shameless hussy.

Mrs. Walker had been right all along.

They were *all* right.

She could tell by his smug grin he found some sort of perverse pleasure in watching her drool over his cock. So thick, dark, and engorged, it seemed ready to explode once again. Mockingly, the heavy beast angled downward at her as though waiting to burrow deep within her pussy.

He returned his pistol to its rightful place. Then he stuffed his hard-on back in his buckskins and spoke in a slow drawl. "Show's over."

Bastard, she raged in her mind as her eyes locked with his, followed by her new name for herself, *Hussy*. The blush on her face deepened.

After redoing his laces, he adjusted his holster. "That is, unless you changed your mind...again?" he offered with a grin. "In that case, I insist on knowing your name."

She shot him a look to assure him she wouldn't be changing her mind anytime soon.

"You...you said you would ride out."

"Word of advice before I go: draw a gun, pull the trigger. Hesitate, and you're dead. Lucky for you, I don't go round killing women. Anyone else, and you would've been dead as soon as you reached for my gun."

Megan grasped the sudden realization and a lump caught in her throat. At any moment, he could have taken the gun from her knowing full well, she wasn't going to use it on him. He spoke of killing with such ease, as though it was second nature to him.

"Who are you?" The question left her mouth before she could stop it.

"A lone rider passing through. Like I said miss, I mean you no harm." His bass voice remained reserved. Although he appeared to be sincere, the profound soreness between her thighs proved otherwise. It hurt like hell.

"If you don't mind, I'd like to know who I've had the pleasure of..." He cleared his throat, "...spending my time with."

For a moment, she considered his request. He was a drifter, and so far, had kept his word. No real tragedy had befallen her. She'd never see him again. What harm could there be in revealing her name? "Megan Spawn."

His brows deepened in a curious scowl.

"Miss?" he asked with a cautionary note in his tone. His eyes studied her as if he were sizing her up.

She crossed her arms over her chest, averted his obscure gaze and feigned interest in visually locating the whereabouts of a chirping cricket nearby. "That's missus. Mrs. Reed Spawn."

He nearly fell over with robust laughter so uncontained that birds took flight, disengaging leaves from branches in their haste. Crisp, new leaves floated out of the darkening sky around them in a slow descent to mother earth.

With growing contempt, she watched him as he continued to laugh. She wondered what was so hilarious. So what if she were a married woman? The title of missus also applied to widows, which she was soon to become, barely two weeks into her twenty-third year. He didn't know her circumstance. And more importantly, it wasn't any of his concern.

He walked back to where he'd left his hat on the ground, chuckling as he went. In seething rage, she followed several feet behind.

"I fail to see the humor," she said rather snippily.

He picked up his hat and brushed the leaves off, then he turned to face her. Plopping the hat back on his head, he offered his hand. "Allow me to introduce myself. I'm Devin Spawn, your son."

Everything went black.

Dazedly, her heavy eyelids opened sometime later. She found herself leaning against his broad chest, perched on his massive thigh as he knelt with one knee in the grass. Her first thought was she must have fainted. Suddenly she became aware of blatant heat penetrating the thin layer of fabric, branding her hip. Afraid to look down, she realized she was virtually sitting on his penis. Feverish shivers of excitement and need, instead of fear and anger, sent her senses scrambling for clarity.

"Perhaps I should have said your stepson, Mother." Devin grinned, and she cringed, shooting him a 'go to hell, and this time, stay there' look that only broadened his smile.

"Take your hands off me." She came to her feet, slapped his hands away and took several steps back.

"Whatever you say...Mother." He straightened. "Although I won't complain if you care to put your hands on me again, minus the gun of course."

"Stop calling me that," she snapped, feeling her cheeks heat with shame.

* * * *

Devin turned to retrieve her dress from the tree stump, remembering the last time he rode through the area over eight years ago. His father was married to another woman—of that, he was certain. This had to be wife number three. One thing for sure, his father knew how to pick 'em.

This one was young enough to be Reed's daughter. Hell, at twenty-nine he was much older and he was Reed's first born.

"Reed married you fresh outta diapers?" He asked without looking at her as he picked up the dress.

"Not that it's any of your concern. I was eighteen when we married five years ago." Her lips drew into a thin, tight pink line.

Dress in his hand, he strolled toward her. With a few shakes, he let loose fallen leaves and whatever else may have crawled inside. His gaze traveled over her with new regard. At least she wasn't a mere child. "Are you daft, woman, out here alone, unprotected?"

"I have protection or at least, I thought I did. My gun is in the pocket of my dress." With a flippant wave of her hand, she indicated the blue calico in his tight grip.

He searched the garment pockets until he found the small pistol with a pearl handle, sized to fit the palm of a woman. He held it up with his thumb and index finger. "Protecting you from what, rabbits? That's about all this peashooter is gonna kill."

"I'm not out to kill anyone," she stated with proud condemnation. Her eyes suddenly narrowed when he stuck her pistol in his pocket.

"Where guns are concerned, it's shoot to kill. If the boys would've been with me I'd run out of lead dropping 'em like flies just to keep 'em offa you. With the way you were swimming in the river, even a preacher man would've turned a deaf ear to the holy gospel to partake in the sin 'tween those legs."

"A...a gentleman would have turned away," she chastised vehemently.

"Don't waste your breath trying to fool yourself. We both know there ain't a damn thing gentlemanly about me. You were showing the goods and I was looking 'em over."

"Well I hope you took a nice, long look, 'cause that was the last."

"Looked, touched, felt..." He brought the finger he had inserted inside her to his nose and inhaled deeply. Then swirled his tongue along it seductively, licking every inch. Her eyes widened. His lust filled eyes challenged her to look away. Finally, he added, "Smelled and tasted. My father is a helluva lucky man. You have a damn fine pussy, Mother."

"Stop calling me that," she bit out furiously. The heat on her cheeks spread to her throat.

"You don't mind my talkin' 'bout your pussy, so long as I don't call you Mother."

"Yes, no, yes, no, stop calling me Mother and stop talking about my..." She clamped her mouth shut and crossed her arms beneath her breasts in an obvious fit of outrage. The shift dipped dangerously low, stretching the thin material over the hard, pink peaks.

He quirked a brow, and his gaze rested brazenly on the bunched up mounds of flesh as he gave her a moment to finish, knowing that was one sentence going by way of the wind.

"Reed should know better than let you out of the house at night practically naked," he chastised yet kept his tone and expression unattached. This seemed to infuriate her even more from the way her eyes were burning daggers in him.

"I was properly clothed when I left. If you would have given me my dress when I asked, I would be so now."

"You didn't have a stitch on when I rode up. And with the way you were acting, didn't give a flip if anyone was around." He threw the dress at her, causing her damp hair to whip up at the abrupt burst of wind.

Beet-red skin turned to vivid scarlet under his blatant scrutiny. He watched silently as she slipped her dress over her head and encountered difficulty getting her hands through the twisted sleeves when the bulky material caught around her shoulders.

For a moment, he lost his mind, thought about offering assistance but promptly came to his senses. During her minor struggle, his gaze never strayed from the waist down. He sighed wearily, frustrated at the fact he still wanted her. She turned her back to him and gave him a nice view of her round ass through the thin shift. Somehow, she managed to work her arms through the correct holes and button the tiny green beads running down the front.

He rolled his eyes but held his tongue, annoyed by her sudden pretense at modesty. It was a bit too late. He knew his mother as intimately as his father did. Couldn't help but speculate how many others knew Mrs. Spawn, as well. He began to wonder if his father was even alive.

"How is he?"

She glanced fleetingly over her shoulder. He noted her expression suddenly changed, took on a sorrowful ambiance. After the last button was completed, she turned to face him and finally answered, "I'm grateful he lasted this long."

Mother dear thought her words would shock him, beget some sort of emotional response. He could tell she grievously disappointed. He didn't care one way or the other. As long as Reed was alive, he was going to get what he came for.

"I've heard so much about you. You're—"

"A vicious killer, a lowlife thief, Indian savage, no-account bastard, or the closest description yet, the Devil's Spawn," he finished for her.

For a quiet moment, he studied her. She simply stared back at him, as if thunderstruck by the self-description of which he was neither ashamed nor proud.

At last, she calmly stated, "I was going to say you're finally here. He's been waiting for you."

Cautiously, his eyes narrowed as she sat on the tree stump and slipped on her shoes, unsure of whether to believe her. Perhaps his father sent word, after all. If so, his gut instinct for the first time would have been wrong.

A faint smile curled her lips and the dimples on her cheeks deepened. "Would you like to meet your sisters?"

Slender hips swayed gently under the calico as she made her way to the wagon. He followed silently.

Standing next to the buckboard, she gestured inside. He rested his hands along the railing and peered into the wagon. The tops of two small, blond heads peeked out from under several blankets. If they were girls, it was sure hard to tell from the wrapped bundles.

"What's wrong with them?"

"They're asleep."

To him, they looked dead, but he kept the morbid perversity to himself. It became clear to him why she didn't run, fight, or scream. As long as they quietly slept, remained out of view, they were safe from harm.

From the corner of his eye, he admired the courage and inner strength in one so young and undeniably delicate. The way of the untamed frontier was survival. Mrs. Spawn did what she had to in order to survive, held her tongue like a trained mute while he tried to have his wicked way with her.

A pity he didn't succeed completely.

His stepmother was damned lucky though that he was the one who stumbled across her and not some other no-account murderer. Certainly she would have been raped and tortured. Dependent upon who ran across them, the girls might have been turned into Indian slaves or killed by desperados.

His gaze drifted to the sleeping bundles, doubting Mrs. Spawn would agree with his assessment as to her good fortune.

First and foremost, if he found his mother out in the woods spreading her legs for some other man beside his father, the man would be dead instantly. Present company excluded. Then, he would do something he had never done before—kill the bitch.

No one cheats a Spawn.

Her soft, melodious voice dragged him from his disturbing speculation. He turned his attention to her as she climbed onto the high seat in front of the wagon and took the reins in her hands.

* * * *

Megan caught sight of where he was looking, nowhere near her face. With a huff, she smoothed her skirt and covered her exposed ankles drawing his eyes to hers as she stared at him disapprovingly.

"I asked if you were passing through." Inwardly, she prayed he said yes with no thought of stopping by the ranch. Why else would he be there? She held her breath.

He cupped a hand to his mouth and made what sounded to her like a convincingly realistic birdcall.

She glanced at the deep blue sky, searching the canopy of tree branches, expected some sort of bird to come flying out of nowhere and rest upon his shoulder.

Much to her amazement, within seconds, an extremely large golden horse, black from the knees down, appeared and quietly made its way to his master's side. He took the dangling reins in his hand.

Devin stroked the horse's nose with a gentleness Megan found so out of place for the veritable giant. From her guess, he stood nearly seven feet tall and was endowed with a well-muscled physique and strength to match. Her extended family member appeared to be capable of bringing instant death to both man and beast with his hands alone.

Yet, strangely enough, he continued brush a hand tenderly along the horse's nose and neck until the golden animal seemed to purr like a kitten. In one smooth motion that took her by surprise yet again, Devin hopped on the horse with the grace and agility of a well-practiced rodeo rider half his size.

"Seeing how you're in a hurry to be rid of me, *Mother*." She cringed. "Let's get this over with. Lead. I'll follow."

The wagon lunged forward, and she couldn't help but be reminded of who he was and what they'd done by his use of the word "mother" as if the tingling, stickiness, and soreness between her thighs weren't reminder enough. She clamped her legs together as a shudder of lusty awareness passed through her body and more of her own juices added to his.

* * * *

Devin followed behind in silence until they neared the ranch. The little girls in the back, he assumed, were accustomed to the rough journey since they remained sound asleep. As they turned the bend leading to the front of the sprawling ranch, he noticed two saddled horses tied to the hitching post in the courtyard. His trained gaze intuitively searched the perimeter. To his immediate right was the barn and corral. Just beyond a bunkhouse and vegetable garden. In front was the well-lit, single-story plank house he had seen only once before. To his left was a grove of pecan trees and the outhouse.

He hurried to the front of the wagon, jerked on the reins and brought it to a halt.

"Who's there?" His wary eyes read her thoughts, intent on leaving her no doubt he expected the truth and would settle for nothing less.

"It's just Doctor Keeling and his assistant, Caleb Walker. The doctor comes over at least once a week to check on Reed. It's the only time the girls and I go to the river. The only fun they have since…" Her eyes misted over and her voice trailed off.

The quarter moon reached overhead, its light shining bright, radiating in her eyes. He'd be a fool to believe what he saw was genuine. Something was out of sorts when it came to his stepmother. She didn't look and certainly didn't act like the wife of a husband who was at death's door.

Then again, what the hell did he know about how wives behaved?

Over his shoulder, he glanced back at the house, then at her. The explanation was believable at least. With a golden price riding on his head, there was no space for risks.

"Get rid of them. Quick. Say a word about me, and they're dead."

She gasped. Her face turned pale.

He noticed her mouth move and waited. Nothing came out. "Go on. I'll be listening." He slapped the mare's rump, and it lunged forward. "Their lives are in your hands."

Chapter 3

As Megan wheeled the wagon in front of the house, a chilly forewarning began to roost. Her body shook with fright. What if they noticed she was nervous? What if Devin misconstrued something Caleb said? Surely he wouldn't kill them. Deep down, she knew he meant every shrill word.

Dear God, she prayed for strength.

"You're late, I was about to go search for you." Caleb Walker's frantic voice reached her from the doorway as he came barreling out of the house.

The wagon came to a creaky stop. She looked at her dearest childhood friend, and terror shook her body. The past years had been exceedingly noble to him. Caleb had grown taller, much more breathtakingly handsome and refined in his finely tailored three-piece suit. His splendid, chiseled features and exquisite deep blue eyes, along with his charm and grace, only added to what one could assume was perfection—God's true intent at the male species. In an effort to gather strength and courage, anything to keep the man that touched her heart; alive, she closed her eyes and inhaled deeply.

"I was worried about you." His voice thrummed with emotion as he practically yanked her off the wagon into his tight embrace. "You've never been this late before."

Quickly, she pushed away from Caleb and stepped back. Worried, her eyes roamed the dark shadows cloaking the various structures, looking for a sign. He was out there lurking, watching, and listening.

"You're trembling."

"I'm cold. I was swimming. My hair is wet," she rambled. To avert his questioning gaze and hide her shakiness, she fumbled with the chaotic bun at the nape of her neck. She paid no mind to the loose tendrils dancing in the light breeze around her shoulders. The back of her dress was soaked from her partially dried hair, which further aggravated the unpleasant situation.

"How does one get grass in their hair from swimming?" Caleb asked as he picked blades of grass from her tousled hair.

"Caleb, I can't answer all these questions." She swatted his hand away. An inappropriate thrill blazed through her at the picture the answer brought to her mind. *Hussy.* She hurried to the back of the buckboard. "I'm tired, cold, and wet. Please, help me with Shelby and Emma. I want to get them inside."

"Yes, yes, of course." Brows in a tight knit, he stared at her. "Are you sure you're okay?"

She could feel Devin's eyes watching her. He was near. Of that, she was certain. And if she wasn't careful, dear, sweet, worried Caleb was as good as dead. Her pulse raced.

"I'm fine, really. The girls need to get to bed, and I want to check on Reed," she reassured him after taking a calming breath.

"Very well, though next time, I'm accompanying you. It's not safe to be out by yourself."

"I'm not by myself. I have the girls with me and my gun." Her hand went to her pocket and suddenly realized it wasn't there. Devin kept it. She tried to swallow her heart back down her throat.

"Precisely why you and the girls should not be alone." He scooped up six-year-old Shelby and handed the wrapped bundle to Megan.

"Look at you." His gaze raked over her disapprovingly from head to toe. "You look ready to swoon. How would you protect yourself against a gang of outlaws? Let's not forget the reason the mountains are called Apache Mountains."

"I didn't come across either," she countered nervously. *Does one outlaw constitute a lie?* she wondered as he gathered eight-year-old Emma in his arms and followed her into the house. Who she had encountered was far worse in her mind than any red-skinned savage or ruthless band of outlaws.

The ruffian was not only dangerous and deadly, he was related. And if that was not horrendous enough, he was ruggedly handsome and kissed so sensuously, all her resistance vanished. She'd found herself not only instinctively responding, but yearning for him something fierce, which aggravated her to no end.

"Consider yourself fortunate," Caleb said as his booted foot kicked the door open. He stepped aside to let her pass first. Once inside, he kicked the door closed.

"Doctor Keeling," she called out, ignoring Caleb's ongoing rant about the dangers of a single woman traveling alone with two small children.

"In here." The portly older gentleman's soothing voice traveled from Reed's bedroom.

"I apologize for my tardiness. How is Reed?"

With Shelby cradled in her arms, Megan strolled into Reed's bedroom while Caleb left to put Emma to bed. She flashed the doctor a warm smile that quickly vanished when her gaze fell upon her husband lying motionless on the bed: skin and bones, his skin ghastly, the color of death. Yet the man had a will of iron. He clung to life with every last breath in his emaciated body, refusing to relinquish life until his only surviving son returned.

Devin Spawn, the most notorious, ruthless, double-gun cutthroat to roam the western frontier.

As luck would have it, he'd finally arrived.

What would happen now?

She knew in her heart it was the only reason Reed remained alive. He'd told her many times he wanted to see Devin one last time, set the story straight before he died. His son deserved to know the truth.

Day after day, week after week, month after month after his second wife, Ella, died, he'd stop by the Silver Nugget saloon while in town for supplies. Nursing the same mug of beer for hours on end sometimes, reminiscing with Megan while she mopped the floor, wiped the tables, or washed the dishes. Sometimes, he'd follow her outside while she did laundry.

No matter where she was, Reed would seek her out. After the first few visits, she started looking forward to his company. Reed was the only person who was truly kind to her, expected nothing in return except a sympathetic ear. Their chats continued until he unexpectedly asked her to marry him days before her eighteenth birthday.

Ecstatic at the prospect of never setting foot in the Silver Nugget again or becoming one of Jazelle's girls on her eighteenth birthday, she graciously accepted.

They left together that same night, went straight to the preacher, and never looked back.

That was, until Reed's condition became increasingly worse. Her memory and realization of what the future held also became increasingly apparent and terrifying her due to the resemblance to her past.

The enormity of Devin's arrival sent shivers rippling through her body for more reasons than the obvious. Sure, he was so utterly masculine that if most men stood beside him, they would be reduced to mere boys. The potent male heat radiating from his body was intoxicating. His silver eyes were strikingly seductive, and in a blazing fury, awakened a need in her she laid to rest long ago. The most impressive, potently virile part of him that embedded forever in her memory was beyond compare, beyond description, and stole her breath away. The thought of it trembled her heart and stimulated places she didn't even know existed with an overwhelming arousal that transcended her knowledge and dazed her consciousness.

She brushed each carnal desire, stark image, and wayward thought aside. Instead, she worried how his presence would impact Reed's condition. After all, awaiting Devin's arrival was the sole reason Reed held on. If he passed on now, what would become of the girls? Unfortunately, she had a good idea of what the future held for her, and she wanted no part of it.

What of Shelby and Emma? Who would take them in? Would they be safe? Would they end up like her, working at the Silver Nugget Saloon or upstairs in Jazelle's Place?

Doctor Keeling sat in a wooden chair beside the bed, his expression full of kindness and understanding.

"Don't fret none," he said in a comforting tone. "Doing my job. Besides, you and the girls need a break. Just wish I could come by more often to lend you a hand. Glad Caleb's here to help you out. Now, you go on and put Shelby to bed. We'll talk when you're done."

With a smile, she offered her thanks. Leaving the doctor, she carried the sleeping child into their bedroom. The room was simply furnished with two twin beds, a dresser and mirror, small table and chair, and two chests, one for each of the girls. On the wall, she hung a single shelf and filled with books. That was her contribution to the girl's education since taking over their upbringing.

* * * *

Caleb looked up at her as he pulled the covers over Emma, now sleeping snugly in the bed closest to the door. He smiled and pulled the covers back, making room for Shelby.

At the Spawn ranch often enough, he knew their sleeping arrangements. For the time being, they suited him just fine. Shelby and Emma shared one twin bed, and Megan slept in the other whenever she found the time.

"Here, let me help you," he offered, moving to take Shelby from her arms.

"Quite all right, I have her. Thank you." She moved past him and settled the small girl next to her big sister, tucking them both in.

He sighed out of frustration as he watched her kiss them both on the forehead. No matter how hard he tried, she refused his assistance. Sooner or later, she was going to need him, and he was ready. For now, he was biding his time and waiting for the inevitable. A horrid way to look at it, but such was life.

Reed was going to die any day now. And he was ready to take her husband's place in every way possible.

Take care of her, provide for the children. Oh, yes, love her the way she deserved to be loved.

From the first day laid eyes on her, a scared, bony thirteen-year-old girl who lost her family in an Indian raid, he loved her. That would never change.

If only she gave him a chance to make up for what his parents had done. The day his father found them doing more than playing in the horse stable, his mother shipped him off to Europe. Not once did he forget her, stop loving her, nor stop dreaming of the day they would eventually marry. News of Megan marrying a man old enough to be her father turned those dreams into nightmares.

After completing his medical education abroad, he returned to Tejas a year ago when his own father fell ill. He intended to relocate to Boston after his father later died and begin his own practice, along with a close friend he met in school. Reed suffering his first stroke halted his plans. He remained in Tejas in order to be of assistance, help in any way he could as Megan cared for her ailing husband.

When Reed suffered his second stroke, he vowed he wouldn't leave without her, aware it was a matter of time before she was a widow. Months later, he was still waiting, his patience running thin.

Soon, he kept telling himself, she would be his bride, then his lover.

For now, he had to settle on being her friend.

He closed the bedroom door and locked it as she crossed the room. She gave him a look of 'not again' as though expecting his weekly 'will you marry me?' plea.

"Listen to me. You've lost so much weight you're almost as gaunt as Reed. Your dress is practically falling off you." He hoped she would see the concern in his expression, the heartfelt desire and willingness to take care of her and the girls, and come to her senses. Intentions of a good friend, or any way she would have him. Unwilling to watch her suffer, he wanted to be there for her.

"Thanks. You're much too kind," she said wearily. She straightened the scooped neckline hanging off her shoulder, causing the front of her bodice to dip dangerously low and reveal the swell of her taut bosom sitting high on her chest.

"Wasn't meant as a compliment," he said roughly, struggling to resist the pathetic urge to look down and try to catch a peek at her breasts.

"None taken."

"Those circles under your eyes are more noticeable. You look ready to fall over any moment from exhaustion or malnutrition. Take your pick. Why don't you admit you need help?"

"And you're the one to help me?"

"Yes. If you'll stop being stubborn."

"What would your mother say? That woman hates me."

"Something she'll have to deal with. All that really matters is how I feel about you."

"Not tonight. I'm tired. Doc is waiting for me." She closed her eyes, and released a heavy sigh.

"Then when?" He grabbed her by the shoulders, because she really did look about ready to fall over from exhaustion. The movement shifted her neckline lower, and just like a man, he used the opportunity to glimpse the pink tips of her pale breasts, visible through the low, gaping neckline. He felt a stirring in his groin. His heated voice suddenly took on a strained quality. "When can we discuss our future?"

"Lower your voice, please." She glanced at the sleeping girls. "You'll wake them," she whispered.

"We both know after they spent the afternoon swimming, they'll sleep so deeply, a tornado wouldn't wake them."

They both knew it was true. Even now, he could hear Shelby's light snoring. There was no way she could get around it—he knew the running of her household backwards and forwards. Each morning he came by to take the girls to school. Then he returned for coffee and grown-up conversation afterwards. He was certain she enjoyed the pleasure of his company, probably more than she dared admit. Always a chivalrous gentleman, he kept it innocuous, but tonight was different. He was unable to brush off that sense of doom he felt when she didn't return on time.

"Tonight, I'll take your advice and get to sleep as soon as you and Doc leave. I promise." She tried to shrug out from under his grasp, but he held his ground and tightened his grip slightly.

"You know good and well you'll constantly wake up throughout the night to check on Reed. The man's practically de—"

"What a horrid thing to say," she snapped, cutting him short.

"Forgive me." His hands slid down her slender arms, then released her. "My patience is on edge tonight. When you didn't return, I was so worried about you. That's all. Why don't I return tonight after I see Doc into town? That way, you can get rest, and I'll watch Reed."

"Caleb, we're not kids any longer." She looked up at him.

He saw a sadness in her eyes as if she wanted to cry. A bitter reminder of their childhood innocence, their lost youth stolen. A pitiful feeling he shared but never revealed. He wanted to take hold of her until the pain and disappointment subsided and make up for those lost years.

"What would people say? It wouldn't be right."

Out of frustration, he exhaled deeply. "Meg, I'm here all the time. Practically everyone in town knows how I feel about you."

"I'm a married woman. What is Dr. Keeling thinking, the two of us locked away in my bedroom while he sits with my sick husband?"

"Doc knows Reed's condition. Knows my intentions are honorable. He doesn't gossip."

"Does this fall under doctor/patient confidentiality?" Her voice held a touch of amusement, and he concluded he was finally getting through to her.

He grinned. "You can call it that if you wish."

"You're incorrigible. What will I do with you?" She shook her head and amusement rang in her voice.

"It's what I can do with you that matters." There was no mistaking the sultriness in his tone.

"Not tonight, Caleb. Tomorrow."

"You promise." The pink flush on her cheeks made his blood boil and his chest puff with hope.

"You're impossible." She swatted her hand across his chest playfully.

He caught it and held it close to his heart. He wanted her to hear his heart beating for her.

"I don't know how you ever passed medical school," she said, "with your mind always in your britches."

"Passed Female Anatomy with an all-time high score, thanks to you and my britches."

"Glad to be of service." She smiled sheepishly.

Gently, his fingers nudged her chin upward. He focused on her soft, hazel eyes as they glimmered with longing. She may have been teasing, but he knew she was remembering being his first patient so long ago, just as he was. How could her body ever forget his touch, his hands caressing her young, developing breasts, his naive fingers on her unsullied flesh exploring every heated inch and the warmth of his lips on hers anymore than he could?

"Any time you're ready for your exam, I'll be glad to demonstrate my professional skills," he offered softly.

"Perhaps tomorrow. For now, let me pass. Doc is waiting on me," she said quickly, ducking away from him.

"Till tomorrow, milady," he whispered close to her ear as he leaned over and opened the door. He bowed and waved her through. Caleb immediately contemplated removing that godawful dress. Sparks of blazing arousal leapt from his cock to his balls at the thought of what he would do next.

"After you drop off the girls at school, we'll talk."

"Talk?" He jerked upright, glaring at her back as she made her way to Reed's room.

For a moment, he really thought they'd made headway. Tomorrow sounded promising. Now, he wasn't so sure tomorrow wouldn't end up like any other morning—leaving him stonewalled and blue-balled.

* * * *

Megan chuckled quietly, aware Caleb would be deeply offended if she laughed outright. She loved him too much to ever cause him any amount of distress. However, there was no room in her life to give him what he wanted. At least, not now. Her smile fainted once again as she stepped inside Reed's bedroom.

Doctor Keeling moved toward her. With one last look over his shoulder at the sleeping invalid a breath shy from death, he turned to her and softly murmured, "Still no change, I'm afraid. Continue to keep his last days comfortable as best you can."

Caleb came up right behind her. He remained silent as he stared at the frail man's body. She took comfort knowing he was there.

"You've been doing a mighty fine job. He's clean, no bed sores, and you're keeping plenty liquids in him. Reed's a lucky man to have you for..." Doc paused, cast Caleb a fleeting glance, then smiled at her. "...a nurse."

"Thank you, Doc." She feigned a smile in return. The entire town probably thought Caleb Walker was her bedmate. For the second time tonight, she may as well spread her legs, and this time, let Caleb take her. Get it over with. At least then, he would finish what he started long ago. Perhaps the rumors, or more like half-truths, would end.

"The girls and I work hard to ensure his comfort. I would ask you to stay while I make a fresh pot of coffee, but they were having so much fun, we stayed later than usual. It's left us all tired, though. I hope you understand." She felt a wee bit guilty for blaming the girls for her wanton misdeed, but they couldn't tell from her sincere apologetic expression.

"Perfectly. You get plenty of rest." He followed her past the kitchen into the great room.

"Come, Caleb, let the young lady sleep tonight." He gave Caleb a wink and patted him affectionately on the back.

Caleb took one look at her and grinned ear to ear. She felt her cheeks heat from embarrassment. The man must want everyone to suspect they were more than friends. In a way, they were.

"Goodnight, gentlemen," she bid cheerfully after they exchanged a few pleasantries and mounted their horses. She remained on the porch for a moment to watch them ride away. Their shadows, one tall and refined and the other short and rotund, disappeared around the bend before she returned inside.

Shaking her head at the outrageousness, Caleb didn't even try to hide the fact he would return in the morning to take the girls to school or clear up the doctor's esoteric hint as to why she was not getting enough rest.

It wasn't as if her reputation was untarnished. Everyone knew she used to work at Jazelle's, though not as an upstairs girl. But that didn't stop men from making crude remarks on those few occasions she ventured into town alone, or the way women turned their noses as she passed. Probably the reason Dr. Keeling assumed she allowed Caleb liberties. The thought made her blood boil.

Older and wiser now, the thought of escaping into another marriage out of necessity was not appealing. The last thing she needed was to be indebted to another man, even one she cared for.

Never again.

Besides, it seemed that whole sex thing between a man and a woman was more painful than it was worth. There had to be something wrong with those rare women at Jazelle's who seemed to find pleasure in an act so animalistic. On many occasions, she witnessed the horses and other farm animals copulating. Though the act itself was rather interesting, nature's way of bringing new life into the world, the animals didn't appear to enjoy it. Climb on, climb off. It was all over in seconds.

Perhaps Mrs. Walker was right all along: carnal knowledge was work of the devil.

That didn't explain kissing. Kissing was different, very different. It made her weak and breathy, ache in some places and wet in others. Yet it always left her unsatisfied somehow, made her yearn for something more, something just out of reach that she could never seem to grasp. Exactly what that was, she hadn't figured it out just yet. Like when she inserted her fingers in her vagina, it made her skin tingle and her pulse race, nothing more.

But when Devin touched her...

Dear Lord, she had to forget him, put him out of her mind completely.

Think only of her and Shelby and Emma. What would happen to them after Reed passed? Marriage wasn't exactly an option she was partial to. No, instead, she planned to take the girls and make a new life elsewhere. Start fresh and independently. Somewhere no one ever heard of Megan Adams or Mrs. Reed Spawn.

Maybe even change their names. At least, that was the plan after her debt was paid off. An ordeal she was not looking forward to.

As usual, the house turned quiet after the girls were tucked in. Collecting Caleb's cup and saucer from the long rectangular dining table in the center of the great room, she left them in the copper tub she used as a sink. As she retrieved the doctor's coffee cup from the small table next to Reed's bed, she watched the gentle rise and fall of his chest. The movement was so imperceptible. Sadly, she wondered how many days were left for the once-robust man.

Though she never loved him as a husband, she loved him dearly in a fatherly sense.

Reed was always there for her. Never asked for anything in return. He opened his home despite everything that happened. He trusted her with the care of his two daughters.

The third and final stroke a couple of months ago left him unable to move or speak and only able to open his eyes and stare in silence at the world passing by.

She missed their conversations over coffee while they sat on the porch and watched the girls play in the yard. Missed his generous spirit and sense of humor. The unconditional acceptance.

The comfortable arrangement was ideal. She truly looked forward to standing by his side and helping as the girls matured into prosperous young ladies. With the understanding it meant relinquishing any chance of ever falling in love, getting married, and having a family of her own.

Reed, Shelby, and Emma—they were her family now.

She was happy and content with her choice, for as long as it lasted.

Ready to pass out from exhaustion, she stepped into the kitchen with Doc's half-empty coffee cup in hand. Her featherbed called out to her. As she rounded the edge of the kitchen counter, her gaze caught sight of the imposing dark silhouette filling the opened front entryway. Devin entered the house so quietly it caught her off guard. Her heart skipped a beat, and the cup slipped out of her hand, breaking in three as it hit the floor. Cold coffee splattered the front of her calico.

He actually needed to dip his head to clear the doorframe. His powerful demeanor, part animal, part diabolical, and one hundred percent male, undersized the house instantly.

Her eyes roamed the towering length of him as he bolted the door. Cloaked in a dark and dangerous mystique, she couldn't pull her gaze from him.

As he turned, the dim lit kerosene lantern hanging over the table did little to reveal the features hidden behind a full beard and mustache of cinnamon brown that blended gloriously into a thatch of wavy, shoulder length hair that spilled out of his hat that concealed his penetrating silver eyes she remembered so well.

She continued to stare. Luckily for her—or was it unlucky?—his perfectly-lined, ruby lips were in plain sight and invoked the recent memory of their riverside amour. Her knees went weak, yet she could not stop her gaze from drifting over every manly muscle from his broad shoulders, flat abdomen to his massive thighs, and long legs, straight down to his large, moccasin-clad feet. She finally rested her gaze on the most riveting part of him that inundated her sensibilities, shattered her control, tempted her beyond reason, and made her conscious of her own compromised femininity.

* * * *

Devin's entire body tightened with a familiar ache at the intense way she stared at him. He felt like a hungry wolverine who hadn't eaten in ages…or been properly fucked. He clenched his teeth and fought to stifle the tension building deep inside his loins. No, he did not come here to fuck his stepmother. No matter how much it appeared she wanted or needed it, and he sure as hell wanted to give it to her. There was only one reason he was here. Then, he would high-tail it out of Dodge.

He needed to hear his father tell him in his own words. Why? Why did he give Devin away? Why had he never wanted him?

"Where is he?" His tone impatient and rough, too rough to sit well with a man who prided himself on always being in control, absent of emotion, and bound by no familial ties.

She motioned toward the open bedroom door behind her.

Without a word or so much as a glance, he strode past her. Silently, like a pillar of cold, hard stone, he soaked in the sight of the motionless, dying body lying on the bed.

His father.

The man who brought him into this wretched world.

The very same man who gave him away the day he was born.

He felt…what did he feel? Nothing. No, he felt cheated. This man, practically on the other side of death's door, could tell him nothing.

He'd ridden two weeks straight, crossed the desolate desert plains, scoured mountains, went without sleep and food to reach the territory of Tejas in time to stare at a corpse.

"May I get you anything?" Megan asked softly from near the doorway.

"Leave us," he ordered quietly. He heard the rustle of skirts, and as she turned to leave, he added, "Close the door."

Chapter 4

Megan awoke with a start. With a jagged swipe of her fingers, she wiped the sleep from her eyes. She glanced out the lace-covered window. A pale resemblance of dawn streaked the fading blue. That meant only one thing. She overslept. Hastily, she jumped out of the small, twin-sized bed. When was the last time, if ever, she'd overslept?

She rushed to the dresser to find something to wear. On the cold floor, she stood in her bare feet, rummaging through the dresser drawers. She caught sight of her reflection in the looking glass, and paused.

Seldom did she ever take a moment to consider her appearance.

Barely touching the dark circles under her eyes with her fingertips, she frowned. The crinkling furrow did little to help the bleakness tainting her once creamy complexion and youthful good looks. She should be so vain to believe Caleb whenever he remarked her beauty was unrivaled.

Of course, he'd told her the very opposite last night. And judging from her appearance this morning, he was right.

With her palms screening her cavernous cheeks, she felt much older than her twenty-three years. Her gaze dropped to the small swell in front of her sleeping gown. As slender as a willow, her figure was that of a girl much younger. She lacked the voluptuous curves she always wished her body would develop. The red robin had taken its sweet time to call, waiting until she was fourteen. She cupped what was left of her small breasts. They'd lost some of their roundness during the past months. She wondered if the reason she never quite fully developed was her woman-time only flowed every other month.

Taking a cautionary glance at the girls' reflection in the mirror, her pulse quickened. She lifted the hem of her gown above her hips once she was satisfied they were still sound asleep. Her head tilted slowly from side to side. She examined the sparsely covered mound between her narrow hips.

There was more pale flesh than golden curls. She couldn't help but ponder what he thought when he looked at her.

As if her body remembered the pleasure of last night, his fingers stroking her intimate flesh, she felt her pussy throb with arousal. An unmistakable heat rushed through her veins. She felt her nipples harden and brush against the front of her gown. They ached for his touch.

Biting her lower lip, she raised her gaze to the sleeping bundles in the mirror once more and tentatively lowered one of her hands. She parted the pouting lips with her fingers, revealing the inner flesh, slightly red and still sore from last night's unpleasant incident, the brazen assault on her shattered senses and an illicit assault on her willing body.

"*...even a preacher man would've turned a deaf ear to the holy gospel to partake in the sin 'tween those legs.*"

His heated words echoed in her mind. A thrill of the forbidden washed over her at the mere thought of his huge cock, hard and long, yearning to be inside her. He'd been unable to resist the carnal temptation he said she presented, or how he struggled to restrain the depth of his overwhelming passion as he strained to pierce her flesh with the bulky, flared tip of his cock. The memory of those few minutes lying in the grass made her juices pour forth.

"Dear God," she breathed on a gasp, releasing the gown abruptly and shutting her eyes. Why did she feel this way?. How could her body respond so easily by just by thinking of the man? How could she warm at the thought of his touch, and tingle and moisten at the sight of him?

She braced her hands on the dresser, breathing in ragged pants, and she stared at her flushed reflection. There was no way she desired him, would not allow herself to desire him. He was Reed's son, for Christ's sake.

Evil. The epitome of pure evil.

There was a slim chance she could very well be carrying his baby. No innocent herself, she knew where babies came from and was well aware the tragedies of bearing a fatherless child.

At Jazelle's, she learned a thing or two from the women about preventing pregnancy. Later, when she was alone, she would mix her herbs and wash herself of his seed. She'd have done it as soon as she returned home, but conceiving was highly unlikely. She hadn't had a flow in several months due to her recent bout of stress-induced weight loss from the lack of eating properly or perhaps her failure get much sleep. What little food they had, she made sure the girls ate first. Often, that meant she did without meat, even if she was lucky enough to shoot a bird or trap a rabbit that day.

She picked up the brush to try and tame the unruly ringlets that had become a frizzy, tangled mass during the night. With another glance in the mirror, she put the brush down, deciding she didn't have time to mess with her hair when the cow needed to be milked, water hauled, eggs collected, and breakfast made before the girls were off to school. Hastily, she gathered her hair in a loose knot atop her head and searched through the open drawer for something suitable to wear.

All her clothes were threadbare from too many washings and no longer fit properly. She didn't even have time to make new clothes for her and the girls. Even if she did, there was no money to buy material.

Sadly, she sighed. Had her life truly come to this?

She was once a happy, precocious little girl with parents rich only in love for her, and a younger brother whom she adored. She'd been taken in by Reed, who provided security and hope for a future. Soon, she would be left vulnerable. Without the protection provided by a marriage license. Prey to any man. One thing was clear. If she didn't move away, with her reputation, she would definitely be in need of a bigger gun.

Unshed tears welled in her eyes at the memory of her long lost family and her current situation. She held her chin high. "No use thinking about them. Ain't going to bring them back. Nor change things," she whispered to her reflection with a bold gleam rising in her eyes.

To persevere, she had to be strong, refuse to submit to helplessness or hopelessness.

If she survived the savagery of an Indian raid, living with an overbearing, fanatical religious simpleton, four years in a bordello, five years married to a man, she didn't love, raising two kids on her own and caring for an invalid husband, then by God Almighty, she could survive anything.

Her choice for the day was an oversized, faded green blouse and brown skirt. On her way out to the privy, she shot a glance at the closed door to Reed's bedroom. By the time she reached the barn doors, her pulse raced. In less than an hour and a half, Caleb would arrive like clockwork to ride the girls to school.

She squatted on the low stool beside the milking cow, both hands reaching out and latched onto swollen udders. The bucket started to fill with milk while she speculated why Devin hadn't already left. Perhaps he intended to leave after breakfast. She crinkled her forehead as she tried to hold on to that last shred of hope.

The cow snorted and swatted its tail as Megan's fingers twisted and squeezed its udders distractedly.

Their small town was just like others. Gossip and tales of Devin Spawn's exploits ran rampant. Whenever a bank was robbed or man shot down, the news hit the wires, and the saloon filled with the wildest and most gruesome stories ever told. Besides herself, no one knew the notorious outlaw was Reed's son. No one probably would believe it if Reed himself stood on the church steps on Sunday morning, rang the bell, and announced to anyone who would listen the cold-blooded murderer was his flesh and blood.

A genteel, honest, law-abiding citizen who helped his fellow neighbor whether he was asked or not, if he saw a need, someone struggling or going without, Reed Spawn was there.

It wasn't that Reed was ashamed of Devin—more like he was ashamed of himself. Guilt-ridden, he held himself accountable for the misfortune befallen his first born.

During weekly visits to the Silver Nugget, Reed confided his inner most thoughts. He spoke of Devin and the love he still held for his boy's mother, Grace, the true love of his life. Sometimes, he would also speak fondly of his second wife, Ella.

Devin's unflinching eyes, brute strength, quick draw, and cold heartedness crowded every claim. Not one person, including Reed, ever mentioned how breathtakingly handsome he was or the overwhelming power of his sexuality, the sensuousness of his mouth or softness of his hands. Then again, if he stole your horse or bank safe full of money, or filled a neighbor with lead, a person may tend to slight those trifling qualities.

* * * *

Dressed and ready for school, Shelby and Emma were ordered to quietly sit at the table like good little girls and finish their breakfast. Meanwhile, she absently tended the garden, waiting for Caleb to appear.

Every few seconds, she'd glance at the dirt road on the side of the barn, searching for a cloud of dust, a sure sign a hoarse approached. If Devin's threat still held salt, Caleb's fate more than likely continued to rest in her hands.

For once, she wished Caleb was not a man of his word. Since he took his biblical name to heart, it was highly unlikely.

The thought sent a chill down her spine. If rumors were true, could Reed's son be heartless, shoot and kill an innocent man without recourse or provocation, with no regard for human compassion or life itself?

Her blood ran cold.

* * * *

Devin's eyelids fluttered as his ears picked up the faint sound of movement across the plank floorboards. He sensed he was not alone. His eyes remained closed and breathing steady as the faint sound neared.

Devin had settled back low in the armchair next to Reed's bed. Sometime in the wee hours of the morning, he had fallen asleep, his. arms dangling over the sides, long legs stretched out in front of him.

The vibration was too faint for a grown man, and the scent wasn't that of a woman. Certain it wasn't Megan, his right hand slowly journeyed to his pistol, fingers curling around the butt.

In a flash, he bolted upright in the chair, colt cocked, out of leather, and by his side. His gut wrenched at the sight in front of him. One more second, and his two sisters, whom he'd completely forgotten about, seeing as how he only saw the tops of their heads last night, would have been dead.

He gulped down the lump in his throat and returned the gun to its rightful place. Unaccustomed to being in such close proximity to children, for once, he didn't know what to do or say. He stared at them, overwhelmingly dumbfounded.

The bigger girl sat on the foot of the bed, staring wide-eyed at him as though she was ready to bolt at any moment. The smaller one stood by his side, her arm frozen mid-air as though she was about to touch his whiskers.

His brows drew together as the little one brought both hands to her mouth and started to giggle. The other one looked on warily.

The hand-hewn wood creaked under the tension as he clutched the chair arms in a death grip. The older one, with long, blonde pigtails, a button nose, and tight-lipped with familiar silver eyes looked older and wiser beyond her minimal years. The youngster, with a head full of silken curls, big round blue eyes, cute little nose and cherubic cheeks, appeared the opposite of what was considered proper for nineteenth-century children. Obedient. There was little calm and quiet to the bubbly child, who beamed with a naughty and rebelliousness spirit in her eyes.

These two tiny creatures were his half-sisters.

His gaze narrowed as the oldest continued her appraisal with the intensity of a hawk.

The smallest was the first to speak, and she did so with a guileless exuberance that he found unnerving. "Megan says you're our brother. My best friend in the whole wide world has a brother. They play together. Will you play with me?"

"Shelby," Emma's small voice rang out, chastising her younger sister and drawing her attention, albeit temporarily. "He's too big." Her eyes swept over him with an air of disapproval, and she quickly concluded, "And too old."

With a slight tilt of his head, he glanced in Emma's direction, raising a brow.

"I don't mind, Emma." Shelby moved closer to Devin's side, and when her pudgy palm landed on his hand, he stiffened.

Damn it if the little girl wasn't scaring the living shit out of him. He quickly wondered if this was how other men felt in his presence. For the first time in his life, he understood their unease.

"He'd be good for climbing trees."

His gaze jumped from one girl to the other while they discussed his merits between themselves, as if he wasn't even in the room. He wished he wasn't.

"Megan says he won't be round long 'nough."

"We can play hide-n-seek while he's here."

"He's visiting Pawpaw, not you."

Devin noticed the little girl's disposition changed instantly. Her bottom lip puffed out. Her big, blue eyes cut to her father, lying eerily still on the large bed.

"He's sick." Her innocent voice sounded both pained and worried, yet there was a touch of hope glistening in her eyes even he could comprehend.

"He's dying," Emma corrected Shelby in a remarkably stern tone. She pointed in Devin's direction. "And he's leaving, so don't go getting used to the idea of a brother."

Very little escaped Devin's intuitiveness, and there was a hurt so deep in the girl, it drowned the childhood right out. A troubling so intense for one so young, it showed in the stiffness in her form, harsh sound of her voice, and in the dark aura emanating from her stone-cold heart. Was he describing the young girl who shared the color of his eyes, or himself? The likeness was uncanny.

A large, round tear formed in Shelby's sky-blue eyes. "You goin' way?"

Devin watched the tear slide gently down her pink cheek until it trailed down her chin, then fell, leaving a small wet spot on the front of her yolk-colored dress. He glanced at Emma, sitting with her hands crossed daintily in her lap, a challenge in her eye as though daring him to deny.

He faced Shelby and replied with a single nod.

"Told ya, Shelby." Emma's face radiated with smug satisfaction as a new, bigger tear formed in Shelby's eye. "They all leave."

Devin watched Emma with an intense regard and realized she wouldn't stop the torment until her younger sibling was left as bereft as she. At that moment it came to him, he was clearly a new pawn in an old game. A game of torment she probably used often.

"Damnation, I've heard enough." He rose out of his seat, and the one called Shelby bolted out the door.

"He said a soap word," Shelby screamed over and over as she ran through the house.

"Don't tell," Emma called out after Shelby, but it was too late, as the swift girl had already thrown open the front door and dashed outside.

His full attention was riveted on Emma as she slowly swung her legs off the mattress. She stood at the end of the bed. Her hands gripped the round knob on the end of the short bedpost.

"You're not afraid of me." Now that they were alone, she didn't have to put up a brave front for her little sister, and he could tell she was clearly terrified.

She hesitated for a moment. He could almost see her mulling over whether or not to tell the truth. Slowly, she shook her head.

"Why not?" He took a step closer.

Her head drew back and she looked way, way up at him until she had to take two steps backward.

After a big gulp, she confided, "Cause you're in trouble. Shelby's a squealer. She's a tellin' Megan you said a soap word. Then, you'll get it."

He laughed, which seemed to confuse the little girl. Apparently, punishment for uttering a "soap word" was severe enough that even he should be shaking in his moccasins. "What of your misdeed?"

She stared at him in wide-eyed wonder.

"You were told to stay out of this room." He gathered at least that much from the girls' effort to keep their shaky introduction private.

Her eyes narrowed in defiance.

"It's my home, and you can't tell me what to do," she shouted.

In a stern tone meant to intimidate, not frighten the child, he ordered, "Leave, now."

She glanced at her father. Reed's eyes flickered. "No," she shouted defiantly.

"Get out of here before I pick you up by your pigtails and toss you out the window," he said with a bit more emphasis. To prove his point, he took a step closer and reached for her ponytail.

He chuckled as Emma ran out of the house, screaming for Megan. Flicking his wrist, he closed the door. This time he locked it. He resumed his seat and took Reed's hand. Despite his father's eyes being closed, Devin began where he left off last night, recounting the less gruesome and noteworthy misadventures in the wilderness.

* * * *

"I told you girls, best stay out of his way while he's here. Calm down, Emma." Megan brushed wayward strands of hair off the quivering child's forehead in an attempt to settle her nerves. She understood all too well just what effect the virile bushwhacker had on the female psyche. What she didn't know was how it seemed to transcend through the generations.

"You gonna make him eat soap, Megan?" Shelby yanked on her skirt, looking up at her eagerly, eyes full of expectation.

The sound of hooves turned them around. Caleb was trotting around the bend.

Megan dropped to her knees, gathering the girls in her embrace. "Now girls, we aren't supposed to breathe a word of this to Caleb. Remember what I told you earlier?"

The girls nodded in unison, acknowledging their brother's visit was to remain a secret, even after he left. Megan promised that if neither girl spoke a word to anyone, in one month, each would receive a half-pound of rock candy. As they licked their lips and their eyes took on a greedy quality, she was sure they would keep their word.

With a nervous glance toward the front door, Megan stood and shook the dust from her skirt. She brushed a few wayward strands of hair behind her ear, and prayed silently for a quick departure.

Her praying was disturbed midway when Shelby yanked harder on her skirt. "But Megan, he said a soap word."

She managed a nervous smile. "Not to worry, Shelby. He doesn't know the house rules. I'll speak to him. Okay?"

"Okay!" She nodded happily, as if satisfied at least he was going to get a good talking to, and not she or Emma for a change.

Both girls ran up to meet Caleb as he dismounted. He hugged and kissed them both as they squealed with delight, the blatant display of affection conveying equally.

"Good morning, Caleb. If you don't mind, the girls need to get to school early this morning."

With Shelby propped in one arm and holding Emma by the hand with the other, he sauntered to the garden. Megan knelt down and began to yank swiftly at the weeds, desperate to appear occupied.

"No time for coffee this morning?" His tone was casual, yet the suggestive undertone was clear, reminding her of last night's conversation as he gave her a quick wink.

"Afraid not. The girls are ready. Right, girls?" The hint was apparent, and she dreaded what would happen when he returned shortly, expecting if not coffee, then a whole lot more.

In unison, they both nodded and replied with a quick and unusually polite, "Yes, Uncle Caleb."

"Very well, if higher learning is their pursuit, who am I to dawdle?"

He placed Shelby in the front of the saddle first, then lifted Emma up and sat her directly behind her sister before remounting. The girls were small enough to easily fit in front of him.

With a lusty gleam in his eye, stirring a part of Megan that had no business being stirred, he tipped the brim of his hat, turned his reins, and off they went.

Breathing a sigh of relief, she relaxed the tight-fisted grip on her skirt she hadn't even realized she held.

* * * *

The distinct sound of a rider garnered his attention. Devin watched the friendly interaction between his father's wife, his father's children, and another man from the kitchen window. Not just any man, one he deemed too handsome for his own good. He was the same fellow that dashed out of the house last night and threw his arms around Megan when she rode up.

A bile bitter taste rose in his mouth as his lips tensed with scorn.

Blond hair and blue eyes were wasted on men, better served on a woman for when a man looked into her sultry eyes while he fucked her. Pretty Boy was too much of a dandy, clean and proper, dressed in an Eastern-style suit complete with vest and tie. He was out of place in the untamed frontier. Same as an Indian in a loincloth would be in the big city. This was where manhood was based on how tough a man was, how fast he could draw, and how much whiskey he could drink. From the looks of it, one shot of rot would do Pretty Boy in.

Once again, proof God didn't exist—worthless good looks on an even more worthless man.

Just then, Megan walked through the front door and paused in her tracks when she noticed he was leaning against the kitchen counter. His deceptive, mellow stance didn't quite fit the bitter reproach he felt.

"I..." From the way she stammered, Devin figured she knew he'd at least witnessed the other man's departure. "Would you like breakfast?" She reached for the egg basket on the table. "How do you take your eggs?"

"I'm not hungry."

He couldn't remember exactly when he'd eaten his last good meal. Aside from what he scrounged during his trek to Tejas, it was probably two weeks ago. Awakening to find little girls staring him down, his father's condition no better, and now, Pretty Boy eyeing his father's wife rendered all thoughts of food pointless. The bitterness still lingered on his tongue and wrenched his innards.

"Coffee? I can make a fresh pot." She hurried to the pot sitting on the stove. "Won't take but a minute."

"Maybe later. I'm going for a ride." He took two steps past her and stilled when she shouted unexpectedly for him to wait.

A nervous energy had her rushing into Reed's room. Puzzled, he watched her kneel before a wooden chest sitting in the corner of the room.

It seemed she located what she was searching for, a sealed letter Reed wrote before he fell ill. She briefly explained how he told her about it after his first stroke and her promise to give it to Devin if he showed up. When she handed it to him, she asked if he wanted her to read it. He looked at her coldly, stuffed it in his pocket, and walked away.

On the way outside, he cursed her to hell and back and felt a twinge, a very minor twinge, of remorse when he noted his horse, Deuce, had already been supplied with oats and fresh water.

For half a sliver of a woman, she possessed unparalleled nerve and courage. She'd assumed he was not only illiterate, but deaf and blind to not notice the other man and offer no explanation as to why the good doctor's assistant behaved as though he retained ownership of the family while Reed lay dying inside.

There was one sure thing he knew about women—the effect they had on a man. That sinful look a man gets in his eye when all he wants to do is bend her over, throw up her skirts, and burrow so deep into her snow-colored mounds that no one would be able to find him until the first defrost of spring. Hell, it was spring, and Pretty Boy definitely wanted to be buried.

And Devin was more than willing to make his wish come true. Bury him six foot under, that is.

* * * *

Devin had been gone no less than thirty minutes by the time Caleb returned. As usual, she heard him waltz into the Spawn home as though he lived there. He smiled, charming as ever, as Megan exited Reed's room, holding a plate with a half-empty bowl of vegetable broth.

"How about that cup of coffee?" he asked, tossing his brown Stetson over his shoulder. It latched onto a peg of the hat rack near the door. He settled into an armless chair at the table and his gaze trailed over her boldly, appreciatively.

Megan felt the simmer of sexual awareness deep in her womb. The sheer potency of his maleness stroked the long-forgotten fire Devin awakened. She was shocked how readily her body now stirred with sensuality, when only this time yesterday, the presence of strikingly good-looking Caleb purely warmed her heart.

She cleared her throat and stepped over to the sink. Her face flushed with embarrassment. She felt the heat coursing through her veins at the unmistakable attraction.

"Caleb, there is nothing better I'd like to do all day than sit around with you drinking coffee. But Reed needs his morning bath," she replied calmly.

"Let's skip the coffee and go straight to what we both long for," he suggested. His voice was low, filled with wicked intent as he made his way to the small kitchen.

Stunned by his boldness, she swirled around. A shiver of alarm raced through her. Her gaze darted toward Reed's bedroom door, as if expecting him to barge out and defend her honor in light of the other man's crude remark.

With that same boyishly wicked grin she had seen numerous times in the past, he was there, trapping her between his arms against the sink. A familiar lust shone in his eyes as he peered down at her, only inches from her upturned face.

"It's been too long, Megan," he said softly. "I've been a very patient man. I've not laid a hand on you since…"

His voice trailed off. She gasped when he lifted her tiny frame effortlessly, sitting her on the edge of the counter.

She felt the arousal emanating from the only true love of her life. Try as she might, she could not ignore the answering sensations surging through her quivering body. The need in his beautiful blue eyes weakened her resolve, her strength to resist the carnal temptation of her heathen flesh.

"Please, Meg," he pleaded. His warm lips brushed over her cheek and along the delicate curve of her throat, making her moan softly. He stood between her legs, pressing his upper body into hers. One hand cupped her buttocks, grinding the thickness of his arousal into her pussy lips, the heat penetrating the layers of fabric and sending a jolt of sinuous vibration coursing through her veins. His other hand traveled beneath the layers, searing her skin. Through her stockings, she felt the heat of his fingers running over her calves and inching upwards.

His gaze darkened with lust. His hands smoothed up her bare thighs. "You're not wearing pantalets."

"Caleb," she breathed with arousal, but in her mind, she begged him to stop. For more reasons than one, this was wrong. Yet her body arched into his. She felt his hand touch the skin of her upper thigh, and she parted her legs even wider, allowing him full access.

"Oh, yes." He groaned roughly into the base of her neck, kissing and licking the skin. His cock throbbed against her sensitive tissue. She gasped when his fingers fondled the silken curls over her mound. "Oh, God, how I've missed you," he struggled to speak, his fingers lowering to the slick crack. Her thick, creamy essence coated his fingers, which teased the outer folds of her pussy.

She whimpered, fighting the urge to push against his hand. She lost. Her aching pussy, drenched with anticipation, wanted him there. Her hips shifted upward, sliding his fingers along the swollen folds, closer to the waiting entrance.

Something that sounded like rough words or a primitive groan escaped his throat. He buried his head against her neck and suckled on the responsive tendons. Excitement flared inside her. He recalled that always made her nipples pucker. Her breasts ached for his mouth. She grew dazed when he parted the female folds, and a thumb circled her engorged clit. Megan arched, moaning and thrusting against his hand. Her juices coated his fingers even more, and her cunt throbbed at his intimate touch. She felt him trace the outline of her channel, probing, preparing for entry.

His breath was hot against the sensitized skin on her neck. Wildly wicked sensations ripped through her body, pulsating from her wet channel to her swollen breasts and hard nipples that ached for his touch. Megan gasped at the wondrous melting sensation of his finger nudging her entrance. He teased and tempted her beyond reason, a trace inside sanity.

That was all she needed.

One last flicker of sensibility reminded her she loved Caleb too much to put him in danger. Despite how it would hurt and disappoint him, not to mention confuse him. She had to put a stop to what was happening. The madness.

"No," she shouted with a strangled breath, easily pushing him away in stunned bewilderment. She hopped off the counter quickly and hurried across the room on wobbly legs. She stood on the other side of the table, trembling, desperate to put as much distance between them as the room afforded. "No, Caleb, we can't."

"Megan," he pleaded, sounding both shocked and confused, the fiery arousal still burning bright in his eyes. "Why the hell not? It's not like it's the first time I ever touched you."

The hurt clouded her gaze. This was Caleb—sweet, gentle Caleb asking her to do the unthinkable.

"I'm married. Don't you understand?" she cried out.

"In name only." The exasperation showed clearly on his face, frustration heating his voice.

"As long as Reed's alive, I won't be unfaithful."

"Meg, please, I'm begging you. The man's been holding on for months. Look at me." He gestured at the huge bulge tenting his finely tailored trousers. "I don't know how much longer I can wait."

This was quite different from the last time she saw Caleb naked. Her eyes gaped downward at the impressive sight. The memory of Devin's enormous cock pointing straight at her in the darkness, tempting her, calling to her and promising her unimaginable pleasure, flooded her mind. The tip of her pink tongue licked her lips; every nerve ending in her body trembled with awareness, raged with unmet need.

"I know you want to. I can see it in your eyes." He started to move across the room.

"Stop, Caleb, please." She held out a staying hand, her breathing erratic to the point that she sounded they way she felt—weak. "It doesn't matter what I want. As long as my husband lives, I'll not bed another man."

Dear God, she surmised what she and Devin did out in the woods wasn't technically considered adultery if he failed to enter her completely. The thought made her pulse race and her wanton vagina moisten and throb in response. Oh, sweet mercy, she was going to burn in hell for her sinful ways.

"Lest you forget the pleasure we can give one another without fornication."

"Caleb!" The memories came flooding back. She burned with mortification.

"Very well, Megan, I'll wait for you as long as I have to. Thinking of you, dreaming of you, being near you will have to do for now."

She felt tears pushing behind her eyes. He looked crestfallen. A gentleman, though, he kept his distance.

For that, she was grateful.

"I think its best if you leave now," she gently suggested, not knowing how much more of a strain on her emotions she could handle.

With a glance over his shoulder, he retrieved his hat. The look upon his crestfallen face reminded her of a scolded puppy retreating with his tail between his legs. Poor, Caleb. It was for his own good that she turned him away. His very life depended on it. He returned the Stetson to the coveted position atop his finely molded head with its crop of blond waves, and turned to face her.

"I love you, Megan Adams." He pronounced each word slowly, deliberately.

Use of her maiden name was a vivid, intimate revival of when they explored an innocent, young love within each other's arms.

Her heart sank.

"You'll always be the only woman for me."

Without waiting for a reply, he walked out the door.

She wanted to die.

Chapter 5

Deuce ambled along aimlessly while his master found he exhibited some semblance of a conscience after all. In the middle of the vast countryside, the air was clean, crisp and timeless and called to mind all-too-familiar memories better left buried.

What had he accomplished by returning? This place, this land, was never his home. He didn't belong here. Reed couldn't even speak, though his fading gray eyes were filled with sincerity, almost a pleading.

He gritted his teeth, realizing there was no chance of redemption, of understanding why he was brought into this world, to be given away the same day.

The anger and resentment was so profound, it squeezed his chest and swelled the nerves along his temples and neck.

Devin recalled the ten years he'd lived with his two spinster aunts. They tried their best to turn him into a respectable lad of good breeding. They'd hired the best nannies which he'd always managed to frighten away with his unsavory antics. Refused to wear the starched clothes they bought him in place of his worn jeans and tattered shirts. They sent him to the fanciest schools, each of which threw him out as easily as the mop water.

"Where did we go wrong?" he'd heard them ask when they thought he wasn't listening. Such was the reason he found himself on a locomotive headed west after he nearly killed a boy two years his senior for pushing a girl to the ground at the park. He didn't know the girl or the boy. Something inside him clicked when he saw her hit the dirt and then cry. He charged the boy, kept pounding the other lad's head into the ground until two men came running and pulled him off the body, beaten into a bloody heap.

Devin's gaze drifted over the rolling grass gently swaying in the soft breeze as he thought of what transpired afterward.

* * * *

Nineteen years ago, on a clear day much like today, Devin watched the world of vivid greens and browns whiz by the window, the chugging of the iron wheels lulling him to sleep as the train headed to nowhere.

There was no trouble remembering the masked gunmen shouting their way down the narrow passageway between the rows of seats, rousing him sharply from his slumber. At first, he thought it exciting, the Wild West he heard so much about come to life before his youthful eyes. Guns drawn, the train robbers separated. Each took a coach. With a handkerchief concealing his nose and mouth, the remaining gunman ordered the occupants to give up their belongings or die.

It was the most thrilling experience of his young life. True to form, when everyone was told to put their faces down, he ignored the command and watched in amazement as the desperado collected wallets, watches, and jewelry. One young lady didn't want to hand over her newly acquired wedding ring so easily. Disregarding her husband's pleas, she'd foolishly sat on her hand in a futile attempt to conceal the diamond on her finger. The tall, slender masked man grabbed her by the wrist and dragged her down the aisle.

Devin took one look at her husband, ash white and near fainting, then the poor lady crying hysterically, and something inside him clicked once more.

Without thought or concern for life or limb, Devin lunged over his seat. He knocked into the gunmen, causing him to release his grip on both woman and gun. The poor woman ran for cover, leaving Devin punching and kicking the outlaw. As loud as his ten-year-old lungs would allow he warned the outlaw to leave the woman alone.

Each time the train robber tried to stand, Devin knocked him down. The outlaw scrambled for the gun that had fallen beneath a seat. With no holds barred, he kicked Devin hard into the aisle. Standing, he slipped the hammer on his Colt and took aim. Devin rose, ready to pounce again.

"Stretch," a booming voice rang out, filling the compartment with a tense silence. Riveted, all eyes turned toward the opposite the end of the cabin. A large hand reached down and lifted Devin by the collar.

Devin turned mid-air and looked up at his future.

John Laredo was an older, formidable force. Not one to reckon with. A scar graced his left cheek from ear to mouth. He had black eyes that warned a man to stay away, scraggly gray hair, and weathered skin that spoke of years of a life of crime and living to tell about it. There was no fear in the mountain man. He went without a mask and walked like he owned the place.

Ol' John found what he always wanted that day—the son he never had. A boy with enough guts and fury to rival his own, to carry on death and destruction with a vengeance. "From the looks of it," Ol' John boasted, "the kid still has lots of growing up to do." Oversized and strong, Devin's body hadn't caught up to the rest of him. The leader of the infamous Laredo Gang couldn't have been happier with his spoils.

Tied up and thrown over an extra horse, he left that day with the gang that soon became his family, and he'd never lived a civilized life again.

* * * *

Devin swung his leg over Deuce and eased out of the saddle. He allowed the horse to ramble at will underneath the shade of a large oak tree, nibbling the lush carpet of grass. Devin stretched out nearby, propping his head on his hat in the knee-deep grass. He gazed up at the puffy white clouds drifting in the pale blue sky, the memory of the sole time he spoke to Reed stirred an unknown emotion—regret.

On a whim, Devin rode through Tejas close to eight years ago. He'd had no intent to stop until he noticed the boy about the age of five or six running in the yard. Something he didn't care to identify tugged at him as he recalled seeing his father in person for the first time, recognizing him from the pictures his aunties kept around the house. Reed was a tall, well-built man who looked like he could hold his own. A faint smile tilted Devin's lips at the fond recollection.

He'd never forget the look on his father's face when he introduced himself, nor the look when he rode out less than an hour later. Twenty-one at the time, he wasn't about to start taking advice from a man he didn't even know, who'd discarded him like an old boot, then tried to tell him to change his lawless ways. *Find a good woman and settle down*, Reed had the nerve to tell him. There wasn't a man alive who'd dare tell Devin Spawn how to handle his business without risking his life, and Reed wanted to interfere, convert his ways.

Galled by the memory, Devin muttered an obscenity. For some odd reason, he remembered the little curly-haired girl ranting something about a soap word. That, in turn, brought to mind the letter Megan had given him. From inside his pocket, he pulled out the letter. An aged, imprinted 'S' held the pages sealed. Breaking the wax stamp, he glanced at the hard lines and sharp angles of the script and guessed Reed handwrote it. He sat up and leaned back against the rough bark of the tree, then began to read the two-page letter.

By the time he finished, his brow furrowed in a deep scowl, every muscle tensed, and his gut wrenched.

Devin bolted for Deuce and galloped like the wind toward the ranch.

* * * *

Megan's stomach tightened as the front door pushed open with such a loud bang, it sliced fiercely through the silence. Next she heard what she could only assume were Devin's heavy, purposeful footsteps headed her way. The man had terrible timing. Reed's bathwater was sure to get cold, all because his son was heartless, bitter, and apparently riled up about something. Why did he even bother to return at all?

Her fingers gripped the warm, wet washcloth in her hand. Riveted on the doorway, she held her breath, waiting for his inevitable appearance.

Fury emanated from him in thick waves. He stepped aside from the doorway, his presence daunting, intimidating and dangerous. Suddenly, she realized before her was the real Devil's Spawn. The overwhelming sense of power and aggression he evoked left no trace of the silver-eyed, sensuous man with lush lips by the river. Every rumor regarding the legendary force came to life in horrific detail. Eyes wild, dark, and blazing with rage turned her blood cold as she tried to remain calm and show no fear in the face of evil.

He ordered her to leave. From the anger shading his voice, she did not intend to object. Not knowing if his anger was directed at her, Reed, or some other outside source, she wasn't about to leave her husband lying naked— exposed and completely vulnerable. With her back to him, she took her time covering Reed's frail body with a sheet, then a thick blanket, and finally prop his pillow.

With forced calm, she walked out of the room without so much as a glance his way.

Once she crossed the threshold, he slammed the door shut. The gust of wind lifted her skirt and cooled her ankles.

She hadn't known him very long, but she knew anger when she saw it. Devin was beyond angry. Best if she left him alone. She never imagined a person could possess so much fury, and the intensity was frightening. It left her wondering what trials and tribulations a young boy alone in the world had to endure to end up a demon other men feared.

Outside on the porch, Megan inhaled the fresh spring air deeply into her lungs. She lifted her face to the warmth of the sun and tied the sunbonnet she kept near the front door. While the sun lightly kissed her skin, she had no desire to resemble weather-beaten animal hide, so she diligently wore her bonnet. Circles under her eyes, freckles on her nose, dimple cheeks— besides her dowdy clothes, she didn't need anything else adding to the homeliness into which she had been born. She doubted anyone with more than one weak eye would even glance at a short, plain, hazel-eyed, scrawny female with unruly spiral curls lost somewhere between brown and blond, who looked more girlish than womanly. Certain the fondness they developed long ago blinded Caleb. She was dubious whenever he told her she was pretty, especially now that she lost what little shape she used to have.

Perhaps for the very reason Devin wanted to kiss her the evening they met—frontier women were scarce. Average two females per one hundred men meant there were some desperate men seeking female companionship.

Jazelle's Place would not be hurting for business any time soon.

For the second time today, she caught herself thinking of her appearance.

Flippantly, she shrugged her shoulders and set off to work in the garden. There were too many chores to let Devin Spawn upset her or brooding over her homely looks to hinder supper from being on the table.

* * * *

"Why?" Devin grunted pacing the room. His chest rose with each ragged, frustrated breath. "How dare you ask this of me? You send me away, and now, you ask for the impossible. The most ludicrous."

He stopped and glared at Reed, wrapped snuggly in the bed, motionless.

"Why, damn you? Why?"

He stepped closer to the bed and looked straight into Reed's eyes.

"Do you not know who I am? What I have become and all that I have done?"

Reed's silver eyes blinked wearily in response.

"Speak to me. Speak to me. Tell me why."

The question went unanswered.

Devin waited, his own silver eyes imploring, begging for some type of response.

Reed's eyes fluttered, and then closed for the final time.

"Don't do this to me," he growled tightly with pent-up emotion. He grabbed his father by the shoulders and shook him vigorously. As if by sheer force of will, Devin could shake life back into the dead man. "Breathe, damn you. Breathe."

Reed's head flopped boneless until Devin realized it was useless. He let him go. Once more, his father had deserted him.

This time, for good.

He didn't know how long he sat on the edge of the bed, staring absently at the lifeless body.

In deep thought, he remained stock-still until he heard the front door open and the light steps of Megan cross the puncheon floor.

Devin took a deep breath and stood.

* * * *

Megan decided it was best to act uninterested, ignore the brooding tyrant. She went about her business, rinsing the fresh-picked vegetables in the kitchen sink. She kept her back to him as he took a seat at the table.

"Got a moment?" He said blandly as she cast a brief glance his way. From under the table, he kicked out the chair across from his, indicating for her to join him.

"Not really," she said, returning her full attention to the vegetables. "I have—"

"Don't wait for a written invite." Devin's tone elicited a prompt response.

With a sigh, she wiped her hands on the ragged-edged cheesecloth tied around her waist in place of an apron. From across the room, she glared at him. She tried in vain to swallow her indignation through tight lips. Failing, she replied saucily, "Such a warm request. Only a fool spurns a skunk."

From the corner of her eye, she could tell he wasn't the least bit pleased by her insolence by the way his eyes crinkled at the corners as though he was only able to stomach looking at her in tiny increments.

To spite him she ignored the token chair and chose to sit in the armchair at the head of the table. She clasped her hands tightly in her lap. After the first good night's sleep in eight months, she felt a renewed confidence this morning. She considered herself strong enough to resist the sexual magnetism of such a horrendous brute. As long as those silvery eyes didn't gaze upon her dreamily, and he remained callous, didn't bathe, and left before nightfall, it would be easier than tying a bobcat with a piece of string.

Satisfied and content with her fortitude, she smiled.

"Don't go tryin' to apple pie me."

She blinked, and her polite smile faltered. Well, callousness was one less risk factor she need worry about.

"Have you read it?" He tossed the crumpled letter on the table.

Megan took a deep breath. From the dark look he was giving her and the seriousness of his tone, there would be no chance for dreamy eyes or whispered endearments, she surmised a bit wistfully.

In silence, she eyed the letter sitting in the middle of the table. She lifted her chin and replied in the most haughty tone she could muster, "No, but I have an idea." *And a thought: how about a bath?*

The law favored men. Women were deemed mere possessions. Reed often mentioned he wanted his son to inherit the ranch, as was customary. If it were true, Devin Spawn could put her out in the street, with or without the girls. That was the reason she told Shelby and Emma he was their half-brother. Though only six and eight, respectively, and they had a right to know their future was in his hands. As was hers, to a certain degree.

Megan could walk away, but not without Shelby and Emma.

"Reed was under the impression you need protecting."

Her eyes narrowed, certain she heard him incorrectly.

"Surely you meant Emma and Shelby."

"No, Mrs. Spawn. You."

"Me?" she snapped, aghast by the absurdity.

"Yes. And he wants me to do the protecting."

Clearly, this was even more absurd than the last statement. Was this the cause of his foul mood? She took a steadying breath as her fingers covered her gaped mouth. Befuddled, she didn't know what to think or say.

"Don't fret. I have no intent on following his request. Not now, not ever."

Most unladylike, she slumped back in her chair—from relief, outrage, shock, she didn't know.

"I'm neither savior nor babysitter."

Insulted, that's what she was. Her blood boiled at the iciness of his tone. How dare he demean her with flagrant, contemptuous rudeness? She didn't ask him to come. Now that he was here, she didn't want him to stay. Moreover, she did not need him to babysit her.

Her back straightened and her hands gripped the chair arms firmly. The challenging move rearranged her loose-fitting blouse. "Perfect, since there is no need for either one here. I'm a woman, Mr. Spawn, not an imbecile. I'm perfectly capable of caring for myself."

Scowling, Devin drew in a deep breath.

She became aware his gaze focused on the neckline draped over one shoulder, baring an immodest portion of her skin and the embroidered edge of her chemise. Disheveled ringlets hung over her shoulders and down her back. A slight flush heated her cheeks, yet she refused to cower. She fought the urge to tuck her hair in place or adjust her clothes.

Megan seethed, but her stomach tightened with an odd sensation.

Was he just going to sit there and stare at her? Come to think of it. The way he looked at her was below suspicious. As if, he remembered the feel of her body beneath his. Her insides began to melt at the memory of his touch. His gaze drifted lower. She felt her breasts swell, press uncomfortably against the green blouse. Her nipples hardened underneath the thin layers. He seemed to undress her layer by layer with his lascivious gaze. An arousing torrent of desire ran up and down her body and settled near her lap.

For land's sakes, if she didn't say something soon, from the look in his face, he'd have her stripped naked soon.

"Now that's settled. What of Shelby and Emma?" she muttered, unable to finish the rest of her thoughts regarding their future.

He settled back in his seat, bumping his hat off his forehead.

She blinked. There were those glorious, silvery spheres of temptation, staring back at her intensely. A maelstrom of thoughts clouded her mind and enticed her senses. The full force of his gaze could not be ignored, nor the surge of heat touching parts of her that ached with need. Why did her traitorous body respond so readily, as if she had no control? All he had to do was give her that look, and her legs would fall open. Damn him! Why was he still here?

"Yours to do as you see fit."

Finally, he spoke. She breathed a sigh of relief. In the event of Reed's untimely death, she'd keep the children. More importantly, Devin would move on. A faint smile tugged at her lips. If he got up and left now, it wouldn't be soon enough. She didn't know how much more of him she could handle.

"Nothing would please me more than to raise the girls as my own. When the time comes, rest assured, I'll do right by them. They'll be loved and sheltered as best as possible." Megan noted his demeanor was aloof, despite her reassurance. Had she imagined his interest in her? Wishful thinking on her part? Outlandish! Of course not. "All that I ask, Mr. Spawn, is to refrain from using a colorful vocabulary and leave your firearms at the door while you are under this roof."

His eyes narrowed ever so slightly. "You can cut out the bullshit formality, Mrs. Spawn. You and I are 'bout as intimate as two can get. And as for my gunbelt, again, you should know I seldom take it off, no matter where I am or what the fuck I'm doing."

Deliberately using foul language, referencing last night—not once but twice, and out and out refusing her polite request to leave his weapons at the door was downright insulting and disrespectful. The man was a scoundrel. Worse than a scoundrel, he was, he was...Oh hell, she couldn't think of what was worse than a scoundrel, but whatever it was, Devin Spawn was ten-fold. It just made her that much more determined not to give him the benefit of a reaction.

"Well, Mr. Spawn," she replied politely, "I seem to recall your word as a gentleman. If the rules of this household are too stringent for you to follow, then I suggest you continue your journey as promised."

Dear Lord, the man was a murderous outlaw. The rules of polite society didn't apply. No one could handle him, let alone govern control. As long as they were to exist under the same roof, she couldn't ignore him. She couldn't pretend he wasn't the most seductive, handsome, dangerous man to ever set foot of God's green earth or deny how she envisioned what he looked like without buckskins, or how the heat of his touch melted her resistance, scorched her skin. How his lush lips took her breath. His kisses sent a surge of steamy liquid down her thighs.

Nor could she forget her foolishness in thinking his finger was his penis, or the pain when the actual thick, huge thing almost ripped her sensitive flesh in two.

Devin Spawn had to go. There wasn't any question about it.

His steely gaze locked with hers in a match of wills. He appeared in perfect control of his emotions. Made her feel the sexual attraction was purely one-sided, which only irritated her further.

After a tense moment of silence, she felt triumphant when he looked away first.

Rather impolite, she thought when he reached out and crumpled the letter. He stuffed it inside the pocket of his jacket and drawled in his usual deep resonate tone, without the least bit of inflection, "My word is 'bout good as the ink on this here paper in an August downpour. I'll leave when I damn well please."

His eyes seemed to light up, amused, when she shot him a go-to-hell look. If her nails were longer, she would claw his eyes out.

"You must be a simple-minded fool to take the word of a stranger while you stand in front of him naked."

Megan felt her face turn beet red first, and the rest of her body soon followed. A knot of anger twisted her stomach. She clamped her hands in her lap to squelch the desire to throw something at him, seeing how there wasn't anything within reach except a chair.

"If a fool is willing to do anything out of desperation to save the lives of two innocent, young children, then yes, I am a fool. I would have done almost anything you or any other blood-thirsty savage asked of me if it meant they wouldn't be harmed."

The overwhelming temperature of her emotions brought her close to tears. She needed to get away.

"If you'll excuse me, I need to finish Reed's bath," she said contemptuously as she pushed her chair under the table.

"Don't bother. He's dead."

"Reed," she barely whispered, glancing toward his bedroom door before her legs gave out.

* * * *

Devin saw it coming. He'd be damned if he caught her. There was no way he'd fulfill his father's dying wish. He plain refused to do it. No matter how quick on his feet he was or how many other females he saved from a fate much worse during his lifetime.

Not her.

Not Megan Spawn.

Not Reed's young, impetuous widow.

No matter how tantalizing a distraction, he wouldn't touch her with his bow and lance at a distance of five hundred yards.

Slowly rising from his seat, he looked down at her limp body.

All he asked for was a kiss. What she offered went well beyond her impassioned claim out of necessity to save the children. Lust, pure and undeniable, drove her.

If she wanted nothing to do with him, going so far as tell him to leave, he'd be damned if he picked her up off the floor. As far as he figured, that fell under the protection category.

The hard, throbbing bulge in his buckskins was just going to have to find another itch to scratch. He stepped over her on his way outside.

He'd seen plenty "go-to-hell" looks in his days, but none that quite matched her intensity. He found it laughable and surprisingly refreshing.

Hell, he had a mind to stay put just to spite her. To break that façade of composure until she was begging him to fuck her again, screaming as he shoved every last inch of his cock into her tight little pussy. The harder, the better. Treat her like every other whore he'd ever fucked. He'd make no allowances for his dainty stepmother, so tiny she most likely fit in the palm of his hand.

As he rode into town, he decided to stay long enough to give Reed a proper burial: a preacher man, a pine box, and perhaps a flower or two. Lay him to rest next to Devin's mother on the hill behind the house. He figured another day at the most. That should rattle the young widow's bones once she picked herself off the floor.

Chapter 6

With detailed instructions on how to care for his prized possession, Devin left Deuce at the livery. He sought the undertaker and arranged for Reed's funeral. Immediately, Devin sent the thin, balding man out to the ranch to retrieve the body before his sisters returned from school.

When informed the customary waiting period for burial was three days, he was not too chipper about the delay. He offered to pay extra to speed things up, which the stubborn old man refused. He had only two choices, to shoot the bastard and bury Reed himself, or to stick around and ensure his father received a proper sendoff. Unfortunately, his choice meant sticking around longer than expected. Damn.

Given directions from the man at the livery, he crossed the dusty roads and made his way to the bathhouse for a hot bath, close shave, and clean clothes. With only a few hours sleep last night and wearing the same filthy garments the past two weeks in the saddle, he was not only hungry and tuckered out, but disgusted with his own reeking filth.

An hour later, he stood in the bathhouse corridor, feeling like a new man. He tossed his saddlebags over his shoulder, rifle in hand. Disregarding the bath attendees' hospitable suggestions where to go for a hearty meal, he headed straight for the saloon to find some grub.

Not in the mood for mingling with civilized folks, he seldom interacted with decent, law-abiding citizens, unless one considered crossing them in his line of work "interaction."

Dressed in black britches, charcoal gray shirt, gray cowboy hat, and black snake-skinned boots, he turned the heads of the females, young and old along the boardwalk. Mexican, Indian, and white, it did not matter. He was accustomed to eliciting interest from both men and women—for completely different reasons, of course.

Something about the way he walked, his bearing, cleared the boardwalk. It stirred a frenzied buzz among the men. Though no one would guess his identity, he had the mark plain as day as to what he was.

Devin tried to be inconspicuous. He'd left his bow and lance back at the ranch. He was the only gunslinger in the west known to be equally skilled in Indian weaponry, double six-shooters, and Bowie knifes.

By nature, he ignored women who didn't look like they'd ruffle their skirts, even if the price was right. From the corner of his eye, he sized up the men. Most looked like they didn't know which way a bullet exited a gun, and therefore, he deemed them tenderfoot. If anyone had the misfortune to recognize him then it was time for target practice.

What was wrong with this town? There wasn't a formidable foe in the whole damn place. With only one main street, several blocks long, it was too small for someone like him to get lost. He could get into a whole heck of a lot of trouble if not careful.

Devin wandered over to the Silver Nugget saloon and pushed open the batwings. He stepped to one side, and put his back to the wall. An unconscious move out of years of ingrained behavior since one never knew where enemies lurked.

At this time of day, there were a dozen locals spread at the tables and a few lined up at the bar. Most turned and looked over the new arrival to see if they recognized him. Once they made up their mind, the majority returned to their drinks, card game, or bar girls. He shot a warning glance at the few remaining gawkers. They quickly followed suit, going about their business.

Noise blared in the smoke-filled saloon as the piano player battered the timeworn keys on a rickety piano in the corner of a small stage, making what only the player could deem music. Devin cringed as the sound pierced his eardrums. He made up his mind right then-and-there to find the farthest table, or else, put everyone out of their misery and shoot the hell-raiser. The piano player was sure to raise the dead. With Reed freshly departed, Devin wanted no chances at seeing his father walk any time soon.

He ambled up to the end of the bar and rested one foot on the leg rail. With an elbow on freshly polished mahogany, he motioned to the barkeep with a single nod.

"What's your interest?" the barkeep asked, making his way down the long bar.

"That's after I eat."

The bartender grinned. "Until then, what you drinking?"

"Whiskey, and no watered-down shit."

The barkeep's face crinkled as though insulted. Without a word, he placed the frothy glass in front of Devin.

Devin slipped him a coin, which he picked up as soon as it hit wood.

"How much?"

"For what?" the barkeep asked curiously.

Devin tilted his head in the direction of the piano player. "For him to shut the fuck up."

"Mister, if you don't like the music, just say so."

"Just did." He took a long swig.

The barkeep called out to the musician, told him to take a break.

The piano man closed shop so fast, Devin figured he didn't like listening to himself, either. The barkeep's brow knit in a tight row as he studied Devin's clean-shaven face.

"Ya look familiar. Do I know you?"

Devin restrained the urge to laugh as the man struggled to place him. On his way to the bathhouse, he'd taken note of the post office, bank, and jail. Habit. Eyes like a hawk, he spotted his missive hanging outside the post office from across the street. He already knew what it said. The same wanted poster was in his pocket neatly folded.

Ten thousand dollars in gold for Devin Spawn–alive.

He hated the drawing. It didn't do him justice. The ears were too big and eyes were wrong. Too close together. He looked dirty and unshaven. At least they accurately listed his wrongdoings.

"No."

"Been in town 'fore?"

"No."

"Ya look awfully familiar. Like I've seen ya somewheres 'fore." The barkeep grimaced, slowly shaking his head in deep contemplation.

As usual, his hat sat low on his forehead, shading the silver eyes known to make lesser men wince. There was little chance of Devin being recognized. Unless he took off his hat, and he only did that while in the intimate company of women.

"Take a seat yonder." The barkeep gestured to a few empty tables in the far-off corner, where a lone diner was finishing his meal. Devin offered few words, making it difficult to place him. With a steely gaze, he watched as the burly man scratched his head, scowling as he wracked his brain. "I'll send someone to take yer order."

"Keep 'em coming." Devin raised his glass, indicating he didn't want an empty glass, and started to walk away.

"Mister," the barkeep called, and Devin cautiously turned with one thought on his mind. The grip on his rifle changed slightly. Bartenders usually kept a shotgun behind the bar. If the man finally recognized him, he wouldn't have to worry about serving drinks where he was going.

"After, go through that door ov'r yonder." He pointed to an unmarked door in the center of the back wall and grinned. "The ladies will tend to whatever interests you got."

Devin offered a slight nod of thanks.

No sooner had Devin settled into a small round table a few down from the other diner, his back to the wall, when he was greeted by an old woman. She had brown, leathery skin, dried from the sun and wrinkled to a crisp. Her silver hair was tied in a severe bun on top of her head, yet her yellow smile, or what was left of it, was genuinely friendly.

"Howdy mister. What can I get for you this fine afternoon?"

"Anything edible. I'm hungry, not picky."

She chuckled. "Man with a hearty appetite deserves someum' special. Got some mighty nice steaks in couple of hours 'go."

"Good. Along with whatever else you have."

"What'll it be? Green beans, mashed taters with gravy, beans, corn, carrots, biscuits, or cornbread?"

"Everything."

Her dark blue eyes roamed over him boldly. With legs too long to fit under the table and shoulders broad as the tabletop was wide, he was used to being gawked at like some kind of circus act. If only he earned a nickel every time. Her appraisal lit up her eyes and put a mischievous grin on her face.

"Reckon ya got's a place to tote it all."

"You bring it. I'll eat it."

Her smile broadened.

"Coming right up, mister," she said, hurrying off to the kitchen with vigor in her step.

In his element, his gaze wandered the room. None of the drinkers posed a threat. From what he could tell, they were cowboys and drifters, most wearing a gun for show, from the looks of it. When Devin glanced to his right, the bartender was still studying his profile.

Abruptly, the man realized he chose the wrong stranger to infringe upon his privacy by the facial indication Devin gave him. The bartender went back to wiping the used glasses with his soiled apron, setting them among the unused ones.

Devin finished off his glass in two swallows.

Before the empty glass hit the table, a sweet-smelling barmaid strolled up to Devin's side with drink in hand. Her heavy bosom flounced with each exaggerated movement of her hips. She took a seat without an invite.

He greeted her with a cold, hard gaze, a warning her presence was unappreciated. She slid the mug across the table. Despite the twinge of fear glinting in her green eyes, she remained. His first thought was she must really be hard up for money. That or she figured he was the only one in the room who looked like he knew how to hit that female spot just right.

She leaned over the table, somehow managed to squeeze her arms together, pressing the plump swells of her breasts until they spilled over the tight confines of her bodice and the tops of her brown areolas appeared.

It was definitely the latter, which didn't surprise him none. Men that knew how to ease a woman's needs had a certain air about them. He saw the excitement flare inside her at the prospect of well-charted territory.

Scarlet red lips curled into a smile, and he felt the coldness in his expression slowly drift away. His cock barely stirred as her nipples strained against the satin dress she wore. She was too easy, too perfumed, too whorish, if that was even possible.

"Looking for company?" She batted the dark lashes framing her heavily made-up eyes in a manner meant to seduce him, implying she would be up for anything. He played out this scene dozens, if not hundreds of times, in joints notches above this two-bit, flea-ridden hellhole.

"Later," he curtly answered, surprised her blatant offer didn't tempt him as it should have.

"I'm here now, big guy." She practically cooed so provocatively, he wanted to ram his cock down her throat just to see how accommodating she could be.

Instead, he replied evenly, "After I eat." He put the emphasis on "after." Bathed, a good meal in his belly, and a few drinks, the Cannon wouldn't fail him. Not again. Not like it did last night with... Shit! He was thinking about her again.

"Might be tied up later." She batted her eyelashes, reached across the table, and slipped a deft finger under the cuff of his sleeve. He felt her sharply manicured nails rake over the fine hairs on his forearm.

A single brow rose, and a smile tilted his lips. He wondered what she'd do if she really found herself tied up later. His slight smile disappeared when he remembered he left his rope on his saddle back at the livery. Damn.

From years of practice, he could tie a woman to a bed with a single rope in a matter of seconds. It used to be a sport whenever his gang rode into a town where there weren't enough women to go round. Lined up, his men would time him. They'd hoot and holler as Devin went from room to room. The women were of disreputable virtue, paid well for the special bonus, which added to the already overly excited ruffians. Even in the fanciest parlor houses, so-called gentlemen forgot their manners behind closed doors. Whores in run-down cribs fared no better. However, he never allowed his men to inflict violence, rape, or poke without paying. Everything else was free bidding.

From the saddlebag draped across his thigh, he retrieved a gold coin, and placed it on the table.

Her interest seemed to perk up as she reached for the coin. His palm was there before she could grab it. Disappointment shone in her eyes as she stared at him.

"I said, later."

She casually shrugged her shoulders, red waves falling over her bosom. "Suit yourself, sweetheart. The name's Hattie. I'll be waiting for you upstairs."

Hattie rose from the table, and walked away in the manner in which she arrived.

Devin watched the swing of her robust hips until they disappeared behind the closed doorway. No real beauty, but she'd do. Nice and plump, like he preferred. Her breasts were big enough to warm his cock while she sucked on the head. He'd ride those hips hard until she was saddle sore. Then, he'd flip her over and lose himself in the taboo entrance between those fleshy mounds.

Out of view, the faint interest easily dissipated. He was able to return his full attention to the room.

His decision to stay out of Tejas while his father was alive worked in his favor. No one knew him. With anonymity, he had free reign to come and go as he pleased.

Except now that Reed was gone, there was no reason to stay or keep out of trouble. Yet the more he thought about it, the deeper a scowl creased his brow. There were two reasons, perhaps three. He lifted his glass to his mouth then downed the entire contents in one long swig.

Damn if she wasn't sneaking in on his thoughts again. The memory of his father's lifeless body continued to taunt him. Big hazel eyes glazed over at the mere mention of Reed's death. Her dainty body sprawled on the floor as he walked past. Did she love him? It was common for girls as young as fifteen and sixteen to marry. How old was she when they married? Was their marriage real? Were they man and wife in every way? Was that little curly-top girl their love child?

Lost in thought, he didn't even notice when the barkeep came over with a refill.

Devin was certain the older girl belonged to his second wife. The woman had been carrying a babe about a few weeks old on his first and only visit years ago. Their oldest child, Reed's second son, must have died some time ago. Probably the same time his second wife did. Who knows?

It didn't matter.

Nothing mattered anymore.

As soon as the funeral was over, he was running himself out of town with no intention of ever looking back.

Dear Mother could take up with Pretty Boy for all Devin cared. Torment him. Let him believe he was going to get the fucking of his life, just to have her squeeze them slick, taut muscles, force him to spill before the head of his cock made it past the tiny slit.

Bloody-hell! He groaned, envisioning her dainty, warm body splayed wantonly for Pretty Boy. The thought riled his blood. Devin shook his head.

Certainly, he didn't care if that dandy plunged into the tightest, hottest pussy to grip a man's cock.

Devin's head rolled backward. He closed his eyes, lingering on the vision of Megan's dainty form, posed seductively on a bed of grass. Her chemise bunched below her underarms while he worked a finger inside her moist heat. Wet and ready for him. He felt the lasting heat of her small hand inside his buckskins, stroking and tempting his aching cock until he was ready to explode. He could still feel her slender legs cradling him as he inched his way into the tightest cunt ever. Not even virgins he deflowered as a well-endowed teenager were that tight.

His hips lifted slightly from his seat, whilst he imagined thrusting inside her, impaling all twelve inches in one hard thrust. He needed to hear her scream in pleasure, have her hips rising to meet his, feel her climax milking him until he filled her body with his seed.

A distinct aroma forced his eyes open as the cook put three plates in front of him. One plate was filled a thick, juicy steak, one overflowed with all the fixin's, and the last was piled with cornbread and biscuits.

He inhaled sharply and read the appraisal in the old woman's gaze.

"Musta been some dream. There's willin' women over yonder can make it reality." She flashed her gap-toothed grin, pointing toward the famed center door.

He was amazed the old woman still held a knack for spotting lust in a man's eye.

"Right now, sugar, you're all the woman I need," he offered truthfully, not knowing if he was hungrier or hornier. Either way, he was in the right place to satisfy both needs.

After handing over the utensils wrapped in a napkin, she brashly replied, "Iffin I was forty years sprier an' my bosom were up here." She cupped her breasts and lifted the sagging flesh high on her chest. "I might believe ya and give ya a wild, woolly ride."

Devin shook his head and laughed. "I'm afraid if you were a mite younger and your breasts were sitting up high, you'd be more woman than this ol' boy could crawl into." He leaned over and swatted her ass playfully.

"Sunny, I doubt there's a woman alive you couldn't handle. You enjoy. I'll be back to check on ya."

"Ma'am, if you made it, I'll enjoy it."

Laughing, she made her way back to the kitchen.

Devin wasted no time cleaning off all three plates and emptying three more glasses of whiskey. He expected the food to be a notch above trail grub. It was surprisingly good.

* * * *

Once he settled his account with the barkeep, he learned the old woman's name was Ida Boyd. Mrs. Boyd looked about ready to fall over when he walked into the kitchen and handed her a tip bigger than she made in a year.

With no desire to hear the extent of her graciousness, he excused himself and made a hasty retreat toward the unmarked door.

The makeshift hallway that connected the two abutting buildings was long. It gave a fellow plenty of time to think. A robust, scantily clad brown-haired woman who showed her years of experience despite the heavy makeup caked on her face greeted him on the other end.

The one thing he hated about whores was their makeup. It never failed to smear as they worked up a sweat. Even worse, it rubbed off on him. Why couldn't a woman be self-assured enough walk around bare-faced? Some men preferred a natural appearance, as though she just stepped out of the river.

"Hello, cowboy," the mature woman said in a baritone voice that sounded strangely seductive for a woman. Then again, maybe it was that thinking he did in the long corridor that had him questioning why he was here in the first place. "May I be of service?"

Brazenly, her eager gaze trailed up and down his length. He was well aware when it stopped at his groin. Even without an erection, he knew she was getting an eyeful by the way her eyes glimmered with lusty satisfaction.

"You're a big one," she gasped, smiling wickedly.

"Where's Hattie?" If a big old woman started to sound sexy to him, then it had been entirely too long since he rammed his cock into the heated depths of womanly flesh. He needed to fuck something, anything before he went plum loco.

"Whom shall I say is calling?"

"A man starved for pussy."

At his unabashed response, the woman didn't even blink. She named her price and he paid. With an overt sigh of regret, she gestured toward the staircase. "Hunger no more. Room twenty-one is down the hall to your left."

He started up the stairs as she offered, "Name's Madame Jazelle. I own this here establishment. Let me know if I may assist with any *unmet* needs."

With a tip of his hat, he climbed the steps three at a time.

* * * *

Hattie was, indeed, waiting for him, sprawled on her back on a comfy bed. There wasn't much else to the room besides a small table, chair, and trunk where each girl usually kept all the belongings she owned in the world, including clothes. From what he could tell even before she threw back the flimsy covering, she was naked under the satin bed sheet.

Devin wasn't one for wasting time or making small talk. A swift kick and the door behind him shut. He didn't bother to take off his hat, gun belt, or anything else, for that matter.

Hattie was pushed back into the mattress with her legs spread wide, three fingers in her dripping pussy. The rosy tips of her heavy breasts received much-needed attention as he took turns cupping each breast and sucking the stiff peaks.

He sucked on one breast and pinched the hard knot on the other between his fingers. Her eyes closed. She arched against him, gasping with delight while his thumb mimicked the motion on her clit.

Her hips gyrated on the bed as he admired the bountiful view in his grasp. Big breasts were always a temptation too good to pass. Hattie's were full and firm with plump nipples. Then why had their taste not made his mouth salivate or hunger for more?

The blasted situation irritated him. He wasn't here to please her—at least, not until he was assured she was able to reciprocate, give as well as take, that was for damn sure.

Unmoved by the ease his hands alone could cause a pleasurable response, afford a prostitute the luxury of forgetting her one and only objective: his gratification. Devin released her abruptly to her unabashed disappointment, moving to the edge of the bed. He directed her to his groin with a nod of his head and demanded curtly, "Take it out."

With a heavy sigh, she followed orders. He leaned back and spread his thighs to allow her plenty of room. She knelt between them. Without hesitation, her manicured hands went to the buckle on his holster. His hand closed over hers.

"Not yet," he rasped, the primitive urge resonating in his ears. The surge of his blood rushed downward. Clearly indicating his intent, he moved her hand to the fly of his britches. This had better be good. He needed it too damned much.

He watched her bite her lip with growing frustration they both seemed to feel. Her fingers struggled to push the buttons through the holes of the uncompromising fabric, stretched beyond its limit. "Damn, you're big," she hissed, grimacing and forgoing the well-versed voice of seduction.

When his rock-hard cock finally sprang free, the bulbous head bobbed forward with anticipation, nearly hitting her in the face. She stumbled backwards, flat on her plump ass. "Holy shit, cowboy, you're too damned big."

Hattie gawked at the exceptionally long, thick shaft pointed directly at her. "There's no way in hell that horse dick is coming near me. You ain't ripping my pussy in two," she shrieked, clamping her legs tightly.

Normally, his reaction would have been one of humor and understanding. Today, he was on a dire mission, growing more painful and critically urgent by each passing second.

Miss Hattie was a baseborn whore with a stretched-out pussy probably the size of the Colorado Rockies. Here she was, acting unceremoniously like a fresh, scared, untried virgin on her wedding night.

So what if he was hung like a horse? A damned twelve inches long and nearly eight round. Tarnation! He was in a whorehouse, not out by the river with a sniveling tease. He came here to be fucked, and he wasn't leaving until he was good and fucked.

Though not known for urbane charm and benevolence, he proved how hot, horny, and ornery he really was. "Bitch, are we gonna fuck or not? If not, get the hell out of here and find me a loose cunt I can bury my dick in," he exploded at the top of his lungs, not caring if the people in the next town heard him.

Not a second was wasted. Hattie yanked the sheet off the bed and wrapped it around her shoulders. She scrambled out the door quickly.

Down the hallway, curious onlookers came out of their rooms, all similarly wrapped in sheets or pulling on their pants and undergarments. He heard her cursing, complaining, telling all who would listen that she wasn't going to let him rip apart her moneymaker with that beast between his legs and let him leave her high and dry.

Devin was undone by a newfound level of malcontent at an old situation replayed countless times since he became a fully developed teenager with an insatiable appetite, who practically fed entirely off whorehouses. He fell back on the linen-covered mattress with a loud plop, arms extended at his sides, hat falling to the side.

* * * *

Madame Jazelle was no fool. Once she learned of the delicate situation and who the unassuaged patron was, she stepped lively to address the problem by any means necessary.

She rushed down the carpeted hallway to allay the ruckus, directing the other paying customers back to their rooms. Money didn't exchange hands if services weren't rendered. If men weren't flat on their back or holding a mug in their hand, then no one earned a plug nickel.

The position of sole proprietor of one of the best run brothels in the Tejas Territory was a feat accomplished by shrewd business sense and an even keener understanding of the male consciousness.

A starved patron is how he'd referred to himself. The man was no ordinary customer. Everyone from outlaws, to docile husbands, to innocent bucks, with an occasional preacher or passing politician, patronized her establishment.

The girl who stepped forward and volunteered to service him called him simply "The Cannon," and Jazelle knew who he really was. The assured confidence in his walk, steely eyes, and authoritative presence had 'ruthless' written all over him. Clearly, he was someone who wasn't afraid of shooting up what she worked so hard on and spent so many years building if his itch wasn't aptly scratched.

Even though she carried a pistol in the specially made garter strapped to her thigh, and the bartender downstairs kept a sawed-off shotgun under the bar, they would be no match for the likes of him. Their spineless Sheriff would be the first to run for cover once the lead flew.

Within minutes, Madame Jazelle stood solicitously inside the doorway, apologizing profusely, offering her often-used lie used to rectify most situations. Hattie was new and he was not to be discouraged. Her customers always left satisfied. Guaranteed.

"I have just the girl for you, sir." She motioned down the hallway to hurry Hattie's replacement along. "Says she knows you."

She took note of the glorious sight stemming from his groin as it reached toward the ceiling and added quickly in a tone that disclosed her heightened discriminating arousal, "If this one doesn't work out, I'll do you myself, on the house."

It was the first time she'd made such an offer during her twenty-five year career history. She eyed him with a certainty from a woman's standpoint hell-bent on seeking pure pleasure rather than an entrepreneurial concern.

* * * *

Devin flatly ignored her last comment. He lifted his head off the mattress, brows arched in curiosity. Someone in Tejas knew him. Before he could speak, a long-legged, golden-haired, blue-eyed beauty appeared in the doorway. Dressed in a black gown with pink ribbon ties down the front and a plunging corset that served to boost her ample breasts to their place of honor, he recognized Cheri instantly.

Propped on his elbows, they passed a knowing glance. Thin lips painted rosy red curled into a wickedly sinful grin, directed at Devin. Her eyes filled with unspoken promise and down-right carnal intent.

Cheri placed her hand on Madame Jazelle's shoulder and gently tried to encourage her out the door. "I'll take it from here."

Hesitating, Madame Jazelle looked Cheri over as though she was sizing her up and then glanced toward Devin. Devin nodded his approval. With a sigh of relief and a last offer to let her know if he needed anything, she left the two of them alone.

Cheri locked the door, giggling like a little girl who just found her favorite toy. With her back to the door, her blue eyes rose to meet his, glistening with serious arousal now. He watched as she languidly undid the first bow of her gown, revealing the cleft of her bosom.

"Devin, I knew it was you. Only one man could fit Hattie's description. I thought you were playing Indians."

Her hourglass figure swayed provocatively under the sensuous swirl of gauze as she neared the bed. The second bow, then a third came undone, exposing her uplifted breasts and corset-covered abdomen.

He sat upright. The flare of sheer male lust heated his blood. She stopped several feet in front of him, beyond his reach, in case he decided to grab her. A real professional, she knew exactly what she was doing. Another tease. It made his cock even harder.

Her hand dropped to the last tied bow, above the apex of her thighs. She twirled the pink ribbons with a single finger. He was going to lose his mind. With that steamy look in her eye, he knew she savored the anticipation and delighted in what little control she imagined holding over him. He let her have that, at least for now.

Over a year had passed since they were last together in Montana. Known for her shaved pussy and ability to give good head, he mused why he didn't seek her out a long time ago. Voluptuousness was just what he needed, a means to forget a wisp of a beauty.

When his eyes locked with hers, he blurted the first thing that came to his mind. "What are you doing here?" Not that he was complaining. He was more surprised at his luck to find one of his favorites in a dump, compared to the fancy Titillate Trove. The high-class brothel was not only lavish, it boasted the most beautiful, highly skilled, and well-paid women that only men with weighed-downed pockets could afford.

"I could ask the same of you," she responded softly, drawing the last tie loose and allowing the gown to fall from her shoulders to the floor in a whispering swish.

Her smile flourished as his gaze raked over her body, bare except for the lacy corset. The small gap between them narrowed. She ventured cautiously, "I heard you avoided Tejas like the plague."

She straddled his thighs carefully. Worked her knees under the holster strapped to his hips as his hands intuitively caught her around the waist.

"Is that why you're here? Hiding from me?" Roughly, his hands gripped her buttocks, pulling her shaved pussy in line with his cock. He felt the heat and moisture of her plump vaginal lips coating his cock, and grinned with relief.

Her fingers wasted no time attempting to unbutton his shirt. "Sweetheart, do I look like I'm hiding?"

In a display of strength, brawn, and dominance, he flipped her flat on her back and impaled her with one savage thrust. She screamed at the fury of the powerful invasion, acting out of bodily reflex, but he didn't care. He needed this, hard and deep and savage. He was dying to forget hazel eyes, cone-shaped breasts, and a sweet, pink cunt. The only way was to slam into another hot pussy that was open, willing, and eager to consume his aching shaft.

He growled as her tight, unprepared pussy muscles clamped around him at the brutal intrusion. She bucked against him, her protesting muscles relaxing as he continued to slam his cock into her with long, hard thrusts.

Her fingers curled around the wrought-iron bars in the headboard to prevent her head from hitting them as her body thrashed beneath him. She arched her hips, tightened against him. He knew she was close to coming, moaning as though this was her first real fuck in a long time. His hands braced on the wall above the headboard, he drove harder, deeper, desperate to ease the insane torment boiling inside him.

"Devin, don't stop," she screamed, and he knew he was hitting that perfect spot that always sent her careening over the edge. "Oh, yes."

"Stop? I'm only beginning," he growled roughly. Each orgasmic spasm gripped his cock erotically as he plunged furiously inside her heated wetness. Her cries drove him higher as he tore through her flesh. Her cunt drenched him as she thrashed beneath him.

The bedsprings creaked viciously, and the headboard thumped loudly against the wall. The grunting, huffing, and puffing split the paper thin-walls letting everyone know he finally was getting the fucking he came for.

He felt her pale, long thighs wrap around his hips as she rose to meet his pounding thrusts with a matching fervor of her own. Her body trembled with desire beneath his. He held himself above her, bracing his hands on either side of her shoulders. Hoping she'd forget the potency of his arousal, the dominating, lustful desires he was known for. Inwardly, he cringed when he felt her hands around his neck. She wanted to draw him closer. The raw, hungry look in her eyes was unmistakable.

He wanted to keep this what it was, a sex act and nothing more than a way to release pent-up frustration from the past six celibate months. This longest dry spell ever had damned near drove him crazy, drove him into the arms of his stepmother.

As always, one woman was as good as the next. He kissed, sucked, and fucked them all. Paid and left until the next time. No ties. No emotions. Sometimes, no names.

Devin stared at the sun-faded wallpaper in front on him, ignoring her silent plea. He longed for the moment when the edge of oblivion freed him. Everything he needed was here: a warm body with big breasts, and wet pussy to bury his cock deep inside. It did little to ease the dark shadows tearing at him. It was never like this before. A blinding agony struck him. In the past, the solace that usually came with sex was non-existent. He drove harder, each driving stroke ripped a wild, abandoned groan from her throat.

Oddly, he had no desire to kiss Cheri, though he'd often spent hours in joyful bliss with her whenever in Montana. Although she was only twenty-six, her line of work had begun to manifest, rendering her appearance to be much older.

Still quite appealing, her ready and willing, cock-loving pussy suited his purpose quite pleasurably. Cheri was accustomed to a certain degree of attentiveness and passion from him. Without it, her perceptive curiosity would arise. Though this was entirely a business arrangement and she was well-trained submissively, he dreaded the possibility of having to explain his fragmentary enthusiasm out of obligation to their long-standing acquaintance.

His gaze fell to her rose-painted lips, open in expectation. He shut his eyes, covered her mouth with his and visualized perfect pink lips, full and pouting. The kiss was hard, devouring. He claimed her mouth in an intoxicating, passionate kiss that spoke of unquenchable yearning, possessive desire and unfathomable emptiness.

* * * *

Cheri tried to keep up with the intensity of both rhythms as he plunged harder, faster, deeper into both orifices. His tongue pushed against her tonsils as she fought for each breath. Her inner muscles stretched wide to accept each powerful, frenzied thrust as her body buckled helplessly.

A second orgasm built deep in her loins. She tightened her vaginal muscles and squeezed his cock in an erotic grip that drew his balls tight. Her hands clutched the fabric covering his back, pulling her body up to his and ground her throbbing pussy into his groin. Her breasts flattened against his muscled chest. The rough material of his shirt scratched her tender nipples sensuously and she ignored the sting through the pleasure as her head banged against the wrought iron rails.

The intensity of his feral lust raged out of control. She had never seen him like this before. He thrust inside her over and over again, like a man hell-bent on dying. Beads of perspiration formed on his forehead. Sweat dripped down his back, dampening the fabric within her tight-fisted grip.

And then, it hit. Her body tightened as her pussy spasmed around his penetrating flesh, milking him, gripping him as her juices gushed, soaking her thighs.

She cried out into his mouth. He refused to release his stronghold until she felt his own climax spurt from him, filling her with one powerful explosion after another as every muscle on his body convulsed.

In the far corner of her brain, she heard his guttural cry. He thrust into her one last time before he fell into a dead heap over her weakened form, without so much as a thought of crushing her under his weight.

Several minutes later, as her heartbeat returned to normal, she murmured through strangled breaths, "Sweetie, I can't breathe."

Without a word, he rolled his two-hundred-plus frame off her, breaking their intimate contact. Chest heaving between ragged breaths, eyes still closed, he just lay there.

She propped herself on one elbow, and began to brush sweat-dampened strands of auburn hair from his beaded brow. Cheri took in every detail as her gaze ran down his long length. He hadn't even taken off his boots, let alone his holster, and his hat had fallen off the bed during their lewd tussle.

Bold as she was experienced, she muttered, half-amused and a bit indulgent, "If you wanted to fantasize, you should have told me. I would've played along."

Opening his glazed eyes, he cast a bewildered sideways glance. "What in the hell are you talking 'bout?"

"Sweetheart, this wasn't your style." She rolled onto her hip and leaned over, slowly stroking her hand along his left arm. Her breasts spilled over the top of her corset that now hung loosely around her waist, due to their zealousness.

The movement seemed to hold his attention, but only for a moment much to her chagrin.

"Whoever she is, she's wrapped you good." The Cannon, she remembered, possessed enough stamina to share with a dozen others. Always ensured a female was ready to take him by bringing her to orgasm after orgasm before entering her. Most importantly, he never climaxed so quickly, no matter how long he'd been out in the wilderness.

"Cheri?" The tone alone demanded an explanation.

"Megan," she answered.

He shot off the bed, staring at her with a wild disturbing look that told her he had no earthly clue as to what she referred.

"When you shot your wad, you called me Megan," she offered as further clarification.

He did something else that both surprised and pleased her. Cursing, he quickly undressed, tossing the garments around the room as fast as he could take them off.

Not one to be overdressed, she happily followed suit and unlaced her corset.

"Cheri," Devin ordered, "find a friend."

She smiled. Ah, the Devin Spawn she knew so well. The Cannon.

In a flash, she jumped off the bed, pulled on her flimsy gown, though it did little to conceal the naked flesh bouncing underneath. She took the time to tie a single bow at the waist before rushing toward the door.

"Cheri," he called out, taking off his britches.

With her hand on the lock, she turned to face him.

"Bring two."

Chapter 7

In the dark of night, Devin stood on the porch steps and listened to the sounds coming from inside the well-lit Spawn ranch after he settled Deuce in the barn.

When he left Madame Jazelle's, he was the most well-sated, contented customer to have paid for a broke bed, busted chair, and hole in the wall. Not to forget the hanging light fixture one of the girls used for a swing.

His troubles were forgotten until the small whimpers permeated the quiet night sky. He glanced over his shoulder in the direction of the barn, telling himself there was still time. Wouldn't take much to saddle up Deuce and ride on out. Megan didn't want him here. She didn't need him any more than he needed her in his life. And those kids. Little girls. What good were they?

Trouble.

That's what they were, pure Trouble with a capital T.

The whole bunch of them. Nothing but trouble.

Yet something kept him here, drew him. There was no reason to return. Yet he did, not understanding exactly why. In town, he'd mounted his horse. Without realizing it, he had led Deuce here.

"Must be the oats," he huffed under his breath, grinding his teeth.

He'd decided long ago it was best if he not question his misfortune. He strolled inside and hung his saddlebags on a hook near the door.

"Devin," Shelby exclaimed, jumping off Megan's lap. The little girl ran toward him, big tears streaming down her eyes.

Rifle in hand, he froze, unprepared when Shelby grabbed onto his leg. "Pawpaw's gone to heaven," she cried.

He glanced at Megan, seated on the Victorian-style couch against the wall that connected to the girls' room. Signs that she, too, spent the day crying were fresh upon her face. Her gaze turned icy. Her mouth thinned to a narrow line. The assistance he sought from her clearly was not forthcoming. Well, at least she hadn't changed her mind about wanting him around.

Emma was seated at the table, hands perfectly crossed in her lap, little legs dangling off the chair, crossed daintily at the ankle. Not a flicker of emotion shone in the girl's eyes as they slowly joined his before quickly returning to resume their position, staring into the empty space before her.

His full attention dropped to the tiny, curly-haired package at his feet.

He lifted her in one arm, and carried her outside.

"Devin, I knew you'd come back. Emma said you wouldn't. But I told her you was," she whimpered, big tears filling her eyes.

When they reached the middle of the front yard, he stopped. He dried her tears with a gentle wipe of his thumb.

"Look up, and tell me what you see."

Shelby wiped her messy nose with the back of her hand. She blinked up at the dark sky, then at Devin, shrugging her shoulders, she quietly replied, "Nothing."

"Ah, look again," he encouraged her softly.

Big blue eyes darted upward. "Stars. I see lots of stars."

"You know what those stars are?"

She shook her head.

"The Indians believe each one is a spirit."

"Angels."

"Yes," he hesitated. That word didn't sit well with him. Not a damn thing concerning sacred matters agreed with him. "Angels." The word grated off his tongue. "Your father—"

"Our father," she corrected.

His eyes narrowed. The girl was giving him no breaks. "Our father's spirit is up there watching over you right now."

"Megan says Pawpaw is in heaven."

"Nighttime is when the spirits come closer to watch over you while you sleep."

"Which one is Pawpaw?"

"That one. The great big one." He pointed to the North Star. Picked out the most obvious, ensuring she'd be able to find it if she ever cared to look for it again. That is, if she believed him. "He was a big man. Now, he's a big spirit."

Shelby's big blue eyes became even larger. "Not as big as you."

Devin tipped his hat back and couldn't help but grin.

"If anyone tells you different, you tell me. I'll set 'em straight."

His gaze roamed to the front porch, where Megan was standing with an arm around Emma's shoulder, quietly observing them.

Emma had a smug look on her face as if she knew the last part was meant for her. It was.

"You 'bout ready to head back inside?"

"Not yet, please. I wanna stay here so's he can see me plain. Pawpaw might be missin' me."

"Suit yourself." He would have called her by name, if only he remembered what it was.

Devin strolled the yard with her nestled in one arm. Her gaze never drifted away from the biggest, brightest star in the black sky.

Luckily, for him, he remembered the story from when an old Indian woman used it to console the young daughter of a warrior who died on a buffalo hunt. At the time, he dismissed her words, returning to whatever task he was doing. Somehow, though, the tale came flooding back in his time of crisis.

Nearly an hour later, arm growing numb from being in one position so long, he carried the sleeping child inside.

"Where does she belong?" He looked at Megan, curled up on the couch with her mending. Apparently, she'd sent Emma to bed and waited on him to ensure he didn't run off with the kid, or who knows what. That was the problem with the world—no trust.

"I'll take her," she said plainly, reaching for Shelby as she neared.

"Point me in the right direction. I'll do it." He glanced at the sleeping child, not ready to hand over the small blonde bundle just yet. He had never held a child before. She was sort of cute and soft, like a furry critter right before he skinned it.

"Shelby belongs with me, Mr. Spawn. I wouldn't want you bothered any more than necessary." Her voice was the same melodious tone, yet the coldness in her eyes was anything but harmonious.

Devin deposited the child in Megan's arms. Her message was loud and clear. She took his words to heart.

He paced the floor in Reed's bedroom, *his* room for the time being.

They were his sisters. His flesh and blood. Two tiny little girls. What did he know about raising girls? Not a damn thing.

He knew women. That's all. More like how to pleasure them. Aside from that, he didn't know a damn thing about them, either. Megan was a woman, experienced with kids. He couldn't care for one without the other.

Frowning, Devin rubbed his jaw. Who said anything about caring for them? There was no call to be wasting time worrying over them.

"Ah, shit, I'm going to bed," he grumbled, kicking off his boots.

Chapter 8

The aroma of potatoes and eggs frying woke Devin. Yawning, he stretched his limbs toward the four bedposts. It had been a long time since he'd actually slept in a real bed. No one except Cheri knew who he was. Her continued loyalty and silence would be well-rewarded in more than monetary gains. The threat of a bounty hunter tracking him to the ranch was slim. Last night he'd slept with both eyes closed.

His feet stuck out from under the sheet draped over his mid-section. He patted the comfy, yet firm mattress. There was plenty of room for three of him, with room to grow.

He grinned.

Obviously, his father knew the added benefits of a large, sturdy bed.

From the wedding picture his aunts had hung in his childhood room, Reed stood over six feet, not much taller than his mother did. Devin took after her, his aunts had always told him. Grace was a beautiful, well-built woman with dark, reddish-brown hair and eyes that lit up a room. She had a bold fire in her spirit that attracted Reed instantly, despite her unladylike height.

This custom bed must have been made for them. He sighed wearily, glancing at the empty space by his side. He wondered what the current Mrs. Spawn would look like lying naked by his side, the heat of her adorable little body warming his, innocent eyes darkened with arousal as she gazed up at him. He imagined her soft lips panting for breath, her sweet pussy slick and hot, ready for penetration as he moved over her and plunged his hard flesh into the tightness of her fragile body.

He groaned, staring at the sheet tented over his groin. *Shit.* He couldn't go outside looking like this. For damn sure, he wasn't about to act like a snot-nose kid and dirty the sheets, then have her wash them, knowing what he had done and not dare guess he was thinking of her when he did it.

His gaze turned upward to the straight pattern of nails holding up the ceiling. He thought of Big Grizzly, the bear that had nearly killed him. Much younger then, believing he was unrivaled, he'd left his rifle and holster near his campsite. The bear came out of nowhere before Devin picked up the danger signals Deuce gave off. Caught bathing in the stream, there was barely enough time to grab his dagger. Big Grizzly was dead, and he'd been mauled, left plumb naked, with hardly strength left to climb on Deuce before passing out. If it had not been for Deuce leading him to the Comanche widow of Ol' John, and the Indian herbs and cures she applied to kill the infection, he would have died for sure.

* * * *

"Smells good."

Megan and the girls turned at the same time toward the source of the deep, groggy voice that filled the great room. Her expression remained cool and level, but her body heated and stomach fluttered with arousing betrayal.

So what if he found time to bathe and shave? Revealed what she feared most, glorious features to go with those glorious silver eyes. Apparently, he also found time to go into town yesterday and come back fresh as a fiddle and smelling of cheap perfume.

"Devin," Shelby said happily.

Emma gave the well-muscled form dressed in black a quick, dismissive glance before stuffing a fork full of scrambled eggs in her mouth.

Good for you, Megan praised Emma's fortitude.

Shelby was easily swayed by a childish need for a male figure in her life, but not Emma, and Megan was no silly schoolchild. She knew exactly where the grieving son sought comfort for his loss. There was only one place in town that bought that florid perfume by the gallon.

Not only was he a lying, thieving, murdering scallywag, he was a cheating, womanizing, lily-livered pig who could rot in the infernal fires of eternal damnation for all she cared.

He ran a hand through his thick, auburn head of hair, stretching his shirt over his broad shoulders, and her heart sped up. She recalled the peephole at Jazelle's. She would have given anything to have been there last night and steal a glimpse of those hard muscles forcing apart female legs, his massive cock poised to conquer. The thought caused her pussy to tighten in need. In the best interest of her sanity, she shifted her stare to the girls once more.

"Have a seat. I'll fix you a plate." She turned her back to him, her voice coming out unsuitably strained.

Feeling somewhat refreshed after a second night without waking every hour to check on Reed, she fought the urge to smile. So what if it had been a long while since a man walked out of that room in the morning seeking breakfast? Moreover, never a man rough around the edges. Confident from his shoulder-length hair slicked back to black boots polished to a high-shine, she had to admit he looked both sexy and dangerous.

What was she thinking? He *was* dangerous. A danger to her nerves, a danger to her already raw emotions, a danger to their future, not to mention a danger to her weak, traitorous body that possessed a mind of its own. A mind that wanted him, craved him on sight.

"Sit by me," Shelby piped up excitedly.

From the corner of her eye, Megan watched him take a seat next to Shelby as she went to the sideboard for an extra plate. The sight of his tight, round rump made her feel both wanton and guilty for staring. A widow less than twenty-four hours, and already she lusted after another man—her stepson no less.

Had she no shame?

Of course not. She had been a married woman out by the river, and that hadn't stopped her from spreading her legs. *Hussy.*

Once again, she gave in to lusty temptation and studied his every move. He looked down at Shelby, and then across the table at Emma. Poor Emma, Megan thought to herself as the little girl continued to quietly eat her food, pretending Devin didn't exist. Megan knew all too well Emma waged a losing battle. Devin's presence was too daunting, too overwhelming a physical force for anyone to dismiss.

"Sleep well?" he asked Shelby.

"Oh yes, I dreamt of stars and angels."

His brow shot up, as if he was taken aback by her reply.

"Do you think Pawpaw will be here tonight?"

"Ask your sister." He titled his head in Emma's direction and managed a half-quirked smile. Megan noticed an amused glint in his gaze as she filled a cup with coffee.

Emma considered him a moment, turned up her nose, then simply replied, "Guess so, Shelby." She went right on eating.

In one hand, Megan held his plate level with her waist, and in the other, she balanced a cup and saucer. He watched her approach the table, his silvery gaze intense and appreciative. Appreciative in the sense she was a woman, not that she was about to feed him. She noticed his eyes were focused about six inches above the plate heaped with eggs and potatoes.

"Oh, goodie, I can't wait." Shelby tugged on his sleeve, diverting his attention away from her once again.

Megan took a shallow breath of relief. Her insides melted from his mouth-watering proximity as she set his plate in front of him, along with the coffee cup and saucer.

"Will you help me find him tonight?" Shelby asked softly, her dark blue eyes full of hope. Megan watched tensely, hoping by some small miracle he would let her down gently. Both girls had already suffered enough disappointment in their lives without Devin Spawn adding to their misery.

"Sure," he agreed loudly, as though he wanted to ensure Megan heard him.

Her body stiffened. That meant he was staying. Her pulse raced. She rounded the corner of the table, cautiously glancing at him. Beneath her lashes, she detected a faint grin curl the corners of his lush lips. Suddenly, she wanted to feel those soft lips on hers.

"Hope you like your coffee black. We seem to have run out of sugar." Hastily, she resumed her seat next to the one Emma had vacated earlier. Seated across from him gave her a small degree of comfort, the wide table between them providing a false sense of security.

"We haven't had sugar in a long time." Shelby held out her two little arms wide to indicate the lengthy timeframe.

At times, Shelby was too honest. Megan frowned slightly. Devin was not the type to miss anything. In case of further inquiry, she hid behind her coffee cup as she took a hurried sip.

"I prefer cream." His deep, male voice drew her and their eyes met across the table. A blush heated her cheeks as he pretended to wipe something from his bottom lip with his finger. The devilish move was meant to evoke memories of their riverside dalliance. Sexual intent glittered in his gaze.

Her unease was replaced by the memory of his finger moving inside her, sending a shocking flare of arousal rushing through her body. She blinked nervously. As though that minor effort could counter her heart pounding in her chest. Dear Lord, not even in front of the girls did the potency of his sexuality diminish.

"We don't have cream, either," Shelby offered matter-of-factly.

He broke eye contact with her and stared down at Shelby, as if annoyed by the childish interruption when evidently more mature matters filled his mind. "You have a cow, don't you?"

Shelby nodded enthusiastically.

"Then you have cream."

"Shelby, let him eat in peace." Unable to cover the note of exasperation in her voice, she would just have to deal with it. Abruptly, she left the table. If he saw it as a pathetic attempt to escape him, so be it. She needed to flee and she didn't care if he realized it or not. "Help Emma clear the table."

Both girls jumped out of their seat and hurriedly did as requested.

Megan kept them busy cleaning the kitchen while he finished eating alone. She sent brave little Shelby to collect his dishes after he picked off the last bite of potatoes.

"Care for more coffee?" Megan asked calmly from a guarded distance across the room.

* * * *

Devin shook his head.

"I'm going into town. Need any supplies while I'm there?"

Last night he slept soundly for a change, deep enough to dream of moistened skin glistening in the moonlight lying on a blanket of green, dark blonde hair the color of honey splayed wantonly around a delicate oval face flushed with arousal, arms outstretched and legs parted in a silent plea. He'd awakened in the morning to envision her beside him in a big lonely bed only to sit across from her at the breakfast table surrounded by little girls wasn't exactly what he expected or needed.

What he needed was to get as far away from her as possible.

Devil's Pact   105

He wanted to ride into town and find solace in the arms of Cheri, Pearl, and Violet. Who knew when he would return? At least the trip could be beneficial in more ways than one.

"No thanks," she said dryly. Unexpectedly, he detected a slight stiffening of her shoulders as she rinsed soapsuds from the plate in her tense grip.

"But Megan, there's lots of stuff we need," Shelby offered helpfully.

Megan quickly shushed the little girl.

His gaze darted to Shelby, who pouted, and then narrowed on Megan. "Which is it, yes or no?" he asked Megan sternly, rising from the table. She was hiding something beyond her pride and disapproval of his unwarranted presence. There was no doubt it was just a matter of time before he found out what it was.

"Perhaps, we can use an item or two." From the nervous glint in her eye, the admittance came under duress.

"Can I go with you to town?" Shelby ran to his side.

He looked down at the little girl and shifted his gaze toward the reserved Emma, drying the dishes next to Megan.

"Only if your sister joins us."

Emma turned to face him.

He looked at her square in the eye, waiting for her expectant decline.

Her eyes widened with a surprisingly defiant glint.

"Oh, Emma, please," Shelby shouted over and over again as she jumped up and down excitedly.

"Okay." Emma's innocent reply brought a happy shriek from Shelby, but he was positive the smug smile on her face was for his benefit alone.

"Shit," he muttered under his breath. He didn't think the little muskrat would say yes.

"Are you sure they won't be too much trouble?" The worry straining Megan's voice was palpable.

Hell, yes, they'll be trouble, he wanted to yell. Looking down her nose at him, what she really meant to ask was "would that be wise?" Did she expect, him to corrupt the lil' darlings in one afternoon? Maybe she thought he'd teach the girls how to shoot on the way into town, take what they needed without paying, or steal a few horses on the way home. His next words shocked even him. "Not at all."

Soon, he would be kicking himself. He exhaled deeply. Shelby ran into her room cheerily to look for her sunbonnet. Emma followed primly, with her slender nose in the air.

Dammit. He really needed to visit Jazelle's again. Asleep under the same roof and sitting across from hazel eyes, pretty pink lips, and pert little breasts was too much for his rejected libido to handle. Now, stopping at the saloon and drowning his frustration was out of the question. He cursed inwardly.

"Very well, I'll make a list."

He watched, burning to possess her, as she moved to her writing desk. Her tiny waist and the small curve of her hips and rounded bottom swayed enticingly. She was dressed in a faded brown muslin dress that looked like it was about to slide off her slender shoulders. It took all his control not to throw her on the table, rip that dreary dress from her body and sink between her trim legs.

"I'll be outside." His was voice rigid as he stalked into the bright morning sun, eager to breathe space unscented by females. Three of them: small, smaller and smallest. How did his father do it?

"Easy," he muttered aloud. "He got to fuck *small* every night." In a sudden fit of rage, he kicked at the dirt, sending a cloud of dust and rocks barreling into the barn wall with resounding clunks.

* * * *

Shelby and Emma kept him laughing on the trip home with stories about Megan's arrival at the ranch, their lack of knowledge regarding the farm and cooking techniques. Their teacher's attempt to teach the boys how to dance with girls was also amusing.

Not once could he remember when he'd laughed so hard. Aside from the stares and whispers from curious townsfolk, it wasn't a bad trip after all, he concluded when they pulled up to the house, the wagon loaded down with supplies. Megan handed him a list with a few items. Thanks to mile-a-minute Shelby, the list grew while they were in town.

Shelby ran inside to show Megan her new rag doll. Emma followed, doing her best not to look just as excited about the new book she'd picked out. Considering her attitude from the get-go, Emma wasn't such a bad kid after all. The kid had spunk. He had to admire her. Though she'd opened up a little, he knew she was holding back. She was a kindred spirit that only he could understand. There was more to the girl waiting to be unleashed—that is, if he took the time and decided to stay awhile.

He shook his head broodingly, leaving the small items on the porch. On his way back, he would carry those in the house for Megan. Leading the wagon to the barn in order to unload the larger supplies for the animals, he wondered about the money situation. The Spawn name had vast holdings in three Eastern banks that he knew of. Unless Reed was the type to squeeze a dollar until it bled, there was no reason for them to do without a damn thing.

It wasn't his place to question Reed's financial habits he decided and pushed the matter aside. He began to unload the wagon. One more day, he reminded himself.

* * * *

"Mr. Spawn, may I have a word with you?" The censure in her voice several minutes later caught his attention, as she hoped it would. If not for a tiny stiffness in his bearing, Megan would have guessed otherwise, from his failure to acknowledge her with as much as a glance.

Without a reply, he continued to unload bags of oats from the wagon and pile them in a corner of the barn as she trailed behind.

"My concern is in regard to your purchases."

As he tossed a sack on the growing pile, he rolled his eyes. Megan ignored his indifference and kept right on talking. "Much more than what was on the list. Are you extending your stay?"

He pulled a bag out of the wagon, pausing long enough to glare at her. She wasn't about to cower. Throwing the bag over his shoulder, he stalked off. She followed a few hurried steps behind.

"Not that I have a right to refuse if you so choose. You see, herein lies my true concern."

He walked faster.

She had to lift the front of her skirt above her ankles as she scurried to keep up with him. The hem of her oversized brown dress dragged in the dirt.

"The girls, you see, Mr. Spawn—Shelby and Emma." She lied. She was eager to have him leave to preserve her sanity. One look at him and her stomach muscles tightened in need. Even now, her breath started to catch. She tried not to notice the sweat glistening on the dark patch of skin beneath his partially unbuttoned shirt or how his rolled sleeves revealed each flexing muscle and corded vein on his strong forearms while he worked. His buckskins clung to every muscle along his powerful thighs and tight rear like a second skin. Such a view made her long to feel his legs wrap around her.

"Their gifts, it's...it's improper. Considering how the money was obtained," she snapped, covering her heightened state of arousal.

When he cast a fierce glance over his shoulder, she knew she'd touched a raw nerve. There was no proud haughtiness lurking in the dark shadows in his eyes often unduly warranted by men living the way of the gun, but she sensed a deep-rooted bitterness.

Not accustomed to running, she paused a moment to catch her breath. Undid the top two buttons of her bodice to fan herself with the loose muslin material in an attempt to cool off and calm her trampled nerves. Her pulse seemed to race beyond control. A lecture was not her intent. No matter the intended duration of his visit, ground rules were in order if she were to survive.

Her breathing restored, driven by determination, she rambled on hurrying to keep pace with his long strides again.

"If you'll be departing as proclaimed, it is best for all involved if you have as little involvement with the girls as possible."

On his way inside the barn he stopped short and she ran right into his back with a resounding grunt. Tossing the bag of oats off his shoulder, he grabbed her roughly by the upper arms.

Startled by his powerful display of dominance, she gasped. Her arms were pinned to her side, toes barely touching the ground, leaving her helpless. Fear and excitement raked over her skin, leaving her terrified at what he would do to her.

"What are doing? Unhand me." She meant to shout, but it came out needy, desperate. Her eyes widened, witnessing the fury in the taut, determined lines in his strong-edge face. The piercing silver in his eyes deepened to dark charcoal. She drew in a ragged breath, and the outdoorsy scent of his hard body filled her nostrils, making her feel faint.

"I've been listening to you yap. Now you listen, and listen well. I'll leave when I damn well please. I'll buy what I damn well please. I'll speak to my own sisters whenever I damn well please. As for where the money came from, it's none of your damn business."

He released her so abruptly she stumbled backwards. She rubbed her arms, not that it hurt, but because the blaze of lust she felt at his rough touch was wickedly intense. It scorched her senses and frightened her. Her chest heaved with shock at the arousal racing through her system and her willingness to accept the extremely intoxicating lust he exuded.

She stared at him, wild-eyed and furious. Without regard, he turned his back to her. Her nerves and emotions were in shambles, rioting while he calmly picked up the bag of oats and swaggered off.

"I...I just didn't want them to get attached, that's all," she stammered feeling as though she'd been reprimanded. His arrogance and mistreatment left her aflame, puzzled. What was she thinking? She'd never treat a rabid dog the way he treated her, much less a child. Megan couldn't take another moment being near him. Part of her wanted to kick him off her land, and something deep inside her wanted to throw herself at him, cling to him and never let go.

She'd lost her mind. There was absolutely no other logical explanation.

Devin Spawn had to leave, and soon.

Terrified by the shocking longing washing through her body, she snarled, "You don't know the first thing about children."

"Hell and damnation, woman," he growled as he swung around. "You don't know when to quit." He tossed the fifty-pound bag of oats aside as if it were a loaf of bread, and with long, purposeful strides, started toward her.

Her heart flipped at the menacing glint in his eyes. In an attempt to escape, she backed up until flush against the barn wall. She was a few feet off from her intended target, the opened barn door to her right.

With a hand braced on either side of her head, he leaned close, trapping her against the wall. His heady, masculine scent was alluring, arousing her weakened system further as his eyes burned into hers.

Unable to drag her eyes away from his, she eyed him nervously. He was much too close. She needed distance. Plenty of distance. Miles and miles of distance. Megan splayed both hands against his chest to shove him away but they stilled the instant her fingers touched his bare, sweat-drenched flesh.

The heat generated from the hard muscles of his chest seared her skin, and the pounding of his heart rivaled her own.

"Don't fret over what you can't control. Bonds don't form in a few days," his tone hard, disciplined. His gaze was dark and intense, yet his full lips parted softly. His handsome face hovered inches from hers as if he wanted to kiss her. A kiss she'd welcome as she had by the river.

"You're right," she breathed, and he blinked as if startled by her assent. Besieged by her desire, hot bolts of arousal and lust raged through her blood straight to her throbbing pussy. The heat of his body whipped around her, mesmerized her and depleted her strength. She felt her knees weaken. She was mad for wanting him, but heaven help her, she did.

"It takes an instant," she whispered, finding her gaze coast to the fullness of his lips, deep rose and lusciously sinful. She wanted to moan at the heated memory of his kiss, the silkiness of his lips and velvet moistness of his tongue. The lingering taste of him left her hungry for more. His nearness stealing what remained of her breath.

As though he read her thoughts, his eyes wandered down the length of her body and settled on the swell of her breasts, visible beneath her gaping neckline.

She felt her nipples hardening from the intensity of his gaze, aching for his caress. Desperate to feel his lips on hers, his touch on her skin, she waited, dying to scream in frustration at the need pulsing through her.

Sexual tension swirled around them in droves, drawing out the lengthy silence, filling the air with their fevered breathing.

When he finally lifted his eyes, the glaze of lust in the heated depths had her heart pounding in her chest. She knew he felt the same. Their instantaneous attraction had ignited at first touch. The desire for more simmered beneath the surface, ready to blaze into a raging inferno of passion. Neither of them could deny the sexual heat sharpening their breathing, heating their skin or darkening their expressions.

Did they dare?

He leaned closer. Her head titled up, and her lips parted in anticipation. Daringly, her fingers slid over his bare skin beneath his shirt. She felt him shudder, his breath growling from deep within his chest. She struggled to keep her eyes open, holding her breath. Desperate, she awaited the heated touch of his soft lips, now only a breath away from hers. So close, she felt the heat of his lips caress hers like a moistened kiss.

"Megan." It was the tiny voice of Shelby, calling from the front porch.

In a fit of rage, his curse cut through the silence like a savage dagger leavening no prisoners. He straightened swiftly and punched the wall to the side of her head. Her eyes closed as the loud bang echoed in her ears, vibrating the debilitated planks at her back. Several cracks formed in the wooden plank in his wake.

Unmet yearning. Oh, yes, she understood devastation all too well. Her own displeasure would drive her to a similar reaction if she claimed the strength. Powerless to her desire, she watched him, unable to move or speak.

He promptly saddled Deuce and raced off, just as Shelby skipped into the barn, new doll in hand.

Chapter 9

Tired and perfectly content after spending the past several hours taking Cheri, Pearl, and Violet in every way imaginable several times until they passed out from exhaustion, Devin was ready to put up with anything. With no desire to remain in town and sleep on a lumpy mattress too small for his long legs, he looked forward to his last night in the luxurious comfort of Reed's oversized bed.

After settling Deuce in the stall for the night, he pushed the front door open, took a step inside, and froze.

"Devin! Don't look," Emma and Shelby shrieked as they tried to cover their nakedness with their little hands while standing in the tin washtub in the middle of the parlor area while Megan rinsed their soapy hair.

He slapped a hand over his eyes, apologizing profusely while he eased out of the house. He felt his way along the wooden door with his free hand.

In shock, he shut the door and stared wide-eyed at it.

Safely on the porch, he shook his head, never realizing little girls could scream so loud. His heart was actually racing. That was one spectacle he didn't want to repeat.

He stormed toward the barn, saddled Deuce, and away they galloped as the cool night air clipped around them.

Little girls didn't do a damn thing for him. Add little sisters, and the mix became that much more appalling.

"Women and children—the whole lot of them aren't worth the time or trouble," he spat.

Months of solitude in the wilderness only intensified his dark desires. His sexual demands were rough, intensely dominant, and sometimes downright abusive. He would never intentionally hurt his partners, but his twelve-inch cannon left first timers raw and aching for days. Like a lust-driven disease he couldn't control, it seeped into his blood and ravaged his system until he was left succumbing to his explosive impulses.

He didn't know how to behave around ladies, instead seeking release with two-bit whores, and often times, Indian squaws, built strong and trained to endure the pain he so often enjoyed inflicting.

Protection!

His father had asked him to protect his beautiful young widow. Did Reed not know what his son had truly become? Who would protect Megan from him? He wanted to fuck her until she screamed, begged him to stop. He wanted to dominate her, to possess her, to tie her up and force her to submit to his every depraved demand.

He was an animal, a savage beast. A beast to be driven back to the seclusion of the wilderness, among other unholy creatures of nature.

Dear frail Megan, so tiny and childlike—if she knew what he wanted to do to her, she would be horrified. Never intentionally would he hurt a woman or child. He'd even gone so far as to take the lives of members of his own gang if they dared tried to harm one in front of him. Megan needn't fear for her life, only her innocent body being dominated by primitive lust so potent, it combined forbidden pleasure and searing pain.

For now, she was safe, but he didn't know how much longer he could contain the fury welling inside him. She was his father's widow, legally his stepmother. It was wrong, even to him, a man who knew no bounds legally or morally. Visions of her in his father's arms ran rampant, eating away at him like a vile poison.

After tomorrow's funeral, he'd turn Deuce's reins to where he belonged, lost in the vast openness of the wilds and never look back.

* * * *

Kerosene lights in the great room were dim, and the house was quiet. Devin breathed a sigh of relief as he approached the porch. It was late, and he and Deuce had ridden for miles. All he wanted to do now was crawl into bed and go to sleep.

With the assumption he'd given them plenty of time to bathe and go bed, he lightly tapped the front door. There was no response. Slowly, he opened it, stepped inside, and took in the dimly lit surroundings. A smile of satisfaction curled his lips as he carefully barred the door behind him, making sure not to make any noise.

Like a mountain lion in sight of his prey he catfooted across the room. Perched slightly on the edge of the couch, he gazed into the bathtub only a foot in front of him.

There, Megan slept, submerged in water just below her breasts, arms resting atop the rim of the large tin bathtub. Both legs bent, leaning to one side, shielding his view of her most intimate charms except the very top curls on her fleshy mound. White rose petals floated softly atop the steaming water.

Her head tilted backward, lips slightly parted, and her honey-colored ringlets cascading to the floor in a silken waterfall. Her skin, flushed from the warmth of the water, glowed in the soft, flickering lights from the fireplace.

His darkened gaze rested on her breasts, and he counted each deep breath as they rose and fell just above the waterline. The nipples, only tiny pink beads waiting to be touched, pinched, nipped, and sucked, centered teasingly in round areolas so pale, they almost blended in with her cream-colored skin.

He lounged back on the sofa, allowing his legs to spread wide. His engorged erection throbbed in his buckskins like a beating drum. A little more than three hours ago, he left not one, not two, but three women back at Jazelle's Place, thoroughly and totally fucked and absolutely certain they wouldn't be able to get out of bed tomorrow.

He sought release to cleanse his mind and satisfy the deep craving to take what wasn't his.

All because of a skinny, flesh-and-bone girl who was too small to be considered a full-grown woman. Though at the moment, judging from the boiling blood surging through his veins, the lust blurring his eyes, and the hefty size of his erection, every necessary quality was in perfect form.

Damn, she was beautiful. Soft firelight blended with shadows, contouring the swell of her breasts and her delicately slender neck. Moistened porcelain skin only enhanced her svelte figure with a sensuality that negated her childlike appearance, much to his satisfaction.

Dammit. He wanted her so bad. His skin was fraught with tension so tight, it vibrated in his eardrums. She was so close, he could feel the heat of her skin caress his and smell the scent of roses and innocence swirling around him.

Unconsciously, he stroked his cock through the material until the pain became unbearable. He gritted his teeth at the memory of her tight, hot wetness gripping him as the flared head stretched her wide. Oh, hell, if he kept this up, the front of his buckskins would be as soaked as she was. It was then he dipped a hand in the warm water and splashed a few drops in her face.

* * * *

Megan jerked her head upright, waking with a start. Her heart beat madly. Slowly, her eyes focused on Devin leaning over the tub. He stared at her, his hand idly making circular motions in the water. She clutched her bent legs to her chest and curled into a tense ball.

"Get out," she snapped, her tone heavy with distaste, jerking her head toward the front door.

He regarded her quietly. The lust, raw and unbridled, blazed in his eyes.

"Why?" Devin sat upright slightly, hands dangling between his parted knees.

"Extend me the same courtesy you extended Shelby and Emma. Allow me to dress out of common decency."

"You've had plenty of time, *mother*."

"The water had to be reheated…" Suddenly forgoing her superfluous need to explain, she changed her tune when the endearment sank in. She shook her head, annoyed by her rambling. "How many times do I have to tell you I'm not you're mother? So please stop calling me that."

"Precisely why I'm staying." His tone was low and provocative as his eyes seemed to melt liberally over her body. He grinned and settled further back into the couch, resting his powerful, muscled arms along the back, extending his long legs on either side of the bathtub. "You're not blood."

Her gaze lowered to his erection, thick and hard, gloriously outlined and strained against his form-fitted buckskins. Without volition, she gasped. He tried hard not to notice how her body trembled with desire and how her eyes grew heavy. Mesmerized, she licked her lips and forgot to breathe feeling a heated wetness gush between her thighs.

"We need to talk."

Her mouth fell open, yet not a sound escaped. Briefly, she met his gaze and dropped it involuntarily to the riveting bulge once again. The grand image of what was beneath bombarded her senses. Amazingly, his cock throbbed under her blatant stare, and she literally heard herself whimper.

Pure lust, clear as day is what she felt. The same as when she looked up at him down by the river and whispered, "*Don't stop.*" Her body was on fire, she could feel the juices of her pussy leaking into the bath water, her desire raising the temperature.

"Megan." His voice sounded pained, heated with arousal as he sat upright.

It drew her attention instantly. The first time he called her by name. Not Mother, not Mrs. Spawn, and not Dimples, but Megan. Dazed by the enchanted music to her ears it took a moment to clear her mind.

Then, she noticed his eyes roaming over her, consuming her as if he fought the temptation to drag her out of the bathtub and pull her into his strong embrace. If he reached for her, took what he wanted, she wouldn't stop him, couldn't stop him. She needed him deep inside her. She wanted him to make her forget the past. Wanted to lose herself in his arms and not even think about the future, just live for the here and now and the pleasure she'd tasted on his lips.

With bated breath, she waited for him to make a move, give her a sign, anything that would give them permission to cross dangerous boundaries beyond sanity's existence.

Say yes.

Reach for me.

Anything.

The dreaded silence lengthened.

Megan stared at him, unable to breathe or move. Forbidden sensuality washed over her in waves. She waited. Waited for him to reach out and take what she was too afraid to give.

His expression was pained, frustrated and angry, but his eyes blazed with a primitive lust in the dark gray depths. Like a force of steel, he appeared to be fighting his own inner demons.

"Why is the ranch in such ruin?" This was the one question she feared.

Her heart stopped. Nightmares flooded back. She swallowed, gaping at him.

How did he know the ranch had been thriving? Reed was making a name for himself as a well-respected rancher. His illness alone should not have affected the running of the ranch.

"I want the truth." He sounded as impatient and frustrated as he looked.

"Now?" she asked hesitantly. All she wanted to do was scream never, not now, not ever.

"Yes, now. Tell me what happened."

"Can't this wait till tomorrow, or at least until I'm dressed?" she ventured in a tone that was both low and guarded.

"You've kept me waiting long enough. I would've have asked you earlier. Listening to your nonsense drove me away." His dark brows deepened in a scowl.

"Back to Jazelle's," she bit out and chided herself silently for showing the remote hint of jealously. She held no claim over him. He could do what he pleased. Apparently, he had, visiting Jazelle's twice in two days and returning smelling like he'd bathed in cheap perfume. *Horny toad bastard.*

"Don't try my patience," he replied instantly. "I guarantee you'll regret the consequences. I won't ask you again." His deep voice resonated with warning.

Further backward she sank, her backside butted tightly against the tub. She stared at her trembling kneecaps and took a deep breath. There was no getting around it—she either answered him or else turned into a prune. *Only specifics. Don't offer more than necessary.*

"After Reed's second stroke, he wasn't able to get around much. The field hands started to ask questions about the outlook of the ranch. I tried to assure them things would work out."

"Go on. Tell me, what happened to the cattle?"

"I rode out to the fields every now and then to check on things and noticed the cattle weren't being branded properly. I brought it up with the foreman. He said he would take care of it. They stalled with excuses. Insisted the hands wanted to be paid up front. I paid what I could, but they said it wasn't enough. I didn't have any more money. One day, they were gone."

"Who was gone?" His questioning gaze turned to annoyance, as if she wasn't providing answers fast enough.

"Everything. The foreman, the field hands, the cattle, pigs, everything."

"What happened?" His jaw tensed

"They took them."

"The hands?" he asked with a cold finality, and her pulse raced.

"They took every last head of cattle and supplies and everything else they could carry."

"Where did they go?" Devin's face turned to stone.

A vision of a tombstone flashed before her eyes. If she read the look in his eye correctly, whomever she mentioned would be dead before tomorrow's sunrise. A chill ran down her spine.

"It doesn't matter. It's too late now. Don't you see? You'll never get them back. They won't let you." Fear and remembrance shrouded her eyes.

"Who, Megan? Who?" he growled.

"He won't let you. They'll kill you as soon as you set foot on his property. It's no use. Don't even ask. They're gone."

"I'll be the judge of that. This ranch is mine now. No one cheats a Spawn. Tell me, what is his name?"

"Devin, he has hired guns for hands. He owns the Sheriff. It'll do no good. You'll only start more trouble for me and the girls. Please, let it go."

"I'll not ask you again. Either you tell me, or I'll drag you out of that tub as-is. We'll ride all over town till we find every last damn head of cattle and the sorry-assed bastard who was fool enough to think he could cheat a Spawn and get away with it."

"Hardin. Leroy Hardin." The name rolled off her tongue as though it was the most contemptuous, tainted, hated name to ever pass her lips. "Owns the ranch budding ours."

In a flash, he grabbed his rifle off the rack and headed for the door.

"Devin," she cried out, terrified, jumping to her feet. "They'll kill you."

"They'll try." He turned and faced her. His brows arched in surprise.

"Even if you survive, what will happen after you leave? The girls and I will still be here. Hardin will still be our neighbor." Her voice filled with concern and fear for not only him, but herself and the girls.

"What are you willing to offer to keep me here?" His darkening gaze roamed openly over her body, causing her to look down at herself. She gasped, suddenly realizing she was naked. She plopped back in the tub, sending water splashing over the sides in big waves as her body burned with humiliation.

"That's what I thought." His voice turned cold as he stormed into the darkness.

* * * *

Like a moonless phantom, he would creep in silently and kill them. Slaughter 'em one by one as they slept. Fifty, one hundred, the number was unimportant. He wanted to murder every one of the bastards. Moreover, he could.

If it weren't for Megan's tormented face haunting him. She'd just stood there with a pleading, worried look on her face, arms by her sides, completely nude and dripping wet. Water streamed down the peaks of her round breasts, the sparse thatch of dark blond curls matted, dribbled water between the hollow of her trim thighs and trickles of droplets slid down her smooth belly and slender legs.

At the sight, his cock had grown hard instantly. With the way he felt, it wouldn't have done either of them any good if he stayed. The only thing on his mind now was red. Blood red. His wrath would be directed at those deserving.

He understood all too well range wars between neighboring ranches could get pretty ugly, especially with cattle rustling involved. But to cheat a defenseless woman! A Spawn, no less. There was hell to pay, and it was up to him to collect.

The truth of her words burned in his ears. Tomorrow after Reed was laid to rest, she and the girls would remain to face the aftermath alone. It wouldn't be right.

Hell, when did he grow a fucking conscious?

His sight was set for the most grandiose spread nearby. He found the large, two-story adobe ranch house easily. It was lit enough to give off the impression activity was still taking place inside. Outside the home and around the outlying parameter, several lowlife ruffians patrolled, armed and alert.

Though not alert enough to spot him as he crawled through an upstairs window. With a whispered instruction and quick nod from his master, Deuce sauntered off into the night's blackened shadows.

Once inside, Devin acclimated to the darkness rather well. As he suspected, judging from the size and amount of windows on the outside, this had to be Leroy Hardin's bedroom. It was large, took up an entire end of the second floor. It was decorated rather comfortably with dark, masculine furniture and a huge bed butted up against the windows.

Devin opened the bedroom door a crack and concentrated for a minute on the jumble of male voices coming from downstairs. Satisfied he was at the right place, he closed the door. There was nothing else to do but wait for his host.

He positioned himself in the far left corner of the room, opposite the direction light would fall from the opened doorway.

His wait was not long. Keenly, he listened to the advance of footsteps over the carpeted hallway and the soft muttering of voices, one male and one female. He heard the distinct male voice wish someone a goodnight and then a rustle of skirts, as though the female leaned over to kiss him farewell.

Accustomed to execution of his duties at night, he eased a bowie knife from a sheath strapped to his calf. He waited, not moving a muscle, for the right moment as the knob turned and the door opened. From the hallway light, he could distinguish a, tall, slender, balding man step into the room and close the door behind him as he reached for the oil sconce.

With a resounding thud, the knife pierced the red plaid wallpaper inches from Leroy Hardin's hand, just before he touched the wall sconce.

"I wouldn't do that if I were you." Devin's deep voice warned instantaneously as Hardin reached for his gun. Another knife pierced the door inches away from his now stilled hand above the six-shooter strapped to the man's hip.

"Wouldn't do that, either." His tone was now a vicious warning.

Mr. Hardin raised both hands in the air, squinting as if trying to make out the dark figure and voice coming from the darkness while he stood in the faint ambient light shining through the windows.

"My boys will—" he started arrogantly.

"Find your throat slashed," Devin finished for him, guessing the gutless man was ready to shout for backup. He hired gunslingers to do the dirty work he was either incapable of doing or didn't want to dirty his hands with.

"What do you want?" Hardin bit out.

"Make amends amongst neighbors."

"Neighbors use the front door." Hardin's tone was quick and sarcastic.

"Backdoor's more to my liking."

"Do you mind if I sit?" He nodded in the direction of the plush side chair near the window closest to the lamp outside. "My legs are tiring out."

"Nice chair. Wouldn't want you to stain it." Devin could hear the man's deep exhalation at the implicit threat.

"Start talking," Hardin said bluntly, standing absolutely still.

"I'm here on behalf of the Spawn Ranch."

"I have no beef with Reed," he snapped back.

"I say you do."

"Look here, mister. Don't know what you heard—"

"Heard you took some cattle didn't belong to you from an ailing old man and his wife," Devin interrupted.

"Whatever yarn she wove is a lie. No one round here listens to a two-bit whor—" The knife slicing the top of his ear off halted the ending of his sentence. Instinctively, Hardin's hand went to what was left of his bloodied ear, and he grunted.

"Speak out of line again, and the next will cut out your fool tongue." Devin spewed pure hatred, and Leroy Hardin's eyes widened as he swallowed harshly, blood gushing from the gash in his ear, spilling down his arm.

"Where's the cattle?"

"Done drove 'em to Louisiana."

"Mighty neighborly of you to go through the trouble. Mrs. Spawn will appreciate the money from the bill of sale you made on her behalf."

"Why, I—" Hardin stammered.

"You have a problem with that?"

"No. No, of course not. Don't have that kind of money lying around."

"Bank's open tomorrow. She'll wait till then."

"Look here, she doesn't know what's owed her. We can make some sort of deal. I like how you handle things. Ride for me. I'll pay you well."

"Wouldn't you like to know who you're hiring?"

"Doesn't matter. I could use a fella like you 'round." Hardin's tone grew in confidence.

"Turn on the light," Devin instructed in a throaty whisper, smoldering in the darkness.

Steadily, Hardin reached for the oil sconce ensuring no moves were misjudged. As the light filled the room, his face went pale when he faced Devin.

Devin had leaned casually in the corner with a foot planted on the wall behind him. He nudged the brim of his hat off his forehead to give Leroy a good, long look.

"Name's Spawn…Devin Spawn," he drawled.

Leroy Hardin's face turned a nasty shade of green, and his eyes bulged in their sockets.

No doubt, Leroy Hardin had heard a story or two. Within gun sight of the devil himself, Hardin should be guessing right about now he was damned lucky to still be alive.

Across the room, Devin moved but kept his eyes on the other man. He extracted the knife near the wall sconce. Hardin flinched.

"Seeing as how I own the ranch," Devin stated matter-of-factly in his deep, calculated tone as he reclaimed the knife near Hardin's hip and returned both to their sheaths, "don't think I'll be able to take…" He pulled the blooded knife that sliced through the man's ear from the door and wiped it on Hardin's upper arm. "You up on your generous offer."

Devin stepped back, and returned the bowie knife to the sheath strapped to his waist. "You have till noon tomorrow to make amends."

Chapter 10

Devin chose the cover of the pecan trees to the right of the ranch house, a position to give him a clear view, unrestricted shot and cover from approaching riders from different angles. The small hill behind the barn and larger hills behind the house meant riders had to travel over the hills, or take the dirt trail leading to the house and risk detection. A bigger risk to anyone sneaking up tonight would be to angle across the open land to the left of the house or cut through the pecan trees, where he could easily hear them. Whichever way they chose, he could see them, yet they couldn't see him. Thanks to his Comanche friends, he was a master at blending into his surroundings and moving about undetected.

He didn't bother to go inside and inform Megan of the situation. She'd find out soon enough when the fireworks began if Mr. Hardin didn't take kindly to Devin's suggestion.

There was nothing else for him to do but wait.

When the stars dimmed and the blackened sky turned to gentle hues of yellow and blue, he couldn't help but bemoan his annoyance. If Hardin started in on him, as Devin hoped he would, then he could finish off the no-account scum.

Appears Mrs. Megan Spawn was coming into some money.

"Lucky bastard gets another day," he grumbled as he drifted silently into the house, bearing an armload of firewood for the hearth and a bucket of water to make a pot of coffee before Megan woke up. Since he wasn't able to get any sleep, he needed the jolt a hot cup of black coffee supplied.

His sense of hearing was acute. The squeak of the mattress told him she'd climbed out of bed. Moreover, the shuffling of tiny feet slipping into her house slippers and rustle of clothing as she donned her robe lent an intimacy to his mind's eye. The light patter over the wooden planks moving toward the bedroom door made him more anxious than he had a right to be.

He sat in the chair positioned near the parlor window, his gaze focused on the landscape before him.

He gathered from her startled gasp when she opened the bedroom door that she was very surprised to see him alive. With his back to her, she couldn't see the smirk on his face.

"Morning," he offered quietly without turning around.

She rushed to his side, a white eyelet robe wrapped tightly around her small frame. Underneath, an oversized, long-sleeved eyelet nightgown buttoned to the neck dragged on the floor.

Did none of her clothes fit properly? he wondered. Her long, honey-colored ringlets tousled down her back and over her shoulders. Her face was drawn, and there were dark shadows under her eyes. From the looks of it, he could tell she'd had a rough night.

"Devin," she breathed. Her eyes seemed to absorb him like a venerated apparition. As if requiring reassurance he was real and not a dream, she laid a hand on his shoulder

He stared at the dainty hand resting on his shoulder and followed it up to her eyes. The heat of that one little unexpected touch burned right through his clothes and stirred his groin. Covered from neck to her toes, she looked damned sexier than any naked, sprawled-out, highfalutin whore he'd ever laid eyes on.

"Made coffee," he offered, dropping his gaze once again to the small hand searing his flesh through his clothing because he couldn't bare to look at her a moment longer without touching her.

* * * *

Megan looked where he did, withdrawing her hand from his shoulder quickly. She tucked the robe tightly under her neck, suddenly feeling as exposed as last night when she stood in the washtub. The intensity of his silvery eyes washed over like heated waves, seeping through her pores and ignited what she could only name as forbidden arousal.

The only fate worse than Devin Spawn's death would be his continued existence on the Reed Ranch.

Dear God, how would she manage to ignore this man when she could scarcely breathe whenever he was near?

"What happened?" she asked uneasily, afraid to acknowledge last night's vexing exchange had truly transpired, but she had to know. She held her breath, and waited.

"Son-of-a-bitch is still alive." His voice weighed heavily with distaste. "He'll pony up."

A miserable dread filled her soul at his declaration. Her tightening heart gripped her. *Hardin is alive.* She wanted to get away from Devin's searching eyes, but he followed her to the kitchen,

"Since he hasn't done so by now, I doubt he'll trouble you again."

Since he hasn't done so by now. She paused mid-motion, reaching for one of the cups stacked on the shelf. Her body stiffened.

"Whether I'm here or not, he's aware the ranch is mine."

His voice brought her out of her reverie. She swung to face him, cup clutched in a death grip to her chest, and practically shrieked, "Are you certain?"

"Only way to be certain is to return and kill the slimy snake." Devin leaned his hip against the counter, arms crossed over his chest. He tilted his head, his silver eyes studying her. As though he could read her thoughts and see the fear gripping her soul, he goaded, "A nod will do."

Briefly closing her eyes, she shook her head. Though she didn't want anything more than to see Leroy Hardin get what he deserved, if she said yes, that would make her no better than him.

"No, if you scared him well enough to leave me—the ranch alone, that suffices." She breathed a sigh of relief.

Reputation alone could ward off a lesser man. Face to face with solid-muscled, six-foot-nine Devin Spawn was menacing to all others. Truly, she wanted to know what he'd done to the morally reprehensible man, but held her tongue.

"Sure?" he asked.

"Quite," she replied, pouring a cup of coffee. "I'll start breakfast as soon as I change," she added quickly to change the subject. To avoid further discussion, she took a sip of coffee while hurrying to her room. She really meant to visit the chamber pot, but those silvery eyes followed her everywhere. The last thing she wanted to do was give him any ideas of watching her in the most compromising of positions. The man had seen her do everything else. She needed some element of mystery.

* * * *

After breakfast, he heard them in the distance, felt the faint rumble beneath his feet. Riders, seventy or more, approached fast from the north at least five miles away.

Hardin's ranch was to the east. Without question, Devin knew it wasn't him. There was only one other possibility. On intuition alone, he finished hitching the wagon for Megan and the girls, who were inside dressing for the funeral. When that was done, he made his way to the barn.

Deuce was clamoring in his stall, seemingly aware of the impending situation.

"You're ready to fly." He walked over to his horse and stroked his nose, calming him down. "Not this time, fella. Best if you stay behind."

He saddled up one of Reed's stallions. Whether it was an act of bravery or gutlessness, he decided against going into the house to retrieve his rifle.

Outside of the barn, he mounted the black stallion and stared at the ranch house for a good long while.

No need for goodbyes.

Who knew if he would ever return?

One thing for certain, he wasn't one to run. In the past, he would have stayed and fought. Not now. Not with the girls nearby. Today, he'd face his future head on. With the decision settled, he flew north to whatever lay ahead.

* * * *

Megan heard a horse gallop off and ventured outside to investigate. Devin was nowhere to be found. Deuce was in his stall, and Shadow, Reed's favorite horse, was missing, along with Devin's saddle.

The wagon was already hitched and ready for her and the girls. He had given his word that he would follow them to the funeral. With the services to begin less than an hour from now, her imagination ran rampant. If he showed up smelling of stale flowers again, she'd shoot him on sight and bury his whoring remains next to Reed. In a huff, she climbed the steps leading to the porch.

As she reached the front door, she heard the rumbling of hooves charging wildly through the bend and swung around. Her heart stopped the moment she saw Leroy Hardin riding in her direction, with eight of his men following closely behind.

"I'm looking for Mr. Spawn," he stated abruptly, pulling to a stop in front of her while a few of his men spread around the yard, their trigger hands perilously close to their firearms.

"Reed has passed on. Funeral is this morning." Her eyes swept over the men. A few of them she didn't recognize. A couple used to work for Reed. And the one by his side, Rusty, she hated almost as much as she hated Hardin.

"My business is with Reed's son, Devin Spawn."

"I expect him back shortly," she lied, but his sort of scum didn't deserve the truth. Hardin's left ear was bandaged, and she couldn't help but speculate Devin's involvement. She would have felt a sense of morbid satisfaction, except upon hearing Devin wasn't there, Hardin's guarded gaze turned malicious.

Her stomach churned.

At a half shake of Hardin's head, Rusty leapt from his saddle and joined her on the porch.

"Nice to see ya again, Megan." Hardin's right-hand man grinned, displaying his tobacco stained teeth as he leaned in to pass her an envelope. His foul onion breath and squalid odor assailed her nostrils. She turned her face away from his, and took a step back.

Rusty gave a raucous laugh that raked Megan's ears.

Inwardly, she flinched. That laugh echoed in the deep recesses of her memory. Her teeth clenched. She fought to hold back the tears threatening her eyes.

Rusty leaned in closer to drop the plain white envelope by the hem of her skirt. He whispered, "You's a widow now. Lots of lonesome nights ahead, huh?"

Without waiting for a reply, the red-haired gunslick jumped back on his horse.

"Tell Mr. Spawn I hope it is to his satisfaction." Hardin's cool tone sounded forced, and the evocative look he gave her was anything but cordial.

As soon as they turned the reins on their horses, she ran inside and heaved her breakfast in the chamber pot.

* * * *

It wasn't long before Devin reached them. From his estimate, there were closer to one hundred riders, an entire well-armed regiment of blue sitting straight in their saddles.

Now, that's mighty strange, Devin thought. He was expecting a U.S. Marshal and a shitload of trailing posse, not the United States Calvary. He was fully aware the army abstained from civic affairs, concentrating mainly on Indian and Mexico relations in these parts. That's when they bothered to venture this far south, since there weren't very many white settlements in what was still considered Mexico.

As soon as they spotted him, the first squadron followed orders, prepared to fire. Their rifles jerked in a straight row like a tightly strung clothesline, every barrel pointed at him.

Without a break in stride, he held his course until he reached what he assumed was the commanding officer off to the side of the front line. He brought the black horse to a snorting, dusty stop in front of a stern, gray-haired man in full military garb. Devin grinned. "Mornin'."

"Devin Spawn, you're under arrest." The captain faced his second-in-command by his side and ordered their prisoner be searched, stripped of all weapons and hands bound.

"Mind if I ask why the military has taken a fancy to me?" Devin inquired directly, maintaining his calm demeanor as several soldiers approached him cautiously.

"You may take it up with my superior officer, Colonel Thomas O'Roake."

"Where is this Thomas fellow?" He asked informally, just to piss off the stuffy officer.

Captain Derby sneered at him. "Colonel O'Roake is at Camp Griffin. We shall arrive tomorrow evening."

* * * *

The following evening, Devin and his captors descended upon Camp Griffin. A bugle rang out, heralding their approach. Immediately, Captain Derby rushed him inside the colonel's office. Colonel O'Roake sat behind a large maple desk, with several officers seated nearby.

"Mr. Spawn, have a seat, please."

Devin glanced around the room. He was the one with a ten-thousand-dollar hide. Nonetheless, the tension these rigid military men exuded couldn't be sliced with a razor-sharp knife. The fine hairs on the back of his neck raised in heightened awareness. The bounty money, the Indian trader, and the twist of fate tied to Reed's decline—it all boiled down to this.

Like a good soldier, shackled, weaponless, and out of uniform, he plopped in the chair indicated directly in front of the colonel's desk.

Without delay, the colonel placed the wanted poster in front of him. Devin eyed it dismissively.

"These posters have been forwarded around the country."

"I have one. Don't like the drawing much. Doesn't quite capture my eyes."

The colonel regarded him fleetingly and continued to speak. "As noted, it states alive. The constraint can easily be revised."

"Why bother? You already have me under arrest." He shrugged his shoulders and rattled the shackles binding his arms behind his back to prove his point.

"Mr. Spawn," the Colonel stated heatedly, "my orders come from the top. Personally, I am appalled to sit across from a lawless, vicious killer who has no regard for human decency. I wouldn't trust you with my worst enemy's mangy mutt, let alone your word, but your skills are legendary."

Were all prisoners treated this way? Devin wondered. His gaze darted to the other men seated in the room, who were listening very intently while scrutinizing his every move. Tied up and unarmed, what did they really expect him to do? Well, he could think of a few things.

Leaning back in his chair, he exhaled deeply to give the impression he was bored. It didn't sit well with the colonel, whose tone grew agitated.

"Your association with the Laredo Gang is why you are here. Although you haven't ridden with them for a few years, you may be aware of their actions. Your reputation as a fearless marksman and tracker exceed—"

"Quit fluffing my feathers," Devin interrupted gruffly. "What is it you want?"

"My directive is to petition you to track down the Laredo Gang."

"Why?"

"They raided a wagon shipment of ours. Murdered the entire garrison of fifty men. The wagons carried enough rifles and ammunition to arm the entire Cheyenne nation. That's where we suspect they're headed. The Chickasaws and Choctaws are refusing to sign a treaty to cede their land in Mississippi and relocate to a reservation. We have word if the Cheyenne get hold of the arsenal beforehand, the other tribes, along with the Potawatami, will join them. We'll have a bloodbath on our hands. Hundreds of innocent lives, women and children, will be lost."

"What's my part?" Devin didn't fault the Chickasaws or Choctaws. No man wants to be run off his land. He figured the men in the room hadn't dragged him here for his opinion.

"Track them, dispose of them and return military weaponry."

"And?"

"If you agree to assist your government in this very delicate matter, you will receive the reward money for the return of the weapons and each member you bring to justice. In addition, President Adams will grant a full pardon."

"If I don't?"

"In the event you consent and fail to follow through, then "dead" will be added to the poster, and the award will be increased. You'll spend the remainder of your days looking over your shoulder. We both know there won't be too many of those."

Devin quirked a brow. The Colonel didn't know him too well.

"You've gone through an awful lot of trouble to find me. I missed my own father's funeral."

"We hope it's been worth it. What's your answer?"

"Why the hell not? I could use the target practice."

"We'll discuss the plans tonight. I'll have supper brought in for you." With a brief a nod from Colonel O'Roake, a low-ranking officer left the room to fulfill the meal request. "How many troops will you require? Lieutenant Allen will assign them immediately."

A young man stood, tall and stiff as a pine tree. Devin eyed him disapprovingly, assumed the spiffy toy soldier was Lieutenant Allen. He shook his head. It amazed him how the colonel didn't even have to snap his fingers, and yet, these boys still jumped at the slightest provocation. If he ever joined the army, he doubted not more than an hour would pass before he punched someone's nose in at the first order.

"How many wagons?" Devin's eyes narrowed on the colonel.

"There are four wagons. Three loaded with rifles and one with ammunition. We estimate one hundred, perhaps two hundred troops should suffice?"

"Four."

"Four hundred? We don't have that many troops available. It will—"

"Do you have a doctor here?" Devin glanced up at the straight-arrow Lieutenant Allen, standing a few feet from him.

"Yes, do you feel ill?" A worried looked creased the Lieutenant's face.

"Colonel O'Roake needs his hearing checked." He faced O'Roake. "I said four, as in four men. Best shots available, if you want them back alive."

"Four men? That's preposterous. We have reports there are nearly thirty men riding in the Laredo Gang."

"Four men," Devin repeated. "Take off these damned cuffs, and we'll leave within the hour. After I collect my horse back at the ranch, I'll go after 'em."

With a nod from the colonel, Captain Derby quickly removed Devin's shackles.

"You'll need to eat and rest after the journey, and we have plenty of horses," Colonel O'Roake said matter-of-factly. "You may choose—"

"My horse or the deal is off. We leave tonight, or the deal is off."

* * * *

Later that evening, Megan still hadn't managed to dress for bed. Settled on the couch for the past hour, frowning with worry, she stirred her spoon in the cup of cold coffee. The girls were snuggled in their beds, and she'd sent a persistent, yet thoughtful Caleb away earlier that day.

With Reed laid to rest yesterday afternoon, there was no reason for Caleb to call daily in the pretense of a medical capacity. The only thing his presence accomplished was to feed the rumor mill.

Leroy Hardin's bank draft was deposited. Mr. Pierson, the banker, told her it would take several days before the money cleared. *"Bank regulations,"* he said with a smirk. More like Hardin up to his old tricks, she figured after hearing the rumor. The army had arrested the notorious outlaw, Devin Spawn, just outside of town. It was all the townsfolk paying their last respects to Reed wanted to discuss. If it were true, she'd never see a cent of the money Hardin earned from selling off Reed's cattle.

The money would really come in handy. Debts paid sooner than expected, insuring her and the girl's safety. With enough money left over to move if she decided. At least the issue of remarrying could be dealt with in due time.

Caleb Walker was her childhood sweetheart, best friend, and a kind, gentle man who loved her in return. She'd loved him since the moment she laid eyes on him as he slinked down the stairs the day Doctor Keeling dragged her, kicking and screaming with shock and fright, through the Walker's front door. It was the day after a rescue team searched the raided stagecoach and found her, the only survivor. She lost her father, pregnant mother, and younger brother, including the two drivers and a few other passengers. She was scared, dirty and downright scrawny. He was all arms and legs, with a mop of blond curls in permanent disarray and a smile filled with hope and joy. But his eyes, like brilliant sapphires, touched her heart instantly.

They became joined at the hip.

Only thirteen and alone in the world, she felt safe, secure, and loved with him. A love that intensified as the weeks passed. Deep and profound, strong enough for a young girl to risk her belief in propriety and do the inconceivable.

Her parents had been deeply in love, eager for a large family. Why couldn't she and Caleb have the same? Sometimes late at night, when her parents thought she and her brother were asleep, she'd sneak a peek at them cuddling in their bed. Or she lay awake and listen to their subdued moans as her body warmed.

Privacy in their one-room house back east was non-existent. Once in a while, the covers would slip off their joined bodies, giving her a good idea how she and her baby brother came to be.

With a teenaged exuberance, she longed to share the same intimacy with Caleb.

By the time they reached fourteen, they were cuddling like her parents used to. At least, at the time, she thought it was the same. Mr. Walker caught them in the horse stable. Mrs. Walker put Caleb on the next train to Europe to live with relatives, threw her out of their house, and warned every decent family in town not to take her in unless they wanted to board a trollop. Their husbands and sons would become ensnared by the witchery of a temptress with sin in her soul and lust on her mind and become tainted with mercenary desires. With a claim like that, no one dared take her in.

If not for Mrs. Walker's bitter hate and Megan's memory of the outcome of that fateful afternoon, there wasn't a doubt she and Caleb would be married at this point. As it was, Caleb never learned the entire lurid details of what transpired after he was dragged from the house.

Ten years later, she still didn't have the strength or desire to tell him.

For the next four years, her life had been full of dread and uncertainty, back-breaking work, and later, indoctrination. A true test of her trust, faith, and moral fiber, she resigned herself to live behind the only door opened to her, a sinkhole of depravity—Jazelle's Place.

And so it was as she sat on the couch in deep thought, unsure why Devin Spawn rode off two days ago. Certain there wasn't a man alive who could take on Devin, she refused to believe the rumor. It didn't seem like him to give up so easily without a fight. It just had to be sensationalism. No matter what, it didn't explain why he missed Reed's funeral, deserted them without a word. From the beginning, he said he was only passing through and was neither baby sitter nor protector. At least he could have said goodbye.

Her parents never had the opportunity to say goodbye. Reed passed away, unable to speak. Now, Devin was gone.

If the rumors where true, she'd be left with only one conclusion. Hardin's check would never clear. With her debt unpaid, she'd be left no choice but to return to Jazelle's.

Caught up in musing, the sharp knock at the door made her jump. When the Sheriff's voice rang out, her first consideration was Devin. Her next was the absurdity of Sheriff Tucker showing up with news of Devin Spawn, when no one other than Leroy Hardin was certain he was Reed's son.

The alarm going off in her head was too late as she opened the door. To her wide-eyed shock, a bold hand shoved her inside while another aimed a pistol at her, and a booted foot kicked the door wide open. As the scream left her mouth, a familiar red-headed figure rushed inside. His large, calloused hand covered her mouth as he pinned her arm behind her back and pushed her against the wall.

"Soon, you'll be screaming for a different reason, Megan," he snickered against her throat, his whiskey and tobacco breath throttling her senses, chilling her blood. She shook her head furiously, her eyes wide with fear as the sheriff and two more men pushed their way into the house.

The girls! Her heart pounded against her chest. *Not the girls!*

She kicked and clawed, biting the hand ground into her face as all four men pinned her to the floor, gagged her, and tied her up.

Please, dear God, not the girls!

Once subdued, Rusty tossed her hog-tied body over his saddle, mounted, and settled her deviously across his lap. He rode off, talking about old times, her skirt flying in the breeze. Tears of shame, humiliation, regret, and unknown fear spilled from her eyes.

This was her fault. Whatever happened to her was the least of her worries. But the girls. Whatever happened to the girls was her fault. She was the only one to blame. If not for her wanton nature, none of this would be happening. A flood of raw, angry, frightful emotions bubbled deep inside, tightening her throat as she choked on her sobs.

Rusty urged his horse into a brisk trot. He started laughing when the jarring sensations forced her belly against his erection. Disgusted, she could taste her stomach fluids as they descended through her upside-down body. Her body stiffened as she felt his calloused palm trail down her back through the layers of fabric.

Chapter 11

The moon, a faint sliver, hung amid the changing hues lingering in the sunset. A magnificent display of colors danced over the pinons and grassy slopes. Oblivious to the serenity, Devin flew at breakneck speed across the wild, brushy country toward the ranch. The four baffled, uniformed soldiers and packhorse kept the frantic pace at a modest distance.

Devin didn't know how he knew. He just did. Just like he didn't question where his next breath came from, he also didn't question his intuition. It kept him alive. It revealed things to him no else could see, hear, or even understand. Since he arrived at Camp Griffin, he felt compelled to return to the ranch for reasons beyond Deuce.

As the rambling ranch house came into view, his gut wrenched. There were no lights. Megan always kept the kerosene fixture above the table on low at night.

With barely a break in gait, he jumped off the black stallion. In two long strides, he was up the walk.

The door was ajar.

His heart pounded.

In one leap, he was over the porch and through the front door, pistol in hand. Finely honed silvery eyes acclimated to the surroundings instantly. The signs were there, the ones that had plagued him for the past two days. Megan and the girls were in trouble.

The hearth was cold. A full cup of coffee sat on the small, round table next to the couch. The girl's beds were unmade, sheets tossed haphazardly on the floor.

Before the sergeant and his men gathered a breath to speak to him as they entered the house, Devin grabbed his rifle from the rack and dashed past them on his way to the barn.

A touch of respite washed over him when he spotted Deuce clamoring in his stall, hungry and feisty, but none the worse for wear. The horse caught sight of Devin. Straight away Deuce snorted his discontent.

Devin wasted no time exchanging saddles. Reed's old saddle was already strapped down on the black stallion by the time Sergeant Major walked in, followed by the three soldiers.

"Mr. Spawn, is everything all right? Will we be staying here the night? We've been riding hard for two days, the men and horses need rest." Sergeant Major's tone was direct and cool.

In a sidelong glance, Devin noticed the wariness in the man's gaze. The officer eyed the rifle, then the two saddled horses.

"Need to go into town. I'll be back. Follow. Stay. It's up to you." Devin already knew they would follow. Come hell or high water, he was going to find Megan and the girls and bring them back. No one was going to stop him. Of that, he was confident.

* * * *

With the military breathing over his shoulder, he thought it best not to shoot up the town first, then ask questions. He decided to start with the sheriff and go from there. Follow the trail wherever it led, then start shooting.

In no time at all, he reached Sheriff Tucker's office and barged right in.

The Sheriff was dozing, reclined back in his chair with his legs propped on his desk. With the jarring sound of the door banging open, Sheriff Tucker bolted upright, cursing up a storm at the disturbance.

"Where's Megan Spawn?" Devin demanded heatedly, glaring at the portly older man. His reddened cheeks, blotchy nose, and glazed, red-lined eyes gave off more than a hint of recent alcohol consumption.

"Who the hell wants to know?" Sheriff Tucker bit back with a slur, his beady eyes squinting as he tried to focus on the four soldiers entering his office, then the huge man in front of him.

"Her stepson," he growled. Inwardly, Devin winced. If she heard him now, she'd be madder than a barrel full of rattlers. He didn't like saying it any more than she liked hearing it.

From the way his eyes bulged and darted to the wanted poster hanging on the wall behind his desk, Devin detected the moment Sheriff Tucker realized to whom he spoke—right about the time the color drained from his face.

"She's working," he blurted, his forehead starting to bead with sweat as he glanced at the four soldiers who stood quietly inside the door.

"Where?"

"Don't want no trouble."

Devin slammed his fist on the desk, causing the Sheriff to jerk back a step and everything that wasn't bolted down on the desk to vibrate. "Damn you, little man, tell me where before I beat next week's shit out of you."

"I'll tell you, but you gotta know, it's legal. Either she works, or she's jailed for default on a lawful contract."

Devin grabbed him by the shirt and back-handed him across his face with such force, the shirt ripped right out of Devin's grasp. Sheriff Tucker fell backward into his chair, clutching his crimson cheek.

"You've seen him, officer. Arrest him," he shouted, staring helplessly at Sergeant Major and his men, seemingly afraid to look at Devin again.

"Our orders are to follow this gentleman wherever he travels and assist *him*. We do not interfere in civil matters," the Sergeant responded reverently. Devin leaned over the desk and grabbed the Sheriff by the front of his torn shirt again, yanking him out of his seat.

Sheriff Tucker cowered at the news. This time, he began to tremble. His last thread of hope appeared to vanish along with any shred of his surviving dignity.

Devin's hand came up, and Sheriff Tucker blurted, "Jazelle's. She's at Jazelle's."

Sheriff Tucker was breathing raggedly, eyes glazed with fear as Devin released him. Abruptly, he slumped back into his chair, thankful for the reprieve. Devin thought the good-for-nothing sheriff looked 'bout ready to whistle Dixie and dance a jig if Devin felt a hankering to request.

"Emma and Shelby?"

"Shelby is at the Garrison farm, and Emma is over at the Johnson's place, behind the café."

* * * *

Very few dared disturb Madame Jazelle while she tallied the week's receipts. Everything happened at once at the loud bash brought on by the door to her private office being kicked open. Anger raced her blood and her gaze shot up. Underneath the desk, she threw up her skirt, reaching for the derringer strapped to her thigh, set to shoot the trespasser.

Her eyes widened and her hand stilled. Jazelle instantly recognized the forceful Cannon from his two previous visits. Another dilemma with one of the girls, she surmised. With a relaxed smile on her face, she sat back in her chair, positive she had the perfect remedy—new blood.

However, she intended to save the coveted arrival for her most discriminating client who expected to utilize the girl exclusively. Since he was out of town at the moment, there was no harm earning a little extra on the side. If the price was right, a profitable deal more to her liking was always attainable. Her excitement increased as the dollar signs flittered in front of her.

Known only by "Cannon," she couldn't very well call him that, so she greeted him in her usual seductive tone. "Darling, there's a favorable outcome to every entanglement." She liked the play on words.

"Where is she?"

"Who?"

"You know who the hell I'm talking about," Devin growled.

"Cheri?" she asked with a valid air of curiosity. Inwardly Jazelle grumbled, thrown briefly by the dark challenge in her formidable client's voice.

"Megan Spawn."

"Word travels fast. Interested in the new girl? It'll cost you."

"I ain't fucking paying for kin." His muscles tightened every line taut in his face.

"Sorry, sweetie, this one you are." Madame Jazelle took a deep, steadying breath as her pulse sped out of control. Her mind raced. Hardin promised good money for the girl, and she wasn't about to let Megan slip away so easily.

"Like hell I am." He loomed over her desk, wiped it desk clean with one sweep of his arm.

She gasped, watched with chagrin as the night's receipts scattered across the floor, along with the tiffany lamp, ink bottle, her favorite shot glass, and everything else.

"Assuming you're Devin, then your pa should have enlightened you about your stepmother." Practically shaking in her chair, she fought to control her nerves. She could hear her own voice quaver. She hadn't become a successful proprietor by allowing anyone to see her sweat, backing down from a fight, or letting someone pull a fast one over her, and she wasn't about to start now.

"Look here, bitch. I don't know what the fuck you're trying to pull, but you have two seconds. I always wondered what it would be like to skin a woman alive." She stared at the huge hand curling over the handle of the long blade sheathed at his waist. "One."

Her wide eyes shot from the long blade to the fiery warning in his black gaze. She swallowed hard, gripped with fear.

"Fine, I'll tell you." She was fond of her skin just the way it was—every flabby roll and wrinkle. Hardin's deal failed to provide round-the-clock protection, though the eager beaver expected to show up later tonight to partake in widow Spawn's delights in privacy after her customers left. Hardin assured her Megan Spawn's stepson, the notorious gunslinger, had been arrested. Had she known the outlaw was the same man standing in front of her, Jazelle would have thought long and hard before dragging Megan back.

"Megan worked for me before she married your pa. I put a roof over her head, fed her, and clothed her. Could have made lots of money off that gal. Still can. Men pay top dollar for young and attractive girls, with fresh little—"

"Take care of what you say." His tone was a cold warning, and she heeded every word.

Madame Jazelle countered with a sneer. He might be wearing a lethal collection of weapons designed for considerable harm, but she had the supply to his demand. That pretty much kept her in charge of the situation. "All I'm saying is, Reed offered to buy her, and I accepted. He'd been paying for her since day one. Still owes me money, and I ain't letting her go until I collect every damn cent. Whether she earns it on her back or you pay up, doesn't matter to me."

"How much?"

"Fifteen thousand."

"Fifteen thousand! What, you dress her in diamonds?"

"Interest, sweetie," she bit back with smug satisfaction. At her age, the thrill of negotiation aroused her more than sex. "Either you pay the full amount, or for a tidy sum, we can work you around her other clients."

He pulled out a pouch tucked in the inside pocket of his jacket. It plopped with a deep thud in the middle of her desk. "Keep the change," he said dryly.

Her eyes widened with sheer ecstasy. She knew the sound of gold when she heard it. And baby, that was the sweet knock of pure gold, and lots of it.

"Sweetie, she's all yours." Her voice hummed with elation as she started to pull out gold nugget after gold nugget, lining them along the top of her desk. "Truth of the matter, I'm glad you're taking her off my hands. She's been spitting fire from hell ever since she stepped foot in this place. Hasn't worked out like I hoped."

"Where is she?" he demanded menacingly, towering over her desk.

"Up front in the saloon, probably scaring off the customers," she offered happily, hauling a scale from the bottom drawer to the top of her desk.

"Come near her again, and you won't live long enough to see this hellhole go up in smoke."

Madame Jazelle's gaze rose to meet his. For once, she was rendered speechless at the icy viciousness in his tone. Never would she forget the look in his eyes, black orbs boring the conviction behind the pledge before he stormed out the room.

* * * *

"Ah, Sarge, can't we have at least one drink? Colonel don't hafta know," Corporal Sam Webster grumbled at the same time Devin was learning of Megan's whereabouts. Sam glanced forlornly at the bar where the soldiers sat in a corner table in the saloon, nursing their glasses of water.

"We're on duty. When you become Sergeant Major, you drink all the whiskey and beer you want. For now, we have to keep our wits about us."

"Why, the Laredo gang ain't round these parts," Trooper Vic Morrow piped up, frowning as he pushed his glass of untouched water in the center of the table and crossed his arms over his chest in objection.

"They're not the ones concerning me at present. If Spawn doesn't come through that door within the next five minutes like he said," Sergeant Major nodded his head toward the connecting door that led to Jazelle's Place, "we're going to have to go after him. And fellas, it's gonna take all four of us to handle him."

"Don't knows 'bout you guys, but I'd rather have a double dose of honey any night than the best whiskey any ol' town has to offer." The three other soldiers followed Sergeant Edgar Toledo's line of vision to the newest attraction at the Silver Nugget.

They smiled and mumbled their agreements at the petite figure dressed in a mid-calf red satin skirt with black ruffles, black fishnet stockings, and a black-and-white corset that pushed up her small breasts dangerously above the plunging neckline. So low, it looked as if one wrong move and her nipples would pop out. Golden-colored hair curled atop her head with several loose tendrils falling down her back and around her shoulders.

"Can't I stay in town whilst the rest of you go back to the Spawn ranch? I'll be back in the morning, I swear, Sarge."

"You're the randiest rooster in the hen house, Toledo. I've noticed that one—" Sergeant Major responded just before Corporal Webster interrupted.

"A fella can't help but notice a warm body ripe for the plucking," Webster added grinning at Toledo.

"And Toledo wansta do the plucking," Trooper Morrow joked.

"Plucking ain't what I had in mind." Toledo elbowed Morrow in the arm, snickering. "Mores like fucking."

"Well, you fellas can forget it. Since we sat down, she hasn't been overly friendly to anyone. Don't think she's setting her sights on your sorry flat butt, Toledo. And besides, we ain't got the time."

"My butt ain't what I was gonna use. B'sides, only needs a few minutes with a real man to set her straight, not that drunk she's with now." Toledo grimaced as they all intently watched the ruckus unfolding several tables away.

* * * *

For the hundredth time today, Megan tried to sidestep groping hands as she deposited a whiskey bottle on the table with a loud thump. She would have succeeded in her hasty escape if not for the persistence of her current patron.

"Chickie, where's ya scurrying to?" The drunk rose out of his seat slightly, grabbing her by the arm. The three other cowboys sitting at the card table laughed when he yanked her across his lap.

"Unhand me. You have your whiskey. That's all you're getting from me," she hissed as she attempted to unhook his tight grasp from around her waist.

"Tonight, I'm lucky at cards and gettin' luckier with the ladies."

"Don't see no ladies round here, Hoss," a buddy from across the table sneered.

"This is one lady who'll be passing you up," Megan declared heatedly as she attempted to stand.

"Not so fast," he muttered, tightening his grip. He pulled her back onto his lap and kissed her on the neck. She slapped his face, yelling vehemently for him to let her go. Her loud voiced captured the attention of another saloon girl walking nearby.

"Hoss, why you wasting time on a rattle-boned mouse?" Hattie said sweetly, draping an arm around his shoulder, staring at the large pile of money sitting in front of the drunkard. With her hand on Megan's forehead, she pushed Megan's face from Hoss, who was leaving a slobbering trail down Megan's neck.

Megan gave off a shrill noise and her neck jerked sideways.

Hoss grinned up at the other woman. His body swayed in its seat. The other men looked on, baring stained-toothed sneers.

"She'd be nothin' but a worthless poke." Hattie pulled Megan off Hoss's lap by the hair, knocking her to the floor.

Megan shrieked and landed on her rump with a loud thud, several of her light golden strands dangling from the other woman's long fingers.

With mixed emotions, Megan scrambled to her feet. The other woman happily took her place on Hoss's lap. Part of her was thankful for her replacement, yet her temper escalated by the unceremoniously removal of herself. Unruly customers came with the job. It was to be expected. If she had to work here for who knew how long, then there was no way she was going to allow the other females to trample over her.

"Who ya calling worthless, you festering barrel of lard?" Megan hollered, yanking the other woman's red hair until she was halfway off Hoss's lap.

The redhead screeched, clutching at Megan's wrist frantically.

The men started hollering and laughing. Hoss grabbed Hattie's plump ass and shoved her forward. She landed on Megan, and they both tumbled to the floor while several other patrons started to gather around the quarreling females.

Megan tried to push the woman off, but estimated Hattie had at least a good thirty pounds or more on her big-boned frame. The other female straddled her, twisting painted fingers in Megan's updo, and banged her head against the wooden floor.

With all her might, Megan made a fist and landed a punch across the woman's right cheek. Megan rolled the woman off as the redhead fell sideways, crying out. They continued to roll on the floor—arms flaying, legs kicking, clothes ripping, and hair flying.

The entire crowd gathered around, including the soldiers. Enthusiastic men pushed the tables and chairs out of the way as the tumbling mass rolled across the floor. They went right along with the women, hooting and hollering, giving them plenty of space to carry on. Some were even taking bets as to who was going to win.

Toledo whooped the loudest when Megan's strap busted and her left breast popped out, so firm, it scarcely bounced when the satin-striped corset ripped apart, soon followed by the other breast.

The buxom redhead spared no modesty as her robust tits spilled out of her torn neckline. Legs kicked in the air, hiking her skirt up around her waist, revealing her bare ass and proof she wasn't a natural redhead.

* * * *

In a rage, Devin barged through the crowd, knocking people over in the process. He shouldered his way to the center and reached down into the middle of the fracas to scoop Megan up with a single arm wrapped around her waist.

The crowd booed and shouted their protests. As soon as he shot them a warning look, most quieted down.

Swiftly, Hattie scrambled to her feet. She took a blind swing at Megan.

With a mild nudge of his hand on her forehead, Hattie fell to the floor landing on her butt with a grunt. She gaped up at Devin through her tousled red locks. Recognition soon shadowed her wide-eyed expression. She scuttled backwards on her hindquarters. Apparently, coming to her senses and forgoing the fight. She quickly covered her bottom half with what was left of her skirt.

Megan continued to flail, kicking and screaming at an invisible opponent. Obviously, she didn't realize he was holding her. He balanced her on his hip, ignoring the verbal and physical tumult.

The remaining patrons seemed to possess enough sense to recognize the ferocity in his gaze. They quieted down and backed off as he turned to walk away.

Evidently, Hoss, not known for his good judgment—whether inebriated or not—choose that moment to confront Devin, who towered over him a good foot and a half.

"Looky here, chum, this ain't no cern of yurs. These tarts were a fightin' ov'r me an the win'er getsta ride me pony," Hoss slurred, drawing his gun and waving it in the vicinity of Devin.

With a single, powerful right, he knocked Hoss clear off his feet. The man landed on a table several yards away. Devin stalked toward the kitchen with Megan buried under his arm.

"Let go of me. Take your hands off me," Megan shouted, scratching at the hand cupped around her bared breasts. She seemed unappreciative to be concealed from raunchy, bug-eyed onlookers.

"Cannon." The sultry voice of Cheri rang out behind him, making him stop in his tracks right before he entered the kitchen.

"Still like it rough, I see. Is this the Megan I've heard so much about?" Cheri gave him a saucy wink, reminding him of the time he'd called out Megan's name while pumping sperm in Cheri's pussy.

Megan finally ceased screaming and fighting, and he knew she was listening to Cheri. He caught her glancing backward from her bent-over position and noticed the sudden heated glare as her eyes took in the overly made-up woman, half-dressed in a pink and black-satin low-cut gown that left nothing to the imagination.

His lips thinned into a grim line. He tightened his grip possessively on the small bundle safely tucked under his arm. The scathing warning in his eyes went unheeded as Cheri suggested seductively without so much as a pause, "The girls and I wouldn't mind a fourth."

He caught sight of the soldiers making a beeline toward them. *Oh hell, just what I need. An audience.* Not likely to tell Cheri to 'fuck off' in case he was ever in need of her services again, he replied in his deep, blunt tone, "Not tonight."

"What is she talking about?" Megan's tone was quarrelsome, as though mindful the voluptuous woman plied her wares upstairs. He suspected she already guessed by now they were on intimate terms.

"Shut up," Devin ordered, ducking through the kitchen maze of stoves, tables, chopping blocks, and racks hanging from the low ceiling filled with pots and pans.

"Put me down." Megan protested, squirming so her nipples tickled his palm.

"Where can we be alone?" he asked his new friend, Mrs. Boyd.

"Ov'r yonder." Mrs. Boyd quickly pointed down the narrow hallway toward the storeroom.

"We don't want to be disturbed."

"No one comes in my kitchen unless I let's 'em in," Mrs. Boyd replied in an keyed up tone before heading to block the kitchen door with a iron pan in one hand and wooden rolling pin in the other.

With a swift kick, the door to the small, dusty room opened. One more kick, and it shut with a boom.

* * * *

Promptly released, Megan stumbled backwards and struggled to cover her exposed bosom with the scraps of material remaining from her torn top. Assured not enough material survived for the job, she settled for crossing both arms over her breasts, meager in comparison to buxom Cheri. At least what she did have were perfectly round, perched high on her chest, and were as firm as her rounded behind—unlike Cheri, who was going soft on both ends and the middle.

"What the hell do you think you're doing?" He barred the doorway, stuffing his hands in the pockets of his jacket, eyes roaming over her angrily. "I'm gone for a few days, and this is where you wind up? Whoring? Shelby and Emma? Thought you wanted to care for them. Was this how you figured going about it?"

"You know nothing of the situation."

"You were a whore when my father married you. Couldn't wait to come back and spread your legs? Is that why you were in such a hurry to be rid of me?"

"No, it's not like that," she bit out. The stabbing accusation struck her with alarm.

"I favor a good tale and a good fuck as much as the next fella. Start talking, or I'll handle you like any other piece of ass in the place and finish ripping off what's left of your clothes."

"There's rules. Everyone pays up front. Besides, I'm working in the saloon, not upstairs alongside Cheri." She tossed him a dismissive look and attempted to walk past him, well aware she tempted fate.

"Where the hell do you think you're going?" He caught her roughly by her upper arms and held her, looked down at her with half-crazed eyes. "Back outside like that?"

Despite her fear, her body trembled with anger. She would be damned if she allowed him a sign of weakness. She showed an inkling of disgrace as his heated gaze roamed freely over her bare breasts. Her puckered nipples were so hard, they ached from what she wanted to believe was the cool air outside and not the wild flutter in her belly.

"Fuck the rules. Within two minutes, you'll be face-down on a mat upstairs." His breathing escalated, and her heart pounded with excitement. He pulled her closer, just enough so the hard peaks brushed against his cloth covered stomach. She knew he heard her breath catch, saw the flush on her cheekbones that matched his. For an insane moment, she found herself wanting to press against him, rub her half-naked body against his. Oh, dear Lord, what was she thinking? His harsh, unsympathetic tone broke into her delirious reverie. "Rules don't apply to a bunch of randy cowboys after they done got an eyeful and their bellies are full up with whiskey."

"I'd rather take my chances outside than listen to you degrade me." She turned up her nose, and looked away, refusing to be governed by him or any other man, to see the lust in his eyes or acknowledge her own pitiable desire, nor the untold need for his protection.

"I'm gonna do a whole helluva lot more than that. I done took up where my father left off." Megan glared at him. "'Cept I paid in full for you. Mother dear, I own you."

"That can't be. It was too much," she whispered in shock, unsure of what she was even saying. Her head started to spin—or was it the room?

"There's something we can agree on." He released her, stuffing his hands back in his pockets. "Fifteen thousand for your skinny ass is robbery."

For the briefest of moments she hesitated, eyed him defiantly. No one owned her as though a piece of property. "A thief should know. I didn't ask for a protector, or for your handouts."

His brow darkened. "Reed did."

"As I recall, you refused his request."

"I'm not here on your behalf."

"Did I interrupt your nightly visit to that…that harlot?" She clamped her mouth shut, mortified to hear herself whine like a jealous wife. His eyes glittered in a smiling fashion aware of her envy.

"If not for Shelby and Emma, I'd leave you here, where you belong to rot."

"Leave me here, then. Walk away. I'll make amends by myself. Get the girls back on my terms," she grumbled. The fact he didn't flinch, affirm or even try to deny her charge angered her more than his taking a lover. After all, their brief encounter was less than satisfying, mildly passionate, more pain than pleasure. Cheri could keep the brute and that, that glorious thing between his thighs. Oh, no, she was mistaken—not that.

"Done tried that and you failed miserably. They need a mother, and you're the only one they know. Stay here and this town will run you out before they ever return those girls. Of course, if you don't care for them…" He trailed off.

"I love them," she snapped tensely, in fear of losing them. "There isn't anything I wouldn't do for those girls. They're all that I have."

"Prove it?"

"How?"

"Return to the ranch and continue mothering them."

"And where will you be?" she asked with disdain.

"About."

"Lurk roundabouts as their babysitter. Keep an eye on me so I don't sneak off again." she sneered, resenting the way he defied her without bating an eyelash.

The awkward moment of silence told her she was way off the mark. Under the wide, charcoal brim, his dark brows arched faintly. "Not exactly. I'll help however I can. My interest leans more towards Reed's entitlements."

"What do you mean?" She eyed him cautiously, ignoring the lust burning in his piercing silver eyes.

"Share your bed." His voice was silky smooth unlike the huge bulge she glimpsed visibly throbbing in this britches that presaged his wicked intent.

"Have you lost your mind?" She felt her cheeks flame at his barefaced sexual offer. A shameful offer that aroused and terrified her, slammed into her eager cunt.

"As far as I see it, you don't have much choice. Pay me off, or do what I say. What's it gonna be?"

"Reed and I were husband and wife. I can't simply fall into your bed. I don't even like you." With a need all its own, her body tightened with sexual awareness.

"And with Reed, it was love at first sight? Humph. Sex is strictly a means of scratching an itch, no emotion involved. That's how I like it, that's how I aim to keep it. Forgot your whoring days, you'll get used to it again."

"You've gone mad." She shook her head nervously, panic-stricken.

"It's getting late, and we have to collect the girls. They've been broken up."

"Who said I've agreed to your less-than-idyllic offer?"

His silvery gaze flickered amusedly, softened, and then darkened as it swept up and down the length of her. In a fluid motion, his muscled arms caught her by the waist, brought her flush against his body. The heat of his massive body seared her bare flesh. She drew in a startled breath and grew dizzy by his strength and scent, so utterly male and so deliciously pleasing.

Before she could mumble a protest he captured her mouth in a kiss so heated and carnal, it took her breath. She melted in his arms, accepted his sweet mouth, his sensuous lips, and his gifted tongue. Her body trembled with fiery sensations deep within her belly. Afraid of collapsing at any moment, she clutched the fabric over his biceps for support.

She moaned her need in his mouth as the warmth of one hand molded her breast in a sensual caress and the other splayed over the curve of her buttocks, lifting her slightly against his erection. The heat from his hard cock warmed her partially exposed belly.

Furious is what she should feel for not fighting, resisting his arrogant dominance. Instead, she climbed atop his feet, reaching up, grinding her mound against his engorged cock, thick and hard between their bodies. A burst of lust curled through her, moisture settled between her thighs preparing her body for whatever he wanted.

Megan shuddered at the depth of his passion. He kissed her hungrily and she kissed back, as if long-departed lovers reunited. His fingers milked her nipple. An erotic flame raced from her breast to her trembling vagina, frightening her as he squeezed the sensitive bud firmly, a slight tug of pain/pleasure driving her insane with a shocking flood of arousal.

That edge of pain threw her into a maelstrom of sensations and she nipped his lip hard. Sent his lust spiraling as he deepened the kiss, his tongue spearing her mouth forcefully. Both his hands roamed down her back, clutching her tightly to him.

She felt his entire body tighten with need. He seemed to fight for control over his body, emotions, sensations, as though a dark fury raged within him. Terrified of the lust pulsing through her own body, the overwhelming need to be possessed by him, and the thought of him struggling to restrain the sexual urges he spoke of earlier, the ease at which he could dominate her with his overpowering strength.

Just as abruptly as he grabbed her, he released her, his breath quick and ragged as her own. His eyes were dark, glazed with lust, a wild intent. With the tip of his tongue, he tasted the blood trickling from his nipped lip. He raised a brow in a sinful tribute.

She stepped backward, claiming much needed distance, took a deep breath to calm her shattered nerves and her wet pussy throbbed in frustration.

"Jazelle doesn't want you, and I saw why. Bad for business." He shook his head broodingly, and she couldn't help but wonder exactly what he knew of her sordid past.

"Other than walking the streets, you don't have an option, unless you got twenty thousand hiding in here pretty good." With a dash of jollity in his tone, he reached over and lifted her tattered skirt, the black laced ruffle partially torn from the hem flipped up with the movement brushing against her belly. "Cause I sure didn't feel it."

"It was fifteen." Indignant, she swatted at his hand while keeping one arm draped over her breasts in a vain attempt at modesty. Though he just felt her up, that didn't mean he could have free reign. If only her body was as easily governable as her intentions.

"Interest."

"Vile, despicable, arrogant varmint," she spat.

"For someone nipple deep in arrears, you shouldn't be name-calling. Now let's get a move on. It's getting late, and we need to get to bed." He grinned, and she fumed at his overtly suggestive statement.

"When...how will we determine my obligation has been satisfied?" Fury growing by leaps and bounds, unable to allow him to strip her of the last bit of dignity by granting him full control over the matter. It was her life, her body they were discussing. She needed some resemblance of authority no matter how minuscule.

"Going rate here can be doubled." He frowned, glanced briefly around the small, cramped storeroom, dusty shelves stocked with kitchen supplies. His eyes narrowed, disapprovingly. "Hell, even tripled. I don't give a damn. As long as you do whatever I say. No matter what I ask. No don't sit well with me. Disobey, and I'll add on."

Her eyes flared at the implications of his well-heeled promise. At the triple rate, it would take over three years to work off twenty thousand dollars, depending upon his sexual appetite. If she judged from his daily visit to Jazelle's, it meant he'd want to have his wicked way with her every night. If she dared tell him no, then she'd be at his mercy for several years. Dear Lord, the thought of him so enormously endowed, sharing a bed, being intimate, sent ripples through her body. It frightened and excited her at the same time. Did she even want to tell him no? Yes, of course, she hated him, or so she kept reminding herself.

"What shall I receive in return?" she muttered, pushing away the thought of his lips on hers, his large hands caressing her body, holding her close, touching her where an ache suddenly throbbed uncontrollably between her thighs.

"Reckon my name alone oughta do ya. No one in these parts will dare harass you or the girls again. You'll have a roof over your head, plenty of food, and money to buy you and girls new clothes that fit. Run the ranch, turn it into a goat farm, or knit all day. I don't give a damn as long as you pull up your skirt and spread your legs when I tell you."

She made a small whimper at his callousness, total arrogance based on the truth of the facts. Even so, the reality, plain as day, gripped her senses. Her imagination began to soar at the thought of being forced to submit to him. Her head began to spin with anger, humiliation, and fear, and though she didn't want to admit, anticipation and arousal, as well. Unshed tears filled her eyes.

Devin's unanticipated move caught her by supreme shock, undid her last fragment of emotional control. He removed his jacket, and carefully arranged it around her. Gently, he brushed what was left of her styled updo from her face. He bent down and tenderly brushed his lips along her temple and whispered, "Don't cry, Megan. I'll keep you safe."

Familiar with his foul language, overt confidence, sultry good looks, and dangerous demeanor, along with the reputation to back it up, she thought she could cope with whatever he dished out. His pity and shred of compassion was entirely unexpected. So out of the realm of his cold, hardened character, the floodgates unlocked, and every suppressed tear since her parents' deaths released.

Megan rested her head over the beating of his heart, clinging to him in a manner that seemed desperate, needy. She sagged against him like a limp rag doll. He gathered her up in his arms and made his way outside to the waiting horses and soldiers in the back alley.

Moments earlier, she'd wanted to hate him forever. Now, she wanted to believe him. His strength, powerful and infallible. His warmth, comforting and full of hope. His scent, so utterly masculine and tantalizing, enveloped her senses. Tears streamed down her cheeks non-stop. It had been far too long since she felt truly safe, yet somehow, deep down, she knew without a doubt if anyone could keep her safe, it was Devin Spawn.

Chapter 12

It was well past midnight by the time they drew up at the ranch with the girls in tow. Sergeant Toledo quickly dismounted seconds before Devin, who held Shelby tucked in one arm sound asleep. Sergeant Major grimaced as Toledo beat Devin to Megan's side.

With growing concern, Sergeant Major watched her smile graciously at Toledo as he offered to help Emma down from Megan's lap. Wrapped in Devin's oversized buckskin jacket, it almost completely covered the woman's ripped red satin saloon dress. As if Toledo remembered the firm breasts every man back at the saloon had gotten an eyeful of, his hands tried to slip underneath while helping her off the horse.

Taking note of Devin's scowl, Sergeant Major shared expressive glances with Trooper Morrow and Corporal Webster. In a deep, pensive mood, he shook his head. It didn't take a genius to figure out the young widow bore a new claim. A shroud of fury masked the notorious gunslinger even a blind man could witness.

Quietly they reined their horses to the hitching post and dismounted. No one said much of anything. They followed Devin and started up the steps. Once Megan was inside with the girls, Devin stood in the middle of the porch, rifle in hand. He blocked their further advancement with a warning glare.

"Ya'll sleep in the barn. We pull out at dawn. Take care of my horses." He swung on his heels and strode inside. They heard him bolt the door.

At his audacity of subjecting them to a night in the barn, they gaped and scowled at each other for a curt second. Morrow and Webster mumbled a heated protest.

"Well, you heard the man, Toledo," Sergeant Major finally barked, hastily untying his horse from the hitching post.

"Me? Why me? I got more rank than Morrow and Webster," he bit back, yanking the leather strap free from the post as the two other men chuckled, doing the same.

"You the one wanna be so helpful. Help with their horses," Sergeant Major ordered, leading his horse to the barn without so much as a glance over his shoulder. Gravely mindful Sergeant Edgar Toledo's one-track mind got him into more trouble than a porcupine had bristles, and with results equally sharp and destructive.

* * * *

"Where are the guests? Megan asked, coming out of the girls' bedroom with extra blankets in her hand as Devin finished bolting the door. His rifle rested next to the doorjamb.

"Barn." He turned to face her, tossed his hat on the wooden dining table in front of him. He combed his fingers leisurely through his dense, shoulder-length mane.

"There are two beds in the loft upstairs. We have plenty of room, as well as blankets and pillows for them to sleep comfortably."

"They're sleeping in the barn." He undid his gunbelt and hung it on a peg near the door, then started to undo the knife collection strapped to his legs and waist.

Her eyes roved over him nervously as she watched each weapon freed from his massive body. She couldn't help but wonder why a man who obviously was capable of killing someone with his bare hands would need so many superfluous weapons. "They're soldiers. It's impolite," she muttered, pulling her gaze away from the growing pile of fate sheathed on the table.

"Dimples, I'm not changing my mind. We have business to attend. After the girls are settled, come to bed."

"Tonight, I..." Megan stammered, blinking in surprise.

"Saying no?" His eyes narrowed and lips tightened.

"Of course not, it's just that—" Already, he challenged her. Her pulse raced madly. She was treading on dangerous ground.

"I'll be waiting in our bedroom." It was a restrained, yet effective order.

Her heart thundered against her ribs as she watched the door to Reed's bedroom close behind him. There was no evading what was coming. She felt her legs weaken. His reference to "our bedroom" didn't escape her.

Apparently, he didn't care Emma was still awake, four cavalrymen were outside, and Reed barely dead a week. Her immoral reputation as a former employee of a whorehouse was all that interested him. That, and how best to recoup the money he'd paid out.

Megan checked on Shelby one last time and found her tucked in and fast asleep. She kissed Emma good night. In an attempt to prolong the inevitable, she offered to read a bedtime story. On the verge of falling asleep, Emma declined.

There was no other way to dawdle, she concluded with a pout. The beginnings of a smile began to tug at her lips. An idea occurred to her. If Devin wanted her, he was going to have to work at seeing her naked.

Taking her time, she changed into her long-sleeved eyelet nightgown and robe, ensuring each button was securely fastened on both garments. Underneath, she wore her pantalets, stockings and garters, and burdensome corset. Though her breasts were smaller because of her loss of weight, they were still as firm and pert as when they first sprouted. Rarely did she use the pinching contraption, except for propriety sake whenever she ventured into town.

Megan stood outside her new bedroom and prayed for courage. Inhaling deeply, she reached out and opened the door.

She gasped and stood stock-still, staring wide-eyed and breathless.

Awed.

"Come in and lock the door behind you," he instructed quietly, sprawled on the expansive bed. He was propped up on one elbow, stripped raw, and stroking his glorious hard-on slowly. Each movement of his fingers up and down the thick, purple-veined stalk and around the mushroom-shaped head mesmerized her, made her tremble with need. She felt naked and completely exposed despite the layers of clothes.

Megan couldn't move. An uncontrollable fire raged through her bloodstream.

Dear God in heaven, she couldn't even breathe, let alone make out what his moving lips uttered. All she managed was to stare. Every nude male she'd ever seen before, including Reed and young Caleb, were merely adolescents, boys in training with aspirations someday to develop into what lay before her. Devin Spawn was the true embodiment of the adult male form in its finest, powerfully built grandeur and well-endowed magnificence.

Broad, honed shoulders, heavily built arms, rippled chest, taut abdomen, and long muscular thighs parted slightly as his hand dropped to his scrotum, running his thumb over the full, oversized sacs. His rock-hard erection reached proudly for the ceiling.

"I'm waiting."

The commanding voice brought her out of her trance-like state. Through a haze, she saw the primitive hunger blazing in his heavy-lidded gaze. His broad chest rose and fell roughly. She licked her lips. She wanted him, heaven help her, despite who and what he was. She wanted him kissing her, touching her, making love to her. Oh, yes, thrusting that big cock inside her, especially that. Most definitely that.

His lips curled into a wicked grin after she locked the door behind her.

"Take off your clothes," he rasped. His voice was tight with arousal as he sat up, resting on pillows propped against the wooden headboard. His legs spread wide and a large, tanned hand stroked the thick shaft firmly while the other massaged his balls.

Aware her every movement was trailed by his intense silvery gaze, her entire body trembled, fingers shaking excitedly at the buttons. She regretted her flawed button idea, not realizing she was the one who would eventually undo each and every button painstakingly as he watched and waited, sitting three feet in front of her in the nude, playing with himself.

"Good girl," he whispered when she undid the last button on the robe. "Let it drop to the floor." She followed orders, and the cotton garment fluttered to the floor around her feet in a puffy white cloud. "From now on, when you come to me, don't wear it."

She looked up at him, disconcerted by the demand. A bitter reminder she could refuse him nothing. Forced to submit to his desires, she was his private whore, but oddly enough, the idea didn't terrify her or make her feel sullied as it should have. It made her insides warm and her outsides tingly.

"Don't stop. Take off the gown."

Her gaze lowered to the extensive string of tiny pearl buttons from underneath her neck to the last button on the hem resting on the pine planks.

She wiggled her toes in her house slippers, testing for feeling as her legs grew weak. She took a deep breath before starting the next series of buttons. Her bosom rose with each ragged breath, as did her anticipation level. Thankfully, she found comfort in wearing the corset. At least her aroused nipples, straining against the constricting garment, couldn't be seen.

What was he going to do to her, especially with that humongous thing between his legs? The memory of their first encounter by the river flashed before her eyes. She could feel the warm liquid escaping from her pussy as she thought of that thick, hard fleshy cock tearing between her thighs once more.

Hypnotically, she was drawn to his penis. Awestruck by the sheer size of it, a soft moan escaped her lips and captured his attention. He looked up from where her fingers were working mid-chest and seemed to notice what she eyed. He grinned. "My cock gets hard when I think about you, Dimples. Come here." He sat on the edge of the bed.

She hesitated briefly, realized there wasn't a choice in the matter, and moved between his parted thighs. The warmth of his body and manly scent whirled around her, shattering her resolve, causing her failing resistance to dwindle further. Uncomfortably, she swallowed the large lump in her throat, trying hard to keep her eyes above his shoulders.

"Don't be shy. After all, you're no virgin. A token bride, hand selected from all the whores at Jazelle's." For a moment, he paused. A look of frustration washed over him and vanished just as quickly.

Obviously lewd thoughts crossed his mind. She winced, recalling the peephole at Jazelle's. Did he imagine her servicing other men? Why would he even care?

"Probably know more than I do," he hissed, his voice rising in annoyance suddenly, confusing her even more. "Touch it."

"I...I worked in...in the kitchen," she stammered, locking her eyes with his. A dismal excuse, but it explained her lack of experience. Her body burned with embarrassment and shame, ashamed that she wanted to please him. To do all those things she witnessed and more. Despite her fear of ravishment in the process, she craved that glorious weapon between his thighs. Timidly, she crossed her arms behind her, glanced down fleetingly at his erection, and then stared frantically into his eyes, darkened with lust. She nibbled her lower lip. "I never..."

Her explanation trailed off. The blood pumped rapidly through her system, gritting her teeth worriedly. She'd never be able to please him the way perhaps Cheri had.

"Reed knew I never worked upstairs when he married me," she blurted anxiously.

His eyes flared with seething rage. Before she knew what was happening, he grabbed her gown and ripped it open, tearing it from her body. She shrieked, shocked and frightened by his abrupt, almost violent actions. His large hands curled over her shoulders, with little effort, he pushed her to her knees.

"I said, touch it," he grumbled. His eyes were dark and wild, chest heaving, nostrils flaring as he stared down at her. She trembled in her pantalets and corset, kneeling between his legs. Pieces of the ripped gown scattered on the floor.

She peered up at him, saw the angry fire smoldering in his coal-black eyes. What had she said or done to anger him? Even though her fingers ached to fulfill his request and satisfy her curiosity, her shaking hand hesitantly reached toward his cock in the midst of its bed of dark curls. She closed her eyes as her hand neared. He groaned unexpectedly when she finally touched the tip of the engorged head.

At the velvet softness, her eyes darted open. It was hot and throbbed in frustration at her passive touch. Her fingers ran gently over the crimson head and she marveled as it twitched.

A moment ago, he'd frightened her when she sensed him losing control, an extreme force driving him to madness. She shuddered now, wondering what it would be like to experience that unleashed passion pumping deep inside her. A hot liquid heat surged between her thighs, primed and ready. She groaned at the thought.

"You like my cock, don't you?" he rasped, as though struggling to sound normal.

Through her lashes, she glanced up at him and blushed, too mortified to reply, she enjoyed herself tremendously. His cock, as he called it, was beautiful. The only word she could think of to describe such a magnificent piece of male flesh. It was very thick, and velvet soft, yet hard and deep red and swollen with bluish veins running along its length. The capped head with the tiny hole in the center secreted a small amount of fluid, tempting her taste buds.

"Say it, Megan," he persuaded softly. "Cock. I want to hear you."

"Cock," she whispered faintly, running a single finger around the ridged head, feeling a little confident he derived pleasure from her touch.

"Very good. Get used to saying it, because I'm going to talk about your sweet pussy when I fuck you. I want to hear you scream how much you want my cock stretching and thrusting into your dripping wet pussy."

Megan's jaw dropped in carnal shock. She burned a beet red from head to toe. Everything in his expression told her he was serious. He expected her to use explicit words she never imagined passing through her lips. Worse soap words imaginable.

"You're doing a good job. Nice, gentle touch. You'll find I prefer it harder—the rougher, the better. Grip my cock with your hand. Rub it up and down the shaft."

"It's too big," she muttered, her hand halfway around the wide girth. The heat of his flesh was intense in her hand as it pulsed in her grasp.

"Use both hands, one at a time, and move your hand up toward the head."

She followed his instructions, fingers circling tightly around the base, moving upward and over the head as the other hand circled the bottom. Over and over again, she moved her hands over his penis until he groaned, "Oh, yes, baby, just like that."

A sense of satisfaction washed over her at her strange erotic influence over him. She noticed his eyes close and his hips rock slightly while she continued to stroke his cock. More fluid dripped from the tip, and she couldn't help herself. Didn't know what made her do it. A flood of hot arousal, raw hunger, assailed her. Utterly lost in his gorgeous, naked maleness, the hard length in her grip, as of this moment she ruled him. In an instant, she bent down and licked the droplet off with the tip of her tongue. It tasted exotic, unique, like the man himself.

"Shit, Dimples," he growled, eyes flaring open. He stared into her eyes as she smiled up at him, beaming with unspoken promises. Fascinated by his response, she willingly licked the thick-ridged tip of his shaft, lapped at the fluid collecting on the end. A tortured hunger to taste every hard, thick succulent inch of him overcame her inhibitions. "Keep it up. Don't stop. Use that tongue of yours."

She flattened her tongue, swirled it over, around the head, and up and down the thick stalk, bathing his hot flesh with her saliva. She was eager to please him and taste more of his tangy essence.

* * * *

"You're fantastic." Devin's voice was tight, strained with the need to bury his cock down her slender throat. He could tell she lacked experience though. Her eagerness to please him made up for any deficiency. Amazedly, she sucked, licked, and tasted him as if his was the first cock she ever touched. Perhaps it had just been too long since she had a good fucking. He closed his eyes, fighting the resentment, not wanting to imagine her doing this or anything else with his father.

"Oh, yes." He trembled, opening his eyes. He watched her tiny hands squeezing and tightening around his thick length, pleasuring him until his scrotum drew tight, until he battled with himself to hold back. One hand gripped her hair, holding her head as the other grabbed the base of his cock and rubbed it over her greedy tongue and lips. "Lick it, taste it, get used to it, because you're going to be drinking a whole lot of my come soon."

Her tongue followed his movements, darted over the head as if she was starving for him to fill her hungry mouth. In utter fascination, he stared as her hand covered his, stopping him, showing him what she wanted. He nearly lost his mind when she fed the swollen head into her mouth, felt her pearly teeth raking the sensitive flesh. He let out a guttural groan, an animalistic noise of exquisite pain, bodily desperation, and hot-blooded arousal.

The wet suckling sounds filled the room. Shamelessly her tongue stroked, licked and tasted the hard flesh in her grasp. She stuffed the wide head into the tight grip of her velvety mouth and pulled it out with a loud pop, repeatedly until he groaned in pleasure.

"Suck it. Use your tongue." He stared at her, smoothing a hand over her cheek, dimples filled to capacity with the head of his cock, her tongue raking the underside of his flesh. Never in a million years could he have guessed this half-woman, half-child could make him, a man known to last for hours, want to come so quickly. But damn, he struggled to hold back as she suddenly drew back. He watched, groaning from the ravenous need as her pink lips and red tongue nibbled on the veins along his hard flesh.

"Shit," he growled when her mouth stretched wide over the head and it disappeared between her taut lips. She devoured him vigorously, sucked hungrily. Like a wild woman bewitched, she couldn't seem to get enough of him. Her heated moans of desire vibrated over the bulging head buried in her moist cavern while her hands continued to stroke the long length of his throbbing cock.

"Fuck yes, Megan." His hips lifted off the bed as his head fell back. "Grab my balls, tight. I want you to feel my sperm shoot from them. That's it, baby," he groaned when her hand grabbed his swollen, aching-for-release scrotum. Her fingers rolled over each ball, mimicking the maneuver she saw him perform earlier. "Oh, yes. I'm almost there. Stroke faster, harder. Keep the grip tight and your mouth open."

He felt her hand tighten around him and start to move up and down his length faster. Her fingers squeezed his balls hard, and her mouth opened wider, keeping the tip of the head perched on her tongue as it fluttered over the sensitive vein underneath.

His fingers tightened their grip on her head as his hips lifted off the bed. "Don't stop. I'm coming. I'm coming," he growled, fingers twisted in her hair, and as he hoped, the slight pain spurred Megan to suckle harder, stroke faster. Her whimpers of pleasure vibrated over his imbedded flesh.

"Swallow it," he ordered with a ragged breath, holding her head still, his body shuddering with the explosion rippling through him. The head of his cock buried in her mouth, she tightened her grip, swallowing as each load spurted down her throat in hot gushes. "Swallow my come, baby."

Eyes shut, he felt her searing strokes glide over his length and the moistness of her silky tongue lap softly at the last drops of come seeping from the hole. He opened his eyes, released his grip and pulled his still-erect penis back.

Her eyes glazed, darkened with the greedy need raging through her system. He smiled down at her. She loved it. He was unable to believe how lucky he was to have her at his beck and call. In spite of the conditions, he was going to enjoy her luscious body immensely.

"That was amazing."

She smiled at the compliment, and as if not wanting to waste any, wiped drops of come dripping down the corner of her swollen, rosy-tinged lips with the tip of her tongue.

"Now, it's your turn," he murmured, ignoring the maddening urge to fuck her, to thrust hard and bury himself deep in her depths that blazed through his blood, nearly destroying his control.

"No, we can't," she blurted, scooting back on her heels.

Confusion and disappointment tightened his body. The blood pounded hard in his veins, his abandoned cock jerking in the air, hungry for more the instant she withdrew. She wanted him. His offer to share her bed wasn't totally abhorrent as she let on. He had seen the fiery excitement in her eyes, smelled her arousal, felt her body's need in his arms, yet now she was truly frightened.

"It's wrong. Something bad will happen to you if you put that," she muttered, glancing at his penis, then at him, "inside me."

Devin had no intention to fuck her tonight, if that was all she feared. Her blatant refusal was cause for punishment, but what she said made no sense. He half-moaned in annoyance, his body far from satisfied. "What in the hell are you babbling about?"

"Reed." She averted his gaze, eyes lowering to her clasped hands on her lap. "It was because of me he suffered his first stroke."

He grimaced but remained silent, studying her intently. His hand rested on his parted thighs, his hard-on, aching for another type of satiation, hung heavily between his legs.

"We were together in bed when he suddenly collapsed. That night I was about to perform my wifely duty. I guess it was too much for him. Coupling is for procreation only. We weren't—at least, I wasn't trying to conceive. What we did was morally wrong, and it was entirely my fault. I'm a bad, evil, wicked person. And if you try to take me, the same result shall befall you."

For a long moment, he didn't say a word, just held her anxious, terrified gaze. After a while, he calmly stated, "You were raised to believe sex is solely for conceiving and all else is uncalled-for, therefore leading to Reed's tragic illness."

She nodded, appearing relieved he fully understood.

He wanted to laugh at the absurdity, except she actually believed it. His eyes narrowed. "What we just did, you sucking my cock, doesn't apply."

She shrugged her shoulders.

"Hate to admit this, but I've been humping like a jackrabbit most of my life, and I ain't been sick a day."

"Different for men, I suppose. Nonetheless, I've been warned against the perils of partaking in the pleasures of the human flesh. The circumstances of my," she paused, frowned faintly, "sinful nature led to your father's death. I wouldn't want to take further chances."

"Who told you you had a sinful nature?"

"It's not important." Her lashes lowered to half mast.

"If I didn't think it wasn't important, I wouldn't have asked. Now tell me. I won't repeat myself."

"The woman who raised me after my parents were killed."

In a few hours, he would be tracking down the Laredo Gang, living in his saddle, going without food and sleep. There was no time for her life story or everything he wanted to do to the cute delectable body in front of him. Except she looked so miserably entrenched in the antiquated, misguided sexual teachings and past ordeals dealt in childhood. He doubted she would ever enjoy whatever he did to her until she got over her guilt and any instilled taboos. Apparently, there were plenty.

"Perhaps we should start at the beginning." He drew her up by the shoulders, and together, they sat propped on the pillows against the headboard. She trembled, nestling alongside his chest. He wrapped an arm around her. One hand slowly started to undo the front laces of her corset. "Don't mind me. Talk while I keep my hands occupied."

Her eyes widened as though surprised of his adeptness at such a taxing undertaking as women's lacings.

"When I was thirteen," she started, her voice catching as the top three laces came undone, "my family attempted to move here from the East by wagon. We were attacked by savages."

"Indians?" he asked, and she slanted him a look as though galled he truly required further clarification. In his line of work, he ran across savages from every race imaginable though most people reserved that term for red-skinned people.

"Yes, savages," she repeated, the animosity heavy in her tone. "They killed my father, mother who was five months pregnant, and my younger brother, who was almost seven. A family took me in." She paused, taking a deep gulp as her corset, half-undone, gaped open, and her breasts bounced out.

"The lady of the house was church-going. After a while, she didn't take kindly to me. She claimed I possessed a sinful nature and would only beget calamitous troubles if I allowed myself to give in to the carnality of the flesh."

As he undid the last of the laces, he noticed her eyes close. He lifted her slightly from his chest, slid the corset from underneath. Her breathing deepened, and his fingers ached, mouth watered to sample the taut nipples, rock-solid beads atop the sweetest, creamiest confections he'd ever seen.

"Unable to trust me around her family," she resumed and her voice quivered. Looking up at him with big eyes, he suspected she was growing anxious, probably waiting impatiently for him to do something, anything. Instead, he just he held her. His arm wrapped around her small waist, hand rested beneath her breast while the other strummed fingers atop his thigh. He watched her, listening. "She turned me out when I was fourteen. That's how I wound up at Jazelle's. I did laundry, cooked, cleaned, whatever needed doing until two days shy of my eighteenth birthday, when Reed—"

"Okay, I heard enough," he stopped her in an effort to avoid the bitter reminder his father had bedded her first. Incredibly, she must have been a virgin when they married. The sorry-assed, lucky bastard. It wasn't the idea she worked at a whorehouse that angered him, yet he felt a strange sense of relief that a stream of men hadn't bedded her. It was the fact she'd married his father. The old man who gave him away at birth, then took a girl young enough to be his daughter as his wife. She shared his bed. The same bed they were going to use. His only recourse, from what he gathered Reed's technique as a lover was, evidently, nowhere near his. Sex only for baby making, what nonsense, Devin mused. If he believed that, he would have been dead long ago.

"Slide out of your pantalets. I want to explain how your body reacts in lessons we'll both enjoy."

As though already familiar with what was hiding under her pantalets, she cast him a reproachful glance.

He grinned, his most notable, sinfully erotic grin, and she obeyed, despite the look on her face.

She tossed the garment over the side of bed, and sat upright, legs extended straight out, totally nude except for her stockings. A deep, red blush covered her from head to toe.

"Relax. I won't hurt you. You might even like it. Lay back." He gazed at her nakedness. His cock throbbed at the erotic display of innocence and wantonness.

"Only whores like that sort of thing. Married women do it because they have to." She did as he directed, stiff as a board, hands crossed over her belly and legs squeezed tightly together, staring straight up at the ceiling.

"You don't look relaxed." He shifted her hands to her sides and stretched out alongside her. "Married or not, if sex between a man and woman wasn't supposed to be enjoyable, then your body would have been made differently."

"What do you mean?"

"Aside from babies popping out from between a woman's legs and suckling at her tit, a female's body was made for pleasure—her own, as well as a man's."

"Sounds like more wind than a bull in green corn time."

He took her words as a challenge and grinned at the thought of how he was about to change the doubting expression of her face. "Taking my cock in your mouth and stroking me was a hell of a lot more satisfying than whacking off alone in the woods. Believe me."

Her eyes snapped to meet his, and he saw that look of doubt intensify.

"Satisfying for the man, but what of the female?"

He quirked a brow in surprise, and a smile crossed his lips to assure her she was about to find out.

"Allow me to demonstrate. If I do something you enjoy, by all means, tell me. I'll continue, but only if you ask. Same applies if I do something that hurts or you don't like. Let me know, and I'll stop. Can you agree to that?"

* * * *

"Yes," Megan barely managed to whisper. Was he crazy? All he had to do was look at her with those incredibly sensuous, silver eyes and she melted. Her body shivered with anticipation and the fear instilled by Mrs. Walker.

He started by brushing a lock of hair from her shoulder, drawing it behind her ear. She inhaled on a gasp when he nibbled her ear, the warmth of his breath tantalizing the skin along the curve of her throat. His tongue lined the shape and he nipped the lobe. It was heavenly to give herself to him, trust in him. She sighed and closed her eyes. Her head fell to the side freeing his mouth to kiss along her jaw line and down the curve of her neck to the slope of her shoulder.

Her chest rose with each deep breath, and her nipples puckered and ached for his touch. He brushed wet, hot kisses along her chest, down the cleft of her breasts. When he captured her breasts with his hands, possessing them with long, knowing fingers, and teased the crests with his thumbs, she whimpered softly. He squeezed the tender mounds firmly, drew a sensitive tip into his mouth, and lapped it greedily with his tongue.

She cried out, jutting her breast eagerly toward his mouth.

"Do you like that?" he asked, drawing back just enough to speak. Insatiably, he suckled the hardened nipple without waiting for a reply.

Apparently, even he didn't hear her faint reply, because he moved to the next breast. She felt his hand knead one breast and cup the other while he devoured the globe almost entirely in his hungry, moist mouth. Her body writhed beneath him and dim whimpers escaped her throat. Still, she couldn't bring herself to tell him to stop or keep going. His hands glided down her belly as his tongue and lips trailed a fiery path of desire, lower and lower.

His weight shifted, she felt him move further down the bed while his hands caressed her hips, encouraged her legs to part freely as he planted kisses atop her mound.

Her whimpers grew in volume, and he held her down with one hand on her hip as she wiggled her bottom toward him instinctively.

"Open your legs," he ordered with a rough, strained voice of authority. Unable to resist, she parted her legs a minute degree. "More. Spread them wider."

As her thighs separated further, the bed shifted once again under his weight as he moved between them. He hooked his hands beneath her knees, dragged her toward him until her legs were upon his shoulders, leaving only her upper back, outstretched arms and a long trail of hair remaining on the bed. He curled his arms over her hips to hold her still.

"What are you doing?" she murmured through closed eyes, unable to see, only feel, unaware of what was about to happen only aware of the all-consuming desire to be his. Too aroused to open her eyes, her cunt swollen and slick with her own arousal, she was willing to beg for what she craved, except she didn't know exactly what to beg for.

"Partaking in your carnal flesh." Fingers combed through her pubic curls as his palm curled over her mound.

She felt him opened her labia wide, spreading her wantonly, helplessly to his view. Her tender flesh was his for the taking. "Devin," she moaned. Her body trembled with excitement, burned out of control.

"Yes," he groaned as she felt two probing fingers sweep over her clit and along her aching entrance, driving her arousal higher.

She moaned harshly, her body arching upward, his face only inches from that most intimate part of her.

"What's wrong, Megan? Don't like what I'm doing?" She felt him again, and this time, his silky fingers flickered over her clit longer, teased the narrow slit of her pussy. "Do you want me to stop?"

Her head thrashed on the pillow as the strange sensations collided within her body. Her senses shattered as an intense, fiery longing struck between her legs. She struggled to breathe as she wiggled her hips, discovered the pleasure increased when she bore down on his fingers.

When he gradually slid a finger through the slick entrance, she cried out at the lingering sensation that assaulted the core between her thighs, quenching the burning ache momentarily before it raged into a full-blown fiery inferno. Her body stiffened as her thighs tightened on either side of his head.

"If you like what I'm doing, tell me, or I'll move on," he murmured as his finger began moving inside her with ease. Her intense arousal lubricated the tight passage, accepting his possession of her.

She tried to catch her breath, answer, make sense of the pleasure driving her crazy, mad with desire, when all she was supposed to feel was shame.

Yet there was no iniquity or embarrassment, just utter bliss. She wanted, needed, yearned, had to have more.

"Devin," she called out his name softly, arching her hips toward his face as his mouth replaced the finger that had been strumming her clit. She could feel the moisture of her arousal trickling from her body and coating the finger thrusting in the tight channel, driving her wild. She was anxious for him to continue fanning the flame he ignited within her, to keep his tongue swirling over the root of her desire, sending hot currents from her clit to every pulsing nerve in her body.

"Say it, Megan," he gasped hoarsely, and she felt his breath hot against her vagina, his tongue plunge into the searing depths already taut around his embedded finger, suckling her throbbing flesh.

Hands clutching the bed sheets, she knew what he wanted to hear. The hot need built, tormenting her sensitized body until she wanted to scream for him to never stop. Knowing he would stop if she didn't answer. "Please," she breathed.

His thrusting finger paused, and he gave her one last lick before he rasped tightly, "Please what?"

Her gaze collided with his. With his nose just over her mound, she could feel his breath heaving hotly on her sensitive flesh. His tongue slowly flicked back and forth over the sensitive pebble while he seemed to wait for her reply. His pupils were enlarged, black with desire, face flushed with arousal. Her chest heaved. She gasped for each breath, and she knew he was just as lost in the pinnacle of madness.

"Don't stop." Her head dropped to her shoulder, and she cried out weakly as his ravenous mouth continued its onslaught, and his finger buried deep inside her. The heated blood in her veins coursed through her body, centering where his tongue intensified its manipulation, sending more hot juices flowing from her inner recesses.

His hand cupped a breast and his fingers tweaked the hard nipple, giving her a flash of sensation bordering between pain and pleasure. His mouth and tongue didn't stop their torment on her clit. Her body was on fire, and something strange, wonderful, uncontrollable was happening, taking over her body like never before. Bolts of pure bliss, jarring pleasure shot through her as her body jerked with its first earth-shattering orgasm ever. She screamed, body convulsing with ultimate pleasure and felt his hands tightening on her hips, pulling her tightly against him.

He didn't stop. He continued sweeping his tongue over her sensitive folds, greedily suckling the creamy essence from her climax. His embedded finger fucked her hole with increased vigor, in and out, as the pulsing sensations barraged her diluted body. She felt another powerful culmination build deep inside her womb. His mouth focused, the adept hardness of his finger slid inside her tight, slick folds deeper and faster, while his other hand clutched and squeezed her breasts and nipples.

Small moans died against the pillow as she buried her flushed face. The second explosion pummeled through her, terrifying her. The pleasure was too intense, the need too carnal and emotions too weakening, and she was rendered powerless to control her body or thoughts.

However, the onslaught continued, despite the swollen root of painful, sensitive nerves. He kept tending the array of lustful manipulations, harder and faster. Increasing the pressure and rhythm and shattered her last sense of reality. The rich essence of yet another release flowed from her body into his mouth. His lips and tongue drank from her moist flesh faster than the juices seeped from her trembling cunt. She was dazed, breathing shallow, no longer conscious when one orgasm ended and the next began.

Like a voracious, wild animal, his blissful onslaught, nonstop sensations overwhelmed her senses with the unending pace that dazed her mind. Her inner muscles quivered. Body trembled with spasm after spasm while he devoured the honeyed cream like a starving beast feasting on her bare flesh.

She was so weak, she thought she was going to die. Then, it hit her with a reprehensible awareness. He wasn't going to stop. He would persist until she spoke up, told him what she wanted.

Unable to endure such burning, intense pleasure a moment longer, she struggled to find strength. "Stop," she breathed weakly, her eyes too heavy to open.

Relieved, she gasped for breath when he drew back. Her hazy eyes fluttered open briefly. He lowered her limp body to the bed and stretched out alongside her. He pulled her against the heat of his large, sheltering body, wrapped his arms around her, and draped his thigh over her hips, dragging her even closer. A hand smoothed her honey-colored hair off her dampened forehead. "I was beginning to think you really didn't want me to stop."

His breath was warm against the curve of her throat. She could hear the amusement in his voice and smell her heady scent of arousal on his lips. If she had the strength, she'd smack him. Shoot him with his own gun. *Later,* she told herself. *I'll shoot him later.* She closed her eyes and nestled her weary head in the crook of his shoulder.

"Your pussy is so sweet, your cream so rich and luscious. I could go on forever," he whispered in her ear, his hands caressing her breasts. With his voice low and deep, he told her she was beautiful, praised her body and how she brought him so much pleasure. Went on and on whispering ways he'd bestow pleasure beyond her wildest dreams, do wicked, naughty things to her, used explicit words that heated her blood.

Okay, maybe she wouldn't shoot him, but she could still smack him.

* * * *

"So you tried to kill me by giving yourself to me the night we met?" Devin asked minutes later, after sensing the solidity of her body and breathing return to normal. His tone held no hint of emotion or judgment.

He detected a faint shudder race through her body. Her wariness and hesitation were apparent when she glanced up at him, as though she dreaded answering his question.

By her lack of response and guilty look, he guessed her answer was yes. Of all the ways for someone to take his life, that was the one way he would want to go if the choice was his.

"Unfortunately for you, your attempt at death by seduction failed."

He held her close, to at least give some sort of confirmation he wasn't about to toss her out the door—at least, not yet.

"There could be one of two reasons." Biting her lip, she paused briefly and averted his gaze. "Most likely, because I lack feelings toward you."

"You loved him?" His body tensed. Fortunately, seemly entrenched in her own web of trepidation, she failed to notice his apprehension.

Her breath caught in her throat. Eyelashes fluttering, she cast him a quick sideways glance, as if surprised he would ask such a question.

Especially while they were lying naked in Reed's bed, and after what just transpired.

"Reed?"

"Who else?"

"I...of course...I loved him."

"What's the second reason?"

"You and I didn't really...complete the act," she responded sheepishly. Her eyes flittered toward his cock, dark in contrast as it lay across the pale skin of her abdomen. Its thick length reached from one sharp hip bone just beyond the next on the other side.

"I came inside you," he said. Looking up at him, she turned beet-red at his reminder of her behavior that evening. "What more is there?"

He studied her cavalierly, waited to hear if she dared mention his ineptness at fully consummating the act, only able to bury the head of his cock in her hot, wet channel. Even he was disappointed with the outcome. He had never come so fast. In frustrated agony the next day, he'd run into the waiting arms of three seasoned whores.

She shrugged her shoulders, causing her swollen breasts to rise and fall, brushing her peaked nipples against his bare arm, drawing his attention and making his cock twitch upon her belly.

"To test at least part of your theory, we'll try again." His lips curled into a lazy smirk, gliding his hand lower over her narrow hipbone, along her slender thigh.

She gasped, "What?"

Drawing her leg over his hip, he shifted her body gently until her back cradled against his abdomen, her buttocks pressed into his groin. The length of his cock tucked into her labia lips, the slick juices readily coating his flesh. He lowered her leg, the head and several inches of the shaft extended past the dark blond nest between her thighs.

He knew she couldn't take her eyes away from the erotic sight. Hell, it was hard for him not to stare, not to give in to temptation and bury himself deep in the hot, wet heat he'd just tasted. A small sound from deep in his throat drifted past his gritted teeth as he felt her thighs clench around his hardness. Her pussy lips drench him with sweet, hot liquid. He was certain the carnal temptation was mutual when she bore down on the thick erection, as though aching to have him touch that spot, to give her that wonderful pleasure once more—only this time, with his cock.

He wanted nothing more than to give her what he sensed she desperately needed. It took all his determination, his last drop of control, and every bit of his willpower to hold off.

"Not tonight," he hissed through gritted teeth, grasping her hand fisted in the sheets and bringing it to his cock. He drew her tiny palm around the solid stump throbbing between her clenched thighs. It jerked, and he groaned. He shifted his free hand underneath her torso, curled his arms around her and cupped her breasts, claiming ownership. He shut his eyes and burrowed her head under his chin, murmuring wearily, "I need my rest. And I fully get you're not in love with me any more than I'm in love with you. However, we most certainly will complete the act when I return, and if I'm still alive afterwards, who knows? We may do it again."

He knew.

Precisely why he was willing to put up with purple balls the size of coconuts, use the pent-up frustration to his advantage to heighten the awareness of every sense, use the savage hunger to kill every last member of the Laredo Gang.

When he was done, he'd return and release every ounce of raging testosterone inside her.

It may take hours, days to satisfy his voracious appetite, but he was going to have her anywhere, any time, any way he chose.

"Be forewarned. Now that I know you're a picked-over wildflower, I'll not make allowances like I did that night out by the river."

Chapter 13

The following morning, Megan awoke as the rush of dawn flowed through the sheer lace curtains. She was weary, ravenous, naked and still trembling from the unbelievable memory. Who knew what they did could be such a workout? It drained her energy more so than the hard labor she performed daily on the ranch and for an entirely different reason.

She turned on her side, inhaled the lingering male scent and warmth in the indentation beside her. She was disappointed his presence would soon be another faded memory. There wasn't a note, no goodbye, nothing. That was to be expected. Their relationship, if she could call it that, wasn't based on respect, courtship, or even friendship, just sex.

The racy thought sent a shiver of forbidden excitement pulsing over her skin and arousal slamming into her pussy.

If the pleasure she'd experienced last night was any indication, their depraved arrangement wouldn't be half-bad. She'd gain her freedom in a most delightfully wicked way, take the girls and move away after they parted ways. If she avoided pregnancy, no one would be the wiser. After all, she was a widow—no one expected her to be an innocent virgin, or would ever suspect she was sharing a bed with her deceased husband's outlaw son. Very few people even knew he was at the ranch.

Nor did Devin ever need know that when she touched him, took his thick cock in her mouth and drank his liquid essence, she loved every magnificent, rigid, luscious inch of it. Aside from her fears and wariness, she couldn't wait to part her legs and surrender her docile body to his complete control.

She felt giddy, her flesh tingling. Aware it was just a matter of time before she no longer had to deny herself, her body. The needs and desires burned hotter and brighter wherever he touched.

* * * *

After the bank draft cleared the following day, things soon went back to normal. Rumor had it Leroy Hardin got wind of Devin's return and decided for health reasons it was best not to risk going against the notorious gunslinger.

Money made things easier as the weeks slowly dragged along. The girls gradually adjusted to life without their father. The first week was the hardest. With Devin absent, they felt doubly abandoned. At least Shelby did. Emma remained to herself, no matter how hard Megan tried to reach her.

Devin had offered no details or expected return. He'd only admitted there was a job to do. Nonetheless, if the army was involved, it couldn't have been good. Troops spent their time fighting Indians. She was well aware how vicious an opponent they could be. In truth, she could offer no worthy reply to their inquiries if their brother would ever come back.

Megan submerged herself in the daily duties of running the farm. She kept herself and the girls busy and tried not to think about him. Shelby and Emma were each sewn new outfits and had new shoes. Additional animals and supplies were purchased. Workers were hired to fix the leaky barn roof and the loose stones in the main chimneystack and other odd jobs that slipped to the wayside during Reed's illness.

She even bought enough material to sew two black dresses to wear during her mourning period and started a third. She couldn't help but wonder what the proper mourning period was for a widow who was eagerly waiting to be fucked by her deceased husband's son. Each time she closed her eyes, the heated memory of taking his fiery erection in her mouth evoked a warm gush of liquid that soaked her pantalets.

The cold, lonely nights were spent dreaming hotly of Devin's return. She awoke each morning alone, lustful, and with her fingers buried in her seeping wetness. Devin had introduced her body to unknown pleasure and awakened forgotten desires. Desires that needed relief, needed to be assuaged with his touch, his mouth, his tongue. Her fingers were a poor substitute as she tried to ease the burning ache that increased with each passing day and discomfiting night, but it wasn't the same. She needed the man.

A few days ago, Caleb had paid a welcomed visit. Not one for frequenting Jazelle's whorehouse or the Silver Nugget saloon, he failed to realize she worked there. No man in town doing business with his family's bank or concerned one day they may be in need of his medical services, dared mention that his enamored was a harlot.

It was her own fault, really, she surmised. The night they took her away, she'd asked him earlier that day to leave and graciously suggested he not stop by so frequently. Concerned for his reputation, respectable gentlemen that he was, his presence at her house would cause gossip and only add fuel to the fiery disposition his mother already harbored toward her.

They sat on the front porch, talking and laughing over coffee one afternoon while the girls played in the yard, like old times with Reed, as though they were a family. From the corner of her eye, she stole glances at Caleb. No longer was he a lanky, unfledged boy of fourteen. He'd filled out nicely, tall, muscular with broad shoulders and looked distinguished in his tailored suit and tie. The perfect spring sky was no match for his deep blue eyes. Undeniably, Caleb was a very handsome man. Downright gorgeous. She was flattered that his interest in her never faltered. The sexual attraction still was there, simmering now, waiting to rekindle, but not blazing out of control, like it did for Devin. Nevertheless, it was there.

When the intense blue depths of his amorous gaze caught hers, she felt the lusty awareness burn deep inside her womb. Incredibly, she wished he would never stop looking at her that way, never stop wanting her. Never stop loving her. She wanted to take him in her mouth as she did Devin. Suckle Caleb's flesh until he spilled over her tongue. That was something they never did in the past, anxious to share her new skills with him and more, to make up for the past and look toward an impossible future.

For both their sakes, it was up to her to stem the forbidden desires and carnal lust that had torn them apart in the first place and was predestined to keep them apart.

If only circumstances were different, they would have married, moved away, and started their own family. There was no doubt in her mind they could have been extremely happy together.

This ranch, Shelby and Emma, along with Devin, were her life now, and she was going to make the best of it.

Regretfully, when the memory of Caleb's warm, tender kisses upon her lips, soft caresses kneading her breasts, and gentle touches probing her virginal pussy became unbearable, she sent him away. She hid from him what kept them apart, a dark past his parents were part of and she couldn't forget.

* * * *

"Ya think he's a coming back?" Morrow asked, looking over at Sergeant Major sitting gloomily on a log next to their campfire.

The scowl on Sergeant Major's face deepened. He poked the embers, stirring the flames with a long twig in his hand. "Why wouldn't he?" he grumbled, trying to sound convincing though he wasn't certain.

"Can't trust a man like that." Webster joined in.

"He's got more to lose than the rest of us."

"Hell, we're the one's sittin' here like ducks wait'n for the firing squad. I don't see his neck nowhere's round." Morrow balked, spitting a wad of snuff into the fire.

Sergeant Major glared at him. "He's tracking 'em."

"What we gonna do iffin he don't show?" Webster's expression didn't hide the fact he was worried. Sergeant Major sympathized. Four men facing nearly thirty gunslingers at once wasn't an everyday event. Even though he and Webster were sure shots, even he couldn't stomach the odds.

"Sure as hell ain't gonna run. We got orders." Sergeant Major growled a long moment later, adding the twig to the flames as he sat up and eyed the rest of the men.

"Keeping the bastard in our sight wuz part of them orders. You's the one let 'em go off by himself," Webster huffed.

"One of us shoulda gone with him." Morrow shook his head soberly.

"I don't recall you's volunteering to tag along," Sergeant Major reminded him, pissed off his men were second-guessing him. "Remember, two trackers can be spotted easier than one."

"Yup, I'll remember once the lead starts flying."

"Tarnation, what the hell you yellowbellies worked up 'bout?" Toledo hollered, lifting his hat of his face as he raised his head from the saddle where he slept, not far from the fire. "A guy can't sleep with ya'll gums yapping like ol' bitties."

"Go back to sleep. Toledo. Ain't no one talkin' to ya," replied Webster.

Toledo drew up on his elbows, a quirky smile on his boyish, freckled face. "When you go on disturbin' a man dreaming of romance, he got's a right to speak his piece."

Sergeant Major rolled his eyes to the night sky and sighed. Wasn't there anything else on the hormone-driven young buck's mind?

"I reckon we take aim and shoot up the motherfuckers so's I can get back to that cherry in Tejas." Toledo sat up, leaned on the tree butted against his saddle.

Sergeant Major straightened, thrown by Toledo's remark. The nineteen-year-old was a fine horseman and a damn good shot, but hadn't the sense of a sick mule if he was talking about the Spawn woman.

"You know the one. The shoestring hellion. I figger she'd be a fireball in bed. With an ass that small, fancy how tight her twat—Ouch!" he barked, rubbing his shoulder precisely where Sergeant Major had aimed the blunt-edged rock. "What the hell you do that fer?" He grimaced, still rubbing his shoulder.

"Best quit your figuring. Find another snatch to poke your dick into. That one's taken," Sergeant Major warned.

"By who? She's newly widowed."

"You're young, and if ya got a hankering on growing old, you best take my advice and figure on another gal." Sergeant Major snapped, gritting his teeth. The lad was his responsibility. A worried furrow creased his brow.

"You gonna interfere with a man and his love life, Sarge?" Morrow asked jokingly.

He bit back at Morrow, with a dismissive gesture directed at Toledo. "We ain't here for romance. And I ain't gonna take up for him when he's faced with the wrath of a double-barreled, gun-toting lunatic seeking vengeance."

"You ain't talking 'bout that Spawn fellow? That's her stepson." Toledo gave him a questioning glance.

"I love my ma, but I don't pine after her like that," Webster admitted, grinning ear to ear. Morrow, seated beside him, chuckled.

"Ah, I ain't scared of him. Never believed nine-tenths of them stories 'bout him no way. He didn't even shoot that boozehound back at the saloon."

"Wouldn't have been a fair fight. The man stood a foot in front of him and still would've missed 'em with the way his six-iron was a waving."

"Well, I would have shot the scalawag jest fer pointin' it at me."

"Takes more guts to go against a pointed pistol with just your fist," offered Morrow pointedly.

"Doesn't make you more of a man if you ain't fighting fair. 'Sides, his hands were full of your woman," Webster said just before he and Morrow busted out laughing.

Toledo fumed.

Some time later, when the four of them sat around the fire chatting, Devin stepped out of the darkness without a sound.

"Everything done?" The deep voice caught them off guard. Sergeant Major stopped breathing as he and Morrow instinctively reached for the pistols strapped to their hips. Webster leaned toward his rifle, slanted on the log.

Toledo, across from Morrow and Webster, gaped at Devin. Appeared frozen in his seat.

Devin moved closer to the fire.

Sergeant Major breathed a sigh of relief. Dropped his hands between his spread legs, away from his gun, and was elated he didn't have to use it. He felt damned lucky Devin was on their side. If not, they'd all be goners.

"Yes. I've set the gun powder, and the guys built and buried the trap like you suggested." Sergeant Major replied, glancing over at Morrow and Webster, who oddly continued to look nervous.

"Good. Then we're ready."

"Did you locate them?"

"Their camp's not far from here. They'll be here round mid-afternoon."

"How many?"

"Just over thirty. I counted five wagons, not four."

Major, Webster, and Morrow exchanged knowing glances at one another.

Sergeant Major calmly stated, "Colonel must have been misinformed."

It was too dark to see his eyes, but the Sergeant Major felt the heat of Devin's piercing gaze studying him intently.

"You sure they're coming this way?" Sergeant Major quickly asked as a means to distract Devin's attention from the extra wagon.

"What's the best way to get where you want to go?" Devin replied, his brows drawn into a tight knit.

A befuddled look shadowed Webster's face, as though it was a trick question. After a slight hesitation, he replied, "The main road."

"And if the law's after you?"

"The back road," Toledo smugly jumped right in.

"So if you were smart, knew the law was gunning for you down the back road, and not fool enough to venture along the open main road, which way would you go?"

"Find my own trail," Morrow answered, not wanting to be left out of the conversation.

"Off the beaten path," Sergeant Major suggested.

"Ain't nothin' more beaten and rough than a canyon full of rocks amid pinon pines. Can't maneuver loaded-down wagons 'round trees, over earth softened by leaves and pine needles. Gives 'em one way in and one way out. Where we'll be, waiting to ambush 'em."

"Seems like we oughta meet 'em out in the open like honorable soldiers, stead of ambushing 'em like a bunch of savage Injuns."

"Get within gun sight of them, and that blue uniform will be red before you ever break leather. Only live by one rule—my rule. If a man is out for my blood, I'll fight him any damn way I please. I aim to win."

"We all know what to do tomorrow. Why don't we try to get some rest?" Sergeant Major ignored Toledo's comment, knowing Devin was correct. It left him wondering, if that was the case, why didn't he shoot the old man at the saloon? "Devin, we have some beans 'n beef left if you're hungry."

"No thanks. I'm standing watch."

"They're camped miles away. No reason for ya to go without sleep or eatin'."

"Yeah, you can pull up your gear by the fire, keep the coyotes away," Morrow offered.

"Also ruins your night vision. If I get hungry, I have jerky in my saddle bag." Devin started back toward the trees.

"Spawn," Toledo called out, and Devin turned with a huff.

Sergeant Major glared at Toledo, praying the lad developed sweet reason within the last hour and took their advice to heart.

"Thought we could chew the fat a little?" He held out his cigarette makings, and Devin shook his head. "Seeing how this will all be over after tomorrow, I got to thinking."

Major covered his eyes with his hand and slowly shook his head in disbelief.

Toledo continued. "Perhaps you and I can get to know one another."

"Why?"

Webster shot him a 'shut the fuck up' look that Toledo answered with a wide-tooth grin and kept right on talking.

"So when you head back home, I thought I'd ride with you. So's to keep you company."

"Why?"

"Got a hanker to learn ranchin'."

"Don't need tagalongs and don't know a damn thing 'bout ranching."

"Sorta hoping you'd do the honors of introducing me to your stepma, Mrs. Spawn. Seeing she's a wi—"

Reflexes quicker than the eye could follow, Devin lunged over the fire while he slipped the hammer on the pistol in one hand and the bowie knife sheathed at his waist in the other. A reflexive move Sergeant Major suspected was repeated dozens of times throughout Devin's ill-famed life. The razor-sharp knife held against Toledo's jugular sliced through the top layer of skin, drawing blood, as Toledo laid flat on his back, eyes bulging and face ghost-white. Devin loomed over him, his knee deeply ground in the man's chest.

Major, Morrow, and Webster made sure their hands were in plain sight in response to the gun pointed at them, making no quick moves.

"Listen up. If so much as a flicker of interest sparks your eye, I'll cut out your gizzards and feed 'em to the coyotes and have your worthless heart for breakfast." Devin glanced over his shoulders. "And if the rest of you try to stop me, you'll meet the same fate."

"We're government soldiers. You can't shoot us," muttered Morrow.

"No one will ever know what happened to ya," he replied in a voice as cold and dangerous as the fury burning in his eyes as they cut to Morrow, then back to Toledo. "Take it as a warning. I'll spare your plug ugly face, only 'cause I need you alive."

Major released the breath caught in his throat, thankful Devin was man enough to admit he needed the extra gun power.

"I don't haul no wagons. Don't matter who they're for," Devin added gruffly.

Major frowned.

The man was impossible. It made sense now why he'd requested only four soldiers to drive back four wagons. Devin intended to kill the members of the Laredo gang himself, and if he, Toledo, Morrow or Webster got in his way, he'd kill them, also. The Colonel, along with everyone else, would suspect they died in the skirmish.

He swallowed hard and cursed Toledo's untamed libido under his breath.

Chapter 14

The radiant yellow, pink and blue hues of dawn revealed the rocky shadows of the cliffs and valley below as Devin rode to the top of the canyon. He listened for clues of what lay ahead but heard only birds, scrambling iguanas, and other small wildlife scurrying about as he reached the level ground above.

Morning's first burst of sunlight filtered over the mountain peaks to the east in a brilliant display of burnt red and fiery gold. From here, he could see the countryside, miles of open prairie land, sloping mountaintops, and the lush pine forest below, where Major and the others were finishing their coffee and breakfast of bacon and biscuits. The bright morning gave him a clear view of the serene calm soon to be disturbed. When Bush and his bunch rode up, Devin would know.

He sought a nice shady spot under a tree and he securely tied Deuce, an act seldom required. "Sorry, fella, you might get spooked when the gunpowder goes off," he explained, running a gentle hand through the horse's golden mane.

Deuce whickered, shook his head, and kicked up a puff of dust, as if in protest.

"It's for your own damn good." Devin walked away, grinning. "Don't need to hear shit from you too."

The men assigned to him needed reassurance and coddling, ever since he found the Laredo Gang's trail a few days ago. Hell. That was a woman's job, not his. If they asked one more stupid-assed question, he swore he'd kill them all and finish the task himself.

Several hours of waiting were ahead. He tried not to think about almond-shaped, hazel-brown eyes gazing up at him, darkened with arousal, as he peered over the edge of the cliff. He grimaced as the soft whispers of *please* and *don't stop* clouded his memory and stirred his loins.

He picked up a rock and hurled it over the side of the cliff, just to have something to do. Seldom did he ever play a fool's game, lived in the past, or allow his mind to ponder the future. What was that scrawny girl doing to him? He shook his head, tried to ignore the images of pink lips clenched around his cock, tight mouth suckling on the head, and moist tongue licking it just right. He recalled her hands stroking his shaft, gripping his balls, or her swollen red pussy lips slick with juice that tasted sweeter then the finest honey or the way the ...

Shit, he grumbled. It wasn't working. No matter how hard he tried to forget the image of the head of his cock filling Megan's greedy mouth, pink lips stretched to the limit by his thick stalk, he couldn't. The erotic scent and taste of her honeyed cream as he licked and sucked her sweet cunt lingered with him. His breath ragged, cock pulsing, aching at the memory of her tight vaginal muscles clamped on his embedded finger as her body trembled with climax after climax. He shuddered at the harsh, fiery need to be inside her. The highly erotic memories enveloped him, made his raging lust heighten to the point his hardened cock was painfully unbearable.

Devin moved away from the cliff's edge. Tugging anxiously at the buckskin laces, he freed his aching, stone-hard erection.

His entire body tensed as he gripped his cock and stroked it roughly. He closed his eyes, went with the image that plagued his mind since the evening they met. Megan's pale body spread out on a bed of grass, her wanton gaze looking up at him, opened for him, accepting him freely. Only this time, he buried his cock into her tight, wet, hot flesh to the hilt, drove into her over and over again as her tiny, fragile body writhed beneath his, until she begged him to fuck her harder, plunge deeper, make her come.

Devin, he remembered her frail voice breathing his name as he ate the endless supply of her cream from her throbbing pussy. He stroked quicker and harder, tightened his grip. He imagined her pussy spasm around his cock and heard her climactic cries. Pressure built deep at the base of his spine. He gritted his teeth to suppress the ferocious wail rising from his gut as his cock exploded, spurting his release several feet in front of him. The intense sensation rocked him.

With his clean hand, he wiped the sweat off his brow, then stared at the other hand coated with his sticky seed. Spewing obscenities, he stuffed his cock into his buckskins, still hard and yearning for the real thing.

What did she do to him?

He never wanted a woman so badly in his life, especially one so unripe. Voluptuous women with curves to grab on to so that he could ride for hours were more his style. Not soft, creamy skin firm over sharp bones, pert, round breasts with nipples no bigger than a raindrop, and an intoxicating smile of white pearls beneath luscious pink velvet ribbons with deep dimples under the apples of her cheeks. It was enough to rattle a man's stirrups—and those eyes. At first glance, sweet and innocent. Yet those hazel depths reached beyond a man's soul, deep into his darkest desires.

There was only one other way to temporarily assuage the dark demons, the barbarous need within—blood. He could taste it, smell it, and he felt it in his marrow. His hands clenched into tight fists, itching, ready, waiting eagerly for what was to come. Like a man possessed, his silver gaze turned cold and deadly at the realization that in a couple of hours, at least one dark desire would be satisfied.

Today, he would kill.

* * * *

The sun dipped mid-way along the western skyline as Devin calculated, mid-afternoon when the three ruffians rode ahead of the others. They made their way through the canyon, peering hard, scouring the cliffs toward a narrow canyon with steep walls—the perfect stop to make a stand. Devin knew it well. As did members of the gang. They often used it after their lawlessness, the rocky carpet made it nearly impossible for a posse to trail them.

It lay on a direct course into Cheyenne-infested country. Men with any brains steered clear of the area. After Devin stepped down, Bush became the self-proclaimed leader. They intended to exchange the weapons for gold. The Colonel didn't have to tell him that. He already knew the only logical explanation why so many rustlers would take up with Bush to swindle the federal government.

He'd introduced Zach Bush and a few others to the Cheyenne Chief years ago after they robbed a bank and needed a place to hole up. They hunted, ate and drank with the warriors, and even screwed their women. The Cheyenne never mentioned gold around outsiders. It was a closely guarded secret. They knew what would happen if word ever leaked that gold was buried on their land.

Small gold pockets existed in the Black Hills, smack dab in the middle of Comanche territory. Ol' John, the man who'd snatched him from the train, married a Comanche woman. They spent winters living amongst them. After Ol' John died, Devin returned her to her people and continued to visit, even after she passed years later. Considered family, the Comanche allowed him to take what he needed as long as he didn't reveal its place of origin. To this day, he kept his word, only taking enough when he ventured into town for food, drink, women, a hot bath, and close shave. It had been a fluke that he'd hauled more than enough to pay off Megan's debt.

He harbored no ill will against the Indians and he counted many his friends. Even so, he couldn't idly stand by while rifles and ammunition fell into their hands. Hundreds of women and children would lose their lives on both sides. That was something he'd never allow.

The look in Megan's eyes as she recounted the tragic circumstances of her parents' deaths strongly reiterated he was doing the right thing. Not for honor, because he damn well knew there wasn't a shred of honor in his bones. He was a cold-blooded murderer and no-account thief, and if there was a holy man above, only he and Lucifer below knew all Devin had done.

It sure wasn't for the bounty or to save his skin. Ten thousand or ten million, he didn't give a damn one way or the other. Let the vultures come after him. More call to perfect his accuracy and speed.

His two aunties taught him it was inexcusable and unforgivable to harm an innocent, even one he didn't know. Now, all he could think of was Shelby and Emma. Two of the littlest mops of blond curls, big eyes, and button noses he'd ever seen. They were his blood, and he'd go to hell and back to protect them.

Then there was Megan. Sweet-smelling, smooth, creamy skin, warm and firm petite body scarcely curved in the right places, slick, open, and aching eagerly just for him. Damn, he was getting hard again just thinking about her. With a stiff shake of his head, he tamped down the arousal creeping into his lust-starved blood, and turned his attention below.

It was a matter of patience and timing. Devin kept his head low, rifle tucked under his belly as he lay on the ground. He instructed the other men to do the same, no chance for sunlight to reflect off silver parts, alerting anyone to their presence. He looked to his right at Sergeant Major lying low, some forty feet away.

Major gave him an acknowledging nod.

Devin smiled inwardly, recalling his final words before Toledo took his spot at the end of the canyon near the gunpowder, Morrow across to his left and Webster on the other side toward the center of the canyon, where the trap was set.

When the last hoof passes the mark, light the fuse and count to ten slowly. On seven, take aim. Eight, fire. Nine, Webster pulls the rope, triggering the trap—a fence high enough to stop a horse from jumping over made out of sharpened branches that Webster and Morrow built and buried under the rocky terrain to trap them in. *On ten, the fireworks go off, and the dance begins.*

Choose your partner well, he'd instructed, and they looked at him foolishly. He explained one free shot was all they were getting. The task of facing over thirty skilled gunslicks wasn't for the faint at heart. Each man below could detect a shooters whereabouts by the direction of the bullets flying, and the shooters' accuracy and deadly potential by the men falling. They'd be firing back with a single intent on their mind—survival.

Every sense heightened. He listened to the horses ride up one end of the canyon and back again. Soon after, the wagons and other riders descended upon the narrow. Once they passed the center point, a wide-open canyon, they were sure to lower their guard. Their eyes were focused on the exit, toward the gold just beyond death's door. At that point their life was no longer in their hands.

Devin fed off his adrenaline, blood racing as the final horse's leg stepped over the mark. Like a well-oiled machine with the fuse lit, they each started counting. On six, they pulled out their rifles, took aim on seven, and on eight, five shots rang out. Five men below toppled from their saddles, dead before they hit the rocks.

Devin took out Bush with a shot right between the eyes. "Stinkin' bastard," he muttered. "Never did like you." The man had an aversion for baths, and Devin hated the smell of him.

On nine, Webster triggered the fence, which sprang up at a sixty-degree angle while the horses buckled. The outlaws, in a confused fray, bolted for cover behind the wagons as the gunpowder went off on ten.

The jarring blasts ricocheted through the narrow canyon, ending the way to freedom as the walls tumbled down, forever blocking the exit.

Devin capitalized on the tumult and waylay, picked out Gil, the best shot in the bunch. Gil, cinched up tight as though trying to get his horse under control, more than likely had no clue what hit him a moment later. He was dead before the projectile exited his brain.

Shot after shot rang out as the echoes reverberated, and the canyon filled with dust from the panicked horses' hooves, and the gunpowder mingled in the clouds. The lowlifes below were felled like flies with deadly accuracy.

Frank, the next sure shot, met Devin's deadly fate while the Major and his men took two men each. It was then they pulled off the fifth wagon's tarp.

Devin's eyes flared at the distinct shape of three small cannons filtered through the smoky haze. He recognized Creed, a sorry excuse for a human, harmful to every living creature, including beast, as he loaded the iron ball down the barrel.

Creed went down, and Earl, a back-shooting scoundrel, took his place. Devin only had seconds to reload before the cannon now aimed at him fired. Why in the hell, he wondered, did someone name him after a deadly weapon? Where was the resemblance?

The bullet struck Earl in the right eye just before the fiery cannonball barreled toward Devin. With not a moment to spare, he scrambled from the edge of the cliff. Shards of rocks raised by the impact peppered his face.

Seconds later, by the time Devin reached the edge of the cliff, the cannon was reloaded. He took aim and downed the nuisance. A scant second passed before Bruno climbed the wagon and kicked the dead man aside as he lit the charge. Bruno received the same lot, but held on long enough to direct the cannon toward Devin before his limp body tumbled off the wagon.

Devin reloaded, knew his position was made once again. He rolled several feet before the second blast tore away the earth he'd warmed moments ago. Gunslingers worth a lick stayed alive by intuitively sensing an opponent's mastery and ingenuity. He was certain the surviving men below knew who was about to send them to hell.

Dead, dying and wounded sprawled on the rocks as the tiny red rivers flowing through the cracks grew in number. The cries and moans rose through the dust and heat of the sun-filled sky as the assault continued.

Outlaw after outlaw collapsed. Devin kept up the ruthless pace, downing a man with each blast, until the number dwindled to just over a handful. They pulled back. The first rider galloped at full speed and sailed over the barricade with ease.

Devin's eyes widened with outrage. His hands clenched the heated rifle as he started to call for Deuce while quickly reloading. He suddenly remembered his horse was good and tied. Without a moment to spare, he jumped to his feet as the second horse took flight. He cursed Webster and Morrow. Even at this distance, he could tell the height of the fence fell short of his order.

At full speed Devin ran, jumping over rocks, fallen logs and large cracks in the dried-up mountain cliff. He propped the rifle against his shoulder and took aim. It was dead on. The rider slumped out of his saddle and landed on the pointed spikes, piercing his rotund belly as his horse glided over the fence.

The following rustler was luckier. Devin, jumping over what appeared to be a long-abandoned campfire consisting of a small pile of rocks and ash remnants, faltered as he landed. The second bullet was off, piercing the back of the rider's arm. His horse rode fast. The wounded man joined the others already nearing the mouth, desperately racing towards the refuge of the nearby canopy of pinon trees.

Devin was good, but he wasn't that good. He had to pause and reload once again, knowing it would take all of three seconds. Three seconds he didn't have to spare, as the horses galloped at full speed, closer and closer to escape.

He raised the rifle to his shoulder, sighted off the distance over several hundred yards. The target was at a downward slope and rode fast, almost a quarter a mile away. Slowly, Devin pulled the trigger. The black cowboy hat flew off as blood, bone and brain tissue splattered out of the unrecognizable rustler.

Once more, he cocked the hammer of the second barrel and raised his rifle.

"Spawn," Major shouted, grabbing his arm. "They're gone. We got the wagons."

"Outta my way," Devin growled, elbowing the Major on the side of his face and knocking him to the ground.

It was an impossible shot from atop the dusty mountain. He could barely see the outlaw taking up the rear, quickly descending upon the trees. For a moment, it looked as if he was about to get away cleanly. Devin stared straight down the barrel, nostrils flared as he took a deep breath and held it.

Devin slowly, ever so slowly, began to squeeze the trigger. As if in slow motion, he tracked the bullet until it reached its intended target. The outlaw didn't have a chance.

"You knew about the cannons." Devin turned toward the Major. The viciousness of his tone yanked the man out of his awe-inspired trance as the Major continued to gape in the direction of the poor son of a bitch who toppled from the saddle a moment before his horse disappeared behind the trees.

"Colonel ordered us not to tell you," Major said. "He thought you wouldn't go through with the deal if you knew how heavily armed they were."

"And the fucking fence? It's a good two feet shorter than I told them to build."

Major shrugged his shoulders. "Didn't know. Toledo and I were working on the gunpowder. I'm as surprised as you are."

Devin stalked toward Deuce, spewing venom the likes of which Sergeant Major must never have heard come out of one man in all his forty years, judging from his face.

In no time, Devin met up with Webster and Morrow as they walked among the dead or dying men scattered along the narrows.

He swung out of the saddle, the purpose is his stride evident, the look in his eye deadly.

"Sorry-assed bastard," he growled, coming up to Webster. "Next time I tell you to do something, do it." His fist landed between Webster's eyes. Webster was out before his butt hit the rocky earth.

Morrow was trembling when Devin turned and shouted, "Same goes for you." Devin felt teeth loosening and nose crushing under his fist, just a scant second before Morrow fell flat on his back.

Toledo turned white as a sheet. "Uh," he muttered as Devin started to walk away.

Devin cut him a cold glare.

"What 'bout the wounded?"

"Leave 'em."

Toledo's jaw dropped in disbelief.

"We ain't got time for this shit," Devin grumbled, finishing off the wounded and dying, knowing they wouldn't survive the long trek back to camp. He'd do the same for a wounded horse, but hell, it was a generosity his kind didn't deserve.

Time was of the essence. If any Cheyenne were within hearing distance, they'd be on their way. While on friendly terms, Devin wasn't about to wait around to try and explain to over a thousand angry Indians why they weren't getting their weapons.

As it was, thanks to Morrow and Webster, there were survivors. The double-crossed gunslingers would be gunning for him. They were probably angrier than the Indians ever would be and thinking of ways to get even. Always one for finishing what he started, he'd trail them and finish the job when time permitted. For now, they needed to put as much distance between them and the nearby Cheyenne as possible.

* * * *

Devin and the four soldiers rode into camp with the five wagons, two of which Toledo pulled with his team of eight horses. Behind were the two dozen or so horses the dead gunslicks no longer needed.

Curious onlookers beamed with shock, excitement and revelry. Some joined the parade of sorts at the gate and followed all the way to the livery.

"Colonel? Colonel O'Roake, they're here!" exclaimed the young private as he ran into the Colonel's office, saluting hastily in the process when he noticed the high-ranking officials sitting around the conference table to the right of the large room.

"Who?" Colonel O'Roake asked, waving off the salute and forgiving the overzealous interruption.

"Spawn and the other men."

The colonel dashed to the window, along with several of the other men at the table.

"They're all here."

"They made it." Colonel O'Roake's remark was more of an astonished statement of disbelief than a question.

"Yes, sir. Fit as a fiddle, 'cept for a slash across Toledo's throat and the bruises."

"A few cuts and bruises are to be expected after what they've been through," the General said, glancing over his shoulder at the private.

"Begging your pardon, General. Toledo says he got it shaving. Morrow's busted nose and missing tooth was from tripping over a rock, and Webster has two black eyes."

"What happened to *him*?"

The private, standing at attention and staring straight ahead, tried hard not to laugh, but a slight grin curled his lips. "Ran into a tree."

"Sergeant Major?" the Colonel queried warily.

"Black-and-blue cheek. Got it from walking into the side of a mountain."

General Simms, two Lieutenant Generals, a few other colonels discussed the outlandish reasons for injury in the line of battle amongst each other. The colonel was almost afraid to ask as a knot twisted deep in his gut. "Mr. Spawn?"

"He's headed this way. Don't look none too happy."

A scant moment later, Devin stormed past everyone in the officer's headquarters and didn't stop as he entered the Colonel's office.

"Mr. Spawn..." the colonel began, smiling graciously though he was surprised to see him alive and even more stunned to learn he was successful. Truth be told, he was somewhat fearful of the man closing in on him with a wild, intent look about him.

"You lying bastard," Devin interrupted heatedly.

The colonel only had time to blink before everything faded to black.

Devin sucker-punched the well-starched and heavily decorated officer. He glared at the limp body sprawled on the floor and coolly added, "Worthless piece of dog shit. No one lies to a Spawn."

A hush swept over the room. The private backed out quietly, suspecting someone may have a fool idea about ordering him to apprehend Spawn.

General Simms studied the formidable man, aptly referred to as the Devil's Spawn. This was the first time he had seen him, but certainly not the first time he'd heard of him. The weaponry alone strapped to his person was enough to wipe out each person in the room. He stood there, huge and tough, waiting for a challenger. There was no fear, no nerves, nothing but daring, guts and hard, muscled brawn.

The General weaved through the other men gathered about the window. Carefully, he stepped over the Colonel, and met Devin in the middle of the room. "Allow me, Mr. Spawn, to be the first to extend my congratulations, since it appears Colonel O'Roake has tripped over a rug and is unable to thank you properly for a job well done."

Devin's eyes narrowed.

General Simms followed the intense silvery eyes taking in the gold stars and stripes decorating his uniform. They exchanged a knowing look, seeing how there probably wasn't a rug in the entire building, let alone the room they were in.

Chapter 15

"Is that the only reason for your rejection the past month?" Caleb held Megan's hands tightly clasped between his, sitting across from her at the table in frustration, the look of utter despair upon his face.

"Yes," Megan meekly replied, not fully aware why she couldn't bring herself to send Caleb away for good. Dressed in widow's weeds, she'd used Reed as a feeble excuse not to marry him instead of searching deep for the real reason.

He moved around the table, sat on the edge, one leg planted on the floor and the other dangling. Easing her up by the shoulders, he pulled her into his warm embrace.

"Meg," Caleb pleaded softly. "If it's true, I'll submit to your request, wait as long as necessary till you forget what you were even mourning."

He lifted her chin toward his face.

Filled with sorrow, her eyes slowly rose to meet his. The shadow of anguish clouded the blue eyes, the whisper of hope clinging beyond the depths, and the love forever engrained in his soul. Suddenly, she found herself wanting to be lost in his gaze. Swept away by whatever bound them together for an eternity.

"Ask me to wait. Tell me you love me, and I'll be patient, though it will kill me more each day not to be able to hold you like this." His arm tightened around her as he kissed her forehead gently.

The warmth of his lips seared her skin, made her shiver with a puzzling lusty awareness that awakened her fear. She had a very real fear that stringing Caleb along was wrong, might hurt him emotionally and place him in danger physically. If her depraved lust, the sinful nature Mrs. Walker had warned against, was the cause of Reed's condition, then she refused to take that risk with Caleb. Wrong or not, it was a risk she was willing to take with

Devin. There was no love between them, only hot-blooded lust that she could not deny. If anything happened to Caleb, the love of her life, she would simply perish.

Before she allowed him to go further, ignoring the longing in her saddened heart, she slipped out of his embrace and put distance between them.

"Oh, Caleb, don't ask me when you already know how I feel. It wouldn't be fair to make you wait when I don't know if I'll ever be prepared to marry again."

"That's for me to decide." His poignant tone tore at her heart as he slowly walked to where she stood at the opposite end of the long rectangular table.

* * * *

Standing on the front porch, Devin decided he'd heard enough during the past couple of minutes. He hadn't covered hundreds of miles in two days without stopping, exhausting his prized Deuce to near death, to listen while another man professed his love for Megan.

He stepped inside.

"Step away from her and draw." Any man fool enough to traipse on his property, risked a double-barrel offense. Both hands were ready for Pretty Boy's slightest move.

Apparently, neither seemed to hear the door open, but Megan and Caleb no doubt heard the cold finality of the threat that turned their attention.

"Devin," Megan gasped on a breathless note.

"Who are you?" Caleb shouted, glaring at Devin for the first time.

"I should be asking the questions, seeing how you're in my house."

"Yours?" His bewildered gaze shot to Megan, then back to Devin.

"But it don't matter who the hell you are, since you'll be dead soon." Devin drew his shooter, gestured for Caleb to move away from Megan. "Like I said, step away."

"Devin, no," Megan shouted frantically, jumping in front of Caleb. "He's a doctor. He's not carrying a gun."

"You know this man?" Caleb appeared more surprised at learning she knew him than at the threat on his life.

"He's Reed's son. Devin Spawn," She answered nervously, staring at Devin as he removed one of the knives strapped to his calf and threw it on the table. It came to rest in front of Caleb. "What are you doing?"

Without answering, Devin tossed the other revolver beside the knife.

"Choose how you want to die, Pretty Boy."

Caleb's eyes narrowed.

Devin noticed the other man's fist clench, and his whole body seemed to stiffen at the use of "Pretty Boy."

"Devin, I don't know what you're thinking, but Caleb is a childhood friend. That's all." Megan looked up at Caleb, and the plea in her eyes told him to be quiet and let her speak if he wanted to live.

Devin could tell the man wasn't about to step down from a fight, not when his masculinity was challenged.

"Don't lie on my account. I can take care of myself." Caleb brushed her aside, stepping to the table to choose his weapon. He stared Devin in the eye and declared with firm confidence, "I plan on marrying her."

Devin laughed. It was a chilly, harsh laugh meant to provoke, but there wasn't a flicker of humor in his steely gaze. "Before I kill you, you should know how futile your death will be. Tell him, Megan."

Caleb turned to Megan, and Devin noticed the shame, humiliation and fear shrouding her eyes. She remained speechless.

"Tell me what?" He glared questioningly at Devin.

"I own her. Bought and paid for her. So you see, she's not free to marry you or anyone else."

"Name your price."

"She's not for sale."

"What do you want?"

"To get this over with."

"Caleb," Megan pleaded, "don't be a fool. He'll kill you. The man's a walking death machine."

Inwardly, Devin smiled at the compliment—or was it meant as an insult?

"Megan, you don't think you're worth dying for? I'm only doing what I should have done long ago, defend you against my parents."

"You were a young boy. What could you have done?"

"I'm a man now, and I won't make the same mistake twice."

"It's too late. There are things about me you don't know. I'll never be free to marry you. I belong to Devin now."

Even Devin sensed how her words punctured the other man's heart. The rather touching interlude between the two displayed an intimacy beyond mere friends, and quite beyond innocent childhood friends, as she so heatedly professed. Megan Adams Spawn apparently held more secrets he had yet to discover.

"Then, my dear, there is no reason to live." Caleb turned and reached for the knife, knowing by the time he lifted it he'd probably be dead.

Clearly, Pretty Boy wanted to die. Devin realized he was serious. The man truly loved Megan. How unfortunate.

With his hand covering the handle, Caleb paused, looked up, and stared at him.

Devin quickly surmised if he killed Caleb, Megan would never truly be his. Her body, yes, but all else would be forever lost to him. It was in that instant Devin realized he wanted much more from her than he dared confess. Megan was creeping into his disreputable soul in a way that made his blood boil with an unquenchable need, made him yearn for the solitude of the wilderness, and at the same time, take her into his arms and never let go.

Did Caleb feel the same?

Caleb picked up the knife, stood solid, as if waiting to be gunned down by the man who claimed his woman.

Oh, hell yes, Pretty Boy was in the same hellish existence.

Despite his strong disposition toward his formidable opponent, measured by degree of Megan's affection, not lethal propensity, Devin could never kill Caleb.

"Leave, before I change my mind." Devin kept his expression reserved, his tone dangerously low and absolute. He watched Caleb's gaze flicker, as if contemplating his own fate at Devin's most gracious offer to extend his life another day. His grip tightened on the handle, as though calculating the effort to direct it toward his nemesis. There wasn't a hell of a lot of calculating with a six-shooter already cocked and pointed directly at him. With a reputable speed unsurpassed, the man would be a fool to doubt he'd be dead in an instant and have Megan only in the afterlife.

Devin could see Caleb struggle with his decision to live or die—either way, he'd lose. If he made the wrong choice, Devin would lose, also.

His best option, transfer the upper hand to his opponent. Devin returned his pistol to leather, shocking Caleb and Megan.

A test of sorts to see what Megan thought of him. Not limiting gallantry to Caleb for willingly laying his life on the line over a miniature porcelain figurine of a woman, albeit a beautiful one, the tables were now turned. As if putting his gun away wasn't daring enough, carefully he unbuckled and untied his double belt. He tossed it off to the side of the table in a rare feat he'd afforded no man before.

Unarmed, he waited for Caleb's next move as they stood eye-to-eye.

Pretty Boy must choose between becoming a cold-blooded murderer or what some considered a fate worse than death—defeat.

The intense silence shrouded them in a black eerie cloud and dragged on as neither of them backed down.

* * * *

Megan was the first to speak, her voice tinged with terror.

"Caleb, please," she begged. Despite the trembling of her fingers, she tried to pry his tight-fisted grip from the knife. "I've made my choice. Please try to understand. You'll find someone else."

Caleb looked down at her, his face going pale for the first time. He studied her face for what seemed like an eternity, as though searching for a hint of the person he once knew, the young girl he fell in love with years ago. The one he still worshipped.

"I love only you, Megan Adams." He turned, knife still in hand, stormed out of the door, and swung upon his horse.

Megan clung to the doorjamb, watching as Caleb disappeared around the bend in a cloud of dust. Suddenly, she felt cold, alone and completely empty. Tears streamed down her cheeks.

"So tell me, Dimples," Devin's deep voice drew her around. "Just how friendly were you two?"

Hatred burned into her mind. Overlooking his brassiness, she stepped away from the door and shot him a look the likes of which he probably wouldn't soon forget.

"Let's get one thing straight, Devil Child, or whatever the hell they call you. I only said that for Caleb's sake."

"Which part?" he asked in a calm, matter-of-fact tone.

"My belonging to you," she spewed, wiping away tears with a rough swipe of her fingers. "You don't own me. Not now, not ever. I'll not be the property of another man. So you see, Mr. Spawn, I'm only here for the girls. As soon as I can, I'm taking them away. I'll get as far from you as humanly possible."

"It's Devil's Spawn. I suppose it has the same meaning, though. I prefer the way you say it. Definitely has a nice ring to it. Devil Child." His voice was a relentless tease, and she fumed, anger spreading through her system.

Her gaze dropped to the gunbelt on the table.

"Don't even think about it," he warned, all traces of humor removed from his voice.

She clenched her fist in the folds of her skirt. "Why don't you jump on that monstrosity you call a horse and ride on out of here? I'll be glad to be rid of you."

"Don't go lying, Dimples." His voice turned low, suggestive. "There's something you want from me. A reason you agreed to return to the ranch. The real reason you sent Pretty Boy packing. Since the first night we met in the woods by the river, you've wanted it." He moved around the table, but his eyes never left hers.

She started to back away in the opposite direction, her heart pounding like the beat of a drum. Her body reacted viscerally to his husky tone, the raw arousal in his silvery gaze. The sensual bow of his lips brought to mind the pleasure he'd shown her on their last night together.

"When you look at me, I see it in your eyes. I can see it in your eyes this very instant."

"I...I don't know what you're talking about." Every glorious detail of that night, the vivid image of him sprawled naked in the middle of their bed, turned her blood hot. She glanced downward. The bulge in the front of his buckskins grew before her eyes. A flare of heated desire raced down her spine. She bumped into a chair behind her and let out a startled gasp, her breath coming in spurts.

"I've wanted the same thing. I've dreamt about it, imagined it and thought about it more times than I care to admit. How it would feel to be inside—"

"You're wrong." Her eyes widened, watching him advance, the dark intent in his gaze dizzying to her senses. "I don't want anything of yours."

"Oh, no, Dimples, you want it bad, as bad as I want it. Want me to show you how bad I want to be inside you?"

Yes. She shook her head.

His hands worked the laces of his buckskins. "How bad I want to fill your sweet pussy, to have you in my arms beneath me."

Unable to move, her feet were rooted to the floor. Her wide-eyed gaze was riveted to the enormous bulge straining the thin material for freedom. Her fingers curled tightly around the back of the chair. Reflexively, she bit her lip and moaned, a soft, pitiful moan as he peeled apart the butter-colored fabric, revealing the solid erection beneath.

"See how bad I want to feel your tight pussy gripping my cock as you come." He held his cock at the wide base, stroked the thick length slowly with the other hand. It pointed directly at her, seemed to call her, tempt, promise and warn her all at the same time. It lured her to heavenly bliss or the perils of hell, she wasn't sure which.

"Come here, Dimples," he spoke softly as he beckoned her with a wave of his hand, directing her to the chair he'd pulled away from the table.

Mesmerized, weakened by her own arousal, she took a cautious step toward him. Lord help her, because alone she could not resist the temptation he presented. Megan hesitated, drew in a deep breath. She took another step and then froze when he advanced.

With his left hand resting on the small of her back, he guided her the rest of the way. Another small moan of desire escaped her lips when the head of his cock brushed against her elbow. The heat seared her skin, daring her to touch it as the distinct scent of his arousal overwhelmed her senses.

"Sit." He held the chair. Automatically she did as requested. "I won't hurt you."

Her eyes grew even wider, noting his erection was directly within eye level, only inches from her face as he stood in front of her. She swallowed hard and licked her lips.

* * * *

Talk about control. Devin wanted grab her hair and ram his rod down her throat until he hit rock-bottom. That wouldn't do Megan any good. He wanted to please her, ravage and fuck her, make her forget Pretty Boy and take her to a place only he knew. Limbo, a state of oblivion bordering heaven and hell.

From what little experience they shared, he knew she wouldn't be able to handle what he had in mind. He had to go slow. Her small, tight vagina wasn't accustomed to his demands. This was going to require patience, a lot of patience, and he was not a man known for patience when it came to appeasing his dark, sexual desires.

Not wanting to treat her like a common whore, a grimace lined his face. Unsure how to a treat lady, his breathing altered by his pulsing need, while he reflected he wasn't exactly built for one as dainty as Megan.

She was Devin Spawn's woman now, and he was just going to have to control the bestial unrestrained lust raging in his blood. He liked the sound of that—his woman.

At least, until he had his fill of her Then, he would be on his way.

He never stayed in one place long. No woman ever managed to change his ways. Not his aunties, the Comanche woman John married, the pretty squaws who fired up his peace pipe, hot-and-spicy Mexican senoritas, or the enamored soiled doves who promised an endless supply of free goodies if he settled with them.

He enjoyed his freedom too much, lived his self-indulgent days coming and going whenever he pleased.

Megan was surely a passing fancy, someone he wanted for the moment, though the desire was beyond comprehension, out of place for a loner who never needed anyone.

Perhaps it was the death of his father, the idea another man wanted her, or the selfishness coming from some sort of perceived ownership, seeing how he'd paid good money for her. Reason could be simply a physical attraction. One look at the petite, taut body, pert breasts inflating the front of her dress, those pouty, pink lips that could grip a man's cock tight in her inviting mouth and suck him bone dry, or kiss so softly and passionately, a man could feel the burn clear to his toes.

Whatever the reason, he'd stay a few days, no more.

He sat directly in front of her, legs on either side of hers, his cock practically resting in her lap.

* * * *

Unable to pull her eyes from the erotic site, her body trembled. Megan was barely aware as he gathered up the hem of her skirt. She clasped her knees together when she felt the heat of his hands on her skin just below the hem of pantalets. The throbbing between her thighs intensified.

"Tell me." He spoke softly, the heat of his arousal darkening his charcoaled gaze and deepening his tone. "What *did* you two do?"

Her head jerked up. Momentary shock ripped through her. He asked about Caleb.

"Tell me."

She couldn't bring herself to speak the truth. The warmth of his fingertips scorched the curves of her calves as they inched higher over the thin material.

After her failure to respond, he asked again.

"We..." she gasped, closing her eyes briefly when his hands rounded her knees.

His hands stilled, and she knew he was waiting for her answer.

"We didn't have relations."

"You and he never fucked?" His voice was surprisingly low, almost soft she thought.

Mortified, she shook her head.

"Say it. I want to hear you say it." The palms of his hands continued their slow journey up her thighs.

"No, we never..." She paused. With no desire to put what she and Caleb shared in such degrading terms, yet unsure the beast under the calm mask could understand the depth of their love, she chose, "had sex."

"What *have* you shared?" His hands trailed over her hips, dipping behind her to cup the roundness of her buttocks as they rested on the wooden seat.

"Must I tell you?" She trembled. The memories, his proximity, and her own lusty awareness were too much.

His hands stilled once again. "Remember our agreement. You are not to deny me anything. Never tell me no. I'll guarantee you'll not like the consequences."

Her mouth clamped shut. Not only did she not want to share the beautiful memories of her time with Caleb, she didn't want to recall something that could never be.

"I'm waiting."

For an instant, she considered just what those consequences he spoke of may be. His large hands once again rested on her knees, squeezed them with a minute degree of pressure, a subtle warning of the tremendous reserve of additional strength. It helped her decide. She began quietly, hesitantly, "We—he used to touch me."

He looked into her eyes, and she dropped her gaze to her lap. With his hands still underneath her skirt, he parted her knees slightly. His voice was low, a rough velvet device of seduction. "Where? Where did he touch you?"

She hesitated, fighting the wave of moisture and the quiver between her thighs, desperately trying to ignore his cock jerking above her skirt. "There...between my legs."

"Your thighs?" His hands roamed slowly up her inner thighs.

"Higher," she breathed, closing her eyes, parting her legs to ease his voyage as the ache between her thighs intensified.

"Here?" he asked as his fingers kneaded the soft flesh of her upper thighs over her pantalets.

"Higher." The overwhelming excitement, the desire had her shivering.

His large hand splayed over her covered mound as his fingers grazed the sparse curls poking through the timeworn fabric. "Here?"

"Lower," she moaned on a sigh. Her heart beat furiously as his fingers crept steadily closer to her weeping flesh.

"Here?" he asked sensually, finding the correct location. Her body jerked when he fingered her cotton-clad pussy, drenched with the tell-tale sign of her arousal.

"Yes," she gasped, arching her back a tad, a silent plea for him to sink his finger inside and ease the ache, the need.

"Did you like it?" he whispered in a heated, suggestive manner. His fingers stroked the throbbing wetness lightly through the thin layer.

"It was nice." A long moan escaped her when his fingers moved in a circular motion above her labia with a firm pressure.

His brow rose in a skeptical fashion and a single digit eased between the covered outer lips. "When was the last time he touched you?"

"Fourteen," she murmured struggling to keep her eyes open. She squirmed as the divine sensations took over.

"Days, weeks?" Devin penetrated the folds of her greedy pussy as deep as the constricting material would allow, provoking a loud gasp of pleasure from her.

She bit her lip. The power and heat emanating from him made her quiver. Waiting for her reply, he watched her bosom rise and fall with each shallow breath. Her gaze dropped to his cock, which twitched precariously on her lap. With the desire to end the inquiry, to have his delicious, hard, impossibly wide cock fill her and quench the ache in her pussy, she softly replied, "I was fourteen."

He yanked his hands from between her legs and jerked down her skirt so rapidly, she sat up, puzzled by his reaction. Her breathing still shallow and a flush covered her cheeks and spread down to her chest.

"At what age did he begin?" he asked, clearly incensed, leaving her little option but to tell the truth.

"Thirteen," she blurted, feeling awkward, thwarted by the intimate contact so rude and abruptly taken away.

He stood up so fast, the chair fell backward. Hastily, he stuffed his erection back into his buckskins. "The bastard took advantage of you."

"It wasn't like that." She shook her head, trembling with confusion, in panic at the searing eyes staring down at her.

"I should have killed him," he growled fiercely.

That would never happen, not while she lived. She needed to reassure Devin with the truth. "We were both young. Caleb is only six months older than me."

She remembered it like it was yesterday. After all these years, it was comforting to confide in someone finally. She told him almost everything.

* * * *

Caleb's parents—the most logical choice, since they were the wealthiest family in town—took her in after the raid, which killed her parents, her brother, and their chance for a better future in a developing frontier. Heartbroken and withdrawn while living in the only two-story house in town at the time, she seldom spoke to the conservative banker or his pristine wife. Mrs. Walker's time was spent either with a small group of society women, praying at church, or patronizing the dressmaker to have the latest European designs replicated to fit her overly round figure.

Caleb was the only one to go out of his way to be friendly, drawing her out of her shell little by little each day. Soon, she was as comfortable with him as she had been with her own six-year old brother, Trevor.

One beautiful, summer day, the sky was blue, the sun bright and hot beaming down on them as they walked home from school. She suggested they take a dip in the river. "It would be delightfully refreshing," she exclaimed, running down the grassy knoll toward the river. She laughed and taunted Caleb as he yelled after her his mother's consequence if they dirtied their tailor-made clothes.

"We'll take them off, silly," she replied, unbuttoning her blouse and flying it above her head like a kite.

Caleb ran after her, catching sight of her dressed only in her chemise as she jumped in the water. Against his better judgment, he stripped out of his clothes, and wearing only his long johns, he dived in.

After their exhilarating swim, she coyly explained they needed to wait until their undergarments dried, or risk soaking their clothes and having his mother discover what they'd done. Following her advice, he hung their wet garments over a low-lying branch to dry.

Both naked and wet as newborns, she curled into a ball. For the sake of modesty, Caleb sat far away from her. Megan complained she was cold.

Gallant even then, Caleb wrapped his arms around her, used his body to warm hers. So close, their bare moist flesh touching made her ache in places a young girl should have no knowledge of.

Her tiny, pebble sized nipples were hard, and when he noticed, she explained they did that whenever she was cold. In an attempt to warm her as she artfully suggested, he rubbed his hands over them. When his untapped cock became hard, he stopped, turned red with embarrassment.

Megan just smiled as her own budding body tingled with enlightenment.

She liked his hands touching her.

She liked it a lot.

And so it began. Megan Adams introduced Caleb Walker to carnal temptation, seduced him on the way home each day from school after they frolicked in the river. She'd whimper about the coldness, knowing chivalrously he'd offer to warm her. Certain body parts were often colder than others, allowing his hands more time to explore and heat her up each afternoon. Finally, they stopped swimming altogether, stretched out in the grass, and kissed while he touched her emerging breasts and that most intimate of all places, between her thighs. With one finger inside her, sometimes, he would take his developing penis in his hand and stoke it until a white fluid spilled out. Other times, he would lie on top of her, rubbing against her until the sticky stuff would squirt between their bodies.

Curious and eager to understand exactly what happened to him and why something like that never happened to her, she offered to stroke him until the explosion that always made him shudder and groan, as though in some sort of pain he seemed to enjoy, spilled in her hands.

Caleb Walker's mother, a devout Christian, preached to Megan nightly that carnal delights of the body were the Devil's work. She warned Megan to pray for strength, to turn away from wicked, sinful temptations of the flesh, never realizing Megan led her precious son down the immoral avenue of lust, a sensual awakening they both couldn't resist any more than Adam resisted the forbidden fruit in the Garden of Eden. Their young bodies touched, explored, come alive under the warmth of the afternoon sun. All the while, Caleb whispered in her ear how beautiful she was, how they'd always be together, and how much he loved her. Sweet words she longed to hear, sentiments she returned wholeheartedly.

* * * *

"You seduced him?" Devin watched her in absorption.

Her shallow breathing, the subtle rise and fall of her breasts, the gentle parting of her lips and the heated flush on her cheeks revealed, as she retold the story that it aroused her to no end.

Megan tried to smile, not realizing she somehow managed a wide-eyed innocence. Once again, she witnessed the spark of arousal darkening his gaze.

"Take off your dress."

"What?"

"You heard me."

Megan stood on legs turned to mush and started to fumble with the hooks on her black dress. She felt her body tremble with sensual awareness, could see the lust intensify, glaze his eyes as he focused intently on her fingers. As each hook came undone, his breathing became harsher. She shrugged out of the black dress, letting it fall to the floor around her feet and heard his swift intake of breath.

She looked down, realized the sun shining brightly through the open door made the homespun linen chemise transparent much to Devin's satisfaction. His lips curled into a sexy, sinful temptation, provoking her desire to view his nakedness. Boldly, she allowed her gaze to travel to the distinct outline at his groin. The thick bulge reached up his abdomen at a sharp angle, the darkened flesh visible through the unlaced fly. It grew to even greater proportions as he continued to devour her with his eyes.

As though he couldn't bear another second of her being scantily covered, he ordered in a tone strangled with desire, "Finish undressing."

Without hesitation, too caught up in her own wanton need, the fierce throbbing between her legs sending her mind reeling, she did as ordered, drawing the thin garment over her head. She tossed it aside and kicked the dress from around her feet.

Every nerve ending awakened, her entire body trembled with growing sexual excitement and nervousness. She stood in front of him wearing only her pantalets and stockings, arms by her sides. She felt the warmth of the sun from the open door heating her bare breasts and couldn't help but wonder if the sight of her small, underdeveloped body pleased him.

Her fingers hooked on her waistband and she wiggled out of her pantalets, already soaked with her arousal. Kicked off her slippers, she tossed the final garment aside and stood naked except for her stockings, awaiting his next request.

"Remove your stockings."

Bending forward slightly, her hands clasped her thighs to slide off the stockings.

"No."

Immediately, she stilled at the gruff, strained order.

"Put one foot on the chair," he ordered.

A surging rush of pleasure rippled through her body as his intent became clear. She placed her right foot on the seat of the chair, giving him an clear view of her wide, bared pussy as it throbbed and glistened with her desire. The action made her feel wickedly seductive, downright brazen. She eased the stocking slowly off her leg with one hand, conscious of where his gaze was riveted.

Aware his eyes never left sight of the swollen, tender flesh between her legs, she moved to the other side of the chair. Her excitement grew. Angling her leg wide, she revealed what she knew he wanted to see, to touch, to taste, to possess. A soft sigh escaped as she lost the struggle to contain the gush of hot, sticky liquid seeping from her aching cunt. She took her time pulling away the final stocking.

"Lie down on the table." His voice was thick and rough, sultry.

Her body trembled with anticipation, entranced by the sexual heat enveloping her. She did what he asked. Her back lengthwise, on the smooth, well-worn oak, she waited, wondering when and where he would touch her first. What he would do to her? She lay perfectly still, submitting to her own meekness.

Chapter 16

"Show me." His tone was rough with lust, aroused by her stark obedience, eagerness to please him. A dark part of him wanted her to resist, challenge him to tell him no. Only then would he fulfill his depraved desire to completely dominate her, to force her into submission.

Her eyes searched his for an explanation.

"Show me how he touched you. I want to know, to understand."

It was downright wrong, cruel to ask. Strangely, he had to know everything she shared with Pretty Boy. Whatever occurred between her and his father was their business. He didn't even want to think about it.

Thoughts of the other man tortured him.

Devin needed to know if he possessed a hold on her heart with the undeniable command of a youthful first love that one never forgets. Or was it infused by a more mature desire, brought on by a man and woman in the throes of ecstasy? Or was it what he desperately wanted to believe she was, a woman with flagrant sensuality, a need imbedded at birth infused in her blood to be awakened at a young age, and luckily for Pretty Boy, he was the recipient of her budding passion and nothing more?

He resented the unfamiliar stab of jealousy raging through him—not that she wasn't a virgin, but that she had a past outside of marriage at such a tender age. If he had known of her when he passed through town eight years ago, he would have stayed when his father asked him.

Back then, she would have been a girl of fourteen or fifteen, and he the leader of the notorious Laredo Gang at twenty-one. Waiting for her to grow up, to develop into a woman capable of meeting his needs, would have been pure agony.

Then, he remembered Pretty Boy, a young kid himself, the first to sample such delights. Fortunate bastard. Devin might still kill him just for beating him to the punch.

Alongside the table, his gaze swept over every detail. In a month's passing, she'd blossomed and now filled out the widow's weeds she wore. He speculated the unending stress of caring for his invalid father no longer kept her up nights, freed her days to care for herself. The supplies and food he'd purchased assisted in the beguiling changes within her. Her delicate, oval face glowed, her cheeks were no longer sunken, nor were her eyes, filled with dark shadows. Their glistening hazel depths could not be hidden behind her long, thick lashes. Her perfect lips curled upwards at the corners, as though waiting for any excuse for a smile to grace her expression. Even her dimples were more prominent.

When he came upon her floating in the river, she'd been straight as a pine tree, bony as a carcass drying out in the desert. Though still quite frail in comparison to most females to which accustomed, she now had the curves of a woman. Gone were the cone-shaped breasts, replaced with softly rounded breasts, the peaks hard little pebbles begging for his touch, and her waist, still tiny, now curved gently into rounded hips.

He witnessed the shivers of excitement wash over her body, heard her soft, rasping breathing. Blood rushed to this groin, and quite impossibly, he grew yet another painful inch as his heated gaze beheld the only glimpse of heaven a devil of his breeding would ever know, the sparse curls covering the pouting folds of feminine temptation that drove men mad with desire.

Before him was a real woman, despite her miniature stature, well aware of the ingrained lustful desires that reddened her blood and the pure, unadulterated sensuality that radiated from her pores. Her innate sexual nature knew no bounds in spite of the attempt to conform her to societal standards.

A noticeable shudder shook her dainty frame as he took her hand in his, and with the other, encouraged her to part her outstretched legs. He guided her hand to the dark blond fuzz nestled between her slender thighs and whispered in a ragged breath, "Show me how he touched you."

He thought he would go mad, lose control when a single finger disappeared between her glistening lips, withdrew completely, and sank back again.

In silence for what seemed like an eternity, he watched her legs part wider, her breathing increase, yet the pumping momentum remained the same.

Unable to take anymore, he murmured raggedly, "What else did he do?"

For a moment, she paused before her left hand covered her breast and gently caressed the creamy mound as her fingers rolled over the puckered nipple.

"What else? What else did he do?"

Eyes completely glazed, her mouth opened slightly as if to speak. A soft moan escaped.

Her hard breathing was proof she was taking pleasure in her touch as she had in the river the day they first met. Today, he felt as he did that day, on the other side of madness, the threat of losing control immense. He understood why Pretty Boy preferred death to life without ever sampling such potent, exquisite sensuality.

Finally, she spoke without stopping the enchanting caresses. "He would touch himself."

He held her gaze. The look in her eyes was that of a woman seeking pleasure. She was his for the taking, offering her nakedness to him, and he was rock-hard, about to go mad with wanting her.

"Sometimes, he would let me touch him," she continued in a tone that spoke volumes, her gaze filled with sinful intent.

Within moments, he stripped out of his clothes, sent them flying in every direction with the speed and agility of one whose very life depended on precise, subhuman actions.

Unconcerned that the doorway at his back was open, he was comfortable in his own skin, with his own primal sexuality. A shameless gasp escaped her lips as her gaze dropped to that part of him that stood out and beckoned her, bursting to possess her. Anxious or afraid, she bit her lip and clamped her thighs together, capturing her right hand between her legs. He loved how the sight of him affected her.

"Give me your hand."

She hesitated. Her body shuddered with what he hoped was excitement. Finally, after a long pause, she offered the hand on her breast, the one farthest from him.

In complete wonderment, he chuckled inwardly at her innocence. For a widow who began her sexual foray at a tender age and grew up in brothel, she was the most inexperienced "experienced" woman he knew.

"The other hand."

Their eyes locked when he grasped her raised hand. He sucked the finger, slick with her juices, into his mouth. He tasted her essence, swirling his tongue around and around until she whimpered. She watched him draw each finger into his mouth, wetting them sufficiently for what he had in mind.

His body stiffened as he lowered her hand to this cock. He groaned, fought to control his release, his primitive need for possession as her moist, slender fingers inflamed him with her heated touch. Steadily, he guided his hand over hers to demonstrate exactly what he wanted her to do.

As if recalling what he liked, her hand began to move of its own accord. She stroked up and down the thick shaft in a tight-fisted grip. He groaned, closed his eyes at the sensations that jutted from his groin to the far corners of his body.

"Don't stop. Whatever you do, don't stop until I tell you." Devin's hips started to thrust as Megan stroked faster and harder, the heat flared stronger and stronger.

His hands cupped both breasts, his tongue glided over the rigid, pointed nipples. He suckled one nipple, then the other into his mouth as she moaned with pleasure, her body arching against his mouth. She was divine, pure heavenly sweetness. His body ached with an insatiable need to devour the firm, ripe flesh. Every part of her luscious body spread out on the table before him, like a feast for him alone to dine on, to satiate the ferocious hunger within.

Her small hand, only able to go halfway around the wide girth, pumped feverishly, stroking the sensitive ridge along the underside, bringing him perilously close. He groaned against her breast, nipping the tight bud between his teeth.

He heard her cry out as the piercing sensation slammed through her system, knew she was racked with arousal so hot, her skin burned and glistened with beads of passion. That extra bite of pain with her pleasure brought her to a brink of discovery, urged him to progress further. His grip on her nipples tightened, twisting lightly as the tip of his tongue licked the hard, tiny pebbles. She whimpered. Her body shuddered, pushing against his hands and mouth. He smiled on the inside, cock excitedly throbbing in her grasp on the outside.

He wanted more. His hand descended lower.

Her hips jerked in response as his fingers probed the hot wetness between her thighs. With a knowing touch, his thumb stroked her engorged clit, and she exploded instantly, sending her screaming, buckling on the table. Her grip on his cock tightened, squeezing him hard, causing him to grunt with approval.

Without shame and full of egotistical male pride, he asked the one question to which he already knew the answer.

"Did he ever touch you like that?" His longest finger penetrated the entrance to her silken depths, pushed past the slick muscles of her tight vagina causing her to gasp sharply. He sucked, nipped, and kissed the sensitive tendon along the smooth curve of her throat.

"Oh, God, no," she barely managed to breathe.

"Again?"

"Yes…yes…again."

His hunger increased as she spread her legs wider, allowed him complete access to her hot, dripping pussy. She rocked her hips against his hand, encouraged him to thrust deeper as he slowly worked his finger inside the wet heat of her tight passage. He heard her moaning. His gaze remained transfixed between her gyrating hips as he eased deeper, faster into her throbbing wetness.

Propelled by a lust-filled urgency, he added another finger, preparing her for what was to come, working the double thickness deeper in her slick flesh as her muscles clenched around him. His cock was thicker than her slender forearm, its head bigger than her fist. He needed to get at least three fingers within her tight, tiny passage before attempting the impossible.

He felt her slim arms clutch the edge of the table, releasing her stronghold on his erection. Her hips arched, she cried out at the unexpected invasion, yet her pussy was accepting the intruder greedily, the spongy, moist flesh opening for him. One hand tightened on her nipples while his fingers drove into her heated passage. Instinctively, she pulled her thighs together, moaned and panted with pleasure.

"You stopped." He wasn't too disappointed. Her grip was too rough and fast—just the way he liked it, a problem, considering how close she brought him.

"I'm sorry," she panted.

"Don't be. There's plenty of time for that later. For now, concentrate on what I'm doing. How it feels."

"How can I not?"

He chuckled.

Expertly, he alternated between thrusts and strokes, curls and twists with the expertise of one trained on how to give pleasure at a very early age from those who knew—women. Tutelage from the most beautiful, gifted women at the most expensive parlor houses lasted several years until his size began to overwhelm them, and his desire sometimes crossed the delicate balance between pain and pleasure. Thus, he took to paying for his encounters.

This time, it was Megan he was pleasing, not some whore he cared nothing about. He had to make it good. Make her want him next time.

His lips covered hers with swift urgency, bestowing the agonizing need coursing through his veins. Astonishingly, she accepted his tongue as it darted between her lips, greedily suckling the taste of him until he moaned with satisfaction.

He resumed caressing her breasts, massaging her aching nipples as he enticed her, coaxing her slick pussy into submission. He applied pressure on the swollen nub beneath his thumb and brought her to a rapid climax. She bucked on the table and cried out his name, giving him a sense of satisfaction he had no right to feel once again as the second outburst overtook her, drenching his embedded fingers.

Quickly, he built a third climax out of an irrational sense of rivalry, driven by the need to possess her mind, body, heart and soul.

There was only one way to do that.

Megan moaned harshly and went entirely rigid when he pushed a third finger past the tight barrier. He didn't give her a moment to adjust. The triple thickness drove in and out furiously while his thumb stroked her arousal to a new level of intensity. The sudden explosion had her twisting on the table, her keen wail filling the house, traveling outside and rising in the heat of the sun.

His hands hooked beneath her knees, positioned her across the table so her bottom was just past the edge. He leaned down, spread her dripping nether lips wide and inhaled her scent, like the petals of a beautiful rose opened, fragrant and inviting to touch.

Keeping his tongue rigid, he swept over the moist flesh top to bottom, tasting the sweet cream of her pleasure. After a quick intake of breath, he heard her follow it with a long gasp as he flicked her clitoris and caressed the entrance to her body with his tongue.

"Oh, yes," she whimpered, and he knew she was his. Megan was finally his.

He moved between her legs as they dangled boneless off the table, brushed tender kisses along her jaw line as he whispered, "You're mine, Megan. I'll erase every memory of every man who ever touched you. After today, you'll desire only me."

Her hands clasped his face, pulled him down, and she claimed him with her mouth in a fierce, passionate kiss that assailed his senses. The heady scent of her desire filled his nostrils. Felt the warmth of her breath on his cheek.

His lips and tongue mingled with hers in an erotic dance, music all their own that neither wanted to end. She sucked his tongue into her mouth. Her lips were warm and soft. He could taste her frenzied need, her lustful desire. Knew she was ready when he took hold of his cock and positioned it at the entrance of the slick hotness between her thighs and she arched her hips, accepting him.

"It's time," he said roughly, staring into her glazed eyes so dark, they were almost black.

The tip of his cock pulsed against her throbbing core, and he fought the urge to plunge himself deep inside her wet, hot tender flesh.

"Yes." She shifted her hips in expectation, not knowing the true extent of what her dainty body asked. His desperate need to tear into her, damn the consequences, as he took what he wanted assailed his senses. He needed control, to think of her.

She panted, "Oh, yes."

"Megan," he groaned. "I won't lie to you. It's going to hurt like hell. It'll pass. Then, you'll be mine."

He felt her body tense at his heated proclamation, saw the alarm washing over her.

"Relax, and it'll go easier. Your sweet pussy is hot and wet for me. I've got to have it now." His voice was deep, ruthless and as desperate as his need to have her.

"Devin, you're so...so big. You didn't fit before." She blinked up at him, the trepidation gleaming in her eyes as he nudged against the tiny opening. "I'm afraid."

"My fault I didn't prepare you. You're ready now, and I can't wait any longer," he groaned, heard the lust straining his voice. No longer was holding back an option as her tight vaginal muscles began to stretch, gripping his cock.

"Devin," she cried, fear shining bright in her eyes as he fought to push the head into searing heat, achingly tight.

He stroked her swollen clit until she panted and arched her hips into his. She trembled like a virgin, her slick velvety muscles dragging almost painfully against his flesh while he inched his way inside. He groaned when the head finally sank past the most blissful, hottest grip imaginable.

"It hurts," she screamed as he eased his cock inside her, nestled deeper between the soaked lips of her throbbing pussy. Despite her cries of protest, the gush of juices lubricating his cock told him she was eager, ready and willing to experience the cannon.

"Get used to the feel of me." He struggled to breathe as the incredible heat tightened around his flesh, sucked him in. Moving his hips gently, he stroked the narrow entrance, feeding his cock slowly to her. "It'll pass. I promise."

"You're too big, Devin. I can't. I can't."

"Relax, baby." He stilled, afraid of hurting her as he felt her body tense completely. Less than half his cock lodged into the tight heat as fought back the incredible urge to bury himself to the hilt. The hot, silky depth of her cunt drove him mad with desire, pushed him beyond control.

"You're tearing me apart," she cried out in fear, but her muscles gave way, her inner body clutched his hard, driving flesh.

"Pleasure will override the pain," he groaned raggedly. The pad of his thumb massaged her swollen clit while he took her breast in his mouth. His tongue mimicked the movements against her nipple. She moaned and twisted, her hips bucked toward his allowing his cock deeper into the hot confines of her pulsating cunt.

"Good girl." He inched inside the tight sheath by small degrees. He suckled the curve of her neck, branded her with his passion. His fingers tugged on her nipples, a bite of pain to enflame her desire, exciting him further as her inner muscles gripped the thick shaft. Her juices gushed over his cock. "Damn, your pussy's so wet."

Short, shallow thrusts in and out, until his cock was more than halfway inside. He was nearly ready to burst, to die from the sparks of fire radiating from where their flesh joined. "So hot and tight."

"Oh, Devin…that feels… that feels…wonderful," she muttered between long, breathy moans.

"Doesn't hurt?" His voice was a ragged groan as he shifted slightly, lowered his gaze to where her throbbing flesh stretched taut around the wide girth of his cock. Only a few rigid inches remained between them. *Damn, what a pretty sight.*

"A little," she gasped, closing her eyes tightly. "Am I filled with you yet?"

"Almost." He didn't want to lie to her—the widest part, the base, was yet to come.

Her eyes widened as if to say, *There's more?*

"You'll learn how a big cock can pleasure you in a way nothing else can." He really meant *no one* else, especially Pretty Boy. He ground his cock deeper into her hot channel as the muscles tightened and sucked his hardness in. With the way she panted, her hips wiggled and her cunt throbbed and creamed, she was ready to take him on. He was amazed at how such a frail sliver of a woman's pussy drove him to a madness he was on the verge of losing.

"Hurry, Devin. I want all of you. To be filled with you," she begged, as if she, too, was unable to restrain herself. As though this was her first experience at fulfillment, an excuse to unleash the wanton woman buried deep inside. He felt her stretched to the max, muscles clench the massive cock, that was his burden to bear and he could have exploded right then and there.

"You want it, baby? You want my big cock inside you?" Pure animal lust and male pride filled his voice.

"Yes, yes," she panted, her breathing labored, her face dazed with arousal.

"Say it. Let me know what you want." He rocked in and out sinuously, giving her a glimpse, a taste of what she asked for. Dying to give it all to her.

"I want you inside me." Her hips gyrated under him, her voice a soft, seductive whisper.

At her heated words, he pulled away slightly, pleased to see her flushed body pulsate with need, her nipples taut, eyes glittering with lust.

"My cock. Say it, and I'll give it to you, baby."

She closed her eyes as though afraid to ask, beg, demand what she wanted. Sprawled out buck-naked on the dining table with a man's cock buried between her legs in front of the opened front door in the middle of the afternoon. Not exactly, the best time suddenly to become bashful, he thought.

Her eyes snapped open, and he read the sexual request, found it too difficult to refuse. It tempted him beyond reason when she gasped on a breathless whisper, "I want your cock inside me."

He lost control. He withdrew, kept the head buried, then rammed the full twelve inches into her until his balls slammed against her ass. She screamed, came instantly. Her body bolted off the table, her orgasm pouring over his cock.

"Hell yes," he growled fiercely. He rode her hard, unable to control the white-hot intense pleasure ravaging his system. He pushed past sensitive tissue, stretched her, filled her, and drove her need as he stroked her spasming womb with each powerful thrust.

Her hips instinctively rose to meet thrusts so savage they were almost brutal. He couldn't get enough of her, never imagined it could be like this. She bucked against him frantically, as though she fought to keep up, to ride him just as hard.

He pummeled into her with abandon. His growls drowned out her cries. His grip tightened beneath her knees, holding her legs wide, stretching her beyond limit as he lifted her hips off the table to deepen his penetration.

Her cries turned into moans, her hips meeting his every thrust with a savage fury of her own. Her tiny upper body withering on the table with each driving stroke, each time his scrotum pounded against the fleshy mounds of her rear, exciting him further.

"You're fucking fantastic. Your pussy is like a silk glove. I could stay here forever."

"Devin, it's happening again." Her tiny voice was a strangled, blissful warning.

"Yeah, baby, come for me. Let me feel your pussy milk my cock." His thrust became more urgent, dying to feel her tight walls milk him again. Like a caged animal, he rammed into her, lifting her off the table with each wild thrust. Striving for a freedom he didn't dare imagine before.

Within his grasp, he felt her stiffen. She screamed as the orgasm ripped through her. She gasped for breath, convulsing against him, perspiration coating her body.

"Yeah, that's my girl," he growled, feeling her slick pulsing, inner walls squeeze him. He drove his hardened strength into her without mercy. He caught her by the nape of her neck as her body jerked wildly, her explosion gushing around his cock.

"Don't stop," he shouted, releasing her as he felt her vaginal muscles begin to relax.

"Come for me again, baby." He never felt such a sensation before, her hot, tight slickness gripping him like a second skin so damned tight, it was painful. A pain he willingly endured. Her climax pulsed around him, tightened and released his engorged flesh as though hundreds of fingers milked the blood out of him. He wanted to feel it again. He needed to feel it again.

Greedily, he raked her sensitive clit, still throbbing from her last climax, sent her spiraling instantly. He barely gave her time to recover from the last. Her head thrashed, arms braced at her sides, the solid table the only semblance of steady permanence.

He felt her tiny body shudder, hot, wet and open for him. His hard, driving thrusts never faltered, in and out, harder, faster and deeper. Between her cries of pleasure, she gasped for breath.

"Devin, please," she begged between the incessant spasms that rocked her body, and soaked his embedded flesh. The sounds and aroma of sex swirled through the warm afternoon air, firing his lust further.

"Not yet, Megan, don't ask me to stop." *Not when I'm finally fucking your sweet pussy,* he wanted to shout so the whole world heard. *Knew she was his.*

"Please, Devin, I'm begging you."

Thwarted, but aware it was Megan's first time with the Cannon, he placed her legs over his shoulders and braced his hands above her shoulders to keep her from sliding off the table.

"Come with me," he groaned before capturing her mouth in a heated kiss. He drove into her slickness, faster and deeper and harder still, brought her once again to an exploding release that drenched him. His own bone-shaking climax tore through him as he slammed into her swollen hot depths. His cock shook violently as he shot his seed into the voracious cunt that tantalized him erotically, brought him so much satisfaction like never before.

His body tightened, shuddered. He threw his head back and ground out her name as the last drop of the seemingly endless stream filled her quivering, sated body.

Resting the full weight of his body on his forearms, he slowly withdrew from her and moments later when he felt strong enough to move, kissed her softly on her moistened forehead.

* * * *

Megan slowly opened her eyes. Her lids felt so incredibly heavy, it took effort. Turning her head slightly to the left, she caught sight of the thick, heavy-weighted flesh reaching half-way down his thighs while he crossed the room to pick up his clothes and the menacing weapons discarded in haste.

Lazily, she propped herself on her elbows. A hen pecked in the front yard. The warmth of the sun on her naked body, the beads of perspiration shimmering on her skin made her feel wanton. Her gaze lowered to her breasts, the pink tips and pale skin now rosy red and flushed from his overzealous kisses. Dropping her gaze to her parted legs dangling over the edge of the table, the curly hairs drenched with their cum also covered her thighs. She blushed at her own brazenness, sprawled lewdly in front of the open door in broad daylight. Anyone walking up the front porch would stare straight at her gaping pussy.

She had done it. Her body tingled with awareness, savoring the delicious indiscretion. She'd given herself to him and more surprising, he managed to survive. She survived.

Megan found it hard to believe such a huge penis fit in her small body. It was an experience beyond comprehension, farthest from reality and more magnificent than her dreams. Devin was beyond compare.

Her eyes were drawn to him. Where did it all go? Through the peephole at Jazelle's, she gawked in envy, anticipation, trepidation, and only admitted to herself excitement and arousal. Every size, shape, and color poked in front of her. Big, small, and downright puny, but none came close to oversized Devin Spawn.

Even his body—tall, broad, and rock-hard, rippled with muscles, tanned by the sun gods themselves—was a grand study in masculine perfection.

Perfection that drove her to near insanity, a delightful terror that made her pussy start to throb and grow wet with desire, something Megan would have thought outlandish minutes ago. Granted, the man was her dead husband's son, the most dangerous, notorious, wanted outlaw in the entire western frontier.

Despite it all, stronger impulses prevailed. She wanted him.

Filled with a strange twinge of excitement and nervousness she could not explain, she stared, unable to take her eyes off him.

"Do you like what you see?"

He caught her ogling. The flushed heat of her skin stirred her blood at the wickedly, sexual look in his eyes. His bluntness shouldn't have come as a surprise, considering what just happened. Like some mythical hawk, he could probably read the shameless thoughts running through her mind.

"*Like* is so...unsuitable." She heard the shaky catch in her voice.

"What's on your mind, Dimples?" he asked offhandedly, holding a gun in one hand and holster in the other, standing naked as a jaybird near the end of the table. She watched him return the pistol to its leather home and run a calm hand along each bullet on the belt, as though a naked, willing woman spread out on the dining table was an everyday occurrence.

Studying the limp pecker between his long, muscled legs made her drool. He looked up and smiled, seemed to take immense pleasure in her open curiosity and appraisal of his intrinsic male anatomy.

Feeling more forward than the first time she sat in Caleb's lap and touched his hard flesh, she boldly replied, "I can't rightly explain it. One word comes to mind—hunger."

His brows rose, stunned by her unabashed honesty.

"One look at you, and I hunger for your touch. Hunger to have you inside me again, feed me every last inch as I swallow you whole."

Leaving his guns on the table, he moved closer. Her breath caught as his hands glided up her knees to her upper thighs and then stilled.

"Don't be shy with me. Say exactly what's on your mind. I'll give you whatever you want." He took hold of his penis, and it began to swell. She groaned as she felt him rub the tip over her flesh, still tender, sensitive from their intimacy. "If you want my cock inside you, filling that hot pussy of yours, then say so."

"Devin," she breathed, her heavy-lidded eyes met his as she lifted her hips toward him in response.

"Damn, girl, keep looking at me like that, and I'll fucking lose it. Look at you." His lips tightened into a thin line when she winced as his fingers slowly slid through the slick crease of her pussy. "You're tired. Can't even sit up, let alone go another round, though I admire your appetite."

Biting back her disappointment, moaning softly, she lay back and closed her eyes. Strong hands curled around her waist as Devin pulled her forward. Enveloped in his masculine scent of arousal, her nipples brushed against the hard expanse of his bare chest, causing her to gasp.

He held her body tightly against his, the heat of his skin steamy against her weak, moist flesh. Sensitized to his touch, his muscled strength felt comforting, reassuring, and unbelievably arousing.

"Look at me." Their eyes locked. His hands cupped her buttocks, pulling her tightly against his steel hard erection. "I'm ready. I'll always be ready for you. But in case you didn't realize it, I fucked that pretty pussy of yours raw. When you hop off this here table and try to walk, you'll feel it. There's a few things you need to learn about me, and it will suit you well to remember. Don't ever tell me no or lie to me. And I don't like quickies."

She blinked. What was that supposed to mean?

"I like my women always ready for me. From now on, don't wear any so-called unmentionables."

"Wh…what?" she muttered unsure if she understood correctly.

"No pantalets, no chemise, no nothing."

No decent woman went without at least a chemise. For a while, she went without pantalets. After she lost so much weight, they kept sliding down her hips. Now that she regained her weight, to go without pantalets was kind of wickedly illicit, and though she didn't want to admit it, highly erotic, to walk around all day wearing nothing beneath her dress.

For purely sexual reasons, he wanted access to her body at any time, day or night. The lusty thought sent a warm gush of liquid to the intimate area he was now grinding with the tip of the engorged steel rod in his hand.

From the wicked gleam in his eye to the sultry grin curling his lips, he gathered the idea exited her, though she tried to look shocked and embarrassed by the request. Her pussy coating his cock with a bucket load of cream told him otherwise. Her reaction to each indecent proposal, accepting them without question shockingly aroused her instead of scaring her into rejection. What else would he ask of her?

Along the slope of her throat, he brushed kisses, whispered, "Whenever I feel like spanking your bare ass, sucking your tits, or eating your cunt, I will."

Her body stiffened slightly in his arms in response to his choice of words.

She shrieked when he nipped at her shoulder with his teeth and released her.

"Put only your dress back on. Get some rest for tonight."

"Tonight," she repeated, perplexed by what was to occur later in the evening.

"That wounded passage is sore, Dimples. We'll work on your stamina another night. Tonight, you get to suck my cock, and I'll eat your pussy. Give your insides time to recover."

An excruciating sensation struck her inner recesses at the memory of his lips and tongue consuming her ravenously. She quickly calculated the hours.

Moving away from the table, he pulled on his buckskins. "I'll pick up the girls and take them into town for their evening meal."

Megan eased off the table and let out a loud groan, feeling as though someone had pounded her body with fists. The aches and pains were numerous. She grabbed the wooden edge as her legs started to give out.

"Can you make it?" He actually looked concerned as he watched her strained effort to move. She did her best to hide the suffocating pain. Taking an awkward step, she lost the battle.

"Oh my." She leaned her bare buttocks against the table, afraid to bend over to pick up her dress for fear of never being able to stand upright again. She stood absolutely still. Closing her eyes, a throbbing ache of a strictly painful persuasion rippled through her body.

A scant moment later, he was by her side, wrapping his solid arms protectively around her.

For a critical moment, she couldn't believe she almost begged him to take her again. Had she lose her mind? Thankful at least he had sense. Or was it his experience with plowing into females whenever he wanted? He seemed to know an awful lot about how she felt even before she did. Recalled the times he returned from town smelling of cheap perfume. That Cheri woman at Jazelle's was on first-name basis. Not even first names. She called him something else. What was it? Did he have a cute nickname for her? Perhaps Floppy Tits? Did he leave those girls sore? Was he concerned about their well-being afterward?

"Leave me alone," she hissed, trying to shrug out of his embrace. The sudden rage of jealously caught her off-guard, added to her resentment.

Ignoring her protests, he cradled her in his arms and carried her into the bedroom.

"Consider this your first and only warning."

"I'm not telling you no," she countered stubbornly. "I've ran this ranch for months alone, I believe I can mange to walk from one room to the next alone."

Averting his eyes, she hid the grimace straining her face as he deposited her gently on the bed. There was no way she'd let him know the extent of soreness setting in.

Nothing seemed to escape his keen vision.

"Like hell you can. If I had the time, I'd make you soak in a hot tub. For now, get rest. When I return with the girls, I'll bring in the tub."

He left the room before she could voice an argument.

"Till then," he added, returning with only her dress. She wondered what he did with the other garments. "Stay in bed."

He took the quilt folded at the end of the bed and covered her with it.

"I'm not a child." She pulled the cover up to her neck and gritted her teeth. Shocked even that small movement renewed the aches shooting through her arms.

"That's why I fucked you. If you were a child, we wouldn't be having this conversation."

Chapter 17

Megan felt as if her body was perched on the losing side of a battlefield. However, each time she thought of yesterday afternoon, it tingled with a rush of desire that rekindled her hunger for his powerful body. Maybe the sizzling need wouldn't be so unbearable if she'd stayed awake after soaking in the steaming hot bath last night.

Devin waking her before dawn by licking the tender folds between her legs, bringing her to one orgasm after the next, made up for her disappointment.

In return, he showed her how to take more of his cock in her mouth— what he referred to as "face fucking".

She found it immensely enjoyable and was actually good at it. Almost half his thick stalk fit in her mouth. While squeezing his balls, his hands tightened in her hair, the prickling of pain sent fiery pulses rushing through her system, straight to her empty pussy. It flared her appetite, had her sucking harder until he came twice. Hungrily, she swallowed every drop of his hot release.

The warmth of his body, the beat of his heart against her chest as he held her close made her want to stay in bed forever. The sun climbed over the horizon and beamed like a beacon through the lace curtain, warning her reality existed and what she felt was transitory.

Over breakfast, Shelby mentioned Ms. Rosalinda, their teacher, had joined the three of them for supper at the café yesterday. Ms. Rosalinda was a nice enough young lady. Pretty in a tall, blond, hourglass sort of way, but not one for socializing outside her close circle of well-heeled friends.

Of course, Devin brushed the encounter off, saying Shelby insisted Ms. Rosalinda join them after the teacher practically invited herself. Not wanting to cause undo suspicion, he went along with the child's request.

Since there was no reason to turn green over an innocent dinner, she let the subject drop and went about her day. Devin tried his hand at taking care of the animals, and Megan stayed mainly in the house, only going outside to pick vegetables for lunch and supper.

Most of the day, she was on pins and needles, expecting him at any moment to do what he so vehemently threatened—lift her skirt and take her.

To her chagrin, the man was an absolute total contradiction.

As she moved around the house, wearing nothing under her widow's weeds, her body quivered with anticipation. She was dying to work on her stamina, to try out her new suckling skills once more, or have him fill her aching pussy with his cock.

What did he do? He stayed away. He actually stayed away. When he came in for lunch, he hardly glanced at her. Right afterward, he hurried out the door, mumbling about the weather.

By late afternoon, it began to rain. When it was time for bed, she questioned if he would even want to sleep with her again, much less touch her and keep her warm on such a cold and windy night.

What changed? Did she do something wrong? Was she too inexperienced to please him? Was she too skinny? Too short? Not pretty enough?

Whatever it was, she hoped it wasn't her inability to keep up with his carnal desires. The man was intensely sexual and possessed unparallel stamina. She doubted she'd ever be able to keep up. Was a lofty debt enough to keep him around longer?

All sorts of asinine thoughts left her so distracted, she hadn't noticed it was thundering outside when she walked in the girls' bedroom.

Megan's jaw dropped, and she froze mid-step. She not only noticed the pink flush covering her bare arms in her short-sleeved dress, she felt her entire body warm instantly, responding with undeniable lust.

"Megan, come here and look at Devin's scars," Shelby hollered excitedly, standing on Emma's bed and indicating the part her hands made in Devin's wavy auburn locks.

"And the one's on his back." Even Emma seemed tickled as she ran her hand over his bare back. He sat naked from the waist up on Emma's bed. This presented Megan with ample opportunity to admire his masculine form, a well-defined, bulging v-shape which narrowed to his trim hips.

Shifting slightly to face her, he smiled sheepishly, and her breath stilled in her chest.

There were so many prominent features on the man. She never noticed the three scars carved into his muscular back. But then again, she had been too busy staring at what was between his legs to look anywhere else. The tapered scars were long, ran almost from the left side to the other at an angle.

"A bear did 'em, Megan." Shelby's eyes were wide with excitement

"Yes, and Devin killed him." Emma actually appeared impressed by the uncommon feat of heroism.

"And the Indian woman..." Shelby turned to Devin. "What was her name?"

"Bird Whisperer," Devin volunteered with a moderately low tone.

"Yeah, her. She made him all better. It was a good story. You missed it, Megan."

Taking a deep, calming breath, she met his gaze. The glimmer of humility caught her by surprise.

"I hardly think a tale on bears and *Indians* is appropriate for children before bed."

The tone in her voice told Devin she wasn't happy with his topic of choice. Not that he was boasting. He just couldn't bring himself to read the ten-cent fantasy novels when he'd lived the real adventure. There were learned lessons, beneficial to even young girls and a stubborn woman who looked like a kid herself.

"Perhaps she's right, girls." He stood and grabbed his shirt off the bed. When she first walked through the door, he caught a glimpse of the sexual arousal bright in her eyes. It left him feeling too exposed. Too aware of every frustrating second that had passed since his cock exploded in the tight depths of her sweet pussy.

In the morning, Megan had sucked him down her slender throat deep enough that he came twice. It was good. Damned good. However, he was greedy, downright demanding, and he wanted more. A helluva lot more. He fed off her honey-flavored climaxes until she begged him to stop. Dying to ride her again, he parted the slick folds of her tiny vagina and realized the extent of his depraved abuse. Her swollen, tender insides were streaked raw from the driving fury inflicted by the monstrous weapon between his legs. *Damn.* Sometimes, he felt cursed.

Until her battered body recovered, he needed to stay away from her.

Hell, it would be better just to stay away from her entirely. They were so mismatched, it was ridiculous. Her fragile body was never going to get used to the likes of him and his depraved ways. He should get out while the getting was good.

The girls pouted, and he shrugged. He found Shelby's quivering lower lip endearing. It was Emma's soulful eyes mirroring his that tugged at him.

"Don't worry. I'll come up with another story tomorrow," he added, slipping on his shirt.

"Oh, goody," they both cheered.

"You gonna tuck us in, Devin?" Shelby asked, scrambling to her bed.

"Only if you get under the covers right now."

From the corner of his eye Devin watched Megan return to the sewing she left on the side table next to the sofa, while the girls jumped under the blankets and waited for him.

"All right, who wants to be first?"

After he tucked them both in, he let them kiss him good night. Heading toward the door, Shelby stopped him.

"Devin, why doesn't Megan sleep with us anymore?"

Thrown for a loop by her unexpected question, he hesitated. "She keeps me company," he finally answered after taking a deep, restorative breath.

"She never kept Pawpaw company," Emma added bluntly, looking at him with her big, inquisitive eyes.

"You mean, since he took ill?" Devin corrected, standing at the foot of Emma's bed.

"Even before then," Emma explained, and a sudden realization struck him hard.

"This used to be her bed ever since she came to live with us. I used to sleep over there." Shelby pointed to Emma's bed. "She was too scared to sleep alone in the loft."

"Ever since you and the soldiers brought us home, she stopped sleeping with us." Emma's tone was direct, accusatory, placing the blame entirely on him.

"What's the matter, she don't like us anymore?" Shelby looked hurt.

"Of course she does," Devin supplied, feeling a small pinch of guilt at taking their bedmate away from them. Yet despite their apparent distress, he needed Megan more and wasn't about to restore the previous sleeping order. "You girls are growing up and need your own space. My bed is big enough for two. Megan has more room to sleep comfortable with me."

"But Megan is not much bigger than Emma. She can fit."

As usual, Shelby was giving him no breaks, and Emma was staring him down with her intensely observant silver gaze.

"Yes, but sometimes grownups need to be alone."

"Do ya'll kiss?" Shelby bolted upright, eyes wide, eager for his reply.

He swallowed the lump in his suddenly dry throat. "Huh?"

"I saw Miss Rosalinda let this cowboy kiss her when I was supposed to be playing at recess one time."

Devin arched a brow. "Oh?" he replied, simply for lack of anything better to contribute to such a declaration.

"Miss Rosalinda has lots of male callers during recess." Emma joined in, as though wanting to be included in the discussion that was leaving him more uncomfortable by the second.

"Uh, good for her." He scratched his head. "I think you two should go to sleep now. We'll finish this…talk some other time." Without waiting to hear more of their age-inappropriate schoolyard gossip he left the room and closed the door behind him.

"I need to talk to you," he stated as he walked toward the front door.

Megan looked up from her seat on the couch. Putting her sewing items aside, she casually replied, "Go right ahead. I'm listening."

He opened the front door, and a blast of cold night air rushed inside. "Outside. I don't want the girls to hear."

The sounds of heavy rain inundated the large room. Thunder and lightning lit up the night sky, matching his mood.

"I'll get my wrap."

With her crocheted shawl tight around her shoulders, they stood side by side on the front porch. Silent. Staring into the dark openness in front of them as the rain came down in thick sheets. The harsh pounding of pellets on the roof necessitated the need to speak above a whisper.

"You lied to me," he finally spoke in a low, matter-of-fact tone that belied the deeper emotions bubbling in a confused pursuit of truth beneath the surface of his skin.

"What are you talking about?"

Out of the corner of his eye, he saw the slight tilt of her head. Curiously, she looked up at him. "You led me to believe you were a virgin when you married Reed. That he was the only one. You lied." He turned to face her. "You're nothing but a whore."

"I don't know what you're talking about."

"You never loved him. What did you do, marry him for his money?"

"Devin, no. I...I did. You have to believe me. I did love him."

She was lying. She had to be lying. Her avid response was too real, too learned, her need too great, her lust too strong. He glared at her in a long moment of disbelief. He wanted to believe she was innocent, not a whore who enjoyed spreading her legs for men.

He grabbed her by the shoulders. "If you loved him, why did it take you five years to go to him? If what you said was true about the night he had his stroke."

"It's true. I went to him that night."

"Why only *that* night? What about all the other nights? Who have you been with?" Unable to control the doubts, the questions, his need to possess her in a way no other man had, his fingers tightened around her slender shoulders as he shook her.

She searched his face frantically. The fear in her eyes was real. Unable to control the crazed sense of rage, he ignored it. "Stop, Devin. You're hurting me."

The pent-up, frenzied tension gripped him, took strong hold and wouldn't let go. His hands stilled, yet unknowingly his fingers were digging into her flesh. "I'll do more than that if you don't answer me."

"Let me go, please," her feeble voice trembled, and her body cringed beneath his hands.

As he towered over her, he stared down into her pained expression and decided he was moments away from potentially hurting her. The one woman who dared touch beyond the physical, made him feel beyond his dark lust, made him want, yearn, and imagine more than his ruthless lot deserved, and he was about to harm her.

Gritting his teeth, he released her and moved to the opposite end of the porch. His rage turned his blood to lava. His heartbeat was so loud he heard it over the thunder and rain battering through the darkness. Megan lied to him. Perhaps she lied about everything—Caleb, his father, her family, what she did at Jazelle's.

* * * *

Leaning against the porch rail, Megan caught her breath as the stitch in her arms ebbed. Her raw, quivering nerves were on edge. Devin had reached a higher level of anger, surpassing the day Reed passed away.

Turning from the wet, windy gloom closing in on her, she looked at him. With his broad back to her, the fury emanating from him was daunting, his strength impressive and intimidating. Truth was on her side, and that had to count for something. "Devin, if you calm down, I'll tell you everything."

He turned to face her, his stony expression unmoved. The front of his clothes were splattered with rain. Keeping his distance, he just stared with a cold finality that sent a shiver down her spine straight to her toes.

"I loved Reed." Her voice trembled.

In the darkness, aided by a flash of lightning, she noticed his eyes narrow, as though he didn't believe her.

"I loved him like a father. He was the only one who had been kind to me. He took me away from Jazelle's, married me because that was the only way to keep me safe."

"Safe from what? That bastard Pretty Boy?"

The stinging rain against the wooden porch planks reminded her of the shrill laughter that rang in her ears when she was dragged behind Jazelle's washing shed. The flash of lightning was hideous like the glowing whites of his eyes as he bent over her, held her down until his boss finished with her. Her stomach churned. For support, a false sense of strength and permanence, she leaned her back against the porch beam.

"Everything I said about Caleb was true. We never...you know." She lowered her gaze, hiding the disappointment and shame that Caleb was not the one. "His mother threw me out of the house, mainly 'cause..." Her voice trailed off.

"Cuz why?"

"Mr. Walker." She turned her back to him, held onto the thick, rough-hewn beam and stared up into the blackened, starless night, allowed the rain to pummel her face and the front of her dress. "My monthly flow started that day. Caleb was curious. We hid in the carriage house. I had my skirts pulled up around my waist and...that's when Mr. Walker found us. He ordered Caleb inside, said he was gonna teach me a lesson, take a switch to me. He tossed me over his knee, threw my skirt over my head, and pulled down my pantalets. 'Cept he never got a switch. He kept rubbing his hand over my bottom and...and..."

"I get the picture," he quietly offered.

"That's when Mrs. Walker came outside. She blamed me. They shipped Caleb to boarding school. Jazelle was the only one willing to take me in. Every day, Jazelle reminded me that once I was old enough, I'd work upstairs with the other girls. Jazelle forced me to look through a peephole at women and male customers to learn. Days before my eighteenth birthday, when I was to start working upstairs, your father offered to marry me. Reed said I was a good girl." At the memory of what prompted Reed's sacrificial proposal, a big sob overpowered the rain shower as she buried her face in her hands.

Devin remained quiet until her composure returned a few moments later. She prayed he assumed it was Mr. Walker. What his wife caught him doing was shameful enough, but he didn't do the unthinkable. Her tormentor came much later.

"I didn't learn Reed paid Jazelle to marry me until after his first stroke, when he told me about the letter." She wiped the tears and raindrops from her drenched face. "I never told anyone about Mr. Walker touching me—not Reed, not even Caleb. I did tell Reed about Caleb. I let him believe Caleb was the sole reason his mother sent me away."

"Megan, what about the night Reed suffered his stroke?"

She closed her eyes, raised her face, let the rain sting her skin to hide her tears. Oh, how she wished that night never occurred. She inhaled deeply and she turned to look at him.

"Reed treated me like a daughter. Grateful at last to have a real home, I thought it was the only way to show my appreciation. I crawled into his bed. He woke up, shocked to find me there."

Devin moved his lips as if to speak. Before he said anything to stop her, she revealed even more.

"Reed turned me away."

"What?"

"He said that wasn't the reason he married me. He wanted me to be part of the family, but not as his wife. Ashamed by what I tried to do, I started to cry. I wanted to die. To comfort me, he put his arms around me. That's when he had his stroke."

"And you think you were the reason for his stroke."

"If I didn't go to him that night, lewdly surprise him, he never would have gotten sick."

"You don't know that. The man was old. Who knows how many ailments he had? Don't go blaming yourself for something you didn't cause."

Though Reed was seldom sick, she desperately wanted to believe Devin. She blamed herself for so long—for Caleb, for Reed, for everything.

* * * *

There was one question nagging Devin she had yet to answer. The most important unanswered question heated his blood made him irrational and disintegrated what little control remained.

"Who is it, Megan?"

With a puzzled expression, she stared at him.

"Your lover. Who is he?" Acting on instinct, what she revealed he took as truth. She'd been a virgin when she married Reed, yet a virgin no more. Of that, he was certain. No virgin, even one who saw the things she had responded the way she did out by the river. She'd been eager to part her legs for him. She wanted him to fuck her too damned much that night and not out of an ill-conceived deadly notion. He knew better than believe it was due to tenderness or charming seduction on his part. That just wasn't him, and it seemed to suit her fine. In addition, the one telltale sign notable in all virgins, the one no woman could ever fake, was nonexistent.

Pretty Boy took after his father—neither had any sense when it came to women. Touching, that was all either of them were good for. Too bad the elder Mr. Walker was dead, or Devin would pay him a grisly visit tonight.

That left only one other person. The one she failed to mention. Probably the one she waited for out by the river while the girls slept nearby. The get together was ideal. Once a week, the doctor and Caleb would care for Reed while she snuck off using the girls as her excuse and meet her lover for a little sportin' out in the woods.

"I…I…don't have one." She shook her head. "There isn't anyone."

"Don't lie to me."

"Devin, please. I'm not lying. You have to believe me."

"Then explain why you weren't exactly virginal if I'm the only man who's ever fucked you."

He sat on the railing, crossed his arms, and waited for her to explain. Taking no notice as the hard rain pelted his back.

"Take my word for it. You're the only one."

"I find it too hard to believe."

Tears began to fill her eyes, yet she didn't say anything for a long, tense moment. "I don't care," she finally whispered so softly, he barely heard her. "I don't care," she cried out louder, running down the porch steps.

"Megan," he yelled after her. Dressed in black, she would have blended in the shadows if not for her pale arms and golden hair piled in a bun at the nape of her neck.

"Never! I don't care what you do. Never again!"

For a long while, all he could do was stare at her while she ran screaming past the garden straight toward the open field. The wind ripped the fringed shawl from her shoulders. Her soaked slippers immersed in the thick mud as she continued her irrational, wayward escape in her bare feet.

"Come back," he hollered as the bolt of lightning and thunder crashed through the bleak darkness.

"Shit." Devin jumped over the railing when he noticed not only did she ignored him, she seemed to be in some frenzied state that had her screaming utter nonsense at the top of her lungs.

"Stop running." He nearly closed the gap with several long strides in his soaking wet moccasins, sloshing in the mud and grass with each hurried stride.

"No, no…not again. You can't force me," she cried as he reached out for her just before he slipped in a puddle. He landed face down with a grunt, sludge and torn blades of grass spattering his face.

It suddenly occurred to him—it wasn't him she ran from. "Megan," he called out, rising to his feet. He had to catch her before lightning struck her or she caught a deadly chill. Silently he fretted over the dreadful thought.

He ran faster and took a dive when he came within a few feet of her. He turned in time and caught her in his arms. They landed with him on his back and her on top.

With all her might, she kicked and clawed, screamed in terror.

"Megan, it's me, Devin." He tried to hold her until she calmed down, but her thin bare arms were so wet, they slipped out of his grip. She pounded his chest, clawed through the thin layer of mud to get to his face. "Megan, it's Devin," he said repeatedly, trying to capture her rain-slick arms.

"Devin," she finally called out to him. "Devin, you're here." She sank against him as if too exhausted to move. Her breathing came fast and her heart pounded so hard he felt it.

"Yes, Megan, I'm here," he whispered soothingly, wrapping his arms around her. "I'm here. Don't worry, no one will hurt you."

"Is he gone? Tell me he's gone. Please." Her small, feeble voice trembled with uncertain anguish, and his chest tightened with a much stronger emotion.

"There's no one but you and me." He held her body against his, brushing wet strands of hair from her face. "Give me his name, that's all I need."

"It'll do no good," she whimpered and his gut clenched in fury. "No one 'round here listens to a two-bit whore."

Devin burned deep in his soul with an inner wrath. His entire body went rigid at those exact words he recalled. It was no range war or cattle rustling among ranches. Reed married her to protect her from the spineless scum who practically owned the town, Leroy Hardin. The man himself was after her, and Reed knew it.

The first opportunity after Reed's death, Hardin probably had Jazelle up the price to force her back to work, only this time as his personal prostitute.

"I'll take you inside." His tone held the grim, cold finality he felt as he made a move to sit up.

She raised her head off his shoulder and laid a hand on his chest to stop him. "I know what you plan to do, but you can't." Her voice strained with suppressed emotions.

He was certain she knew he figured out who it was. "Megan, he hurt you. The bastard will pay."

"I want to forget. It was all but forgotten until I was back at Jazelle's. Devin, if you go over there...I'll have his blood on my hands. I won't be able to forget."

"You can't honestly say if I do nothing, you'll be able to forget." Hell, he'd never forget, and he wasn't even there. Didn't even know when it happened, how many times—nothing. All Devin needed to know was once was more than enough.

She closed her eyes, and this time, he could see the tears and raindrops pouring down her face.

Covering her ears as if to block out the memories, shaking her head vigorously, she cried helplessly, "Devin, please make it go away. Make it stop."

He sat up and put his arms around her. "Let's go home."

"No, now, Devin. I can't wait. Help me forget." Her voice filled with pain, heartache. She tore at his shirt, ripping the soaked material and popping buttons.

"Megan, I need to get you inside before you freeze..." He didn't dare voice his concern, tried to capture her hands, but they were like small, slippery snakes.

He watched, amazed at how fast she tore open the front of her dress. The sight of her creamy breasts, slick with moisture and glowing in a blaze of lightning, stirred him against his will.

"I can't wait, Devin." Straddling him, she lifted her skirt, exposing the plump lips between her thighs. Sitting directly on his rock-hard cock, she ground her pussy into the engorged thickness straining against the front of his saturated buckskins. "Help me to forget. Help me."

"Not like this," he struggled to speak, heard the anguish in her voice. Aware she unconsciously acted aggressive to conquer her fear, when in reality she felt vulnerable and scared. Often he saw the behavior in whores who had been victims of abuse. Either they acted as mere receptacles for a man's cock or they refused to be a victim, sexualized their anger and took on a more aggressive role to reverse the painful memories.

Megan wasn't making his decision any easier by pressing her cunt against his eager hardness, but he never took advantage of a woman's extreme vulnerability before and he sure as hell wasn't about to start now. "You're sore from yesterday. It's too soon. Tomorrow. Wait till tomorrow, and I'll do whatever you want."

"No, Devin. I need you now." She leaned over him, bringing her mouth down to his. Her tongue drove past his lips, devoured him in a needy, urgent kiss that spoke of desperation, loneliness, heartbreak and longing.

"I'm here. Don't worry, I'm not going anywhere." Devin broke their kiss and fought to keep his voice level while he welled with bitter fury, anger and frustration. His wrath was aimed toward the man who dared harm an innocent young girl, yet his inbuilt need for revenge was greater. He'd not be satisfied until retribution time.

"Don't leave me, Devin. Don't ever leave me." Her hands tucked into his loosened shirt. She was so cold, her entire body shook and her teeth chattered.

He didn't reply. Curling his body around hers, he did his best to block the cutting sheets of rain from pelting her.

He carried her inside and stripped them both of their wet clothes. He laid her down on his bearskin in front of the parlor fireplace and built a roaring fire. Then he piled a load of blankets over them, and he used the heat of his body to warm hers. He held her frail body as though she were made of the finest china.

Chapter 18

"Mmmm." Even though he was half asleep, his hips instinctively surged toward a moist heat. A tightening sensation, wetness gripped him, and his cock jerked. "Oh, yes," he moaned groggily as the slow, sensuous glide moved over his erection and enclosed the head of his cock within a hot, velvety cavern. Firm strokes traveled up and down the length.

This was an incredible dream he didn't want to wake from. His breath rose in the pre-dawn hours as the increased pressure rasping against the underside of his cock snapped his eyes open. He stared as Megan opened her hungry mouth and showed him her greedy tongue, lapping that sensitive spot that heightened his raging desire. Damn, he taught her well.

"Good morning to you, too." His rough voice carried a touch of amusement. Her eyes, locked with his, seemed to smile back with mischief. In awe, he watched her warm mouth suck down half his cock. Her full lips drew taut until they were thin, pink lines moving up and down his flesh with a firm suction.

"Oh yeah, that's it. Suck it hard." Voice was low, ragged as his fingers clenched in her hair, setting the rhythmic rise and fall of her head. She moaned over the engorged head, sent heated vibrations up his spine. "Harder, baby, and I'll come for you."

She massaged and tickled his balls, and he knew that's exactly what she wanted, his seed. The understanding stroked his desire, emitting a harsh growl deep in his throat. He increased the tempo, penetrating her mouth with fast and hard thrusts.

"Swallow it," he moaned, holding her head in place as the first jet of hot semen shot down her throat. "I want breakfast, too," he muttered harshly, moments after he laid flat on his back groaning and gasping for air. Eager to return the favor, savor the creamy delights between her thighs he balanced her over his abdomen with her ass toward his face and her pussy hovering over his mouth. Placing a hand along the graceful curve of her back, he lowered her to his chest. "Move for me, baby. Slow and easy. I want to feel those hard nipples brush my skin as I have cream with my sugar."

His mouth feasted on her flesh while she followed instructions, writhing sinuously against his skin. His hands splayed over her buttocks and spread her firm cheeks. His gaze locked on the pristine hole, a fresh shade of pink, wrinkled tightly just inches above his nose. He felt his cock grow hard instantly. She took the rigid tool in her hands, running her tongue and fingers up and down the length. Dear, sweet Megan had no idea what he wanted. Her soft moans turned into whimpers of pleasure when his tongue delved into her hot little cunt as he drove her to a feverish peak.

Afterward, he carried her to bed, parted her legs and plunged inside her docile body. They came together as he drove his cock deep into her silky depths. They repeated the sensual performance several times until they were too exhausted to move.

With his arms wrapped tightly around her, he dozed in and out of consciousness, not sure if what he heard was Megan or a dream.

"Promise me, Devin," she repeated softly.

Lazily, his eyelids slowly opened. He hadn't been dreaming, Megan was really begging him not to kill Hardin. It took a moment to gather his thoughts.

"Megan," he finally said in husky, sleepy tone. "I can't make that promise."

"It happened a long time ago. It's too late for revenge now. It would be murder. Besides, it's his word against mine."

"I don't want to hear it. *I* take your word, and that's all that matters. As for Hardin, he won't ever bother you again." He was wide-awake now, and he felt her body stiffen at the mere mention of his name. The slimy snake definitely had to pay.

"Don't go looking for trouble on account of me." The vision of him strung up or other horrific possibilities flashed before her eyes. He could read them plain as day. There wasn't a man alive with a gun strapped on who didn't have them, only he ignored 'em. "If anything ever happened to you because of me...I...I..." She buried her face in his chest, soft whimpers escaping the tight confines.

Devin didn't say anything for a long while, just held her and listened to the soft sobs as warm tears streamed down his bare chest. He had caused many tears. Never had anyone cried for him.

"All I say is if you don't want me to, I won't go gunning for him. But if the sorry-assed bastard ever comes within sight of me, I'll kill him."

* * * *

No one mentioned Leroy Hardin's name during the days that passed while the scratches she'd clawed on Devin's face healed. She was hardly foolish enough to mistake silence to mean Devin changed his mind—not in the least. He readily escorted the girls to and from school, though Megan was keenly aware of his motives. His efforts to help around the house were an unpredicted touch.

True to his word and much to her delirious gratification, while the girls were at school, he'd pull up her skirts and take her. Wherever he found her, outside in the garden or on all fours scrubbing the floor, or gathering eggs from the coop, as if consumed by a ravenous need, a greedy, uncontrollable lust, he would ravage her. Not a single inhibition resided in his sexual nature. He used illicit words that made her pulse race when he told her what he wanted. He brought her to the edge of depravity and made her beg for what she needed.

Each night they fell asleep only after their bodies were sweaty, exhausted, and thoroughly sated. Intimately they learned each other's bodies, expressing their wants and desires openly as they quietly moved from one carnal position to the next, mindful not to wake the girls. They awoke each morning with a renewed lustful vigor, as though they hadn't fucked each other in years.

Not much house cleaning or garden tending was accomplished, but Megan didn't mind. Her body was in a constant state of arousal. There was no denying she just couldn't seem to get enough of him and that huge, magnificent cock.

Yet, in her heart, she could tell Devin waited for any opportunity to find Leroy Hardin and kill him. With different excuses, he went in town more often. Megan could only wait restlessly until the time came when the two finally crossed paths.

In fear of that day, Megan rushed out of the house as soon as she noticed that Ms. Rosalinda's carriage pulled around the bend. Since Rosalinda's arrival in town after completing finishing school in Georgia last year, she was the town's first schoolmistress. During the past year, not once did she ever come calling, especially on a Sunday.

Shelby and Emma were quite fond of their teacher. They spoke of her often. At twenty, Rosalinda was close in age to Megan, but, they had little in common. The only time they spoke was at the schoolhouse. Though pleasant enough, the young woman struck Megan as the type to seek female companionship only when it benefited her. She preferred her many male admirers instead which suited Megan just fine.

"My, what a pleasant surprise." Megan ignored the butterflies in her stomach and kept her voice pleasant. Standing on the porch, she spoke quickly, before Rosalinda even brought the fancy black carriage to a halt. "Rosalinda, what brings you out on a beautiful Sunday afternoon? I hope the girls haven't been troubling you."

Rosalinda smiled and batted her eyes. To Megan, the pale flush on the well-dressed woman's cheeks made it appear as if she blushed at the inquiry.

"Please forgive me for not coming to pay my respects sooner. I've been meaning to call on you, but I've been so busy with school work and all."

"Thank you," Megan replied, adding a faint smile.

"The girls are no trouble at all. They are such dears. My dearest students, if truth be told," Rosalinda drawled in her well-honed imitation of a Southern belle.

"Thank you again."

"They are so lucky to have you for a mother. God forbid, a poor widow already. Not to old to chase the little darlings sun up to sun down. It's a wonder you don't look more haggard, considering."

"Considering?" Megan tried to keep her tone friendly as her smile disappeared, the insult apparent.

"Losing their father and you lost your dear husband. Perhaps another elderly gentleman may take pity on you and consider you marriageable." Rosalinda's eyes flittered over her and around the yard as though she looked for something or someone. "Having family is so important."

"Yes, of course," Megan replied coolly. Internally, she cringed at the frankness of the belittlement, the glib look sweeping over her body that seemed to compare her small-boned petiteness to Rosalinda's own big-breasted voluptuousness.

"We must look out for one another, being neighbors and all. Comfort one another in time of sorrow, with open arms."

As the other woman became more and more flustered, Megan remained motionless, quiet. She was too busy trying to figure out what Rosalinda wanted.

"If you ever need help, let me know. My assistance is yours. Just ask. My hands will be here. They do anything I ask. Men are so very helpful to a woman in need."

Megan tilted her head in astonishment, unable to believe her ears. Rosalinda described her ranch hands as though they were choirboys and not hired guns, ruthless men after a fast dollar.

"I heard how things were a little rough for you a while back. Thankfully, that's all behind you now, since you have such an able body to help around the house." Rosalinda glanced fleetingly over each shoulder. "It must have come as a quite a delightful surprise to learn your late husband had a son."

Struck with a bolt of clarity, Megan's eyes grew wide.

"Especially one so capable." With a flick of the wrist, her fan snapped open. Rosalinda waved the fan in a fast frenzy trying to cool the obvious flush on her face as if it were the dead of summer and not spring, with a crisp breeze from the north.

If Megan didn't see it for herself, she never would have believed it. With every breath, Rosalinda's large breasts heaved, swelled above the low neckline of her Sunday best. Swollen nipples tented the front of her tight-fitting bodice. She was aroused. The woman was here to see Devin.

"And so helpful. Dev—I mean Mr. Spawn." Rosalinda batted her eyes and laughed, a dainty little chuckle that made Megan want to slap her into next Sunday. Instead, she feigned a smile.

Rosalinda continued. "When he picked up the girls on Friday, he helped me rearrange the bookcases. He left so quickly, I didn't get to thank him properly."

I bet you didn't.

"I was passing this way and thought, how rude it would be of me not to express my gratitude."

"I know how busy you are. Wouldn't want to keep you longer than necessary, I assure you I'll give him your message." Megan was proud of herself. She actually sounded sincere.

"And disgrace my headmistress?" Her tone held a small illusion of chastisement. "Hardly. I was taught it would be much more meaningful if I did it in person."

I bet it would.

"Is he here?" Her eyelashes fluttered once more, maintaining an air of propriety.

"Yes. He's in the barn," Megan replied in a pragmatic tone, grudgingly resentful that the entire town probably saw her as a spent widow with a tainted reputation, whereas, the men all flocked around the prim and proper educator. Were her large breasts the draw?

Rosalinda smiled sweetly. Her eyes lit up, outwardly pleased with her good fortune.

"With the girls," Megan added smugly, watching the disappointment cloud the other woman's blue gaze.

In a big puff of purple satin and lace, bodice perfectly fitted to her lush figure, Rosalinda climbed out of her carriage. She gave Megan a polite nod and made her way to the barn.

Megan stood on the porch she waited until the barn door closed before returning inside. She had no claim over Devin. The only thing he gave her was his body—nothing more.

Rosalinda had reminded her Devin was her stepson. What could she really expect from him—a lifetime commitment? To live in sin together until they grew old? Another week as his lover? Another day? With Devin, one never knew.

All that she knew was she didn't want to lose him.

* * * *

Gritting her teeth, Megan chopped the carrots until they were a mound of orange mush.

"Is that what's for supper?" Emma asked, grimacing at the orange-colored juice streaming down the table into a small puddle on the floor.

"Yuck." Shelby supported her sister's displeasure.

Megan snapped out of her doldrums and stared at the mess in front of her. She sighed, feeling foolish for being jealous in the first place. After all, there was no way to be one hundred percent sure of Rosalinda's reason for visiting Devin. Then again, her greatest concern was Devin finding out who Rosalinda was.

Dumping what had been carrots into the slop bucket for the pigs, she wiped her hands on a damp dishrag. She wished it would be just as easy to wipe away her feelings for Devin as well.

"Girls, let's go outside and gather more carrots."

"Oh, goodie," Shelby exclaimed, running to the sideboard to retrieve the small basket Megan kept on a lower shelf for her to use when she helped in the garden.

Megan took a step outside and stopped short when she saw the black carriage still parked out front.

Her head snapped around to Emma standing right behind her. "Rosalinda's still here?" she asked sharply. How unwise of her to assume because the girls came inside, Rosalinda had left.

"Yes. She's with Devin."

"Are they in the barn?" Megan remained calm, though her nerves were on edge. She pushed the gnawing fear aside. It could all be innocent. They could just be talking. Perhaps Devin hadn't found out yet.

"I dunno. I came in before Shelby. Ask her."

"What did Ms. Rosalinda want?"

Emma shrugged her shoulders. "Something about inviting him to supper at her house."

Her heart skipped a beat. "What did he say?"

"First off, he said no, but Ms. Rosalinda kept talking. Kinda like she does at school. Only this time, I didn't hafta stay to listen."

Shelby skipped out of the house, basket in hand.

"Shelby," Megan blurted loudly when she saw the little girl. Taking a calming breath, she lowered her tone. "Are Devin and Rosalinda still in the barn?"

Her big blue eyes gazed up at Megan. A look of indecision crossed her chubby face. She clamped her lips together, shook her head, and bounced down the stairs.

Megan darted down the steps after her.

"Where are they, Shelby?" She put a staying hand on Shelby's shoulder.

"He told me not to tell."

Devin was new at this game. Megan knew how to work around it. She dropped to her knees in front of Shelby. "Okay, Shelby, I know you don't like it when Emma calls you a squealer."

Shelby's gaze darted to Emma, and she stuck her tongue out at her big sister.

"It's not squealing if I guess. May I try and guess?" Megan coaxed her.

Shelby nodded her head and smiled. Her sparkling eyes looked over Megan's shoulder, straight at the pecan trees to her right.

"Are they picking pecans?"

"Flowers—" Shelby covered her mouth with both chubby hands, her eyes wide.

Megan palmed the girl's cheek, assuring her everything would be okay. Rising to her feet, she started toward the trees.

"Megan," Shelby called after her. "Devin told us not to bother them. They were gonna pick flowers for her father."

Shelby's account made Megan's heart beat faster. Head to toe, her body stiffened. She tried her best to stay calm, moved on wobbly legs toward Shelby. "What did you say?"

"Devin said he couldn't eat supper with her tonight. But he'd show Ms. Rosalinda where to pick some nice flowers so's she can take 'em back home. So's she can let Mr. Hardin know he'll be paying a visit real soon."

For a breathless second, Megan realized her worst fear had come to life. "Girls, go in the house." She rounded them up and all but pushed them down the path to the porch.

"Megan, aren't we gonna pick vegetables?"

"Later, Emma. We'll do it later. Now go inside and don't come out until I return."

She waited until the girls closed the door behind them before running toward the wild heather patch just beyond the pecan trees.

* * * *

Over Rosalinda's lusty cries, Devin sensed Megan coming.

"Shit," he muttered aloud, knowing Shelby had sold him out. He tightened his grip on Rosalinda's hips, thrusting his cock even harder into her well-rounded ass.

"Oh, yes, more, more," Rosalinda begged, pushing back into his groin.

He couldn't stop now, so he gave the lady—and he used the term loosely—what she asked. Spreading her cheeks wide, he surged up, burying every inch deep inside the back entrance.

Rosalinda gasped, her nails digging into the bark of tree she held onto. Without a stitch on, her full breasts swung wildly when he slammed into her.

With the help of crackling branches and dried leaves, Devin focused in the direction he knew Megan would appear. Apparently, she saw no need to sneak up on him. Not that he was making a very good effort to hide from her. At least he didn't want her to catch him with his britches around his ankles while he rammed his cock into another woman's ass.

"Get out of here, Megan," he growled as soon as he saw her through the trees. His heart battered against his chest. She stood a few yards away. He watched the shock and anger washing over her expression and was more than a little surprised her feelings got to him.

Rosalinda stopped her feverish moans. Her gaze followed Devin's line of vision until she came upon Megan standing in the trees. "Oh, fuck," Rosalinda muttered and attempted to scramble for cover.

"Stay," Devin demanded quite forcefully, grasped Rosalinda's breasts and squeezed them hard. Her shriek of painful pleasure went along with the unceasing thrusting up her ass.

"I said, get out of here, Megan, unless you wanna stay and watch." He held her gaze. She remained stock-still for some time. His stomach clenched, and he worried she would never speak to him again. Let alone allow him to touch or come near her again. How would he ever make her understand?

Megan's lips slightly parted and he groaned in disbelief. He watched her cheeks flush a pretty pink, her nipples harden. He couldn't believe it. Somehow, her anger turned to arousal before his eyes. He wanted to go to her, take her in his arms and keep her there forever. Except he couldn't stop, not now, not until he finished the depraved act. That was all it was to him, a means to an end, nothing more. His eyes beseeched her, telling her he wanted her, only her.

His hand lowered to Rosalinda's pussy, angling her hips, offering a better view. He heard Megan's heavy sigh beneath Rosalinda's gasp when he plunged a trio of fingers in her soaked, gaping cunt. His deft thumb strummed her clit, had her screaming as her orgasm rolled through her. Apparently, Rosalinda forgot Megan looked on, rocking back to bury him deeper, intent on her ravenous pleasure. Rosalinda's body shuddered in his tight grip while Megan's eyes transfixed on his cock powering in and out of the forbidden hole between white, fleshy cheeks.

Devin's eyes never left hers. Megan watched wide-eyed and intense, breasts rising with her escalated breathing. Her passionate, glazed expression had his cock thickening, enlarging even more. Rosalinda cried out in orgasmic bliss as he continued to fill her rectum with everything he had, imagining it was Megan in his arms.

At the other woman's renewed heated cries, Megan's gaze rose to meet the telling look in his eyes. Lust, dark and pure, burned bright in her eyes.

Covering her gaping mouth, Megan swirled around and ran.

* * * *

By the time she arrived on the front porch, Megan managed to gather a sense of composure. Restrained, she strolled through the front door. The girls picked carrots and she fixed supper, as though nothing out of the ordinary happened.

Her body still quivered when they sat down to eat. Hurt, anger and jealousy she understood. Confusion and envy replaced her appetite. Unable to think straight, she questioned her innermost beliefs. What was wrong with her? Why wasn't she normal?

She wasn't supposed to be aroused at the sight of Devin fucking another woman. Yet, seeing him, his thick cock ramming into Rosalinda's ass, was so erotic her own pussy trembled in desperate, lusty need. She should want him to take her only. Throw only her into climax. Desire only her. It was her wanton nature. Her depraved, carnal desires consumed her, dominated her senses and frightened her. Megan hated to admit it. The raw, undeniable lust that pulsed through her veins was irrepressible

Devin had that knowing look in his eyes, could tell she was excited, reveled in the other woman's pleasure. His hands gripping those big, lush breasts, his fingers tunneling into that wet cunt had been highly erotic. On a shameless edge of wickedness, she yearned to see him take those pale breasts in his mouth and suck on the hard nipples that stuck out like plump pillows on a huge round bed. She imagined him spread Rosalinda's long, solid thighs and bury himself between her hairy pussy.

When Rosalinda cried out, Megan felt her own slick arousal weep from deep within her pussy. She fought the urge to run to him, push him free and impale herself on the object of her desire. Instead, she ran away in terror and shame, afraid of her own sinful needs, the tantalizing power he held over her, the agonizing truth that no matter what Devin did, she would never stop wanting him.

Annoyed by her irrational behavior, Megan refused to look up when Devin waltzed through the door. In a straightforward tone, he stated he was escorting Ms. Rosalinda home. To avoid speaking, she took a big bite of biscuit and looked the other way. The girls looked on curiously, but she paid no attention when she heard him grab his rifle and an extra box of shells from the rack and hat off the peg on the wall.

Without another word, he walked away.

An hour later, he returned. She ignored him the rest of the evening. He made no effort to acknowledge her, which frustrated her even more. They did not speak up to the time she put the girls to bed and exited the bedroom with an extra blanket and pillow.

"What do you think you're doing?" he asked, staring at her while he leaned against the doorjamb to their bedroom, arms crossed over his chest.

Casually, she walked to the sofa and sat the blanket and pillow down before she turned to look at him.

"You don't think I'm sleeping with you tonight, do you?"

"As a matter of fact, I do."

"Check your facts, Mr. Spawn. You couldn't be more wrong." With everything she had, she spoke to him charmingly which seemed to make him angrier.

"Damn you, Megan, are we starting that bullshit again?" He straightened, hands on hips, giving her a dark, warning glare that sent shivers down her spine. She was determined not to give him the upper hand, no matter the amount of growl in his tone.

"I believe you are the one who started it. And if you don't keep your voice down, you'll wake the girls."

He stomped across the room and took her by the arm.

"Take your hand off me." She tried to dig her fingers under his as they sank into her upper arm. She loathed the fact with the little pressure he exerted, he could do as he pleased with her. She was no match for his well-muscled strength.

"You're not sleeping on the sofa." He dragged her toward the bedroom.

"Then you must be, because I'm certainly not sleeping with you." In no way did she intend to go easily. She shrugged and pulled back every step of the way.

He didn't say another word until he jerked her inside the room and locked the door. "You're getting in that bed, and I don't want to hear another word about it."

"Then cover your ears, 'cause I'm not staying." Moving away from the bed, suddenly too large a presence, she took what she hoped was a formidable stand next to the small, unlit fireplace on the opposite wall.

"I don't give a shit if we fuck tonight or not, but you're sleeping in that bed if I have to tie you to it." He growled, standing by the bed.

Folding her arms across her chest, her eyes darted toward the door.

"Don't try me, Megan." She met the heated intensity of his gaze head-on, the authoritative manner glistening back at her fueling her anger. His tone was low and unyielding as he unbuttoned his shirt and shrugged out of it. "Now take off that dress and climb in bed."

Megan tried not to notice how his sinewy muscles flexed with each movement. Her cheeks grew hot and a flurry of anticipation, need seeped between her thighs when his hands went to his holster buckle. She swallowed hard.

"I rather sleep on the floor than next to a lily-livered skunk like you." At least her voice didn't betray her.

He dropped his holster on the chair next to the bed.

"Stay awake all night. It makes no difference to me." Removing the knife sheathed at his waist, he tossed it amid the holster. "But you're gonna be lying next to me as naked as the day you were born. And it ain't gonna be on the sofa, or the floor, in the barn, or anywhere else but this here fucking bed." He gestured to the bed with a nod.

"You must be confusing me with one of your harlots if you think you can order me to do something I have no intention of ever doing again."

By the way his eyes widened fractionally, she could tell he didn't like the sound of that—not the least bit. Insecurity propelled her furious resentment. She wasn't woman enough to satisfy him. Unable to bear the thought, the desperate fear of losing him, she'd rather send him away than risk him hurting her, waiting until he made her fall in love with him. If she hadn't already. Tears welled in her eyes. She blinked them back.

"I suggest you find comfort with one of them," she continued. "Rosalinda is a tall girl, and perhaps you'll fit in her bed."

"I don't want to sleep with Rosalinda."

"No, you just want to fuck her."

He rolled his eyes and darted a glance at the bedroom door. She felt a sense of triumph. Suddenly, the sofa idea seemed a whole lot more appealing to him, she speculated. If she kept this up, he'd toss her out the room.

"There ain't enough room in her bed for me." He ran his fingers through his hair, drawing her gaze to the solid bicep cording his arm, well-shaped shoulder, broad chest. "Besides, I don't want to fuck her, or anyone else at Jazelle's. I just wanna go to sleep with you by my side. Is that too much to ask?" He sighed as though he realized his mistake, knew the answer before he finished asking the question.

"We'll you sure as hell coulda fooled me. You sound so sure there isn't room in her bed. Tried it out, have you?" Raising a brow, she added in a silky smooth voice. "What—too lumpy?"

"More like too full." His hands dropped to the ties in front of his buckskins. Taking note of the butter-soft fabric taut over his cock, she licked her lips, imagined the thick length sliding between her lips, her tongue licking the bulbous head…

She blinked, resisting the carnal urges rioting through her system brought on by the downy soft fur traveling below his navel. Foreseeing the curly nest below as he continued to untie the laces, she stared at the lace curtain subtly blowing in the breeze.

Before she'd laid eyes on him, there were no throbbing urges, no quivering sensations, no burning desires to have a man's cock buried between her thighs, nor ravenous hunger to feed off him. He did this to her, turned her into a vessel of sin. A veritable sexual slave who craved his touch as a means of life support, begging and pleading for any scrap he tossed her way. Except it wasn't a scrap she wanted, far from it.

"You think its Hardin's peachy disposition or wages bolstering loyalty out at that ranch? If there's a hundred hands riding ov'r yonder, I reckon by now fifty pumped that ass. And the rest are lining up."

"How do you know?" Jerking her head around, she eyed him contemptuously. His acute knowledge of women angered her. How to please them. What they were thinking. What they wanted. How much they wanted him. She particularly hated that.

"The way your little ass wiggles when you walk, and you brush your breasts against me accidentally when you pass. Or lick your lips while watching me from across the room, and your sweet pussy gets soaking wet because you know my dick is already hard just thinking about you."

He gave her a coy glance, but there was nothing demure about his tone. It bubbled over with pure seduction, and her vagina throbbed in response. He knew what he was doing to her. "Oh, yeah, Megan, you were born to fuck, and I was put here to fuck your hot, tight cunt, fast and hard. Just the way you like it. How I'm going to give it to you."

"Who said I wanted you? Go back to Rosalinda. Fuck her," she shouted, ignoring her body's heated betrayal, the fire churning through her bloodstream.

He approached. Her gaze focused on his erection. The swollen tip visible above the loosened waistband, the thick shaft threatened to break free from the partially unlaced confines. A flare of tumultuous arousal shot through her.

He stopped in front of her, tipped her chin with his finger. He held her gaze, stared deep into her eyes and smiled delectably. That sinful smile where he curled only one corner of his lips, the one he knew she that left her breathless.

"Don't even try to lie to me. Your eyes give you away, the flush on your cheeks, nipples poking through your blouse."

His gaze lowered to the front of her dress. She looked down and saw the hard knots straining the cotton fabric. When she looked up, his gaze went to her lips. They parted on their own volition. He was so close, close enough to take her.

"The same as this afternoon, you want it. It turned you on to see my cock impale her ass, but you're too afraid of the intensity of your passion to admit it."

She sighed, helpless to resist the lure of his dark, sultry words, or deny the salacious need for sexual excess. He knew what she felt, knew she visualized them now.

"It arouses you, makes you wet and horny to watch other people fuck."

Her heart raced out of control. She wanted to shut out the truth, the desire blurring her eyes, look away from the lust darkening his gaze. The eroticism of it all was too powerful an aphrodisiac to resist.

"Insatiable Megan wants to be part of the action, don't you? Always hot, eager to have a man's cock between your legs. My cock."

The potency of his carnal magnetism, his deep voice and suggestive words left her feeling exposed, utterly powerless in her need for it, him— everything.

"You can't deny if I lifted your skirt right now, you'd be naked, just the way I want you. I can smell your arousal from here. Your pussy is wet for my cock."

She blinked, as though the trifling feat could erase the betraying signs. How could her body react when she was mad at him? Beyond mad— furious, outraged, yet her traitorous body had a mind and will of its own. It craved every hard, virile inch of his well-honed muscles, especially twelve impressive inches, and he knew it. The arrogant bastard.

Megan loathed herself for being weak, for wanting him so much, for needing him, for loving him. Above all, for allowing him to tempt her while her emotions were in shambles.

"I hate you. I hate you," she cried, beating her fists against his chest. "I hate you."

Devin closed his eyes and took a deep breath and her arms at his side. He stood there like a man and took his due punishment.

As though he sensed she had taken enough aggression out on him after a long while, he grabbed her upper arms and held them down tight by her side. "Megan, stop. I get the picture."

Through the haze of tears streaming down her face, she blinked up at him. Her chest rose with each harsh breath, fingers still throbbed from the force of her blows.

"I'll sleep on the sofa," he said.

Chapter 19

Overall, it was one of Devin's favorite times of the day, when it was cool outside and the sun began its ascent on the horizon. The girls busy getting ready for school, still half-asleep—therefore, creating little noise. After a hearty breakfast, it was his time to enjoy a final cup of coffee in an obscure form of tranquility before saddling the horses. Usually less than two hours earlier, he and Megan would have frolicked through their third or fourth orgasm.

This morning was vastly different. He made his own coffee, not a whiff of breakfast, and his back hurt from crouching his six-nine frame on a four-foot couch. Megan snapped at him when he told her to keep the girls home from school today. Emma and Shelby were so excited, they ran around the house clacking worse than baby chicks. He was horny as hell.

Propping an elbow on the table, he pushed his cup away and buried his face in his hands. Moments later, he looked up when he heard the distinct sound of hooves pounding the dirt in an awful hurry.

"Damn," he shouted. It was earlier than he expected.

"Ah, he said a soap word," Shelby said animatedly.

On his way straight to the bedroom, he reached for the soap Megan kept on the kitchen counter, bit off a large chunk, and swallowed it one gulp, much to the amazement of all three onlookers.

"Someone's here." Emma ran to the front door.

Checking the barrels of each Colt, he strolled out of the room, holster strapped on and tied down. "Keep 'em inside," he directed at Megan without looking at her.

* * * *

"Devin." Megan's voice was rife with urgency, terror as she stared out the kitchen window and saw her neighbor and twelve hands barreling into the front yard. "It's Hardin."

Devin was already standing on the porch.

"Why is Ms. Rosalinda's father here?" Shelby asked with mild curiosity, her head peeking through the crack in the door.

"He don't look nice," Emma added, standing by her sister's side.

Megan ran and pulled the girls away from the door, closing it quickly.

"Never you mind. Get to your room now." She scooted them away. "And stay there."

Her body trembled with heart-wrenching fear. Frantically, she perused the room for the best place to stand when the firing began. Somehow her feet wouldn't move.

Holding on to the edge of table, she stood frozen—listening, praying.

* * * *

"You know why I'm here, Spawn." Hardin brushed away the front hem of his jacket behind his back, and several of his fellow riders did the same. All eyes were on Devin, their hands ready to reach.

"I've been expecting you." With acute awareness, Devin's took in the spaced out crowd. The eyes always gave them away. It wasn't just a job this time, it was personal. Not a member of the Hardin outfit, Devin infringed on their territory. More like he fucked what they considered an unspoken fringe benefit their boss-man probably wasn't even aware of, and *he* definitely wasn't entitled to.

"Wanna step down, or you wanna die where you stand?"

"Nice of you to give me an option." Devin grinned. "There's just one problem, seeing how the girls like to play where you are. I wouldn't wanna saturate the yard."

Hardin's dark eyes turned cold with contempt.

"Name the time and place. I'll be there." Devin glanced at the other men. "They're invited, too."

"The old mill down the river. Know where it is?" Hardin grated with a scowl.

"I'll find it."

"Noon."

Devin gave a nod of consent. He waited until the last rider disappeared around the bend before turning his back.

Stepped through the doorway, he looked up and paused briefly when he saw Megan holding onto the table, gripped with fear.

There wasn't time for explanations. *Later.* He'd make it up to her later. He didn't know how just yet, but he'd figure it out. Megan watched in silence, trancelike as he draped his extra shell belt across his chest, bow over his shoulder. He grabbed his lance case and rifle and headed out the door.

* * * *

Privately, Devin cringed when he heard Megan enter the barn. The frustration was eating away at him. The way she swung with all her might last night, no doubt she was madder than a hornet's nest. Toss in a double dose of fright, and she was akin to lit gunpowder, on a fiery path to destruction. He wished the outcome, the events leading up to it, everything could have been different. As it was, a man had to face his battles head-on, and to hell with the consequences. Fight or retreat, live or perish—it was a matter of timing and opportunity. Not about to back down, his grip tightened on the strap as he continued to saddle Deuce inside the horse's stall. There'd be no sweet lovin' tonight.

"Why? Why did you do it?" Megan asked.

He kept right on preparing Deuce for the ride. "You know why."

"Did you have to fuck her?"

Without a pause, he cast a fleeting glance over his shoulder and returned to the task at hand. "Did you really expect me to wait forever? I saw an opportunity and took it."

"You promised."

"Dammit, Megan." He swung around, resting a hand on the saddle horn. "It was like Hardin knew I was after him. He never came into town. I couldn't wait around forever. Would you rather I stole his money from Pretty Boy's bank or rustle his cattle so's the law would be on his side?" His full pardon was his business. Finally, since the age of twelve when Devin killed his first man, no one hunted him. He was able to walk the streets without having to risk gunning down a trigger-happy lawman. From

Megan's insolent expression, the options laid out did not meet with her approval either.

"So you made sure he'd come after you by raping his daughter."

"Ah, shit," he growled, swinging the stall gate open and walked to where she stood near the front of the barn. "Is that what you think? I didn't rape you when I had the chance. Do you honestly believe I'd rape *that* woman?"

"I don't know what to think…you're…you're…"

"Go on, say it." He stopped a few feet in front of her and waited for her to call him what he was—the worst kind of outlaw known to man, without a conscious, heart, or soul.

It boiled his blood, the way she just stood there, staring up at him with those patronizing hazel eyes like some sort of foreboding angel of despair dressed in black. His judge, jury and executioner packed into a hot little body of pure sinful temptation.

"Yeah, you can't say it, but you sure as hell can think it. Well, let's clear the air. I'll lay it out for you. The virtuous teacher has been dallying with me since the first day I picked up the girls. Which I've done my damnedest to ignore, 'cuz someone else has been meeting my needs."

Megan averted his gaze, but not before he noticed her cheeks turn a bright rose. He touched a nerve that was still sensitive, raw. It gave him a hopeful tremor.

"I didn't invite her here. Had no reason to go anywhere with her. 'Cept when she told me who her father was. If you think I raped her to get Hardin here, you should've stayed longer, perhaps joined us. You would have liked it."

When her hand came up to slap him, he caught it. Every subtle flicker in her eyes revealed her rage, but the thought aroused and tempted her. He never intended to ask it of her. He'd been determined to leave it a sexual fantasy.

"You did enough of that last night."

He released her wrist and went back to Deuce.

"Go inside, Megan."

Yesterday, he'd slammed Rosalinda's ass, but it was Megan he'd thought about, Megan he wanted to hold. It was Megan he wanted to fuck and Megan he wanted to protect. He was positive it wouldn't have made her feel any better to hear that he couldn't bring himself to shoot his seed into the other woman, he kept that tidbit to himself.

It could have all been over with yesterday, and Megan would have figured it out afterwards. Unfortunately, Leroy Hardin was out when his precious daughter arrived home in a wrinkled dress and mussed-up hair.

To ensure word got back to him, Devin put up a good show in front of the hands, who eyed him viciously as they rode up. Mustered up his best gentlemanly air, he helped her out of the carriage and up the steps. As polite as could be, he walked her to the front door. Finally, in a move truer to his nature that no polite gentleman would dare, he grabbed her ass, ground their loins together, and drove his tongue down her throat. Also, in case any of the onlookers had doubts as to what took place prior to their arrival, he cupped her breasts, leaned down, and kissed each one on the bared flesh pushed up and over the low neckline. Only then did she drift inside, flustered and panting for more.

Not once did he consider it using the girl, since they both got what they wanted. Only difference was, Rosalinda was going to lose her father over the trade.

"And so now you get do what you wanted from the beginning—kill Hardin since he cheated a Spawn and stole livestock." Megan stepped closer to the stall.

Devin turned and stared at her. He had forgotten all about the cattle Hardin's men rustled from Reed, mainly due to the ample compensation.

"What if you kill him, and the law strings you up afterwards? What if he or his men kill you? Is that when the killing stops? Who'll protect the girls then? Tell me, what sort of flowers do you want on your grave?"

The truth was always in the eyes.

Megan couldn't believe a man would fight over her. Pretty Boy tried, and she'd sent him away. Desperate to wrap her mind around the notion he'd risked his life over damned cattle instead of her, she blamed herself for Reed. Now, she feared his blood would be on her conscience, as well.

In a deft move, he swung his body over the gate, took her in his arms and, with the crook of his finger under her chin, nudged her to look at him. when she tried to squirm out of his embrace. Her tense bearing altered, waned against the length of his body and his heart clenched. He held her, resisted the suffocating need to yank up her skirt, force her legs apart and penetrate her until she knew she was his.

"There are some things a man has to do." Sugar-coating not being his forte, he wanted to reassure her in some way. She felt so fragile, soft and inviting in his arms, sweet smelling and warm. His hard cock stirred against her belly, and he heard her breathless sign. His voice strained and dropped two levels. "That's just the way it is, Megan. Can't rightly explain so's a woman understands. Nothing is gonna happen to me. To ease your mind, just in case, I owe it to Reed to settle the score. It's just like you said. No one cheats a Spawn."

Tenderly, he kissed her forehead and let her go. He turned, opened the gate and led Deuce outside, mounted and rode off.

Megan was a Spawn.

Hardin cheated her in the worst way a man could cheat a woman.

It was up to him to do what his father didn't even have to ask—protect her.

* * * *

Devin came from behind, circling wide across the river upstream. He'd hidden Deuce within whistling distance, half a mile away, leaving plenty of time to hike back and take up residence high on the hill overlooking the abandoned mill below.

Judging from the size of the shadows the trees cast, he estimated it was close to the eleventh hour when Hardin and his men eventually made their appearance.

He shook his head solemnly. That was the trouble with the world, you couldn't take a man by his word. Hardin said noon, and here he was, showing up an hour early. Can't even trust a crook, and Devin should know—he arrived close to nine.

In his profession, one didn't live long by taking chances. Hardin came early, expecting Devin to show up early.

Unfortunately, for Hardin, he miscalculated.

Back at the ranch, Hardin rode with a dozen back up. From the looks of it, he didn't take too kindly to Devin's brazen assurance and decided to add a few more to the ugly brood.

Two lookouts climbed the roof of what appeared to be an abandoned building. A dozen more spread out in the patch of trees between the road leading to the building and the hill. One made his way to the end of the trees, the most logical choice to position a lookout if Devin did the logical thing and came from the direction they expected.

Leroy Hardin dirtied up his shiny brown boots pacing up and down the dusty, overgrown road. To Devin, the man looked uncomfortable. He could almost see the sweat beading Hardin's forehead. Out of the three-hour head start, an hour remained. Devin saw no reason to add to Hardin's misery with tardiness.

He moved down the hill, blending skillfully with nature's plentiful growth, a technique he'd mastered long ago with the aid of his Comanche friends.

The first to go down were the two on the roof. They didn't know what hit them. Silent arrows pierced their hearts, one by one, leaving Hardin unaware.

In newly sewn moccasins, Devin crawled through the trees undetected. One by one, he introduced each gunslick to his bowie knife. Some either climbed up the trees or hid behind fallen logs or in the dense brush. The more confident remained on their horses and stuck out. Devin took pleasure in sneaking up on them from the front, surprising them right out of their saddles. It made it very easy for him to give 'em a ruby red necklace.

Only two were left, one of which was Hardin. He decided to take care of the last spotter on his way out. After all, it was nearly noon, and there was no need to keep Hardin waiting a moment past.

The last of the blood washed from his blades floated down the river as Deuce answered his whistle and appeared.

With a devilish grin, Devin swung a leg over Deuce, turned rein and headed toward his dancing partner.

In the distance, Hardin appeared to have grown somewhat confident. Devin rode up, amusedly considered the man mistakenly thought he was riding into an ambush. Little did Hardin know only one hired hand remained, and the ill-fated back-shooting ambusher passed the time about a mile away.

Once within pistol range, Devin slid out of his saddle and patted his prized horse's rump to move him out of the way.

"I'm ready whenever you are, Hardin."

From the way Hardin's eyes darted about, Devin guessed the man was starting to realize something wasn't right.

"Or would you rather hear how I fucked Rosalinda's pussy? Might be carrying my child. Who knows, you and I could've been kin someday."

He lied, but Hardin didn't know that. To see the man turning red at the possibility the Devil's Spawn impregnated his daughter was an incalculable pleasure. What a thought to give a dying man.

"Why you no good, dirty bastard," Hardin grated, drawing his revolver.

Two shots rang out, followed by a piercing bellow.

Hardin's bullet had burrowed in the hard packed earth several feet from Devin. He clutched his thumbless hand, cursing Devin to hell and back.

By now, Devin knew the lone hired hand heard the shots and would come to his boss's aid. At least, what was left of him.

Devin strolled up to Hardin. The look of fire in his eye, the taste of blood on his lips and the need to kill on his hands, that's how his men described him when he was about to conquer his opponent. That's how he felt, and that's just what was going to happen.

"I take it you don't wanna hear how she begged me to fill her cunt with my seed. I figured you'd want to hear it from me, seeing how no one would believe the word of a two-bit whore."

Hardin's eyes grew impossibly wide. They both now understood they were here to defend a woman's honor.

Devin grabbed Hardin by the red kerchief tied round his neck. It wasn't a fair fight, thumb missing and all, but the way he figured, it wasn't fair what he'd done to Megan.

Afterwards, he left the bloody, bone-crushed heap still breathing and started to walk away. For Megan's sake, he'd let him live. Devin really did plan to go back and honestly assure her he didn't gun him down.

However, with every step he took, it gnawed at him. There were those who didn't deserve mercy. In his gut, he knew when he started something he *had* to finish it.

"Ah, who the hell am I joshing?" Devin turned and drew. "See you in hell, Hardin." He fired, and Hardin stopped breathing instantly.

He swung around when he heard a sole rider charging toward him. With just enough time to drop and roll, the bullet whirled past his head. His gun already drawn, he sighted quickly and eased the trigger back.

The black cowboy hat flew off as the redhead toppled from his saddle.

Blood spewed from Rusty's mouth. He looked up at Devin and cursed, holding the huge gash in his belly.

Something about the man didn't sit well with Devin.

The way Devin saw it, he had three choices: one, to finish him off cleanly; two, to leave him to whatever found him first whether it be help or critters; or three, to torture him.

"Score's settled." Rusty sneered, not far from eternity.

"How you figure?" The man wanted to go with a clear conscience, so the least he could do was hear him out.

Rusty spit up some blood, a thin red trail dribbling down his grimy cheek. "You fucked Hardin's daughter, and he fucked your pa's woman."

Devin stopped breathing, fury gripping his heart and lungs. Shot a glare at the lifeless body several feet away and had half a mind to shoot Hardin again. He narrowed his eyes on the redheaded cowboy with an instant death wish, lying at his feet. "Hardin was braggin'?"

"Boss didn't make a move without me. I was there at the saloon. Held her down while he got her good. Split that fresh cherry, left her bleeding...." The sound of Rusty's shrill laughter rang in his ears, grated on Devin's fading nerves.

Sliding the long bowie knife from its sheath strapped to his waist, Devin chose option three.

* * * *

Very few attended the funeral of the town's former richest proprietor three days later. Rosalinda concluded her mourning period rather quickly. She took off her black garb the day after they laid her father to rest. The educator went back to school straight off, which caused a stir of impropriety among the biddies in town.

The only thing Devin could come up with was the girl was finally free to stop playing Miss Virginal Belle and let somebody have a stab at that pussy. Her father partly succeeded in keeping her chaste, expecting to acquire the most advantageous, influential marital arrangement in the hopes of gaining respectability. At least, she confided that much while she brazenly tried to get into his britches.

Rosalinda not only gained her freedom, she was now wealthy enough to secure her own destiny. A young, non-chaperoned, horny woman living on a ranch with a bunch of willing men, he could just imagine what that destiny was.

Megan had a tough time coming to terms with Hardin's death. Devin patiently helped her cope best he could. Not until Rosalinda stopped by on her way home from the funeral to tell him out of self-defense, she held no ill will, did Megan finally let him back in their bedroom. Since then, he kept her satisfied at every opportunity.

Once before, she asked him to wipe away the painful memories. He planned to do just that for her and the girls. He built a swing on the side of the house. Let the girls ride Deuce. When they asked how the horse got his name, he explained it looked like he was wearing two pairs of boots—a deuce, and he finished by teaching them the basics of poker. He even joined them on a picnic by the river, where he killed a rattler that frightened Shelby.

After a week passed, they fell into a nice, normal routine. Normalcy left Devin yearning for the wide-open wilderness. There was nothing normal about his life. He was itching to leave, and the sooner the better. He longed to return to where he belonged, to track and dispose of what was left of his old gang. Ol' John always warned, *"Tie up loose ends before turning, or they'll get your back."*

The right moment never seemed to arrive, though. It was always tomorrow. One more night with Megan, and he would leave tomorrow. First thing in the morning, he told himself, after his sweat-drenched body recuperated from sapped strength. By the time lunch rolled by, they were fucking like dogs in heat again. Before he knew it, nighttime crept up on him. Megan had this way of slanting her head, looking up at him through her lashes and wetting those luscious pink lips that told him she was ready to be tucked in bed...or fucked and sucked in bed was more like it.

"Oh, yeah, that's the way, baby, squeeze my cock," he groaned, thrusting deep inside her pussy as she clenched her vaginal muscles, tight heat searing his hard flesh. Tomorrow, he'd leave tomorrow, for certain this time, he told himself.

"Harder Devin, make me come again," she murmured, bucking hard against him, tightening her muscles further. "Ohhh, that feels incredible."

On his knees, he tightened his grip on the headboard, holding his body on the edge of hers. Her legs drawn onto his shoulders, the position allowed a deeper penetration, extreme pleasure. It felt as if his cock plunged into a tight, silk encased path straight to her womb.

"Hold on, baby. I'll fuck your tight cunt just the way you like—good and hard." He groaned, squatting on bed to power his thrusts. He gripped her waist, demonstrated the effect quite nicely as his cock surged into her with a forceful, deep thrust that pushed her head, pillows and all, against the headboard. Her gasp heaved from deep in her throat. She trembled, clung to him, her nails digging along his forearms.

"Yes, yes," she chanted softly as he felt her body tumble closer to ecstasy with each hard stroke inside her quivering flesh.

A sharp knock at the door accompanied the faint voice calling for Devin. They jumped and turned their startled gazes toward their locked bedroom door.

Megan's eyes grew wide. Her legs slid off his shoulders. When she mouthed for him to get off, he shook his head with a mischievous expression to tell her 'no way.'

He went to his knees and blew her a kiss. To quiet the squeaking bed, he slowed his thrusts, maintained the intoxicating sensations. He wanted to keep Megan close without sending her into a screaming frenzy.

"What is it, Shelby?" he asked guardedly after the child called to him once more.

Embarrassed, Megan tried to push him away, her palms sliding over the sweaty planes of his chest. Devin ground his pubic bone against her clit, rocked his cock deep inside her heated depths. Her hands curled around his neck. She arched her back, gasped for breath. He felt her pussy swell, grow wetter and hotter, clench him tightly, knew she was nearing climax.

"Devin, I had a bad dream 'bout snakes."

"There's nothing to be afraid of." He bent down and licked the peak on Megan's breast. "It was only a dream." He licked the other puckered nipple, caught it between his teeth, causing her to gasp in delight. "Go back to sleep," he gritted out between his clenched teeth, keeping the hardened nipple in his mouth. He pointed his tongue and ran the tip over the sensitive flesh, had Megan shoving her breast in his mouth, panting.

Her fingernails raked into his buttocks, encouraging him to thrust harder. "Devin, I'm so close," Megan whispered in a soft, desperate plea.

"I'm scared." Shelby's small voice pervaded the dark room.

"Go back to your room, Shelby. I'll be there in a minute." He withdrew almost completely, plunged inside her snug, heated channel hard enough to let Megan know he was thinking of her and Shelby at the same time, trying to please them both in very different ways, but not hard enough to shake the bed.

"Now, Devin. Come now," Shelby whined impatiently.

"Okay, Shelby," he promised with a grin, climbing out of bed, taking a wide-eyed, still-impaled Megan, with him. "Give me a moment, and I'll be coming."

He stood with his knees slightly bent, clasped Megan's firm rear and surged deep and fast. Since she weighed next to nothing, he easily glided her petite body up and down his length.

She clung to him, pressed her heels into his ass. Long locks of dark gold waved wildly as she leaned back and pressed her clit against his hard abdominal flesh with each long, deep, pistoning stroke.

Sweat dripped down his back. His chest rose and fell harshly with each labored breath. He moved her faster, felt his cock tighten, enlarge, throb. She trembled in his arms, heard her fight to control her whimpers and he knew they would come together.

Megan opened her mouth as if to scream, but instead, locked her teeth tight on his bare shoulder when she came. Her body tensed, shuddered, inner muscles gripped, milked his deeply embedded flesh sensuously, sending him into his own erotic oblivion with one final, hard thrust. He shuddered, gritted his teeth, and fought back the growl of bliss that tore through him while he held her tightly to his chest, his jerking cock spewing his seed into her rippling pussy.

Watching the naughty smile on her flushed face, he laid Megan back on the bed. She quickly threw the covers over her nakedness. Their eyes met in the pale moonlight. Her eyes glittered with erotic bliss and he knew her insatiable need couldn't have withstood a postponement anymore than could his.

He grinned. The look he gave her was of pure male sexual pride and satisfaction. He took the washcloth from the table where Megan always kept a pitcher and basin and wiped away the musky scent of their lovemaking before pulling on his buckskins.

It was more beneficial to satisfy them both than wait until his hard-on subsided. He shook his head as he thought how the sight of his blind snake fighting in his buckskins probably would have frightened Shelby just as much, if not more than the rattler he killed at the picnic.

"Okay, Shelby." Dressed only in his buckskins, he lifted the small child with one arm and closed the door behind him. "Tell me 'bout this dream."

"Yucky, Devin." Her cherubic face crinkled as her short, stubby fingers trailed paths through his sweat-drenched skin. "You're all sweaty."

"I was rushing for you."

A deep frown appeared on her small face. "What happened?" Shelby touched the deep red oval mark on his shoulder. "Did the snake bite you?" Her voice concerned.

His gaze dropped to where she indicated. Caught up in the tight confines of Megan's silken depths, it felt so good he hadn't even realized she took a bite out of him while he filled her pulsating pussy with his release.

He cleared his throat. Abruptly, he changed the subject, carrying Shelby back to her bedroom.

Chapter 20

From the way the situation unraveled days later, one would assume his plan went awry. At least this time, Devin didn't have to fuck Rosalinda, just avail her like one waves a carrot in front of a stubborn donkey. Not that he would ever openly compare Megan to a donkey, but she sure as hell was as stubborn as a mule and feistier than a jackass.

After they dropped the girls off at school, Megan was livid when Rosalinda boldly conveyed her designs with a telling wink. She charged ahead on her brown palomino. Devin deliberately let her believe she was getting away by not rushing after her.

He let Deuce graze on a patch of grass outside and casually strolled through the open barn doors. "Haven't you learned by now not to run from me?"

"Next time you fancy a rendezvous with your flame, leave me out of it." She yanked the heavy-duty saddle off her horse, and with considerable effort, shoved it on its stand. "I'll not have you parading *her* in front of me."

Megan was hot. Each heated word indicated the trip was successful, a step closer to his eventual departure. No matter how many times he buried himself deep inside her supple, inviting passage, it was never enough to satisfy his craving. It left him wanting more, starved for the warmth of her breath mingling with his. Her taste. Her touch. The intoxicating inhalation of her subtle sweet rosy scent mixed with the tantalizing aroma of her desire. The feel of her tiny body shuddering beneath him as he brought her to completion time and time again.

He thought long and hard for days and could come up with only one solution to ensure she and the girls would be safe after he was gone. A solution she would never agree to outright. He'd have to do some groundwork in advance. Then, with properly executed sexual coercion and extreme subtlety, he would succeed.

The sooner the better.

Her intense blaze of passion, the depth of her sensuality, her fiery spirit he could handle. The other raw emotion in her eyes filled his mind with turmoil at the sheer intensity. It overloaded his senses, forced emotions upon him he never knew he had.

His only remaining kin were his two little half-sisters. The last thing he wanted to do was hurt them. If he stayed, it was a recipe for disaster. Kids and outlaws with vile reputations didn't make for good stew. Sure, he told them bedtime stories, took them swimming, and carted them off to school, but Megan had been right from the beginning. Association with a bloodthirsty cutthroat, death on his tail…well, it was just a matter of time before his past caught up. When it did, those innocent girls had to be far away from him.

He stood by her side looking down at her. Megan leaned back against the saddle, arms crossed so tight over her chest it was a wonder she could breathe. Her defiant chin pointed in the opposite direction. Did the woman never look in the mirror? She was unaware of her own beauty. He grew hard just looking at her.

"You've forgotten our agreement. You'll do as I say, or else," he warned sharply. She paid him no mind.

A whirl of dust mounted when she twirled around. She glared at him through the brown haze and snapped viciously, "Do what you want with her, just not in front of me."

He captured her roughly by the upper arms. "If I want you to watch while I fuck her, you will. You seemed to enjoy that."

The fire in her eyes burned bright. If not restrained, he figured she would have tried slapping him by now. She squirmed to get free, and he held her firm, angering her even more.

"Like hell I will. I'd gouge my own eyes before that'll ever happen." She stomped down on his moccasin-clad foot. From her expression, he could tell she grew even angrier when he didn't flinch.

"What if you joined us?" Her eyes suddenly widened, flickered in disbelief, taken aback by the illicit offer, but the gleam told him she was intrigued, aroused as well.

"Would you like that? You, me, and another person fucking at the same time? Would you let them touch you? Our hands on your body, two mouths servicing you, pleasuring you. Think about it, Megan, two people focusing on you, making you hot, wet, screaming in need."

She shook her head in denial, her face flushed. "No, never." Her breathless whisper held no weight of final authority.

"Luckily for you, I don't fancy Rosalinda," he said truthfully, dropping the subject now that he planted the seed in the back on her mind. He held Megan by one arm. She squirmed and protested while he led her to an empty stall. He was confident the untamed passion she hadn't yet learned to control overwhelmed her system, fueled her anger. "It's you I want. Take off that dress and prepare to be punished."

Megan's eyes flared even wider. She stood her ground, puffed her pert breasts in the air, arms rigid by her side. "I'll do no such thing."

His lips twitched at her defiance. It's what made her unique, that lively, bold spirit that entranced him, stirred him undeniably, and made him hotter than hell, harder, and longer than a shotgun barrel. The little nymph, she knew what was doing.

She stood now with both hands on her narrow hips and her hazel eyes held a challenge he was about to take her up on. He smiled and took a step closer, more than a little impressed, actually, that she held the patch of earth beneath her feet.

His hand hooked over the center of her neckline and dragged it all way down in one jarring swoop, popping buttons in all directions.

"My dress," she shrieked as he tore the black cloth from her body. He hated to do it, knowing the work she put into sewing it, but he had his reasons. Damned good ones.

She stood only in her black slippers, the tattered dress scattered at her ankles. He didn't allow her a moment to get her bearings to fight back, or even think. He propped a foot on the second rung of the stall and tossed her over his bent knee.

"Devin," she shrieked. Her legs kicked in the air, shoes flying off her feet. "Put me down."

"Tell me no, this is what you get. I've warned you, time to be punished."

* * * *

"You're not serious." Megan clung to his massive thigh to balance herself and keep from falling face forward into the hard-packed earth only a couple of feet from her head. Her long hair, loosened from her struggles, swept the dirt floor into a cloud of dust that crinkled her nose and made her want to sneeze.

A splayed hand ran along the curve of her back while another held her thighs securely. She tried to move, but the pressure on her back increased.

"What do you think?" he asked her warningly.

She stared over her shoulder, her body trembling in anticipation. Her eyes widened in alarm when she saw him raise a hand. Her heart thundered in her chest, then...

A wail tore from her throat. The piercing sensation of flesh striking tender flesh seared through her body.

"Naughty girls get spanked." As one screamed ended, another began as he slapped her rear again. His splayed palm was large enough it covered her entire bottom. "You're a naughty girl aren't you?"

"No, no," she gasped in shock. She should be fighting mad, terrified, or at least in pain. Instead, she was gushing between her legs, shivers of excitement charging her nerves. He was certain he'd struck her with enough force to tinge, leave his mark of triumph upon her skin.

"What did you say?" His hand smoothed over the round curves of her butt, a finger dipped between the crease, and she stilled.

"I'm a good girl," she murmured softly, trembling. When she felt him stroke the entrance to her anus, her butt cheeks clenched his finger, held him in place. The faint touch evoked a fiery excitement, a darker side of her sexuality. It terrified her.

His other hand came down firmly on her bottom once more, tearing a feverish gasp from her throat. "Come on, Megan. You know you're naughty."

She shook her head, fought the confusion, strong desires and depraved sensations racing through her veins to every nerve ending and straight to her clit. His hands smoothed over her ass again, squeezed the round, tinged cheeks. The tender flesh throbbed, overwhelmed her senses, flared her eagerness. She arched toward him, desperate to have him fill her starving pussy.

"You should have been spanked a long time ago. Watching people fuck through peepholes." At his erotic possession of her, his sensuous incitement, lewd images flashed before her eyes, heating her bloodstream. "Did you play with yourself?"

Yes. "No!" Smack.

"Stick your fingers in your cunt?" His voice was rough, tight with lust.

Yes. A tremor of awareness shot up her spine. She shook her head. Smack.

"Wish you were the one being fucked by all those men?"

Only one. She felt his cock hard and thick against her bare hip. Shaking her head, she moaned, "No."

He smacked her ass again. Hard, soft, she wasn't sure anymore. Her cheeks were stinging now, burning, hot. Her pussy pulsated with shockingly arousing sensations. Liquid heat dripped down her thighs. She needed...she needed...oh, God, she needed so much.

"Did you want to suck on those cocks? Swallow their come?"

Only Caleb's. "No, never."

He came down hard. She jerked against him, his cock tightened, heated her flesh through the fabric. A breathy, desperate whimper escaped her.

"You're lying. I know you too damn well," he accused her darkly.

Shaking her head in denial, she wailed in pleasure/pain as his hand landed on her rear. Her body trembled with arousal from the sharp, stinging bite of pain, from the indecent memories, the erotic dreams each night after she peered through the peephole, often without Jazelle knowing.

"Teasing the school boys."

"No!" Smack.

"Showing them what they couldn't have."

"No!" Smack.

"Flaunting that pretty, little pink pussy in front of them."

Caleb, only Caleb. She shivered, moaned at the hot, sensual, unforgettable memories. Smack.

"Let the young boys touch but never fuck."

"No, no, it was only one," she cried weakly with arousal.

"You admit, then." He sounded pleased. "Say it. Say how naughty you are." His voice was a deep, seductive, dark stimulant.

"Yes, yes. I've been naughty," she murmured, her body hummed with excitement, awaiting the consequences of her confession.

"You liked showing him your pussy." His hand slowly moved over her back, a heated, caressing encouragement.

"Yes," she moaned, drowning in the rising waves of exquisite torture/pleasure.

"His fingers inside you, making you wet, hot, hungry for something more. Hungry for his cock. For him to fuck you."

Memories too numerous, the desperate wanting, the emptiness seared through her trembling body. She couldn't deny she had wanted Caleb. That was so long ago. Another lifetime. Devin was here now, the heat of his cock branding her hip through his buckskins. He was hard, thick and ready, and she needed him now. She opened her mouth to beg for release, and a soft, revealing moan escaped from her lips.

His palm came down on her bottom. Her ass tightened as she cried out. The sensation triggered her cunt to throb and clench in need between her thighs. She felt her juices seeping out of her pussy.

"Spread your legs, Megan. Let me see those pussy lips you let someone else touch," His voice was husky, demanding.

Hesitant, knowing what he would find, she parted her legs slightly, pleading, "Devin, no more, please."

"Only I say when you had enough," he growled, moving his hand between her thighs, forcing them further apart. "And I say I'm only beginning."

Her hips jerked as he easily drove two fingers inside her spasming pussy. He began quick, short little thrusts. Wet and aching with need, she heard a squishy, gushing sound inside in her vagina and burned with embarrassment.

"Damn, you're so wet. I think you like your punishment." She felt his fingers swirl in the thick liquid gathered in the slit. The scent of her arousal reached her as she dangled upside down from his perched thigh.

"No," she gasped faintly but sounded unconvincing to her own ears. She rocked against his hand, working him in deeper, tightening on the impalement, desperate for the release to come.

"Your drenched pussy tells me different." He withdrew his fingers, gathered her juices and slid them to her anal entrance. He taunted the tiny hole, easing a long, breathy moan from her throat. "I wish you could see this pretty ass of yours."

His wicked complement intensified her sexual desire, increased her hunger for him, for anything. She shifted on his thigh, lifted her hips, offering her pussy as sacrifice. A glance at his face showed her the depraved lust darkening his eyes, telling her this was going to be no ordinary reprimand. He wanted, expected more. From the way his expression darkened with wild, lusty intent, he was probably going to get it, whether she gave it to him or not.

"What are you doing?" A flare of unbridled excitement coursed through her veins at the image of his huge cock plunging in Rosalinda's ass. Rosalinda was a big girl, nearly twice her size. The woman probably had plenty of room within those plump cheeks. Whereas her behind was so tiny, there was nowhere else to go but out the proper side.

"I want to fuck this ass of yours," he growled, the furious need apparent. She cried out feeling him nudge past the opening with the tip of a well-lubricated finger, his breathing rough, heavy on her back.

"That's unnatural, dirty. Besides, you'll never fit," she contested, struggling weakly. Her body stiffened as she envisioned the deviant invasion. "You're too big. It hurts when you take me regular." The fear was palpable. He mentioned it a few times in the past, but never went further. Today, he sounded convinced it was time to try.

"I never hear you complain." The smug amusement in his voice was transparent.

"Damn you, Devin." Stretched impossibly wide every time he entered her vagina, immense pleasure overshadowed that flash of pain she grew to relish. He provided a wondrous combination of sensations each time they fucked. She'd never give it up. "You put Deuce to shame with that beast hanging between your legs."

A deep, throaty chortle left his throat. She didn't find it a bit funny. The truth never was. Her new motto: Anything but *that*.

"I'm so fucking hard, I have to have you." Devin lowered her to her feet, released her. He started toward an empty stall, grated in a low, almost pained tone. "Come here."

Once his back was turned, she bolted toward the open barn door.

"Megan," she heard him shout as she ran out the door.

The gravel walkway leading to the porch steps was a foot away. She was almost there, a few more steps. She'd bolt the front door behind her. Lock their bedroom door. Surely he wouldn't break down every door in the house. Or would he? How far would he go to possess her? At the thought of his strength overpowering her, forcing her to submit, an intense, hot flare of passion and excitement raced through her body. She felt her cunt tighten, weep, ache with greedy need. Her legs turned to mush.

His heavy, hurried steps were behind her. She glanced backward. The sight of the rope in his hand caused her to trip over one of rocks lining the path. Crushed gravel dug into the skin of her knees. She scrambled to her feet, wasted not a moment to brush off the dirt or faint traces of blood on her skinned knees.

He was too fast, there before she realized it.

Dear God, no, she thought, as his large, muscled arm scooped her up and hoisted her on his hip. In one long stride, he scoured the steps. With two swift kicks, he opened, and then closed the door behind them.

He ignored her protests, tossed her facedown on the bed. Despite the arousal flooding her body, she struggled with all her might to get away. She kicked and screamed. He held her down easily with one knee scarcely touching her back. "Devin, get off me." Her blood raced as she saw him loop the rope around the front bedpost. "What are you doing?" she screamed at her own helplessness as he tied it to her wrist. She kicked out at him after he removed his knee, but found the move only served his purpose. He grabbed her leg and tied it to a foot-post—first one, then the other. "Have you lost your mind?" Her breathing laborious, her body responded, accepted, craved the depravity. With ease, he restrained her final wrist as she screamed in protest, "Untie me!"

He said nothing.

"Devin," she shouted, her voice confused, shocked, breathlessly excited. She pulled on the rope in all directions, finding little slack, let alone a means of escape. Ripples of fiery lust and carnal suspense raced through her body. She was a small "x" in the middle of a huge target. Helpless. Restrained. Completely at his mercy. "Untie me."

Without a word, he yanked two fluffy white pillows out from under her arms as her body thrashed on the bed. With just enough slack in the rope, he propped them under her hips, lifting her ass in the air.

"What are you doing?" She strained her neck to look back in time to see him release his monstrous dick from his buckskins. Her eyes flared wide, body stiffened, her butt cheeks clenched at the thought of what he was going to do.

"What do you think I'm going to do?" His dark gaze centered between her spread thighs. He just stood there beside the bed, as though he delighted in watching her squirm. The bastard. She watched, licked her lips while he stroked his cock. It throbbed in anticipation, so enormously wide, terribly elongated, the blue veins thick and bulging with blood. The flesh was deep red and velvety hot. It had a determination of its own, as if it reached out to her in search of new adventure, waited eagerly to claim its prize, the last of her innocence.

"No, Devin, you can't. You'll never fit. I'll be ripped in two. I'll never walk again."

He climbed on the bed, laughing. A deep, throaty laugh that sounded as sexy as hell.

"I'm gonna fuck your ass, and you're gonna enjoy it." Her butt clenched. She groaned from the stinging sensation as his splayed hands smoothed along her hips, his thumbs grazing her buttocks as if checking his handiwork.

A sharp blow landed on her tender rump, and she cried out at the pain/pleasure racing over her skin. Her soft, gasping wails went unheeded as several more blows left their mark, heightened her lust to an intolerable level. Her pussy was on fire, her engorged clit throbbing for release. Her breast swollen, nipples ached with agonizing need as she squirmed against the bed. She wondered if she could die for want of fulfillment, pleasure wantonly withheld.

He drove a finger in the hot wetness of her pulsating cunt, drenched with her juices. Megan arched her back, crying out from the insane, torturous arousal spiraling through her weakened body. He pulled back and then thrust deep inside her. He teased, probed, tortured her just enough to bring her close, never enough to send her over. "You need to learn a lesson. Don't ever run from me again. Don't tell me no."

"I'm sorry, Devin." She clenched her vaginal muscles around his buried finger, gripped him tightly, desperate to keep him buried. "It'll never happen again." Her breathing fast, her hips shifted dying to bring his buried hand against her clitoris. "You're scaring me."

"Trust me, Megan. I won't hurt you." His voice harsh, tortured, leaving her unsure if she should believe him, believe he could control the hot need, the intense sexuality that was so much a part of him, the carnal depravity darkening his gaze.

"Damn, you're so beautiful." The bed sank under his weight as he moved between her legs, running his hands along her back, over the curve of her buttocks, and down the backs of her thighs. "Tied up, spread open, wet and hot, and all mine for the taking."

He leaned over, brushed her hair aside, his moist lips burned kisses at her neck. His cock brushed against her ass, the heat of his hard arousal on her flesh made her shudder. He caressed her breasts, milked the nipples with his fingers until they were hard peaks, left her gasping for breath. His hand lowered, graced the rounded globes that still burned from his deftly inflicted discipline, tender touches, soothing, soft whispers upon her tender flesh.

Overcome by the sinful downfall he initiated, desperate to quench the tumultuous ache, the unceasing throbbing he built between her thighs, she pleaded, "Make me come. I can't wait."

"I'll tell you when it's time." Her pitiful wail of disappointment echoed off the walls when he pulled away. "You're too horny. Too greedy." He gripped her hips, and she arched her back, expecting him to thrust his cock into her eagerly awaiting pussy. "You haven't learned your lesson."

"Ahhh," she sighed heavily feeling his hands lower to the slick crease propped up by the pillows in sweet temptation. His fingers held her slick flesh open, his tongue swept from her clit to her anus in a swift motion that had her careening out of control. Once more, and she would come. One more lick of her clit, and she would fall apart, melt away and die. Instead, his pointy, devilish tongue swirled through the swollen folds, penetrated the entrance to her vagina. Obviously, sinfully aware she was on edge, never granted her the climax she sought. Her whimpers needy, hungry, desperate to release the pressure building in her body, she wiggled her pussy upward, pushed her clit closer toward his mouth.

His tongue moved upward, lured her in a wet temptation toward the forbidden back entrance causing her to tremble with an alarming awareness that wracked her body.

"Devin. Rosalinda, I'll watch," she panted frantically. His tongue stilled. "I'll do whatever you want."

"Are you positive?" He sounded hurt, disappointed, his breath hot, heavy against the cleft of her ass.

Unsure what she wanted, terrified of failing, disappointing him, she said nothing.

"You want me doing this to her and not you?" He parted her cheeks and speared the taboo hole with a deep plunge of his tongue, tearing a cry of pleasure from her lips. "Taste her and not you?" he moaned against her pulsing flesh, his heated breath sent ripples below the surface of her skin, flaming her passion. "Pleasure her." He buried a finger in her pussy. "Fuck her and not you." He added a second digit and began a hard, fast rhythm of strokes. "Are you that afraid of my cock hurting you or do you just want it too damned much it scares you?"

Megan tugged on the ropes, heedless to the rough texture as her arms and legs pulled in every direction, dying to get closer to the intimate kiss that felt more wonderful, tempting than it should have. He thrust in tandem with his tongue in her anus and fingers in her cunt, torturing her flesh with carnal delight, never letting her tumble. Until she realized this, too, was part of her licentious punishment.

"Oh, Devin," she breathed, pushing back against his mouth. She felt the building sensation start to take over. *Oh God. Yes.* She was almost there. He withdrew. "No!"

"I don't want her. I want you. I want this," he groaned, voice a strangled plea. Before she realized his carnal intent, a thick, juice-coated finger plunged into her ass.

The harsh invasion had her screaming at the pleasure and pain racing through her system. Hot bolts of desire radiated from her anus as she felt him work the knuckle past the tight ring of muscle.

"Relax," he ordered softly, easing inside the exit. "Your ass is mine. Your body is mine to do with as I please. Think of the pleasure. It will feel so good, Megan, you'll be begging me for it."

Megan gasped for breath, her pussy gushed heatedly at the fiery pinch in her rear, her muscles stretching for the heated invasion. She gave herself over to the rage of lust, her body accepting him, the erotic invasion searing the depths of her ass, blissfully aware soon it would be his cock.

"That's it. Nice and slow." He pressed deeper, worked his way inside her patiently, until he stroked her slow and easy. "Loosen those ass muscles so I can fuck you."

Reality turned into a strange exhilarating, wickedly sinful pleasure. Stretched and full, burning up with erotic flames, hot strokes of desire, she panted his name as he brought her to fiery sensations she never believed possible. She moaned and begged for more, writhed on his finger twisted and thrust in and out.

"You like it, baby. I knew you would."

Her moans grew louder, and she almost missed the torment, needy desperation to please her in his tone. She arched into him, thrashing her head side to side, pushed back on the thick finger wedged inside her rectum.

"Come on, Megan, give it to me. Show me you want it." He halted his strokes, and she understood what he needed. Her acceptance, to know he was giving, not just taking pleasure.

Unable to hold back, she shamelessly rocked against his hand. Slow at first, until she found a nice tempo. Her hips worked up to a fever pitch that had her moaning with lusty pleasure.

"Yeah, baby, that's my girl," Devin growled encouragingly.

Lost in the ecstasy, she rocked faster, pushed back harder, sinking his finger deeper. He groaned deeply when she tightened her anal muscles around his finger. Her cries of red-hot arousal filled the bedroom.

"You're too tight now. When you can take all my fingers, my cock will fuck your ass good and hard," he warned harshly.

"Not again," she rasped at the loss when his hand left her anus, and cried out a second later when it landed firmly on her rear. She reeled from the overriding loss, fought the burning torment, the shameful pleasure stinging her cheeks. The bed shifted as he swung his legs over the edge. Damn him. She was so close. He denied her yet again. Amazed how exquisite, hot the lust flared through her system at being taken in the ass. Even if he didn't touch her clitoris, she would have climaxed. Fucked is what she needed—an orgasm, not another spanking.

"Devin." Her voice panted, pleadingly. She noticed him quickly undressing. *Thank you.* "Hurry, I need you to make me come."

"Not yet, Megan, you've been a naughty girl. Remember, you're being punished."

Her eyes widened in shock and anticipation at the dark sensuality in his tone. Her gaze dropped between his thighs. His grip was tight around the base of the hard stalk that extended between his long muscled legs, a manly vision of fierce temptation.

With two added pillows, he raised her upper body sufficiently for what he had in mind. He positioned the engorged, pulsing head of his cock close to her face. His fingers gripped her hair, pulled her head back. They locked eyes. She caught sight of the wild, feral, purely sexual gleam in his gaze and moisture flowed from deep in her womb.

"Open wide." He ordered, and she obeyed.

She licked her lips when drops of pre-come leaked from the tiny slit on the velvet soft tip. Starved for him, incapable of waiting to taste and lick him. Devour his cock. Eat him whole. Her neck stretched out and her mouth closed over the bulky head, buried it in a tight suckling motion.

"Make me come," he continued. "You don't get yours until after I do. Make it good."

She watched the lust wash over his face. His darkened gaze followed the bulky outline beneath her cheek while she gobbled up more than half his beefy cock down her throat. He knew what he was doing to her was exciting her like never before.

No decent girl should, but she loved his domination. She needed to be at his utter mercy in order to lose that barrier of control that tied her to her past. Forced to submit, do nasty, sinful things or else feeling shame and guilt for wanting to try otherwise. At first, it terrified her. Not out of fear, but the unknown, a sinfully carnal anticipation that left her pussy foaming. She was shocked to discover her sexuality raged to the dark side of depravity, the forbidden. Her mind tried to make sense of the inescapable, unexplainable intense sexual arousal, at taking pleasure in pain. Her own helplessness, willingness to share him with another woman, how insane was that? His refusal to her request was a wondrous joy.

"That's it. *Suck it,* baby, good and hard," he growled, brushing her hair off her face. He stared down at her, his face aflame with lust while her mouth suckled his manly flesh.

Anxious to please, she stretched her lips taut, taking more of his thick flesh into the depths of her mouth.

"Give me what I want." He cupped her breast, tweaked and pinched her hard nipple. She groaned at the small prickle of pain, extra edge of lust. He moaned in approval at the vibration around his flesh. Her mouth sucked hungrily. "Make me come."

"Suck it, baby. Harder." His fingers tightened in her hair, turned her into a wild, lust-starved woman. She tasted, licked, and nipped every thick, hard, virile inch of his iron hard erection, slathered his balls until they glistened with her saliva.

"Ohhh, hell, yes." His expression was one of awe, appreciation, lust, and satisfaction. She felt him tighten; thicken within the confines of her mouth. His engorged scrotum tucked beneath her chin, the musky scent of his arousal heady, captivating. Her tongue swept over the ultra-sensitive ridge along the head. "You're fucking killing me."

Devin held her head with both hands and shut his eyes while he fucked her mouth. His heated thickness glided smooth and fast between her lips. Gently she scraped her teeth along his flesh, giving him the spike of roughness he told her rippled from his cock, up his spine, and straight down to his toes. He groaned, gave a final, hard push deep between her lips, burying almost every inch down her throat. Her gag reflex milked him. Recalled what he taught her, she fought to keep his cock within the tight confines of her throat.

He growled a reminder, holding her head still. "Swallow." His back stiffened as the first spurting jet of his hot semen erupted from his cock, flooded her mouth and shot down her throat. "Suck my cock. Drink my seed."

She felt his entire body shuddered violently as she continued to suckle his hard flesh, swallow his precious nectar. Her lips tightening around his throbbing flesh until he pulled back moments later. His cock had hardly diminished.

"Shit, Megan, you're getting better each day. I can't wait till tomorrow."

"My turn," she said breathlessly, gazing up at him. She licked her swollen lips seductively, hoping to refresh his memory regarding returning the favor.

Swiftly, he changed positions, brushing the tip of his glistening cock over her ass. He growled desperately, "Dammit, I want your ass so bad."

"Devin," was all she said a moment before he impaled her quivering pussy with one savage thrust that propelled her into a fiery wave of explosions, had her shamelessly crying out at the wickedly hot, intense, searing release seemingly flowing endlessly.

The room teemed with sexual scents and sounds, their sweat-glistened bodies slapped ruthlessly against each other once he cut the ropes free. Grunts, moans, and shouts of pleasure mingled as his cock slammed into her. He gripped her bucking hips, showed her no mercy. Gave her what she asked, needed, begged him for and more. Her head thrashed in the crumpled sheets. Harder and harder, he plunged into her flesh until they tumbled together into a sated heap of ecstasy.

By the time they fell into each other's arms, she lost count of the intense climaxes that shattered through her body. As sleep slowly took her, she lay curled against Devin, already deep in slumber. The blissful replay in her mind of begging him to fuck her ass while on all fours, her cunt hovering over his face. He obliged by easing two fingers inside the back entrance while working two fingers in her pussy. Devin drove her into a heated, crazed frenzy by the double penetration while his mouth sucked on her clit. She groaned all over his hard flesh as she tried to lick his balls and jerk off his cock. Unable to feel beyond her pelvic region, she gave up trying to make him come. Her last memory before she finally dozed off was of crying out at the exquisite pleasure.

* * * *

Drowsily, Devin pried one eye half open. Megan, snuggled against him, came into focus. A scant second later, all senses were on heightened alert as a male voice called from outside. The distinct scrape of the front door opening brought Devin's head snapping upward.

Instinctively, he reached over for one of his Colts he'd left on the table next to the bed, always within easy reach.

One foot already firmly planted on the floor and the arm curled under Megan, ready to toss her out of harm's way if need be. The footsteps warned him someone was on the other side of their bedroom door.

* * * *

"Megan?" Caleb's worried voice drifted into the room as he opened the bedroom door. "Are you here?"

With one foot inside the room, the man's jaw dropped, eyes flared. Devin watched the shock turn to outrage on his face. Caleb's eyes narrowed, roved over the scene, from Megan to Devin, the ropes on the floor, then finally to Megan again.

For a gut-wrenching moment, Devin was grateful Megan was asleep, didn't think she could survive the look of disappointment, contempt and a host of other emotions aimed at her. If Caleb made a wrong move, Devin was ready for him. From the way his body strung tight with fury, he doubted Caleb could move.

It seemed Pretty Boy either failed to notice or plum didn't care a gun was pointed at him. Instead, he just stared miserably at Megan's naked flesh. He could tell she had been fucked good and hard.

Carefully, Devin eased his arm from under Megan. She moaned softly in her sleep, curled into a ball in the warm spot he just vacated. Her round bottom, still flushed from her earlier punishment, stared back at Caleb, and Devin couldn't help but wonder what the other man was thinking as his blue eyes widened, darkened with anger.

Devin put the Colt away, jerked on his breeches, and shrugged into his shirt, clearing his throat in the process.

"I...I..." Caleb paused, and shook his head. Disgust hardened his face. He glared angrily at Devin. "The girls. I brought Emma and Shelby home."

Devin ran a hand through his hair, frustrated and mad at himself for forgetting.

Caleb's attention dropped back to Megan. "Rosalinda asked if I could bring them home." His voice cold, bitter, his expression pained. "They hadn't been picked up I...I thought something happened."

"Thanks," Devin replied conversationally, studying Caleb's reaction.

With his hand on the glass doorknob, Caleb took a deep breath. He glanced at Devin, then Megan once more. The disappointment shone heavy in his eyes. His brows drew in a tight scowl. He turned to leave.

"Wait. I was gonna come looking for you. I need to talk to you."

* * * *

For a troubled moment, Caleb didn't know whether to welcome the opportunity to stay without question or take his packed bags and leave Tejas the instant he returned home. Megan lying naked on the bed was a sight he dreamt of for years. A nightly dream where he was by her side, not some vile, vicious murderer. He felt his throat go dry. The bittersweet thought left him with a heavy, aching heart. A deep misery tore at his soul.

He'd loved her since the moment he laid eyes on her. That would never change. To him, she would always be his. Reality was glaring in his face, though, flaming his agonizing resentment. Did she really want this other man? Had she experienced pleasure sharing his bed?

The telling smell of sex hung heavily in the air, shone in the afterglow upon her face, told him she at least had given herself to him. Was this their first time? He prayed to God it was. His hope of a future together faded before his eyes.

Skin was pale, appeared as silky soft as he remembered. Only now, the firm mounds on her backside were marred with a peculiar flush. There was faint bruising on her wrists and ankles, as though... His gaze dropped to the pieces of rope thrown about and then cut sharply to Devin, sitting beside the bed, stuffing his overgrown foot into a moccasin.

Caleb felt his entire body stiffen, his blood race, his heart pound, his fist clench. *Bastard. Heathen. Doer of all things evil.* He grimaced. he wanted to believe that only by force did Devin take her. The rough bastard didn't know a lady should be treated gently, like the delicate creature she was.

Megan seemed to purr and stretch out like a cat. She rolled on her back, sprawled out on the bed, exposing her charms. His pulse raced, his cock grew hard instantly. Her pert breasts reached skyward with each deep breath in total slumber.

He gaze raked over her delicate slimness. He struggled against the instinctive desire overshadowing the rage tensing his body. She looked so beautiful, sweet and innocent. His attention settled on the tender flesh between her well-formed, slender thighs. Her pussy was a deep red, swollen as though it suffered through a severe fucking, hard and selfishly, without tenderness or love, with only the cruelty of male gratification in mind. Those nether lips glistened with *his* semen. A jealous fury ate at Caleb.

Devin covered Megan with a quilt he picked up from the floor. At least the no-account had the decency to do that, Caleb concluded.

Begrudgingly, Caleb followed him outside.

"Devin," the girls both exclaimed happily, seeing them as they stepped off the porch and started down the path. Emma stopped pushing Shelby on the swing. Emma hurried toward him. Shelby jumped off the swing and ran past her big sister.

"Sorry, girls, for not picking you up at school. Megan is napping right now. If both of you go inside and stay real quiet so's she can sleep while I talk to…" he paused, tilted his head in Caleb's direction, and continued, "him, we'll go into town for supper. How's that sound?"

With a heavy sigh, Caleb rolled his eyes. He assumed the legendary outlaw could not commit to memory the name of a man he almost shot in cold blood two weeks ago.

"Oh, goodie." Shelby hopped up and down.

Emma, more sedate, nodded her head excitedly. "Can we get candy?" she asked with a twinkle in her eye.

"You can have anything you want as long as I don't hear a peep outta ya'll."

"Yippee," they shouted, skipping down the rock-lined gravel path. Devin grinned when they quieted down once they reached the steps.

Caleb cringed inwardly. Candy was bad for kids, but who was he to speak up? He wasn't their father. Not even a stepfather, or better yet, their brother. Though they continued to call him Uncle Caleb, he was no longer welcomed in their home. He was nothing to them. Not anymore.

"I fail to comprehend what business you and I can possibly discuss," Caleb said with extreme indignation when Devin gestured to follow him toward the barn.

"That's where you're wrong. You and I have lots in common." Devin turned on his heel, and walked away.

After a moment, Caleb followed, bitterness eating away at him.

When he entered the barn, Caleb noticed Devin bend over and pick up what appeared to be left of Megan's dress. Hatred boiled his blood. The black garment had been ripped to shreds.

With growing contempt, Caleb stood a few feet beyond the entrance, eyed Devin cautiously. Next, Devin retrieved a slipper from a pile of hay inside an empty stall, then he found another atop an old whiskey barrel. He placed both on a shelf, along with the dress.

Caleb didn't know what was going on, but whatever it was, he didn't like it. Not one damned bit. Megan couldn't possibly choose this man over him.

Devin strolled throughout the barn aimlessly, picking up this and that, then putting it back down, as if stalling for time. As Devin moved, Caleb slowly followed, not taking his eyes off him. Devin carried a good hundred pounds or so more than he, with nothing to lose, Caleb willingly faced fear head-on. Unarmed, he had no call to carry a weapon. He led a good life, hadn't an enemy in the world—until now.

"You got it hard for Megan," Devin said, plain as day, coming to a halt. He took a casual stance, leaned a shoulder against a beam several feet to Caleb's right.

Their eyes locked. Caleb failed to get a read on him. His eyes were expressionless. No emotion at all flickered in the silver depths. His calm tone held no clue as to his intentions.

"My feelings for her are of no concern of yours." Caleb kept his voice just as even, fighting the furious urge to attack and defend what should rightly be his.

"I say they are."

"Despite the absurdity of purchasing a human, as you so claim, it does not automatically entitle you to their emotions. Only physically do you have some sort of hold over her. What Megan and I have will last an eternity. When she's free of you, I'll be waiting."

"Wrong again."

Caleb's eyes narrowed. His jaw tightened from the rage searing his soul. Despite his church upbringing, the hatred he felt for the man standing in front of him could not be dismissed.

"Megan says she's in love. That gal can't get enough of me." Devin grabbed his crotch and lewdly rearranged himself.

What a crude, audacious beast, Caleb reflected with loathing.

"Wants me to fuck her morning, noon, and night. I've never seen a wilder filly when she latches on to my cock. Can suck your coffers dry. Then again, you wouldn't know, seeing how she only let you finger-fuck her."

Caleb blazed with fury at the speck of mockery in his tone. Apparently, Megan revealed the precious moments they shared long ago. His stomach churned with horrific hatred, yet his tone remained reserved. "A gentleman should never discuss intimacies."

Devin let out a deep, raunchy chuckle. "If being a gentleman means missing out on sweet pussy like that, hell, you go right on being a helluva gentleman. I'd rather fuck her."

With a roar, Caleb charged toward Devin, lunged in the air. They both landed with a grunt.

* * * *

For a second time, Devin granted this man more than anyone prior, except perhaps Megan. That was the opportunity to actually hurt him, cause him physical harm.

First, he backed away from a gunfight and let Caleb live. This time, he permitted Caleb to release the deep-rooted aggression he harbored since the day they met. The punches didn't worry Devin none. Leaving his holster and knives on the small table in the bedroom, aware Pretty Boy didn't carry a firearm, he didn't expect his life to be in any real danger.

He blocked most of the blows with his elbows and forearms. A few found their way to his face, but even that was tougher than leather and withstood the pain.

Pretty Boy possessed muscle beneath that citified suit.

There was some real effort delivered behind each powerful strike which Devin hadn't fully expected, but found to his liking.

It didn't take too long for him to grow tired of being punched, kicked, jabbed, and prodded without returning a single blow in return.

Devin grabbed hold of Caleb's arms as the man started to jab a right, then a swift left. He twisted a leg over Caleb, immobilized the other man's legs. It required most of his strength to regain the upper hand. With a short grunt of considerable effort, he straddled Caleb and held his arms out to the sides.

"Is it out of your system so's we can really talk now?" Devin's grip tightened on Caleb's arms as he continued to squirm and kick.

"There's nothing to discuss with the likes of you," he bit back fiercely. With a sharp jerk forward, Caleb slammed his head into Devin's, busting his bottom lip.

"Shit, that hurt." Devin licked the blood dribbling down his chin. "If you're not careful, I might start to get mad."

"I'm past mad." Caleb kicked his legs up, then brought them down quickly. Devin was more than amazed to find himself tossed off in the process. Jumping to his feet, Caleb stood, fists raised in a ready stance.

Out of arms' reach, Devin rolled to his feet, held up both hands as if in submission. Caleb wasn't even winded, he noted. A damn good sign.

"Dammit, I'm not here to fight you." Devin moved his voice up an octave, took on an assertive tone.

"Only fight with your weapons," Caleb muttered angrily, swept a glance of disgust up and down his rival. "Shoot unarmed men, eh?"

Devin couldn't help but grin. The man had balls, proof he had made the right decision.

"Now, I wouldn't want to harm Megan's future husband," Devin admitted seriously as he watched the shock registering on Caleb's face.

Chapter 21

"Why are we headed toward the river?" Megan asked out of innocent curiosity as Devin led the wagon down the path that led to river, away from the ranch.

The thoughts running through his mind were anything but innocent.

"Do you trust me, Megan?"

"Seeing how you're not a gentleman of your word, I don't believe I do," she replied teasingly, reminding him of the promise he made when they first met.

Casting a sidelong look, his eyes narrowed. Mischief lit her eyes, mingled with the glaze of arousal. He was already hot and hard for her. He wanted her desperately. Despite the intense ache, the need to possess her, he was just going to have to learn to live without her, learn to ignore that 'Take me—I'm yours' look in her eyes. "If what you're saying is true, then it's time for me to move on."

"Damn you, Devin Spawn, yes. Yes, I trust you, and yes, I love you." Her tone was heavy with exasperation. Hurt clouded her eyes.

He looked away. "Simple yes or no would've done." He hated when she tossed that four-letter word around so easily, while those "soap words" coming out of her pretty, dainty little mouth with ease pleased him greatly. He liked when she used debauched crude words, asking, begging for pleasure, demanding what she wanted with regularity.

With his encouragement, suppressed urges were no longer, and moral pieties were liberated. She was now a woman with a very strong appetite for the pleasures of the flesh, including the most lewd and crude on the menu.

Today was the day.

He smothered a grin. "Then you'll do as I say."

"Don't I always?"

"That's my girl." He gave her that half-grin she seemed to like, the one that made her lick her lips, lift her face toward his as she awaited his kiss. His control was slipping. If she responded the way he expected, then he wouldn't deny her.

"Am I your girl?" Her voice was a sweet whisper, and her hazel eyes glittered in the sun with expectation, delight, and something else that didn't suit him.

He hesitated, and apparently, that didn't sit well with her. The curl of her smile faded.

"Depends," he finally responded in a dry voice as her gaze fell to a far away destination beyond the grasslands. "You wearing the dildo like I asked?"

For over a week, she had been following his instructions, preparing herself for him. She'd used the assortment of dildos he surprised her with one day. They ranged from small to large, but even the largest was nowhere near his size.

He instructed her to insert one every morning after he took the girls to school and leave it inside her ass until he was ready to take it out. As of yesterday, she'd worked her way up to the largest and trained her anal muscles to tighten around the device to keep it in place for hours.

Going about her business with her anus filled throughout the day drove her insane with desire. It heightened her awareness, sensitivity to touch, and every little movement of her body became so much more, a tortuous pleasure all its own. The dildo strengthened both her vaginal and anal muscles to such a degree that she could sit on him and milk his cock just by moving her inner muscles. He wouldn't have to do a thing—but then, his control always got the better of him, and he'd flip her over and go at it.

It was the same as when he'd bend her over wherever he found her and fuck her with the dildos. In the barn, the garden, kitchen counter, leaning against the hen house, up against the horse corral—it didn't matter where. He'd lift her skirt and have his wicked way with her. Never bringing her to climax until their morning chores were done, and they had the rest of the afternoon for a long, delicious fuck fest.

He'd taught her patience, a slow, drawn-out buildup, which amassed a heated, deliciously intense, mind-blowing climax that was worth the wait.

In a constant state of arousal, her every feminine nerve ending came to lascivious, decadent life. He knew her body had hummed, tingled all morning, anticipating what was coming. How intense her orgasms would be when he finally plunged his cock in her aching pussy and buried his fingers in the place considered taboo.

"The ride to school and back has been like sitting on your fingers the entire time. I can't take much more. I'm aching for you to fill me up. Why can't we go home?" Her voice was a desperate invitation for sex.

His cock throbbed, hardened into a painful ache at the image flashing before him. He couldn't wait to get to the river. Joggling the reins, he urged the horse into a speedier gait.

"Patience, Megan. You'll get a lot more. Today, every last painful, disappointing memory from your past will be erased. Any guilt or shame you were made to feel as a child for your God-given desires will be set free. No more hurting, Megan. Today, you start to feel alive again."

This from a man who never uttered those three letters—G-O-D. Damn, what was happening to him?

"Being with you makes me feel alive for the first time. I don't know what you're planning, but you're all that I need. Oh, Devin, I'm so hot and wet right now. You can take me right here on the road. I don't care who sees."

Casting her a quick glance, his steel-hard cock jerked in response to her impassioned proposal. Her body was shivering, no doubt consumed with desire.

Today was definitely the day.

"Since I returned, I've been nothing but honest with you," he ventured softly, painfully aware of the significance of his intent. He knew she harbored no suspicions. "While I'm here, I'm yours. Rest assured, I'll do whatever is necessary to keep you safe, even after I'm gone. On that, you have my word as a man..."

...*who cares for you.* He sighed, unable to utter those last few words. If he truly cared, would he be able to follow through on what was about to take place?

He turned his eyes forward, but he couldn't bring himself to look at her, to see the disappointment shadowing her eyes at the reminder of his eventual departure.

She wanted something from him. Something he couldn't give her.

His love. A home. Family. Safety. Security. An honest future. And all the damned hopes and dreams that went along with it. Everything he knew nothing about. What his kind wasn't entitled to. Didn't deserve.

The past was a wretched dark cloud. No presidential pardon was ever going to change that. The present was a fading existence, and his future he relived many times over at the end of double barrels through the men that fell at his feet. Three years ago, growing weary of commanding a bunch of worthless men, the carnage and injustice, he had climbed on Deuce and rode off. He'd lived in the vastness of the wilds, alone, far away from civilization, decent folk. Society didn't want his kind around, and he sympathized.

In cold blood, he had murdered sons, husbands, and fathers, robbed trains and stagecoaches, stolen horses and cattle. He'd burned homes and more. That was all he knew how to do, and he was damned good at it. The best. No remorse. No apologies. No excuses.

Death and destruction were part of his life.

It was in his blood. He could taste it. Feel it seeping through his veins from birth. A sinister need so corrupt and debauched, it deadened him until he was a hollow shell of a man on the inside.

Only a man with no heart could do what he was about to do.

* * * *

Megan's inquiry was met simply with "a surprise" as Devin led her to a secluded area not far from the river. Nestled into an alcove in the mountains, the only way to get to it was through a dense thicket of trees and overgrowth. The gentle sound of water rustling nearby, birds chirping a sweet melody, and the bristling of leaves in the slight breeze gave her a sense of calm security. However, the crackling of dry leaves heaped under their feet alluded to extreme privacy, an illicit rendezvous. The sunlight labored through the impenetrable canopy of branches. It provided a shadowy light, reminiscent of dusk, an ambiance of allure that tantalized her arousal.

Panic-stricken, she stopped in her tracks when she saw a noose dangling from a solid branch with a blanket spread out underneath. Her pulse raced. She looked up at him and asked nervously, "What's this, Devin?"

"Trust me, Megan." His voice was low, rumbled with intensity. "You know I'll never harm you. Do this for me." He placed a hand to the small of her back, tried to coax her forward.

Not that she was completely frightened. More like cautious, considering they were in the woods. Anyone could happen upon them. She didn't budge, wondered why since the hot throb of anticipation, submission, being dominated was building in her body.

"I know you better than you know yourself," he whispered, leaning down slightly, his breath heating her throat as she felt him move behind her. "I know what you need." Her body trembled as his hand moved over her hip to her mound. "What you crave." His fingers eased between her thighs, pushed into her burning cunt as far as the fabric allowed.

"Let me show you how to awaken those wanton desires." Her breathing rose as she parted her thighs slightly. His fingers stroking her soaked flesh, drenching the material as her body burned. "Satisfy every decadent urge you've kept buried so long." His other hand dipped below her neckline. "Make you scream out in pleasure so intense, it borders on pain."

She gasped and whimpered when he pinched one hard nipple, then the other. The thought of being restrained, fucking out in the open, aroused her, sent a gush of hot liquid between her thighs seeping through the material as both hands continued to probe, caress and stroke the flames of red-hot desire.

"Today, you're going to be fucked like never before." He pressed into her, letting her feel the heat of his erection against the curve of her back. She shimmied against him, moaning with pleasure. "In ways you never imagined."

They both knew if he wanted, he could tie her up without her approval. They weren't back at the ranch, and what he intended—exhibitionism and bondage—fed her newly uninhibited sexual need like never before. It had her body pulsating with lust, arousal so intense, her pussy hadn't stopped throbbing.

"Remove your dress." His voice was rough.

She practically pulled the buttons off her dress. Her chest was beating wildly. She felt his hand beneath the bodice as he rolled her nipple between his fingers.

Megan heard his deep groan, felt his cock jerk in his buckskins as she slid the dress off her shoulders. She looked down. Tanned, long fingers continued to caress the stiff bud as her dress caught on the hand between her thighs before he pulled his hand away. The dress fell to the ground in a brown muslin puddle.

A second later, he thrust two fingers deep inside her. She shrieked in pleasure, twisting and pushing against him. She needed him there by any means. He ground his hand into her cunt until she was on her tiptoes, panting with desperation.

"Come on, Megan," he growled as his fingers worked inside her pussy, gripping greedily. He eased her backward.

Feeling with her feet, she moved back until her toes were on the top arch of his moccasin clad feet, and her heels rested above his ankles. He held her in place as she wiggled her hips, and he pressed the bulk of his erection into the crevice of her rear.

"That's it, baby," he growled, his breath hot against her shoulder as his fingers moved inside her, and his thumb raked over her clit. His cock thrust against her from behind, harder and deeper as he drove her higher and higher while his other fingers teased, pinched, and pulled her aching nipple. "Come, Megan. Give it to me. Let me feel your pussy squeeze my fingers."

Hot, intense sensations invaded her body from both sides. She was panting, trembling, dying in his arms with need as the fiery flames built. She fought for breath as she threw her hands up and around his neck, holding on for dear life as she cried out. Her body tightened and her pussy started to spasm as the pleasure washed over her.

"That's my girl. Come for me. Let me have that sweet cream," he moaned, grinding his cock into her ass and thrusting his fingers deeper into her convulsing depths.

She felt the creamy release leave her body as she melted into the strength of thrusts.

"Oh, yeah, baby. That's it. Shit, Megan," he growled. "Why do you have to be so damned beautiful?" Grinding his aching cock into her back, he eased her back to earth. Both hands moved, and his splayed fingers spanned her entire waist.

"That's a bad thing?" she murmured softly, her body still humming as she leaned back into his erection, hot and hard beneath his buckskins.

"Hell, yes. I can't resist you."

She gave a throaty chuckle as he playfully spanked her on the derriere.

"Come here," he rasped through gritted teeth, leading her by the hand to where the short rope hung from a heavy, low tree limb of a large oak tree. The canopy was just high enough to sustain Devin's height, crowded enough for a morning of steaming hot, wild, reckless sex in seclusion.

"Devin, what if someone comes?" she gasped with a nervous excitement. Her heart felt ready to burst as she padded across the cool, crisp leaves without a stitch on, glancing through the thicket of trees.

He drew her hands overhead and tightened the noose around her wrists.

"I'll shoot all uninvited guests." His voice was quiet, deliberate as he his gaze met hers.

Staring up at him, she couldn't help the drawn-out sigh of longing that escaped. Potent, raw sexuality filled his expression. Hard-core determination emanated from his powerful frame. He was too damned sexy for words. Her poor body didn't stand a chance against all that muscled male virility. It ached for him. She was already soaked, prepared for whatever he pleased.

"Watch me, Megan," he ordered softly as he unbuttoned his shirt, directing her eyes to his burly chest. She licked her lips as he pulled it from the waistband. His tight nipples were hard, centered on well-defined pecs that heaved with each ragged breath. She ached to touch them, to feel them, suck them into her mouth. He tossed the shirt into the vicinity of where her discarded dress was bunched on the cool earth. "I know how much you like to watch."

She did.

He was an especially well-built specimen of pure unadulterated male sensuality at its absolute finest. She was unable to pull her eyes away from each rippling muscle in his arms, shoulders, and along his back as he bent over and pulled off one moccasin, then the next and added them to the growing pile of clothes.

"See what you do to me?"

Her gaze roamed upward as he stood to his full, formidable height, big hands on his hips, feet planted wide apart. She took it all in. He was naked from the waist up. Her restrained hands ached to touch his bronzed flesh. She felt a flutter deep in her stomach. Her gaze traveled downward. Her lips parted in an enthusiastic gasp of delight.

"Damn, Megan, you make me so hard, I lose control." His hands worked the buckle on his double holster. Her attention riveted to the bulge straining beneath his buckskins. The material was so softened from continued wear, the engorged head was clearly outlined, the thick length reaching up his belly. She swallowed hard as his cock jerked in response to her gaze. She wanted him in her mouth, buried deep in her pussy, thrusting inside her, knowing the pleasure he could give her. He dropped his holster and the long-bladed Bowie knife sheathed behind his right six-shooter off to the side, within easy reach. "Are you as ready as I am?"

"Oh, yes. I've been ready all morning," she panted, licking her lips as they twitched in anticipation. Her breath came more rapidly, eager to see the part of him that drove her mad with desire. "Show me, Devin. I want to see how hard you are."

"Show *me*, Megan," he responded. A wicked smile curled his lips as his darkened silvery eyes blazed with sinful intent. She watched his gaze drop between her thighs. Knowing what he wanted, she parted them, Then arched her hips to allow him a clear view of his pussy. It was hot, wet, and throbbing for him. It belonged to him, only him. Whenever he wanted. However he wanted.

"Oh, yeah, Megan," he whispered, quickly unlacing his buckskins. She followed his eyes as they roamed over her exposed body, then focused on her cunt. She felt her breasts swell, nipples tighten, ache for his touch. Her body trembled with need as she spread her thighs further. She wiggled her hips as she felt her knees buckle under his intimate inspection. "Look at those pretty lips, swollen and red, so shiny with your cream. Damn, Megan, just looking at you is about to make me come in my pants," he said heatedly, his thumbs hooking on his waistband, yanking down his buckskins.

She moaned when his engorged cock sprang free.

Kicking out of his buckskins, he quickly tossed them aside and stood completely naked before her. His eyes never left hers. The depth of his emotions took her breath away. "Whatever happened before, it's all yours now, Megan. It wants no one but you," he whispered, holding the huge cock sticking straight out from his body from its lush nest of dark curls with one while stroking it eagerly with the other.

"Hurry, Devin." Her pussy was already drenched when she thought about what he was going to do. Hearing his declaration warmed her heart and touched her soul. It was as close to saying he loved her as possible. It was all she needed to hear. More than she ever hoped for.

"I need you so bad, I can taste it. I can taste your sweet pussy on my tongue." He knelt before her parted legs. His hands smoothed up her trembling thighs.

"Oh, God, yes," she panted as he ran a finger gently over the outer lips. Her pussy clenched and squeezed out more juices down her thighs.

"Like that?"

She whimpered in response, her body swaying forward, encouraging his touch.

"You look so willing. *Are* you willing, Megan, for *anything?*" He looked up at her. His finger circled the entrance of her body, slow and easy.

"Yes. Anything," she breathed, feeling helpless against his tormenting pleasure. She looked down into his eyes, dark and bewitching like pure, mortal sin in glossy charcoal.

"Tell me what you want."

"Devin, please." Spreading her feet farther apart, she arched her hips toward his face. Her body trembled, preparing itself for his lips and that devilishly long, pointed tongue deep inside her vagina, right where she wanted it.

"Please, what?" His voice sounded strangled, desperate as he looked up at her. His thumbs held her quivering flesh apart. She felt the heat of his breath whisper over the folds of her skin.

"Suck me...please," she begged on a breathy moan. "Make me come."

"Gladly." Draping her legs over his shoulders, he cupped her ass as he drove his tongue greedily into her hot cunt. She was gasping, crying out as he teased and licked the moist flesh expertly. He thrust inside the hot recess of her body, feasting on her essence. Her body was on fire, bucking against his mouth.

Constantly, his tongue lapped along the groove of the labia and he thrust the tip inside the lips along the groove around her clit, careful to avoid direct contact, driving her arousal perilously close to the edge. Her whole body shook, desperate for release.

In the far corner of her mind, she knew the whimpers slicing through the serene wooded air were her own. So what if she scared the animals? Let the squirrels find their nuts elsewhere. Hers were right between his legs. She shoved her aching pussy into the heat of his mouth. She shivered each time he came perilously close to that sensitive nub, only to avoid it. He exerted his control over her senses, her release, her body. She needed something, or else she would die, just die from the unending, mindless pleasure.

"Please, suck it. Suck my clit," she begged, feeling every nerve ending shoot currents of fire to her vagina as his tongue slid through the folds of her pussy. The juices traveled down her thighs, forming faster than he could suck them as the slurping, suckling sounds of a hungry man's feast echoed around them.

"I can't take it any longer. Make me come," she begged as he sucked the inner lips into his mouth. His tongue ran along the slit as the burning ache intensified. He probed, teased, tortured the sensitive tissue skillfully, just enough, always just enough to bring her close. Damn him. What was he doing, torturing her with pleasure?

She cried out as her knees buckled on his shoulders when he applied gentle pressure to the dildo buried in her ass. Her thighs clenched around his head, and her upper body fell back, held up by the rope around her wrists.

Her body was on fire as the mindless, relentless sensation raced through her body. Begging, trembling for release, she tried to shift her hips and grind her clit against his tongue when she caught sight of a movement in the trees.

"Devin," she breathed, eyes flaring wide, unsure if it was man or beast. Her body stiffened atop his shoulders. Her pulsed raced in alarm.

His hot tongue thrusting down her vagina was his reply. She bit down on her lip, fighting the continuous delirium that pierced her senses.

"Oh, my God," she shrieked as Caleb came into view. He made his way through the dense trees, heading straight for them.

She felt her body flush with the heat of embarrassment. Caleb couldn't see her like this. What would he think or her? What would he do? What would Devin do? Oh, no. No. No. No. It couldn't be. Not him of all people. Not like this.

She tried to jump off Devin's shoulders, as she fought back tears of shame, dread, humiliation, and utter mortification. His arms were firmly planted atop her thighs, and his grip tightened on her buttocks. Her heart sank.

I'll shoot all uninvited guests.

A suffocating heart-stopping fear gripped her entire being. Caleb was a dead man.

Arms tied, she was entirely at Devin's mercy. His mouth wasn't loosening its hold and his tongue plunged deep inside her pussy. She couldn't run and hide, or even attempt to cover herself.

Shaking her head frantically, she motioned Caleb to stay to away, believing if she shouted a warning, Devin, who was unaware at the moment, would be alerted to his presence.

Their eyes locked as Caleb stepped out of the trees into the confinement of the small alcove. The horror, shame and embarrassment she felt was soon replaced by absolute bewilderment and extreme astonishment as she read the inexplicable sexual arousal in his deep blue eyes.

She recognized that look. She'd seen it often enough just before Devin lifted her skirt and fucked her. The shock of his reaction stirred her blood.

As if she required confirmation, her gaze lowered. Caleb's cock was hard, strained against the front of his well-cut trousers. This wasn't what she expected—not from Caleb. How could he abide another man grinding his face into her pussy, eating her like she was his last meal? It confused her even more. But her body possessed a carnal urge all its own. She felt a flood of moisture seep into Devin's mouth and her vagina throbbed against his lips.

Caleb wasn't taken aback or outraged. He was taking pleasure in what Devin was doing to her. Lust blazed clearly in his eyes, as if he wanted to be between her thighs. He wanted to be next. The wanton thought made her sigh deeply as a surge of sexual awareness coursed through her veins.

As Caleb neared, Devin finally released her. The sudden brush of cool air on her flesh drew a quick intake of breath from her. Disappointment at the loss made her momentarily forget the distress of the situation as her feet touched the blanket.

"Our invited guest has arrived," Devin announced, licking her juices from his slick lips. She felt her entire body burn, flush an embarrassing shade of red. Straightening, Devin turned her to face Caleb, his hands constantly caressing her body.

Filled with questions, heart beating wildly against her ribs, Megan could only gape at Devin. She could form no words or discernable thoughts. His hands roamed over breasts, down her belly, over the curve of her hips, and along the slope of her back, again and again.

"He's here for you, Megan," Devin said softly.

She turned her attention back to Caleb, who stood a foot in front of her. The lust radiating off him was apparent. Love also glowed in his sweet, tender gaze. He was gorgeous. Sometimes, she thought him too good-looking for a man. And he loved her, and part of her would always love him. But why? Why was he here?

"He's loved you since you were kids. Remember how you used to touch each other?" One of Devin's hands found its way to her vagina. His fingers carefully parted the outer folds.

Moaning softly, she closed her eyes when he slid a finger inside her body.

There wasn't a doubt Caleb watched Devin's finger move in and out of her pussy, mimicking the way Caleb used to touch her when they were young teenagers. She could hear the catch in his breath, could almost feel the heat of his body on hers.

"He's the first one to ever kiss your sweet lips and caress your tender breasts," Devin whispered softly. His other hand cupped a breast and his fingers rolled over the hard nipple, causing her moan with need—for what? Caleb? "First to touch your virginal pussy. And you were the first to touch his cock."

Sighing, she licked her lips. She remembered their innocent touches, the warm friction as they rubbed their bodies together. She recalled them holding each other as they kissed in the warm sunlight, lying in the grass after their afternoon swim.

"Megan," Caleb said, "say the word and I'll leave. You'll never see me again."

She opened her eyes slowly and felt her heart shatter. A deep longing in his eyes crushed her spirit, as if he, too, relived the bittersweet memories Devin evoked. The intensity in his blue depths, desperate, scorching. The truth of his words struck her to her very core. He'd walk away, never to return. He'd leave for Boston as he planned. She'd never see her beloved Caleb again. All it would take was a single word, yes or no. Nod or shake.

"Believe that I'll always love you regardless," Caleb said.

"It's up to you, Megan." Devin spoke encouragingly as his finger continued the undemanding in-and-out motion, just as she showed him how Caleb used to touch her, enough to arouse, but not satisfy. Enough to drive her higher.

Him? Which him? Caleb? Devin? Oh dear, Lord, what was he asking?

"If he leaves," Devin continued, "you'll always wonder what could have been. The added pleasure of two pairs of hands caressing you. Two mouths kissing you, and two cocks fucking you."

Megan knew the growing wetness coating his finger told him the idea of having them both excited her tremendously. Her rapid breathing only confirmed it further.

"Caleb looking at your naked body excites you, doesn't it, Megan?"

She swallowed hard. Watched in amazement as Caleb's gaze caressed her body openly, as if he was already making love to her with his eyes. It made her knees weak and her heart swell. Her blood rushed to her throbbing cunt, and arousal churned like never before.

"Answer me, Megan. The idea of him fucking you is making you so wet. My whole hand is covered with your cream."

Struggling for her next breath, she couldn't bring herself to admit the idea both aroused and fascinated her. She didn't have to choose either one. The idea should have horrified her, but strangely, it didn't. Both would take turns satisfying her pussy with their cocks, giving her pleasure. If only she could throw caution to the wind, find the words to speak and tell them what she wanted.

"You want him, Megan. You've always wanted him." Devin's deep voice was suggestive, pure temptation to her weakened senses as he added another finger. The double thickness tore a whimper from her throat. Her hips instinctively rocked against his hand. "Tell him how you'd rather have his cock filling your pussy than my fingers."

Just as she fought to suppress the moan that escaped, the lust consuming her was too much to deny. Meeting Caleb's gaze, she knew her eyes were flaming with desire, as were his. There was no jealously in his expression, only a savage intensity, dark lust glowing hotly. His breathing was harsh, and she knew he wanted her. She knew that he was willing to share her with Devin. The unbridled arousal in his dark gaze drew her eyes downward. His cock jerked, throbbed against the loose black material, as though it was trying to get at her.

She exhaled harshly as the rage of anticipation washed over her, unlike ever before. Her body softened against Devin's. She relinquished total control to him, as the thought of being taken by both men flooded her senses with overwhelming need, longing and flashes of desire.

"Show him what you've deprived him of all these years. What you're so eager to give him now." Standing behind her, he moved his hands to her hips, gently indicating what he meant.

Parting her legs slightly, she closed her eyes and arched her back. She pushed her breasts toward him, aware the mounds of flesh were swollen with need, the nipples tender, hard buds aching for the touch of her lovers.

"That's my girl," Devin whispered softly. "A little more, so Caleb can get a good look at how wet and ready you are for him." Devin's hands cupped her breasts, rolling the nipples between his fingers.

She struggled for breath, heard Caleb moan his consensus. He was staring—of that she was sure as her thighs parted more. She thrust her hips upwards, allowing him a clear view of her wide-open cunt as it throbbed for him.

She whimpered when Caleb ran a finger along her drenched labia, felt him whirl the tip in the moisture gathered between the creases. She kept her eyes closed while Devin kneaded her breasts. She moaned and propelled her pussy against Caleb's hand. Her body shuddered, and she cried out when his finger gently stroked the hood shielding her engorged nub.

No longer frightened, she was too aware of the potent lust emanating from her two handsome lovers. She couldn't deny she wanted them both. She pushed aside any thoughts of impropriety as her body burned with a depraved desire she never believed possible.

She moaned at the temporary loss when Caleb moved away.

"Open your eyes, Megan," Devin ordered, his voice low, tight with arousal. Drawing her eyes open, she watched as he shifted her body slightly in Caleb's direction. Caleb pulled off his jacket and tie as he moved toward the pile of clothes they'd started earlier. "He's a grown man now with needs. And he needs you, just like I need you."

Her heart pounded against her ribs as she watched Caleb undress. He shrugged out of his vest and shirt, revealing just how much he had grown underneath.

"Devin," she gasped from the sexual tingles, searing heat racing to the growing ache between her thighs. Was it wrong to be this aroused by the sight of another man while being held by the one she loved?

What was she thinking? Caleb wasn't just another man. She'd loved him for years.

Straightening her, Devin leaned down and planted kisses along the curve of her throat, whispering softly, assuredly. "There's nothing to be afraid of, Megan. I'm right here. Let Caleb make love to you. That's all I ask."

"Why?" she barely whispered. The single question floated in her mind.

"He loves you, Megan. Let us erase the memories of your past."

Her appreciative eyes never left the magnificently naked male body walking toward her with an assured confidence. Broad shoulders, lean waist, and narrow hips. A body packed with hard muscle. The light dusting of curly blond hair on his chest, trailing to a narrow path down his rippled stomach to an impressively large, stiff cock that was parallel to his stomach. Long and thick, topped with a swollen red mushroom-shaped head. Though a few inches shy of Devin's twelve, Caleb was almost as thick and just as tempting.

A shocking bolt of tormenting need coursed through her body like an electrifying blaze of lightning as her pussy trembled and gushed.

She wanted to lick him head to toe.

* * * *

Caleb took a deep, rough breath.

He couldn't believe what was happening. Megan had actually accepted him. She'd agreed to be fucked by two men at once. If she agreed to that, what else would she consent to? A proposal?

"I'm not a boy any longer." Caleb smiled as he stopped in front of her. He noticed the curious look on her face as he handed a vial of lubricating oil to Devin, then dropped the pouch he brought filled with contraceptive sponges next to Devin's gun belt.

"So I see," she breathed as her eyes drifted downward.

"And I've learned a few tricks." He was mesmerized by her reaction to his nakedness. Her face flushed with sexual desire. Her pupils dilated, nearly black, as the tip of her pink tongue licked her lips sensuously. She was probably unaware of how hard she was staring or how tempting she looked, tied up and helpless, radiating passion. He felt his cock beating like a drum against his belly.

"I can't wait," she murmured breathlessly.

"You won't have to," he said, drifting one hand to a knotted tip on her swollen breast as her chest rose sharply before his eyes. His other hand moved between her thighs, massaging the crease, so wet and slick. Her body shivered in need.

"You're even more beautiful than I remember." He leaned down and softly kissed the gentle curve of her shoulder, and she trembled against him.

She moaned as his finger lingered at the entrance to her inner moist flesh. Obviously, his teasing caress was slowly driving her mad with desire. He could feel her insides throbbing hard, aching to be filled. Megan wanted him, his cock. She wanted them both. She was hot, wet, and ready. The thought made his body shake with an agonizing hunger, a raging desire to plunge deep into her wetness and keep thrusting until she screamed out his name as he brought her to the climax she craved.

"I'm not a girl any longer." Her voice was husky with arousal and her heavy-lidded gaze was clouded with desire. She was tempting him, provoking him, waiting for him to take what she was offered.

"So I see." Lowering his head, his tongue lapped and swirled at the pebble hard nipple as his hand continued teasing her other nipple, and his finger pushed inside the soaked depths of her tight pussy. He began a slow and steady thrusting motion. He heard her panting at the intoxicating triple sensations he inflicted upon her.

"I'm ready whenever you are." Devin smiled knowingly at Caleb when he finally lifted his mouth off Megan's sweet breast several moment later. The nipple, now a rosy red, glistened with his saliva.

"After I take out the dildo, I'm going to fuck your ass, and Caleb is going to fuck your pussy." Devin's voice was low, strained as he kissed and nipped the slope of her shoulder with his teeth.

Her lust-filled moan surprised him, made his temperature rise and his pulse soar. Megan liked a touch of pain with her pleasure, apparently.

"Devin," she whimpered. Caleb watched her body stiffen as Devin steadied her slender hips, coaxing her in a low, hushed whisper. "Relax, Megan. It will be easier."

"It's inside her now?" Caleb asked excitedly, moving behind her. "What an incredible sight," he added, his hand gently caressing her rounded cheeks. His eyes glazed over, and he stared in awe at the end of the ivory dildo lodged completely inside her anus. The thought of her muscles tightly gripping his flesh caused his cock to jerk.

"Take it out," Devin generously offered, as if he understood and shared the need to possess her, to hold claim over her body and bring her joy and pleasure.

Megan's entire body shuddered as Caleb slowly pulled the eight-inch dildo out. Devin had confided he needed to be the first to fuck her virgin hole before he left. After he was gone, Megan would be Caleb's. Seeing to her welfare, he decided to assist in preparing her. Taking her dainty size and frailty into consideration, if Megan was to survive anal sex, more than fingers were required. Thus, he'd lent Devin his souvenir collection of dildos.

In the beginning, it appalled him to learn Devin planned to sodomize Megan like an untamed animal. But each day, Devin stopped by his office before picking up the girls from school. He'd describe her sexual progress in graphic detail. Positions. Quantity of fingers. Which dildo. Climaxes. Screams. Everything. As though he, too, was being prepared. It worked. He anxiously awaited today's arrival. He wanted Megan. Wanted her sweet pussy and her tight ass. He was dying to take her in every way a man could possibly take a woman.

Her body swayed as the first two inches appeared, and Caleb suddenly thrust one inch back in. Megan gasped, her legs noticeably shaking.

Devin braced her swaying hips, his eyes riveted to the sight between her pale cheeks as Caleb continued to slowly fuck her with the dildo, causing her to cry out with pleasure and pant for breath. He continued to pull two inches out, then returned one inch slowly until it was completely free, and she cried out in protest as he momentarily left her.

Discarding the dildo, he started to bend down to pick up the pouch.

"What the hell is that?" Caleb shouted, astonished by the size of Devin's excessively large penis, glistening with lubricant. Devin held it perched over her ass he smoothed over her skin, thumb eagerly stroking the crease as if he couldn't wait.

Megan jerk around, her eyes wide, as if not knowing what to expect behind her.

"Look's who talking. That's no twig." Devin chuckled dimly.

"It's no damn tree trunk, either." Shaking his head, he glanced at the tiny hole between Megan's trim hips, then the heavy stump protruding from Devin's groin, and wondered how she managed to walk straight.

"Boys, if someone doesn't fuck me soon," she warned, her voice hot with lust, "I'm going to scream bloody murder."

They looked at each other.

"You heard the lady," they said in unison, moving into action without hesitation.

Retrieving a sponge from the pouch, Caleb stood between Megan's parted thighs. Devin supported them on his forearms, lifting her honey-coated pussy to their waist level.

"What precautions have you been using?"

"Stop being such a doctor and fuck me," she shamelessly ordered, voice tight with need.

"Patience, love. We have all afternoon." Caleb parted her vagina and pushed the sponge through the tiny opening. Aware Devin looked over her shoulder as Caleb's fingers and sponge disappeared into her tight channel, her slick flesh clenching around his fingers. He could see Devin's grip tighten as she rocked and moaned in his arms. "We can't have you heavy with child."

"Megan just wants to be fucked," Devin growled anxiously as he passed her to Caleb's awaiting arms. "She loves hard cock. Isn't that right, baby?"

Wrapping her legs around his hips, Caleb positioned her hot wetness against his cock. There was a sudden flash of shame in her eyes at Devin's heated charge, but everything about her dazed expression told him it was true. Her burgeoning flagrant scent engulfed him. The heated liquid seeping from her pussy dripped down the length of his erection, filled him with a sudden urgency.

"Kiss me, Meg," Caleb demanded gently. He needed to see love shining brightly in her eyes, to know she wanted him, needed him. That it wasn't lust, but love consuming the two of them. Needed to feel it and taste it. To believe it.

She looked up at him and parted her lips, enticing him.

She was a woman in love. He could see it glowing in her hazel depths for all the world to see, clear as day. She wanted him. After all these years, Megan still wanted him. Megan Adams still loved him.

His lips covered hers. He pulled her body tightly against his, unable to resist the ache a moment longer. He kissed her like a starving man ending a ten-year fast, as if tasting her for the first time. Touching her silky skin, holding her smooth little body in his arms, the heat of her drenched flesh soaked his cock as she dug her heels into his back.

He felt her shudder against him. Her sweet tongue mingled with his in a highly erotic embrace that had them each moaning in bliss. Her slick release of desire coated his cock as she ground her flesh into his. He pushed back, rotating his hips, rasping her clit with his hardness. She shuddered in his arms, which caused him to groan in her mouth. Deepening the kiss, his tongue devoured her, mouth staking his claim on her heart.

His hands ran down her back, spreading her rounded cheeks, baring that tender little hole.

As soon as he felt the tremors radiating through her body and her slick flesh throbbing against his cock, he knew she felt Devin's erection start to stretch the tight muscles of her anus.

* * * *

Devin grinned, aware Caleb was in for a surprise. Megan was far different from the innocent girl he probably remembered from years ago.

He stared at the pink little bud as he gripped his cock, solid and hard, pulsating against the narrow opening as he began to push through, accepting the tip of his cock. Caleb's long fingers were dark against the soft, pale skin pulled apart, the tiny entrance open for him. His body shook with sexual need, to take her until there was nothing left to take.

"Devin, you're too big," she shrieked, and he stilled, not wanting to tear her apart with his raging, out-of-control desires.

Megan, you took my four fingers. Remember?" She nodded, her body trembling in Caleb's arms. "Remember how I parted them inside you? That sensation of fullness? You were screaming, you loved it so much."

"Ahhhhh," she cried out, and he assumed she remembered rocking on his hand, panting, screaming, begging him to use his cock, then going off like a wagon load of gunpowder barreling over a mountain until she fainted in a spent heap.

"You can take me, baby." He touched where their flesh joined, the pink skin around his thickness. "Give this one thing to me." His voice sounded desperate, needy even to him. "I've got to have you." As if he couldn't wait any longer, he inched deeper between her firm, pale mounds as she whimpered softly. "I've got to have this." The one thing he could lay claim to. Say was truly his. That he would be her first. It would bind them together forever. If only in this one way. The only way.

His cock was aching, hard, thicker and larger than any of the dildos he fucked her with over the past week. He could feel her anus opening hesitantly as he worked the head inside her with an unending, steady pressure. In spite of his measures, the entrance was still too tight. He struggled, groaning against the clenching little hole.

Megan cried out. Her body stiffened at the invasion, feeling his massive cock tunneling into her. Helpless to his power, she whimpered against Caleb's shoulder as the pleasure and pinch of pain mixed and mingled. The torrid sensations washed over her, took hold of her senses.

"Relax, Megan," Devin growled, his voice tense, rough with desire. He was struggling to keep control. She had seen what happens when the suppressed fury, the raging need to possess was unleashed. She was aware of the wild, uncontrollable sexual intensity that pushed him over the carnal edge.

She suddenly became frightened. Her body bucked in their arms. "It hurts," she screamed as the first ring of tight muscles submitted willingly. Even so, she protested, twisting furiously. She jerked forward, away from his savage possession. "I can't take you both. Not like this."

"Concentrate. Give yourself over to it. Feel the sensation. Let it happen," Devin coaxed between rasping groans as his fingers dug into her hips. Ignoring her protests, he held her still. His cock sank deeper until she felt the flared head push its way inside her body. Her lusty cries faded around them.

"Meg, you want this," Caleb whispered softly. He rained kisses along her cheek, down her neck and shoulders as he brushed her hair aside. "It's just nerves, my love. Your flesh is malleable. It'll stretch for both of us."

Both of them! Could she really do this? Tightly wedged between their muscled bodies, their sexual heat and their arousing manly scent consumed her.

"Let us give you what you need," Caleb whispered over her increasing moans. Her muscles continued to stretch, surrender as she felt the thick shaft moving inside her, thrusting in and out by small degrees, slow and sure. "Let us bring you pleasure. Let us love you."

Love. They both loved her. "Oh, yes," she moaned, opening her heavy-lidded eyes as she forced her body to relax.

Gasping now, she gave in to the incredible sensation. Imagining the exquisite pleasure to come, she pushed back on the thick intruder burning her with pain and filling her with a fiery excitement. The intense, seductive arousal was so powerful, it drove her need like never before. Her body responded, opening, accepting, parting for the raging need to be dominated, possessed by them both.

"Fuck yes, Megan, that's my girl," Devin groaned as the head of his penis disappeared.

Her muscles gripped him inside the hot inferno of her ass.

"Let me have that ass," Devin said.

She cried out, her head falling back as he buried two more inches inside the tight channel stretching around him. So thick, so hard, so deep and so incredibly tight, she was burning alive.

"Take me, baby." His voice was dark, tortured as he continued to stretch her anal muscles impossibly wide.

She felt at least half of his thick, bulky cock buried in her. She trembled uncontrollably and fought to breathe. There was more to come—much, much more.

"Feel it hot inside you. Hard just for you. Take it all," Devin growled, withdrawing slowly. He pushed in again easily, thick inch by solid inch. Then, as if yielding to his innate sexual desire, he rocked against her, and his strokes steadily increased. "Ease that hole. Let me fuck your ass."

"It burns." Her hips bucked feverishly against Caleb. She rubbed her clit over the heat of his hard cock pressed between them as she felt each degree of Devin's thick shaft stretch her, pull her muscles taut, eventually giving way to the forbidden invasion.

His cock grew even harder inside her. He kept thrusting deeper and deeper, its length never ending. The pain was too hot, intense, searing her, tearing her apart. She wasn't ready. Not for this. She was dying, no longer able to take such pleasure.

"You're killing me," she cried out.

Devin gripped her hips as Caleb pulled back slightly and thrust three long fingers into her swollen cunt. She screamed as the flow of pleasure rippled from her core to every pulsating nerve ending in her body. The forceful shock pushed her further back, lodging his cock deeper in the tight channel.

Devin withdrew slightly, then drove in a little more as she continued to cry out.

Together, as though they did this often, the two men worked her body. Caleb's fingers harshly thrust into her pussy as he squeezed her clit. The biting stab of pain forced her back on Devin's cock as he continued to thrust in and out, expanding the tiny back hole with his incredible thickness.

They both encouraged her, murmuring crude, lewd words that Devin knew spiraled her wantonness out of control, telling her how pleasurably satisfying it was going to feel with two dicks—one fucking her cunt, and the other fucking her ass.

Megan could only scream at the illicit eroticism of it all. It was painful, arousing and shocking. She was shocked at how much she was enjoying the sharp bite of pain each time Caleb squeezed her tender, swollen clit. Did Devin tell him how much she enjoyed being taken roughly? She didn't care if he knew. Not anymore. Her body pressed between two massive walls of pure animal lust, dominating, possessing her completely, wanted to be fucked. All she could do was surrender to her own depraved hunger, her thirst for more. For all they had to give.

"Oh, Devin," she panted as he continued his stabbing thrusts, burying his enormous length in her ass.

"Scream, baby. Let it out," he shouted, as his hand smoothed over her ass, down to what was left of his buried cock protruding from her tight hole.

She felt his fingers, trembling with his lust when they raked over their joined flesh, as if gauging her ability to accept the last few inches of his beefy stalk, the thickest portion yet to enter her. The wide, hard base that rose from his groin, a challenging fantastical creature of flesh and blood, manly desires of the most carnal, sinful variety.

"Fuck me, Devin. Give it all to me," she shouted, driven half-mad, unable to take his short, cautious thrusts any longer. She wanted to feel the pleasure she knew his large cock could bring. "I want your cock filling my ass."

Devin let out an animalistic howl when he quickly pulled out, then savagely impaled her to the hilt. She barely noticed Caleb as he almost lost his balance, caught off guard by Devin's action.

With one deep, penetrating thrust, he claimed her ass. Her screams of pain and pleasure ricocheted off the mountains and down the river.

Caleb wasted no time, positioning his cock at her front entrance. Devin's cock was so engorged, it all but filled both channels.

"Dammit, there's no room," Caleb groaned. His voice rose with lust. His face was a tortured grimace as his straining cocked lodged against her hot, drenched vagina, unable to penetrate the blocked entrance.

"Caleb, hurry. I want feel your cock inside me." Leaning back on Devin's chest, she rested her head on his shoulder and she whimpered at the sensation of Devin's long, thick cock easing out of her tight grip. Her muscles clenched around the still buried head and fought to keep him inside. Unable to control her own depraved desires and protesting the sudden disappointing emptiness, she pushed back and whimpered as her ass swallowed half his swollen erection.

"Easy, baby," Devin growled. She reveled in knowing he was desperate to be buried between her forbidden entrance when he withdrew, but kept the tip wedged snugly between her cheeks.

Caleb slammed into her soaked cunt, hard and deep with a single, powerful thrust. His roaring groan mirrored her cries as she bolted off Devin's chest. Her cries turned into primitive screams of intense arousal and torturous pleasure as Devin's cock rammed back into her, his swollen sac slapping against the bottom of her rear cheeks.

Megan came, that quickly. She shuddered with the intensity of her climax. A part of her was shocked at how she allowed herself to take two men at once. Yet, she burned, inside and out, hungry, starving to satisfy the dark arousal tormenting her with an unbridled lust as the fiery sensations ripped through her.

Both men stilled as the overwhelming vibrations of her pussy walls spiraling in a heated frenzy as her orgasmic burst washed over them. They were both breathing hard, fast and rough, as her tight-fisted inner walls contracted and gripped their cocks erotically with each spasm. Hot cream coated their imbedded flesh.

"Slow." Devin's voice was rough with lust, and he could only get one word out. His body shook with need as the convulsions slowly faded. Her body trembled and her breathing became labored as she felt them there. One buried deep in her pussy, and the other compressed in her tight chamber.

Caleb followed Devin's request, and they both began slow, rhythmic thrusts, letting her get used to the burning sensation of being filled completely by over twenty inches of pure, heated manly flesh.

Lost in her own desperate need, she was vaguely aware of their dark growls of satisfaction, knowing their huge cocks were separated by a thin wall. Hard and throbbing, thrusting against each other in the tight confines of her hips. She didn't move. She didn't have to. The pleasure was so decadent, so hot, and so fucking erotic, her body was aflame with passion, savoring the next climax as she felt it build deep in her womb.

"So tight, Megan," Caleb panted through ragged breaths. "Lord, your pussy is burning me alive."

"She's fucking fantastic," Devin rasped with pure, male sexual pride. "Made for pleasure."

She savored the pleasure as it radiated through her, building a burning ecstasy, a fire so deep, she was melting between them. Two men she loved, totally filling her, indulging her desires, making her whole.

"Oh, yes," she begged as they each drove into her flesh with long, luxurious strokes, again and again. "Don't stop. Don't ever stop fucking me."

Glistening with sweat, her body was perched between theirs, held up by Devin's forearms. Her heated words urged them on, and they began to plunge harder, deeper, faster, gliding her body sinuously between them with each surging thrust.

"Come for us, Megan," Devin groaned, his rasping breath hot against the damp skin along her back as he developed a rhythm all his own. With each powerful thrust, he lifted her off Caleb. Each withdrawal of his dick brought her full body weight down on Caleb's cock, driving her insane.

Gripping her breasts, Caleb squeezed the areolas forward, licking the hard tips as her body thrashed helplessly between theirs.

No longer able to scream, she struggled to breathe as each thrust grew more powerful. The intensity of each downward stroke against her clit when she fell on Caleb's cock shook her body violently. She could feel her orgasm building deep in her womb. She was so hot, so aroused, ready to erupt as the twin sensations washed away all trace of realism. Her focus centered on the all encompassing carnal ecstasy driving into her again and again.

"Oh, yes!" She barely managed to cry out as the intensification collided in a violent crash into oblivion, the maelstrom of sensations numbing reality, to all that was around her except the two glorious cocks still pumping into, spurting their own explosive releases deep inside her tight, stretched channels as her tumultuous orgasm went on and on. First Caleb came, then after a few more forceful thrusts, Devin followed. He held on longer, enjoying the fierce intensity as her inner walls clenched, spasmed, convulsed wildly around his flesh. Each man groaned her name and sang her praises as she milked the last drop of seed from their very cores.

Chapter 22

Megan moaned with disapproval minutes later. Her quivering muscles tightened to keep Caleb buried inside her body as she felt him withdraw from her satisfied nest. She felt boneless, resting her spent body against Devin's chest as he eased her legs from around Caleb's waist. Devin cradled her in his arms. Her eyes slowly opened in time to see Caleb's tight rear as he walked away, the sexual haziness still clouding her gaze. The man was gorgeous coming and going.

"Was it everything I promised?" Devin lips curled into a wicked grin, eyes dark and heavy-lidded.

"More," she whispered, smiling up at him. Her body still vibrated from the exquisite satisfaction.

"Good, because we're not finished with you yet."

She couldn't believe it was physically possible to want so badly. Her clit tingled, swelled, throbbed with anticipation, her pussy moistened with readiness, and her arousal escalated. This was just the beginning.

Caleb joined them, the bundle of clothes under one arm. Silently, she watched him as he stood in front of them. He was still hard. Reaching up, he used Devin's knife to cut the rope free just above her wrists, leaving her hands tied. She felt her cheeks turn hot as he gave her a knowing wink when he caught her staring at his cock.

Devin carried her toward the river, speaking softly, whispering how beautiful she was and the pleasure she brought them both. Caleb followed a few steps behind, toting their belongings.

With her cheek resting against the heat of his chest, she listened to the strong beat of his heart and his sweet words. He told her how they could satisfy her every fantasy, bring her countless pleasure. His soft, male voice stroked her, filling her with excitement and anticipation.

She hadn't even realized they reached the riverbank, that he carried her out to the middle of the river, until Devin lowered her into the cool water. She gasped as her legs entered the water. Her tingling body shivered on the outside and raged with a hot flame on the inside. The mildly flowing current reached just below her breasts. Her nipples hardened instantly as the ripples washed over her belly and legs.

"Remember how I found you, Megan?" Devin's whisper was a soft, seductive cue. "Floating on the water like a beautiful lily. Open, displaying the petal flower in the center. Inviting to touch."

The image of her attempt at masturbation flashed in front of her. In spite of the constant flow of water against her breasts, she could feel the flush of embarrassment burn her face down to her chest.

"There nothing to be ashamed of. It's what brought us together."

Caleb lifted her legs as Devin drew her back, resting her shoulders against his abdomen. His arms curled under her underarms as he rested his hands below her breasts.

She was burning up, trembling, gushing, thinking of what they could possibly do next.

"Float for me, Megan. Like you did that day." They stretched her body over the water at their waist level, allowing her to float as her head rested against Devin, just above the waterline.

Her eyes shifted to the bulbous head of Devin's still-hard erection as Caleb stood beside her and untied her wrists.

"Show me, Megan," Devin urged her once more as Caleb moved past her feet, granting her plenty of room to comply.

Spreading her legs wide, she relaxed her body and floated spread-eagle. She was aware as she did it that Caleb, standing at the opposite end, would see right between her thighs. A hot flare of arousal poured through her. She watched his eyes lower, turn a vivid shade of blue as he focused on the throbbing flesh, soaked with semen, begin to part.

"Yes, baby, that's how you did it." Devin voice was laced with lust. Megan glanced up at him.

Her long hair floated about her shoulders and brushed underneath her back, sending a shudder down her spine. She licked her lips and wondered if her hair tickled his balls or tantalized his cock as it whirled around Devin's groin.

Within the endless expanse of clear blue sky above, the spring sun warmed the top of her naked body. The cool water below chilled her backside while her nipples tightened painfully, yet did little to quench the raging fire of desire burning deep between her thighs.

"Tell us what or who you were thinking about that day, Megan," Caleb said.

Her eyes joined with Caleb's as he moved in the water, closer and closer between her legs. The small, rippling waves splashed gently against the moist flesh of her pussy, dripping with his seed. She ached for him still. Judging from his thick erection jerking above the water, he was in need also.

She'd heard among the woman at Jazelle's that cold water had a negative effect on the male anatomy, but apparently, the laws of nature didn't apply to these two hardened men.

Her eyes widened as Caleb cupped water in his hands and dribbled it over her belly. She quivered as the small droplets rolled off her heated flesh and collected in her navel. The look in his eyes was intoxicating as he gathered water in his hands again. The wet beads fell on her breasts and formed a puddle between the narrow cleft before it began a slow, chilly descent toward her ribcage, down to the concave of her tummy.

A shiver of awareness coursed through her as the heat of Caleb's palm touched her drenched skin. His hand glided over her abdomen, spreading the cool water over her quivering flesh with the tips of fingers. Her thighs tightened as he worked his way lower, his fingers combing through the sparse, matted curls over her mound. She felt her inner flesh melting as his palm covered her soaked flesh.

"Don't be afraid or ashamed to say what's on your mind," Devin encouraged her, his voice deep and thick with lust. Her rock-hard nipples must have been too hard for him to resist. Biting her lip, she watched his hands move straight to her breasts. She closed her eyes, moaning at the dual sensations of pleasure and pain as he teased, pinched, rolled, and pulled the stiff peaks between his fingers. "Tell us."

"Caleb," she whispered in desperation. A spark of desire raced through her body as he pressed his palm against her clit. Opening her eyes, she lost herself in his blue depths. She couldn't take her eyes off him. He seemed to be worshipping her with his gaze, admiring, craving, desiring her as he always did. This time, they could do something about it. "I was thinking of you."

* * * *

"Meg." The sound came out as a strained groan. Caleb had waited so long to hear those words. She longed for him. To hear she thought of him as she pleasured herself, after he tried to do just that so many times, only to have her deny him was beyond heart-wrenching. "You should have told me."

Caleb saw her expression change. She closed her eyes as if to hide her true emotions. He moved closer between her thighs, dying to hold her, To tell her everything would be all right. He would take care of her forever, if only she would let him. If only.

"Caleb, you're here now, partner." Devin's heated tone was suggestive. He snapped Caleb from the past and brought him to the present.

He stopped as he was about to reach for her. He read the approval in Devin's face and finally understood why he was here. Kneeling down in the waist-deep water, it reached just below his shoulders. He placed his hands on the velvet-soft skin of her upper thighs and lifted her. She buckled as her eyes snapped open. He leaned forward, inhaled her sweet, musky scent before he swept his tongue into her heated, drenched flesh with a lusty vigor, from her anus to her clit, up one way and down the other.

"Caleb" she panted as he stared up at her from between her thighs.

He parted her slick, hot flesh and licked the thick juice seeping from her body with the tip of his tongue.

Megan cried out, shivering and squirming in his grasp. He tightened his grip on her thighs, pushing them apart as he felt her trying to draw them together in need. Feasting on her sweet cream, he speared his tongue into her silken depths.

"Tell him what you want," Devin whispered, his own breathing rough, coming as fast as hers. "Let him know what you need."

Caleb drove his tongue deeper, lapping her rich nectar as it flowed from her body, waiting to hear what she would say. His eyes never left her face. She was beautiful in her pleasure—skin flushed, lips parted, breasts heaving, nipples plump between Devin's fingers as he tweaked them roughly.

"Ohhhh," she breathed, bearing down on the pull of his tongue. Her body arched toward their caresses. "Suck me. Make me come."

Caleb wanted to do that and more. Pulling back the hood over the swollen knot of nerves, he covered her clit with his mouth and sucked it hard. She cried out as lust claimed her. He felt her body tremble, stiffen, contract, gush, finally buckle as her orgasm crashed through her body. She crushed her pulsating flesh against his mouth, clamped her legs tightly over his shoulders as Devin's hands moved under her to keep her thrashing body above water.

Lord help him, Caleb couldn't get enough of her. Her body. Her skin. Her breasts. Her lips. The most intimate part of her was honey on his lips, hot to his touch, liquid on his mouth, full and ripe for the taking. Her release overflowed, and he hungered to lick, taste and swallow every drop. Pushing her thighs apart, he buried his mouth deep between the slick, swollen folds and his tongue plunged in the hot depths of her cunt.

Building yet another climax right behind the first, he continued to drive his tongue into her throbbing pussy as she whimpered and splashed in the water. Tasting his release mixed with her sweet essence heightened his lust as his cock bobbed beneath the water. Her heady scent of arousal filled his nostrils and surged his need to devour her.

With a single finger, he stroked the throbbing nub of delight. She came instantly, screaming toward the heavens. "Suck harder," she screamed over and over. Her body convulsed as the waves of hot, slick fluid poured out of her, and cool river water splashed over her.

Sucking, kissing, tasting, savoring her sweet cream, he brought her to one more climatic ride before they carried her out of the water. They laid her limp body over the blankets spread out in the grass that he had prepared earlier.

He stretched out on the blanket as Devin lifted her body, still pliable and filled with their release. Holding his cock steady, he aimed it toward the hole Devin loosened. Waited anxiously as Devin lowered her small, rounded ass over him. Using one hand, Caleb parted her cheeks and guided his cock into the small entrance.

"Push down on me, Megan," Caleb groaned, and she moaned as he felt her anal muscles open to receive his erection. He grimaced in agony as Devin eased her downward slowly.

Caleb could see the determination torturing Devin's face and dismissed the other emotions he saw. Concentrating on Megan, he felt her tremble as the engorged head of his cock was gripped tightly in her heated passage.

"Oh, God." Consumed with lust, forgoing slow, he pushed deep into the tight heat of her body, stretching the tiny back entrance once again as she cried out. He felt each ring of muscle give way as all nine inches disappeared into her hot recess as far as he could go. His voice was hoarse as he instructed her to lie back on top of his body. "You're so tight. A dream, Megan. Your sweet little ass is pure joy, a dream come true."

Without waiting for Devin, he started to thrust his hips up, plunging his rigid flesh in and out of her tightness. His hands covered her tender breasts, caressing and squeezing the hard nipples firmly until she writhed above him. Moving with slow, easy thrusts, he watched Devin curiously and listened to the continuous stream of her soft, passionate moans.

* * * *

Standing with his bare feet firmly planted on either side of their entwined legs, Devin looked down into her dark, heavy-lidded eyes, glazed with lust, a raw hunger that told him he had done his job well. Dainty, fragile Megan, a mere sliver of a woman, was ready for anything. Lifting her legs, he spread them obscenely wide. Dropping his gaze from the generous film of moisture coating her swollen, clandestine lips, he became transfixed by the sight of Caleb's big, reddish cock pumping slowly in her small ass. He didn't know if it was more erotic to watch Caleb fuck her or join in.

He joined in, but not before Devin brought her slender legs together and stared as the tiny hole stretched for Caleb's thick cock as it slid in and out. The thick juices seeped out of her swollen cunt, coating the wide shaft embedded between her pale cheeks, easing the passage into her tight channel. The sight made him want to ram deep inside the wet heat of her pussy, tear into her, ride her hard and long until she forgot Pretty Boy even existed.

She wasn't his, though. Megan could never be his. Not even in this lust-filled moment did he have any claim over her. There was only one thing he could do—take what he wanted and leave.

Motioning for Caleb to stop his thrusts, Devin tightened his hands on her ankles. Yanking her legs up and down vigorously, he churned her like soft butter. He slapped her pale ass against Caleb's groin repeatedly. Her body trembled above Caleb's as they both moaned and groaned, their eyes shut as the sensations washed over them. He swallowed tightly as Caleb's large hands dug into her tender breasts, the hardened, rosy peaks visible between his splayed fingers. Scowling, Devin felt his cock jerk in need, need for her tight, hot pussy.

Her cries turned into one long stream of wicked pleasure. No longer could he hold off.

Wrapping her legs around his waist, he positioned the throbbing tip of his hard-on at the front entrance. He rose over her, kissed her with a fiery passion that spoke volumes and thrusting his tongue greedily into the sweet cavern of her mouth.

Throwing her dainty arms around his neck in a desperate, needy embrace, she met his kiss with an urgency all her own that told him no matter what, she was his and his alone. Moaning with pleasure, her body arched against his. Drawing an arm around her waist, he pulled her tightly to his chest, breaking Caleb's hold. He felt the firmness of her breasts against his flesh, the pointed tips rasped against his skin.

In answer to her ravenous sexual appetite, he sank his engorged cock into her soaked, impossibly small pussy, made even smaller by Caleb's cock buried on the other side of the thin membrane separating the two narrow channels. A strangled cry left her throat as her body culminated with another orgasm. She panted and moaned into his mouth as he began a rhythm of powerful, long strokes, so deep and potent that he wanted, needed her to feel him all the way to her core. He thrust in and out of her spasming wetness, frantically, urgently with a forceful possession. Each luxurious, erotic movement brought her closer and told her what he never could.

Megan was sandwiched between their large bodies, her slender arms and legs wrapped around him as the suctioning sounds of naked flesh slick with river water slapping against naked flesh increased. His balls relentlessly smacked her quivering bottom. Their male groans of sinful arousal along with the racy scent of carnal lust and sweat filled the air, mixed with Megan's sweet moans and whimpers as he reared back and took what wasn't his over and over again.

He felt her body tighten yet again. He rocked against her, pounded into her body, driving her toward the edge and beyond. Over his lusty grunts, he barely heard the soft moans of pleasure pass through her lips as her release spilled over his cock, and her body rippled, shuddered, and undulated beneath his. When he exploded, somewhere in the midst as each hot spurt, he heard Caleb call out to Megan.

Devin was still hard. Lying on the same grassy spot where he first touched the sweet paradise between her thighs, the only piece of heaven he'd ever known, left him with an unquenchable need he had yet to completely satisfy. He lifted her off Caleb and laid her on her stomach, jerked her legs apart, and sank his cock, slick from their mingled cream, between her ass cheeks.

She cried out softly as she arched her buttocks upward and spread her legs wider.

"Oh, yes, Megan," he growled, thrusting harder, deeper and faster with a wild abandoned fury. "My cock in your ass, that's what you want. Fucking you hard."

* * * *

Clutching clumps of grass as her fingers dug into the cool, soft green carpet, Megan closed her eyes and let the sensations wash over her. She panted as the ache mounted deep in her womb. Squeezing her anal muscles around his hard, thick flesh, she pushed back to meet each unrelenting, glorious thrusts. She loved it. Loved his massive cock deep inside her body. Loved the way his strength dominated her, possessed her. Loved the man. She was his for the taking.

"Nooo," she managed to protest softly when she felt Devin shudder, his cock jerking and pumping inside her as hot spurts filled her already overflowing ass. She felt the thick, sticky liquid weeping down her thighs. But she was so close, the aching flesh between her thighs was empty, her clit throbbed, demanded more. "Not yet."

Reaching underneath, he stroked her clit, and she found what she needed, Soft cries of pleasure raked through the grass as she stretched out her chin over the plush green carpet, wallowing in the ecstasy racing in her body from head to toe.

As if he too was satisfied, with a deep, guttural growl, Devin crammed himself against her buttocks. He held himself there as he spilled his hot seed. A tiny gasp reared up her throat as she felt his fingers slip between the crevice of their bodies and gently cosset the joining point of their flesh just before he moved away.

Glancing over her shoulder as Devin withdrew, she saw Caleb stroking his cock back to life. He quickly replaced Devin between her thighs. Without effort, she complied as he rolled her on her back. He lifted her legs over his shoulders and impaled her with one deep thrust. Moaning and gushing, she felt her muscles grip his flesh exquisitely. The thick length pulsed deep inside her.

Weak, spent, reeling from one orgasm after another, Megan could only gasp for breath. She blinked up at the blue sky, dazed with pleasure as her body soared with blissful sensations. His pace was fast, faster, then even faster, until their bodies were slamming together, and their releases shattered his pounding rhythm and shook their bodies.

Devin and Caleb didn't stop there.

Their dark arousal, the intense, insatiable need filled their lusty expressions and coursed hotly through their bodies like a palpable second layer of gluttonous flesh. She yielded her nakedness to their potent desires and virile sexuality. Their cocks, still hard and long, pumped pure pleasure inside her. Her body instinctively responded, accepted them, serviced them, tumbled with carnal lust as they moved between her thighs. Together. Individually. All she could do was lie back and writhe in pleasure as they possessed her, spread her legs, turned her this way and that way, over and over again, until she floated away in a wondrous aftermath.

* * * *

Minutes, hours, days later, she didn't know. Frankly, she didn't care which as they carried her to the river. They washed the scent of forbidden sex off their bodies. She was semi-conscious, not knowing who held her as hands soaped every inch of her body.

At first, their touch was gentle, cleansing and relaxing, extremely soothing to her sweat-drenched skin as the rosy scent of her favorite soap served as a symbolism of reality. Gradually, the lathered hands and fingers became more probing, sexual, insistent, demanding. Quietly, she let the familiar sensations literally wash over her. Completely exhausted, her eyes remained closed as one hand drove three thick, long fingers between her swollen lips, another strummed her clit, and yet another finger teased her anus beneath the water. Two mouths covered her aching nipples. She panted as her body thrashed in the water, as in a glorious dream she couldn't awake from. She heard a faint, far-off feminine voice weakly chant, "Yes, yes, yes." It was her own voice.

Just when she thought she was going to die from the pleasure, her legs were wrapped around someone's waist, and her body leaned against a broad chest. Her head fell back on someone's shoulder as either Devin or Caleb's cock, she didn't care whose, answered the throbbing, burning ache, the tormenting need in her pussy with one deep thrust. A scant second later, another cock impaled her to the hilt in her ass. Propped between their bodies, their thrusts and hands on her hips and thighs kept her above the water as it splashed relentlessly with each uncontained movement. Having climaxed several times earlier, Caleb's and Devin's next releases were long in coming. By that time, her body had been overwhelmed by their lusty demands three more ecstatically draining times. She fought her weakness, the daze clouding her senses, desperate to keep up with their inexhaustible desires to serve their prowess.

Eventually, she lost consciousness.

Chapter 23

Putting away the breakfast dishes, Megan happened to glance out the kitchen window and notice Devin dismount Deuce, fluid muscle and power inciting the common maneuver to one of perfection.

It never failed to amaze her how two huge creatures could move about with such graceful agility. Normally, she could hear riders approach before she could see them when they turned around the bend of the small hill behind the barn. Yet Devin and Deuce seemed mountain-bred—part Indian, part ghost. As though on winged feet, people couldn't see or hear them until they were in front of them.

Back from dropping Shelby and Emma off at the start of another school week, Devin's tall, stocky frame dwarfed the amazing animal. An unusual breed of horse, never had she seen one so large and well taken care of before. Reed had paid special attention to his horses, as well. He had believed all animals were innocent creatures of God, and it was man's right to care for them, only taking the lives of those necessary to feed his family.

Devin's relationship went beyond that. It was downright awe-inspiring. Even now, as she watched him make his way toward the barn to unsaddle Deuce, they were talking to one another. At least, Devin was talking, and Deuce nodded, shaking his head as though he was not only understanding, but actually answering.

It was then she heard a rider approach and caught sight of Caleb riding up.

She was surprised he would show up so soon after what occurred Friday.

She placed a hand to her belly as the butterflies fluttered. Memories of their wonderful experience by the river were still fresh. Luckily for her, she resisted temptation in the past. If she had known what a fabulous, experienced lover Caleb had become, she may not have been able to resist him, as she had during her marriage to Reed. Then again, they could have been married, and she wouldn't have missed out on ten years of making love to him.

The last thing she could recall was her bath turning into another bout of two wickedly handsome men with two large, hard cocks pumping into her. Strangely, not knowing what happened after she passed out didn't frighten her. It only added a sense on naughtiness. The recall sent a flood of hot liquid between her thighs.

Waking up several hours later that day as the sun faded behind the hills, wrapped snuggly in a pile of blankets, she was the most satisfied woman alive, despite being a tad sore below the waist. Her chores were done, the girls home from school and fed. Devin even helped with their homework.

In addition to her father, Reed and Caleb were the only two men she ever trusted. After a very tumultuous beginning, she'd grown to trust Devin equally.

The men glanced out the window, then exchanged a few words before Devin headed toward the barn. Caleb made his way toward the house, pausing to tie his horse to the hitching post in front of the porch.

Grabbing the coffee pot she'd placed in the cupboard moments earlier, she filled it with water from the barrel near the sink. Placing the coffee pot on the potbellied stove, she struck a match and lit a flame under the pot, knowing Caleb liked his coffee hot and fresh.

Being able to share herself so intimately with Caleb was a once–in-a-lifetime opportunity she didn't regret. It was something she'd treasure 'til the day she died. How was she going to contain herself each time she looked at him, knowing what was beneath that suit and tie? Her mouth went dry.

It was wicked of her to participate, to even have allowed Devin to tie her up. She'd learned from experience how being forced to submit to the forbidden was highly erotic. The giddy excitement, anticipation of the unknown, of being dominated once again added an extra carnal edge to her pleasure. Who knew she favored a deep-rooted desire for depravity? And the addition of gorgeous Caleb, her first love, intensified the pleasure immensely.

She expected it would never occur again, which suited her fine. After all, Devin was more than enough to handle. His appetite was insatiable, his mouth and tongue delicious, his long fingers and smooth hands devilishly attentive, and his hefty twelve-inch cock impressively skilled.

Then again, Caleb's thick nine-incher wasn't anything to laugh at. He didn't lie when he said he'd learned a thing or two since they were teenagers. She'd just have to learn to live and be satisfied with the wickedly sinful memory permanently ingrained in her mind.

Devin never fully explained why he allowed it to happen. The only explanation she could think of was erasing the memories of young teenagers fumbling through their first sexual experience.

Caleb would always be a part of her. She'd love him forever. If pressed, she'd be unable to deny she thought about him often the past few days. Each time, it left her tingling and wet, pulse racing as her temperature rose.

Last night, when the girls were sound asleep, and she and Devin were safe behind locked doors, she asked him to use a dildo while he fucked her. Of course, he obliged without hesitation or question. Closing her eyes, she imagined Caleb in bed with them, both their cocks thrusting deep inside her, stretching, filling, pleasuring her again.

It was her secret, certain it would never happen twice. Decent folk didn't do that sort of thing. It went against everything she believed. And Caleb—well, Caleb was brought up respectable and proper. A real gentleman in every sense of the word.

Dressed in her Sunday best, his mother would fall down and die if she ever found out he cavorted with the likes of her. *"Devil's work."* Would be Mrs. Walker's final words.

It shocked her that he'd participated in the first place. Since he did, she'd cherish the memory. She'd commit his glorious body, magnificent cock, skilled hands, and delightful tongue to her dreams. Where he would live forever.

Devin Spawn, her notorious outlaw, had stolen her heart. As stubborn, ornery and wary as he was, she knew deep down he cared for her, though he would never admit to such.

If only he showed her half as much affection as he paid that horse of his, she'd be the happiest woman alive. And the most sexually satisfied, she thought with a grin. A ripple of lust settled between her thighs.

"Morning, Meg. What are you grinning about?" Caleb smiled warmly as he walked through the front door. Taking his hat off, he hung it on an empty peg next to the doorframe, where she kept her sunbonnet. As usual he was dressed in a European style suit and tie—doctor attire, he liked to call it.

Her cheeks warmed at the uneasiness of being caught daydreaming of Devin's enormous cock, she quickly turned and reached for the coffee tin on the counter.

"Not much. Just how nice it's been this spring. Not too hot, not too cold. Perfect weather, don't you agree? I'm making you a fresh pot of coffee. Take a seat. It'll be ready soon."

"Day seems nice enough so far. Hoping it will improve as the day progresses." He stepped into the kitchen, leaned his backside against the counter next to her. Removing the measuring cup from a hook underneath the shelf, she allowed her gaze from underneath her lashes to travel from his muscled thigh up to the part in his jacket. Her fingers ached to touch the worthy hump in his trousers to make it widen, elongate.

"Oh," she muttered, tearing her gaze away. The kitchen suddenly felt smaller, confined. "You have something exciting planned for this afternoon?" Her voice sounded shaky, coinciding with the weakness in her fingers. "Courting one of the young ladies in town?" She fumbled with the tin lid. Damn thing wouldn't open.

Frustrated, she blew out harsh breath as he reached over to take the container. His hand brushed hers, warm and smooth, evoking carnal images.

Swallowing hard, she moved to the stove and peeked under the lid of the coffeepot to check if the water was ready.

"Not likely," he said as the lid popped open behind her. "Since I already have a girl."

"Really?" Megan swirled around to face him, smiling. She should be excited by the prospect Caleb had finally found a nice girl. It would make things easier if he had a woman of his own. She felt a stab of jealousy at the thought of him making love to another woman. Her smile waned, and she tried to keep her voice cheery, or at least interested. "Tell me all about her."

"Well, she's about so high." He raised a hand in front of him, slightly leveled with her height. "Hair is really pretty, the soft, silky kind a man likes to curl around his fingers. Prettiest eyes, the kind he'd want to look into for the rest of his born days."

As he spoke, the softness, warmth in his eyes changed. The beautiful blue deepened, turned sensual. He was a man, if not in love, definitely in lust with a woman. She was saddened, that look was meant for another. Yet she couldn't stop the sexual stirrings deep inside her womb.

"Sounds like you're really smitten, Caleb. I'm happy for you." Her voice was subdued. She ignored how aroused she was at the thought of him gazing into her own eyes as he thrust his big cock inside her instead of another woman. She made her way to the counter, careful to keep a safe foot between them. She measured enough coffee for three into a measuring cup. She hated herself for being selfish. Where was her loyalty? What did that say about their friendship?

"Are you, Meg?" he asked her gently, his gaze questioning.

"Of course. Why wouldn't I be?" Glancing sideways, she gave him a brief smile. She felt her face begin to flush at the intensity in his gaze. "You're entitled to happiness like any one else." She tried her best to sound sincere and cover any trace of envy as she looked into his eyes. There was a longing there that confused her.

"I'm delighted you agree." His eyes lit up with keen appreciation as he grinned. "I haven't told you the best part."

"She's well-to-do?" She asked playfully, looking away from his boyish grin that warmed her heart and weakened her knees. Taking a deep breath, she rose on her toes and reached for two cups and saucers from the overhead shelf.

He slowly moved directly behind her. "Her figure." His voice was suddenly low, seductive.

Her head popped to attention at the inappropriateness. Men usually didn't discuss their female friend's shape with another woman. That was reserved for tawdry banter amid men.

"Tiny waist," he continued as his hands encircled her waist.

"Caleb," she gasped, dropping the cups on the counter. She covered his hands with hers as she tried to pull them away.

"Firm breasts that fit nicely in my mouth." His large hands glided upwards until they surged over the swell of her breasts. She wore nothing underneath her clothes, so he kneaded them easily through the thin cotton blouse. Her chest heaved from alarm as he sandwiched her between him and the counter. She stilled, her hands above his feeling the heat of his skin pressing into her breasts.

"Caleb." Her voice was a soft whisper. She was too stunned to say anything else. Bracing her hands against the counter, she felt him, hard and thick, pressing into the small of her back, his fingers squeezing, pinching and tweaking the hard peaks of her breasts roughly. The flare of pain curled through her system like raging fire.

She closed her eyes on a breathless cry. *Devin.*

"After the other day, you're mine, Meg." His lips whispered over her neck, voice heated with arousal. "Don't you realize that?"

She made a low moaning sound as he continued to tease her nipples, forcing them to pucker, drawing them out, making the tips plump, easier to grasp through the thin fabric. Resting her head against his chest, she stared up at the ceiling. Her body shivered as she arched her back and pressed her breast against his palms.

His masculine scent of arousal melted her resistance. Using his thigh, he parted her legs slightly, pressed the length of his engorged cock between her buttocks. She gasped as the movement bore down on the dildo Devin had inserted before he rolled out of bed, sending ripples of lust racing through her body, had her pussy throbbing with need.

Why was this happening? Her body was responding, enjoying his touch so readily. Strangely, she craved his body, his touch, as she shamefully reveled in the knowledge he wanted her, not some other woman. The anticipation of another man pleasuring her both scared and excited her. It was improper, weak to yield to all appetites of the flesh and carnal passions of the body.

The absolute epitome of a gentleman, only once did Caleb make an inappropriate advance toward her while married to Reed.

Where's Devin? Why hasn't he come inside?

Her breath deepened as she felt his hand begin to lift her skirt, the warmth of his breath caressing her neck. Her body trembled. Shutting her eyes, she tightened her inner muscles, tried to control the warm proof of her arousal seeping from her vagina, coating the entrance in preparation.

"Caleb," she whimpered, feeling the heat of his fingers on her bare skin, feather soft as they moved slowly up her thigh. Her body was on fire, engulfed in lust.

"Megan, let me touch you." His voice was husky, laced with passion. He brushed soft kisses along the curve of her neck. She shivered as his fingers inched perilously closer to the hot, throbbing folds of her moist, tender flesh. "Let me love you."

Love? Devin! She fought for breath, fought her betrayal, fought for control, fought the wickedness.

His hand stilled at the narrow juncture of her thighs as he encouraged her away from the counter to grant him complete access. She squirmed in his grip as he tried to ease her back, his fingers barely touching the soft curls of her drenched lips. "Stop it, Caleb!"

Backing away swiftly, she found herself butted against her bedroom door. Her hands gripped the doorframe, her knees shaky under her skirt. If she couldn't guess it by the huge bulge tenting his trousers, his roving hands, the wicked intent in his eyes was unmistakable. He wasn't here for coffee.

"We belong together. We both know it. I read it in your eyes the other day." His voice was ragged, tense as he stared at her pleadingly.

She swallowed her unease. The truth in his words was a harsh slap to her senses. "What occurred the other day was nice." She wrapped her arms over her waist as her stomach tightened.

"The weather's nice, Meg." His expression was wild, frustrated. "What took place between us was entirely different. We made love."

"That wasn't love. That was sex." Her breathing was coming a little too fast, voice sounded a little too weak as her arousal ebbed away slowly. She tried to regain her composure, To sound convincing and firm in her denial.

"Then allow me to make love to you now," he whispered, coming dangerously close.

"A wonderful memory." She held up a staying hand, realizing she was a step away from entering her bedroom—the bed. Caleb was too close. Unable to resist the temptation, the memories, her gaze ran the deliciously long length of his body and settled on the hard, prominent appendage straining against his trousers. She blinked, drew her eyes upward. Her voice came out strangled. "It's time we move on."

"I know you want me. That you still love me." Hurt, sexual frustration, anger, and a host of other emotions blazed in his eyes.

Her heart clenched. She suffered the error of giving into temptation.

"There's no moving on without you," he added with conviction.

"That's nonsense. Devin is going to walk inside any second now." Her gaze dashed toward the front door, half expecting it to swing open. "You know how surly he can be," she said with emphasis, fearful Devin would walk in and find them together in a compromised position.

His eyes narrowed, heavy-lidded and dark. "Devin's not coming." His voice chilled.

"What?"

"We have an agreement."

Her eyes widened. "An agreement? What sort of agreement?" she asked quietly, almost too afraid to even ask the question or hear the answer.

"Finding out you don't know him as well as you thought," he replied judgmentally. His eyes turned mysteriously dark, disapproving.

"Caleb, you can't just waltz into my home, grope me, and tell me it's acceptable because you have an *agreement.*"

"Think about it, Meg." He leaned against the opposite counter and crossed his arms over his chest. "Devin ties you up in the woods, and he invites me to fuck you. You were in and out of consciousness, and neither of us wanted to stop. He drove the wagon while I sucked your sweet pussy in the back. It was a long ride home, Megan. There was lots of cream to keep be busy."

Shocked by his bitterness and nonchalance, she stared at him in disbelief. His gaze lowered to below her waist, and she felt her face flush in embarrassment. His summation consumed her. Her senses were in chaos. The flesh between her thighs ached with need, as if her soaked vagina recalled what she could not.

"You don't remember, do you?" He paused a moment, as if waiting for a reply. "I come over today, and he agrees not to interrupt us. What sort of agreement do you think it is?"

Her gaze darted out the kitchen window. The barn doors were closed. They were never closed during the day. No sign of Devin. Her heart sank, her body trembled. What agreement could they have possibly made that would keep him away? He had allow Caleb liberties, free reign over her body?

"He knows?" Her voice was a questioning murmur.

"Not only does he know, but the idea was entirely his."

"It can't be!" she shrieked, too bewildered to say more. She knew all too well about Devin's so-called agreements. Her indebtedness to him. His perverse sexual desires. Carnal appetite so insatiable, it required more than one of Jazelle's soiled doves to satisfy.

"Devin wanted to kill me when he found me talking to you." His voice softened, turned tender as he crossed the kitchen. "What do you think he would do if he found me making love to you? Think about it, Megan. Why else would I be here, if not for him?" He made a move to reach for her, a gesture of comfort.

She shrank back and buried her face in her hands. Caleb had never been cruel before. What changed? What the hell was happening to her life? She was shaking. Her mind raced with unanswered questions. One truth reigned supreme: Devin would murder anyone who touched her without his permission.

At the realization, she stared at Caleb. As far as she knew, their relationship was based on honesty. Devin? What did she really know about him?

"Caleb, tell me truthfully." She searched his expression for answers. Anything to end the turmoil. "What agreement binds you and Devin?"

"Ask him." There was a severity to this voice despite the low, calm tone.

"Very well," she snapped, pushing away from the door. Fury and confusion pulsed through her veins. She needed answers, not the damned combination to his family's bank vault. "Seeing how you're afraid to tell me."

"The truth should come from him," he cut her off sharply.

Grabbing an old dishtowel near the sink, she used it to take the coffeepot, now bubbling loudly, off the stove before rushing out the door.

* * * *

The sound of the barn door banging against the outside wall caught Devin's immediate attention. His head jerked around from where he stood inside Deuce's stall, brushing the golden coat with long, caring strokes.

His eyes narrowed suspiciously from Megan, who was storming towards him, to Caleb, who followed a few feet behind with a troubled look upon his face.

"Is there a problem, Megan?" he asked in his normal deep, nonchalant tone, brushing Deuce as though he didn't have a care in the world.

She stood in front of the stall, hands on hips, tapping her foot anxiously. Her almond-shaped eyes were small slits, but the fury raging out of them was full-blown.

"Depends on if what Caleb said is true," she bit back. Her lips were set in a rigid pink line.

"How am I supposed to know what Caleb said?" He replied, sweeping a brief glance in her direction. "We barely spoke three words to each other this morning." He ignored her as he continued to brush Deuce.

"You sorry son-of-a-bitch," she lashed out furiously.

"Whoa, girl." His head shot up, a brow faintly arched in amusement. "That's a damn soap word if I ever heard one." He grinned and strolled toward the exit.

"Did you or did you not send Caleb inside to fuck me?" Her hands fisted in her skirts. She looked about ready to snap his head off. With or without her teeth. *Ouch!*

He paused momentarily midway as he opened the gate and glanced at Caleb. Locking the gate behind him, he calmly walked past her to a nearby shelf, where the grooming supplies were kept. He tossed the brush in the box that held several other brushes in various sizes and styles of bristles. Finally, he turned and faced her, crossing his arms over his chest and studying her casually.

Her tiny body might have been stiff with anger and her words shockingly heated, but he absorbed the denial she fought to hide shining in her hazel depths. He knew the inner workings of her body, the ease of her passion. Whatever happened in the house, arousal flowed through her system. That was for damn sure. Her small breasts were swollen, lushly constrained in her form-fitted white blouse. The areolas, typically as pale as her breasts, now a rosy pink, clearly visible through the thin cotton material. And any man with eyes could see the pearl ornaments gracing the center of her firm globes, heedless her arousal was so gloriously displayed. It made his mouth water.

"Is that what he said?" He finally spoke.

"Yes," she snapped, casting a fleeting glance at Caleb, as though expecting him to deny his words.

"Does Caleb lie?" he inquired.

"No," she responded.

"Then I guess it's true." As always, his tone remained the quintessential sound of smoothness. She came expecting his denial, a fight. But he refused to give her what she wanted. Not about this. Their safety, hers and the girls' was at stake, and he plumb refused to back down on the issue. He'd push it and keep pushing it until she finally agreed. Even if that meant tying her down in front of the preacher.

Caleb shook his head as he leaned against one of the larger beams in the center of the barn. Evidently, he could see his marriage disappearing before his eyes. Poor bastard.

"You lying, yellow-livered heathen!" she sneered.

With a slow blink, his eyes rested on hers. "What exactly is it that I'm supposed to have lied about?" he asked curiously. No matter how despicable his actions, he hadn't lied to her.

"Why you took me to the river. Just so you and Caleb could have your wicked way." He could see the tears forming, clouding her eyes. She blinked. A futile attempt to hold them back. "You never cared a lick about me."

He dropped his arms to his side and his entire body stiffened.

"That's a lie, Megan," he protested. "What I told you was the truth. I wanted him to..." he paused, unsure how to explain what he was truly feeling. His intentions were honorable, at least to him. Darting a brief glance at Caleb, then back to her, he stared at the solitary tear running down her cheek. "I asked Caleb to marry you." Another tear fell, and he swallowed tightly. "I had to be certain you'd accept." Then another. He took a deep breath, then blew out slowly. "I wanted to accustom you to the idea of being with him." The tears flowed now, and for the first time in his life, he felt the nastiness of remorse seep into his unscrupulous soul.

* * * *

Speechless, Megan gaped at Devin for what seemed like an eternity.

The tension in the barn escalated, oxygen vanishing.

His response was not even close to what she expected. She didn't really know what she'd expected—definitely not this.

After Rosalinda, she vowed never to shed tears over Devin Spawn. She felt her face turn ten shades of red as the fury swelled to intolerable levels. She clenched her fists at her sides. *Damn him.* She wished she was a man. She'd show him a thing or two.

Turning to Caleb, she glared at him. Was no one immune to the devil's temptation?

Wiping the tears from her eyes, she took a deep, steadying breath. "And you agreed to this?" Her voice sounded like a pitiful murmur.

"I've always wanted to marry you. I asked you to wait for me, but you married Reed, instead. It was the only way I could ever have you."

"Was that the agreement? For us to get married, and you take me and the girls away from here? Out of the way, so we would no longer trouble the notorious Mr. Spawn?"

* * * *

Casting his gaze downward, Caleb couldn't bring himself to admit the final part of their agreement. Suddenly felt guilty for his part in betraying Megan's trust.

When Devin first asked him to marry Megan, he was shocked and suspicious. He believed the man had lost his mind. After his persistence, Caleb decided to hear him out. Megan and the girls' safety was a major concern. For whatever peculiar reason, Devin trusted him.

Caleb wanted Megan. For ten years, there wasn't a day that passed when he didn't want her. He was willing to take her on any terms. If Megan loved Devin, then by God, she loved Devin. She was the type of woman who loved deeply, wholly, with all her heart. It broke his heart to hear she loved another. It made him realize he had lost her forever. Devin's carnal idea gave him a flicker of hope, though it was too incredible, too wicked, too debased to even consider.

Nevertheless, he and Devin did the unthinkable, the unforgivable. They took that first step and redirected the love she had grown to feel for Devin toward him. They'd rekindled the flame they started long ago.

Truth be told, he wanted her to agree. He was willing to marry her under any terms. If that meant sharing her occasionally with another man, so be it. He had seen the heated look in her eyes, heard her feminine cries of bliss as her arousal endlessly flowed from her body, saw her reach out to them, seeking and begging for them to satisfy her, the immense pleasure they both brought her. He would do anything to bring her that much happiness every day if he could.

Now, here he was with nothing to lose but the only woman he would ever love.

From across the wide expanse of the barn, Caleb eyed Devin. His expression remained unruffled, his manner easy, truth seen only in his eyes. Each of them accepted blame inwardly. Though Caleb could not outwardly admit to such deception, he knew it showed in every tense muscle, in his despair. Devin, a master of dissembling, appeared at ease, whereas Caleb's gut wrenched.

He lowered his gaze to the fine layer of dust on the front of his black shoes. He couldn't bring himself to look at her, to see the hurt and anger he caused, aware she just scratched the surface.

* * * *

"What else, Caleb?" Judging from the look on Caleb's face, Megan was certain more stipulations applied.

"What constitutes this so-called agreement?" Megan shouted, turning toward Devin after waiting a moment for the response that was not forthcoming. Caleb put it all on Devin's shoulders. Why not? They were broad enough.

"I'll support you if need be. However, Caleb is to remain on the ranch with you and the girls."

"With blood money. No thank you. And why would you care where we lived? You won't be here."

"Whenever I return, I want you here with me." His voice was surprisingly calm, sincere. As if what he asked was common circumstance.

Her jaw dropped. She felt the blood rush from her face as the air left her lungs. She glanced over her shoulder at Caleb. He looked guilty as sin.

She titled her head around to Devin. "Do I understand you correctly? You want to marry me off to Caleb, *and* you want me here waiting for you whenever you decide to return?"

"It's the only way I'll be assured of your safety." There was no emotion, no warmth in his voice or expression. No 'I love you.' Not even a 'I'm sorta fond of you.' Nothing. He was inhuman.

Megan felt her temperature rise, the well of rage bottomless.

Devin wanted to turn her into a whore, at his constant disposal. Continue to use her after she took a solemn vow before God, pledged her love and fidelity to another. All under the disguise of a preconceived deception for her well-being. He was insane.

"No wonder they call you the Devil's Spawn. You're nothing but a heartless bastard, lower than a snake's belly. You're not concerned for my safety, just your own twisted perversions. Why pay for a two-bit whore, when you can gallop into town whenever you damn well please and fuck another man's wife?"

She turned her vengeance on Caleb, stormed to within a few feet in front of him. "As for you, Caleb Walker, have you no conscience? What would your priggish mother say? Maybe the three of us can fuck in your bedroom while your mother and the pastor's wife have tea downstairs after church services on Sunday. Seeing how you agreed to this pact with the devil, how's this Sunday? She can pray for our redemption afterwards."

"Megan—" Caleb bellowed, discernibly shocked by the depth of her anger. Caleb knew she disliked his mother, but not nearly as much Mrs. Walker disapproved of her. Even so, she'd never spoken cruelly of the woman until now.

"Damn you both to hell," she shouted, cutting Caleb off before he could get another word in.

In a swirl, she swung around and headed for the door. Mindful Caleb moved toward her in an effort to calm her down, always the considerate gentlemen. The epithet negated the circumstance. Before he could reach her, she noted Devin's saddlebags hanging from a hook on the wall near the door, his rifle resting underneath.

Lost in the heat of madness surging up in her, she grabbed the rifle. The clicking sound of it engaging was cold and deadly, as she swung it around and aimed it directly at Caleb.

"Take off your clothes," she demanded.

"Megan, let's talk about this. Put the rifle down." Caleb froze in his tracks, hands in the air in supplication. His eyes wide, alarmed.

"Too late for talking. Now take off your clothes." She glared at Caleb, waiting as her lips tightened, and she felt her teeth grinding. She frowned when he didn't make a move. Decidedly, he required convincing.

"Someone once told me if you pull a gun, pull the trigger. Don't think I'll do it? Try me."

"Megan," Devin shouted, stepping toward her. She shot him a quick glance, warning him she had taken his advice to heart.

Raising the rifle, she pulled the trigger. The roar ripped through the roof, leaving a hole the size of a watermelon in its wake. With one hand, she cocked the second barrel. Devin's dark brows rose faintly, moved by her adeptness.

"You only have one shot left," Devin pointed out smugly.

"One's all I need for the bastard who doesn't do as I say." Aiming the rifle directly in the middle of Devin's chest, her eyes narrowed on his.

"Which one of you is that going to be?" Her eyes darted to Caleb, then back toward Devin. "Keep your hands up," she warned Devin. "Now strip."

With a smirk on his face, Devin made a move to unbutton his shirt.

"Not you." She ordered, wiping the smirk right off Devin's face just as if she slapped him.

Silver eyes burned fiercely as he looked at Caleb, who shrugged his shoulders and slipped off his jacket.

"I should have shot the both of you when I had the chance. You, Caleb, for making a pact with devil. As it is, I'm going to let you make love to me nice and slow. Just like in your little agreement. *You* get to watch." The last heated words aimed at Devin.

"It's kinda hard getting hard with a rifle pointed at you. If you know what I mean," Caleb said.

"Shut up, Caleb, and take your pants off. I shouldn't even be speaking to you." She glared at Devin. "And *you*, Devin, so eager to leave. What were you going to do out here in the barn while Caleb was inside fucking me? Were you planning on feeding the chickens and listening? Were you waiting for me to scream when he rammed his cock inside me? Or were you going to peek through the window and watch him spread my legs?"

"Damn, Megan, be reasonable," Devin growled.

"It's time to pay the devil's price. Answer me." She raised the rifle to her shoulder, her voice steadfast and harsh even to her ears. She hoped it had the appropriate effect. She stared down the barrel, aimed dead center on Devin's chest and her finger eased on the trigger.

"Oh, fuck, you want to know? I'll tell you the damn truth. I don't know what the hell I was gonna do other than pretend the shit wasn't happening." A suppressed storm resonated in his voice.

It was comforting to hear, but hardly enough to change her mind.

"Well, it's happening, and you're going to watch. And there isn't a damn thing you can do about it. I want the picture of Caleb making love to me fixed in your mind after you're gone, eating away at you." She paused. "I ought to shoot Deuce. Let's see how you get away then." She pointed the rifle at Devin's horse, the one thing she was certain he loved.

Deuce shook his head vigorously and whickered in heated protest as he stomped his leg into the hay-strewn floor, kicking up a large cloud of dust and straw.

"Megan," Devin shouted, taking a frantic step toward her, as if ready to dive in front of the rifle if need be, to save the horse that carried him out of death's door many a time. This time, he was going to need more than a horse, she gloated inwardly.

"Seems at least there's one male in this barn with a lick of sense." She redirected the barrel toward Devin, taking note of Caleb pulling off his underpants and placing them neatly with the rest of his clothes and shoes on a bale of hay directly behind him. He was truly a fine figure of a man.

Devin breathed a sign of relief as Deuce began to calm down.

"Pick up a crate and get your ass over here, Caleb." She nodded in the direction of the wooden crates stacked against the back wall of the barn.

"I think I'm going to need a little more sweet talking than that to get me in the mood." Plumb naked from head to toe, Caleb went to retrieve a crate.

She noticed Devin glance at Caleb, who was limp between the legs, and saw him grit his teeth in a struggle to contain his laughter. She pursed her lips, frowning as Devin cleared his throat, as if readying himself to attempt to rectify the situation, save Caleb from the humiliation of trying to appease her, when the poor man couldn't even get it up. How wrong could he be?

"Megan, there's no reason to be angry with Caleb." His voice as smooth as silk, cajoling, as if discussing spilt milk, seeming unperturbed because once again his life lay in her hands, she thought, resentful of his inability to show real emotion for anything else besides that damned horse of his. "He was only doing as I asked."

"Everyone always does what Devin Spawn wants. Not any more. Not this girl."

"No need in trying to defend me," Caleb said. "If I didn't want to marry Megan, I never would have agreed to the arrangement. First, you threaten to kill me, and now Megan does the same thing. If I can't have her, one of you might as well put a bullet through me and put me out of my misery."

"How very gallant, Caleb. Put the crate there in the middle of the floor and sit down. Or you may get your wish." With a nod of her head, she indicated a spot a few feet in front of her, directly centered in the barn spotlighted by the sunshine beaming through the open door in the otherwise dimly lit interior. "Seeing how you're so taken with me, I'm surprised you're having trouble. Perhaps Devin can be of assistance."

"Like hell I will. You can fucking shoot my brains out. I don't give a shit," Devin yelled with a deep scowl, nostrils flaring, dark eyes blazing with fury.

"I'll shoot my own brains out before I let him touch me." Caleb pointed wildly at Devin before he jumped up, his handsome, sculptured features flushed with anger.

"Calm down, boys. I was just funning." She giggled, enjoying the invigorating power she held over them.

"Don't taunt a man like that. You're liable to get hurt," Devin warned, his silver eyes brooding, dangerous.

"I may never get it up now," Caleb stated edgily as he sat back down on the crate, running agitated fingers through his blond waves.

"That's my problem, Caleb, not yours." She joined him in the center of the barn.

"Devin, I want you to take a seat on one of the crates in the back. I'll leave the choice up to you." She waited for him to move, and when he did, she thought of something. "Wait. Take your holster off nice and slow, using only one hand. Doesn't matter which, since you're fast with both."

"Fast...or *good*, Megan?" He moved a hand to his gun belt. His thumb rested on the buckle. He dangled his fingers over the fly, drawing her attention to the clear outline of his penis beneath his buckskins.

"Smart ass," she yelled. Even flaccid, it was larger than most men erect, and she could feel the shameless tingle between her legs.

"Bitch," he retorted, yanking off his gun belt.

"Bastard." Her eyes narrowed on him as he hung his holster on a nearby nail hammered at a slant in the wall.

"Mother."

Her eyes flared. That one word was worse than any other name he could ever call her.

"You'll pay for that, Devin. Mark my words," she seethed.

"I'm shaking in my..." His eyes fell downward to his long leggings, dressed half-Indian today, his clothing of choice. Tossing it in her face, knowing how she despised anything about the red-skinned people who killed her family. He concluded with a slow deliberate coldness, "...moccasins."

"You're the lowest, most murderous scum in a pair of moccasins," she bit back, fanning the deadly flame.

"At least I don't have to hold a gun to someone to make them fuck me," he replied insolently.

"You'll say anything to stop me. Sorry, it won't work. Stand up, Caleb."

"Don't know how you two begin sex. Usually, I prefer a more cordial environment at the very least." Placing his hands against his thighs, Caleb pushed off slowly, rising as though it was the last thing in the world he wanted to do.

"In case you didn't know, I'm a pretty good shot," she told Devin pleasantly. "Take a seat and enjoy the show." She moved next to Caleb, rested the rifle butt on her hip.

"Squirrels and bunnies don't count." His deep voice riddled with sarcasm as he trudged toward the back of the barn.

Ignoring his last remark, she grabbed Caleb's flaccid penis and began to stroke it nice and slow.

From the corner of her eye, she observed Caleb eyeing the rifle in her hand. He blew out a frustrated breath. Even though the barrel wasn't pointed at him, if he tried to take it from her, one wrong move, and the finger she rested on the trigger would send a hole through Devin. Whether she meant to or not. She hadn't decided.

"Megan, I doubt this is going to work," Caleb said flatly, eyeing his lack of response despite her well-intentioned ministrations. Thanks to the distance, she saw rather than heard Devin chuckle at Caleb's inability to perform up to rigid standards.

"Take off my clothes, and be quick about it," she instructed curtly. The amused grin and mockery flickering in Devin's eyes faded.

With a quick glance at Devin, Caleb swallowed hard, then did as instructed. She gestured for him to stand by her side to keep her line of vision directly on Devin. She was aware his anger rolled off him in waves, directed at her. She ignored it as she felt Caleb's fingers brush the skin just above her neckline as he undid the top button.

Buttons opened one by one. Slowly, he spread her white cotton blouse apart. When he reached the final bottom, he pulled the hem from her waistband. She straightened her spine as Caleb looked on appreciatively.

Caleb moved behind her, helped her work one arm free, then the next as she switched the rifle to her other hip. Tossing the shirt to the ground in his haste, he immediately began to unhook her gray skirt.

She kept her eyes glued to Devin's. She could see what it was doing to him as he was forced to witness another man prepare to take her. As her skirt fell to ground in a puff of dust, she held her gaze steadfast. Devin's heated gaze narrowed on her face and he appeared to struggle against the urge to take in her nakedness.

"Touch me," she demanded, kicking the skirt aside and placing her left foot on the crate. She tilted her hips forward, exposing the flesh between her thighs fully to Devin's view as Caleb knelt down in front of the crate. She moved her right foot and hip back slightly, enabling the slick moisture of her arousal to glisten in the sunlight.

"Do what you want. Just don't make me come. Not yet," she ordered plain as day.

When she felt a finger trace the slick crease between her labia, she winched, tried to contain the sudden fiery sensations racing through her. She fought the moan as he reached up and gently spread her lips wide, parted the throbbing, swollen flesh to Devin's view. There was no way she could control the surging gush of pleasure flowing as his fingers leisurely stroked the entrance until she was hot, aching, moving against his hand. Or the quivering of her body when he finally drove his fingers into her pussy over and over again, heating her blood, boiling her desire, melting her control. She could feel her nipples tighten, her breast swell, the juices flowing down her thighs.

Her eyes felt heavy with lust, clouded with need. She could barely make out Devin's far-off shadow. If she didn't stop Caleb soon, this would all be for nothing. Devin would never learn a lesson. People were emotional beings, capable of feeling joy, sadness, pain, and love. At times, the worst suffering was the inner hurt that lingered long after any physical injury healed. He had no right to buy and sell her like cattle, pick a husband for her, use her whenever he decided to stroll into town.

Being indebted to him was one thing. Sexual slavery was entirely different.

She'd show him he held no claim over her.

That he could hurt like any other flesh and blood human with a pulse.

That the Devil's Spawn wasn't indomitable.

And she was the one to prove it to him.

"Enough, Caleb," she panted, trembling, hovering on the brink of orgasm as he teased her clit with deliberate care.

"Take it out. I want you to fuck my ass." On shaky legs, she moved in front of him, more than a little disappointed Devin wouldn't observe Caleb removing the dildo, choosing to be taken in the rear, knowing how incited Devin was by even the thought of taking her anally.

This was for Devin, all for Devin. If she found some degree of gratification in having a gorgeous man's cock pumping up her ass, it was pudding in the pie.

She stiffened, took a deep breath as she felt his hand spread her cheeks apart and another begin to pull on the medium-sized dildo. Tightening her hold the rifle with both hands, she fought the shudder roaring through her body as Caleb slowly slid it out. He twisted it leisurely, as if letting her feel every smooth, hard inch of ivory as it left the heat of her body. She restrained a moan as he pulled the device free and tossed it aside. She heard his long, drawn-out breath as he smoothed a hand over her buttocks, trailing a finger along the crevice.

"Sit back down on the crate," she instructed, her voice off-balance. Hearing the creaking movement of the weight of his body settling on the wooden crate, she stepped backwards until each foot was planted on the outside of his. Parting her legs nice and wide, ensuring Devin would have a good view of Caleb's cock as it stretched her tight hole.

She squatted over his lap. "Push that fat cock up my ass, Caleb." She was determined, whether she felt it or not, to act the whore. She'd Give Devin the best show twenty thousand dollars afforded. Though it was becoming increasingly harder to make out his features, her eyes remained on him.

"Megan, let me get you ready first." Caleb's breathing altered, rightly affected by his performance thus far. She could hear the sexual hunger and raw lust in his voice, feel the tension in his hands and the heat from his body. "You're still tight and I don't have lubricant."

Sighing, she rolled her eyes. Was this normal? She was driven by depravity, impassioned anger, forcing a man to have sex with her to the point she couldn't wait to prepare her own body for the assault.

She clinched her butt cheeks together as Caleb's fingers slid over her aching pussy, collecting the proof of her arousal and spreading it to her anus. Over and over again, his fingers gathered her juices and prepared the back entrance. He dipped a finger in the hole with each pass, then another finger, and finally another. He spread her muscles with his thick, long fingers, testing her readiness.

Her body trembled. Her legs shook. She was on fire, ready to beg, cry out in agonized need. Her vision was barely able to focus through the sexual haze. Devin's expression was strained, his darkened gaze centered on Caleb's intimate action. The heat of his breath rose around him like steam.

If this wasn't normal, then to hell with mundane—she'd settle for abnormal any day.

"Caleb," she breathed, then moaned at the ineffective attempt to order him to hurry, hearing the desperate plea vibrating in her tone instead.

Unable to suppress the soft moans when she felt the tip of his thick, engorged cock press against the entrance to where sanity was eventually lost, where man for centuries succumbed to greed and lust.

"Stuff it inside me. I want your big, juicy cock to fuck me hard." Her body tensed as she felt her cheeks being wedged apart, the heat of his cock pushing into her ass, spreading the taut ring of muscles. Through her cry, she heard Caleb groan as he pushed the swollen head past, into the depths of anus. She wiggled her hips, pushing back on him and screamed with added emphasis, "Oh, yes, Caleb. Your cock feels soooo good."

Caleb slid his hands under her arms, careful not to disturb the grip she held over the trigger. He cupped her breasts, fingers bearing down on her flesh.

"Pinch my nipples," she ordered loud enough to reach the back of the barn.

He caressed, teased and squeezed her nipples as he eased her further down his shaft.

"Yes...yes...like that," she panted. "Ohhh...you do that soooo well. Yes, Caleb, let me have it," she moaned as he impaled her, thrust the last few inches with a hard, fast force, his balls slapping against her cheeks. "Oh, God...yesssss."

"Harder...harder. You're...the...best." She was treading on dangerous territory, playing with live ammo, literally. At the moment, it was inconsequential. Devin lived in the here and now. So would she. She could feel every hard, thick, heated inch of Caleb's flesh sliding in and out of her body, burning her alive, driving her need higher and higher. "I love your cock in my ass."

Bouncing up and down on his lap, her breasts jiggled beneath his firm grasp. He thrust his hips upwards, faster and faster, harder and harder, deeper and deeper. She forgot her act and began to feel the fiery sensations, the throbbing ache, pulsing want, torturous need coiling deep within. Her cries of pleasure, the desire, became real.

"Fuck me, Caleb. Fuck me," she screamed, dropping the rifle to the ground. Her hands clenched at his thighs for support, nails digging into his flesh as she moved against him, driving his cock deeper. She needed him deeper, deep enough to fill her completely, stroke her very vitals, touch her heart and soul.

"Oh God, Megan," Caleb growled. He moved one hand to her throbbing flesh between her thighs. She cried out as he sank three fingers inside the soaked depths. He started to thrust inside her body in rhythm to the plunging fire from behind. "You're so tight. So good."

"Yes, yes. Make me come," she begged, tossing one hand behind his neck, clinging to him. Supporting her back against his chest, she balanced her feet on his thighs, spread her legs even further apart. Arching her hips, she rocked against him, pushing him even deeper inside her body. Moving her other hand, she covered the hand plunging in her pussy. Guiding his palm to her clit as she pushed down on his engorged cock. She tightened her inner walls, squeezing him with each deep thrust, the pressure, pleasure, fire raged deep inside her womb.

She turned her head. Releasing her breast, Caleb's fingers curled in her hair, bringing her mouth to his. She moaned, whimpered into his devouring kiss. Their tongues mating with an erotic energy that only fed the flames igniting deep in the center of her very core. Her clit throbbed for relief, her cunt ached with desire as she desperately sought completion, to feed the lustful craving tormenting her aroused senses.

She whimpered in Caleb's mouth as the first spasm overtook her, shaking her body as she thrashed recklessly on his lap. His thick erection still plunged inside her body, his hand still drew pleasure between her tightening thighs. Clinging to him as her body stiffened, the ecstasy tore through her system, washing away her sanity. She couldn't find the strength to scream as she felt the flow of her eruption seeping through her clenching inner muscles.

Devin was beyond furious. The erotic sight was unbearable, pure torture and extremely dangerous to his control. Megan had no clue what she was doing. Treading on the devil's playground wasn't for the faint at heart. His raging fury tightened every fiber in his body as he watched Caleb balance her luscious, tiny, pale form over his large red cock. He wanted to yank her off his lap, drag her off by the hair like a primitive caveman, clubbing anything that would dare come between him and his woman.

His woman!

That was a laugh.

He'd planned this. He'd practically begged Caleb to take her. And now that it was happening, it was killing him.

He wanted to look away, shut his eyes, leave. His blood coursed through his body. He couldn't move. Something deep, dark, and sinister rooted him to where he sat.

Leaving him no choice but to watch Megan straddled on Caleb's lap, thighs wide, flesh bared wantonly. Her swollen, rosy lips drenched with her desire, throbbed with need as Caleb's cock disappeared into her tight ass while a hand kneaded her breast and another tunneled into her pussy.

He could see the desperation on her face, almost feel the greedy lust taking over her body, the tormenting, ravenous need, the want. Her body was searching, struggling, not only for completion, but a means to quench its insatiable hunger. She wanted him. No matter what position, no matter how she moved, pushed herself down on Caleb or how deep or hard he thrust, it would never be enough to satisfy her the way he could.

To stay and watch as she helplessly sought her pleasure, gave into her lust, submitted another to ram into her and not able to touch her, pleasure her, to bury himself inside the hot, lush, ripeness of her sweet, little body was pure hell.

Devin stood, hot, hard, hungry and aching for a woman, unable to remain another moment. Their sounds of pleasure, her climatic cries swirled around him like a dark, stormy cloud. It aroused the hell out of him. He stalked off toward the barn doors with every intention of leaving. Cheri and her obliging friends at Jazelle's crossed his mind. He pushed the thought away just as quick.

As he passed the erotic floor show, the musky scent of her arousal struck him. Incited him. Weakened him. His gaze roamed over her smooth, silken skin, now flushed with passion, glistening with perspiration, trembling with her release. Caleb cupped a firm, round breast in a tight grasp as she whimpered into his mouth. He knew all too well what Caleb was feeling as her vaginal muscles milked his coated fingers, the heat of the narrow canal tightening around his cock, as spasm chased spasm. The knowledge only added fuel to a carnal fire burning so hot, it charred the gates of hell.

Picking up the discarded rifle, he returned the safety before tossing it into a far-off hay stack in the corner of the barn. Undoing his laces, he freed his cock. It felt stone-hard and hot as he tried to wrap his hand around the girth. Heavy in his grip, his flesh ached, throbbed in agony from the lust raging through his body, clouding his senses.

His fingers clenched in her hair, pulling her free from Caleb's mouth. She gave a small shriek of surprise, confusion, shock as he forced her head back to face his.

His chest heaved as hazel eyes, heavy-lidded with arousal, looked up into his. She provoked him, pushed him too far, shattered his control. Now, it was the time to pay the ultimate price. The moment her eyes widened— glazed with fear, shock, and something else that speared his soul—he knew she realized the error of her ways, the depraved desires she tempted.

"Oh, God," she breathed so softly, he almost didn't hear. Her eyes lowered to his hand. She stared and her lips parted, releasing a small whimper. Anticipation, need, fear, nerves? It didn't matter. She was sucking him, regardless.

"That's right, baby. You want to play with a man's weapon. Play a man's game. I'll show you how it's done." He could see her body trembling, shuddering at the savage warning in his voice, the primitive lust vibrating in the tone. He pulled her forward, and her passion-filled whimper nearly destroyed him.

Caleb grabbed her hips as he continued to thrust and plunge toward culmination. His tortured expression edged in fervor, desperate in his quest. Devin ignored him. What he intended could be done with Caleb's cock still buried deep within her curvy rump.

"Suck it," Devin growled wickedly. Slowly, she parted her lips, leaned in closer. Her luscious, pink lips were a warm breath away from the swollen tip. He sucked in a deep breath and held it. He watched as her eyes narrowed on the drop of pre-cum escaping from the tiny hole. He exhaled slowly.

"Take it in your mouth and suck it. And be quick about it." He used her words against her, ordering her like she ordered Caleb, except with a level of intensity only he could provide.

The pointed tip of her tongue swept over the slit, licked the droplet off the head of his cock. The hard flesh twitched with pleasure and expectation in his tight grasp. He gritted his teeth, struggling to control the groan of pleasure rumbling deep in his throat. She mustn't know how much he needed this. How much he wanted to bury himself in her hot little mouth. How much he wanted her. How desperately he needed her. No woman would ever be allowed to hold that kind of power over him. Not Megan, not anyone.

Her eyes flickered with smugness as more fluid seeped from the end.

Devin was far from satisfied. The need too great, too intense. Too damned agonizing.

"Not fast enough, Megan." Moving both hands, his fingers curled around her hair, holding her face steady. He thrust into her partially open mouth, pushed roughly past her moist, warm lips. She gagged as half of his erection slid through her mouth, hit the back of her throat. He groaned, shuddered involuntarily as her spasms massaged his cock. "Make it good," he growled harshly. "Suck it hard until I come in that sharp mouth."

Relaxing her throat muscles, she moaned over his flesh, and he relished every subtle nuance. She didn't have to be told what he liked. Sucking on his cock several times a day, she already knew. Pulling back slightly, she had that, 'I'm going to suck you so good you'll be begging' look on her face.

He wasn't about to let her take the lead.

"Use your tongue, Megan," he demanded as he pulled out completely. He halted her moan of protest as he pushed further back in, causing her to gag once more. He paused until he could feel her tongue bathing his hard flesh with her salvia, easing the way for him to slide between her lips.

"Swallow like I taught you," he groaned ruggedly as he withdrew, then pushed back forcefully. He stayed in the hot, moist confines of her mouth until the milking reflex in her throat subsided. She swallowed more of his length down her throat, slurping on his flesh with her hot tongue.

"Oh, shit! I'm coming," he heard Caleb groan as lust exploded through his body. Jerking so severely with his release, Megan shook, raked her teeth over his sensitive flesh as he slid past her lips. Devin closed his eyes, groaning fiercely as the tremors heightened the wild, primal lust pulsing through his body, tormenting his ragged senses until he wanted to scream, die from sharp edge of pain that was sheer pleasure.

Slowly, he opened his eyes as he felt Caleb reposition Megan. He didn't have to imagine the need to possess, hunger for more. He'd lived it every day since he met her. He watched Caleb stand, knees slightly bent to accommodate for her small size. Maintaining their contact, Caleb tightened his grip on her hips and started thrusting into her once more with a newfound fury.

Bending over her back, legs braced wide, Caleb drove into her. She had to stretch her slender neck, arch her head backward to keep Devin's flesh buried in her mouth. Her gasps and moans massaged him, poured fiery sensations of excess arousal through his body. Each of Caleb's hard thrusts sent her plunging forward, impaling his cock further than ever before in her overstretched, overfilled mouth.

"Yeah, baby," Devin growled in shocked astonishment, total carnal bliss as most of him nearly disappeared down her throat. The tight spasms clenched around him as she fought, struggled to swallow every inflamed inch.

"Suck it, baby. Take it all." He found Caleb's rhythm. With each powerful thrust from behind, Devin surged forward, plunging as much of his erection down her slippery throat as she could take. His tight scrotum slapped against her chin. He watched, amazed, overjoyed, crazed with lust as she shut her eyes, drew her lips taut around him as if in deep concentration. He was intent to give, as well as receive pleasure. An exquisite sight, and intense erotic sensations overwhelmed him as she suckled him hungrily, moaning and gasping as though she couldn't get enough of him.

"Open your eyes, baby. Look at me while you suck my cock." Devin's fingers tightened in her hair.

She groaned, her eyes snapping open. Their eyes locked. Her hazel gaze was heavy-lidded, darkened with arousal, glazed with desire and the depths flared with incitement at the prickling pain only he knew she loved so well. She ran her tongue along the pulsing head as he pulled out and sucked it hard each time he pushed in.

"Harder, suck, harder," he said.

She did as she was told, driving him insane with unspeakable lust. He held her face still as he began to thrust his hips, fucking her mouth with his cock as hard and deep as he would her body. He groaned with pleasure and drove into the heat of her velvet depths as he felt her nails digging into his buckskin-clad buttocks, nearly tearing through the softened leather.

"I'm going to come, Megan," Devin warned with a deep growl, forgoing all aspect of control as she tightened her suction, relaxing her throat as he slid in so deep, he'd swear his cock went past her shoulders. She sucked down most of his long length, and he crammed her hungry, greedy mouth over and over again. His scrotum tightened, filled with his seed, the sensations shooting up his spine, tearing through his cock.

In a haze of erotic pleasure, he was vaguely aware of Caleb's final thrust rocking Megan. Devin's own body arched and shuddered, his chest ready to burst and legs give out as his climax pushed forward, tore through. He shouted for Megan to swallow. His body convulsing, trembling against her mouth as he held her face to his groin, her lips light around the base, damp curls tickling her skin. His guttural roar bounced off the barn walls as his hot seed shot down her throat in thick spurts. Caleb's own shout of pleasure sliced through the air, which was thickened with their sexual scent, the heat of their passion, and their cries of pleasure.

Chapter 24

"Devin, I did as you asked," Megan muttered weakly, seeing the fire burning bright in his charcoal gaze as he stared down at her. She wiped the traces of his semen from the corners of her lips and felt Caleb's harsh breathing warm on her back, his arms wrapped around her waist, cock snugly inside her anus.

"Pointing a rifle at me is doing as I asked? Hardly," Devin replied darkly.

"I'm sorry Devin." Megan quivered.

"Hell, if it was just me, I could probably forgive you. But you threatened Deuce, Megan. No one does that and lives." He was still breathing ragged, deep, from the sustained vigor of the sexual act. The look in his eyes summed up in one word—dangerous.

Deuce lifted his head and neighed his full agreement, a bewitching mockery from within his stall.

Her eyes widened, a sense of fright spread through her. Without question, Caleb was struck by the gravity behind the warning. Breathing still labored, he straightened, and their bodies parted. Placing a calming, tender hand on her hip, he moved her to his side and stepped in front of her, shielding her with his naked body.

Her hands shook on his forearms as she peered around the refuge of Caleb's side toward Devin. The scent of their recent passion was thick, heavy in the air, as was the threat. Formidable danger loomed in front of her by way of sheer brawn and strength.

"Uh, Devin, don't you think you're being a little too harsh?" Caleb asked. "It's only a horse."

The look in Devin's eyes was a fatal warning. Caleb's next word would be his last.

"Deuce is no fucking horse. He's my partner. Only thing that's kept me alive all these years. You kill him, you better damn well have killed me first." His voice came hot and ominous from his broad chest as it rose with a violent turbulence.

She swallowed the knot in her throat and felt Caleb stiffen under her palms. This was her fight, not his. Death was preferable than witnessing Caleb harmed by any means. "I know what he means to you." she murmured softly, seductively, appealing to the overly abundant, innate sexuality pulsing through his veins, if not the man himself. "I never would have shot him. I was mad enough to shoot you, but never Deuce."

"Doesn't matter. What's done is done. You have to be punished, Megan."

"Your certainly can't kill her," Caleb protested vehemently.

She watched Devin in awe. Raw carnality shone in his hardened gaze, yet his muscled body was taut with deep-rooted anger. At times, even *he* could not control it either. She hoped this was not one of those occasions. Tension carved in his hard-edged expression, torn between the passionate emotions separated by a fine line.

Fully clothed, with only the front of buckskins undone, his cock hung heavily between his muscled thighs, nestled between two massive balls. Devin stood eye–to-eye in front of Caleb. He dominated the naked man with his brawn, height and disproportionate level of attire.

Her heart sped up. He knew what that fury raging through his system, that powerful dominance he exuded, and the raw sexual magnetism blazing in his eyes did to her.

"Stand aside, Caleb." Devin's voice was low, firm and held that air of authority that made lesser men flinch.

"I can't do that. I won't let you hurt Megan." He stood unyielding.

Megan glanced up at him, more than a little impressed. She was definitely flattered and touched he would risk all for her. Her gaze flicked back and forth as they stared each other down. Neither would submit.

The tension these two, tall, powerful, handsome men oozed washed over her, made her hotly aware of her own delicate femininity. Any normal person would have been terrified, frightened for their own safety. Not her. Instead, she was tempted, excited, aroused by her pathetic need and lust-filled desires, have her body, passion, lust swept away by all that manly strength, sexual virility and masterful dominance.

"Megan's been punished before. She knows what to expect," he said to Caleb, but his gaze never left her.

Caleb eyes lowered toward her. She blinked up at him, feeling strangely shy as heat flushed her face. She was embarrassed at having her secret shame exposed, ashamed because she felt decadently wicked, realizing how Devin planned to punish her.

Hesitantly, she shifted her gaze. "Devin..." she whispered, feeling vulnerable, helpless under her own depraved weaknesses. Each time Caleb looked at her, he saw Megan Adams, a young, innocent fourteen-year-old girl, naïve in the ways of life. That girl no longer existed.

"Tell him, Megan. It doesn't hurt...too much." His voice was soft, suggestive. His smile wicked, sinful. The look in his eyes intense, searing, burning awareness inside her body.

She shouldn't be responding to the threat of pain. Heaven help her, she was. Treacherously, her clit throbbed, and the liquid heat started to seep down her vagina, easing the way in anticipation. Feeling her breasts tighten, she glanced down and saw her nipples, rock-hard little peaks bursting from darkened areolas. Biting her lip, she knew Devin was vividly aware. His wicked punishment excited her, despite the mild pain he inflicted. It only heightened her arousal, her need for more. Always for more.

Devin's smile was one of triumph as she stepped from behind Caleb and accepted the hand he held out.

* * * *

Puzzled by Megan's lack of protest, Caleb watched as Devin led her dainty nude form to the back wall where the wooden crates were stacked. She was so small and fragile, so utterly helpless and so very wanton. Her lips were swollen. Her long, golden ringlets, in disarray from Devin's exuberant treatment, fell loosely over her shoulders and down her back.

And as she walked away, his gaze smoothed over the long sweep of her graceful back, narrow hips and perfectly rounded buttocks. Her skin was like fresh untouched cream. He glimpsed the little rosette between her cheeks as her curved hips swayed with each step, reddened, loosened and seeping with his semen. His cock stirred, thickened and elongated instantly.

Spirit of a whore, heart of an ingénue, and body of a goddess.

"Like sitting on crates, Megan?" Devin queried in his well-modulated voice as he took a seat on the double-stacked crates, where he'd sat during her sinful display designed to make him jealous.

Caleb was no fool. Because she suffered so deeply, Megan sexually used him to lash out the only way she knew how, and he enjoyed every damned moment. Except now. Wary. Now, he didn't know what was going to happen as he heard Devin calmly order, "You know what to do, Megan."

"Devin, please. I won't do it again. I promise." A hint of fear mixed with lust flickered in her gaze. It piqued his interest.

"No, Megan. It's too late for promises."

Despite her protests, he could see the effect the threat of punishment triggered. Her face flushed with arousal, and her nipples tightened on her swollen mounds. Without even looking or touching, he knew she was soaked. He could hardly control his own excitement or anticipation of what was coming. He was undeniably hot.

She shrieked when Devin grabbed her by the arm and pulled her onto his lap. The tips of the brown leather slippers she still wore barely touched the ground.

Caleb's eyes grew wide as Devin raised his hand, and the sound of flesh slapping bared flesh again and again coursed through him like a torrent of scorching lava. The heat built a fire in his loins, straight to his throbbing cock as his beloved Megan cried out. Her small body trembled, jerked, bucked against Devin as the stinging force branded her ass.

Although he was an active member of a Parisian club that catered to every sexual deviant perversion imaginable, Caleb never partook. Occasionally he passed rooms where the more aggressive domineering or bondage venues were available. He lacked the desire to participate. Megan, so tiny and frail in comparison to the well-tanned, massiveness of Devin looming over her, was daunting, erotic, breathtaking. Demanding submission, Devin's deep voice a formidable persuasion, was riveting.

Little pale cheeks burned crimson as she continued to cry out. Cries devoid of protest, filled with pleasure, sinful decadence as each blow against the other man's large palm landed on her bare bottom. Her body arching against him, breasts thrusting forward as her head and hair tossing wildly.

"Open your legs, Megan. Let me see how much you dislike what I'm doing." Devin's voice was a dangerous whisper as he ran a caressing hand along her back. Impelled by recklessness, a thrill of forbidden pleasure, Caleb found himself unable to look away.

Shamelessly, she parted her legs so wide, her slippers fell off her uplifted feet. As if propelled by a dark, carnal need, she brazenly arched her ass in the air and. rocked her belly against Devin's lap. Moaning as though she was asking, begging to be touched, spanked, or fucked with each wiggle of her ass.

His body was tight with sexual tension, need. Tormented by raging lust and an undreamt craving for something dark, carnal unlike anything he'd ever felt before. Caleb made his way behind Megan as his heart sped up. He had to look. Impatient. Eager. Desperate to see for himself the effectiveness of Devin's punishment.

Caleb's cock was painfully hard as he stroked it, staring a few feet from Megan's gaping pussy. Her aromatic juices slid down her thighs. He was so hot, on fire, ready to erupt and flood the earth with molten lava. Could only imagine what effect it was having on Devin. Clearly Megan, though she cried out, moaned and gasped in feigned protest. She breathed hard, flushed with arousal, body glistening with perspiration, her soaked cunt gaped open, ready and willing to accept whatever penance Devin dished out.

Holy shit, he was fucking enjoying her punishment immensely.

She shrieked when Devin buried a finger in her hot, tiny recess and bucked harshly against his lap. She groaned harshly from deep within the other man's throat, and Caleb could only assume she landed on his cock.

"Damn, Megan, you're sopping wet," Devin muttered heatedly as another slap landed on her tender bottom, burned a bright red.

Caleb's fingers itched to feel the heat of her tinged skin. He didn't need a finger inside her to realize how damp she was. He could see her delicious, thick cream collecting in the swollen folds of her pussy, trailing down her thighs, drenching Devin's buckskins. He heard the sopping noises when the dark, thick finger swirled in the tiny hole. Her rear rose and thrust blindly in the air. Her red cheeks clenched the hand in need under the ravaging assault upon her most delicate flesh.

"I can smell you from here. You're enjoying your punishment too damned much." Caleb couldn't remove his eyes from the imbedded finger caressing the sensitive flesh inside her body as she pushed back on Devin's hand. She moaned like a wild banshee. He could see the tension, the need in her body, hear it in her voice as she hovered near the brink just beyond reason. "Bad, naughty girls like to be spanked."

A loud whimper of protest escaped her lips as Devin completely withdrew his glistening finger. In a passion-filled haze, his eyes went to Devin. Lust and darkness shone in the other man's eyes. Devin passed him a knowing glance, inviting, approving. Entranced, Caleb stepped closer.

Megan groaned contentedly when Caleb dipped a finger into the heated, silken depths of her cunt as another slap singed her cheeks. The sharp sound echoed in his mind, pounded in his heart. He felt her narrow channel grip him tightly, clenching in need. A flare of heat rushed to his erection, now jerking against his abdomen.

"Oh, Devin, please," she cried out, her thighs tightening around his hand, holding him there. Barely able to breathe, he stared at the faint imprint on her curved cheek.

"You've been a very naughty girl, Megan. Deservedly so, your comeuppance will be more severe this time," Devin said. Another blow landed on her clenched cheeks.

Caleb twisted his finger inside the tight heat. Creamy hot liquid flowed from deep with her quivering body as her pussy continually gripped him. He wanted to ram inside her body, unable to fathom how Devin controlled himself.

"Your penalty should be harsh enough to atone for what you did to me and Caleb. Not to mention Deuce." His voice was a harsh growl, throbbed fiercely with primal lust.

In time to the sharp sting landing on her bottom, Caleb curled the digit buried inside her, teased the sensitive spot on the front of her vaginal wall as her vaginal walls constricted tightly. He sent new sensations rippling through her body as she trembled and cried out in desperation.

"I hate you, Devin," she panted, her voice raw with emotion as she tightened her arms around his thigh. Caleb watched her as she rocked her body against Devin's cock. She squirmed, writhed against him. Moved to press her breasts hard against Devin's thigh, rake her puckered nipples against the leather fabric while pushing back on his imbedded finger, grinding against his hand, seeking pleasure, her release.

Caleb swallowed in absolute wonder as he continued to move inside the hot, tight, soaked depths of her throbbing cunt. Never had he seen a woman so hell-bent on receiving pleasure, so accepting of dominance or the sharp bite of pain and complete sexual submission. She was eager in her unbridled lust, free in her fiery passion, intense in her carnal desires. His sweet Megan spread her legs like an absolute sex goddess, a sexual slave, a nymphet consumed with sexual excesses. The debased realization and understanding blew away his rationale, made him lust for her.

"Then why are you rubbing your belly against my cock?" Devin grinned, a most wicked, sinful grin. He heard her scream when the next blow struck the firm globes, already reddened, glowing from the enforced pleasure that had her gushing over his hand.

"I can't take much more of this," she groaned, her voice vibrating with need, her body trembling.

"Megan, your dripping wet pussy tells us you can." Devin's voice was low, pulsing tightly as he ran a hand along the arch of her back and landed another blow on her ass.

* * * *

Megan's eyes flared open. A finger deep inside her. A hand caressing her tender backside, as if inspecting in its handiwork. Another gently traced the line along her spine, sending a shiver of pleasure straight to her pussy.

Caleb.

Lost in her own carnal desire, she'd completely forgotten about Caleb. It was his finger swirling in her cunt, inflicting his own sweet discipline. She whimpered, reveling in his participation, his acceptance and the intimate connection thrusting inside her body.

"To prove to Caleb I'm not a complete jackass, we'll change the direction of your punishment." Devin's voice was tinged with lust, heated and dark, warning her of what was to come. Caleb withdrew his finger from the hot confines she gripped him sensuously with to keep him in place.

"No, Devin—" she whimpered, then clamped her mouth shut. She realized the mistake she'd made in telling him no. She screamed in delirious pleasure as the blow, a biting sting of erotic sensation, came down on her sopping wet pussy, and slammed into her clit, sounding more like sloshing than slapping. One more. One more, and she would explode, die in her orgasmic release. *Please*, she begged silently. *One more.*

"Megan, you know better than to tell me no. For that, we'll show you no mercy," he growled hotly.

Her breath caught. She felt his erection jerk, hot and hard against her stomach as he said the heated words. A flurry of alarm mingled with excitement rushed through her. The intense rush of lust pounded through her veins, igniting every nerve.

"Stand up and bend over." He shifted her off his lap.

She did as he demanded without hesitation. Turning so her back was to Devin, she bent over. Her entire body quivered, every fiber on fire, waiting, imagining what she would be forced to submit to.

"Farther, Megan. Spread your legs farther apart. We want to see your soaked pussy."

Instead of trembling with mortification at her continued sexual degradation, Caleb baring witness brought an unknown edge of unparalleled fiery heat and dark lust flaring through her body. An unknown, depraved desire pushed her beyond explanation. She wanted it. Ached for it. Whatever they had to give—hard, fast, rough, torment, pleasure, pain—she wanted it all and more. Already breathing in shallow pants, she felt her bare feet slide further along the ground, leaving long tracks in the dirt.

"Good, Megan. Now spread your cheeks for me," Devin demanded.

Doing as he asked, aware he and Caleb stood side-by-side, mesmerized by the provocative sight of her bent over. He knew her pussy lips were open, the intimate folds dripping. The 'pearl of her pleasure,' as Devin liked to call it when sucking it between his lips, was engorged and pulsing like a treasure waiting to be taken, at the very tip of her flesh.

Her heart raced out of control. She could hear their harsh breathing, their moans, the jerky movements as both men began to stroke themselves when she reached back. Her hands gripped her tender buttocks, and she winced at the searing sensation tearing through her system. Grimacing, she parted her tinged cheeks, feeling the hole still dripping with Caleb's cream. The twisted bun at the nape of her neck now undone, her hair fell over her shoulders and along her back. She arched, the peaks of her breasts thrust forward. The sweep of her hair was a welcomed touch to her sensitized nipples.

In her mind, she pictured what they saw: dark blond curls nestled between white flesh spread wide open, revealing the gaping entrances, the ultimate temptation of sin, a promise of pleasure, swollen, dripping, and throbbing for them, theirs for the taking. She shuddered on a breathless whimper, hardly able to wait.

"An exceptionally sinful pose. Don't you agree, Caleb?"

She held her breath, waiting for Caleb's response. All she heard was a heavy, manly groan of approval.

"Close your eyes, Megan. Don't move, no matter what. Don't move," Devin warned heatedly, and she obeyed, listening intently to their muted whispers, unable to distinguish what they were saying.

"Concentrate. Just feel," Devin whispered, and she obeyed, surrendering to the deep, seductive sound of his voice coming through the darkness behind her heavy, closed lids. Always obeying Devin, she could do no more. Then, she felt them and thought she would lose what was left of her mind. Four large hands began to caress every inch of her body sinuously. They glided over her arms, back, breasts, belly, up and down her legs, pleasuring her everywhere except where the fire raged brighter than ever before. Her body shivered and pulsated, her desperate moans echoing around them.

Each nerve and cell erupted as warm fingers and hot hands teased and kneaded, pinching a trail of fiery sensations along the way until she thought she could take no more.

Suddenly, lips added a new, torturous dimension. Moist, soft, demanding and heated. Their tongues ran under the swell of her flesh where her buttocks met thighs and deliciously along the small of her back, burning a path down her thighs, sending shock waves through her sensitized lips. They licked and tasting the cream flowing down the flesh of her inner thighs.

Her body responded instinctively, cried out as her nipples were squeezed and tweaked, encased in the hot, wetness of their mouths. She bucked as she felt hands and moist, warm lips roving over her rear, and fingers and wet tongues teasing her cleft, tightening as tender fingers touched her inner thighs, throbbing at the slightest caress to the slick folds she struggled with each passing moment to keep parted. She whimpered at the passion roused from touch alone.

No inch of her body remained untouched except where she was the wettest, ached the strongest and felt the greatest need. Hands, fingers, lips, and tongues tormenting her with sensuous agony until she was too weak to hold her decadent pose a moment longer. Certain she would faint dead away from the extremely licentious torture, it suddenly stopped.

"You're lucky you like your ass filled with cock, because that's all your getting." Grabbing her hips, Devin's voice, roughened with arousal, brought her back to awareness.

"Please, Devin, I want to come. I need to come," she begged helplessly, not caring how she sounded. Only conscious of the hunger, the burning need throbbing between her thighs.

"Not yet, Megan. Not until Caleb and I are done with you." Careful to avoid the most sensitive areas of her vagina, he coated her anus with her slick cream.

"I'm taking your tight ass, and you're going to suck Caleb. Make it good, Megan. Show him how much you like to suck cock." She was vaguely aware of Caleb moving away to wash himself. She felt Devin's fingers dip into the quivering well she still held open and cried out. She bit down on her lip as he held her still. With a firm hand on her hip, he continued to gather the collection of thick cream from her vagina, spreading it to her anus. Over and over again, he repeated the torture, always sure not to touch the sensitive nub that ached for his touch. His thick, long fingers drove her beyond insane, wild and delirious with her need as he drove into the hole between her cheeks. She heard him groan roughly as he prepared his cock with her juices. The thought of him taking her without being well-lubed, his huge cock tearing into her, pounding inside her small body, made her legs shake, pussy tighten and weep in expectation. She was scared, frightened of being ripped in two. She was dying for it.

"Suck him hard. Make him come," Devin growled, and she knew he was just as hot, excited, aroused and desperate as she was.

She closed her eyes, the memory of having two cocks burned vividly. The pleasure was so wonderfully intense, nothing else compared. What Devin planned was pure agony, and she craved it, needed it, wanted it desperately. Two enormous cocks filling her, stretching her incredibly, driving her mad with desire. Neither intended to bring her release, only heighten her immense arousal.

"Remember," Devin said, "you don't get yours until we get ours."

A scant moment later, the swollen head of his iron-hard erection rubbed against the entry of her anus. Her body was already relaxed, prepared. Her channel slackened and filled with Caleb's semen. She pushed back against the flared head and heard a hard, male groan as the entrance stretched, begging for the swollen head to drive inside her.

"Oh, you want you it bad. Don't you, baby?" Devin rasped, his voice heavy with lust.

Megan no longer cared if they shared her body or her passion. Knowing as soon as their need was met, the relentless buildup of pain, agonizing pleasure leading to her impending orgasm would be more intense, burn hotter and be all-consuming. Devin taught her that lesson, and she learned to accept, crave and beg for the dark, sinful extreme.

Her eyes snapped open as she felt the bulging head of his cock nudging the entrance from behind. Caleb was in front of her, holding his thick, hard flesh in his hands inches away from her mouth.

There was no time to react. Megan screamed at the rip of burning pain and white-hot, searing pleasure shattered her system, tore through her body at the sudden invasion of Devin's extreme impalement. With one hard thrust and a deep growl, Devin lifted her off the ground, holding beneath where her legs bent. Her scream was muffled by the sound of Caleb's rough groan as he plunged his cock into her mouth, his hands reaching under her, holding her up as he clutched her breasts.

Devin, six-foot-nine of pure power and brawn and carved of muscle, Caleb, at six-three to her mere size, made it easy for them to suspended her between their two bodies like a pendulum. Her body raged with a fire burning out of control. She clung onto Caleb's hips as her legs curled around Devin's solid buckskin-clad ones.

Caleb made no allowances for his size, as if he figured if she managed to take Devin's twelve inches, then she should adeptly swallow his thick, nine-inch dick. She didn't want to disappoint. She swallowed his hard thickness greedily down her hungry throat, sucking the flared head of his cock with her cheeks and lavishing it with her tongue as he drove in and out of her mouth.

Megan could feel her anal muscles stretching, clenching at his wide, hard flesh, his fingers tightening on her hips as he split her in two. Hard, deep, brutal thrusts, on the edge of being violent, tore through her sanity, heightened her pleasure, her need. Devin incited her toward an intensity beyond her realm, pleasure and pain so uncontrolled, unexpected, it both terrified and made her want to scream for more. Her entire pussy throbbed, so swollen and hypersensitive, and her sheen-covered body shuddered desperately.

Moaning hungrily, savagely around the solid, hot flesh pumping between her lips, she tightened her mouth on him, slurping greedily, tempting him to fuck her mouth harder, eager to taste his rich seed.

Their fiery thrusts were deep and fast, sending her into a total abyss. She felt as though one colossal cock was thrusting inside her from one end to the other, setting her entire body ablaze with burning liquid. An insatiable need for more that all she could do was accept the heated, carnal, depraved sensations washing artfully over her until she was giving as much as she was getting.

Her filled mouth suctioned tightly around Caleb's cock as he plunged deeper. She stroked the same sensitive spot that drove Devin over the edge. She could taste Caleb's release on her tongue as his flesh pulsated in her mouth. She rocked back hard, clenching her anal muscles tightly around Devin's huge erection, driving him beyond his own control. She felt his body start to tighten, his cock swell, expand in her anus. She heard their male cries of lustful pleasure, deep desires of release being fulfilled with each gut-wrenching movement.

She didn't stop as jets of hot, thick semen shot down her throat. Devin held her tightly, shuddering violently against her from the extreme intensity of his ejaculation.

Their heated, primal shouts of passion so intense, they crashed through the slats in the paneled barn walls, echoing through the pasture like men being burned alive at the stake. Even the horses became agitated and jumped in their stalls.

Caleb was spent. He leaned against the nearest column, his breath coming in harsh, fast pants. Devin pulled her into his arms, possessively wrapped one over her breast and the other crossing her belly, resting his hand low on her hip, their connection still intact. His ragged breath warmed her glistened skin.

"Damn, Megan. I believe you really want to kill me," he muttered between breaths.

Giving him a moment to catch his breath, she took comfort in his warmth, his need to hold onto her as though he couldn't ever let her go. If not for the never-ending ache between her thighs, she would have been satisfied to remain in his arms forever just as they were. But the hunger, the need still throbbed for relief. Once she sensed some resemblance of equilibrium was returning, she whispered, "Devin."

"I know, darling," he said with complete understanding. Cradling her into his embrace, he carried her like a small child into the house.

* * * *

Reaching the bedroom, Devin sat her on the edge of the bed. Crossing the room, he took a washcloth and dipped it in the wash basin, then wrung out the excess water. He turned and found Megan staring at him. The wealth of emotions clouding her eyes took his breath away.

He plopped down beside her. She smiled up at him, and again, he was struck by the sheer intensity of the unbridled passion blazing in the hazel depths. This passion was not of a sexual nature, one that made him more than uncomfortable. For a minute, he tried to dismiss his unease as he struggled inwardly for composure. Yet the unfamiliar stirring tempering his defenses would not release its stronghold on him so easily.

"I hope I didn't hurt you?" he asked after took a deep, calming breath. He tenderly wiped the gleam off her brow with the wash cloth. Feeling guilty for behaving like the brute he was, he smiled at her and whispered, "Can you forgive me if I did?"

"I love you, Devin Spawn." Her soft voice was filled with emotions he knew were misdirected. He was undeserving. Unworthy. Nevertheless, her warm words were heartfelt and true. He couldn't return them. Hearing them was tearing him apart.

"I know, Megan Spawn," he replied gently. Lowering his head, he watched her eyes as they lowered to his lips. He leaned in closer. Slanting his lips over hers, he kissed her. A soft, gentle brush of his lips against the warm moistness of hers, so brief, it almost didn't seem real. Only her breathless sigh told him she felt, understood the unspoken words. "I know."

The tension in the room was too much for him. Suffocating. He felt like his chest was about to explode. Eager, downright desperate to change the mood, he fell back on the bed. Tossing his legs over the edge, he stretched out, careful not to kick her in the process. Taking his cock in hand, he hurriedly cleaned up. Flinging the rag on the floor, he ran two expert strokes along the length and ran his fingers along the sensitive underside of the head.

"I could do that for you," she whispered seductively, the tips of her fingers tugging gently on buckskin fly where his hands were diligently working.

"You've done enough," he drawled seductively. *More than you'll ever know.* He gave her a look that let her know he was deliciously sated and about ready for sin.

Megan giggled as he magically came to life before her eyes. He was long, thick, and hard as stone. Perfect to suit her needs.

"It's all yours, Megan." He kept his voice low, a sensuous enticement to the unbridled passion was the message he wanted to convey. It was all he had to offer. "For you to ride as long as you want. At least, until it's time to pick up the girls."

"Can I at least undress you first?" Curling the corners of her lips, she arched a brow in a playful, teasing manner that displayed her adorable dimples. A look that touched parts of him that had no business being touched.

"You can do to me whatever the hell pleases you." He smiled, parting his legs and stretching out his arms, indicating he was all hers for the taking. He didn't have the strength or desire to deny her.

"No interference." She had a wicked gleam in her eye, and he grinned. If he wasn't already hard, that look would have done the trick.

"None from me," he assured her, about ready to pass out from exhaustion. In a tiny package called Megan, he'd met his match.

Slowly, she undressed him. He moved and shifted around as necessary as she pulled off everything in her way. And apparently, everything was in her way, including the sweat dripping from his skin—she wiped that away, too.

When she was done, his breathing escalated as her lips began to kiss every inch of his skin. He closed his eyes, moaning quietly as he felt the warmth and tenderness of her lips, the moistness of her hot little tongue roaming upon his skin. Softly, tenderly, she caressed his entire body with the heat of her body and hands as she moved over him.

He laid back submissively, grimacing with his own need. Lust raged through his bloodstream. Minutes ago, he thought he would pass out from exhaustion, sleep for a year. Now, he wanted her so badly, his heartbeat pounded in his ears. Clenching his fists in the blankets, he fought to remain still.

This was her time. He had given his word, to let her do with him as she pleased.

So this was love: so tender, so gentle and so caring. The emotion so heartfelt and strong, it permeated into his very core, transcended even his most rigid boundaries.

He never imagined one person could possess so much love.

And it was aimed at him.

This must be heaven, he concluded as she straddled him. She braced her palms on his chest, and he stared at her in silence as she raised her hips over his cock. Slowly she lowered herself until he was wrapped in her moist heat. He groaned harshly, battling his inner demons. Holding his hips still took a helluva lot of control, but he managed.

Instantly, she cried out his name. She clung to him as her body exploded and drenched his flesh with the first of many climatic releases. He kept his hands to himself as she kissed his eyelids, nose, behind the ears, the curve of his throat, everywhere but his mouth. As if knowing if she did, he would want to take over, and she would probably let him.

He lay there, fighting the dominant male instinct. She enjoyed her feminine instinct to please. And please she did. Leaving him with no choice but to ignore his raging hard-on as it swelled, throbbed for wet-heat, ached to ram into her tight body as she paced herself. She fought the instinctive urge to pound deep and hard as she convulsed, milked him within her velvet depths each time she took her pleasure. She rocked over his body slow and easy, with long, steady strokes. It nearly destroyed him, but he lay there and let her take what she needed.

Deep down, he knew she desperately wanted to feel his love, needed a part of him she could only have if she took it from him. He felt like a selfish bastard for always taking from someone so willing to give of herself, with one desire in return, what he did not possess, a heart, worthy of receiving as well as giving love.

In a way, by his acceptance, he was sending her a message loud and clear.

* * * *

Throughout the next two weeks, whenever the girls were in school, Caleb continued to come. Come in her mouth, her pussy, her ass, over her belly and face. She thought it strange at first, but he seemed to enjoy rubbing his cream into her skin. He delighted in the least of the perverse acts they performed as they licked various parts of each others' bodies. Devin would have none of it. He wanted her to swallow every last drop of his seed, or fill her body, as though wanting to keep a part of him inside her for as long a possible.

It took her a while before she was completely comfortable accepting both of them. After all, it was unusual. Final acceptance ultimately would mean she agreed to marry Caleb. Devin would ride off, believing all was well. Her life would be spent waiting for his return, if he decided to return. The thought left her sad, confused, strangely alone, and very afraid of what would happen if she made the wrong choice.

Through the peephole at Jazelle's, she'd watched cowboys short on cash resort to sharing a whore, presenting a whole new world of pleasure to her. Usually, they sat in the room and watched. While waiting, sometimes the more anxious touched either themselves or the women. Or else waited impatiently in the hallway for their turn, hollering through the door for their partner to 'poke n' go,' 'rush the flow'.

This was entirely different. Devin and Caleb were both handsome, muscled, well-endowed with thick, long, juicy cocks. And they both knew what to do with them. At the same time, their hands, mouths, lips, tongues, and fingers worked sensuous magic. They left her breathless, satisfied and begging for more. Their stamina was a gift of nature. They could both go on for hours. They'd take turns pleasuring her until she awoke hours later in a sated, sexual daze. She suspected a male rivalry, competition of sorts, but didn't dare bring it up for fear of spoiling her fun.

Devin was the exact opposite of Caleb. Rough to his gentle. Hard and fast to slow and easy. Her body enjoyed, responded, and climaxed to both. However, Caleb was learning what really stoked her fire to mammoth proportions, could see how the sharp bite of pain mixed with pleasure broke all sexual boundaries, intensifying her orgasms into earth-shattering explosions and made her go absolutely wild with depraved lust.

By the end of the second week, she was ready and primed for her two lovers.

Previously, Devin started their trysts by getting her so insanely aroused alone in their bedroom that when Caleb appeared sometime later, she was drunk with lust. She didn't care if the whole town bought tickets to watch her suck and fuck both their cocks, lick and tease their assholes. She was tossed and turned, bent and spread, spanked and tied in every position imaginable. Finally she'd ride them into frenzy until they exploded from the sheer pleasure of it all.

Not today—it was her turn to be in charge.

She kept a watch out for Caleb. As soon as she saw him ride up, she rushed to her bedroom. It was her way of telling them she accepted their so-called 'agreement.' Her mind wasn't made up about the marriage part yet, but she was willing to take it one step at a time. After all, what girl wouldn't want two exquisitely handsome men fawning over her?

* * * *

"Megan," Devin called for her as he walked through the front entryway.

Caleb followed two steps behind and settled on the couch, resting his foot over his knee.

"Shit, Megan," Devin muttered, taken aback at the site on the bed after he opened the bedroom door. His cock stiffened, jerked in his britches as his mouth went dry.

Caleb rushed across the room and glanced over Devin's shoulder.

Devin stood unmoved, gaping, eyes glued between Megan's legs. She was completely naked, sprawled on the bed. Her legs spread wide, with one dildo buried in her ass and another pumping between the pinks folds, glistening with her juices. The expression on her face was purely erotic. She looked so beautiful, so wanton, lost in her own pleasure, need.

   Caleb brushed past Devin, his jacket already removed. The rest of his clothes soon followed.

   Snapping out of his daze, Devin scrambled out of his clothes, popping buttons and ripping material in the hasty process.

   "I can't wait." Megan's heavy-lidded gaze rose to Devin, then Caleb. "I want you both, now."

   Caleb rolled her on her side, drew one of her legs over his shoulder, jerked the dildo from her ass, and impaled her with one deep thrust. Her cry of pleasure filled the room as her body bolted off the bed. Her hands gripped the sheets. Curling his fingers around the dildo in her cunt, he matched the pounding in her ass and had her screaming with each deep penetrating thrust the side position allowed.

   "Is this what you want, Meg?" Caleb growled, plunging into both passages with fiery abandon.

   "Yes, Caleb, fuck me. Fuck me hard," she cried out, bucking her hips against him.

   Devin kept an eye on her. She was so caught up with the double sensations, so aroused and consumed with lust, she hadn't realized what he was doing. He propped the large mirror that hung above the dresser onto the chair he had dragged closer to the bed. He positioned it at an angle for her to witness all the action, top to bottom.

   Kneeling on the front of the bed, he held his cock to her lips. "I want you to watch while you suck me. See how beautiful you look. See what you do to us, Megan."

   She took him in her mouth, and he groaned roughly, feeling the hot, wetness surround his flesh. He glanced over his shoulder into the mirror, watching her. She stared as her mouth moved up and down the thick red shaft she held in her small hands. Her lips stretched taut. Her cheeks filled with the engorged head of his cock as she suckled deep and hard, then slow and easy. His fingers gripped in her hair, until she moaned from the sensuous bite of pleasure and pain the tugging elicited.

   He noticed her gaze lower toward Caleb's thick cock sliding in and out of her tiny ass, his hand ramming the ivory dildo between her pink, swollen lips. The vision was so erotic, so wicked, he could have come right then.

Moving his hand to one of her breasts, he squeezed and released the hard nipple crowning the swollen mound as she moaned over his plunging shaft.

"Suck my dick, Megan. Harder, and I'll make you come," Devin promised, as he continued to watch her in the mirror.

Her face was flushed, eyes glazed with passion as her body moved against them in a heated frenzy. Moving a hand to his balls, she squeezed them hard, rolling them with her hands just the way he liked. He groaned as his blood pulsed with lust, hot and intense. She tightened the grip of her mouth, her tongue flickering the sensitive flesh on the underside that always sent him to where he wanted to go. She was sucking him as if she were starving, as if they hadn't feasted on one another only hours ago. As if she could never get enough of his spicy juice. He sure as hell couldn't get enough of hers.

"Yeah, baby, suck it hard." Reaching down, he cupped the other breast, teasing the puckered tip with his thumb while stroking her clit with the other hand. He felt her body tightening, saw goose bumps covering her skin. He increased his thrusts as Megan's mouth clamped down on his cock, her hand tightened around his scrotum as it filled with his seed.

She came instantly, screaming with pleasure over the head of his cock throbbing in her mouth. As the first burst of semen erupted, she swallowed him down her throat almost entirely. He growled furiously as his explosion flowed down her throat.

Devin's entire body shook as he seemed to endlessly spill down the silken depths of her sweet, hot mouth. Caleb groaned out her name as he shuddered between her legs, filling her ass with his release.

Wasting no time, Devin flipped her over and turned her around. Bringing her to her knees, he jerked her thighs apart and took her ass in one deep plunge. Caleb wiped himself with the washcloth from the small table before slid his cock between her waiting lips.

"You like all your holes filled," Devin growled, replacing the dildo lodged in her pussy with two long, thick fingers. "You like being naughty. Show us, Megan, how naughty you can be." He slapped her ass.

* * * *

Pulling back from Caleb's cock for a moment, Megan wanted to coerce Devin, tempt him. See how far he would go and how much she would enjoy the ride. "Is that all you have? I thought you wanted to fuck me. *You* look in the mirror while Caleb's juicy cock fucks my mouth," she ordered, provoking the wicked flame of passion stroked by their ingrained male rivalry.

Digging her fingernails in Caleb's ass, she swallowed all of him greedily, hungrily as though she were starving. She was playing with fire, and she knew it.

"Don't try me, Megan," Devin warned harshly. The sharp sting of his hand on her flesh ripped through her body, more intense than usual, sure to leave a mark until tomorrow.

She beamed, lust flaring through her body. His cock pummeled into her anal depths with fierce potency as his hands held her in place, the sensations so intense, she burned from the inside out, drowning in the pleasure as he drove deeper and deeper. She wanted more. To feel him lose control. She wanted him to dominate her, love her the only way he knew how.

"You could get hurt. I'll tear your ass apart," Devin said.

Darting her eyes to the mirror, she stared as Caleb's balls slapped against her chin. He dug his fingers in her hair and face-fucked her with the same heated passion he just fucked her ass with. She rocked back on Devin's cock and fingers with a fiery passion. She released Caleb's cock while she wiggled her ass, tempting Devin further. "Ya'll too tired from yesterday? What's a girl gotta do to get a proper fucking?"

He spanked her again, harder. "You're asking for it, Megan."

Her pussy tightened, gripping at the emptiness in desperation. Her mouth clenched around the thick flesh, swallowing the entire cock in her mouth. Caleb groaned, his body shuddering and his fingers tugging at her hair wrapped around his fingers.

"Again, Devin," Caleb growled through gritted teeth, holding her face between his hands. His thrusts increased, plunging deeper down her throat.

She struggled to contain his throbbing flesh, her mouth gripping him harder. Dying to show them both who was in charge for a change.

"She's sucking my cock like never before," Caleb said. "Spank her again, harder."

Devin's hand came down again and again. She jerked as the painful sensations of utter pleasure tore through her body, sent streaks of lightning straight to her clit. Caleb threw his head back, shutting his eyes, groaning as she tightened her lips, her mouth and tongue suckling him harder and deeper as her fingertip swirled around his anus.

"Get ready, Meg, I'm coming," Caleb shouted just as he stiffened. His entire body trembled, hot jets of cream shot down her throat.

Devin took hold of her hips and pummeled her with wild abandon, hard, furious, heated thrusts unlike anything she'd felt before. Caleb's softening cock plopping out of her mouth as she moaned and groaned holding onto the bed. Her body thrashed back and forth, her hips swiveled and ground against him. She couldn't grab the bed—it seemed to move with her as his cock drove faster and faster, until she wanted to scream at the vicious extremity she had no idea existed. Her body was shattering, vibrating, fighting the agonizing pleasure overwhelming her senses. It was too much, too harsh for her tender backside.

He reared back and roared her name, as if overcome by the power of his release rocking his tall frame. Thrusting, he shook his beefy stalk inside her as though to make sure he didn't miss releasing a single drop in the depths before he withdrew. He left her quivering and burning with pulsating pleasure, her body glistening with perspiration and tingling with renewed vigor.

Sighing, he leaned back against the wall with his eyes closed, chest heaving roughly. She struggled to her feet to stand on the bed. She moved in front of him, watching as drops of sweat dripped from his forehead. Looking down, she smiled. Amazingly, he was still hard. He usually didn't soften until after he came at least twice—sometimes three times, which suited her just fine. Considering Caleb and Devin both climaxed and she didn't, she was ready to go again.

Grabbing hold of the slick erection poking straight out between his legs, she informed him confidently, "I'm not finished with you yet."

Chapter 25

"Bears."

"Wolf."

"Bears!"

"Wolf!"

"Girls," Megan chided Shelby and Emma gently as their squabble over which bedtime story they wanted to hear from Devin escalated. "One of your story books would be more appropriate than tall Indian tales."

"Megan," Shelby pouted, her bottom lip curing exaggeratedly almost to her chin. "We like the stories. They're excitin'."

Megan glanced over at Devin reproachfully, arching an eyebrow.

He quickly lowered his head and tried his best to look preoccupied as he went back to cleaning his six-shooters at the table. He seemed to decide it was best to button his lip, keeping out of the way of arguing females, no matter their size.

Moving to his side, she whispered in his ear, "Coward."

As she made a move to step away, he took hold of her wrist. With a gentle tug, he pulled her close. His breath was a warm whisper upon her neck. "My courage, along with my strength, was drained outta me this afternoon."

Blushing at the remembrance of the heated, lustful afternoon they shared with Caleb, she let her free hand casually drop to his lap. Her fingers lightly brushed the soft fabric over his penis. He nearly bolted out of his seat, eyes darting to where the girls sat on the sofa brushing their hair, unaware.

She stared as he stirred to hardness. Her own body grew wet, preparing itself. He mumbled in a low tone through gritted teeth, "Shit, Megan, I gotta tell 'em a story. What the hell are you doing to me?" He looked up at her, eyes darkening with arousal, despite the exasperation in his tone.

Staring back at him, she licked her lips. Teasing. Tempting. His gaze dropped to her hand moving over his erection as he swallowed tightly. Her finger was slender enough to slip under the bulging fabric between buttons. She scraped the hot, bare flesh beneath with her nail and heard his long intake of breath.

Playing unfair is what she was doing. Sometimes, that was all a woman could do to get her way. Never had he touched her inappropriately in front of the girls. They passed plenty of knowing glances, whispered heated words to one another, "accidentally" rubbed legs under the dining table or brushed hands as they passed the mashed potatoes. Like an old married couple, they never argued or touched in front of the children.

"One of my stories," she suggested innocently, blocking the girls' view with her full skirt. She felt his cock jerk as her finger slipped in further. He sighed roughly as she ran the tip over a thick vein.

"Whatever you say." His knuckles turned white as he gripped the edge of the table trying to regain control of the part of his body with a mind of its own. Veins in his temples tightened as he shot her a brooding sideways glance.

Megan withdrew her finger and patted the bulge affectionately. She allowed her hand to linger a moment longer than necessary. The heat of his hard flesh burned through his britches and seared her skin. The flesh between her thighs, now slick with her arousal, tightened with awareness. Another hour, and they would be alone, naked and in each other's arms. She felt giddy at the thought.

She turned and walked away, smiling triumphantly. "Okay, time for bed, girls. Devin's going to read you the story about the fairy princess."

Megan held back her laughter when she heard the heavy sigh of frustration behind her.

"Give him a few minutes to put things in order. He'll come tuck you in," she added, unable to suppress the amusement ringing in her voice.

* * * *

"Do we hafta hear *that* story?" Shelby mumbled when Devin pulled the worn book with a frayed binding and torn pages from the girls' bookshelf hanging on the wall.

"'Fraid so." He shrugged his shoulders. Leaning over, he tucked the blanket around her after she fell back, letting her head plop on the pillow.

He took a seat at the end of Emma's bed and cast a fleeting glance over his shoulder toward the bedroom door to see if Megan was within listening distance. The coast was clear.

"Tonight, it's her story. On the way home from school tomorrow, I'll tell you a new one about a skunk."

"Oh, boy," cheered Shelby.

Raising a quieting finger to his lips, he shook his head. Shelby giggled, then immediately quieted down.

"Don't let Megan know. She don't like you tellin' them stories on account of them Injuns stole her baby brother, Trevor," Emma informed him with big silver eyes that gleamed with excitement. He estimated they must have heard the story hundreds of times, the images conjured by the raid that took place over ten years ago were still vivid in their innocent, childhood minds, more in fascination than in fear.

Devin treated her with a puzzled look at that interesting tidbit of information. He understood Megan's brother had been killed along with her parents. Perhaps Emma misunderstood Megan regarding the tragedy. Grisly details may have been deliberately left out, so as not to frighten the girls more than necessary. Either way, he didn't press further. But the question lingered.

* * * *

It took reading the princess story twice before Emma and Shelby finally dozed off. Afterward, he found Megan in their bedroom soaking in the bathtub.

Locking the door behind him, Devin strode across the room and took a seat on the end of the bed. Resting an arm on his thigh, he leaned over and bobbed the rose petals floating in the bathwater with his index finger.

"You know, you could join me," she whispered innocently. Abruptly, he raised his gaze and their eyes locked. Dwelling on instinct, he had been unaware of her presence. He couldn't say the same about her. The look in her eyes was anything but innocent. She was more than aware of his being there. "Unless you're content playing with rose petals?"

"Megan." He held his tone low, reserved, devoid of sexual innuendo. He paused, unsure how to broach the delicate subject, brushed aside the vivid arousal stark in her eyes as she blinked up at him, face flush, lips slightly parted in invitation. He rubbed his brow, and as usual, quickly decided to take his customary approach. Face it head on. Bluntly. "Why didn't you tell me the Comanche took your brother?"

She looked like someone had doused her with ice water. Her skin riddled with goose bumps from head to toe. Her face turned pale and her jaw dropped.

His gut wrenched. He felt like a heel at the pain swirling in her eyes, memories relived by the mere mention of that fateful day. He reached out to comfort her. She pulled back instantly. He was not sure if it was out of distaste or anger. He could see the emotions flooding her eyes, the fear, tension drawing her expression taut.

"I apologize for my lack of whatever the hell you wanna call it. I'm no sweet talker." He scowled, keeping his tone straightforward, yet low, trying to smooth the damage already done.

Closing her eyes, she sank low in the big, round tub, drawing the water below her chin. She inhaled deeply, paused, and then released it before meeting his gaze.

"It's all in the past. I'd rather not discuss it anymore." She averted her gaze once more, staring instead at the top of her knees peeking just above the waterline.

"You may hate me for this, Megan, but I gotta ask. After tonight, if you want, I'll never mention it again." He took a deep breath. "What happened that day?"

"Devin, there's nothing to talk about. He's gone. My family is gone." Her voice shook with emotion, the tears welling in her eyes.

"Trust me on this, Megan." He couldn't bear for her to look at him that way, to intentionally cause her pain and upset her. But there was a reason. He needed to know. There was a chance her brother could still be alive. Many young children had been taken over the years by various tribes. Beyond the physical, their real families would no longer recognize them. Dependent upon who was doing the telling, lucky ones were raised among them. They lived like the red-skinned savages they were now considered by outsiders. Devin knew several. "Sometimes it helps to talk about it. What did he look like? Did he have hazel eyes like yours, or were they blue?"

Sitting up, she closed her eyes once again as if picturing her baby brother.

"Blue," she described lovingly, a long moment later. "His eyes were blue, and his hair blond. So blond, it was almost white."

He swallowed, hard. His heart raced, but he kept his expression somber, eyes unreadable.

Raising her gaze to his, she nipped her bottom lip. "All that I have left…"

Devin held his breath.

"…is one red slipper my mother made for him."

He choked on the lump swelling in his throat.

"Are you okay?" The water splashed in and over the tin bathtub as she kneeled in the center, reached out, and placed a hand on his knee. For a moment, he stared at the dainty, feminine hand, wet and warm on his thigh. Through it all, she still wanted to comfort him. His chest clenched. He didn't even deserve to be in the same room with her.

Clearing his throat, he rose to his feet and crossed the dimly lit room. False hope wasn't what she needed now. There was a chance he knew where to locate her brother. He wasn't about to let on until he was positive. The sooner, the better. Megan had already been through enough heartbreak.

Eyes steady on the black spaces filled the lace curtain cutouts on the far window, which lent an elusive shade as the single candle glowed on a table next to the bed. Lost in his thoughts, he didn't know how much time passed before he calmly unbuttoned his shirt. "Sorry, Megan, if I upset you. I promise I'll never mention it again." If things went as he hoped, it would be one promise he'd gladly break.

After a long pause, he was suddenly became aware of the silence.

His gaze returned to her as he shrugged out of his shirt. He sat on the bed and kicked off his boots, peeled off his socks and lethal trappings. From where he was, he could only see above the rim of the tin tub. He watched her as she sat curled and down low in the tub. The back of her head rested on the edge, and her eyes were closed. Her golden hair was dry and loose ringlets flowed on the outside of the tub. Her slender shoulders covered in dew glistened in the candlelight. Arms rested along the rim on either side as the steam rose above the water, wrapping her in a soft, heated fog.

He felt sinful, depraved stirrings deep in his belly. Damn, he wanted her so badly, he ached with raw need until he couldn't stand the pain. His body was hot and hard, as if he and Caleb hadn't already put her through enough this afternoon. He didn't know where he found the strength, the fucking stamina. But one look at her, and he could lose himself within her tight little body for hours. Apparently, Caleb felt the same, because he, too, kept her busy, screaming through orgasm after orgasm. They both did. Now, the poor thing was tired, 'bout ready to fall asleep in the bathwater.

Feeling a bit mischievous in addition to the hot-blooded arousal pumping in his blood, he moved to the side of the tub, wearing only his britches.

Her creamy complexion was pinkish from the warmth. Her breasts rose gently. Her nipples were tiny beads almost blending with her areolas. Her stomach was a smooth curve, meager curls between her thighs, did little to conceal the entrance to her sweet treasure.

He smiled down at her, ignoring the lust consuming him. The throbbing stiffness demanded a different kind of wet heat than what she sat in. "Hand me the soap. I'll lather you up." His voice was low, but effective.

Her eyes fluttered open, blinking away the slumberous haze. "Mmm," she purred drowsily, smiling up at him. Her expression was still relaxed, sleepy as she sat up. Suddenly, her gaze came alive with sexual awareness as she noticed his bare chest, the painful past all but forgotten. She licked her lips as he watched her eyes lower, knew exactly where she headed. "Why don't you join me?" Her voice was breathy, seductive.

His brow rose. He tilted his head to get a good, long look. She spread her bent legs, baring the swollen lips of her cunt and the faint bruising marring her pale thighs. He cringed on the inside, realizing he'd done that to her. Fucking her hard while she stared in the mirror as his cock tore into her. She still had not recovered. At times, he was unable to control the fiercely dominate sexuality he had been cursed with. Inhuman urges and dark desires. Damned, depraved is what he was, befitting the wild beast aching between his thighs, demanding attention.

Not tonight, he told himself, gritting his teeth and fighting back his unnatural needs. "This big ol' body ain't gonna fit in that tin cup."

She rose, and he allowed his eyes to rove over every dripping wet inch of female perfection. Latching on to his waistband, she pulled him close. His gaze snapped to her hand as she cupped his cock and then squeezed, causing him to groan. "We can both stand."

Looking down at her, he could see the fiery arousal blazing in her eyes, hear her breath quicken. Leaning in closer, she pressed her breasts against his abdomen. He breathed out roughly as he felt the heat of her slick mounds sink into his flesh. His hard-on grew harder as her hand moved up and down his length. He felt his cock jerk beneath her fingers as she raked him with her nails through the fabric.

"Megan," he growled, trying to remain in control of the untamed lust slamming through his system. "Don't think we hafta fuck every night. Thought you might want a breather. Caleb and I were a little rough on you this afternoon. Didn't mean to hurt you, but it's hard holding back. 'Specially when you talk dirty. Try to order us. You know how men get." He shook his head and grinned, trying to lighten the situation and take her mind and hand off his cock before he did what her bruised body wasn't ready for.

Megan felt the blush rise to her cheeks as she looked up at him. She could see the raw lust in his gaze, as well as the concern. There was an undeniable rivalry for her affections between them. It became even more apparent when she had watched them both in the mirror. Lust had washed over them, strained their expression, darkened their eyes, demanding in their thrusts as they rode her for hours. She couldn't tell one to do something without inciting the other. She loved it. She relished the intense wicked sensations they aroused within her. Devin knew it. Just as she knew him.

His eyes widened and darkened as she slowly worked the buttons of his fly. She heard his breath catch as she spread the edges apart, heard his groan of relief as she reached in the tight confines and pulled his thick, hard, flesh free

"Devin, I loved what you and Caleb did," she assured him softly. His eyes were closed, his face flush with arousal. His male scent was enticing, surrounding her with desire. "I'm not complaining." Holding him with one hand, she stroked him with the other. His hips thrusting slightly toward her, had her pussy clenching in need. "Besides, who said I wanted gentle?"

"You're not sore?" His voice was strained, desperate, his expression no better. The pulsing heat in her hand extended all the way to her clit. He was hard, eager to thrust into her. She couldn't help but be moved by his sacrifice. Despite the fact he wanted her, he was willing to go without. But could she?

It took both hands to curl around the shaft in her grasp. "Look at this thing." She waved the flared tip up at him as his flustered gaze dropped downward. Her hands looked so small, childlike in comparison to the manly flesh throbbing in her small grip. Thick and heavy, hot and hard, silky smooth, she loved the feel of it, holding it in her hands, pushing it between her... "It's like sticking my arm up my privates. I'm always gonna be sore."

He grimaced, muttering what sounded like two-bar soap words under his breath.

"A soreness I can't live without. Along with it comes a whole lotta pleasure." She smiled, smearing the droplet of semen seeping from tiny slit over the velvet soft flesh. It jerked in her hands, and she resisted the urge to take him in her mouth. She glanced up at him, put a little force in her voice. "So if you don't take off your britches and give me what I want, then I'm gonna—"

"What are you gonna do? Punish me?" His gaze softened, held a wicked gleam, and the blood pumping through her veins raced.

Take a whip to him, tie him up, make him wait to take his release while she pleasured him to the brink. He'd enjoy it all. Devin liked it hard and rough. When she made love to him, he seemed to enjoy slow and easy, as well. Even fucking Caleb in front of him eventually worked in his favor. There was no way to punish him.

"Perhaps you're right," she said with feigned sincerity, trying her best to stuff his hard-on back in his britches as his questioning gaze narrowed on her. "After all the romping we've done." She closed his fly best should could, then gave up, leaving the bulging length rising along his abdomen. She waved the task off and looked up at him, fluttering her eyelashes, so very innocently. "My obligations should be settled in full. I think I'll find a man with a much smaller cock that won't leave me so sore."

"Like hell you will." His voice was a fierce, angry growl as he plucked her out of the water and tossed her on the bed.

She gasped his name, landing in an ungainly sprawl in the middle of the huge bed. The wild look in his eyes made her heart speed up with excitement. She was shocked at how a vain, foolish threat could, shatter his control, affect him so deeply, seemingly pierce his very consciousness.

"It's never been 'bout the money." He wrestled out of his pants, his voice rough and dangerous as his heated gaze washed over her, sending a ripple of arousal crashing through her senses. She scooted back on the bed, closer to the pile of pillows running the width along the top. "You coulda sent me packing after the first time. Deep down, we both knew it."

Wetting her lips, she parted her thighs and arched her hips. She was prepared to take him. She was soaked and aching for him. Her breath came quick and her heart pounded in her chest as her eyes followed every muscled movement. He climbed on the bed, a dangerous mountain lion in heat. The long and powerful muscles of his thighs contracting as he moved over her on all fours.

She knew he could no longer contain the fury lacing his arousal. It burned bright, emanated off him in heated waves. She could feel it searing her damp skin from the inside out.

Caught off guard, she wasn't afraid, only somewhat wary. She knew he'd never hurt her. That the rage, his lust, the desperate flame of need would only add to their depraved pleasure, heighten the sensations, intensify her orgasm. Still, the only other time he had come close to being this angry was the rifle incident. She had pushed him too far once again. To a new level of tortured lust, a dark carnal fury surged out of control that added an edge of erotic desire and flared her own desperate need.

"It's always been 'bout this," He growled, his voice husky, furious. Rising between her thighs, he gripped her hips. His thighs pushed hers further apart. Instinctively, her muscles tightened as she felt the swollen head of his cock lodged at the narrow slit of her body.

"This is what you want."

She cried out as he pushed inside her, deep and hard. He stretched the soft folds, filled the narrow passage, immersing her in an instant climax. She fought for breath, trembling from the extreme pleasure spiraling through her. She fed on the hard and deep strokes plunging inside her convulsing pussy.

"I can feel your tight pussy gripping me, your orgasm coating me, making it easy for me to fuck you longer. You and me. We were made for each other." He was breathing rough, fighting to regain a resemblance of control as his body tore into hers. "Say it, Megan," he ordered, his voice a desperate, tormented plea.

Whimpering, she felt every thick inch of his heated flesh pull her apart, stretch her muscles, filling her vagina clear to her womb with each powerful, deep thrust.

"Say it."

"Yes...yes," she panted. "I've wanted you from the beginning." On a hard, hot penetration, she bucked against him, her body on fire. She wasn't ready for this. Not this. His thrusts too intense, ramming against her hips, sending her sliding across the bed. His cock drove deeper into her womb, burning her insides. The pleasure seared her senses, piercing her tender flesh to the point it was almost painful. She wasn't sure if she could handle more, but was willing to die trying. "Oh, Lord, yes. Like this."

"You can't ever leave me."

She shook her head and threw her hands around his neck. Her fingers twisted in his auburn locks. She fought to grab onto anything as he drove deeper, her head pushing the pillows into the headboard.

"I'll find you. No matter where you go. I'll find you." He stared down at her, his gaze dark, crazed, dangerous.

She could only arch against him and answer him with her body. That's where she wanted to be. Wanted him.

"Anyone else, and I'll kill 'em. You know I'll kill any man who touches you."

Then why had he brought Caleb into the relationship?

"Devin...Devin," she breathed between heavy gasps for air. "I don't want anyone else. Just you...like this." Her breasts were swollen, her nipples so hard, they hurt. She felt the hunger and arousal grow deep in her core, caught sight of the desperate, tortured lust blazing deep in his eyes and something else. She gasped, couldn't believe what she saw in his darkened depths, as though someone else, something else entirely, animalistic, savage, obsessed to the point of madness beyond human.

"Like this, Megan." He tightened his hold on her hips, withdrew completely, then quickly thrust in hard and deep. Her inner muscles protested, gripping him, tightening around his heated flesh "And this." She trembled beneath the strength of his penetration of her, felt the sensations multiply, pressure intensify, the pleasure heighten deep in her body. "And this," he growled with dark sexuality as he pulled out then pushed in again, harder and fiercer than ever before. "And this."

Her head thrashed on the bed. It was happening again—so tight, so close. She gasped for breath. Her hips bucked to meet each savage, forceful thrust tearing into her, he pounded into her sensitive clit. She fought back the screams of carnal pleasure and the hot and frenzied sensations washing over her. Her vaginal muscles spasmed around him, the never-ending release draining from her body, weakening her as the maddening, torturous eroticism continued.

Riding the flow of passion, she could feel the total dominance and extreme sexuality coiling in his veins. He needed to possess her as surely as the sweat dripped from his body, in his every feral impalement that seemed to rip her apart, pierce her heart, and claim her soul, in the heat of his words. Yet even as it took over her body, left her breathless, she wanted to beg for more.

"No talk of small dicks. They can't give you what I can. No one knows you like I do. You've got a taste of my cock, so big it stretches your pussy. Rubs against your clit. You come as soon as I stick it in your tight pussy." His voice was harsh, agonized as he slammed into her drenched cunt with brutal abandon. The liquid heat centered where their bodies joined, filled the room with sopping sounds of rhythmic possession. One hand tightened behind her neck to keep her from crashing into the headboard and another dug into her hip to hold her in place. "I can only give you pleasure like that. Satisfy those desires that frighten other women. You want them. Need them. Crave 'em. You can't ever go back."

"Fuck me! Fuck me hard. My pussy, my mouth. My ass. Wherever! I want only you." Her blood was on fire, the raging lust coursing through her body as the pleasure strengthened inside her. Clinging to him, she closed her eyes and gave herself over to the madness. The large bed shook beneath them with each powerful thrust that drove her lust higher. The driving force, burning pain, insanely intense pleasure between her thighs swept her into a maelstrom of exploding sensations throughout her body, tossing her closer to ecstasy. "I love you, Devin."

His mouth took hers in a possessive kiss that stole her breath. She moaned against him, tongue to tongue, savoring his taste, devouring him with her hunger. She laid her claim as her pussy tightened and her body stiffened beneath him, seeking the lustful pitch over the edge that would send her senses careering into orgasmic oblivion.

He pulled back, then rammed himself into her, hard and forceful. She exploded, her scream drowning in his mouth. Her nails dug in the hard muscles along his back and her legs tightened around his waist. Another hard, hot penetration, and she felt his cock swell, thicken, harden. With a potent, powerful thrust, she felt hot jets of semen spurt down her cavernous depths, filling her as her vaginal muscles milked him, clenched his pulsing cock. His lusty cry of erotic pleasure joined hers as his body jerked with his fierce climax. He collapsed upon her, grunting her name, burying his face in the curve of her throat.

His heart beat wildly and his breath was warm and rough against her skin. His arms wrapped tightly around her. Their connection was intact, more than physical. Megan felt him. She was surrounded by him. His strength. His heat. His scent. His possession. His surrender.

Chapter 26

"Devin left over a week ago, Megan. He didn't tell you when he'd return. This is what he wanted. When are you going to realize it?"

Megan stared absently at the cold cup of coffee sitting in front of her as she sat across from Caleb. She shook her head wistfully, refusing to answer and admit Caleb was right.

After their most impassioned night of lovemaking, Devin had fallen asleep with his arms wrapped around her, holding her close throughout the night. She believed it meant he changed his mind about leaving. Shocked her the following morning when out of the blue, he announced he was going away and didn't know when he'd return. They exchanged a few heated words, which left no doubt in her mind Devin wanted her to go through with the pact he and Caleb had made. He took the girls to school that morning, and she hadn't seen him since. He left her only with memories after the passion marks on her neck and breasts faded. The bruises on her thighs and rear and the tenderness between her thighs faded days later.

"Did he at least tell you where he was going?"

"No," she answered softly without raising her gaze. Thoughts of Devin jumbled in her mind. Always of Devin.

"He didn't tell you where he was going or when he'd return. It could be next week, next year. You don't know." His tone was somber.

A short silence ensued. He sighed heavily.

She sat there, didn't move. She traced the floral pattern on her coffee cup with her eyes and remembered his scent, the feel of his flesh in her hands, his taste on her lips…

"Its time you and I were married." Caleb's voice was soft, cajoling as he posed the one question she didn't want to hear.

Abruptly, she raised her gaze. The words hung heavy between them, draining the air from her lungs.

"You need the protection of a husband."

She could hear the concern in his voice and see the love in his eyes, a love that was mirrored in hers. She knew he was right. The answer he longed to hear was on the tip of her tongue. Her heart was winning the battle over her conscience, she couldn't form the single syllable.

"The girls need a father. Your closest neighbors are Rosalinda and her ranch hands. We know what sort they are. I'm surprised Rosalinda has kept them around."

Megan covered her mouth daintily as though she'd belched. Instead she hid the smirk, threatening to turn into a full-fledged laugh. Apparently, Caleb didn't know what sort of gal Rosalinda was.

Crossing her hands in her lap, she managed half a smile and wondered why she couldn't come right out and say yes. Five years ago, there wouldn't have been any hesitation. Caleb was handsome. Gorgeous. She needed him. Wanted him. Loved him. Dreamt of him for nearly ten years.

"Are you sure you still want to marry me?"

Caleb stood and walked around the table. Her heart fluttered as she watched him. His dark navy suit that set off the blue in his eyes and made his blond hair shine like fine silk. Noticeable underneath the fashionable trousers, the subtle flex of his large, muscular thighs had her fingers itching to feel him. Dear Lord, she thought, never had she seen a man look so good in and out of his clothes. Devin was handsome in a rugged, primal sort of way that made her tremble. Caleb turned her insides to warm mush.

With his hands on her upper arms, he encouraged her to stand. She did so readily, turning into the comfort of his embrace as he urged her around to face him.

"Megan," he said softly.

She closed her eyes, laid her head against his chest and sighed.

He smoothed her hair with his hand, then tucked her head under his chin protectively. "After all we've been through, you still have doubts?"

Her greatest fear was hearing shame or disappointment in his voice. Hearing only tenderness pierced her heart. She had lost him once. She fought the tears welling behind her eyes at the thought of losing him again. She didn't know if she could survive a permanent separation. She dreaded her task but she needed to know. Pulling away enough to look at him, she gingerly whispered, "You're willing to share me with another man."

Caleb didn't hesitate. "Yes. Honestly, it's not the most desirous of arrangements. What man wouldn't want you for himself?"

She studied his expression. Unbelievably, his gaze held love and understanding. In the depths, there was an unexpected flare of arousal. The thought of sharing her with another man seemed to incite his deepest wanton spirit even as he spoke. Devin had taken it upon himself to not only corrupt her, launch her into an existence of dark and depraved sexual excesses, cravings for the most carnal passions, but he'd dragged Caleb into this as well. Her body started to tingle with her own lust-filled desires and the memories of their last impassioned encounter.

"But if it's the only way you'd agree to marry me, then yes, a thousand times, yes."

Releasing the breath she held, she felt a single tear roll down her cheek. Caleb was beyond belief. She felt guilty, ashamed. It was her fault he was involved in this deplorable situation. He was too good for her. Despite feeling undeserving, she couldn't turn him away. She was unable to deny she wanted him too damned much. She flattened her hands against the hard planes of his chest, the muscled contours beneath his shirt, and melted into his strength. The warmth of his hands and the sheer proximity of his body were arousing a familiar heat and ache between her thighs. Lust, plain and hot, pulsed through her body.

It had been eleven days, two hours, and fifteen minutes since she allowed herself to feel anything. Eleven days, two hours, and fifteen minutes since she allowed anyone to touch her. Eleven days, two hours and fifteen minutes since Devin left her. She wanted Caleb to touch her, hold onto her and never let her go.

"Oh, Caleb," she breathed, gliding her arms underneath his jacket and around his waist, drawing him closer. She inhaled the fresh masculine scent of him, reveled in the broad length of his virile body pressed hard against hers. She felt her breasts swell and her nipples harden beneath her blouse. Moving against him, she scraped the peaks of her breasts over the layers of fabric separating them, letting him feel her arousal, her need for him. "Heaven help me. I want to say yes, but I need more time. Please try and understand."

He closed his eyes and groaned as his hands splayed, running down her back. Cupping the curve of her bottom, he flattened her against his erection.

"How can you ask me to wait when I ache each night dying to make love to you? I wake every morning dreaming of you by my side."

It broke her heart to hear the pain and anguish in his voice, to know she was the cause of his sorrow was unbearable. Yet she couldn't stop thinking of her love for Devin. She wanted to scream at the injustice of it all. Scream that she wanted him. Wanted them both. Needed them both. She couldn't possibly say yes to one without risk losing the other. Deep down, she knew it. And Caleb had to have known it, also. Their pact couldn't possibly work, no matter how much they wanted it to.

"It's like asking me to choose between Shelby and Emma. I love them both. I can't give up either one." Megan was an Adams, and Adamses were known to face insurmountable odds head-on. They always held true to her roots. At this moment, she wanted to run, to hide her face in the pillows and cry come cold September.

His held her, and as she moved, it tightened, preventing her from walking away as she did the past week each time he brought up the subject of marriage. She looked up at him and had to blink when she saw the torment, the desperate longing radiating in the deep blue pools.

"I'm not asking you to give him up. Only to love me while I'm with you."

His voice was soft and sweet, conveying the words she longed to hear. He lowered his head, and she lifted her face, parting her lips in anticipation. She knew it was coming. Truthfully, she looked forward to it. She wanted to feel something, anything other than the heartache tearing her soul apart. His hot, moist tongue slipped between her inviting lips, stroking her desire. She moaned softly as he kissed her hard, hungrily and desperately.

On tiptoes, she flung her hands around his neck, lifting herself as she drank greedily from his mouth. She yielded to the eroticism as his tongue tangled with hers. She rubbed against the hard length pressed into her belly. He pulled her closer, grinding his cock into the vee of her thighs. Her little whimper melted between their mouths as her body burned with lust and her cunt tightened with need.

She arched against him as his hand cupped her breast, kneading the mound in the heat of his palm. Her body was responding, hot and wet for him. Preparing itself for him. His fingers gripped the peak, caressing and pulling the bud beneath the flimsy material, tearing a gasp from her throat as shivers of awareness and pure excitement raced down her spine.

She felt his thick shaft throb against her as he rocked his hips into hers. Holding her close with his hand on the small of her back, he encouraged her backward, toward her bedroom.

Breaking the feverish kiss, she pulled away. She swallowed tightly, starting at him. Her body was saying yes, but her heart was saying no. That was *their* bedroom. Hers and Devin's.

He ran an agitated hand through his hair. His eyes flared with shock, confusion. He growled, "Megan, you're killing me. What's wrong now?" He sounded ready to boil over with need. The suppressed lust drew his body tight.

Without a word, she led him by the hand to the sofa. The heat of his skin seared her flesh. She was so aware of his presence beside her, the sexual tension rushing through their bodies, her knees grew weak. Her breathing came fast and shallow. There was no denying what was about to happen. What she had to do.

She took a seat on the small sofa and patted the space next to her. Caleb sat beside her, the vivid hunger stark in his eyes. "Kiss me, Caleb," she whispered. No sooner than she finished the last word, she felt the soft warmth of his lips on hers.

* * * *

Caleb kissed her softly, gently. Tasting her sweetness, savoring her warmth, her rosy fragrance imbued in her smooth skin as he fought the need to devour her with his hunger. She slowly allowed her desire to dispel any hesitation or wariness. Rather than demand her acceptance, he wanted her to surrender to him willingly.

"Meg," he breathed against her cheek as his lips moved to the spot behind her ear that made her moan and her nipples harden. He remembered her body so well, the touches that made her shiver. Her left nipple was more sensitive than her right. He remembered how her hips would jerk as he curled his finger inside her body. She'd whimper, body flush, and her juices would soak his hand. He didn't know how to bring her relief then, but he sure as hell knew now. Between nips and soft suckles, he lapped the spot with his tongue. She shuddered beneath him, and he confessed, "I need you."

"I want you," he whispered, as his tongue stroked along the curve of her neck and his hand caressed her shoulder, slipping round to caress her breast and tease the tip straining the fabric. His other hand undid the bottoms of her blouse. He felt her trembling. The swollen mounds of her breast heaved with each rasp of breath as the buttons came undone one by one. She called his name on a soft moan.

Brushing the cotton material aside, he watched the sensual glimmer deepen in her eyes as he trailed soft kisses from the swell of one breast to the other. He cupped the perfectly firm mounds with both hands and smiled when she arched toward him.

"Caleb," she panted as he licked a wet path down the cleft, his thumbs raking over the hard, pink tips. His mouth captured the right, then the left pointed bud in his mouth. He suckled them until she gasped. Her fingers clenched in his hair, drawing him harder on her breast.

He groaned, aflame with lust as he felt her hips swaying against him. He knew her resistance was vanishing and was fighting to control his own. He was overcome with his need to love her, To show her the tenderness, heavenly surrender he longed to bestow. He gently lowered her against the rounded arm of the couch. She was so trusting, lush and innocent, hot and sweet as she stretched out on the cushions. The need, desire, the desperation was so great, he could barely breathe.

His hand dropped to capture the hem of her skirt and raised it bit by bit. His fingers skimmed over her legs as he crushed the voluminous calico over her hips. On their own volition, her legs parted as he glided his palm over her hip and slid his hand between her thighs. Impatiently, she arched her hips off the sofa to meet his probing fingers as they stroked the slick crease and moved through the thick cream gathered at the tiny entrance to her vagina. His mouth watered, caressing the enticing flesh leisurely as she wiggled, sighed and moaned seductively.

Megan panted his name and bucked against his hand as he slowly pushed his way into the tight, hot flesh between her thighs. "Oh, yes," she gasped, shuddering, arching in enjoyment.

Dear Lord, he didn't know if could survive another moment without taking her. Her pussy was so hot, so wet and ready for him. He clenched his fingers greedily as he stroked her slow and easy. The look in her dazed eyes was utter lust, carnal heat staring back at him. She was so lost in her own pleasure, her skin flushing as she gasped for breath, her breasts rising and falling in his grasp.

"Oh, Megan, you're so beautiful," he groaned, wrenched with arousal as he kissed, nibbled with his teeth and licked his way to her other breast. He dropped to his knees between her thighs.

Rolling the tight nipple between his lips, he shifted her leg along the back cushion of the sofa, allowing the other to remain on the floor. He leaned back just enough to devour the wanton site with his gaze for a breathless moment. Her blouse open, pale breasts reddened from his kisses, her eyes dark with desire was purely hypnotic. Her skirt gathered around her waist and her legs parted wide, spreading the glistening vaginal lips. He was bursting to possess her, his intense need escalated to nothing short of a painful suffering, total agony.

She called his name as he added a third finger to the heated passage. Her muscles gripped him erotically. He moved slowly within her, building her arousal by minute degrees, prolonging the moment. Guiding her hand to her breast, he persuaded in a deep, rough voice that spoke of his own lusty desperation. "Touch your breasts."

The passion in his darkening eyes equaled hers as Megan did as he asked. Bringing one hand tentatively, then the other hand to her breasts, she kneaded the perfectly rounded mounds of pale flesh, pinching and pulling the hard peaks toward him as she licked her lips as if anxious to have him take them in his mouth. Too breathless to speak, she offered herself to him, and he yielded, his teeth gently rasping at the tender flesh, making her shudder with carnal enjoyment.

"Come for me, Megan," he ordered, as the throbbing, agonizing ache in his cock threatened his senses and all rationale. He struggled to control the breath heaving from his chest. He couldn't resist the sight of his fingers crowding the pink, glistening folds of her sweet pussy. The soft moistness, the fiery heat surrounded him as the tiny hole opened and closed when he moved in and out. She lay there in complete submission, breathy moans rising from her throat as he brought her pleasure.

"I want to see you come just for me," he growled. Stroking his thumb over her clit, he pushed in deeper and faster into her wetness, a never-ending rhythm. "To know what it would be like, loving you. Just the two of us."

"Caleb," she cried as he stroked faster. Her hips thrust against his hand.

He felt her slick, inner muscles tighten around his impalement. He watched as she closed her eyes. Her head rolled against the padded arm as he felt the first convulsion ripple through her body.

"That's it, my love. Come for me." He couldn't take his eyes off her as her body continued to shudder on the thick cushions as each spasm gripped his fingers, sending a sea of her sweet honey over his hand. "Just for me."

"Caleb, Caleb," she panted over and over again, and he couldn't help but feel a gratifying sense of triumph. As she basked in her pleasure, his fingers still buried within the heat of her tiny, hot body, he was bursting to possess her. He deliberately held back, a testament to placing her needs before his. He was willing to forever put her desires before his.

He devoured her dripping pussy. She cried out as he licked the juices from the quivering folds tightening around his fingers. His mouth came down hard, sucked the tender knot of nerves with unending pressure. His fingers thrust, filled her cunt so fast and deep, she twisted and bucked beneath him.

She captured his head between her thighs and wrapped her ankles around his back. Her fingers clenched in his hair. His other hand cupped her breast. His fingers caressed the swollen globe and nipple. He felt her back arch, her body tighten as she called out. He gazed up as she tossed her head, screaming his name when the climatic sensations fired through her body once more.

Immersed in the aftermath of her orgasm, she lay back on the sofa. Her eyes were closed and her lips gently parted. He could see the lingering sensations still rippling through her body as he kept his gaze on her while he unbuttoned his trousers and pushed them down his hips.

He rose over her and positioned himself between her thighs. He was unable to control the harsh groan rumbling from deep in his throat as he stroked the head of his cock over her sweat-soaked flesh, splayed so prominently in front of him. He didn't even try to stop the heated growl as he pushed the swollen tip into the tight slit of her hot little cunt.

Her eyes darted open, and she glared at him in shock. "Wait, Caleb."

He stilled, confused by her reaction, worried he may have hurt her.

She dropped her legs to the floor and sat up and quickly.

He stared at her, his palms resting on her thighs, very much aware of the pinch of her heated muscles searing the flesh lodged at the entrance of her body. "What's wrong?"

"I…we can't." She moved back on the couch, closing her thighs as their bodies separated. She looked frantic, as though she wanted to escape him, as if he was about to do something evil, vile to her person. It damned near destroyed him.

Outraged, he stood up, yanked his trousers up, annoyed, frustrated, and surprised by her rejection.

"Don't be cross with me," she pleaded and rose off the sofa. As he turned from her, she grabbed him by the belt.

He didn't know where he was going, but he sure as hell couldn't stay there. He didn't want to look at her.

"I need more time," she whispered tenderly.

He felt her palm on his cheek as she urged him to look at her. Her voice was a cry for understanding. The sadness cut through him like a knife. He stared up at the ceiling, his chest clenching in bitterness. How long did she expect him to wait? He was a man, not a book gathering dust on the shelf until someone found interest in strumming through the pages.

"Please, Caleb."

He shook his head, unable to speak. Afraid of what would come out of his mouth if he dared. He felt her move and release her hands from his body as he made a move to walk away.

"Caleb," she called out. The tenderness in her voice made him stop.

"Please look at me," she whispered.

When he turned, his jaw dropped. His heart slammed into his feet as the blood rushed to his cock. She was naked, her clothes lying at her feet. He watched in stunned silence, mesmerized, as she stepped out of the calico puddle and her shoes and crossed the small distance between them. He swallowed tightly, staring at the wicked gleam in her eye, the raw intent blazing up at him.

She dropped to her knees in front of him, lowered his unbuttoned trousers around his ankles. He could only stare down at her. His breath caught in his throat as the blood pumped hard and fast through his system. The flesh between his thighs throbbed and ached like never before.

"Anything else but that," she murmured, licking her lips so seductively, he wanted to come right then and there. She was too sexy for her own good. He felt his cock jerk violently as her small hands wrapped around him.

A harsh groan raked through his throat as he felt the heat of her tongue swirl over the head, just before her mouth enveloped him within her moist cavern.

"Oh, God! Yes, Megan." His fingers coiled in her hair as the entire length of his cock disappeared between her taut lips.

* * * *

"You told Running Bull you stay two moons, three moons. Why we leave early?" Rising Sun asked, propping on an elbow on his side, stretched out on woven leather skins. Devin was keenly aware the other man watched him out of curiosity as he lay on his blanket, with his head resting on his saddle. He stared blankly at the stars glimmering in the night sky.

He'd informed Running Bull he intended to spend time with them, to stay for the next buffalo hunt and celebrate afterwards. When he up and decided to leave one morning, Running Bull asked no questions, to his relief. After all, his visits were seldom long. But this visit was different.

"Good thing we've been practicing. Your English is getting better."

"We always speak English when you stay at camp. Now want answer question," pressed Rising Sun.

Devin didn't like being watched, and he sure as hell didn't like being questioned. He felt the tense set of his jaw, his mouth turn grim and a stiffness of his entire bearing. Rising Sun was Running Bull's nephew. Devin himself had always treated the boy with the respect deserving of his close relationship to the chief. In a way, Devin always held a special kinship for him. Since there weren't very many blue-eyed warriors running around camp, he'd taken the child under his personal wing long ago. What the Comanche's didn't teach him, Devin did. He held his temper.

"There are some things a man doesn't want to discuss," he said simply.

When he'd left the ranch three weeks ago, he meant to stay away at least two months, perhaps more, to prove to himself his unexplained feelings for

Megan were based purely on proximity. She was the only woman he ever spent any length of time with, other than to satisfy his carnal urges. Even then, it was never longer than a few days at the most. He thought out of sight meant out of his mind, then out of his system.

Unfortunately, it was the exact opposite. Once he left, he could think of nothing else. He wished it had been Caleb making love to her. At least it would have been understandable, explainable. Lust was easier to deal with. Watching another man pleasure her added an erotic thrill he hadn't expected. He shared plenty of whores in his time. None of that compared. Didn't even come close.

Her surrender and her complete submission to his desires were instinctive. It excited the hell out of him. Not because he liked to take charge, but because she accepted his demands out of love. Out of her love for him, she obeyed willingly. Cold-hearted bastard that he was, he used her emotions against her and turned her toward another.

No, instead of thinking of her sweet, little body in the throes of ecstasy, he thought of her in general. How her hazel eyes would light up whenever he walked into a room. The sound of her laughter, her smooth skin with the lingering fragrance of roses. The smile ready on her lips and the way her dimples creased her cheeks. What really got him, churned his insides until he lost his appetite, drove him insane, made him want to lose himself in the midst of the any willing woman, was his reaction to her. Everything—the air, the surroundings, the sun, even the damn flowers in her garden— everything would seem to glow brighter whenever she walked by.

As if that wasn't enough on his mind, he worried constantly if she and the girls were safe. When he returned, would he find her and Caleb in their marital bed, leaving him to sleep alone and share only stolen moments with her?

The thought turned his blood cold. It was for the best, but that didn't mean he had to like the solution. Even if it was his idea, It was the only way to keep her safe in the long run. Caleb was the settling down type. In Devin's line of work, someone always had a beef with him. If it was known he had a family, they'd be targets for damn sure. He wasn't worried about himself. A family was different. There would never have a peaceful moment again.

Caleb had to marry her, plain and simple. And he was just going to have to learn to live with the idea she was another man's wife. That is, after he went back and gave her a proper goodbye.

One last time, he consoled himself.

"Tell me of her." Rising Sun sat up and wrapped his blanket around his shoulders, blocking out the cool night breeze drifting through the New Mexico Mountains.

Devin's brows rose at Rising Sun's question. There were so many ways to answer that question, most of which were pretty darn intimate. Playing it safe, he offered, "What do you wanna know?"

"What she look like?"

"An angel."

Rising Sun laughed heartily. "Crazy Buffalo Hunter seen angel before?"

Devin grinned, then broke into the chuckle he couldn't hold back a moment longer. "Can't say I ever have, but if I did, I'm purty sure it'll be the spitting image of Megan."

"Me-gan," the tall, muscular Comanche said slowly, pronouncing each syllable correctly.

"How 'bout we start using your name, Trevor?"

"Tre-vor," he repeated slowly. Jumping to his feet, he strode around the camp fire. Chest puffed out, repeating his name out loud. His waist-length hair, blackened with colored wax and braided with beads, blew in the air.

"First thing we need to do when we get into town is buy you some britches. Get rid of that thing." Devin gestured to his loin cloth.

Rising Sun stopped and turned toward Devin as he lifted the square strip of hide covering his groin. "What wrong with it?"

Devin rolled his eyes as the other man exposed the only part of his body that had been covered. "For one thing—" Devin averted his gaze. Staring at the crackling flames a few feet away, Devin informed him of the impending drawback of meeting his sister. "There are little girls back home. You can't show off your man parts any time you feel like it. White people are funny that way.

"You no care at camp. We all take bath in river—men, women and children. We bang, bang, others see." He shrugged his shoulders flippantly, as if walking around practically nude and having sex in a room full of people were normal.

Devin grinned, cognizant of the customs Trevor had grown up with. "Yeah, but when I'm living amongst my own kind, I wear my buckskins. You'll need to do the same."

"Me no like."

"You're a grown man. It's your choice to stay or not. Meet her, then make up your mind. After all these years, she still thinks about you."

"No remember her."

Devin reached over to his saddlebags next to his rifle and pulled out a little red slipper. Sitting it atop his palm, he held out his arm. "Small enough to fit this thing. I doubt you'd remember."

"How you know from that we share blood?" Squinting his eyes, he jerked his chin at Devin's outstretched arm.

Tossing the slipper in the air, Devin caught it in his grasp and put it away. "Not too many Comanche are sporting pale blue eyes. I kinda figured there was a story behind it. Running Bull told me long ago how he saved you from a raiding party. Back then, your head was covered in blond hair so pale, it looked like the sun was shining off of you. Thus the name Rising Sun. He gave you to his sister after her husband and son were killed." He shrugged his shoulders. "I just happened to remember his story sounded a lot like hers, that's all. I'm grateful to you for agreeing to come with me," Devin confessed, stretching out once more on his blanket, his tone revealing none of the deeper emotions he felt as he thought how fate worked.

If not for the color of his hair, Trevor's life would have ended at six. Comanches worshipped the sun. All it took was one look, and Running Bull believed the sun spirit sent him for his sister. He saved the boy instead of taking revenge for the death of his brother-in-law, nephew, and several others needlessly killed by white soldiers as they slept. All for the sake of their land.

"Running Bull your blood brother. I know you long time. I do it for you."

"Whatever the reason, thanks. We'll be there in a few days. After you meet your sister, you'll be thanking me."

* * * *

"Barkeep," growled Rico, waving his empty glass in the air.

"So what you think? We rob this here bank?" Chewy spit a wad of snuff on the saloon floor.

The bartender looked angry as he eyed the mess as he made his way to their table with a tray of beer mugs.

"Town looks quiet," Pablo added in a Mexican accent. "The sheriff, he snoring when I passed his winda."

"We need cash since that Spawn fella messed us over." Big Louie took a long swig of the beer the bartender had just placed in front of him.

The five men stopped talking for a moment as the bartender placed filled mugs in front of them.

Rico waited until the bartender was no longer within listening distance before he grumbled, "Yeah, I told you the bastard was in on it."

"How the hell was I supposed to know he hooked up with the law?"

"Who you think shot me and your brother from a cliff over five hundred yards away? Those army fellas in blue can't pick a flea off a tick like he can." Dutch's face cringed into a fierce scowl as he rubbed his crudely bandaged arm.

"We gotta find him," said Big Louie, crudely wiping the yellowish liquid dripping from the corners of his mouth down his chin.

"It ain't gonna make up for when the red-skinned savages hang our scalps on their poles for goin' back on our deal," Chewy reminded them.

"Sure as hell make me feel a shitload better knowing he's kissing dirt," added Rico.

"Hey boys." Cheri sauntered over to their table and draped a slender arm around Rico and Dutch's shoulders. "Tejas is sure becoming popular lately."

"Whoa, Cheri," Rico called out in shock as he tilted his head around, running his eyes up and down the womanly figure bent over his shoulder. "Whatcha doin' here in these parts? Last I seen you, you wuz working Montana." He glanced around the table. The other men who knew her were just as surprised to see her, and the two who didn't know her sure looked like they wanted to.

"A girl needs different scenery now and then. Seems no matter where I go, I can't get away from you boys. Ya'll here doing business with Devin?"

"Devin?" Rico shot Dutch a telling glance. Dutch looked over at the other fellows around the table, who were all staring at Cheri. Some of their glances were appreciative, some questioning. For a moment, she appeared alarmed at mentioning his name and seemed to notice their surprise at hearing Devin was in Tejas.

"Oh, you mean Spawn," Rico corrected quickly with broken laughter. "Yeah, we're early. Ain't expecting us till 'morrow. Maybe you can tell us where we can find 'em. Save 'em the trip of coming into town."

The wrinkle crinkling her forehead eased as Cheri smiled. "How about we go upstairs and make a little deal?"

There was nothing Rico wanted more. He felt her full breasts rub against his shoulders as she stood behind him, gliding the palms of her hands down his arms.

Oh, yeah. He wanted to jam his cock into Devin's favorite whore every which way and then some. He recalled how she climbed on a gambling table one night in front of everyone so he could mount her. The bitch's pussy was so greedy for Devin, she didn't care who watched as he shoved that fence pole between his legs into her dripping cunt. Rico wanted to shove his fist up her greedy little twat. Force her to scream for Devin's as he fist-fucked her good and hard.

"I recall you used to be his favorite. Sure he ain't upstairs waitin' on us?" Dutch asked, raising a speculative eyebrow as his eyes narrowed on her. Rico understood his unease. Where Devin was concerned, nothing was left to chance. That is, if a fellow wanted to live.

"Since his pa passed, he hasn't been 'round much. A girl needs some lovin'. Helps keep me in silk."

"I didn't know he had a real pa. Always thought the earth just opened up and spit the son of a bitch out," Chewy joked as he spit another wad of tobacco. The others laughed.

"We ain't got too much money. You takin' us all on for old times sake?" Rico grinned.

Her eyes roamed over the five men seated around the table. She smiled faintly. "Pick one. He can come back and tell ya'll all about it. For a dollar more, one of you can watch."

* * * *

"Girls, time to wash up for supper," Megan called out to them from the end of the gravel path that led to the porch, her hand resting on the hitching post. Shelby looked up from where she sat in the grass playing with her doll as Emma swung back and forth on the tree swing nearby.

Megan moved both hands to her hip, a deliberate act to promote obedience. She waited for the girls to show a sign they were going to do as instructed. Emma dragged her feet in the dirt to slow the swing down. Shelby stood up and twirled round with her doll, as though they were dancing.

Confident they would soon make their way inside, she strolled up the path. Pausing on the steps, she swirled around when she heard the sound of approaching horses.

There were five of them. She counted the riders through the cloud of dust as they galloped toward her. As soon as they neared the barn, her heart began to race. They didn't look friendly. In fact, they looked like the most filthy, despicable characters she had ever seen.

"Girls," she screamed, running down the steps and over the grass, skipping the path altogether as she attempted to dash around the corner of the house to where the girls were playing.

A large, black horse blocked her path. The bearded rider aimed his gun at her, freezing her where she stood for several seconds. She noticed another rider take off behind the house, one left to check the barn, one headed for the bunkhouse, and the biggest one rode to where Shelby and Emma were.

Her eyes widened, and her heart leapt in her throat as she saw Emma kick the man in his shin. Unfazed, he sneered at the small child's effort.

"Where is he?" The bearded man's voice carried an intense edge of what she could only describe as hell-bent on killing. His arms were crossed casually over his thigh as he shifted in his saddle to stare down at her, but the gun in his hand pointed inches from her head was every bit deadly.

Instantly, she knew who "he" was. Outwardly, she tried to remain calm, but she could feel her hands and knees shaking. Looking past the lethal steel, she held his dark, steady gaze. His beady eyes were barely visible from under the dark hat and thick facial hair that seemed to hide all but his nose and the top half of his grimy cheeks. *Relax.* She took a deep breath. "I don't know."

She heard Shelby and Emma scream and flashed her attention in their direction. Incredible fear ripped through her body. The big man had picked them up, each precious, blond-headed child tucked under a sweaty armpit. He was of average height and packed a barrel for a belly. All that excess flesh strained the buttons on the front of his grimy shirt. Absolutely disgusting. He possessed a big, wide face with sweat dripping from his thickly creased forehead. His fat cheeks were already red from the little effort he expended thus far.

"Leave them alone," she demanded at the top of her lungs as she ran around the horse blocking her path. She screamed shocked when the bearded nab jumped off his horse and yanked her by the hair, flinging her to the ground.

With one large hand, he grabbed her by her shoulder and pulled her to her feet. "Where's Spawn?" he snarled, fisting the material tightly in his grip, drawing her close enough to distinguish the rough lines etched in his face, caked with sweat and dirt, his strong, crooked nose and thick, black, bushy eyebrows over squinty brown eyes.

"I told you, I don't know," she bit back insistently, taking her chances she wouldn't be tossed again, or worse.

"Megan," cried both girls helplessly as the big man came around the corner. He grinned as he carried them in his tight grip, their small feet kicking in the air. *Dear God*, she prayed, *keep them safe.*

"Don't hurt them, please," she begged the bearded man as he restrained her. For her humbling effort, she received a blank stare. Squirming, she tried to worm out of the man's tight-fisted grasp. He held her in place easily, exerting little physical effort. She felt utterly useless, inconsequential.

"We only want him. Tell me where he's at, and I'll let ya'll go." His voice was cold and determined, but it held no truth, Megan decided.

"I already told you I don't know where he is or when he's coming back."

"His horse ain't here," hollered the third man as he returned from the barn, his horse trailing behind.

The other two riders rejoined them. She sighed with relief the focus was no longer on her. She took a good look at the men as they approached. When—and that was a huge "when"—they came out of this alive, she wanted to be able to give detailed descriptions to the authorities. Sheriff

Tucker may not come to her rescue, but surely she could find a Marshall in a neighboring town to tail after them and hang 'em high.

"Not in the back," said the fourth man, a Mexican.

"Ain't in the bunkhouse," added the fifth man as he shook his head, as though disappointed they didn't find Devin.

"What about the house?" asked the big man with the barrel belly as Shelby and Emma wiggled and fussed within his grip.

"He ain't there, or we woulda heard him by now," the bearded man replied flatly.

"Don't hurt none to check." The big man shrugged his huge shoulders. The girls' blond curls bounced up and down in the process.

The bearded man looked at the squirming girls. "Stand over yonder where he can see iffin he's in the house." He indicated the gravel path leading up the porch with a jerk of his head. "They's our insurance we get out of this alive."

Megan's gut wrenched at the thought they'd use children as shields. She wanted to use the gun in her pocket. If they were half as fast as Devin, she wouldn't stand a chance. She would be dead and the girls left to their mercy. And they weren't exactly the hospitable sort.

"You two go in and take a gander." The bearded man gestured toward the Mexican and the fifth man, still sitting atop their horses. Guns drawn, the two men followed orders. "If you see him, tell 'em we got his ma and sisters keepin' us company. Sure hope you're tellin' the truth, or you'll be the first to go." He grinned and stuck his gun in her ribs as if she required further persuasion.

She flicked her face from his, fought back her tears as unfathomable fear turned her blood to ice. Her insides were void of all warmth, causing the hair on her arms and neck to perk up. Looking back at the girls, she thought it was good at least they stopped crying for the time being. But they were still very much afraid. How was she going to help them when it appeared there was no way to help herself? A woman and two children against five vicious outlaws didn't leave many alternatives.

It seemed like an eternity passed as the men searched the house, as opposed to the reality of a couple of minutes until they reappeared back on the porch.

"Ain't no one inside," the fifth man grumbled.

The bearded man's grip tightened on her shoulder as he shook her with forceful emphasis. "How long he's been gone?" Impatience thundered loud in his voice.

"Uh." She contemplated telling them the truth. They might leave if they found out he might not be back for weeks. The chance was slim, but it was all she had. "Several weeks. He didn't say where he was going or when he'd return. That's the truth."

"We know he ain't been to see Cheri," the fifth man announced as he and the Mexican laughed, nudging each other as they exchanged telling glances.

Megan cringed on the inside. Cheri was more than a passing fancy, clearly a long-standing business acquaintance. With her and the girls' lives at stake, now was not the time for petty jealousy to rear its ugly head. She found a twinge of relief learning he hadn't been to see her recently. When Devin left, he'd apparently left them both.

The third man gave a short laugh, then muttered to no one in particular. "Just like the bastard. Never stays in one place long enough for his crap to dry."

"Told you this was a stupid idea. We wastin' time." The Mexican shook his head, grimacing as he took off his hat to wipe the sweat off his brow.

"Ain't got nothing better to do." The third man stuffed his mouth with a wad of tobacco and chewed away. He was tall, slender and wiry with a pinched weasel-like face covered with brown stubble. Megan noticed the scraggly hair poking out from under his faded gray hat. If it ever saw the sight of soap, he may just as well be blond. Then again, it may be the tobacco turning his hair and skin a tatty shade of brownish-orange.

"Shoulda been holdin' up a bank," griped the Mexican.

"We can do that later. For now, we owe him for screwing us. Don't forget, he shot Dutch and killed Big Lou's brother."

"Yeah, I want the sunuvabitch," the fifth man, probably Dutch, growled furiously.

Megan listened in horror, her heart thundering in her chest. Her legs were shaking so violently, if the bearded man holding her up let go, she would be a puddle on the grass. She glanced at the girls once more, aware they'd heard the men's intentions. They renewed their struggling under their confinement, dreadful comprehension and alarm blazing in their eyes. She bit back the tears welling in her eyes, determined no to succumb to her own vulnerability.

"What of me cousin Jorge? He kill 'em, too," the Mexican reminded them.

"Ah, I never liked the damned idiot," the bearded man confided, which made the Mexican curse in Spanish. No one paid much attention, except for her. She didn't have to speak the language to realize the man sought revenge. Each man seemed to seek vengeance for Devin's past transgressions.

Though the Mexican had a toothy grin, his small brown eyes were sharp, quick to flare with anger. His hair was dark and straight. It hung past his shoulders and his sun-burned skin was almost red. The short, pudgy man could easily be mistaken for an Apache. In particular, he was older than the others. She estimated near his forties. The rest were probably in their thirties. Only the round one looked to be in his twenties.

"I say we stay and wait. There's food in the house. We got here in time for supper." Dutch rubbed his wounded arm and stared at Megan. The look was nothing nice. It sent an alarming sense of panic through her body. Her nerves tensed with dread. He continued to scrutinize her with his lewd gaze, letting her know there was more on his mind than twisting his thumbs waiting for Devin to show.

"Sounds like a damn good idea to me," the bearded one said, climbing up the stairs. He dragged Megan along as the men followed them into the house. Tossing glances over her shoulder, she noticed the man, presumably Big Lou, let the girls down and grabbed them by their arms as he led them inside. Her captor took her along as he walked to the middle of the parlor area, looking around in undisguised repulsion as if knowing everything he saw, the comforts of a real home, all belonged to Devin.

Megan heard the girls' small shouts of protests, and her stomach tightened. She tried to turn toward the door, but turned into another hard body, instead. With a small gasp, she braced herself, and her eyes lifted as if in slow motion, settling eye-level on the dried blood which seeped through the tattered rags wrapped around his upper arm.

"What we gonna do with her, Rico?" Dutch picked up a misplaced lock of hair from Megan's shoulder and twirled it around his finger. Clenching her teeth, she winced automatically. She glanced downward. Suddenly dissatisfied, she revealed the slight weakness as he callously snorted. Men like these thrived on intimidation, the fear of others, and the thought only deepened her determination not to show her fear.

Like Devin, he wore a bowie knife on his hip. Unlike Devin, his knife wasn't as long, nor was the bulge tenting his denim trousers as big. The very idea of him made her want to vomit. He was, however, about six foot, rather stocky and muscular with ruthless blue eyes and dirty blond hair. At his left thigh was a six-shooter tied down low. He looked like one of those menaces perfectly at home in a bar brawl or clearing Main street at sun-up. If not for his arm, compliments of Devin, she would have pictured him on the winning side, no matter the venue.

Megan turned up her eyes at him, saw the wicked intent beaming in the darkness of his heated gaze. And for once, she wanted Devin here, to shoot the bastard dead where he stood. Finish the job he started. Lord help her, she almost didn't recognize herself.

The bearded man, Rico, released her, and she wasted no time removing herself from the vicinity of Dutch. She gave him a bold stare as she moved toward the table where the girls were standing next to the big fellow. She willed herself not show him, any of them, an ounce of her emotions.

"She'll be our dessert. Seeing how it was Spawn's fault we ain't got 'nough money for sporting with Cheri and the other whores." The tobacco-chewing one dropped his hand to his crotch as he sat on the edge of the table, his eyes boldly roving up and down her body.

Judging from the bulging crease he stroked over his faded trail pants, Megan could tell he was already hard. A harsh shiver of disgust and loathing began deep in her belly. On their own volition, her trembling thighs clamped together. Her hands went to her belly as her stomach churned. Before the day was out, she was sure her breakfast would see the light of day once more.

Did outlaws stay hard? Was horniness a result of or prerequisite for the violent trades of life? They were just gonna have to satisfy their sweet tooth elsewhere. She'd not be a substitute for a cheap whore.

If money was what they lacked, she would gladly give them every cent she had, if it meant leaving her and the girls alone. Somehow, she doubted lust and money were their greatest needs. If they asked her, she'd tell them what they needed. Every last one of the scum looked like they hadn't seen a bar of soap in ages. They smelled like it, too.

Big Lou instructed Emma and Shelby to sit quietly on the sofa. They clutched one another in silence, but the shadows in their eyes spoke volumes. Megan was ordered to serve as they took a seat around the table. She offered the girls soothing looks of encouragement as she moved around the kitchen, the only means of comforting them at the moment.

The gunmen apparently didn't feel a necessity to hold back their brazen appraisal of her while they joked about what they wanted for dessert. She thought for sure she was going to throw up as her stomach continued to turn inside out at the lewd details. All the while, she prayed the girls didn't know what they were discussing. From the looks in their shocked expressions, she suspected they had a clue.

"Not until Spawn is good and dead," informed Rico after several minutes of their raunchy discussion.

"What the hell you talkin' 'bout?" shouted Dutch bitterly.

"It ain't fair seein' how you gotsta fuck Cheri and we didn't." Tobacco spat a big wad of it over his shoulder and roughly wiped the dark dribble from his chin with the cuff of his soiled shirt.

"No tellin' how long we gonna be waiting. A man needs to beat the beast with two backs, amigo. Ain't got no goat or sheep round these parts. Whatcha 'spect us to do?" the Mexican complained.

Megan held onto her breakfast.

"I said no. We keep the bitch in one piece. When Spawn rides up—" he tilted his head toward the girls crouched together in the corner of the sofa, "and they ain't round, he'll burn the place down. We'll never get us a chance to kill 'em."

"Hell. You talk like you're scared of the man. There's five of us. We can take 'em."

"You jackass. There was over thirty, and now, we're down to five on account of him. Dutch gots a bullet in the arm. You never rode with the sorry-assed bastard."

Rico looked around the table at the other men who rode with Devin when he was the leader of the Laredo Gang. "Tell 'em," he shouted.

A couple of the men grimaced, as if they recalled Devin's misdeeds, of which they did not seem in any rush to discuss.

The Mexican shook his head and muttered gravely, "They no call him el Diablo for nada." His eyes darted to Megan as she brought the pot of stew and sat it in the middle of table and left. "He goes crazy if you tryin' hurt a woman or kids in front of him. Cut your heart out and eat it for breakfast."

"Likes the sight of blood. Would bathe in it if there was enough."

Megan felt herself turning cold as her eyes widened. She caught hold of the sideboard as she felt her legs go weak at the bloodcurdling comment.

"And you're gonna tell me he has a warm spot for dogs too, I bet." Big Lou dipped his hand in the stew, drew out a carrot, and plopped it in his mouth.

"Hell, I don't know 'bout no damned dogs, but I've seen 'em shoot a man for leaning on his fucking horse."

The plate Megan just pulled off the shelf crashed on the floor and the men all turned to look at her.

"Dammit, woman," Rico growled. "We're starving. What's taking so long?"

"You act like savages. Eat with your hands for all I care," she snapped, afraid to hear another ill word against the man she loved.

"Best keep your mouth shut. There's things we can do to ya under that there dress can be hidden from Spawn's sight. I'll let the boys have at 'cha if ya keep it up."

The men jeered and laughed at her expense. Doing her best to ignore them, she picked up the broken pieces and threw them away. Taking a deep, calming breath, she gathered a stack of bowls and spoons. They couldn't be talking about *her* Devin Spawn. Devin wouldn't. He couldn't possibly be capable. Sadly, she knew it was hard to separate fact from fiction.

"I'll sleep better knowing we got one up on his ass, long as we got them."

She watched with rising contempt as Rico, who appeared to be the leader, spoke to Dutch.

"After we shoot him," he continued, "you can have first crack. I don't give a shit what ya do to her after."

Dutch grinned, a most vile sort of sneer, as she approached the table. Her stomach heaved. Turning as she felt his blatant gaze roam over her, she tried not to be obvious as she swallowed down the acidic fluid finding its way up her throat.

"I just wanna see him dead for stealing our gold out from under us. Till then, leave 'em be. And that goes for the rest of you's." Rico shot a challenging glance around the table.

As she scooped out a heaping spoonful of stew into a bowl and sat it in front of the Mexican, she took some comfort knowing they were safe for the moment. At least, until Devin showed up, and who knew when that would be?

Chapter 27

The house was eerily quiet. Too quiet. It was late, well past midnight. Megan was exhausted, but refused to give in to sleep. She and the girls were on her bed, fully clothed. Outside, the faint footsteps of the large, round man everyone openly referred to as Big Lou could be heard as he kept watch, pacing up and down the porch. Her eyelids grew heavy as the cadence of his steps lulled her. She fought her weariness to stay awake and keep a safe eye on the sleeping girls beside her.

Rico, the leader of the wild bunch of heathens, was asleep in the girls room, along with the one they called Dutch. Upstairs in the loft slept the other two.

In the wee hours of the morning, her body was emotionally drained and plain worn out. Submitting, she nodded in and out of consciousness, sitting with her back against the headboard.

The forceful hand on her mouth jolted every nerve into extreme panic mode as her eyes flew open. Dawn was hours away, and the single candle on the side table had burned out long ago, making it nearly impossible to distinguish her assailant. Directly, she was dragged off the bed. Her head slammed into the floor as she landed on her back with a thud. Her mouth opened to scream. The pressure of his rough, calloused hand was firm, hindering all sound. She scratched and clawed at his face. She felt his hand under her skirt, on her knee, then her thigh as she twisted and turned. She saw the whites of his eyes widen as he discovered she wasn't wearing pantalets.

"Fight me, bitch. I like it." Dutch's hot breath was clammy on her skin as the most evil of voices rustled at her ear. The hand on his good arm forced her legs apart as he tried to push his way between her thighs. Her nails tore into his skin, gathering flesh and blood beneath her fingernails. Still, he proceeded, dragging his hand toward her mound. As he inched closer, her heart pumped furiously, her eyes bulged in their sockets as her mind raced for answers.

She bent her leg to knee him in the groin. Dutch must have sensed her intent and moved over her, trapping her legs apart as his thighs straddled hers. The weight of his body, heavy on hers, barred her from moving. His hand went from between her thighs to his belt buckle. "Before I kill him, I'm gonna let him know how I fucked his ma."

That would never happen. She'd rather die first than allow him to have his way with her. Pulling her hand back as far as she could, with sheer force of will, she rammed his nose with the hard edge of her palm. At the same time, she opened her mouth and clamped her teeth down hard on the fleshy pad of his palm. Megan tasted blood on her tongue and felt it smear against her hand.

"Shit," he yelled out, doubling over on his side, his thigh lying across her hips. With all the might she could afforded, she pushed him off her body the rest of the way.

Megan quickly scrambled out from under him, rushing to her feet.

She stepped out of his grasp quickly as he reached out to grab her. Nervously, she searched her pocket and drew out her palm-sized pistol. Holding it with both hands as she shook from the fright, terror beyond comprehension gripping her, she pulled the trigger.

"Dammit," he roared clutching his shoulder, the same side as his wounded arm. The blood gushed between his fingers.

The girls woke up screaming, their frantic gazes soaking up the situation in the poorly lit room. They looked from Megan standing at the foot of the bed holding a gun to the man coming to his feet next to the bed.

Rico rushed into the room, bringing the faint light from the kitchen as he opened the door. He was dressed only in jeans, and his bare chest and most of his back was covered in black, wiry hair. He grabbed the pistol out of her hand and struck her across the face with his other hand.

Megan fell to the floor with a grunt as a striking bolt of pain assailed her senses. White sparks flashed before her eyes. She fought the urge to scream and show how afraid she truly was.

By then, the other three men were gawking through the open doorway.

"Damn bitch shot me."

"Shit, look what you made me do." Rico pointed the pistol at Megan who lay on the floor.

Shooting him an insolent glance, she ignored their squabble as she went back to surveying the damage. Lightly touching her throbbing cheekbone, she felt the swelling starting to set in. Running her tongue along her gumlines, she checked for loosened teeth. Determining there were none, she thanked her lucky star. The other stars—surely a person required more than one—must have been busy shining over someone else this particular night.

"Why didn't you fucking stay away?" Rico raged on, sounding as though he was ready to take his partner out for crossing him.

"The bitch shot me. Why you screaming at me?"

"What you want me to do about it? Hell, I ain't no fuckin' doctor. You got one bullet in ya. What's one more? We need her alive, not you."

"So it's like that?"

"Hell, yes." He looked down at her again. Megan could feel his eyes on her as she sat up. She was aware he was concerned the faint beginnings of a bruise were starting to show. The man was afraid of Devin. "Try it again, and you'll find yourself tied up."

He glanced over his shoulder at the girls as they held onto one another, crying uncontrollably.

"Shut the fuck up." He turned and walked out of the room. Entering the kitchen, he muttered, "Since you're awake, fix us some grub. I'm hungry."

Cursing, Dutch stormed out of the room. He shot a dangerous glare in her direction.

Megan raced behind him on her way to provide what comfort she could to Shelby and Emma. She felt a sense of triumph glimpsing the scratches across his cheeks, his bloody, busted nose, and his shirt soaked in red as he held onto his shoulder. Unfortunately, the shot only grazed him. She felt no remorse in wishing the damage could have been worse.

* * * *

"Megan, I'm scared." Shelby's soft voice trembled with fear as she gripped Megan's hand tightly on her lap.

"I'm hungry. They didn't let us have no lunch," Emma said curtly, arms crossed over her chest, scowling at the three men seated at the table. They were drinking Reed's leftover whiskey they'd found in the sideboard.

"Girls, we have to be strong," she whispered with conviction. "For now, we'll do as they say until I can come up with a way to get out of this." If only she believed it was that simple.

Patting Shelby's hand, Megan rose from the sofa. "The girls need to eat. I'll start supper," she announced decisively, hoping her conviction held some weight in the matter.

"I say when it's time to eat." Rico shifted in his chair and looked over at her, as if angered by the interruption.

With the greatest of difficulties, she stood her ground and held his gaze.

His cold eyes flashed to the girls, then back to Megan. "Boys, ya hungry?"

One grumbled something about how he could use a little food. The other shrugged his shoulders flippantly, and she could have slapped away his indifference right then and there.

Turning back to his drink and the cards in his hand, Rico ordered gruffly, "My men are hungry. Cook 'em something."

* * * *

Pablo barreled through the front door. "Rider comin'."

Megan swung around from the pot of chicken stew she was stirring on the stove and stretched her neck to look out the window. Her heart raced. Devin was the first dreadful thought that filled her mind.

Rico ran to the kitchen window, and the other three rushed to look out of the parlor window.

"Who is it?" Rico asked, pistol already directed at whomever it was riding up to the house.

Pablo dragged her by the arm to the parlor window. She couldn't hide her grimace as his fingers bit down hard on her flesh, pinching the skin of her upper arm.

Casting a glance out the window, she gasped in terror as Caleb dismounted. Taking the reins in his hand, he tied his horse to the hitching post at the end of the walkway. A habitual practice repeated dozens of times, only now, she dreaded his familiarity. She prayed he would change his mind about visiting and ride away.

"Who is he?" Rico repeated in a hushed, insistent voice. His grip tightened on her arm, twisted, urging her to speak up.

"Devin's brother," she lied quickly. If they believed he was related, hopefully, just hopefully, it would be enough to keep him alive. Shelby and Emma already called him "uncle", so the lie wasn't too farfetched.

Rico and his men passed questioning glances. Wordlessly, Rico gestured to the others. From the signals, Megan knew it wasn't good.

Forced to sit on the sofa with the girls, she flung her arms around them and held them to her bosom as her blood raced and her body trembled. Closing her eyes, she prayed silently for Caleb's life to be spared.

Her eyes darted open as soon as she heard the mundane sound of a hand touching the wooden door handle. Unable to breathe or move, she stared as the door was abruptly snatched from Caleb's hand and swung open. The rifle pointed at his chest brought his hands up automatically as he was ordered inside.

"Who the hell are you? Where's Megan?"

Caleb's questions went unanswered.

Once he stepped a foot inside, the man hiding behind the door struck him behind the head with his gun.

* * * *

Groaning, Caleb gradually regained consciousness. Instinctively, he wanted to reach behind his head where the throbbing was the worse. His eyes snapped open when he realized his hands were tied behind his back. The rope tight around his chest kept him firmly planted in a wooden chair, while the restraints at his ankles prohibited the last of his freedom. The reality of the situation began to sink in as he started to remember two gruesome characters greeting him at the door before everything faded to black.

"Caleb," Megan whispered as he continued to test the strength of his restraints. Her faint voice captured his attention.

He looked over his shoulder and noticed Megan, Shelby, and Emma huddled together on the sofa. He looked them over intently as he blinked away the haze. Pure, unchecked fury seized him as he took in the black bruise marring Megan's beautiful cheek. All sense of right and wrong took a drastic, sharp turn toward the worst kind of wrong. The wrong there was no turning back from.

"We're fine. No damage. But you've been out for almost an hour," she continued to whisper. Her eyes darted occasionally to the four men seated at the table drinking and playing cards. "They're looking for Devin. I told them you are his brother."

He blinked away the haze and ignored the misery behind his head to listen to her.

"It was the only thing I could think of to keep you alive. Apparently, the only thing murderers fear is another murderer. If we're not alive when he returns," she paused and seemed to contemplate the last of that sentence before she finished. "They're afraid of what he might do to them."

Speculatively, his eyes roamed from man to man. At least he could sympathize with their thought process from firsthand experience. Devin wasn't the sort of man to be taken lightly. Judging from the fierce looks of these brutes, they, too, probably went unchallenged. What did that indubitably say about Devin?

"How long have they been here?" he whispered, biting back the rage surging through his veins.

"Since yesterday afternoon."

"Dear, Lord," he muttered fiercely. "How long are they planning to wait?"

"As long as it takes. I told them—" Megan stopped speaking immediately when she heard the men talking.

"What are we gonna do with 'em?" Chewy glanced in their direction.

"Sure as heck don't look like Spawn," Dutch observed, staring at Caleb over the top of his cards.

"Kinda looks like them little girls. They's all got the same yella' hair." Big Lou ran a hand over his own balding head.

Crinkling his eyes, Pablo rubbed his whiskered chin. "I smell a rat."

"Ah, what you smell is your own stink. I can smell your dirty brown ass from here." Dutch gathered the cards in his hands and tossed them in the center of the table as he rocked on the back legs of his chair.

Pablo stood abruptly, the chair legs screeching back across the wooden floor. He flicked his cigarette at him, causing the other man's eyes to darken as they rose to meet the unspoken challenge in his.

Dropping his hands to his sides as if ready to reach, Dutch made a move to stand up. He stopped midway when Chewy barked loud enough to garner the attention of everyone in the room. "I wanna listen to what he's got to say." Dutch grunted offhandedly, then lowered back in his chair.

* * * *

Megan swallowed down her unease as she watched Chewy make his way toward them. Pablo took his seat, talking to the other men still seated around the table. "Past hour, I've been keeping my eye on her. There's something not right with them two. If he's Devin brother, how in the hell can she be Devin's ma?"

"Stupid ass, different ma's. Cheri said she was young." Rico bit off the end of a cigar and spit it out. He struck a match on the bottom of his dusty black boot and lit the cigar.

Chewy stood in front of her, hands on his hips. He tapped the butt of the pistol holstered at his waist. Looking away, she tried to appear oblivious to his presence. He seemed to be scrutinizing every inch of her body, from the lopsided bun of her hair to the wrinkled hem of the dress she'd worn for the past two days.

"Who the hell you call stupid? I know that. What riles me is the way she looks at him. Like she sweet on him or something."

Frowning, Dutch rose from his seat. "What's wrong? Your ma never paid no 'tention to ya?" He didn't wait for a response as he moved away.

Rico and Big Lou laughed. Pablo fumed.

Chewy's eyes shifted, narrowed on Dutch as he came to a halt by his side.

Dutch stared at Megan, grinning all the while. She was quite familiar with that crude smirk, and it made her blood boil with contempt. "I might've not beaten on my ma if she looked half as good as her."

Megan shrugged back as Dutch picked up a loose ringlet off her shoulder. She glared up at him as he twirled the naturally spiral lock of hair around his finger. He seemed to derive pleasure watching her hair wrap tightly around his finger, as though it were a phallic symbol to sate his disturbingly sick needs.

"Take your hands off her," Caleb warned.

Megan closed her eyes briefly, praying Caleb didn't do anything foolish. She already knew they were only trying to torment her with their raunchy teasing. Nothing more.

The two men turned and looked at him with intense regard as a tense hush descended momentarily. Her heart sped up.

"And if we don't?" Dutch asked coolly.

"You ain't in no position to be making no threats," Chewy reminded him bluntly.

"Untie me, and then we'll talk," Caleb smoothly replied with a challenge in his voice.

"Smart-ass mouth like Devin," Rico remarked, sitting back in his chair. He propped his long legs on the edge of the table and crossed his ankles, as if enjoying the afternoon's entertainment.

Dutch released her hair. His fingers went beneath her chin as his eyes remained on Caleb. She jerked back, causing him to face her with disapproval in his dark gaze.

Megan felt Shelby's grip on her hand tighten as the young girl leaned in closer.

"You and her got something going on?" Dutch's gaze dropped to her chest as she struggled to control her escalated breathing. Megan tried her best to hold her breath entirely to avoid drawing more attention to her already heaving breasts. Grateful for a change her small breasts weren't as obvious, assumingly more enticing than, say, Cheri's rising mountain tops.

Before Caleb could speak, Megan blurted, "He's a preacher."

All five men laughed.

Caleb clamped his mouth shut. He seemed to do his best not to look amused himself as he cast her a quick, bewildered look.

"If that don't beat all. The devil has a preacher for kin," Chewy remarked, chuckling as he walked back to the table.

Dutch took a step back, resting his hands on the shell belt strapped low on his hip. Disgust swept over his expression as he stared at Caleb. "Hell, that don't mean a damn thing. I've seen plenty of preachers in whorehouses.

I even fucked one of them so-called nuns. Course, she prayed the whole time."

"'Wuz it cuz your pecker's too little, or you just plain sorry when it comes to pleasing women?" Chewy's voice held no mockery, and Megan found that amusing in itself.

"You go to hell, amigo, if he real holy man." Pablo made a quick sign of the cross over his chest, as if that meager gesture would atone for his sins.

"I assure you, I've never been to a house of ill-repute in my life," Caleb said.

Megan wondered if Caleb's eloquently proclaimed statement was a lie. At least he sounded convincing, which made it easier for her to accept.

Dutch turned his attention to Megan, ignoring the comments of his cohorts. This time, he brushed the hair away from her face and allowed his fingers to stroke her skin.

She flinched. The clammy feel of his flesh, his putrid scent assaulted her senses. She would shoot him again if Rico hadn't take her gun away.

"You ain't gotta go far when you got this at home" Dutch said. "No wonder Devin hasn't been visiting Cheri lately. Keeping it in the family. What's that called?"

"Incest," Rico supplied, with a nod of his head toward the fat man across the table. "Big Lou here can tell you all about it."

Megan heard Big Lou let out a raucous snicker, and she could only cower at the sickening implication.

Dutch's lips curled into a vile sneer, as he chuckled. "Yeah, that's it. Momma must really be something. Tell me." He glanced at Caleb and seemed to pause for effect, which only made her insides flip-flop. "What she like?"

"I told you to get your filthy hands off her," Caleb growled. He jumped to his feet, lunging at Dutch and taking the chair strapped to his back with them as they tumbled to the floor.

The four men at the table emptied their seats instantly.

Megan's heart beat so fast, she felt the vibration in her toes. Her entire body trembled, shook as she held onto the girls. They started to cry, witnessing Caleb being carried off.

Pablo was ordered to stay and keep an eye on them. Standing at the window close to the sofa, he gave her a half-English, half-Spanish account of the action. Excitedly, he threw blows at a ghost figure in front of him. He glanced at her periodically, either to make sure she stayed put or to judge her reaction—she didn't know which.

She closed her eyes and tried desperately to shut down her emotions. Covering the girls ears so they wouldn't hear over their muted whimpers, the disturbing sounds of wood breaking, harsh grunts, and coarse moans as blow after powerful blow, kick after swift kick found its target.

Megan couldn't take it anymore. The mindless torture was driving her insane. Running through the open doorway, she screamed, "Stop it! You're killing him."

Pablo tried to pull her from the porch post she held onto with a death grip. She watched in horror as the tangled mass of men rolled on the ground, knowing Caleb was somewhere on the bottom.

"Please," she begged. Burning tears rolled down her face, not really knowing what she begged for as Pablo unclenched her hands and dragged her back inside. "No! No! Let me go," she cried, and to her amazement, he released her once they were back inside.

Emma and Shelby ran to her. Throwing her arms around them, she pulled them close. Thankful they were there, or else she would have surely sunk to the floor.

Somehow, she made it to her writing desk against the wall. Her entire body shook furiously. She leaned her hip against it for support. She was unable to breathe when two men carried Caleb inside a few minutes later. They held him up by the underarms with his hands still bound behind his back, feet dragging along the floor.

They dropped his bloody, limp body in front of the sofa, as though he was just another of their discarded cigarette butts or Chewy's spent wad of chewing tobacco, and they simply walked away.

Emma stared at Caleb, silent tears running down her cheeks. Shelby looked up at Megan, her chubby, round face drenched with tears.

Fighting the sob bubbling in the pit of her stomach, Megan wiped her own tears away. She dried her wet fingers with a swipe of her skirt.

She took the girls by the hand. "Come with me, girls." Resolved to remain calm for their sake, Megan pushed aside her fear and anger with the greatest of difficulty. Ignoring the cold, bitter, warning stares from the men, she led them to her bedroom. Once inside, she sat them on the edge of the bed and instructed them to remain quiet and wait for her. She walked into the kitchen, filled a bowl with water, and grabbed a dishtowel off the counter. Calmly, and with the shreds of dignity she could muster, she made her way across the room.

"What the hell do you think you're doing?" Rico inquired sharply as she passed the dining table.

Without so much as a pause, she kept walking until she reached Caleb. "I'll not leave him like this." She knelt down and began to gingerly wiped away the blood starting to congeal around his right eye, which had already doubled in size.

"Wait'll Spawn show's up. You'll need a bigger bowl," mumbled Dutch with wry amusement.

A few of the men chortled.

"I'll use my mop bucket after Devin finishes with ya'll."

The room fell silent for a moment.

"Crazy, bitch," grunted Rico under his breath after the stifling pause.

* * * *

"Ohhh," Caleb groaned, forcing his eyelids open. One stubborn eye didn't seem to want to open but a crack, and it hurt. A lot. In fact, every bone in his body protested the minimalist movement.

He was blearily aware of Megan's movements as she laid her sewing on the side table and slid off the sofa to sit beside him on the floor.

Caleb became aware of the pillow under his head and a blanket covering his aching body. He smiled up at Megan. He instantly wanted to reach out and soothe the bruise that all but covered her cheek, kiss her softly, ease the sadness, worry in her eyes and make love to her until she was drowning in pleasure, trembling with climatic bliss. He doubted he'd survive the effort it would require. "How long was I out this time?"

"It's no time to joke, Caleb." The frantic look in her eyes was no laughing matter. She was terribly afraid and for good reason. It didn't matter how long he had slept. He was in deadly danger, and Megan and girls were in much worse. He didn't even want to think about it. Time was running out.

"You're right," he muttered, grimacing as he tried to push himself up onto his elbows. With his hands still tied behind his back, he found the task difficult. The piercing stab of pain tearing through his chest warned him at least one, if not more ribs were bruised, maybe even cracked or broken.

"Lay still, Caleb," she ordered quietly. Her gaze dissected his every move with wariness. Concern deepened in her eyes. "The men are all outside. One's on the porch. And the girls are in my room. I didn't want them to see you like this."

"There's a knife in my right boot. I want you to cut the rope." He managed to sound more authoritative than he felt. Damn outlaws. Not one of them bothered to untie him, even the odds, make it a fairer fight. What did he expect? They were walking around with lust in their eyes, hard-ons in their jeans, and revenge on their mind.

He preferred they work off their energy on him instead of on Megan. He'd managed several good blows with his thick skull, elbows, knees, and whatever body parts he rammed into flesh and bones. He was built to survive whatever they dished out. Megan, he wasn't so sure.

Her eyes widened in shock. "You can't be serious."

"It's the only way. They think I'm hurt. They won't be expecting it."

"Uh, Caleb, you *are* hurt." She stared at him as though he'd lost his mind.

He frowned, ignoring the tormenting pain deep in his bones. "Megan, we don't have time to argue. Cut me free. Where is Reed's rifle?"

She glanced over her shoulder as they heard a wooden plank creak from a shift of weight out on the porch. She sighed deeply before turning back to him. He read the sudden edge of urgency in her eyes and fumed with fury. Big Lou, on the other side of the wall, scared her. He frightened her more than the other men. After the earlier disclosure, he understood why.

"They found it." He stared as her dainty hand disappeared under the blanket. Her eyes flittered back and forth from the open doorway to her concealed hand. As her fingers moved over his legs, his body tensed. The warmth of her fingers seared his skin through the fabric. Lust, hot and addictive, pulsed through his system and clouded his mind with a different, more intense, tormented agony. He sighed roughly and felt his cock stiffen outright when she pulled his trouser leg over his boot and slipped her soft hand inside the cool leather in search of the sheathed knife.

At the sound of his blatant demonstration of arousal at so minor a stimulant, she turned around. He watched as her brows rose in mock amusement, but there was a flicker of undeniable passion in the hazel depths. He shrugged his shoulders innocently. In his present condition, there wasn't much else he could do as she tucked the knife under the blanket, near his hip.

"And your gun," he breathed harshly, fighting the consuming lust threatening to burst against his trousers with or without her assistance.

"They took it." She rolled him over slightly, cutting through the rope tightly bound around his wrists.

Closing his eyes, he groaned through gritted teeth, positive more than one rib clamored for sympathy. If even one rib was broken and he made a wrong move, the ragged bone could pierce his lung, a chance he was willing to take for Megan's sake.

There wasn't any way of knowing when Devin would return. Sooner or later, the men were going to tire of waiting. Their only chance of survival was if he could get his hands on a gun. He knew it and suspected Megan knew it, as well.

"We have to think of a way to get the one with a sling close. I believe I can manage to take his gun from him."

"I shot him in the shoulder," she confessed as his hands finally came free. "That's why I told them you were a preacher. They would have made you patch him up. So he can turn around and shoot Devin. I couldn't stand for that."

Lying back, he rubbed the rope burns on his wrists under the blankets. It was common knowledge even the notorious gunslingers seldom shot down a doctor in the event their services where ever required. After the bruise they gave Megan, he wouldn't have lifted a finger to help.

"A school teacher would have been more believable than a preacher." His intent wasn't to chastise or be overly critical of her quick wit. Not in the least. At the present moment, he aimed to relieve her mind of their dire circumstances. Even if for just a moment. "Perhaps even a lawyer. I don't exactly look like the most holiest of men."

At the wicked gleam in his eye and huskiness in his voice, Megan rolled her eyes. "Caleb, you're too weak to be thinking about that now," she said in a chiding tone, low enough so the man on the porch wouldn't hear.

"Stick your hand back under the blanket. You'll find out how weak I am." He grinned. A most delicious grin that made the flesh between her thighs throb with acute awareness and her body flush with desire as her gaze lowered. The long, thick outline was quite noticeable underneath the smooth, thin cotton blanket covering his hips.

She smiled at him, remembering how a few days ago while the girls were in school, he made her come twice with just a flick of his tongue. Oh, how long ago it seemed. "Don't men ever think of anything else?"

"No," he answered quickly in a seductive whisper that made her shiver. She felt her breasts swell and, her nipples harden with longing. Saw his eyes lower to the peaks she knew were straining against the front of her bodice. His awareness of her response darkened his gaze. The tip of his tongue slid between his lush lips, slowly stroked over the top, then wet the full bottom lip, as though eager to repeat the motion on her nipples. She couldn't help but moan helplessly at the sight, desperate to have those lips on her.

"But I guess I have to, so we can get out of this mess and finally get ourselves married. I'm looking forward to our wedding night." His voice was rough and the flare of desire, the burning need in his heavy-lidded eyes only heightened her lust for him. Her body ached for him, his touch, kiss, his everlasting love.

Despite their dire situation and the inappropriateness of the moment, she could not help but think about being married to Caleb. Truthfully, she'd looked forward to their wedding night since the age of thirteen. At night, while living in Jazelle's attic, she wondered what it would be like to have Caleb already warming the sheets as she crawled into bed, doing to her what those men downstairs did to the women she watched through the peepholes. Now that she knew, a flare of arousal pulsed through her body and heated her blood.

"Told you we didn't kill 'em," Chewy shouted as he entered the house, causing Megan to jump and jerk back the hand reaching underneath the blanket. He spoke over his shoulder at Big Lou, who continued to keep watch on the porch. For a moment, he regarded Caleb with icy contempt.

"He just woke up," Megan said hastily, rising to her feet after quickly rearranging the blanket to hide Caleb's proof his virility prevailed despite his physical limitations. She took a deep breath to regain her composure at being caught ready to stick her hand under Caleb's blanket in an attempt to make him forget his troubles. At least, that's what she was trying to convince herself was the sole reason. "I was about to get him something to eat."

"Why don't you fix something for lunch so's we can all eat." He dipped the cup he removed from the shelf over the counter into the water barrel. He drained the contents in one long gulp, then let out a deep belch.

Glancing downward fleetingly, she slowly kicked the protruding knife handle under the blanket with her tip of her shoe. Her skirt shielded the small movement.

"Certainly," she replied rather pleasantly, crossing her arms over her chest as she made her way to the kitchen. "It shouldn't take me long at all."

Chapter 28

"Whoa!" Devin signaled, holding up a staying hand late in the afternoon as he and Rising Sun made their way down the rode leading to the ranch house. His line of vision narrowed as his eyes swept over the yard, taking in every detail. The hens were loose, clucking like they hadn't eaten in days. Megan's garden hadn't been weeded in some time. No horses exercised in the corral. Plenty of foot traffic in front of the house. Large prints, akin to male footprints. Numerous male prints littered the dirt courtyard. And for a beautiful, sunny Saturday afternoon, instead of playing outside, the girls were nowhere to be seen.

With a head jerk, he motioned for Rising Sun to pull back.

They did so quickly, lifting little dust in their wake as Devin scanned the hill on his right and the grove of trees off to his left. Habit. Ensuring they hadn't been spotted, in case someone was on the lookout.

"Something's not right." Devin racked his brain for an answer as to why he hadn't listened to his gut instinct the past few days. Caught up in thinking of Megan, he brushed aside every alarm going off in his mind, chalking it up to unmanageable lust. He was so horny, so frustrated, and so damned lonely. Hell, he was just plain miserable since he left her nearly a month ago. Out of desperation to preserve his sanity, he ignored the signals.

Try as he might, no longer could he blame his carnal urges. Suddenly acknowledging Deuce's rough gait the past couple of miles. *Shit.* His damned horse had sensed danger before he did.

He hoped he was in time.

Rising Sun regarded him silently.

Scowling in anger and frustration, Devin looked over at his companion and grumbled decisively. "They're in trouble."

He steered a course straight behind the barn. Rising Sun followed.

* * * *

"No matter how many times I walk past, he's more interested in their card game." Megan slumped back on the sofa, resting her head against her hand, her elbow propped on the padded arm. Her tone held a touch of exasperation. She bit her lip, as if in deep concentration.

Caleb could only imagine the thoughts crossing her mind at what else to do to attract Dutch's attention other than falling on his lap. He sighed heavily, disappointed and angry with himself for not being more help. Can't push a wagon in front of the horse once the wheel's broke.

He shook his head out of frustration. Megan needed him, not the love, comfort, or pleasure he could provide. Strength. Protection. Guts and Glory. That and more was what she needed. Right now, he only had an ungodly supply of doubts.

He had fought the excruciating aches and pains tooth and nail to shift himself to his seated position on the floor, leaning his back against the sofa. Late last night, the fever set in. He was burning up, his body constantly beaded with perspiration. Earlier, the pain had taken its toil when he attempted to join her on the sofa. And the burst of strength he called upon for that small repositioning left him drained, gasping for air as he finally gave up and sunk back to the floor. Though he didn't let on to Megan the extent of his internal injuries, he was convinced at least one more reserve of adrenaline remained. After that, he just didn't know.

"Now, that's a fine pickle." He kept his tone serious to capture her undivided attention. She looked down at him, puzzled. "Should I be more offended when he's tearing your clothes off with his eyes, or because he's lost interest? Ouch," he softly feigned distress when she lightly punched his arm.

"You're horrible. I don't know why I love you."

He glanced up at her through his good eye. He heard the amusement in her tone, but it was the sudden fluttering of her long lashes that let him know she didn't realize what she was saying until after she said it.

Smiling, he winked at her with the bad eye since it was practically closed anyway, extending little effort. "I suggest you refrain from talk like that, or I'll have to disclose my unholy side." The thought alone was enough to send his cock into a jerking frenzy under the blanket. No safe time to preen or primp, her hair hadn't been combed in days or her dress changed, yet her eyes sparked, and her skin glowed with a silky radiance. She was absolutely beautiful. As his gaze lingered on the delicacy of her oval face, he struggled to ignore the sexual awareness heating his blood, escalating his blood pressure. This was not the time, nor the place. Well, maybe the place, but definitely not the time.

She had the most endearing smile on her lips and a delightfully pink blush across her cheeks. The remnants of her bruise were a faint blue and yellow, but still noticeable, as was the lusty glimmer in her hazel eyes. Oh, yeah, there were carnal thoughts on her mind, too.

"If you can manage to keep your hands off me, best if we sit tight for the time being." He deliberately spoke in a soft, seductive tone, meant to titillate her the way she had been taunting him ever since yesterday, when she stripped his clothes off from the waist up. Rico complained he didn't want to stare at Caleb's naked chest all damned day. Megan told him he wouldn't need to if they would have kept their hands to themselves. Dutch glared at him viciously every time he walked in the house. Pablo gave her questioning glances. While the others did the only manly thing one does in the situation—turned up their noses and went about their business.

Megan nursed the bumps, bruises and gashes on his arms, chest and back, along with the knot on his head. She wiped him down with a cool, damp rag, nice and slow. So painstakingly slow, it drove him insane. She slid that rag over every inch of his upper body while her fingertips brushed along his skin. He would watch as her eyes darkened with need and her skin pinked with arousal. Her breath caught as his nipples hardened whenever she raked them with her fingernails. By the time she was done, his erection was aching worse than his ribs, throbbing for relief. She would lick her lips and stare hungrily as it jerked underneath the blanket under her intense gaze.

And last night, the little vixen had to have been horny as hell. Everyone else was asleep except the guy on watch duty. About ready to pass out himself from sensory overload, he felt her hand slip under the blanket, cup his cock and squeeze. His entire body tightened as a bolt of heat shot from his cock up to his spine, down to his toes. Good, Lord, he almost came right then and there. As if she didn't know what she was doing, she smiled sweetly, stood up, and went to bed. If he didn't know any better, he would have sworn he heard her moan as she masturbated herself to sleep. It was probably wishful thinking on his part. Because if it were true, with the way the others were walking around with hard-ons of their own, there would have been hell to pay if they heard.

"Don't want to fight them all again." Smirking, he cast her a telling sidelong glance

Megan raised both her brows amusedly and hid her grin behind her hand. Her cheeks flushed a bright red, and he knew she got the message.

"Let him come to us," he advised, returning to the pressing issue at hand as his gaze lowered to the two little buds pressing proudly against her bodice. He was about to tell her what he was going to do to her after they got out of this as his eyes lifted and noticed she nodded in agreement.

Her head suddenly jerked up, and they both turned around when Emma came out of the bedroom, calling for her.

* * * *

"Whadda ya want, kid?" Rico asked, placing his cards face down in front of him.

Megan immediately stood, her eyes wide with alarm by the menacing tone in his voice.

"I hafta go," Emma stated simply.

"Go where?" Chewy's expression evoked ridicule from the other men.

"Jackass, she hasta take a piss," Dutch muttered.

"I'll take her." Megan rushed across the room, pulse racing out of control.

Before she reached Emma, Pablo jumped in front of her and grabbed Emma by the arm. "I take her."

"The chamber pot is in the closet. It's no trouble." Her eyes darted from Emma to Pablo.

"It's startin' to stink like piss round here. I takin' her to the shitter outside."

Megan felt her heart sink. "No," she practically shouted, not caring her outburst drew glares from the other men. "I'll take her. I promise we won't try to run. You can even walk with us, if you prefer."

He pushed past Megan, taking Emma with him as she squirmed in his restrictive grasp.

"Pablo, come right back. Don't try nuttin' funny." Rico picked up his cards and returned his attention to the poker game.

Pablo chuckled while the door closed behind him and Emma.

Megan stared at the door, her body going numb.

* * * *

"Judging from them saddles, I know who they are," Devin said gruffly, peering through the hole in the barn wall as he studied the house for signs of Megan and the girls.

"What they want?" Rising Sun asked, crouched beside him.

"They ain't here to wish me happy birthday."

"You and me get them." Rising Sun held up his rifle, the dark shadow in his eyes instantly recognizable.

Devin gave a single nod. "We need a plan—" He stopped talking when movement on the porch caught the corner of his eye. "Shit," he muttered. "The bastard has Emma."

They watched as Pablo and Emma walked toward the outhouse.

As soon as Emma slipped inside the small structure, Devin sprinted toward the window in the back of the barn. "Stay here. I'll be back."

* * * *

"I'm ready to go inside now." Emma looked up at the grungy man with wiry whiskers as she stepped out of the outhouse.

Pablo rubbed his jaw, grinning. "You and I go for little walk, eh?" He nodded toward the pecan trees.

"Megan is waiting for me. I'd rather not." Despairingly, she looked at the ranch house.

Emma drew back slightly as his large hand reached out and brushed her hair from her shoulder. "Your mama will not mind if you and me have some fun."

"It's too late to play outside."

"The game I got in mind we play anytime." He grabbed her by the arm and she tried to pull her arm back. His grip tightened. "It'll be our little secret."

"I don't want to go with you," Emma spat, refusing to move.

She squealed as he swung his arm under her, freeing her feet from the ground. He tucked her under his arm, and she opened her mouth to scream for Megan. Nothing came out as he clamped his free hand over her mouth. He hurried behind the trees.

* * * *

Sprinting, Devin didn't pause to think. There was only time to react. Leaping through the air, fingers twisted around the well-worn handle of his large bowie knife. In the same instant he landed on Pablo, he shouted a warning, "Emma, turn away."

With his full weight, he brought Pablo face-down in the earth. As they landed, Pablo lost his hold on Emma. She scurried behind a tree.

Within half a second, Devin's fingernails tore into the man's face as he pulled his head back, the knife slicing his throat from ear to ear, so deep and vicious, his head was almost completely severed.

Before jumping to his feet, he swiped the blade clean on the dead man's shirt and returned it to the sheath at his waist. He spun around anxiously and looked for Emma.

"Emma," he choked with untapped emotions. His voice was rough and his breath came fast as he went to her.

Going to his knees, he yanked her into his embrace and breathed a heavy sigh of relief. His heart pounded in his chest. He closed his eyes, and for the first time in his life, he felt them start to well with tears.

"Devin," she said feebly, drawing her small arms around his neck. She clung to him, and he felt her tiny body yield to the strong, heartfelt emotions abandoned long ago. Every nerve, every fiber shook her tiny frame. The pain, torment, and disenchantment, unbefitting one so young, washed away as the tears flowed in a never-ending stream.

He held for long, powerfully moving minutes as he listed to her tears, felt his own streaming down his face unchecked.

"You're safe now," he finally assured her.

"Don't go. Don't leave me. Everyone leaves me. My ma, my brother, Pawpaw. Please, Devin, don't leave me. I'm scared."

With utmost care, his hands clasped around her face. At last, his searching eyes saw the real Emma, a frightened eight-year-old child, for the first time. As though he looked in a mirror, big, silver eyes looked up at him, frightened of being loved, loving, being abandoned, and of just plain living.

She reminded him of a boy at the age of ten.

Devin swallowed tightly. The lump was lower. He swallowed hard again, but it wouldn't go away.

He pressed her hard into his embrace, unconscious of whether he was hurting her or not, only aware of the need to hold her close, keep her safe, free from all harm. "Dear, sweet Emma," he said soothingly, rocking her gently. "I know you're afraid, but you're safe now. Can you be brave for me while I help Shelby? I won't be far."

"No, Devin," she cried. He didn't want to let her go.

"Listen to me, Emma. Shelby and Megan need me." He stood, picking her up with him. "I'll be back for you. I promise."

Sniffling, Emma nodded. He saw her upper lip stiffen, knew she was trying to be brave as she fought back the tears. His brave little girl, the little sister who shared more than eye color.

"You can help me by telling me how many men there are."

She looked like she wanted to glance over her shoulder at the man lying a few feet away in a pool of blood, as if she needed to make sure it wasn't necessary to count him as one of the bad guys any longer. "Four. Megan shot one of them, but he didn't die."

Damn peashooter, Devin thought to himself. He knew he should have left her with a real gun. One that could do some damage. He had intended to teach Caleb how to use a firearm, but never seemed to get around to it.

"Are Megan and Shelby okay?"

She nodded. "They hurt Caleb real bad."

Frowning at the many implications Caleb's presence connoted, he lowered her to the ground. He turned and allowed one emphatic curse word before facing Emma once more.

Taking a risk, he whistled for Deuce. Trained to follow his master's path, he was not worried Deuce would be spotted. His one concern was the men holding Megan and Shelby captive were familiar with his whistle. The element of surprise would be lost.

"Deuce will be here in a moment, Emma. If I'm not back in an hour, I want you to ride into town. Do you understand?"

"Okay." Her voice was soft as she put up a brave front, wiping the tears from her chubby pink cheeks.

A few moments later, Deuce appeared.

Emma was settled in the saddle as she listened intently to his final instructions.

"No matter what you hear, you stay put. After one hour, he'll take you into town." He patted Deuce, and the horse acknowledged with a whiny nod. "I said that for Deuce's sake. Makes him feel important. Between you and I, I'll be back."

They exchanged a smile.

He turned on his heels.

His total demeanor changed.

No longer Devin the comforter, protector. Devin the big brother, or even Devin the lover, he was now the Devil's Spawn. A distance traversed into a realm beyond human comprehension. It beat in his heart and flowed in his blood, the need and taste for revenge that only spilt blood could satisfy.

He raced over the large hill behind the house, through the open field well beyond the garden, past the bunkhouse, and around the small hill. In a matter of minutes, he reached the barn.

* * * *

Inside the house, Megan's hand dropped to Caleb's shoulder instantly at the faint noise ringing in the distance outside. Her fingers dug into his shoulder as she fell into a trance.

"What is it, Megan?" Caleb looked up at her.

"Did you hear that?" Rico was the first to speak.

"I didn't hear nothin'," Chewy muttered before taking the last gulp of whiskey in the bottle.

"Sounded like a bird." Big Lou shrugged his shoulders.

"That ain't no fuckin' bird." Rico jumped out of his seat and ran to the kitchen window, gun drawn. "That's Spawn."

The other men all stood, pulling their weapons. Two rushed to the parlor window, and Dutch joined Rico at the kitchen window. "You sure it's him?"

"I'd know that call anywhere. That damn friggin' horse is out there, too."

"I don't see nothin'." Chewy squinted his eyes as he cautiously peered out the window.

"Slippery bastard," Rico grumbled heatedly. "He's like a fucking Injun. It's when you don't see him you needs to be worried."

"Grab the girl." Dutch gestured toward Chewy.

"Which one?"

"You idiot," he spat. "That one." He gestured with the pistol toward Megan.

Gripped with fear, she couldn't protest, let alone breathe. Her only awareness was of Devin. He was there. Somewhere outside, he was there.

Chewy yanked her off the sofa by the wrist.

"Leave her alone," Caleb shouted as he started to rise to his feet.

The heel of Chewy's boot landed flush on the side of his face. Caleb fell to the floor with a grunt.

* * * *

Rising Sun examined Devin as his big body squeezed through the window, then straightened to his full height. Though he looked like he fought a war, there wasn't a drop of blood on him or any sign of exertion.

"Little girl okay?"

Devin replied with a single nod as he hunkered on his heels close to where Rising Sun was crouched, watching and listening.

"There are four," he said with brutal authority as he peered through the crack between the wall panels. "No time for war paint, friend, but there will be a battle."

Rising Sun smiled knowingly. Crazy Buffalo Hunter was the type of man he wanted on his side, rather than against him. With death darkening the man's gaze, Rising Sun was assured of victory. And he was used to winning.

"They know I am here." Devin cast a sidelong glance. "You will be their surprise."

"Me no let you down," he replied with certainty.

As Devin explained their attack, the men inside were apparently devising a plan of their own.

"Spawn," Rico hollered from the kitchen window. "I know you're out there. We got your whole family—ma, sister, and your brother."

Rising Sun stared at him questioningly. In the years he had know the man referred to as Devin by his white-skinned peers, he heard of no brother.

Devin shrugged his shoulders. His expression was just as perplexed.

"Let 'em go. It's between you and me. They ain't got nothing to do with it." Devin knew his words were futile. It wasn't the way his sort functioned. Everything was fair game. War was war, and people used every means necessary to win. With one exception, Devin knew where to draw the line. Women and children. That was the solitary difference that distinguished him from the men inside.

"You took from us. We take from you."

"Only yella bellies use females to get what they want. If you want me that bad, I'll meet ya'll front and center. Only let 'em go."

"Nothin' doing, Spawn. I make the rules."

"How do I know they're still alive?" He hoped if they appeared on the porch, maybe, just maybe, they could get away.

The front door swung open. Devin's heart sped up as Chewy appeared in the open doorway, one arm wrapped around Megan's waist. He dismissed the gun pointed at her head, and an incredibly ferocious fury took over his senses as he glared at the bruise on her cheek. Someone did that to her, and all were about to suffer the consequences.

"Here's your ma. Too purty to be any kin of yours." Chewy took a couple of steps forward onto the porch. "Shame for all this to go to waste." His hand slid up her waist slowly.

If Megan still dressed for him, it wouldn't take long for Chewy to realize she wore nothing underneath her blouse. Her breasts were small, round, and perfectly taut, beneath her garments when she moved. Only when aroused did her hard nipples immodestly strain against the fabric. But they could easily be felt if his hand was allowed to continue upward.

He'd not have another man touch what was his. He watched, waited.

"Take your filthy hands off me." Megan squirmed under the roving grasp.

Devin heard the rage in her tone as he watched Chewy's gun-toting hand closely, waiting. Then he saw it, almost an imperceptible move. A minor inch in the right direction. It was all he needed. He took it.

She heard a dull thud in front of her. He knew she didn't know what happened until she looked over at Chewy. He fell half outside and half inside the doorway, a small circular bloodstain in the center of his forehead. He didn't even seem to realize it when she was pulled back inside. But Devin heard the scream, the shock and terror trembling in her voice.

"Three," Devin said simply, turning to Rising Sun. No emotion in his voice. There never was when he had a job to do. "Go. I'll wait for your signal."

With a nod, Rising Sun slipped out the window and vanished.

"You're running out of men, Rico. You can't spend gold if you're dead." Devin moved down a few feet in case they were smart enough to track the vicinity of his voice.

"Can't bushwhack me, Spawn. You ain't got the gold. You give up the guns to the law. You turned on us. Thought we wuz friends."

"I know where I can get my hands on some. More gold than you can spend. Let 'em go, and you ride away. I'll draw ya a map." He relocated again.

They both knew each other was lying. Devin needed to buy time. Nothing else. Just time.

"Won't do no good. Ya know I can't read. I'd rather spit on your grave."

"Haven't you heard, dead men don't spit?" Moving once more, he waited at the double barn doors for the signal.

"Sorry-assed bastard," Rico hollered, as if fed up with Devin's cool-nerved dribble. He fired rounds into the barn sporadically.

Devin ducked and waited.

There it was, a second after the last bullet was fired. The battle cry.

He rushed out the barn doors.

* * * *

"Shit! What the fuck is that?" Dutch hollered as everyone in the room spun around in the direction of the Indian battle cry roaring behind them. The shrill, grotesque pitch sounded like an animal being tortured.

The rifle blast ripped through the momentary silence, and Rico cried out in horrific pain, clutching his shattered guts as he tumbled to the kitchen floor.

Big Lou reached for Megan. Terrified, Megan felt the damp hand clutch her arm. Her stunned gaze rested on Caleb as he clamored to his feet, yielding the knife. He flung his battered body at the man at her side, and she opened her mouth to scream. Nothing came out.

Big Lou grunted, eyes flaring in shock as the knife pierced his protruding belly. Falling to his knees, he only had time to pull the trigger as the Comanche aimed his rifle again and let it rip.

Big Lou's bullet found a target.

Hysteria rose in her as she watched Caleb's tortured expression. He slumped to the floor, a growing pool of blood collecting under him.

* * * *

Devin barged through the door. He spotted Dutch crouched behind the dining table, taking aim at Rising Sun. Without a pause, Devin fired. Dutch dropped like a limp biscuit as Rising Sun's final bullet met its mark, right through Big Lou's sweaty forehead. He came to a final resting spot a few feet from Caleb.

"Megan," Devin breathed. His gaze found her standing over Caleb in stunned disbelief. "Megan," he said again, taking her by the shoulders and urging her to face him. Her eyes never left Caleb. "Megan," he said softly once more, needing assurance she was okay. She was still his.

She finally looked up at him, blankly. "Caleb." Her pitiful tone was a tortured, desperate plea as she slipped out of his arms, then melted to her knees by Caleb's side.

"Megan," Caleb struggled to whisper each laborious word. "I...I always thought you or Devin would be the one to shoot me. Who knew?" He closed his eyes. His breathing became more and more shallow.

"No, Caleb," she cried helplessly, throwing her body over his. "No! You can't leave me."

Rising Sun ran out of the house.

Standing there, speechless, Devin's entire body went numb. He stared, realizing with the utmost certainty, he possessed a heart capable of feeling the most grievous of emotions. Capable of feeling the tormented, gut-wrenching stab of horrendous anguish as Megan ripped his heart out, shred it to pieces, and tossed it aside.

He shut his eyes to the despairing truth lying at his feet.

"Shelby?" he muttered softly, eyes snapping open, as he remembered Megan's wasn't the only life at risk during the bloody melee.

"Shelby," he bellowed, rushing to check the girl's room, calling for her again.

Shelby crawled out from underneath their big bed.

"Here I am, Devin," she cried excitedly, running into his outstretched arms, as though happy to see him as he exited the girls' bedroom, all of them happy it was over.

"Am I ever glad to see you." He scooped her up in a big bear hug and kissed her on both cheeks. "Your sister's alright."

Putting her down quickly, he told her to wait in her room. A room full of dead bodies wasn't the best place for a small child. Once outside, he wasted no time summoning Deuce.

"Devin." Megan's tone was panicky as she ran down the steps. Blood soaked through the front of her dress. "Caleb? Where are going? You can't leave."

Deuce sauntered out from the pecan trees with Emma firm in the saddle.

Devin's jaw was rigid as every bone in his body as he quickly followed suit. He couldn't even bring himself to look at her. "To fetch the doctor."

"You can't leave us here with that...," she paused, her eyes following Rising Sun as he hurried across the yard toward the house. "Him," she exclaimed with outrage, fear and plain disgust.

"Megan," he said forcefully, staring down at her as though it pained him to look at her. It did. "See with what's on the inside, not your eyes. There isn't anyone else I'd leave you with after what just happened than your own brother."

Gasping, Megan hands fell to her stomach. Her entire body started to trembled and her teeth shattered as if she were cold.

Devin knew Caleb was running out of time. If she wanted Caleb to live, there wasn't a minute to spare. As soon as Emma's feet hit the dirt, he jumped on Deuce and rode with the wind.

* * * *

"Where's Shelby?" Emma asked as she clung to Megan.

Megan looked down at the little girl and moved her mouth to speak. Stunned beyond belief, she could not form the words.

"Needle," Rising Sun spoke briskly, gesturing a sewing motion with his hands as he stood on the porch.

"Who's he?" Emma's head tilted with curiosity as she seemed to study the only red-skinned savage she'd ever come into contact with. But then again, he wasn't a savage. Or was he?

Megan's gaze swung around at the unfamiliar, deeply masculine voice. She pored over every intricate detail, from his moccasin clad feet, his long muscular legs, loincloth tied around his trim waist, broad shoulders with two scars on his bare chest, the feather band around his well-honed bicep, beaded necklace and beaded braids in his waist-length hair, so dark it was almost black. A man's body, no longer a boy of six.

It couldn't be.

She felt the air leave her lungs as she let her gaze drift upward.

Eyes, palest of blues, piercing, brilliant as they radiated in sculptured features so scorched by the sun, his skin was nearly red.

His eyes were hauntingly familiar.

"Trevor," she mouthed his name.

"Needle," he repeated. "Now." He swung around and rushed back into the house.

The powerful urgency in his voice struck her. She blinked. The minor movement, along with Emma tugging on her arm, brought her back to a state of awareness.

"Dear God, Caleb." Gathering the layers of her blood-soaked skirt in her hands, she reacted swiftly.

Caleb had already been moved to her bed. His shirt had been removed and used to plug the gushing hole in his side. A bucket of water by the bed, along with the sheets from the girl's beds and odds and ends supplied from nature, were spread out on the table and chair. Trevor pulled close to the bed.

Megan never considered herself squeamish, but as she crossed the room with her sewing kit, saw Caleb's face twist in a tortured grimace as his red-stained flesh was cut with a long, rustic looking blade. She flinched. Trevor's dark fingers dug inside the bloody opening, searching for the bullet, and her stomach started to churn.

Shaking her head, blinking away the cloudy haze, she shook off the unease.

The chances of survival were mighty slim, but any chance was better than none. There was no time to wait on the doctor, lose her nerve, or cry like a baby.

Caleb's life was at stake.

"Here," she said, handing Trevor the threaded needle she'd picked out of her sewing kit. "What else do you need me to do?"

Chapter 29

Doctor Keeling's expression was genuinely grateful as he rose from his seated position beside Caleb, who lay in the middle of the large wood-framed bed. "Mess of trouble he was in two weeks ago, but I'm right proud to say our patient seems to be on the mend."

Doc's gaze swung to Trevor who leaned against the doorjamb, and he added, "Remarkable job you did, broken ribs and all. Maybe one day, you and I can sit a spell and exchange remedies."

Trevor gave a single nod, turned and walked away.

"How's my mother taking it, doc?" Caleb asked curiously. Talk of Devin and the fugitives had circulated like wild fire. Speculation as to why he visited Megan alone in the middle of the afternoon while the girls were supposed to be in school was the stuff people lived for. Juicy gossip of a sexual nature spread like molasses on a hot summer day, went further as it got hotter and much sweeter with time. On the quiet, Doc told him his mother missed church last Sunday. She was too disgraced to show her face after word of him and Megan sharing the same bed, as far back as when he returned from Europe while she was still married to Reed, found its way to her social circle.

It made him all the more determined to marry. To hell what his mother or any of the townfolk thought. He loved Megan, and he was going to marry her. Just as soon as he was able to walk inside the church and was well enough to enjoy the honeymoon.

Megan leaned over him and did her best to fluff the pillow beneath his head. Her breasts hung inches from his face. His mouth watered as his eyes narrowed on the scooped neckline gaped unwittingly. He caught a glimpse of her pert little breasts before she moved away. He smiled up at her, then turned his attention back to the Doc before he did something he wasn't likely to regret.

"As well as can be expected." Doc glanced at Megan, then back to him. The reason for the brooding in his voice was clear. "I'm on my way ov'r yonder to let her know you ought'a be laid up for two or three more weeks, at least."

"That long?" Megan asked grimly, hands on her hips as she stood next to the bed. Her eyes were wide with concern.

"Eager to be rid of me?" he teased even though he knew it was the lengthy recovery period that worried her. When she thought he was asleep, she would kneel beside her cot and pray every night for his full recovery. It made him feel guilty. His prayers always held a more sexual connotation. A man had his priorities.

She plopped down beside him, her mood suddenly changed. It was light, full of warmth and sunshine and polka-dotted rainbows. The Meg he adored. Taking his hand between hers, she drew his hand to her lap, settling their embrace in the warm groove between her thighs. He gritted his teeth when he felt his flesh start to thicken, unable to control his body's response to her. "Of course not. You're welcomed to stay as long as you wish."

If he didn't know better, he would have thought she did it to provoke him, tease him with her womanly wiles, as she had the night his fever was running amuck and he lay practically unconscious on the floor. But her eyes were awash with affection and her smile temptingly sweet. He watched her as she read the need in his gaze, and saw her eyes start to glaze with arousal. Lust coursed through him, hot and fast, as he began to realize her own control was hanging on a thread.

The warmth of her hands and his close proximity to such an intimate part of her body tempted him. It had been too damned long since her tight pussy gripped him, drenched his length with her juices as he drove inside her hot body. His erection throbbed at the memory of the heated depths of her slick vagina. Caleb grinned with the knowledge he was definitely getting better. The blood rushing to his loins was a sure sign everything was in perfect working order—at least, the important stuff.

Caleb's gaze drifted to Doc. His old friend suddenly looked uncomfortable as he eyed the stiff tent sway in the middle of the thin cotton sheet covering Caleb's nearly naked body. He watched as Doc shifted nervously from one foot to the other, trying to discreetly act as if he didn't notice the obvious response to Megan.

As Doc politely smiled at Megan, Caleb looked back at her. His eyes met hers, and he could see the heat and longing in the sparking hazel depths of her eyes.

Megan felt herself faintly blush at the blatant spark in Caleb's deep blue eyes. Poor Doc was desperately trying to ignore the hard pole in the middle of the bed. It was like trying to ignore a steam-snorting, raging bull charging at you in the middle of a pig pen. It was there. Doc knew it, Caleb certainly knew, and the flesh readying itself between her thighs knew it. The only thing left to do was deal. If there were ever any doubts in Doc's mind as to their definition of friendship, they were now dispelled.

"Doc, please let Mrs. Walker know my home is always open to her." Megan smiled warmly, and her entire body suddenly felt warm. She was aware her ease as the sexual tension thickened in the room, lack of widow's weeds, and step toward mending bridges meant her mourning period was definitely over. She was ready to move on, and based strictly on appearances, was doing so with Caleb.

"Every night I leave here, I give her your message. I've told her she's welcomed to join me on my next visit." Frowning, Doc shook his head solemnly.

When she felt Caleb's grip tighten on her hand, she glanced down at him. The flush on his cheeks made her knees weak and her pulse race.

"Megan, you know she'll never come." His voice was sympathetic.

Leaning over, she softly whispered in his ear, "I know. I invite just to spite her."

Chuckling, he responded in a low, suggestive tone only she could hear as she straightened. "You're naughty."

Those two hot words made her body tingle.

"Doc, would you like another cup of coffee before you leave?" she offered graciously.

* * * *

"You can no hide forever in barn." Trevor's voice seemed magnified as it echoed into the dimly lit building as Devin tossed a fork full of hay into the cow's feeding bin. A needless task considering the late hour, performed thrice daily to preoccupy his restless mind.

Devin's head jerked toward the accusatory male tone coming from the opened doorway. It tore him from the carnal thoughts plaguing him consistently. Megan's small body, soft and warm, moving over his, touching him, kissing him, accepting him. His own body moved inside her tight heat, his tongue tasting the sweet nectar from her wet flesh. "Hiding? Who the hell is hiding?" he growled.

"My sister may look like angel, but she no angel. Fiery spirit runs in blood, like me." He smacked his flattened palm against his bare chest in a demonstration of pride. "You want her. Why you no tell her?"

Tapping his hand on top of the wooden handle of the pitch fork, for want of throwing it at him, Devin's eyes narrowed. He'd only been there two weeks. How the hell did Trevor know Megan made Devin's blood boil with lust just by looking at her or thinking about her, that he was dying a slow death from needing her more than he was willing to admit?

He took a deep, harsh breath to temper his faltering control, already so far over the edge he wanted to scream, shoot something. Anything. He grunted, "You're too young to understand."

"Fiercest warrior," Trevor pointed at himself, "captured more coups, killed most buffalo, claimed most women—"

"Yeah, fine and dandy," Devin sharply interrupted, knowing Trevor's list of accomplishments was, indeed, lengthy. If Rising Sun chose to return, he'd soon become one of the youngest chiefs ever. Ironic, considering he was a blue-eyed pale-face with a tan. "Megan's made her choice. She wants Pretty Boy."

By the way confusion washed over Trevor's face, Devin knew he had no clue who Pretty Boy was or that Megan loved him, fucked him every night, was probably sucking his cock right this minute. And he wasn't in the mood for explanations. Not with the thought of the two of them so much in love searing his soul.

"Once he's well enough, I'm getting the hell outta here. You can stay or come with me. I don't give a damn anymore." In a huff, he tossed the fork aside. Dammit. He needed to get away, find clean, unscented air that didn't remind him of Megan each time he breathed.

* * * *

Trevor stepped out of Devin's way as he stalked out of the barn. He noticed Devin pause momentarily when he looked up and noticed Megan and the doctor saying their goodbyes on the porch. Devin's body seemed to stiffen, as if he was fighting to control a driving force beneath.

During the past two weeks, Trevor had learned many things, including he was seventeen winters. And Devin was truthful when he said Megan missed him. His sister accepted him, as did Shelby and Emma. They were patient, kind, and understanding as they struggled to work through the clash of cultures and make up for the lost years with memories—some happy, and some less so.

In no hurry to decide his future, he planned to remain a while longer and allow himself a chance to learn the ways of white people. Live in square houses and try to adjust to wearing trousers. The shaft between his thighs was by no means small and was in the habit of drifting free under his loin cloth. Things down there just didn't seem to fit, bringing to mind the tightly wrapped meat they ate for supper. Sausage. He shook his head as he thought about it. Made no sense to stuff meat back in skin when a woman worked hard at reaping it in the first place. Walking was a hell of a lot more difficult.

Nudging at the denim material covering his groin, Trevor sighed heavily, unable to understand why they hid behind everything. Their eyes. Their clothes. Their emotions. Not saying what needed to be said.

* * * *

Megan observed Doc Keeling's horse trotting along. Doc turned in his saddle and waved a final goodbye as he reached the bend that curved behind the barn.

Megan returned the wave from the porch as he disappeared beyond the hill, and she caught sight of Devin headed toward the water pump. Wrapping her shawl tightly around her shoulders to brace herself against the cool evening breeze, she strolled over. His back was to her, affording her a nice view of his well-curved, tight rear clad in form-fitted denim trousers.

She sighed softly and watched with appreciation as he pumped the handle, then lowered his head under the refreshing waterfall.

"Jumping in the river saves time," she suggested lightly, teasing as she drew closer. She remembered with a smile as a flush of sexual awareness heated her skin, how long ago it seemed since she, Devin, and Caleb took that first wickedly sinful dip in the river. They hadn't been back since. Instead, since returning, Devin took the girls to the river almost every afternoon. That left the two of them little chance to talk, let alone do anything else. Today was no different. They spent the entire afternoon down by the river, which was why the girls were already sleeping like little blonde logs after their trip. She wouldn't hear a peep out of them till tomorrow.

Megan would give anything to sleep that soundly, as though not having a care in the world. She hadn't had a decent night's rest since he left. Even with Caleb visiting, she felt lost, alone and empty the entire time. A tremendous, cavernous need to be held by him, filled by Devin, and loved by him. She needed that most of all. She'd waited with bated breath until he returned. A return that wasn't quite what she anticipated.

The harsh squeak of the rusty iron mechanism as he pumped the handle up and down aggravated the lengthening silence as she stood there, watching the sinewy muscles in his arm and back flex and relax. Water spurted out of the spigot in a steady stream, drenching Devin's thick mass of auburn hair. She wanted to run her hands through the wet strands matted to his face and shoulders and keep running them along the hard length of his body until he finally gave her what she needed.

Straightening, he vigorously shook his head, releasing some of the excess water from his hair. Megan felt cool droplets of water sprinkle over her skin, already pulsing with the sexual need coursing through her nerves, sensitized by his presence. Her body trembled at the sight of him as the water ran down his hard-edged, masculine features, over his broad shoulders, and down his powerful arms and back. His cream-colored shirt clung to him. The soaked fabric molded the hard planes and ridges of his well-honed muscles, giving him a dangerously carnal appearance, taking her breath.

Strangely, it occurred to her he seemed to be doing his best to avoid looking directly at her. With long, sweeping strokes, he smoothed the wet clumps of hair from his forehead as he stared past her. "Caleb will take you to the river anytime you want." Stepping to the side, he completely circumvented her.

"Devin," she bit out, turning to stare at his back as he walked away. She was taken aback by the way the words came out. Mean. Vicious. Cold…final.

His demeanor seemed to stiffen, as did every muscle in his taut body. The distance between them continued to increase. A sense of panic that he was walking away for good suddenly washed over her. She cried out, "What is wrong with you?"

He stopped, but didn't turn to face her.

"We live under the same roof." Hesitantly, she took a few steps toward him. "You can't ignore me. Why won't you speak to me?"

He swung around, and she had to take a step back as the wild look in his eyes stole her breath away, sent a shiver of unease down her spine. "It's pretty damn easy when we don't share the same bed."

His voice, strangled with bitterness, came as quite a shock. It revealed a deep, intense anger and jealousy toward Caleb. The absurdity of the idea confused her. It didn't make sense. She stared up at him. His piercing silver eyes roamed over her heatedly. More frustration shadowed his darkened gaze than the sexual interest she longed for.

"You're the one who offered to bring a cot in the room." Her voice shook with mixed emotions. So soft, she could barely recognize it herself.

* * * *

"What the hell was—" Devin stopped mid-sentence, grimaced, annoyed by the interruption as he noticed Trevor walking nearby on his way inside the house. He pulled at what he could only assume were wedgies up his butt crack. It was nothing nice, suddenly restricting what nature intended to be set free. Known for letting the boys roll free, Devin felt Trevor's pain along with the brutal force of his own.

He noticed Megan did a double take. She stared curiously as Trevor tugged at his each pant leg after every step, shuffling his groin uncomfortably.

With the front door closed behind Trevor, Devin took up where he left off, lowering his voice, fighting to control the hellish existence he found himself in. "Megan, you wouldn't leave Caleb's side. What was I supposed to do? Let you crawl in bed with him? What would the girls think?"

"The girls!" Her eyes flared unbelievably large, her voice rising with frustration. "Since when are you so concerned with the girls? Were you thinking of them the night you tore off my clothes and made me suck your cock? How about when you fucked me on the table, or tied me up and shoved your fingers up my ass?"

"I don't gotta listen to this shit. You wanna fucking share his bed after being with me, you go right ahead." Turning in an intense blaze of anger and lust, he stormed off toward the barn with every intention of leaving for good. The sexual images struck him, tormented, gripped him with a fiery need coursing straight to his cock. In another second, he would be inside her so fast, she wouldn't have time to lift her legs. She was pushing him. And she damned well knew what happened when he was pushed too far.

"Damn you, Devin. Walk away. Leave. Run. Just when you start to feel something. When Shelby and Emma start believing in you."

The anger and desperation vibrated in her voice. But he couldn't stop. He couldn't. He would wind up destroying the only good thing in his life. It was tearing him apart.

"Abandon them. You're good at that. But don't expect me to be here when you return."

Her threat hit him hard, right where it hurt the most. He jerked around. With a few long, purposeful strides, he stood directly in front of her. He stared down at her. It took everything he had left not to grab her, kiss her hard, so she'd take back those vain words. "I don't expect a damn thing from you. You made your choice," he hissed fiercely and was more than a little impressed when she didn't even flinch.

"As I recall," she said firmly with a heaping load of conviction that caught his attention, "you made it for me. I wanted you. You're the one who didn't want me. You handed me over to Caleb. You wanted me to love him, not you. You did everything possible to make sure I did. And because I loved you so much, I let you. He almost died, Devin. What was I supposed to do? Turn my back on him?"

He stared at her, long and hard. How could he argue with the truth?

"Trevor didn't even know who Caleb was. All he knew was what he saw. In a matter of seconds, he made the decision to do everything to save him. Even he understood you don't turn your back on someone in need. Devin…I need you."

I need you too, Megan. More than you'll ever know.

"Go to him, Megan. Caleb needs you more." Nothing had changed. Everything had changed. The underlying reason he needed to leave, why he wanted her to marry Caleb was still there. The only difference was now, he was positively jealous, outraged, aching with misery clear to the marrow. Megan desired Caleb more. She actually wanted to marry him not because he asked, but because she wanted to be his wife. She'd wanted Caleb all along. He could barely stomach the thought.

She looked as though the wind had been knocked out of her. He wanted to reach out and hold her. Comfort her. Tell her…tell her… Tell her the only thing he could, that he was sorry for ever walking into her life.

"I'll only bring you and the girls more hardship and grief. Chewy, Rico, and the other scum aren't the only ones out there. Word will be out soon. There are plenty more bastards itchin' to see me face down. I should know. I'd do the same if I were them."

He turned, and she grabbed his arm. He looked down, where the heat of her small hand burned through the damp fabric, searing his skin. Closing his eyes, he absorbed as much of her warmth, her body, her soul into his flesh as the moment allowed.

"You're not like them, Devin."

His gaze locked with hers. There was so much assurance in her soft voice. He desperately wanted to believe her. "Right. I'm worse."

"No, you're not." She shook her head furiously, as though the harder she shook, the truer the sentiment.

"Tell that to my father. I wasn't even a day old, and already, he didn't want me. He knew."

"How can you say that? Didn't you read the letter? He loved you."

What did she know about love? Because of her, he'd started to feel something other than emptiness, a black hole where his heart should have been. She gave him hope, a reason to wake each morning, to dream of tomorrow, only to leave him longing for what could never be. He jerked his arm from under her grasp.

She pulled back, as if shocked by the coldness of the gesture.

"I thought you said you never read it."

"I...I ran across your papers while doing laundry," she muttered softly. "I saw the President's letter pardoning you. You never told me."

"It's a damn piece of paper. Doesn't matter." He knew what he'd done. How many lives were lost because of him. The faceless men out for revenge. As long as he stayed, Megan and girls would never be safe or secure in their own home.

"Freedom means everything. And what of the lives you saved? All those women and children over the years. Those monsters you rode with would have done horrible things to them if not for you. We wouldn't have lasted five minutes if the fear of your wrath hadn't held them off."

Her tone was emphatic, desperate as she tried to reason with him. It made no difference. He knew what he had to do. Just as he fought against the Laredo Gang, Hardin and his men, his path in life had been thrust upon him. He didn't have a choice. He never had a choice.

"I assume money doesn't matter, either. Is that why you haven't cashed the reward draft? Or did you recover the rifles for another reason?"

"I'm a simple man with simple needs."

"I know about your needs, and believe me, there is nothing simple about them."

Mockery, vindictiveness he could handle, but what she did was far worse. She reminded him, tempted, tortured the hell out of him with her suggestive, husky voice that threatened his last resemblance of control. Those hazel eyes gazing up at him like a love-sick puppy that didn't know when to stay put. She didn't know what she was doing to him. Pushing him too far. Tearing him apart.

"Your father wrote that he loved you. Grace died giving birth to you. But the proclamation of a dying man isn't enough for you. Is it?"

He figured it wasn't much of a question, considering she didn't pause for an answer, and since one wasn't forthcoming, it worked out nice. But she sure as hell was driving him insane, making him hotter and harder with the way she was staring at him. Eating away at him with her dark, sensual eyes, the heat, longing, promises of pleasure reaching into his soul. If she didn't quit soon, he was going to give her what she wanted. Right here, right now. Throw her to the ground and pound away his misery into the wet, hot, tight passage between her thighs. It wouldn't do either of them any good. He'd still leave afterwards.

"What he failed to mention was before your mother died, she made him promise your aunts would raise you."

"Why'd they put me on a train headed to hell?" he groaned between clenched teeth, his voice rough with the unsatisfied lust he knew they both felt.

"Damn you, Devin. You're as hard-headed as…"

He watched in disbelief as her eyes lowered to what must have been the hardest thing that came to her mind. Under her lingering gaze, her face flushed with arousal, his cock throbbed in needy response. He needed to push inside her, fuck her hard, ram into her tight heat until she begged, pleaded, screamed for her release. He heard her soft moan of desire, noticed a shudder wash over her. A dark, primal lust consumed him.

Gritting his teeth, he clenched his fist. The need to hit something, anything was a poor substitute to release his bridled lust and the sexual frustration coursing through his veins. If he didn't find relief soon, he would burst. His chest would literally explode, and his cock would melt inside out from the heat. There was no way in hell he was going to find solace in her hot little body. No matter how much she seemed to need it, want it. Damn her. Damn him for wanting it too.

Her breathing was harsh as her heavy-lidded haze rose to meet his, then nervously looked away. She started anew, her voice quivering in sexual need as she somehow managed to ignore the smirk on his face and the throbbing erection she'd admired moments earlier. "They were supposed to raise you until you were old enough to walk."

Shit. He figured if she could stare at the goods with her nose pressed against the winda and her tongue a hangin', then so could he. He found guilty pleasure gawking at her, seeing how that was all he was allowing himself. He liked how her clothes fit now, nice and snug, showing off her female curves. His gaze settled on her nipples, hard and pleasantly plump. The puckered areolas were distinguishable in the faint remnants of the evening light. Her breasts, firm and full, pushed hard against the tight bodice, straining the buttons down the front of the flimsy material until it looked like they were going to pop open. His mouth watered, his fingers ached, his cock protested, his body throbbed.

"Life was rough back then. Rougher than it is now. Grace didn't give up her life to have you die within your first year. Reed didn't give you away, you stubborn fool. He gave you a chance at life. Your aunts loved you so much, they didn't want to give you up either."

It wasn't working. He was getting too damn horny. With a heavy sigh, he stared past her into the darkness quickly descending upon the rolling field beyond the corral. He tried to think about Big Grizzly, the bear that carved out a chunk of his back. Pretty pink nipples flashed in front of him. Oh, fuck. That wasn't working either. Pretty pink lips, slick with arousal, parted before his eyes. He blinked, blew out a deep breath as he ran his hand roughly through his hair.

"Every year, they put Reed off. It wasn't until you nearly killed that boy they agreed to send you to your father."

He glared at her. How in the hell did she know his life story? "You seem to know a lot about my childhood."

"I should. You're all Reed talked about. After they kidnapped you, he left the ranch. Searched over a year for you. He'd still be searching if it weren't for that old man in a saloon, put a bullet in him. Nearly killed him."

"What old man?" he asked, relying on the heightened awareness of his intuition. He rubbed his pulsating temple as he started to pace back and forth. "Did he ever say what the man looked like?"

"Said he'd never forget his face as long as he lived. Kinda hard to believe, since Reed didn't look at him long. As soon as he walked into the saloon and asked the barkeep about you, he said the man at the end of the bar pulled his gun and shot him. No reason at all. He looked like one of those mountain men with long, white scraggly hair, a scar over his cheek, big and tall."

Devin stopped in his tracks. His heart slammed against his chest as he suddenly remembered that day. It was his third or fourth visit to the brothel upstairs, learning what it meant to be a man. He heard the shot and ran out of the room, yanking up his britches. Ol' John met him in the hallway and told him they needed to use the back exit. *"Trouble brewing,"* was all he offered by way of explanation.

"As soon as Reed recovered, he remarried. He knew one day you would return. When you did, he wanted you to have the family you deserved. A mother, brothers, and sisters. As the years passed, every time a new story rolled in, he paid them no mind. Knew if you found the right woman, you'd settle down. Reed never gave up on you."

His head tilted toward her first, then his body followed as his eyes narrowed on her. "What did you say?"

"Your father never gave up on you."

"No. Before that." He took a few frantic steps closer toward her.

For a brief moment, she recounted her words. Her head tilted sideways as though it just came to her. "About settling down?"

"Yes," he snapped impatiently, eager to hear her explanation. "What did he tell you?"

Shrugging her shoulders, she smiled warily. As if they both understood he considered his father's ideals on salvation less than ideal. "The only way for you to change your lawless ways was if you found the right woman. Said the love of a good woman could make any man hang up his guns."

Reed didn't mention that in the letter. He'd preached the same nonsense over eight years ago when he first passed through Tejas. It's what made him leave. The only way for her to know about it was directly from his father. Bullheaded. Devin refused listen, but it sounded as if she did.

"When did he tell you this?"

"About seven years ago."

"How old were you?"

"Sixteen."

Frowning, he contemplated the ramifications. Reed could not have possibly had Megan in mind. "Marrying age," he mumbled more to himself, but it seemed she heard.

"I suppose. Girls have been known to marry as young as fifteen." Her eyes widened as though she, too, suddenly inferred Reed sought her for him. "You don't suppose?" she asked on a breathless whisper.

Devin shrugged his shoulders, wanting to turn back time, to have a once-in-a-lifetime opportunity to ask his father. Oh. What he would do if it were possible. Nonchalantly, he drawled as if it didn't matter to him either way, "Was he married at the time?"

"No. It was months after Ella and their son passed way with the fever."

"If he wanted you for his wife, he could've done it then. Who knows why he waited to marry you?"

"Devin," she gasped. "Jazelle told me the only reason she took me in was to make money off me by entertaining guests."

Entertaining guests. Nice way of putting it. He stroked his chin to conceal the faint smile that tugged at his lips. A lot of whores had entertained him over the years. Never had he found as much pleasure as he did with Megan. But then, she wasn't a whore. She'd been hand-selected by Reed.

"When Reed found out the Walkers tossed me out of their home, and I was at Jazelle's, he secretly arranged to pay for my services until my eighteenth birthday."

"There you have it." He breathed a little easier, eager to bury the crazy notion his father planned on handing over his virginal wife to him. "My randy old man was only waiting till you were a little older. Didn't want to seem like a desperate lecher."

"No." She shook her head, scowling. "Jazelle was to let me walk away when I turned eighteen. Instead, he married me after what happened with Hardin. Reed explained after his first stroke he agreed to pay Jazelle ten additional years for my freedom. He only paid five before he passed. That's why my debt was so high. Why I had to go back."

Typically, he'd learned from experience, a good whore's career ended near the age of thirty. After that, used and often abused, the lucky ones would end up in seedy crib rows, and the not so lucky ones would end up either on the street or dead. Cheri was getting up in age, and for a moment, he pondered what would become of her. Strictly as a friend, he decided to check on her plans for the future. Oh, hell. He was going soft. He'd never given a rat's ass what happened to a fly on the wall, much less another human being.

With a deep exhalation, he rerouted his thoughts to Hardin. The slimy snake must have known of the arrangement. Once no longer employed by Jazelle, Hardin wouldn't have been able to have his way with Megan so easily. The thought left a bitter, bile taste in his mouth. He had half a mind to dig Hardin up and shoot the bastard again.

"You wanna believe he was some sort of saint. You go right on. I say my father just wanted you for himself."

"Why can't you believe Reed chose me for you? Why else would an honest, married man with a family take notice of a scrawny, scared girl in church one day? Hand over his hard-earned money so no other man would have me? Bring me into his home when he could no longer protect me from afar. Never once lay a hand on me. Ask you to look after me. You can't believe he didn't want me sexually. That he didn't love me that way, because you do. You're too afraid to admit it. Devin Spawn is finally afraid."

He felt as if the world turned upside down. If she touched him, he would literally fall over. Did he love her? He closed his eyes and hoped for a miracle. A bolt of lightning to strike him dead. The ground to split open and bury him alive.

"How does it feel, Devin? It hurts, doesn't it? To want something so bad that you think you don't deserve."

To know. Yes. Hurt? No. He felt no pain through the numbness as the life was sucked right out of him.

His gaze slowly ran over her. She was trembling, her chest rising harshly, a look of desperation etched in her expression as though they just fought a battle. In a way, he figured they did. She'd won.

"I told you before I left, and I'll tell you once more. I'm no rancher, nor do I wanna be. Go inside where you'll be safe. Lock your door and do us both a favor. Stay outta my sight." Turning on his heels, he headed past the barn into the bleakness. Away from Megan. Away from Deuce. Away from himself if he could.

* * * *

"Devin," Megan called sternly.

She thought they'd reached a precarious crossroad. She'd pushed him beyond his limits where he kept his emotions deeply hidden. She expected him to actually search his soul in the heat of the moment and profess what she desperately longed to hear.

Instead, he'd calmly walked away.

"Devin," she repeated moments later, raising her voice to a shrill, desperate cry when she realized he wasn't coming back.

"Devin," she said softly, tears welling in her eyes as the darkness swallowed him whole.

Chapter 30

"Humph," Devin grunted, rolling on his back in the too-small bed. It was late at night, bedsprings squeaking under his weight. Arms dangling over the side, he kicked off the blanket wrapped around his legs, hurled it to the floor with a jerk of his feet. He stretched out naked, the cross breeze filtering through the dual open windows chilled his heated skin.

He hated the loft. He hated the narrow, lumpy mattress. He hated sleeping alone. Hated most of all that no matter how hard he tried, he couldn't stay away.

It wasn't that he expected a thank you for saving their lives. At least she could have looked at him. Brushed a kiss on his cheek. Hell, even a handshake would have been better than pulling out of his arms when he tried to hold her, howling over Caleb. Throwing herself at him. How many tears did one woman possess?

Every waking moment since, Megan seldom left Caleb's side. She spoon-fed him, read to him, brushed his hair and slept in the same room. Hell, she probably held his dick when he took a piss. No telling what they did when she bathed him. The man was laid up with busted ribs, a bullet wound in his side, messed up knee, cuts, and bruises. There wasn't a damn thing wrong with his arms.

Earlier, Devin had walked for miles, waited hours till his hard-on subsided somewhat and sexual tension raking his nerves eased to a manageable degree. When he returned an hour ago, Megan headed straight to bed after he left. She'd been there ever since. The tidbit convinced him more than ever that Caleb held Megan's heart.

Reaching behind him, Devin fisted his pillow with a hard blow, then sunk his head in the indentation. He sighed heavily with frustration. Arms crossed over his chest, feet sticking out the other end, he squinted up at the ceiling. It was dark in the loft, and he could scarcely see Trevor on the other side of the room, let alone count nails in the rafters for a distraction.

If that don't beat all—two naked men in the dark, lying on their beds, and not a dang female between them. He welcomed the darkness. Not because he didn't have to stare at Trevor's naked ass. He seen it plenty of times in the past. Things like that tend to happen after a successful battle or hunt. The finest warriors could pick and choose their partners. Shared in their victory by sharing their women. Conquests, sexual or otherwise, made for one helluva celebration.

Here. Now. The darkness exalted what was going on downstairs.

If Megan didn't love him, if she wanted Caleb more than she wanted him, he figured it was his own damn fault. Like she said, he threw them together. He encouraged her to fuck Caleb good and deep until her juices flowed from her petite body, to suck his thick cock down her slender throat, let him lick her pert breasts and tug at the hard peaks with his teeth, squirt his seed over her beautiful face, plunge into the heated depths of her tight, heart-shaped ass.

Demented pervert that he was, seeing her thrash and scream in need beneath Caleb as he pounded into her intimate flesh again and again only intensified the dark edge of his lust. The flare of arousal in her eyes when Caleb lowered his head, extended his tongue between her wide-spread thighs and ran the tip into the soaked, pink folds of her cunt attested she loved every damned ecstatic, mind-blowing orgasmic minute.

His plan had worked.

It worked like a sweet, juicy peach.

Then why was he so damned pissed off?

His jaw tightened. His stomach tightened. His cock stiffened, jerked upright, emitting a long, wide shadow over his abdomen as the clouds drifted sporadically across the moonbeams.

With a heavy sigh, he realized no matter what he did, what he said, or how hard he tried, he couldn't stop wanting her. Sharing her wasn't the same as sharing other women. Not by a long shot. The others were simply a means to scratch an itch, and there were lots of awfully severe itching spells in the past. Afterwards, he put 'em out of his mind. He couldn't do that with her.

Megan was right. No matter how hard he fought the denial. She was right. How could he have let himself become so damned vulnerable? He muttered a curse under his breath.

When did it happen? He was Devin Spawn, called by many the Devil Incarnate, a blood-thirsty savage who preyed on the weak and stole from the rich.

At least, the myth fit up until three years ago.

Was it possible for someone like him to change?

Could the devil be worthy of love?

Love in return?

Reed, his mother, and aunts all loved him. Hell, even ol' John loved him in his own strange, perverse way, if putting a bullet through his father's gut was any indication. Were they the ones who were wrong, imagined something in him that wasn't there?

His mind filled with haunting regrets, apprehensive thoughts and images of rich pleasure that heated his blood, kept him horny, hot, and aching as sleep continued to evade him.

* * * *

Glancing sideways hours later, Devin observed Trevor's back as his sight adjusted to the faint starlight as the clouds continued to tease the night sky. He chose to ignore the rest of the young man's physique as he made sure his roommate was sound asleep.

Devin mused there were lots of similarities linking them. They were both strong of mind and body, fierce in battle, extremely sexually dominant and passionate about life in general. That's where the similarities started to get blurry. Trevor's passion ran a different course, lent more to a man bound and determined to live life to the fullest on his own terms. For the past nineteen years, Devin lived passionately, as well, harboring a ruthless ferocity. No rules. No regard. His body was already dead on the inside. He had nothing to lose but an empty shell on the outside.

Assured by slow, steady breathing Trevor was out till dawn, Devin sat up and swung his legs off the bed. He couldn't take the madness a moment longer. His mind wanted mental relief. His excruciatingly hard cock demanded physical release. There was only one way to satisfy both needs.

Strong enough to fight ten men at once, yet weak as a mouse when it came to Megan, he had to see her, to hold her, to tell her how he truly felt. He at least owed her that much, and if she warmed up to him, well...

He shrugged into his britches and cat-footed across the room. He dashed a momentary look to Trevor before climbing down the ladder. For Megan's sake, he hoped her baby brother could adjust to clean, decent home life. Because he sure as hell was having a spit load of difficulty.

It wasn't jealously, rivalry or anger welling deep inside him, eating away at him bit by bit. It was an all-consuming need to possess her. That was a strange phenomenon in itself, since he never cared a lick about anything or anyone other than Deuce.

From the moment he'd wrapped his arms around her and his lips touched hers, her warm, tender body pressed against his, he wanted nothing other than to take hold of her body, mind, and soul. All this time, he thought he dominated her, forced her to submit to his sexual demands. Driven by her love for him, she accepted the forbidden taboos thrust upon her. Assumption made it easier to share her sexually. The seduction, ultimate control of her pleasure, the power to govern her sexuality was exhilarating beyond anything he ever felt before. The dominance turned into an erotic craving he couldn't seem to get enough of.

Instead, Megan surrendered of her own accord to her own lust-filled whims. There was no force involved, no hesitancy, no reluctance. She simply yielded to the carnal nature she was born with. She willingly enjoyed the pleasures of the flesh and was probably partaking right now. He brushed aside the notion. It was her business. They were to be married. Husband and wife. Free to do whatever they pleased, and there wasn't a damn thing he could do.

Not even when ol' John dragged him off that train years ago did he beg for his freedom. He gritted his teeth and accepted his fate. But now, he was ready to beg, crawl on his knees. He'd write it out in blood if it came down to that. He'd ask Megan to love him the way he loved her, even if for one night.

Familiar with the layout and needing no aid of light, he maneuvered cautiously around the furniture. Frowning down at the doorknob, he took a deep breath and wrapped his fingers around the carved glass.

It turned, and he exhaled.

* * * *

Devin made a small crack in the door and peered into the dimly lit room. He noted the recognizable figure lying in the middle of the huge bed. Alone. Caleb hadn't moved an inch in the past two weeks. Roots were probably growing out of him. Devin grinned at the musing.

Slowly, he pushed the door open. It creaked, and he winced. In case things worked out tonight, he'd fix that for tomorrow, send the girls back to school and make definite changes to the sleeping arrangements. The agreeable thought made his pulse race.

Taking a step inside the room, a burst of allure ran through him. He felt young, like an impassioned lover desperate to steal a kiss. As if what he was about to do was somehow dangerous, forbidden, illicit. Sneaking into Megan's room in the dead of night, totally unheralded, while the rest of the household was tucked snugly in bed, deep in slumber, including Caleb a few feet away.

His gaze roamed to where Shelby's borrowed bed was situated underneath the open, lace-drawn window. His jaw dropped as he saw Megan, sitting up in the middle of the bed no bigger than the one upstairs, as if she expected him. She was dressed in a thin, homespun shift draped loosely off her shoulder. Long, silken ringlets cascaded over her shoulders and down her back, framing her delicate perfection in gilded gold.

"Megan," he whispered tenderly as their eyes locked. Big, hazel eyes, scorched with passionate longing, blazed sensuously in the soft, luminous glow of a nearby candle.

His heart filled with joy as she bolted out of bed, ran, and then jumped, thrusting her body against his. Wrapping his arms around her tiny waist, he caught her as she flung her arms and legs around him. She buried her face in the curve of his neck, her breath a warm caress against his skin. He sighed heavily, relief washing over him as he felt her melt in his embrace. She whispered softly, "Devin, you came."

"You didn't lock your door." Overcome with mixed emotions and sensations flooding his senses, he could barely get the words out as he inhaled her classic rose scent, fresh and sweet, uniquely hers. He held her tight, recalling every beautiful line of her soft, warm body now pressed exquisitely against his bare chest.

"It's been unlocked since the day you left," she breathed, planting soft, tender kisses along his jaw. He felt her trace the shape of his ear with the hot, moist, pointed tip of her tongue. She knew the sensation always sent shivers down his spine, made the fine hairs on the back of his neck stand on end. He felt his hard flesh thicken and harden even more.

"You're wet." He took a deep, shuddering breath as a flame of possessiveness surged inside him. The material of her shift had ridden up to her hips. Her weeping pussy pressed tightly against the throbbing bulge in his britches. Had she just made love, or was her body preparing for him? His cock throbbed in desperation. The answer no longer mattered. The need was too great. The desire was too strong. He was dying to thrust into the tempting heat of her hot, little body. He groaned in her ear as his teeth nipped at the lobe. "So fucking wet."

"For you," she breathed seductively, rubbing her mound against his stiffness, causing him to grunt as a surge of pleasure coursed through him. "Only for you."

His legs started to go weak. He felt the folds of her labia part as she ground tightly into him. His length lodged snugly between the wet heat of her cunt. Her juices penetrated his britches, coating his cock with liquid heat as she trailed a wet line with the tip of her hot tongue along his neck. The dual sensations were so hot, he felt his blood was on fire. She moaned breathlessly, "You're hard."

"Hard for you," he groaned roughly, bracing his back against the doorjamb. Anxious to fuck her, to ram deep inside her, explode in the velvet, moist depths of her hot, tight cunt. His hands moved past the fabric bunched at her waist. The heat of her flesh seared his skin as he touched the bare curve of her buttocks. Tightening his grip, he rocked forcefully against the slick entrance of her body, thrusting his cock into her clit, causing her to gasp as her body shook. He growled fiercely, "Only for you."

"Are you sure, Devin?" Her trembling voice was a vulnerable plea for confirmation as she clung to him, moved sinuously against him, letting him feel the soft feminine curves of her body. The hard peaks of her breasts branded a fiery path in his skin. "No one else makes you hard?"

"Oh, Megan," he moaned harshly. She closed her eyes as her tongue ravaged his ear between nibbles on his earlobe while he ran his fingers along the crease of her rounded cheeks, descending lower until they met the slick essence thick between her thighs. "You're the one I want. Only one I need."

He kissed her. Hard. Urgent. Her lips already open, welcomed the plunging thrust of his tongue. Greedily, she devoured him, moaning with wild, abandoned hunger. He let her have her way as he coated his fingers, then massaged it into the tiny pucker in her rear, repeating the move over and over again.

She gasped into his mouth. The tight muscles of her anus seemed to protest his invading finger as he scarcely nudged the puckered hole. Torture—the heat and grip of her passage refusing him entry was pure torture on his senses. Tight, too tight for what he wanted. Needed. The sensuous move of her hips against his, grinding against his cock, her supple body arched into his, begging to be taken, didn't help his control. All clarity was lost to him, aware of nothing except the overpowering desire, the voracious want and demanding need to possess.

"I've got to have you," he growled, breaking the kiss as she whimpered in protest. Kicking the door shut behind him, chest rising with each rasping breath, he lowered her to her feet. Jerked the shift over her head in a swift motion, he dragged a breathy gasp of surprise from her.

Tossing the garment aside, hungry for the sight of her, his gaze swept over the feminine contours of her body for a fevered, excited moment. He feasted on her porcelain skin flushed with arousal. Her rounded breasts were swollen, the rosy tips tight knots of longing. Her slender shoulders, the narrowness of her fragile ribcage to the delicate curve of her hipbones, reminded him how insubstantial in weight and form she truly was, yet vital to his very soul, every fiber in his being. The golden fuzz at the apex of her thighs was hardly enough to conceal the tender mound glistening with her desire, tempting his most feral palate, making him utterly ravenous.

His gaze met hers, and the profound intensity of love blazing back at him made his heart clench, flooded his senses with strong, powerful emotions that weakened him and stole his breath.

Damn. He missed her. Needed her. Loved her.

She shrieked like a giddy school girl as he swept her up in his arms and made a shift toward their bed.

"Devin...Caleb?" she reminded him quickly in a hushed whisper as if suspecting he forgot Caleb occupied their bed. Amazingly, he somehow manage to forget they weren't alone. For an instant, he recalled what she'd said, *Wet only for you...*

"If you're worried about waking me, don't bother. I'm wide awake." Caleb groaned, his voice tired, husky.

Devin's gaze darted toward the bed. He felt Megan tense in his arms at the sound of Caleb's voice as she cast a sidelong look toward him. Devin sensed he had been listening, watching them by the arousal deepening his tone and darkening his heavy lidded gaze. There was another indefinable emotion in the blue depths he didn't quite understand.

"At least she permits you to touch her," Caleb said.

Devin heard the longing and desperation in his voice and it confused him further.

"I was beginning to think she had secret aspirations entailing a nunnery," he continued. "She hadn't let me make love to her since you've been gone."

Bewildered by them both, Devin studied her curiously, gauging her slightest reaction. His heart thundered in his chest. "Is that true?"

The silence and tension dragged on for long, breathless seconds. He felt her stiffen slightly and shift uncomfortably.

She glanced up at him, then dropped her gaze timidly, her long lashes fluttered above the delicate bow of her flushed cheeks. "I was waiting till you returned," she admitted sweetly.

Strangely, he detected she was trying to answer in a way not to hurt Caleb's feelings.

Caleb groaned begrudgingly. "It sure as hell ain't been any better since you've been back. Gets pretty damn hard trying to sleep in the same room with that." He gestured toward Megan, naked in his arms. "Breathing her scent. Seeing her naked underneath that sleeping gown." His stared at the white garment strewn on the floor in their haste, then back to them. "Listening to every little sound when she moves in bed. Not being able to touch her. Hard as an iron bar and unable to do anything about it."

Devin chuckled hoarsely. He couldn't help himself. He knew exactly how Caleb felt. Things got just as hard upstairs in the loft.

"I fail to see the humor in the situation," Caleb growled. His voice vibrated roughly with unsated lust.

"Caleb, you're hurt," Megan chided gently, her eyes wide and innocent.

"Does this look like a man who's hurt?" He tossed the bed covers aside. The bottom half of his long underwear was cut low at the waist for easy access to the bandages wrapped tightly around his chest and the wound on the right side of lower abdomen. The remaining portion didn't serve any other purpose than to modestly conceal his groin. Right away, his erection burst free of the loose, red fabric and towered stiffly toward the ceiling.

Devin's brows rose in amused clarity. Here he thought they were going at it like two gophers in a hole the entire time he was gone. He thought Megan *wanted* to marry Caleb and wanted no part of him beyond their immoral pact, tied to him out of obligation.

The knowledge struck him hard and took his breath away. She loved *him*. She wanted *him*. A smiled tugged at his lips, and something tugged at his heart and stirred his lust to a prominent height. Without his permission, she wouldn't let Caleb or any other man make love to her.

Putting her down on her feet, Devin warned darkly, "Megan, you know what happens when you tell either of us no." His eyes never left hers as he started to unfasten the buttons on his fly.

Her eyes widened in shock and lowered to the buttons popping free. Her gaze grew hazy as he spread the cloth wide and his erection sprang free. "Devin," she gasped, breathing hard and fast, as her frantic gaze caught sight of the rising lust driving his dark needs higher. Fear and excitement glimmered in the darkening depths of her eyes. "You can't be serious."

"What do you say, Caleb?" Devin looked over the top of her head at Caleb. "Should Megan be punished?" He held his voice firm, a suggestive beat of arousal deepened the tone at the thought of punishing her, sharing her as he pushed out of his britches. "Should we make her wait for her climax the way she made you wait?"

Caleb stroked his erection with a sure touch, up and down slowly. The flared head throbbed, drawing Megan's gaze. Devin heard her breath catch and smiled. "Shit, I'm so hard now, I'm about ready to burst. Don't think I can wait."

"You don't know what you do to us," Devin told her softly. "To me." He couldn't control his desire any more than Caleb could. His hand ran down her back, cupped her firm bottom and wedged a finger between the taut cheeks, rasping her little pucker and causing her to gasp, her butt cheeks to clench as he encouraged her forward. "Caleb is waiting."

Despite the arousal flushing her skin, escalating her breathing, he felt her hesitancy. He recalled the heated words they exchanged earlier that day. She needed his assurance.

"Suck him, Megan. For me," he said with a gentle and coaxing tone. She glanced up at him, her eyes searching his. He could see the wariness slowly soften, darken, flare into carnal longing and anticipation at the thought of another man pleasuring her. "Take him in your mouth. I want to watch."

As if in a erotic haze, she didn't move. Then, it hit him. She wanted to be ordered, forced to surrender. Despite her feelings for Caleb, she wouldn't accept him on her own. She needed to be dominated as much as he needed submission. Extreme eroticism drove her, as well.

He felt the excess proof of her arousal seeping from her body as he jammed his fingers between her quivering thighs. He drew a ragged breath from her as pulled away just as quickly. She shuddered with sinful desires, dark and deep only he knew she craved. He demanded, "Do it, Megan. Now."

She winced slightly at the power in his voice. He was pleased that it finally made her more receptive, though for now, hesitant. She glanced over her shoulder at him, and he knew from her glazed expression her pussy was creaming with each step. Devin nodded and ordered abruptly, "Suck him good."

The rush of excitement flushed her face at the heated, sexual command and made his cock twitch excitedly.

"Make him spill in your pretty mouth."

At that order, she licked her lips seductively. Her gaze dropped to his cock as if to say she would think of him as she sucked Caleb. Turning with a wicked smile curling her lips, she climbed atop the high, four-post bed.

He shook his head at her audacity, watching her small, rounded ass sway delectably as she crawled on all fours to Caleb. "Swallow every drop."

Caleb spread his legs wide, the dark look in his eyes wicked, carnal. Her fingernails raked over his tightened scrotum as she tugged the long, red underwear down his hips and completely off his legs. She had him groaning in rising pleasure.

"That's my girl," Devin groaned roughly as her thin fingers curled halfway around Caleb, pale and dainty in contrast to the thick, heavily veined, pulsating flesh. Devin fought for control, his own nearly-bursting hardness throbbing, pulsating in agony. He stared at her pink tongue running along the length, dragging a groan from the other man's mouth as his hips lifted slightly.

"Don't move, Caleb," she ordered gently, her breathing coming in quick pants. Placing her palm on his hip as if to hold him down, she brushed a tender kiss on the tip of his cock, causing Caleb to groan even more. "You're still weak."

Devin remained riveted on her wet tongue as she lapped the throbbing cock in her grasp. His own body tense, hot, gripped with erotic desire. Damn, she looked beautiful, so fragile as she knelt over Caleb's muscular physique, with his long, thick shaft rigidly standing upright from his body. She shivered as she prepared to take him in her satiny mouth.

"Stick it in your hot, little mouth. All the way down to his fuckin' balls," Devin growled, tormented by the teasing, lapping sounds. He imagined the heated, glazed look of intent in her eyes as she swirled the flared head with the flat of her tongue just before her mouth sank down the long length all the way to Caleb's balls. Devin's blood soared, his chest tightened, and his cock twitched against his abdomen, reminding him painfully of his own agonizing, burning need.

"Oh, God. Meg," Caleb groaned harshly. His fingers clenched in her hair, giving her the sharp bite of pain they both knew she liked. From the tortured expression on his face, Devin knew Caleb was fighting to control the male instinct to thrust into her hot wetness, fuck her pretty mouth with everything he had. Caleb growled, "Suck it hard."

"You know what to do. Every drop." Devin ordered fiercely and shuddered. A hot flare of intense lust and dark hunger raced through him as her suckling and his groaning increased. Her suckling skills were the best, and he knew exactly what Caleb felt as the inside of her mouth clasped the head tightly, and the tip of her tongue swirled the sensitive underside. Moving behind her, Devin took his cock in a tight-fisted grip.

"Let me see your pussy," Devin growled, and without waiting, he jerked her thighs apart as he sat on the end of bed.

She moaned and her legs trembled as he spread her labia lips wide with his fingers and stared at her swollen clit, the lips dripping with her juices.

His eyes narrowed on the tiny, pink, untouched hole. "Oh, yeah," he breathed heatedly, the erotic, telling vision nearly devastating what remained of his control. "Nice and pink."

His cock jerked in expectancy, and his mouth watered at the thought of what was to come.

Lowering his head within inches of her soaked flesh, Devin inhaled deeply. He filled his lungs with the scent of her arousal, then blew out gradually and watched the reaction. Her body shuddered, thighs trembled, pussy throbbed against his fingers as she moaned over Caleb's erection, causing him to grunt and his body vibrate against the bed.

"Oh, baby. Fragrance of paradise. Now let me taste you," Devin whispered, his own breathing coming rough, impatient as he felt. With one long sweep of his tongue, he stroked her clit and drove deep into the narrow opening, licking her sweet honey into his mouth as she whimpered in pleasure at his intimate kiss.

* * * *

Megan cried out and bucked against his mouth as his devilish tongue speared her rear hole. Devin held onto her hips, wrapping one arm underneath her, clasping a breast as his fingers pinched one, then the other hard peak forcibly, elongating the nipples. Adding an extra sharp bite of pain and fire to the waves of sensations washing over her. His other hand held her open, and he fucked her cunt with his tongue, dipping, licking, and drinking from her heated core like a starving man.

She pushed back against his mouth. Whimpering eagerly over the pulsing flesh on her tongue, desperate to taste him, give him a glimpse of what she felt. Tightening her grip, she moved her hand up and down the length with long, hard strokes as her mouth increased the suction on the head, and her other hand squeezed his balls.

Caleb's cock throbbed in her mouth. She tried to keep their eyes locked, knowing he was nearly ready to fill her mouth with his male heat. The raging desire to satisfy, taste the moist flesh in her mouth made her suckle harder. Her stomach tightened, and her empty vagina clenched around Devin's tongue in desperation as the exquisite pleasure, stroked the need deep in her womb, pushing her closer to the edge.

Lips, tongues, and mouths suckling and licking mixed with moans and groans, filling the darkened room with sounds and smells of heated sex, amplified as Caleb groaned harshly, "I'm coming." He held her head over his exploding cock, spurting a hot stream of semen down her throat as she struggled to keep the suction firm.

The hand on her bottom moved, and a large finger pushed inside her as Devin's suckling mouth latched hungrily onto her clit. Hot, intense flames pierced her tender flesh, exploded from the sensitive knot of nerves throughout her veins in shameful ecstasy. Caleb's spurting cock plopped out of her mouth as she arched back, the blazing sensation ripping though her with explosive, agonizing force as she cried out in erotic bliss. His hand moved from her breast to her waist, holding her weakened, shattering body above Caleb.

Her entire body shuddered. Her fingers tightened around his jerking erection, dragging a guttural cry of pleasure or pain from Caleb—she didn't care, as his heated seed spilled over her hand and his stomach. Her release flowed from her body, preparing her for the invasion to come as she cried out Devin's name. The white-hot, liquid essence she'd tasted moments earlier, that Devin ordered her to swallow, trickled from her lips.

Moaning helplessly with her back leaning against Devin's, she savored the last remnants of her climax tingling through her body. Devin continued to move inside her, long and easy strokes caressing the tender, convulsing muscles with his finger. Her hips slowly rocked into his hand.

"Damn, Megan. You're pussy is hot and dripping wet." His voice was rough, low as he brushed her hair with his cheek. The dark, underlying tone of unsatisfied lust made her vagina spasm with yearning at the thought of him taking her. He lowered her back between Caleb's thighs.

"No one's fucked either hole." Devin sounded awed, amazed that she saved herself for him. His thumbs held her inner lips open, and his fingers spread her cheeks apart. She knew he could tell both entrances hadn't been loosened or touched by anything larger than his finger. That she would be as tight as the day they first met.

"No," she whispered faintly. Staring into Caleb's disappointed face, the pain and passion in his eyes tore at her heart. In giving herself over to Devin's pleasure, she denied Caleb his. Laying his diminished erection in her palm, she began to make up deserting him by licking every spilled drop of sweet essence off his flesh.

"That's changing tonight."

Her eyes snapped to Caleb's at Devin's heated promise. She saw the need in his heavy-lidded gaze. No inhibitions. No jealousy. Only acceptance. Desire. Lust, hot and pure. She couldn't stop the breathless sigh slipping between her lips or the temptation pulsing through her body.

Releasing his hold, Devin began a thrusting motion with a single finger into her vagina, short little jabs. She cried out when he added another finger, which made a sloshing noise as he drove into her juicy vagina. She felt him spread her inner muscles apart, as if testing her readiness. "Your pussy is ready to be fucked. You wanna be fucked, Megan?"

Her body shuddered at the carnal image of either cock taking her, satisfying the tormented need burning deep, deep inside her. She nodded, moaning as her tongue lapped at the tender skin on the tip of Caleb's cock, which began to elongate and stiffen in her grasp. While her hips moved in rhythm to Devin's probing fingers.

"You didn't use a dildo?" He withdrew from her pussy. Her muscles gripped at his slick fingers as she whimpered her disapproval, her body in agony. She moved her hips backward, trying to follow his hand, begging for him to return to the unfilled flesh between her thighs.

"No," she breathed, near tears. She thrust her ass against him as his hands spread her cheeks apart. Lowering her chest, she rubbed Caleb's stiff erection, wet with her saliva over her breasts, pressing the tiny slit on the head against her nipples.

Caleb's lips curled into a wickedly sinful grin as he reached out and cupped her breasts. He gritted his teeth, rolled his fingers over the hard tips, twisting and pulling until she cried out at the edge of pain that fired her pleasure.

"Tight, baby," Devin groaned, roughly prying the anal opening with his finger, well-lubed from her juices. She shifted her buttocks against the shallow intrusion. She was so hot and so horny, dying with intense need.

Her inner muscles gripped him, drew him in. "You're so tight. Too damned tight. Like the first time I stretched your ass."

"Hurry, Devin," she panted breathlessly, alarmed by the wariness in his tone, that he would even suggest, hint at denying her.

"Your ass isn't ready. Not for what I wanna do," he growled. His voice was tight, strained as she felt him slowly work his way inside the narrow channel. "But I need you. I need this."

Her heart beat fast. Her body quivered. She was dying to be filled. She pushed her hips against his hand, sliding down further on his imbedded finger, crying out at the excruciating pleasure stretching her rectum. The wild, hungry need drove her mad with lust.

"Easy, Megan," he hissed fiercely. "I'm about ready to burst as it is. Don't make it harder. Can you wait till I prepare...?"

"Devin," she begged, leveraging her hands in the mattress next to Caleb's hips as she thrust back against Devin, burying his finger deep inside. Her body trembled, her breath came in harsh pants as she forced her anal muscles to open and accept him. She needed to be stretched, filled, fucked, burned alive with ecstasy, not coddled.

"You liked it when my big cock fucked your tiny ass, and Caleb fucked your sweet pussy." He sounded surprised, amazed by her tremulous need to be taken anally, unprepared and so incredibly tight that a single finger barely fit. The protesting muscles stretched, tantalizing, seemed to tempt him to give in to his desire.

"Oh, yes." Her voice trembled with her depraved lust. The incredible desire for the wanton taboo made her want to scream as the fire raged through her blood. Knowing Devin wanted, needed, craved the same only fueled the turbulent flame.

"Say it, Megan. Tell us how much you want it. How much you want two men fucking you."

He wanted to ravage her, plow into her depths with thrusts that matched the out of control fire raging through her body.

"Yes...yes," she panted, thrusting back on Devin's finger and fighting to keep her eyes open and locked on Caleb's. "Fuck me, please. Put your cock in my pussy."

Glancing over her shoulder at Devin, she felt the hot, desperate need stroking her like never before, heating her voice. She ordered him, "Stick your dick in my ass, stretch me. Fuck me hard. Tear me apart."

Closing her eyes to the overpowering arousal pulsing through her body, her head fell back, and her breasts arched upward. "Do it now. Fuck me," she demanded, her weeping pussy aching and her anal muscles pulsing.

"Come here, Meg. I'll give you what you want," Caleb held out his arms as Devin withdrew his finger and moved quickly to the chest where he kept their sexual aids. The raw sensuality in Caleb's expression, the strain to control his need shuddering through his battered body, aroused and weakened her. "I'll fill that pretty pussy of yours."

Shaking, she straddled his hips.

"That's it, Meg. Take it." His hands gripped her hips, guiding her down his erection. Moaning and shaking as she lowered over him. She felt his cock easing deep inside her, stretching her drenched flesh, slick with arousal. "Ease all the way down. Look at it go in."

Leaning over his chest, her gaze lowered to her drenched pussy. Her excess juices leaking over the cock buried between her stretched cunt lips. She watched as the hard, thick flesh, red and thickly veined, disappeared inside her, stretching her, tunneling into her pussy inch by inch as she slowly sank down, shuddering as her body gripped him, clenched around him, his heat searing her in exquisite agony.

The mattress sank under Devin's weight as he moved behind her, taking hold of her hips. Caleb cupped her breasts. Devin's cock, well lubricated with the oil kept in the chest, stood straight out from his groin and throbbed with anticipation. She felt his hot stiffness brush against her back, scorching her sweat-beaded skin. The heaviness, sheer size of it sent a shocking, startling stir of untold lust surging through her system, resounding in her sensitive flesh eager to accept him once again.

"It's gonna hurt." Devin's breath was hard and rough, steamy on her back as he urged her forward. She sighed when he lifted her off the impalement by the hips until only the flared head of Caleb's cock was lodged inside her body. Taking deep breaths, she braced her hands against the headboard to keep herself from hurting Caleb's chest. "You sure you want my cock, Megan?"

"I want both of your big cocks fucking me at same time." Overcome by carnal greed, depraved need flowed beneath her skin and flared through her heated blood. She was beyond stopping, her control non-existent. Already aching, wet, and ready for what was coming, she'd not be denied. Not tonight. Not ever again. "Devin, give it to me."

Devin sighed heavily. Clearly frustrated, unsure of the consequences as she felt the engorged head of his cock throb at the entrance, as if judging the fit.

"Don't hold back," she begged frantically. She trembled as she felt him start to nudge, stretch the tight muscles apart. It made her muscles clench on the tip, barely spearing her pussy. She arched her back, felt like a wild, untamed lion as Caleb moaned, squeezed and pulled the hard peaks of her breasts, sending her to a whole other level of raging carnality. "I can't take slow. Easy. Not now."

"You got it, baby," Devin growled, his grip tightening. "Hold on. Relax." He didn't give her but a breathless moment for second thoughts before he rammed into her channel with one deep, powerful thrust as he pushed her hips down, burying Caleb's cock deep inside her body.

She cried out as the intense pleasure and fiery bite of pain tormenting her flesh, shattered her senses, tore through her shaking body. Caleb groaned. Amid her fluttering lashes, she saw his grimace besieged with lust and knew both passages were overfilled, possessed, gripped their bulging cocks to near painful, intolerable levels.

Devin was motionless, breathing fast and furious. She meant to protest, but instead, opened her mouth and gasped for air. She fought to accustom herself to the heat, thickness completely filling her, stretching her painfully, deliriously wide.

"Megan," Devin groaned harshly, pained. She could tell he was worried, afraid he hurt her by the cries of fierce pleasure tearing from her throat.

Filled with ecstasy, her body speared in two by torturous pleasure, burned alive with lust she answered him the only way she could. She tightly clamped her inner muscles and reared back.

"Fuck, Megan," Devin growled fiercely, taking hold on her hips. He lifted her off Caleb as he withdrew, leaving both heads of their cocks buried inside her, then repeated the move, filling her body to capacity once more as he thrust and pushed hard and deep.

She exploded instantly, And cried out as the shattering release of extreme pleasure spilled between their bodies, drenching them, easing their assault. Her body tightened in ecstasy, her pussy and anus muscles clenching, milking the piercing, driving flesh burning inside her.

Devin didn't hold back. He moved her hips in rhythm as he began to fuck her with hard, deep, powerful strokes. He timed their moves perfectly, understanding their thick erections were too large to fit concurrently inside her smaller, ill-prepared body. Pulling out of her as he impaled her cunt on Caleb's cock to the hilt, had him groaning hard and hips bucking. Then he lifted her weightless body as he buried himself in her ass with brutal strokes, searing her with a fine edge of pleasure and pain that sent her flying higher into carnal bliss.

Before the first orgasm ended, the incredible pleasure gathered deep in her womb once more. Her hair whipped around her face and down her back as her desperate cries of bliss zipped around the room, carried out into the dark of night as the sudden, fierce explosion blazed through her womb.

She felt her vaginal muscles grip, clench the hard, thick flesh invading her suctioning pussy, her anal muscles stretch intolerably wide with each deep, fiery stroke, driving her insane, delirious with eroticism as lust raged through her veins, built up the next orgasmic eruption.

Losing her grip on the headboard, her hands slid to the mattress. Her body brushed Caleb's as she rose on her forearms. He moaned in pleasure or pain, but she was too weak, dazed from desire to question. His strong, powerful arms wrapped around her, drew her close. The scent of his arousal the heat of his body enveloped her, a potent aphrodisiac to her senses.

He moved sensuously beneath her, thrusting his hips, adding to her pleasure. Her overly sensitive clit rubbed against him, triggering her pussy to ignite, streaks of erotic, fiery lightning spearing through her lust-ravaged body.

Gasping for air, she cried tears of joy as Devin drove into her with long, steady strokes that flamed her ass with sweet, fiery pain tinged with desire. Each erotic plunge of the rigid cock below burned the throbbing depths of her pussy as her shuddering body rocked sinuously above Caleb's sweat-drenched frame.

Her body trembled with mind-numbing sensations, front to back, top to bottom. They drove deeper, plunged harder, grew thicker inside her soaked, gripping depths. She could only cry out as each climax washed over her, hotter and brighter than the next.

"That's it, baby. Come for us. Give us your cream," Devin growled. He plowed into her ass harder and deeper with his slick cock as her juices gushed between them.

"Devin, I can't hold back," Caleb panted beneath her.

Forcing her heavy eyelids open, she looked down into his face, twisted in tormented pain and extreme lust with each of Devin's thrusts. In her needy, sexual haze, she realized Devin had orchestrated their erotic pleasure, the raging fire, the dark arousal pulsing through their bodies.

"Brace yourself, Megan," Devin warned, his voice strangled, tight with red-hot, primal lust as he tightened his grip.

Hands fisted into the mattress, she clenched her inner muscles as he began slamming his thick, beefy well-lubed cock in her anus like a mad man.

Harsh male growls of satisfaction and feminine cries of pleasure echoed between them as skin pounded against sweat-drenched skin, plunging into wet, suctioning flesh. The heady scent of sex and lust swirled in the ever-increasing warmth in the thickened air.

* * * *

"Ahhh," Trevor groaned into his pillow, shuddering as his cock spurted hot, sticky sperm over his hand. He remained on his side as his body settled down from the self-inflicted eruption.

There were a lot of willing, young girls eager to pleasure the most esteemed warrior back at camp. It was an honor to lay with one of his stature. Thus, it had been a long time since he stroked himself. But the need had been too great, and he couldn't wait to travel the long distance to camp just for a quick fuck.

He couldn't sleep, though he was able to remain motionless for long stretches at a time, a vital skill when hunting buffalo or enemy. Trevor had lain in bed and tried to ignore Devin as he tossed and turned all night.

With a keen sense of hearing, Trevor heard Devin creep downstairs like a dark shadow. To anyone else, Devin would have gone undetected, but

Trevor's skills were far superior. He heard the door to his sister's bedroom open, and he overheard their impassioned greeting.

That in itself made him hot and horny. It made him want to take a peek downstairs and watch the action. But it was his sister. Even though they were getting to know each other, he wasn't about to witness *every intimate* detail of her life.

He overheard muted voices coming from downstairs, screeching bedsprings, headboard thumping against the wall, the hard moans, deep groans, and lust-filled cries gliding up from the open window below left him aroused and aching. They fired his blood until his own sexual need made him take his hard-on in hand and imagine the warm, ripe, inviting female bodies back home.

He assumed Devin wanted his sister, that their relationship was more than he let on. What he did not know until now was that Devin shared his sister. Evidently, he upheld quite a few Comanche customs.

The devil.

Explicit echoing female cries of release, growls of male gratification brought on by what he deemed intense pleasure derived from mating started again, traveled upstairs. They made his cock twitch, stiffen once more.

He could tell this was going to be a long, frustrating, and restless night. At least, for him.

He rolled onto his back, and his fingers circled his solid erection as a grin tilted his lips.

Perhaps tomorrow, he'd remind Devin not to howl so loud or bang his sister like a well-worn drum. That, or else build thicker walls. He wasn't going to be satisfied with listening to the three of them moaning and groaning every night unless he had his own woman.

If all white women were filled with same fire Devin seemed to share with his sister, perhaps living in a square house wouldn't be so bad after all.

Now if only he could go without britches, life would be perfect.

* * * *

Devin couldn't resist the delectable sight. Megan sprawled in carnal temptation, lying beside Caleb with his arm curled under her shoulder. Her lids closed, and her small breasts heaved with each strangled breath. The intimate flesh between her splayed thighs was swollen and glistening, drenched with proof of their passion.

Taking a seat beside her, he ran his fingers through the thick essence weeping from the crease of her swollen mound. Her pink cunt pulsed in response. He smiled as his cock jerked happily against his thigh.

Breathing harshly, he could feel his heart pounding away in his chest as he slid a finger past the tender folds into the little entrance coated with a big sticky mess. He watched her flesh open, grip him, suck him in.

She sighed softly and wiggled her hips as he buried his finger halfway into the silky, hot confines of her pussy and started a slow and easy thrusting motion.

Damn, he couldn't resist her. As if they hadn't fucked just moments ago, he was still hard, horny and hot as get outta hell.

"Megan, the choice is yours. How do you want it?" His voice came out low and husky, yet the raw desire as to what his needs were sounded pretty damn clear to him. He hoped Megan had the strength to go another round, because his lust tended to back up after long draughts, fortify his stamina and two months going without her was just too fucking long.

Her eyelids fluttered open. Smoldering hazel eyes stared at him adoringly. He felt like the luckiest man alive.

"Make love to me, Devin," she whispered softly.

Shock sucker-punched him in the gut. Hard. It stole the air from his lungs. His hand stilled, and his jaw dropped. For a moment, all he could do was gape at her, the warm, soft glow in her eyes, raw, explicit love was an emotion he couldn't convey.

A strange, intense fear gripped him. He pulled away quickly, rising to his feet.

Silence plummeted in air thickened with the heated scent of their arousal.

His chest clenched as he watched the shift in her gaze. Hurt and disappointment shadowed her expression, tore at his soul. He didn't mean to cause her pain or misery. He loved her too desperately and wholly. He wanted to spend every waking moment and sleeping minute by her side. But wanting and getting were entirely different.

What she asked for was more than he could give, and it terrified the hell out of him. The thought of losing her was more than he could bear.

Deuce had been the only love in his life for as long as he could remember. Caring for his prized horse was straightforward. Bathed and brushed him, fitted new horseshoes regular, took him for long, grazing walks in the sun, led him to clear watering holes, and picked blood-sucking ticks off him with his fingers.

Megan required more than fresh grass and plucking bugs out of her hair. It wasn't about positions anymore, and they both damn well knew it. He was a tired, disgraceful, good–for-nothing outlaw named after the devil, and all that that implied. Could he provide everything she needed? Deserved? Had a woman's right to expect?

Out of love, she had given of herself willingly. Bastard that he was he'd taken all she offered. That and more, much more than he ought to have.

Swallowing the lump in his throat, he tried to tamp down the knot of nerves in his stomach and failed. He looked over at Caleb for reprieve. Assistance. Anything.

Caleb had heard her request and was already staring at him in wide-eyed wonder. He was exhausted and sweat-drenched, nearly ready to pass out. But his expression was profound. There in the darkened, blue depths was an unspoken understanding, '*Be good to her or else*'.

Caleb sighed deeply, then looked down at Megan and managed a weak smile. "Don't mind me. Ya'll 'bout wore me out. Loosened my stitches."

"Caleb," Megan gasped worriedly, pushing up on her elbows as she searched for traces of blood on his bandages. There were none. "Are you all right?" she asked anxiously, sitting up cross-legged, smoothing a hand tenderly over the small portion of his belly that wasn't bandaged.

"After that fucking, I'm tired, that's all." His head rolled to the side, deep in the fluffed pillow. He glanced at her just above the white cotton rise, a sleepy grin across his too-handsome face. "A fellow needs some sleep. I'll be ready for a go tomorrow."

That wasn't what Devin wanted to hear. He didn't miss the well-chosen word. They fucked, and Caleb knew it, accepting Megan's choice. He watched in tense silence as Caleb's eyes closed, and his breathing deepened. The man was asleep in seconds. *Damn*.

Her eyes shifted to him. She waited silently. Looked as though she were holding her breath.

He frowned—couldn't help it. Felt more nervous than he ever imagined possible, and there wasn't a gun, knife or crazed lunatic in the room. Expect maybe for him.

"Megan...I...you know..." He gulped down the lump in his throat. It didn't seem like it was going away. In fact, it seemed to grow larger. Didn't help matters none with the way she was sitting, pink tissue winking at him between her thighs. Maybe if they put some clothes on.

"You know my ways. Rougher, the better. I ain't no gentle partner. Ain't nothing tender 'bout me." He eased back toward the end of the bed, glancing casually around the dark room, wandering where his trousers were.

She rose.

He froze, tilted his head and stared. She floated across the bed, the gentle starlight whispered from outside, softly caressing her glistening, translucent skin. A vision of loveliness.

By the time she stopped in front of him, hot and furious lust raged through his bloodstream. He forgot about his trousers and started to focus on the rigid flesh thumping hard against his abdomen, in cadence with his heart.

Drawing his arms instinctively around her waist, he pulled her close. Heard her startled gasp, felt her body tremble as he smoothed his hands over her rear. The heat, feel of her satin skin sinking into his enticed him, tempted his devilish soul. He closed his eyes and breathed her in, wanting the moment to last forever.

She pressed her petite body against the formidable strength of his, and it nearly crushed his power of control. He was lost, weak as a newborn babe. He shut his eyes tighter and groaned harshly when he felt her small, pert breasts jutted beneath his chin. "Oh, Megan," he breathed, fighting the urge to latch his hungry mouth onto a hot, taut nipple branding his bare flesh. "What are you doing to me?"

Her fingers curled in his hair and pulled his head back. She forced his undivided attention upward as she stared down at him. The look in her eyes played on his chaotic emotions. Dark, sizzling hot arousal had his flesh throbbing, aching for tight, wet heat. Then there was the unbridled love, deep and searing. All his if he dared. If he was brave enough, wanted it bad enough, was willing to sacrifice his soul for it.

"Devin," she whispered, her voice like silk. "Follow your heart. Do what comes naturally."

Shutting his eyes, he moaned like a wounded man left out in the sweltering heat of the desert sun to die. He was so achingly hard, he was dying. His fingers dug into the firm globes of her rear, grinding her mound over the tip of his cock buried snugly between their bodies. It wouldn't take much of a shift to impale her sweet, juicy cunt on the bulging erection nudging at the dripping slit of her heated channel, or toss her on her back, throw her legs over his shoulders, and power home, hard and deep until she screamed, begged for her pleasure.

That's what he wanted it, which in no way resembled what she needed.

He wanted to be the one to bestow everything she desired. More than she ever imagined. What he felt for her went beyond lust, beyond what he couldn't put into words.

Taking a deep breath, he opened his eyes slowly and met the adoration, the hope and stark plea in her gaze. With no desire to be the one to shatter those hopes and dreams, he groaned helplessly, "You know what comes naturally."

"I've shown you before." Her voice was a breathless whisper, sizzling against his heated skin as her warm, moist lips planted soft kisses on his hair, forehead, and over his eyelids. He was going to die where he stood, there was no doubt about it. "How tender, satisfying it could be when two people love each other. Love me the way I love you."

* * * *

"Do you, Megan? Do you love me?" His voice sounded anxious, desperate as though he were begging, demanding her to say yes.

Megan was taken aback, moved to near tears. After so many times, he finally heard, realized the underlying meaning. More spellbinding was that she knew, could tell for the first time he truly felt deep feelings, too.

His body was tense, chest muscles hot and taut against her skin. He was fighting to control the desire coursing through his body for her sake. She looked breathlessly into his darkened eyes, the wild, feral lust glittering in the silver depths that they both craved, thrived on, took their pleasure in.

The thought of all that pent-up emotion, raging lust sent shivers rippling under her skin.

She ignored the thick erection lodged between her thighs, the slick release preparing her body, her quivering pussy eager to be impaled, filled, possessed by him. Always for him. It would be easy to give in to the potent, dark sexuality, the excesses that were so much a part of him. Right now, she needed something else, more. She wanted to pull from him what he kept deeply buried. Yet, she knew it was there, hidden, nearly forgotten below the rough, hardened surface, waiting to be set free.

Megan needed his love.

Light as a feather, she touched his warm, velvet soft lips with the pad of her finger and watched his eyes follow her as she brought it to her lips, then faintly whispered, "From the moment your lips touched mine."

Pure, heartfelt love glazed his eyes, reflected in his expression, and she fought to breathe. He carried her away from the bed, and her heart shattered with happiness into a million little pieces.

Deftly, with little maneuvering, he yanked the thin mattress from the small bed and tossed it on the floor. Gently, oh-so tenderly, he laid her on top. He was stretched alongside her, more of his massively large body on the puncheon floor than the mat. He pulled her into the secure warmth and strength of his powerful embrace.

Snuggling her head under his chin, she wanted him closer. She was dying for his touch, just to be near him as her eyes welled with tears.

"Megan, I...I..." Somehow, his words became lost in the maelstrom of emotions shadowing in his expression. He drew in a long, deep shuddering breath and seemed to abdicate every feeling into action.

He lightly caressed her cheek with his palm. She gazed up at him as a single tear fell from her eyes. Instinctively, her lips parted as his lowered and covered hers with a deep, passionate, sincere kiss that heated her body, embraced her heart and captured her soul.

Megan softened against him. Silent tears rolled down her cheeks as Devin whispered sweet endearments, caressed her skin with a silky, gentle knowing touch, giving her everything she ever dared dream, all she desired and much more at a slow, gentle pace.

"Don't cry," he whispered softly, brushing her tears away with a loving touch. Breathing escalating, she closed her eyes as he moved between her thighs. She felt the heat of his body hovering just above the edge of hers. He was tense, and she could feel his body shaking with restraint as he held his erection wedged at the entrance to her body.

"Open your eyes, Megan," he murmured tenderly. When she did, he slowly entered.

She whimpered openly and her body quivered as she felt him sink into the soaked depths of her passage one inch at a time.

"Do you feel it, Megan?"

"Yes," she moaned, trembling at the blatant emotions burning in his gaze as they joined as one. Without question, she felt what he wanted her to feel. Love.

Buried completely inside, he squeezed her legs together, his thighs outside hers. The position made her vagina feel longer, more snug as her muscles gripped his cock tighter than ever. He rocked against her smoothly, the long, slow strokes of his thick shaft stimulating her clitoris with each glide up and down.

He may not have been able to verbalize it, but she felt it with every deep, slow, gentle thrust, saw it blazing in his eyes. It was in his soft caresses, his tender kisses as he moved against her clit with a slow, steady pressure, building the exquisite sensation deep in her womb as his body continued to adore hers.

She cried out, professing her love as she toppled from an unknown height of pure ecstasy. All else before was but a faint shadow when the strong force of her climax broke over her.

"Megan, I could stay inside you forever," he growled, and she couldn't breathe. Her body was on fire, every nerve ignited, every inch of flesh tingled as the incredible flames of love and desire washed over her again and again. She luxuriated in his heated promise, "Tell me when. I'll never choose to leave you."

"Yes," she panted desperately, closing her eyes. She hungered for more, dwelling in the breathless sensations sailing her away on a blaze of wondrous bliss once more. Her muscles clenched, gripped him sensuously, her deep, intense release unraveled from her body. "Yes."

"That's my girl. Enjoy it, sweetheart. Give yourself to me." She heard him groan as her inflamed body hummed with pleasure, sensitized to his scent, his every touch, every little move. Dear, Lord. She never wanted such heavenly, searing ecstasy to end.

"Let me give you everything you need." His mouth devoured hers. His hands were all over her body, worshiping her. His lips dancing streaks of carnal bliss across her skin. His cock made sweet, delicious, maddening love to her, bringing her one magnificent orgasm after the next until finally her fledging system was overwhelmed with emotions.

"Devin," she whispered on a strangled gasp, dragging her mouth from his. She was so close to the edge of insanity, she thought she would die from glorious pleasure. Trembling beneath him, she lay spent, drenched with perspiration, soaked between her thighs as he maintained his harmonious rhythm in pursuit of her happiness.

"Once more, Megan. Please. Come with me." His voice was deep and rough, strained from containing the raging lust that darkened his gaze, tightened his body.

The knowledge made her heart race, fill, overflow with love. Made her want to weep for him and for herself. She cried out, "Devin, I love you."

Two deep, hard thrusts, and his body joined hers in a sea of carnal ecstasy. Her cry of blissful pleasure swirled between them as she felt hot, thick spurts of his seed fill her pulsing flesh. Shuddering, he fell over her body, his weight braced on his elbows, calling her name.

Minutes later, as the erotic daze gradually faded, he straightened his arms, hands braced on either side of her head. In the dimly lit room, their eyes met, reflecting what they both felt. The significance of their coupling bonded them together, forever and filled an emptiness neither realized existed until they'd met one another.

He planted a soft kiss on her forehead and rolled onto his side, separating their intimate bond. She moaned at the bittersweet loss.

"Why didn't you let Caleb fu…make love to you?" he asked her softly, brushing the dampened locks from her face as he draped a thigh across hers and pulled her possessively against him.

Smoothing her hands up his arms, she glided her fingers over his shoulders, then swirled them in the beaded perspiration on his chest, marveling in his masculine scent. Casting a coy sideways glance and half a smirk, she whispered seductively, "Do you believe I was saving myself for you?"

"You really didn't fuck him." A single dark brow rose faintly as he regarded her with stunned amusement that swelled his male ego judging by the smug grin titling his lips.

She hesitated for effect, letting him think about that for a moment. Even though it sounded more like a statement than a question, she could tell he eagerly awaited her answer. Using her forefingers, she rolled them over his nipples, thrilled they hardened instantly. She pinched them slightly, and he groaned in approval. She glanced up at him when his cock stirred to life across her hips. Everything about him was hard, just the way she wanted. She smiled, feeling her face flush with arousal. "I may have sucked his cock a few times."

"Naughty Megan." His grin turned mischievous, wicked, sexy as sin. "What did Caleb do?"

Megan shifted onto her side, careful to "accidentally" rub against his cock as she whispered in his ear, lewdly describing events that involved her mouth and various body parts, she unexpectedly felt his hard thickness slap her belly. Her vagina tingled, ached with a familiar hunger. Amused their insatiable sexual appetites were well-matched. She grinned against his ear.

After her account, she leaned backward slightly and gazed into his eyes. His expression reflected his complete acceptance, no hint of envy, bitterness, or resentment. Not only did Devin love her, he trusted her.

"Naughty Caleb," Devin teased playfully. His voice husky with arousal, eyes alit with blatant sexual desire so carnal, she breathed a deep sigh in erotic awareness.

Her skin grew hot at the thought of turning him on so easily, by simply describing what she did with someone else.

With the way the three of them carried on, she couldn't believe she managed to blush like a silly school girl. The erotic, primal heat this man generated from a single look was potent, feral and dangerous. Aimed at her. How lucky could one girl get?

"We'll go see the preacher first thing tomorrow."

"Why?" she breathed, caught entirely unaware. Her heart pumped violently in her chest with excitement and anticipation. Dare she dream?

"You know why." His voice was quiet, his face intent. So much so, it made her want to scream with insecurity.

Timidly, she shook her head. "No, Devin…I don't. Tell me." Her harried voice caught. She was afraid to ask. Afraid of being disappointed, confused. Afraid her heart was about to be broken.

"Megan Spawn, I love you." The world stopped, but her head was spinning out of control. "I need you by my side, always. Better believe I know as sure as hell I don't deserve you, but will you marry me?"

"Uh…" Her mind lapsed a brief moment, overcome, stunned, gloriously elated. Tears fell.

The lapse dragged on, and all she could do was blink through the teary, blurry-eyed haze as she tried to focus on the man she wanted to marry—who just so happened to want to marry her.

"Perhaps I shouldn't have put hell and marry in the same sentence. If it'll help, I'll get down on one knee, except I'm already lying buck naked on the floor. Can't get much lower than this."

Giggling, she wiped as many tears as possible from her eyes. Splaying her damp hands on the hard planes of his chest, she reached up and planted a quick kiss on his lips. "I would be honored, Devin Spawn."

He exhaled heavily, relieved.

"To have and hold." He held her gaze as he guided one of her hands to his cock.

"Ohhh, yeeesss," she breathed, draping her leg over his hip as she positioned the engorged head at her opening, spreading her slick folds. She moaned softly as she wiggled her hips until the swollen top was lodged inside. "Till death do us part."

"Till death…" he repeated, grasping her ass tightly as he thrust upward. She shuddered, moaned as he buried himself to the hilt and moved in and out slowly, sensuously. "…do us part."

"Devin," she whispered softly, brushing kisses along his jaw. "What about Caleb?"

Until she saw Caleb lying on the floor in a pool of blood, she hadn't realized how much she truly loved him. It became apparent why she never found the courage or desire to send him away for good. So much of her life was spent loving him. Part of her would have died with him, had it come to that. Leaving her brokenhearted.

If she lost Devin, her soul would have given up entirely.

All would have been lost.

What was wrong with her? How could it be that she wanted to marry Devin, and not be able to give up Caleb?

She felt his body stiffen almost imperceptibly. If she hadn't been in his arms, their bare flesh pressed against one another, she would have missed it entirely.

He rolled onto his back, taking her with him. Her thighs tightened around his hips as she adjusted to the top position. The question was one she thought about long and hard, ever since it was proposed. She blinked down at him, his eyes were dark and heavy-lidded.

"Megan, now's not the time to try and spare my feelings. Do you love Caleb?"

Resting her cheek gently on his chest, worried at his acceptance of the truth, she nodded.

"Look at me, Megan, when you answer," he requested softly.

Lifting her head slowly, she looked into his eyes. There was no anger, no jealousy, only warmth and affection, real, true love glowing in the silver depths.

"He expects to marry me," she said softly.

His eyes narrowed. "Caleb isn't as stubborn and bull-headed as I am. He sees things clear, specially after you kept him waiting two months. If things turn a little hazy tomorrow, we'll *talk* man to man."

"But he asked me years ago to marry him."

"And for whatever reason, you haven't. You said yes to me. They'll be hell to pay if you go an' try to change your mind. Now answer me. Do you love Caleb?"

She nodded first, then whispered a faint "yes," secure in the knowledge Devin Spawn loved her.

"Then Mrs. Spawn, we'll do whatever you want. The pact works both ways. We shook on it, and I never go back on a handshake."

"Oh, Devin, really?" she said excitedly, bouncing on his hips, her inner muscles clenching the steel rod buried deep inside her body, dragging a guttural groan from his throat. Reality set in a scant moment later. He wasn't agreeing to buying a cow or getting a dog. Caleb was another flesh-and-blood man who wanted to love her, also.

She stilled, sitting firmly atop his erection, hands braced on his shoulders. "The three of us together? Forever?"

"Don't see why not." He moved a hand from her waist to where their flesh was joined. His eyes never left hers. As he spoke, he rubbed her clit, gently rocking his hips off the floor and seemingly encouraging her participation.

She moaned faintly as a flare of arousal shot through her body.

"As long as I know you love me, and only because I know he feels about you as I do. If you two married, I planned to stay away from you as long as possible. Rest assured, I would have come around, in time. When I did, I sure as hell would have expected him to keep his side of the pact. Don't get any other ideas. I ain't whoring you. You're gonna be my wife. Any other man even looks at you cross-eyed, and the bastard is dead."

"Can we make it work?" she said excitedly, drowning his face in kisses. "Do anything we want?"

Closing his eyes, he moved both hands to her hips, guiding up and down his thick shaft. "Mmmm, yes," he groaned fiercely, stroking her pussy with short little jabs as his hips lifted them both off the floor.

"So, are we going to Boston?" she asked raggedly, her breathing escalating as she moved her hips in synch to his. "Caleb wants to open a medical practice with a school friend. We'll be safe there. No one will ever think to look for you in Boston."

He grimaced, grinding his cock deep inside her slick flesh. "Megan, do you love me?"

She nodded emphatically and quite happily. Squeezing her inner muscles snugly around his thick length, she sat upright and wailed, "Yes."

"Then show me," he groaned, lying flat on his back, stretching his arms out as if handing her power over of his body, heart, soul, and their future.

She did.

"Oh, God. Yes, baby," he growled. "That's the way."

DEVIL'S PACT

THE END

Siren Publishing, Inc.
www.SirenPublishing.com

Printed in the United States
122049LV00012B/39/P

9 781606 010044